in order for
come into *your* hands, a great number
of unlikely things had to happen.
while it's natural to ask yourself if those things
were 'good' or 'bad', instead look at

THE
GRAVEROBBER'S
SWORD

it this way: they were interesting.
and that chain of interest, I'm sorry
to say, has built up a . tremendous
amount of energy, energy which transferred
into *you* the moment you started reading
this message. (bit of a long spell, sorry
about this) Think about without a chaotic
blotch of curse, I mean blessing, who said
curse? haha definitely not me . sweet
it's done, enjoy!

Copyright © Jesse Jordan 2019.
Published in 2019 by Tablo Publishing.

Tablo
Level 1 / 41-43 Stewart Street,
Richmond, VIC, 3121
Australia

19 20 21 22 23 LMC 10 9 8 7 6 5 4 3 2 1

THE
GRAVEROBBER'S
SWORD

by Jesse Jordan

Published by Tablo

Chapter One

The sword sighed. This was unusual activity for a sword, but Zephelous was an unusual sword. Said to have been forged by Embruin - the dwarven god of creation - as a weapon in the first war, its flawless construction made it immune to the passing of time. As such, the sword tumbled through the centuries, being passed from wielder to wielder until it fell into the hands of an adventurer named Hedge, a mighty wizard on the path to godhood.

When he earned his divinity, Hedge's first act as the God of Knowledge was to transform the indestructible weapon into an immortal teacher; an undying master of combat whose lessons and knowledge could be passed on from wielder to wielder - a guiding hand whose voice would last for centuries as a guiding force of goodness. Destined to seek out heroes, the sword was Hedge's insurance measure against the ever-looming threat that was the forces of darkness.

When the sword gained life, it took a name.

That name was Zephelous.

In its lifetime, it had seen wars of dragons and men, battles that shook the very foundations of reality, and the world come to the brink of apocalypse a dozen times over, always held in the hands of heroes who had won the day.

Zephelous's most recent wielder, a hero named Theus Vraun, had been the sword's favorite. A man respected for his status as a decorated veteran and celebrated for his prowess as a duelist, Theus had proven himself a hero worth remembering throughout the ages - much to Zephelous's contentment.

When Theus felt himself turning old and grey, he took Zephelous and sailed from his home country of Orvand to the continent of Malzen, the so-called 'campaigner's frontier.' With the sword at his side, Theus lived out his life making a comfortable living as a sellsword.

Unfortunately for Zephelous, Theus's death hadn't come at the hands of a worthy opponent or on the field of a glorious battle; it had come from in the form of a mudslide in the middle of a stormy night. A river of mud and stone swept away Theus's campsite one night, killing him instantly. Immune to such damage, Zephelous was swept away as well, and was buried with Theus beneath the earth.

If the sword's sense of the passage of time was correct, it had been almost 80 years since that fateful night. It had taken the better part of a decade for the sword to adjust to being buried in the hands of a dead friend; the rest of the time had been spent honing its latent telepathy into greater psychic abilities in an effort to either free itself or locate someone who might help dig it up.

One of the first things Zephelous had taught itself was the ability to extend its awareness outside of its physical body in a psychic probe - a pulse of awareness that allowed it to sense and reach into the minds around it. It had done so hundreds of times by this point and had yet to find anything more intelligent than a mole.

NOT ENTIRELY TRUE, the sword thought to itself, *THERE WAS A WAYWARD DEER ON ONE OCCASION.* Having nothing better to do than reminisce, Zephelous sent out another psychic probe.

To Zephelous's great surprise, a sentient mind was nearby, registering on its psychic senses like a tiny source of light, a collection of dim stars visible only against the backdrop of complete darkness.

THERE ARE TWO LIKELY REASONS FOR THIS, Zephelous thought, *EITHER THE LIGHT IS DIM BECAUSE THE THINKER IS DULL OR THEIR MIND IS HEAVILY GUARDED.* The sword's extended senses registered the sound of a shovel plunging crisply in to the earth nearby. Zephelous sent another probe out of excitement, this one smaller but more powerful. It honed in on the mind.

WHO GOES THERE? Zephelous asked, sending a telepathic broadcast that would sound as clear as spoken word to its recipient. The digging paused.

Who is in my head? the other mind asked in return. The crispness and clarity of the response hinted at the strength of the mind behind the words, letting Zephelous know indirectly that this was no dullard; this was an intelligent and well guarded mind. Most importantly, it was a voice speaking to Zephelous that wasn't its own.

To the living weapon that had been isolated for so long, this was its own form of sweet sustenance.

Zephelous could also tell that the other had spoken the words verbally as well as in their thoughts - a sign that they were unfamiliar with telepathic communication.

THEY ARE ALL UNFAMILIAR AT FIRST, it thought, *IT BECOMES SECOND NATURE SOON ENOUGH.*

Giddy with excitement, the sword pressed on.

IT IS I, it sent, ZEPHELOUS.

"Ooo-kay," the other responded. "Am I supposed to know what that means?"

The nonchalance of in the other's response gave the sword pause.

HAS ZEPHELOUS BECOME A COMMON NAME?

"Dunno," said the other. "Guess that would depend on what you are."

I AM ZEPHELOUS, said the sword.

"You said that already."

I AM *THE* ZEPHELOUS, the sword clarified, feeling certain this was a misunderstanding. ZEPHELOUS OF THE FIRST AGE, OTHERWISE KNOWN AS THE BLADE THAT CUT DOWN THE GREAT SHADE, THE EDGE ON WHICH THE PLAGUE LEVIATHAN WAS FLAYED! IT IS UPON MY BLADE THAT THE WINGS OF THE GREAT DRAGON YRAGNIMOTH KORIZ'DERAZ WERE SHORN. IT WAS MY SHARPNESS THAT CUT CLEAN INTO THE EYE OF THE GREAT BLIND ONE, RENDERING HIM SO AND EARNING HIM HIS NAME.

"Oh," said the other. "So you're a talking axe or something."

It had been nearly a century since Zephelous had spoken to someone, but it had been several more since the last time it had sputtered.

AN *AXE*? It scoffed. I AM *NO* AXE! I AM *ZEPHELOUS*, THE BLADE WHO--

"Gonna have to cut you off there, because I got that bit the first time around. You're not an axe, you're a Zephelous. Great. I just want to know what a Zephelous is."

I AM A *SWORD*, Zephelous sent, ONE OF GREAT POWER.

"Ah, I see," said the voice. "I'm out."

YOU ARE... OUT?

"Yep, see ya."

I DO NOT UNDERSTAND. WHAT DOES BEING 'OUT' MEAN?

"Means I'm not interested, that I'm walking away now."

YOU WOULD LEAVE ME HERE?

"Sure would. Sure *am*, actually."

FOR WHAT REASON?

"Things always go bad with a talking sword," said the other. "I'm not sure I can leave fast enough, to tell you the truth."

I DO NOT UNDERSTAND, said Zephelous, confused and frustrated. WHAT PREJUDICE COULD ONE HAVE AGAINST A LIVING SWORD?

"Oh, *please*," said the voice. "There's a hundred reasons not to trust a talking sword. You'll end up being haunted or possessed by a demon, or actually being an evil vampire lord looking to take over someone's mind, or some other equally sinister and elaborate bullshit."

I AM A CREATURE OF LIGHT NOT SOME FOUL CREATURE, said

Zephelous, aghast. FOR CENTURIES, I HAVE BEEN A TEACHER, HAVE MOLDED AND SHAPED PERSONS DESTINED FOR GREATNESS INTO HEROES WHO WOULD STAND AGAINST THE FORCES OF DARKNESS THAT LURK IN THE SHADOWS, EAGER TO DEVOUR THE LIGHT.

"How very exciting for you," the mind responded. "Pass."

I BEG YOUR PARDON?

"It means I'm not interested," said the voice. "I'm way too busy for this hero crap you're peddling. I'll have you know that I'm also pretty important, not that you asked."

APOLOGIES, said Zephelous. IN MY EAGERNESS, I BYPASSED INTRODUCTIONS, WHICH WAS HIGHLY RUDE OF ME. MAY I ASK YOUR NAME, TRAVELER?

"I am Kera," said the other. "Otherwise known as Kera No-Clan, She Who Robs Unmarked Graves and Answers to 'You With The Face'."

SHE WHO... SHE WHO WHAT?

"Robs unmarked graves," Kera repeated, no longer a nameless voice. "If I'm being honest, they're not always unmarked. Rich folks like being *real* specific about where they're buried, which is helpful. To me, at least. I also do a lot of tomb runs, ruin looting, battlefield scavenging, and the occasional burial ground desecrating. Most of that stuff is marked somewhere too, but not always. All in all, I'm pretty versatile."

YOU ARE NOT A CAMPAIGNER OR AN ADVENTURER? Zephelous asked. YOU DO NOT SEEK GLORY? The sword heard a low whistle of disbelief.

"There's the understatement of the year," said Kera.

SURELY YOU DESIRE MORE, Zephelous reasoned, feeling its own frustration give way to desperation. YOU MUST ASPIRE TO BE SOMETHING GREATER THAN A GRAVEROBBER. IF YOU DO NOT SEEK TO BE A HERO, PERHAPS I CAN ASSIST YOU ON THE PATH TO BECOMING A LORD OR LADY OF RENOWN?

"Thanks, but no thanks," said Kera. "And it would be lady, not lord. Can you not tell?"

I MUST ADMIT, I AM ABLE TO DETERMINE VERY LITTLE ABOUT YOU, said Zephelous. YOUR MIND IS SURPRISINGLY FORTIFIED.

"Huh," said Kera. "That's good to know."

DO YOU FACE COMBAT ON YOUR... EXPEDITIONS? Zephelous asked, I IMAGINE YOU MUST NEED TO SLAY MANY UNDEAD AS A GRAVEROBBER?

"Not if I can help it," Kera answered. "I prefer to leave the zombie-slaying and ghost-busting to the ratcatchers with god complexes. Although…"

Zephelous could practically feel the wrappings on its hilt tighten with its anticipation as it hung on to Kera's words.

"I was thinking about slaying a ham at month's end."

If Zephelous had a heart, it would have sank at Kera's words. Its frustration and desperation grew, but so too did its desire to be unburied.

I HAVE KNOWN MANY HEROES WITH UNUSUAL ORIGINS, it reasoned to itself. *I HAVE BEEN HELD BY COMMONERS AND CRIMINALS AS OFTEN AS NOBLES AND KNIGHTS, ALWAYS PREVAILING IN MY DUTY. THAT SAID, I CANNOT RECALL A SINGLE HERO WHOSE ORIGINS HAVE INCLUDED GRAVEROBBING…* The sword pondered for a moment. *I SUPPOSE THERE IS A POTENTIAL FOR GREATNESS IN EVERYONE…* Zephelous telepathically observed Kera, tried to see if she had a certain kind of energy it looked for in a wielder, a raw potential that registered on its psychic senses the way heat did to creatures of flesh and blood. It sensed a fire in Kera, a deep well of potential. It resolved to press on.

SURELY YOU MIGHT RECONSIDER?

"The only thing I'm reconsidering at this point was my choice to come dig here," said Kera. "Alright, listen. Do you want out of there or not?"

Zephelous hastily contemplated its options. Kera seemed resistant, combative even, to its mission. Eighty years had been an *awfully* long time to wait for a random encounter like this one. It couldn't help but wonder if it would take another eighty years before the next person might happen by.

I WOULD VERY MUCH LIKE TO BE UNEARTHED, Zephelous said at last.

"Great," said Kera. "Here's my offer: You tell me where you are, and I'll dig you up. Once you're out, I'll dust you off and take a good look at you, then decide if you're worth the hassle of hauling around while I go about the rest of my day. I get to keep you, while you get to be happy about not being buried. If you don't annoy the shit out of me, maybe I'll consider letting you stick around. Otherwise, I'm selling you. If I'm being honest again, that's probably what's going to happen anyway."

WILL YOU SHARPEN MY EDGE?

"Sure."

AND POLISH MY BLADE?

"Why not?"

WILL YOU SHEATH ME BY YOUR HIP AND CARRY ME INTO

BATTLE?

"Let's take it slow," said Kera. "How about we start with you telling me where to dig. After I pull you out and assess the situation a little more, maybe then we can talk about who gets to be sheathed where."

I BELIEVE I CAN WORK WITH THIS, Zephelous thought, GODS KNOW I HAVE WORKED WITH LESS IN THE PAST.

"Well?"

I ACCEPT YOUR OFFER, said Zephelous. I AM SEVEN FEET TO YOUR LEFT, AND APPROXIMATELY EIGHT FEET DOWN.

"Aw, c'mon," Kera complained. "Eight feet down?"

APPROXIMATELY, Zephelous confirmed.

"Do you know how much digging that's going to be?" Kera asked, trudging her way to the spot Zephelous had indicated. "You better be a nice piece of steel."

I AM FAR MORE THAN SOME PIECE OF STEEL, KERA WHO ROBS UNMARKED GRAVES, Zephelous boomed. I AM A WEAPON OF LEGEND, A CONSTANT ALLY OF THE FORCES OF GOOD, A REPEATING ELEMENT WOVEN INTO THE TAPESTRY OF FATE ITSELF.

"Sounds expensive," said Kera, mirth in her voice as she plunged her shovel into the dirt. "Sounds *very* expensive, and expensive is good." She heaved a shovel full of dirt over her shoulder and buried its point once more. "I'm not so sure about this path to greatness, but at least you can help me along the path to the bank."

THE BANK? Zephelous asked.

"Yeah, you know," said Kera, hoisting another load of dirt from above the sword. "Big building, full of gold, none of it mine? Well, not yet, at least. None of it was mine *yesterday*, but as of *today*, I found the *sword that cut down the Shade Leviathan*, or whatever."

THE PLAGUE LEVIATHAN, Zephelous corrected, AND THE GREAT SHADE.

"Even better," said Kera. "I can already hear the gold pieces clinking together. *Do* go on." Another shovel full of dirt was heaved aside. Zephelous's frustration and desperation faded as uncertainty and anxiety took their places.

It did not enjoy these sensations.

Chapter Two

Zephelous's senses didn't include traditional sight, and was limited to seeing the world around it through the eyes of its wielder. It had other senses, senses that were now basking in the first hint of warmth from the sun in almost a century.

GLORIOUS, said Zephelous, its hilt and guard protruding from the earth.

"Enh, you're alright," said Kera, breathing heavily as she leaned on her shovel.

I WAS NOT REFERRING TO MYSELF, said Zephelous, I WAS REFERRING TO THE WARMTH OF THE SUN. IT IS BETTER THAN I REMEMBERED.

"If you say so," said Kera, cracking her neck before standing to plunge the shovel into the ground where the sword was buried.

Plink.

The shovel hit something solid. Kera frowned and tried to remove it, but was stuck fast.

"How did you say you were buried again?"

A LANDSLIDE. IT SWEPT AWAY THE ENTIRE CAMP, INCLUDING THEUS.

"Who is Theus?"

MY PREVIOUS WIELDER, A GRAND DUELIST SO ACCOMPLISHED HE--

"'Previous wielder' was enough, thanks," Kera interrupted, grunting with effort as she fought to pull the shovel back out. "I think I'm caught somewhere between his armor and his ribcage."

STOP, PLEASE! THEUS DESERVED MUCH BETTER THAN THIS.

"You got a better idea?" Kera asked.

TAKE MY HANDLE AND I WILL ASSIST YOU.

"Assist me how?" Kera asked. "By possessing me and taking over my body?"

WHAT? NO, said Zephelous.

"That's what you'd say if you were trying to possess me," Kera countered.

ARE YOU ALWAYS THIS SUSPICIOUS? Zephelous asked, the sword's booming voice tinged with a mix of incredulity and exasperation.

"Absolutely," said Kera. "It's the best way to stay alive. Also, you're a talking sword. We've already established how I feel about that."

THIS LINE OF RHETORIC IS EXHAUSTING, KERA NO-CLAN, Zephelous pleaded. LET US BE FREE OF THIS PLACE. YOU CAN CONTINUE TO DISTRUST ME ON THE ROAD.

"Where is it exactly you think I'm going?" Kera asked.

YOUR PSIONIC SHIELDING PREVENTS ME FROM READING YOUR MIND.

"You can read *minds?* Funny you didn't mention that before."

I AM NOT A TRUE TELEPATH, I CANNOT READ MINDS IN THEIR ENTIRETY, Zephelous answered. I AM ABLE TO PERCEIVE THROUGH THE SENSES OF MY WIELDER, ABLE TO DETECT INTENT AND LITTLE MORE. EVEN IF I WERE A MIND READER, YOURS IS FAR TOO WELL GUARDED.

"Lucky me," said Kera. "How do I know you're telling the truth?"

I SUPPOSE YOU DO NOT, Zephelous admitted. Neither spoke for a moment.

"Besides your whole 'hero thing,' what is it you're after?" Kera asked, breaking the silence.

I DO NOT UNDERSTAND.

"What is it you want to happen after I pull you out? What are you hoping to get out of this? You're *alive*, right? That means there's something you want."

I SUPPOSE.

"What is it?"

WILL YOU FINALLY BEGIN TO TRUST ME IF I TELL YOU WHAT IT IS?

"Uh, no? You're a talking sword that I've known for two hours. You're a *long* way from me coming close to trusting you."

WILL YOU AT LEAST FINALLY TAKE ME FROM THIS PLACE?

"Maybe," said Kera. "Depends on how you answer."

VERY WELL, said Zephelous. IF I WERE TO HAVE A 'WANT,' IT WOULD BE TO FINALLY BE TAKEN AWAY FROM THE CORPSE OF MY DECEASED FRIEND. EIGHTY YEARS IS REMINDER ENOUGH.

Kera let out a high whistle.

"Yeah, alright," said Kera. "But I want you to know you're gone at the first sign of trouble, you understand me?"

PERFECTLY, said Zephelous. Kera took hold of Zephelous's handle with a two-handed grip. The world around the pair appeared in the sword's mind as the graverobber laid her hands on it; the deep browns of the earthen pit, the dull orange glow of the setting sun beyond its rim, the tranquil mauve clouds in the skies above, all painting themselves into a stunning portrait of reality.

IT IS MORE BEAUTIFUL THAN I REMEMBER, Zephelous thought, feeling renewed at the sight of the brilliant ball of flame in the sky.

"Now what?" Kera asked.

NOW WE MUST BECOME ATTUNED TO ONE ANOTHER, said Zephelous.

"And what does that mean?"

IT MEANS THAT YOU MUST BECOME USED TO MY PRESENCE IN YOUR MIND, ENOUGH SO THAT I MAY GAIN PERIPHERAL ACCESS.

"So you do want to read my mind," said Kera.

NO, I MERELY WISH TO HELP YOU IMPROVE.

"You want to improve my mind?"

IN CERTAIN RESPECTS, PERHAPS, said Zephelous. THERE IS MUCH ON WHICH I CAN EDUCATE AND INSTRUCT YOU.

"Like what?"

COMBAT TECHNIQUES, BATTLEFIELD TACTICS, HISTORICAL LESSONS--

"Anything useful?"

COMBAT TECHNIQUES, BATTLEFIELD TAC--

"Stop talking, I don't care about that stuff. How long does attunement take?"

THE PROCESS HAS ALREADY BEGUN.

"That's not really an answer," said Kera. "How will you know when it's finished?"

Kera appeared then in the eye of Zephelous's mind; athletically built, tan skin with gold undertones, brown hair cut short. Her clothes were worn and stained; a belt with bulging pouches hung around her waist, and the only thing that came close to a weapon on her person was a shoulder strap meant to carry her shovel.

IT IS GOOD TO MEET YOU, KERA NO-CLAN.

"Keep it up with the creepy ominous statements and I'm gone."

APOLOGIES, said Zephelous. IF YOU ANGLE THE HANDLE OF THE SHOVEL SO THAT IT IS BENEATH MY CROSSGUARD, YOU SHOULD BE ABLE TO USE IT TO PROVIDE THE ADDITIONAL LEVERAGE REQUIRED TO FREE ME.

"Oh, so you're a *work smarter, not harder* type," said Kera, doing as Zephelous had suggested. "I can live with that."

Wedging the handle of the shovel beneath the guard, Kera knelt down to get beneath and behind it. She shoved upwards as hard as she could, watching the dirt around Zephelous break away a little at a time, the sword being slowly drawn from the earth. The shovel snapped; Zephelous popped free while Kera was sent hurtling into the sidewall of the tunnel. Hunks of soil and sand came loose from the walls and rained down on top of her, sending a cloud of dust into the air.

KERA, ARE YOU ALRIGHT?

"Yeah," Kera said coughing. "I'm fine. Just took a little dirt shower, not a big deal." She coughed again and stood up, using her fingers to rub the dirt from her eyes. After a moment, she stopped and froze in place.

"Uh oh."

WHAT IS IT? Zephelous asked. IS SOMETHING WRONG?

"Yes and no. Mostly no," said Kera, pulling her hands away from her face. The sword's perception of her changed. Her eyes were now voids of white from which technicolor sparks spat out.

"I got dusted."

DUSTED?

"Yeah, dosed with fae ash," said Kera. "You've been alive for eons and eons, but you've never spent time with anyone who got dusted?"

WHAT YOU CALL FAE ASH IS THE REMAINS OF DEAD FAIRIES AND OTHER FAE-KIN, ALL OF WHICH ARE CREATURES OF LIGHT, Zephelous scolded. CONSUMING THEIR REMAINS TO BECOME INTOXICATED IS TABOO AT BEST.

"Best taboo of them all," responded Kera, the white light and eye sparks swirling around her in Zephelous's mind, altering Kera's perception of reality and the sword's as well.

"Do you have any idea how much it's worth?"

YES, said Zephelous, THE LIFE OF A FAE CREATURE.

"*Oooh, so serious,*" said Kera. "Fairies gotta die sometimes, Zeph."

I AM ZEPHELOUS, NOT 'ZEPH'.

"You got it, Zephie."

ZEPHIE?

"I might be a little high," said Kera, walking back to Zephelous to pick it up and inspect it. "You're pretty thick for a longsword."

I AM A GREATSWORD, said Zephelous.

"You don't look that great to me," said Kera. "You look like a bulky, awkward longsword. Your balance looks awful."

I AM A *DWARVEN* GREATSWORD.

"That explains it," said Kera. "I know you said you were from the first age and all, but nowadays we call this kind of design a third age make."

AND WHY IS THAT?

"Dwarves stopped making them around the third age," Kera said with a shrug. "Guess you really are an antique. How about that?"

YOU KNOW SOMETHING ABOUT HISTORY AFTER ALL, said Zephelous. I AM IMPRESSED WITH YOU.

"Don't get excited," said Kera. "It's helpful to know what junk you can sell and what junk you can't. It also helps cut down on how many people can try to rip you off."

I SEE, said Zephelous.

Unable to fit Zephelous into the sling for her shovel, Kera took off her jacket and wrapped Zephelous in it, tying the bundle off with a piece of rope and attaching it to her shoulder strap. With the rest of the rope, she formed into a lasso, throwing it to the lip of the pit to land catch on the handle of another shovel planted deep.

WHY NOT TIE THE ROPE BEFORE DESCENDING?

"And advertise that I'm down here and need this rope? That's asking for trouble."

THE LEVEL OF YOUR PARANOIA IS DEEP AND UNSETTLING.

"It's not paranoia. It's experience," said Kera, hauling on the rope to tighten it. "That ought to do it. Up and out we go."

WHERE ARE WE HEADED?

"The nearest brook I can find," said Kera.

FOR WHAT PURPOSE?

"Well," Kera began, pulling herself up the side of the hole. "Fairies are pretty territorial. Fae clans will live in the same forest until either the forest or the clan dies off."

THIS IS KNOWN, said Zephelous. WHAT IS YOUR POINT?

"My point is," said Kera, crawling over the lip of the tunnel and onto the ground, eyes blazing all the brighter, "that if there's fae ash down there, there's more nearby. Probably a lot more, if I can find the brook they're using as a burial ground."

Zephelous was stunned.

YOU WOULD UNEARTH AN ENTIRE BURIAL PLOT? the sword asked, feeling delirious. DISTURBING THE ETERNAL REST OF INNOCENT CREATURES OF LIGHT, ALL JUST SO YOU CAN CONSUME THEM FOR A *HIGH*, AS YOU PUT IT?

"That's ridiculous, Zeph" said Kera. "I'd never do that."

Zephelous relaxed.

"I'm going to sell most of it. I'm not stupid."

Zephelous wanted to scream.

Chapter Three

IS THERE NOTHING I CAN SAY TO DISSUADE YOU FROM THIS? Zephelous asked as Kera pressed her way deeper into the forest around them.

"Nope."

YOU ARE AWARE THIS AREA IS LIKELY WARDED, YES?

"I'm counting on it," said Kera, pushing a branch aside to peer forward through the thick woods. "They make useful trail markers once you know what to look for. Ironically, being on fae ash makes them stand out."

HOW CONVENIENT FOR YOU.

"It's very convenient, actually."

I WAS USING SARCASM TO DENOTE MY DISPLEASURE.

"I noticed. It wasn't very effective."

Ducking beneath low-hanging boughs, Kera found herself standing in a small clearing in the middle of the woods. Standing in the middle of the clearing was a great oak tree, around which speckled mushrooms grew in dense and colorful clusters. The river broke and forked into two streams which encircled the clearing, forming a natural moat several feet wide. A few large rocks broke through the surface, the water burbling softly as it trickled by.

"How quaint," Kera mused, walking towards the edge of the water.

I RECOGNIZE THIS PLACE, said Zephelous.

"Oh yeah?" Kera asked, peering at the river and the stones. "Is it because it looks exactly like every other idyllic clearing in the middle of the woods?"

NO, said Zephelous. I HAVE BEEN TO THIS PLACE BEFORE. THIS IS WAS THE PLACE THAT THEUS AND I SET OUT FROM BEFORE WE MADE CAMP ON THE DAY HE DIED. THIS IS WHERE WE SPREAD THE ASHES OF MOIRIDIA.

"The what?"

A COMPANION OF THEUS'S. SHE WAS KILLED IN COMBAT, INCINERATED BY A ROGUE DRAGON GONE MAD.

"Dragons kill people. That does happen," Kera said absently, paying more attention to the area around her than the sword's rambling.

I think the river is warded, she thought, the fae ash in her system making the water gleam a little *too* brightly in the setting sun.

The rocks look safe, she realized. *Guess that's how we get across.*

Bending her knees, Kera hopped on to the top of the first rock. She nearly lost her balance, but managed to quick-step across a few smaller stones to land on the far side.

WELL NAVIGATED, Zephelous said begrudgingly.

"What would have happened if I stepped in the water?" Kera asked. "Fairy magic is always old magic. I can't imagine that ward being newer than when you were here."

IT WAS INDEED, Zephelous admitted with a sigh. STEPPING INTO IT WOULD HAVE MADE YOU FORGET THIS PLACE, AND COMPELLED YOU TO LEAVE THE WILDS AND RETURN TO CIVILIZATION.

"That's a bit subjective, isn't it?" Kera said, eyeing the different fungal clusters. She was looking for the telltale glitter present in a mushroom growing above a fae ash pile.

HOW SO?

"What if my definition of civilization is a city across the sea?"

I SUPPOSE YOU WOULD BE COMPELLED TO GO THERE, said Zephelous.

"What if I didn't have the means?" Kera asked, eyes going wide as a flash of light near the base of the great oak caught her eye; two glittering mushrooms, their columns entwined, shone out from between a pair of knotted roots.

I SUPPOSE YOU WOULD BE COMPELLED TO FIND THE MEANS.

"How strongly would I be compelled?" Kera asked.

QUITE, said Zephelous. THE FAE-KIN QUEEN HERSELF IS SAID TO HAVE PUT THE WARDS ON THESE WATERS.

"The fuckin' queen?" Kera repeated, unslinging Zephelous and pulling her shovel around as she made her way to the mushrooms. "Sounds fuckin' serious."

I SAID *FAE-KIN,* I DID NOT SAY *THAT.* I WOULD NEVER BE SO CRASS--

The sound of the shovel plunging into the ground stopped Zephelous mid-sentence.

YOU ARE A DIFFICULT PERSON, KERA NO-CLAN.

"So I've been told," said Kera. "Hey, what's the difference between a talking sword and a pile of fae ash?"

I DO NOT UNDERSTAND.

"It's a joke," Kera explained. "You have to guess. What's the difference between a talking sword and a pile of fae ash?"

I DO NOT KNOW, Zephelous grumbled.

"About seven and a half feet worth of digging," Kera said with a smile, letting her shovel drop to the ground as she got down on her hands and knees in front of the small hole she had dug.

Curious, the sword looked into Kera's senses to see what the graverobber was seeing. To its dismay, Kera was staring at a visible vein of colorful, sparkling glitter that shone through the dirt just a few inches below the surface.

IS THAT…?

"Fae ash," Kera said gleefully.

KERA, PLEASE, THIS IS A SACRED PLACE, Zephelous begged. WHAT YOU ARE LOOKING AT IS LIKELY THE REMAINS OF GREAT FAIRIES OF LEGEND.

"If fairies don't want their dead heroes dug up, maybe they should start burying them deeper than six inches," Kera replied. "Besides, do you have any idea how much an ounce of fae ash is worth? And before you say it again, don't bother with the 'several lives'. These things are dead. They don't mind."

PERHAPS YOU SHOULD BE MORE CONCERNED ABOUT THOSE WHO ARE STILL ALIVE, Zephelous said, sensing a flutter of activity in the trees.

It sent a psychic probe towards the upper reaches of the oak tree, but detected no signs of a thinking mind. There was movement though; the sword was certain.

Kera, meanwhile, was using the fingers of one hand to scoop fae ash out of the hole while rummaging through the pouches on her belt with the other. She produced a small leather bag, and began brushing the ash off of her fingers into the bag. Zephelous's senses tingled again, alerting it to movement closer to the base of the tree.

It looked through Kera's senses again and discovered the source of the movement at last; crawling vines, animated by magic, had made their way down the tree and were snaking their way towards Kera's feet.

AN ENSNARING VINE, it thought, recognizing the magic for what it was. IT SHOULD CAUSE HER NO HARM AND MAY PERHAPS TEACH HER A LESSON.

Kera, meanwhile, tied off the plump bag, now so full of fairy dust it was the size of a grapefruit. Noticing some extra ash on her finger tips, Kera smiled and rubbed it into her eyes. She sat back to rest on her boots as the drug took effect.

"Mmm, that's the stuff," she said dreamily, falling into the relaxed bliss of the fae ash high. "If you tried it, I bet you'd enjoy it."

I DOUBT THAT MOST SINCERELY, Zephelous scolded.

The vines crawled towards Kera's feet like mossy vipers. The graverobber didn't feel them as they wrapped around her boots and legs. Suddenly, they tightened at once.

"What the--"

Kera instinctively snatched Zephelous, suddenly finding herself lifted into the air by the vines to hang upside down like a snared game animal.

DO YOU SEE WHAT YOU HAVE GOTTEN YOURSELF INTO? Zephelous asked. HOW DO YOU PROPOSE TO FREE YOURSELF?

Kera swung wildly, trying to reach up towards her feet to pry the vines off of her boots. In response to Kera's aggression towards them, the vines tightened even further. Their texture became tougher and more bark-like.

"Gods, magic is such bullshit," Kera said, grunting with effort as she struggled. Another tendril of growth reached out towards her, trying to bind itself around her wrists. Kera responded by biting through the plant with a shake of her head, spitting the severed bit out of her mouth and onto the ground. Zephelous slipped from her hand and fell to the ground beneath her in the process.

"Damnit," Kera swore. "You have to know *something* about how I can deal with this stuff, Zeph."

THE FAE AND THEIR KIN ARE CREATURES OF LIGHT, THE ALLIES OF THOSE WHO FORGED ME. AS SUCH, I HAVE NO KNOWLEDGE ON COMBATING THEM, the sword boomed into Kera's mind. WHAT'S MORE, YOU WOULD NOT *NEED* TO KNOW HOW TO FIGHT FAE MAGICS IF YOU HAD CHOSEN NOT TO UNEARTH THE REMAINS OF THEIR DEAD OR HEEDED EVEN *ONE* OF MY WARNINGS.

"Gods," Kera groaned, "you're such a hardass, Zeph."

Kera arched her back as far as she could in an effort to reach her own feet, fighting gravity and inertia in an effort to reach a small blade she kept tucked into the back of her boot for situations like this one.

"Do you even have an ass? I assume you do, based on how full of sh--"

SOMETHING APPROACHES, Zephelous interrupted.

"What kind of something?" Kera asked, managing to wrap her fingers around the handle of the knife at last. Careful not to work in an area that would cut into her boots, she began using the little knife to saw away at the vines.

"What kind of something?" Kera repeated.

I SUSPECT IT MAY BE THE KEEPER OF THIS FAIRY RING, said Zephelous. TRIGGERING WARDS SUCH AS THIS ONE OFTEN ALERTS THOSE WHO ARE MEANT TO GUARD THEM.

"Lovely," said Kera. "Luckily, I'm almost--"

The vine snapped, dumping the woman onto the ground below. Soft as it was, hitting the ground knocked the wind out of Kera.

"*Oof*," she grunted involuntarily, wheezing.

GET UP ON TO YOUR FEET, KERA NO-CLAN, Zephelous commanded.

Go fuck yourself, Zephelous, Kera thought back, wincing in pain.

The tinkle of what sounded like a small bell near Kera's feet caught her attention. Still winded, she glanced down to see its source. A small fairy creature with a face like a hound dog, no more than five inches tall with a sword a little bigger than a toothpick at its side, was hovering in the air just above her boots. Its tiny arms were crossed in front of its chest and the heaving of its shoulders told Kera that the bell tinkling sound was actually the noise it made as it laughed.

"I thought fairies were supposed to be cute," Kera wheezed as she sat up, flinching at the pain in her sides and lower back. "What's with the literal dog face?"

THIS BREED OF FAE IS KNOWN AS A CALAMITY FAIRY, the sword began.

"Ha," said Kera. "I see what you did there. You said breed, and it's got a dog face. Look at you making a joke, Zeph. Good for you."

I DID NOT INTEND TO MAKE A JOKE, said Zephelous. CALAMITY ARE NOT TO BE TRIFLED WITH.

"He's five inches tall, Zeph. What's he going to do?"

Seemingly in response, the calamity stopped laughing, staring intently at Kera as it waved its hands through the air dramatically, flying in a small circle as it did.

"What's it doing?"

I SUSPECT IT IS CASTING A SPELL.

The calamity snapped its fingers and stopped moving, still staring at Kera. The graverobber stared back at the fairy expectantly. When nothing happened, Kera cocked her head.

"Are fairies any good at magic?" Kera asked. "That seemed like a whole lot of hand-waggling for nothing."

FAE-KIN ARE EXCEPTIONALLY GIFTED WITH MAGIC, the sword intoned. WERE I YOU, I WOULD BE VERY CONCERNED.

A branch from the oak tree snapped and fell. The weight of the limb knocked Kera flat once more; its leaves and many smaller branches spreading out in all directions, burying Kera under a mountain of foliage. While she couldn't see the calamity, she could hear it laughing. She ground her teeth.

"That little shit," she cursed. "That thing just tried to kill me."

CALAMITY ARE NOT ESPECIALLY HOSTILE, THEY ARE MERELY TRICKSTERS, Zephelous explained as Kera struggled to free herself. THEY

FIND GREAT AMUSEMENT AT THE MISFORTUNE OF OTHERS AND THEIR MAGICS OFTEN CAUSE TREMENDOUS AMOUNTS OF POOR LUCK.

Kera's face burst through the leaves at last, her nostrils flaring, her eyes wide with anger and white from fae ash. The look on her face combined with her disheveled hair now filled with leaves and twigs, set the calamity laughing even harder. Moving deliberately, Kera reached out through the many leaves and branches and took hold of Zephelous, anger and murderous intent radiating from the woman.

KERA NO-CLAN, YOU MUST NOT KILL THIS FAIRY, Zephelous warned, sensing Kera's building anger. DO NOT FORGET, THEY ARE OUR ALLIES--

"Against the looming metaphor of whatever, whatever. I got it," Kera hissed, using Zephelous to cut away some of the branches pinning her down. Despite its misgivings, Zephelous couldn't help but feel a little happy about being held again.

After clearing away enough brush to have a better range of motion, she took Zephelous with both hands and swung it downwards, using Zephelous's enchanted edge to neatly cut the largest portion of the branch in half, drastically reducing the weight on top of her.

Scrambling to her feet and fighting her way through the remaining brush, Kera growled as a branch recoiled. It snapped her across the face hard enough to draw blood. Kera winced and put her hand over the wound.

The calamity squawked all the more with laughter.

Kera grumbled at the fairy, pulling her hand away from her face. Feeling a stickiness on her fingers, she glanced down to her palm and saw the red of her own blood.

"Alright, you little shit," Kera cursed. "Now you die."

KERA, YOU MUST NOT, Zephelous boomed, THEY ARE--

"Say the words 'allies against the darkness' one more time and I'm going straight back to where I found you and burying you all over again," Kera snapped, eyes narrowing to pinpricks of anger as she glared at the dog-faced calamity.

She lunged at it with an angry shout, swinging Zephelous over her head in a downward slash. To her great displeasure, the calamity easily sidestepped the blow by floating out of reach.

This made Kera overextend her swing, causing her to bury Zephelous's tip in the ground at the base of the tree. Growling, she brought Zephelous up and around in a low slash, aiming at the midsection of the calamity. The calamity dipped low, ducking lazily beneath the swing, chittering to itself all the while.

"Would you stay still, you little shit!?"

ASKING IT TO STAY STILL IS THE SAME AS ASKING IT TO DIE, Zephelous said. YOU WILL LIKELY NOT BE ABLE TO HARM IT. CALAMITY RADIATE AN AURA OF UNLUCK, WHICH CAN CAUSE EVEN AN EXPERT SWORDSMAN TO STRIKE FALSE. YOU ARE DECIDEDLY *NOT* AN EXPERT SWORDSMAN, KERA NO-CLAN.

"Was that an insult?" Kera scowled, sending a combination of jabbing strikes with the sentient sword in the calamity's direction.

The tiny fae kin ducked, sidestepped, and bent low beneath Kera's assault.

MERELY A TRUTHFUL STATEMENT. YOU ARE AN AMATEUR AT BEST.

"Fuck you, Zeph," Kera said, raising a booted foot in an effort to kick the calamity out of the air.

As her foot came down, the calamity drew its tiny sword and charged at Kera's foot, piercing through the leather of her sole and driving its blade clear through Kera's boot so the tip poked out from the other side.

"Son of a bitch - that thing just stabbed me!" Kera exclaimed, pulling her foot back, falling backwards as she lost her balance.

IN ALL FAIRNESS, said Zephelous, YOU HAVE ATTEMPTED TO STAB IT SEVERAL TIMES NOW.

"Well, yeah, but I haven't actually *hit* the thing yet," Kera countered, gingerly placing her foot back on the ground.

The calamity flew up to Kera's eye level and stuck its tongue out at her, its tiny sword flashing as the fairy whipped the weapon through the air in an elaborate flourish. Kera seethed, grinding her teeth in anger. She lunged at the calamity, yelping in surprise as the calamity lunged as well, its sword aimed at her eyes.

Kera stepped back and to the side to get away from the fairy's attack only to promptly trip herself up as her boot snagged in the branches on the ground, causing her to fall flat on her back once more.

Kera sighed as the calamity continued to cackle.

IT IS NOT TOO LATE TO APOLOGIZE AND WITHDRAW, Zephelous suggested. SURELY THE NEED FOR FAE ASH CANNOT BE SO GREAT AS TO RISK CONTINUING THIS ENCOUNTER. Kera's eyes went wide.

"The fae ash," she repeated. "Good thinking, Zeph."

Rolling over onto her knees, she scooped out a hefty fingerful of ash while still holding Zephelous with her other hand.

IN NO WAY WAS IT MY INTENTION TO SUGGEST THIS, Zephelous complained. I CANNOT ADVISE YOU DO THIS, KERA NO-CLAN. NOT ONLY IS IT SACRILEGE, FAE ASH IS A HIGHLY ADDICTIVE SUBSTANCE. ITS EFFECTS ARE SHORT TERM AND CANNOT POSSIBLY--

Kera pressed the dust into her eyes and exhaled happily.

Zephelous groaned.

THIS IS EXTREMELY UNWISE, KERA NO-CLAN.

"It's just a little dusting. It's not a big deal," Kera said, her tone relaxed and easy.

She closed her eyes, waiting to experience the massive head rush she knew was coming.

"Oh, *wow*."

Leaning back, she opened her eyes, revealing dazzling kaleidoscopic light radiating through her orbs, centered in the place where her pupils had been. Seeing the laughing fairy, Kera giggled. Easily, almost lazily, she swung Zephelous through the air with two hands.

The calamity tried to float over the edge of the sword, but Kera rolled Zephelous's grip in her palms, bringing up the flat of the sword to smack the calamity. The dog-faced fairy was sent tumbling through the air before thumping into the trunk of the great tree behind it, sliding down the bark to land in a dizzy heap on the ground.

Deeply pleased with herself, Kera laughed.

"Now *that* was funny," she said, standing up from the branches.

KERA, YOU SHOULD NOT... Zephelous began, its trail of thought disappearing as its consternation gave way to curiosity.

HOW... HOW DID YOU DO THAT?

"Fae ash, baby," Kera explained, her words slurred, a childish grin on her face. "It gives you good luck, *great* luck even, for a short while. I went out on a limb and guessed it might cancel out the calamity's unluck. Guess I was right."

She stepped free of the branches and grinned.

"Ha, *out on a limb*. I'm funny."

BESIDES THE SHEER IMPROPRIETY OF ITS USE, I HAVE HEARD MUCH ABOUT THE NEGATIVE EFFECTS OF FAE ASH, Zephelous commented, concerned for its current wielder. MAGIC DOES NOT COME WITHOUT A PRICE, YOU MUST KNOW THAT BY NOW GIVEN YOUR...

"Line of work?" Kera suggested.

THAT IS NOT HOW I WOULD DESCRIBE IT, said Zephelous, BUT YES.

"I'm honestly not sure," Kera said with a shrug, "I don't usually do it much, but I do sell it from time to time when I can get my hands on it. Come to think of it, this might be the most I have ever done. I'm not worried about it. I'm sure it'll be fine."

THIS DOES NOT BODE WELL, KERA NO-CLAN, Zephelous groaned.

"It'll be *fine*, Zephelous Pointy-Pants."

DO NOT REFER TO ME THUSLY, Zephelous scolded.

Kera made a fake scolding expression, miming the words to Zephelous's admonition.

DO NOT ASSUME THAT BECAUSE I DO NOT HAVE EYES I CANNOT SEE WHAT YOU ARE DOING.

The calamity shook its head, clearing away its dizziness. It looked up at Kera and growled, a tiny and utterly non-threatening sound that made her giggle.

"Aw, look, Zeph," she said, stepping closer to the calamity, "I think it's trying to be scary. You're not so dangerous are you, little guy?"

In response, the calamity let out a high pitched howl, throwing its head back like a pint-sized wolf. Kera laughed and joined it, letting out a howl of her own.

THIS DOES NOT BODE WELL, Zephelous warned. WE MUST RETREAT FROM THIS PLACE AND SHOULD DO SO WITH GREAT HASTE.

"And why should we do that?" Kera asked, giddy and still howling.

THE CALAMITY IS SUMMONING AID.

"What kind of aid?"

IT COULD BE ALL MANNER OF THINGS - FROM A LEGION OF CALAMITY TO A GRAND AUTUMNAL DRAGON.

"So you don't actually *know*, then?" Kera asked.

LET US LEAVE THIS PLACE, KERA, I BEG OF YOU.

"Are you actually worried right now?" Kera asked, the sentient sword's concern reaching her through the joyful delirium of the fae ash. "Like, actually worried, worried?"

SO MUCH OF WHAT YOU SAY IS NONSENSICAL OR REPETITIOUS, Zephelous complained, BUT YES. THE FAE ARE *NOT* TO BE TRIFLED WITH.

"You use the word 'trifled' a lot, you know that?" Kera said, leaning back against the tree, "You should expand your vocabulary. Try saying something like 'shouldn't be messed with', or 'are not to be fucked with'." Kera's eyes suddenly widened, shining with euphoria and childish glee. "Ooh, say a swear word, Zeph! I want to hear you curse."

WHY WOULD I DO THAT? Zephelous asked. WE FACE POTENTIALLY MORTAL DANGER, AND RATHER THAN ASK MY ADVICE ON HOW WE

SHOULD PROCEED, YOU INSTEAD REQUEST THAT I UTTER A CURSE WORD?

"Ha, 'utter'," Kera said, giggling madly, "and yes, you heard me. Say one curse word and we'll do whatever you want for the rest of the day. Just one. I don't care which one. Make it a good one, though."

If Zephelous had a jaw to clench, it would have done so in frustration.

SURELY YOU CANNOT BE SERIOUS.

"Surely I *can* be serious," Kera said, mocking Zephelous's tone and diction.

YOU WILL NOT FLEE IMPENDING DOOM UNLESS I USE A CURSE WORD? Zephelous summarized, hardly believing the situation in which it found itself. WHAT IS WRONG WITH YOU THAT YOU VALUE YOUR LIFE SO LITTLE? HAVE YOU NO GOOD SENSE?

"Maybe I just value a good time over good sense," Kera said with a shrug. "Now, come on. Out with it! Say one swear and we'll run."

FINE, Zephelous conceded, sending a psychic mumble into Kera's mind, the words too indistinct to be heard.

"What was that?" Kera asked, putting a hand to her ear. "I didn't quite catch that, Zeph, you're going to have to speak up."

THIS IS MOST UNDIGNIFIED, Zephelous sputtered, I AM A WEAPON OF LEGEND, NOT SOME FOUL-MOUTHED TAVERN WENCH.

Kera clicked her tongue.

"'Wench' doesn't cut it," said Kera. A buzzing sound from somewhere deeper in the woods caught her attention.

"Better be quick about it, pointy-pants, sounds like something's coming."

I HAVE BEEN WIELDED BY HEROES AND DEMIGODS, Zephelous thought as it grumbled some more. *I HAVE HELPED CARVE PATHS THROUGH BLIGHTED LANDS AND FIGHT BACK AGAINST UNIMAGINABLE EVIL. WHAT HAVE I BEEN REDUCED TO NOW?*

At last, it conceded.

...ARSE, it sent, feeling ashamed of itself. I WAS FORGED TO SAVE LIVES AND TRAIN HEROES, NOT TO SPEAK PROFANITIES LIKE A CHILD. I HOPE YOU ARE SATISFIED NOW. MAY WE LEAVE?

Kera sucked air through her teeth.

"Arse is pretty lame as far as curse words go, but I'll allow it under the circumstances."

Still grinning wide, Kera turned away from the calamity and back towards where she came, only to find herself face to face with a radiant and beautiful woman.

Except she's not a woman, Kera thought, the fae ash in her system letting her see the magic glowing through the woman's skin. *She's faerie.*

The woman's skin was pale and smooth, brimming with orange as the magic shone through like glowing water shining through a woman-shaped tank. Armor made of gleaming chitin sat hovered in place over a dress made of flowing rose petals. A thin sword tinged green as if stained from cutting grass was drawn, pointed at Kera's face.

"Oh, hello," Kera said lamely, raising her hands up in surrender and revealing glittering fingertips.

She stared hard at Kera's eyes and its telltale sparks. After an uncomfortably long time, the faerie woman's eyes snapped shut in a distinctly insect way. She walked a slow circle around Kera, grass stained sword never wavering as she did.

Coming up behind Kera, she raised her sword and tapped it against the side of Zephelous. She paused, then moved back to stand in front of Kera.

"Do my eyes deceive me?" the fae woman asked, her voice musical and ethereal. Her every word seemed accompanied by a ghostly choir. "Is this Zephelous of the First Age I spy?"

Zephelous extended its senses outwards from Kera, reaching for the mind of the fae woman in an attempt to learn who she was. What it found was an old friend.

JILEERA KINGSGUARD? asked an incredulous Zephelous, sending a general telepathic broadcast in order to speak to Jileera.

The fae woman grimaced at Zephelous's message, her face gradually softening to a sad smile.

"I am Kingsguard no longer," said Jileera.

WHAT HAS HAPPENED TO KING VEIM?

"He died, murdered by the Toad King when he swept away the Opal Court."

THAT FIEND.

"The Toad King?" Kera repeated. "Really?"

"It has been an age," Jileera said to Zephelous, ignoring Kera. "I feared you lost, old friend, returned to the mainland with Theus perhaps."

"Old friend?" Kera repeated, "Zeph, do you know this woman?"

IF ONLY THAT WERE THE CASE, the sword said to Jileera, tones of defeat and sadness permeating its broadcast while it also ignored Kera. THEUS WAS KILLED IN A LANDSLIDE SOME WAYS FROM HERE. I WAS BURIED ALONGSIDE HIM."

Jileera's eyes went wide and she lowered her sword.

"Zephelous, that's awful. How long ago did this happen?"

NOT LONG AFTER WE LAST PARTED.

"And you were buried all this time, lying so close to here?" Jileera's shoulders sagged. "Zephelous, I'm so sorry. If I had known, I would have left the woods to come and find you. How did you stand it?"

Jileera stepped forward and reached for Zephelous. Kera took a reactive step back.

"Whoa, lady," she said, placing her free hand on Zephelous's grip, "It's cool that you know each other, but Zephie's mine fair and square. I have salvage rights."

Jileera froze in place. She looked to the sword, an eyebrow raised.

"*Zephie?*" the faerie woman repeated.

SHE HAS TAKEN TO ADDRESSING ME IN THAT MANNER, Zephelous explained, I DID NOT SUGGEST IT NOR DO I CARE FOR IT.

"I should imagine not," Jileera commented, "of all the heroes you've found your way into the hands of, this one strikes me as perhaps the most unusual. You allowed her to consume the fae ash?"

I COULD NOT HAVE PREVENTED HER FROM DOING SO IF I WANTED, Zephelous admitted. HER MIND IS FORMIDABLE.

"Yeah it is," said Kera. "Better watch out."

"How much did she consume?" Jileera asked.

"Enough," said Kera.

A FAIR AMOUNT TOO MUCH, said Zephelous.

"This seems distinctly unheroic, Zephelous," said Jileera.

"Whoa, easy," Kera countered. "Like I told Zeph, I'm not anybody's anything. I'm just a simple graverobber looking to make some coin."

Jileera's eyes narrowed into threatening slits and she ran the blade of her sword along Kera's ash-stained fingers.

"Indeed," she said, her tone serious. "Zephelous, surely you advised her that we are allies against--"

"The darkness that looms," Kera finished for her, rolling her eyes as she did. "Honestly doesn't shut up about it."

KERA, I WOULD ADVISE YOU TO CEASE SPEAKING.

"You advise a lot of things," Kera grumbled.

MOST OF WHICH YOU SEEM TO IGNORE.

"Well, stop being such a grump. Maybe I'll listen to you."

DO YOU REALIZE THAT IF YOU HAD HEEDED EVEN A SINGLE WARNING OR ACCEPTED A SOLITARY SUGGESTION I MADE ON THIS DAY, YOU WOULD BE IN A FAR BETTER POSITION AT THIS MOMENT.

"Do you hear yourself? *If you would have heeded even a single warning...* Nobody talks like that any more, Zephelous, it's 1220. Get with the times, grump."

Jileera followed this exchange, resting her hand on her chin as she did. When she'd had enough, she sheathed her sword and wove her hands in a gently curving motion, tracing a symbol through the air.

When she finished, she brought her hands together in a forceful clap that made no sound. The air around the trio shimmered as a ripple of magic passed through it.

"As amusing and concerning as this development has been, I have no time for it," Jileera began. "Don't try to respond, I've placed an enchantment of silence on both of you. Our laws are old and few - many of them have been broken here today. Zephelous, though your wielder may be willful, our laws see you as an accomplice in her transgressions - something you must have known would happen."

Kera tried to speak, but when she moved her mouth, no sound came out.

Good thing I don't need to make sound to say this, she thought, making a particularly rude hand gesture at Jileera. *Zephelous, can you hear me? Zephelous?*

Jileera blinked impassively at the hand gesture.

"Our laws say there is a price and it must be paid," Jileera said, floating closer to Kera.

The fae woman made a pulling gesture with her hand and Kera found herself entangled by vines. The vines wrapped themselves around her arms and legs, lifting her into the air and bringing her to follow behind Jileera, who was floating through the air towards the edge of the river.

"I will allow the pair of you to leave this place," the fae woman continued, "and I'll even allow you your... ill-gotten gains. As much as it pains me to do so, I feel it would be far more disrespectful to rebury them now."

Zephelous struggled to broadcast a thought, but failed. Jileera shrugged as if she could sense this, offering a sad smile.

"It hasn't been a kind century, old friend," Jileera said. "I'm afraid there's no other punishment that is suitable. Unless you'd prefer I kill her and take you, of course."

Jileera was quiet for a moment.

"I would never," she said at last, gesturing for the vines to bring Kera to the river and forcibly dunking her head into the stream. As Kera kicked and fought against the vines to no avail, Jileera took the bulging bag of fae ash from off Kera's belt, opening it carefully. Looking at the contents, she sighed heavily and dipped a finger. She commanded the vines bring the struggling graverobber up and out of the water.

Kera coughed and spluttered without making a sound, glaring at Jileera all the while. Jileera smiled back and pushed a liberal amount of fae ash into Kera's eyes. She then closed the bag and put it back into Kera's belt.

"I wish you luck on your ongoing quest, Zephelous," Jileera said, commanding the vines to drop Kera on the far side of the river. "I hope, for your sake, that your destiny has not failed you this time."

Kera sat up. Her eyes were glassy spirals of light and a slack jawed grin hung on her face. The world around her was a spiraling haze of color and light. She began to stumble her way out of the woods, chest and shoulders heaving with silent laughter.

Chapter Four

KERA--

"Shh... too loud," Kera groaned, pressing her hands to her temples. The inside of her skull felt like it was trying to bludgeon its way out and Zephelous's booming psychic voice did nothing to help the matter.

"Has no one ever taught you how to whisper?" Kera sat herself up, feeling her body ache every bit as much as her head. The world around her began to spin quickly, too quickly, an overwhelming feeling of nausea making the olive undertones in the skin of the gravedigger turn a vibrant green. She closed her eyes. It didn't help. She turned her head to the side and retched.

YOU ARE UNWELL, KERA NO-CLAN, Zephelous commented, concern apparent in its tone.

"No shit," Kera mumbled, using her hand to wipe stray vomit from her lips before flinging it away. She opened her eyes cautiously, taking stock of her surroundings.

The room she was in was small, no more than ten feet by ten feet and had no visible entrance or exit. The room was dimly lit, but the source of the light wasn't immediately apparent to Kera. After her third time scanning the room in search of a torch, she realized where it was coming from.

The walls are glowing, she thought. *Magic is bullshit.*

She tried to stand, but her legs wouldn't hold her weight. Her attempt made them shake and collapse, bringing her back down to the ground. She held her hands out in front of her face to see if they were shaking too. They were.

"Gods-damn fae ash," she muttered.

IF ONLY SOMEONE HAD REPEATEDLY ADVISED YOU AGAINST CONSUMING SUCH A SUBSTANCE, Zephelous remarked, YOU CAN BARELY STAND IN YOUR PRESENT STATE, NEVERMIND TRYING TO FIGHT.

"Well, what was I supposed to do?" Kera asked. "Stand by and let that stupid calamity get away with being a dick?"

IF BY 'BEING A DICK,' YOU MEAN TO SAY USING ITS NATURAL TALENTS IN AN EFFORT TO WARD OFF YOUR INTENTIONS TO UNEARTH AND CONSUME THE REMAINS OF ITS KIN, THEN YES.

Zephelous's tone was measured as it continued to admonish the impetuous grave robber. FURTHERMORE, WHEN APPROACHED BY THE FAE-KIN WARRIOR--

"What fuckin' warrior?"

I SAID *FAE-KIN*, NOT... THAT.

"Not what?"

THAT WORD.

"Which word?"

THE ONE YOU USE SO *VERY* FREQUENTLY.

"I use a lot of words frequently. You'll have to be a bit more specific."

ARE YOU ONCE AGAIN ATTEMPTING TO GOAD ME INTO CURSING?

"Only if it works."

IT WILL NOT.

"Damn. It was worth a shot. But seriously, what warrior?"

YOU DO NOT RECALL OUR ENCOUNTER WITH JILEERA?

"Who?"

JILEERA, THE FORMER KINGSGUARD, NOW THE WILDKEEPER.

"Yeah, listen - a list of titles really isn't as helpful as you might think it is," Kera grumbled, pressing her palms into her aching eyes.

The tremors in her hands had subsided a little, but not by much.

Kera took a deep breath and tried to stand again. She discovered that while her legs were wobbly and uncooperative, they would hold her weight so long as she braced herself against the wall behind her. Staggering her way to the far end of the room, Kera put as much distance between herself and the foul-smelling puddle of vomit as she could, letting her back slide down the wall until she was sitting once again. Her head felt like a drum being used to pound out a dwarven war song.

Ba-BOOM, ba-BOOM, ba-BOOM, ba-BOOM.

"Gods, I feel like death," Kera groaned, her mouth nauseatingly hot and dry. She let her eyes crawl around the room once more, looking at the floor this time.

"Do you see water anywhere, Zeph? Because I do not."

I LACK EYES, KERA NO-CLAN. I CANNOT 'SEE' ANYTHING.

"You know what I mean, you big grump," Kera said, giving Zephelous's pommel a flick as she did. "So, what happened with this wild warrior I supposedly met?"

SHE CONFRONTED YOU FOR UNEARTHING THE REMAINS OF THE FAIRIES BURIED IN THE GROVE.

"Checks out so far. Then what?"

SHE ADMONISHED YOU AND FORCED YOU INTO THE WARDED WATERS, PLACING A GEAS UPON YOU.

"What's that?"

A MAGICAL COMPULSION, A COMMAND THAT CANNOT BE RESISTED.

"She cursed me, then."

CURSES ARE DARK MAGICS THAT NEGATIVELY AFFECT THOSE THEY ARE PLACED UPON.

"I didn't want to end up in jail with a hangover," Kera countered. "Those are two pretty big negatives, which really makes this geas thing seem like a curse."

IT IS *NOT* A CURSE.

"If you say so. Was she pretty?"

I HAVE NO WAY TO ADEQUATELY GAUGE THIS.

"Oh, c'mon, Zeph," Kera said with a frown. "Centuries of hanging around with all these 'heroes of legend' and you have no concept of ferocious but beautiful battle maidens or ravishing and deadly warrior princesses?"

I AM FAMILIAR WITH FEROCITY AND DEADLINESS, said Zephelous. BEAUTY AS A CONCEPT SEEMS HIGHLY SUBJECTIVE.

"You're impossible to talk to."

WE SEEM TO BE CONVERSING JUST FINE.

Kera sighed.

"Let's try it this way - did you ever encounter any of those women?"

I WAS WIELDED BY BRIGITTE LIONSIRE FOR A TIME, said Zephelous. FROM WHAT I GATHER SHE WAS CONSIDERED TO BE THE EPITOME OF BEAUTY IN ALL THE REALM WHILE SHE LIVED.

"Lionsire… as in, the Lion of War?"

YES, THE VERY SAME, Zephelous responded eagerly, thrilled to have found some common ground with Kera at last. SHE WIELDED ME IN THE GREAT CAMPAIGN TO DEFEAT THE FORCES OF GRELGEROS THE DEPTHLORD.

"Whoever that is," Kera muttered under her breath.

HOW IS IT YOU KNOW OF THE LION OF WAR, BUT KNOW NOTHING ABOUT WHAT IS WIDELY CONSIDERED TO BE HER MOST HEROIC ADVENTURE?

"I'm a graverobber, Zeph. I know lots of stuff about lots of dead people."

AND WHAT DO YOU KNOW OF BRIGITTE?

"Uh, well, she was called the Lion of War," Kera began.

YES, AND?

"Tall, brunètte, blonde highlights, light brown skin, great smile…"

I AM IMPRESSED AND CONFUSED.

"I have that effect on people."

HOW IS IT YOU ARE SO FAMILIAR WITH HER?

"I, ah, acquired some paintings of her a few years ago."

WAS SHE WIELDING ME IN ANY OF THE PAINTINGS? I GREATLY ENJOYED MY TIME WITH HER. SHE WAS AN EXCELLENT STUDENT WHO BECAME A TRUE MASTER OF COMBAT.

"She was not, actually."

OH, Zephelous responded, saddened to hear this. PERHAPS THE DEPICTION WAS BEFORE HER TIME WITH ME. SHE WAS QUITE ADEPT WITH A MAUL AND SHIELD, THE WEAPONS OF HER HOUSE. I ASSUME THOSE WERE DEPICTED?

"Yeah, no. Those weren't there either."

I DO NOT UNDERSTAND, said Zephelous, feeling deeply confused. WHAT WAS SHE HOLDING IN THE PORTRAITS IF NOT ME OR THE ARMS OF HER HOUSE?

"It's, ah, hard to describe," said Kera. "It was also a while ago and I ended up selling them back to the guy I stole them from."

IS IT A WEAPON YOU DO NOT KNOW THE NAME OF? YOUR PSYCHIC SHIELDING IS WEAK IN YOUR PRESENT STATE, GIVE ME A MOMENT AND I WILL VISIT YOUR MEMORIES AND UNCOVER IT FOR YOU.

"Yeaaah, you don't have to do that," Kera said with a grimace. "It's really not a big deal and it probably wasn't her anyway, so…"

IT IS NO TROUBLE, said Zephelous. I HAVE ALREADY… OH.

"Yeah."

I SEE.

"Yeaaah."

While Zephelous' sentience allowed it to experience emotions, it had never before felt embarrassment quite like this. It made a mental note to add that to the ever-growing list of 'first time' experiences it had acquired so far in its brief time with Kera No-Clan.

"So," Kera said while clearing her throat, "would you say Jileera was about as attractive as Brigitte?"

I AM NOT CERTAIN HOW TO MAKE A COMPARISON, AS I HAVE ONLY EVER SEEN JILEERA WITH HER CLOTHES ON.

"Well, yeah, but... wait, was that a joke?" Kera asked, a smile creeping across her face. "Did you just bust my chops a little?"

I DID NOT INTEND TO DAMAGE YOUR CHOPS.

"Of course not."

IT HAS BEEN SOME TIME SINCE I EXPERIENCED A MOMENT OF LEVITY LIKE THIS ONE, said Zephelous. THEUS OFTEN USED HUMOUR WHEN WE FACED DIRE STRAITS.

"I'm not sure that you taking a peek into a dirty corner of my mind counts as being in dire straits, but I'm all for you being less of an old grump of a sword."

I'M AFRAID YOUR SHOCKINGLY EXPLICIT COLLECTION OF PAINTINGS IS NOT THE REASON I REFER TO OUR PRESENT SITUATION AS DIRE.

As Zephelous spoke, a section of the wall opposite Kera slid backwards, moving on rails to reveal a nearly perfect seam. It then rolled to the side, revealing an entrance beyond which two hulking armored figures. They entered the room with polearms at the ready, tips pointed squarely at Kera. Their armor was black and red scalemail, which glinted menacingly in the soft light.

"You must be Dire and Straits," Kera quipped.

A third figure wearing black and red robes with the hood drawn rather than armor, entered the room behind the huge guardsmen. At less than a quarter of the height of the lumbering armored warriors, Kera struggled to suppress a snicker.

He's got to be either a gnome or a halfling, Kera thought, *I won't be able to tell until he lowers that hood.*

When the figure pulled back its hood, he revealed himself as a gnome whose face was a veritable map of wrinkles. Deep lines ran all the way from his chin to his receded hairline. A few wisps of fine silver hair drifted freely on top of a head that was otherwise bald.

With a pronounced throat clearing sound, the old gnome produced a scroll nearly as wide as he was tall and unfurled it, letting it roll away on the floor. He then reached into the pockets of his robe and produced a pair of golden pince-nez glasses and perched them on his bulbous nose before beginning to read.

"Kera No-Clan," the gnome began, his high-pitched voice grating on Kera's ears, adding yet another layer to the pain she felt in her head.

"You stand accused of a number of crimes against both the city and the peoples of Zelwyr."

"Zelwyr?" Kera echoed, "what the hell am I doing in Zelwyr?"

A GOOD AMOUNT OF CRIME, IT SEEMS, said Zephelous.

"I got that, thanks."

"Pardon me?" the gnome asked.

"Nothing," said Kera. "Get on with it."

Clearing his throat once more, the gnome repositioned the parchment in front of his face, obscuring all but the top of his head as he began to read.

"Kera No-Clan, in the week since your arrival here in Zelwyr, you have committed - and are being charged for committing - fourteen counts of destruction of property--"

"I'm sorry, did you say four*teen*? I'm sure you meant four, but I heard *fourteen*."

Moving the parchment aside, the gnome scowled at Kera.

"You heard correctly," he said, glaring at her for a moment longer before ducking back behind the parchment. "As I was saying, fourteen counts of destruction of property, three counts of arson, two counts of theft, five counts of burgling, two counts of rioting, and one count of inciting a tavern brawl. How do you plead?"

"Uhhh," Kera said, drawing a blank. "Zeph?"

"'Zeph' is not a recognized plea," the gnome said with another scowl.

"Zephelous?"

"'Zephelous' is also not an acceptable plea. You may respond by saying either 'guilty' or 'not guilty'. In your case, I would advise--"

"I'll get to you in a minute, little hand of the law," said Kera. The gnome flushed and began to sputter a response, but Kera ignored him. "Zephelous, what the hells?"

WHILE UNDER THE INFLUENCE OF FAE ASH AND THE GEAS OF JILEERA, YOU DID INDEED COMMIT MANY OF THESE CRIMES, Zephelous said. I ATTEMPTED TO STOP YOU ON SEVERAL OCCASIONS, BUT COULD NOT OVERCOME YOUR PSYCHIC SHIELDING.

"You didn't even try to talk me out of it?"

I COULD NOT HAVE BROKEN THE GEAS IF I HAD TRIED, KERA NO-CLAN, Zephelous said, a defeated tone permeating its words. THAT SAID, I TRIED TO ADVISE YOU AGAINST ESCALATING YOUR SHENANIGANS SEVERAL TIMES.

"And?"

YOUR TYPICAL RESPONSE WAS 'GET BENT, POINTY-PANTS'.

"That... makes sense, unfortunately. What happens now?"

"What happens now, young lady," the gnome interjected, "is that you face the trial you quite vehemently requested, the one you invoked by citing laws so ancient that even *I* had forgotten them."

"A trial, that's fine," said Kera. "I've been in front of a few juries. I'll just tearfully explain to the magistrate that I was under the effects of a fairy curse and that I fell and landed in some fae ash. I'll get assigned some community service, which I'll *absolutely* do and *not at all* bail on the first chance I get. Everything will work out."

The gnome rolled the parchment back up with a sinister smile on his face.

"I'm afraid that won't be the case."

"I thought you said I was getting a trial?" Kera asked.

"I did," said the gnome. "But I didn't specify that it would be a court trial. In fact, it will be quite the opposite, as you so *vehemently* requested."

"Oh gods," Kera groaned, "don't say it." The gnome rocked on his heels.

I have a distinct feeling that I know exactly what words are going to come out of this guy's mouth, Kera thought, *and I'm pretty sure I'm going to hate it.*

"As requested, yours will be a trial by combat," the gnome announced, looking far too pleased with himself for Kera's liking. "You will be expected to face off against a champion selected by the chief plaintiff. Because the bulk of the damage was done to the town itself, I claim that right as Steward of Zelwyr."

"Oh, for fuck's sake," Kera cursed. "Why didn't you stop me from doing this, Zeph?"

IT WAS MY SUGGESTION THAT PROMPTED YOU DO SO.

"Of course it was," Kera said, puffing the air out of her lungs. "When does this whole 'trial by combat' begin, exactly?"

The pounding in her head hadn't subsided; it made forming a coherent thought almost impossible. It also made this conversation agonizing. She wanted nothing more than to close her eyes and sleep for days, somewhere far away from this mean little gnome and his awful voice.

Far away from Zephelous too, she thought. *This is what I get for digging up a talking sword. I really should have known better...*

She realized then that the gnome was smiling at her; something about the way the corners of his lips were turned upwards a little *too* sharply told Kera she wasn't going to like what he had to say.

"The trial begins in fifteen minutes."

"*Fifteen minutes?*" Kera repeated, feeling a surge of concern.

 "As in, fifteen minutes from *now*?"

"I believe you'll find that's typically what someone means when they say 'in fifteen minutes.'"

"Zephelous!?"

"You keep saying that word--"

"I do and it keeps not being directed at you," said Kera. "Zephelous, what the *fuck* did you sign me up for?"

The elderly gnome bristled, his face flush with either embarrassment or anger. With a grumble and a snap of his fingers, he wordlessly commanded the armored men to take point on Kera. They advanced towards her, each armored foot fall a cacophony of noise that assaulted Kera's hangover. One of the guards maneuvered behind her and used the shaft of his halberd to prod Kera forward, making her fall in step behind the other guard while she was herded past the grinning gnome and out of the room.

THE COMBAT WILL BE FINE SO LONG AS YOU ALLOW ME CONTROL.

With little choice but to allow herself to be herded down the narrow stone corridor, Kera did her best to take in as many details as she could: the walls and floor were stone and looked ancient, with sconces hanging on the walls every few feet between paintings that depicted scenes from battles Kera didn't recognize.

The smell of her vomit still lingered in the air.

I haven't seen a window yet, she thought. *I'm willing to bet that smell lingers for a looong time.*

"Control of what, exactly?"

"I beg your pardon?" the gnome asked.

"Still not talking to you," Kera said to the gnome, offering a fake smile.

CONTROL OF YOU, OVER YOUR MOTOR FUNCTIONS AND REFLEXES, Zephelous explained. I HAVE OFTEN ACTED ON MY WIELDER'S BEHALF IN TIMES WHEN THEY HAVE BEEN INCAPACITATED.

"Are you saying I'm incapacitated?"

YES, said Zephelous, YOU ARE ABOUT TO VOMIT.

"Yeah right, I feel perfectly fi--"

Kera's stomach turned. Acidic bile made its way up her throat and into her mouth. Fighting the urge to spew it all across the floor, she clenched her jaw shut and swallowed, her eyes watering as she did.

"See?" Kera said. "I'm fine. Completely fine."

THAT WAS AN UNNECESSARY DISPLAY OF BRAVADO, Zephelous said grimly. IT WAS ALSO DEEPLY UNSETTLING.

"You're deeply unsettling."

A MOST WISE RETORT.

"You're a most wise... shut up."

Kera pressed her fingers into her eyes, applying just enough pressure that it helped soothe the drumming. The spinning of the world around her slowed, but dehydration still dulled her senses.

"Is there any chance I can get some water before we do this?" she asked, speaking to her armored escorts and their diminutive leader.

They ignored her entirely.

"Hello? Anyone, anybody?"

"My *deepest* apologies, Kera No-Clan," the gnome said, poking his head around the legs of the man in front of Kera to mock her. "I hadn't realized you were finished speaking to yourself. Perhaps I should say yourselves? Am I speaking to Kera or Zephelous at the moment?"

"It's actually a '*ph*' sound," Kera corrected, her tone sickly sweet, "as in, 'Ze-*phe*-lous' or 'go *ph*-uck yourself.'"

The gnome glared at her, but the guards chuckled.

Wordlessly, he turned away and continued marching.

These guys like jokes, Kera thought to herself, *maybe I can use this.*

"I'll take that as a 'no' on the water," she called out in exaggerated loudness.

Zephelous, I'm too hung over to remember my jokes. Do you have any?

THIS IS LIKELY NOT THE TIME TO BE MAKING JOKES.

This is probably the single best possible time to be making jokes, Kera corrected. *A little reprieve would go a long way right now.*

I SUPPOSE, Zephelous conceded, THAT SAID, WHAT IN OUR BRIEF HISTORY TOGETHER MAKES YOU BELIEVE I WOULD HAVE A JOKE FOR YOU?

Fair enough.

"Hey, have you folks ever heard the ballad about the half-orc knight who went searching for the valley filled with beautiful orc maidens?" Kera began, smiling in spite of herself. "He quested for years and couldn't find it, so he sought out the wisest sage in all the land for advice."

"'*Good sage,* he asked, *I seek the fabled valley of beauteous orcs.*' The sage stroked his beard while pondering the knight's question. '*I'm sorry, good knight,*' the sage said once he'd finished thinking. '*I'm just not sure the female orc chasm exists.*'"

Both guards snickered at this; the one behind her barely suppressing his hearty *ah-huh, ah-huh, ah-huh* of a laugh.

YOU HAVE SIGNIFICANTLY RAISED YOUR STANDING IN THE EYES OF THESE GUARDS, Zephelous remarked.

I could have told you that, Kera thought back.

"Female orc chasm," the gnome muttered, "there's no such thing."

"I pity your wife," said Kera.

The guards erupted with laughter. The gnome turned around and held up a commanding hand in an effort to silence their laughter, which failed miserably. He shook with anger, the veins under the skin of his neck and forehead bulging out.

The gnome threw up his hands and stormed ahead a few feet, hopping up to grab a lever on the wall and pull it down. Another part of the wall slid away, but instead of revealing another cell, this began to let brilliant sunlight shine through its opening. The ground was a lake-sized patch of sand, the border of which was high stone walls.

The guards prodded her through the opening and into the scorching heat beyond, forcing Kera to shield her eyes against the sudden intense brightness. They were still snickering at her joke, much to the gnome's displeasure. Blinking rapidly in an effort to help her eyes adjust faster, Kera stumbled a few feet into the sand. The heat and sunlight seemed to double as she stepped out of the shadow of the wall behind her. Her body ached for water.

"What do you say, folks?" Kera said, turning back to the guards. "It's not much of a final request, but how about some water before I die?"

Still chuckling, the larger of the two guards untied a wineskin from his belt and threw it into the sand at Kera's feet. Kera bent and snatched it up eagerly, unscrewing the top as fast as her hands would let her. She poured it into her mouth so aggressively that she almost choked. The water inside was room temperature, but clean and crisp. She drank until she couldn't swallow any more, then poured some on to her forehead. Her stomach settled, her body rejoicing at being given a liquid that wasn't booze. Wiping a dribble of water from her chin, she looked back at the guard and extended the container towards him, offering to throw it back.

The armored man shook his head.

"You can give it back to me if you don't die," he said, his voice deep and his diction sounding somewhat childish to Kera.

"What if I do die?" Kera asked.

"I'll just take it back off your corpse, I suppose."

"That's mighty altruistic of you," said Kera, taking another drink.

"I don't know about that," said the guard, reaching for the lever once more, "but I do like being honest."

"I can see that."

"Have a good fight."

"I probably won't."

"No," the guard responded with a heavy tone, "You probably will not."

With that, he flipped the lever upwards, the door sliding back into place.

Kera spun slowly in a circle, nursing the wineskin all the while. The walls around her served as the base for an amphitheatre, one that looked shabby and in state of disrepair. Seating space that could have held a thousand spectators only held under a dozen presently. One of them coughed. Another was noisily chewing on something.

"Huh," said Kera, relaxing. The almost non-existent crowd and the general sense of disinterest in the arena gave her hope.

Not what I was expecting, she thought. *This might be okay.*

ARE YOU ALSO DISAPPOINTED? Zephelous asked.

"Why the hells would I be disappointed?" Kera asked, squinting as she scanned the arena, looking to see if she could spot an exit or her opponent. Seeing neither, she shrugged and drained the last of the wineskin.

SURELY YOU KNOW OF THIS PLACE, DO YOU NOT? Zephelous asked, a sense of longing permeating its broadcast. THIS PLACE WAS ONCE A SHIELD FOR THE ENTIRE REALM. LATER, IT WAS A PLACE WHERE WARS WERE SETTLED WITH DOZENS OF TROOPS RATHER THAN THOUSANDS. LATER STILL, IT SERVED AS HEADQUARTERS FOR THE FORCES OF GOOD ALLIED AGAINST--

"Don't you dare finish that sentence," Kera said. "I am too hungover for your crap. You're going to make my head explode."

IMPOSSIBLE, said Zephelous, pausing for a moment before continuing. AT THE VERY LEAST, HIGHLY UNLIKELY.

The telltale sound of the gnome clearing his throat somewhere behind her made Kera turn. Looking up at the stands, she saw the steward standing at a podium that overlooked the arena. She noticed a small set of stairs that led up to the pulpit. She would have laughed if she wasn't positive that it would have made her puke.

"Honorable citizens of Zelwyr," the gnome began.

Kera glanced at the stands once more, counting even less people than before.

I feel like these are less the honorable citizens than the ones who have nothing better to do, she thought.

"The purpose of this gathering is for us all to bear witness to the trial by singular combat requested by the criminal called Kera No-Clan, as is her right. As steward, I have taken the privilege of naming the champion to fight on behalf of Zelwyr. I name Bas Maxus."

The steward flashed a beaming grin at Kera and sat back expectantly.

The arena was still for a long while with only noisy munching as background.

"So, uh," Kera said, breaking the silence, "this means I'm free to go, right?"

"Of course not," the jailer spat. "Where is Bas?"

"How should I know?" Kera asked. "He's your champion, not mine."

"What makes you think I would be asking you?" the jailer hissed.

I bet if I tried hard enough, I could count the veins on that guy's head, Kera thought to herself.

"Charles!" the gnome shouted.

"Here, my lord," said the guard, his voice revealing him to be the same one who had given Kera the water. He shifted his bulk to turn towards the podium.

"What is it?"

"Where is Bas?" the gnome demanded, hands balled into tiny fists. "The executioner needs to be present for an execution."

"Technically, my lord, it's only a trial," Charlie said. "It's really only an execution if she ends up dying."

"If Bas isn't here, go and fetch Arlene.

"Oh," said Charlie, "I guess it is an execution, then."

Kera put her fingers in her mouth and blew a whistle, regretting the ear-splitting noise immediately. Charlie turned to face her. She held up the waterskin, making her intention to throw it clear. Charlie lifted an armored hand to catch it as Kera wound up and lobbed the wineskin in his direction. Her aim was good, but instead of hitting Charlie's hand, it hit him in the chest and ricocheted towards the gnome and hit him on the back of the head.
Kera snorted.

"Sorry about that," she shouted.

"That's alright," Charlie called back, bending over to pick up his container. He gave his armor a quick slap. "I didn't feel a thing. This armour's pretty well built."

"She was talking to me, you gigantic idiot," the steward barked.

"But your lordship," said Charlie, "why would she be talking to you when it's my wineskin?"

The steward trembled with rage and Kera couldn't help herself from smiling.

"Fetch. Arlene. *Now.*"

"Well, alright," said Charlie, "but just so you know, it might take me awhile. Shouldn't be more than a month or so. Arlene's on vacation at the capitol, but I'll go and fetch her at once."

"And you didn't think to mention that earlier?" the gnome said, banging his head on the podium.

"You didn't ask me where she was, your lordship, you only asked me to fetch her." The jailer dug his fingernails into the skin of his cheeks, pulling so forcefully that Kera she could see him scratching his skin raw.

"Get in the arena," the steward said at last.

"But your lordship," the guard said, "I'm not Arlene."

"*Do you really think I don't know that, you simpleton?*" the steward shouted, "just get *in* there and *kill her.* After today, a part of me hopes you die."

"If you say so, your lordship," said Charlie.

Without so much as another word, the massive guard turned and walked straight forward towards the area, ignoring the ten foot fall from the stands to the arena floor entirely. He landed on his feet so firmly and with so little recovery that Kera couldn't help but let her jaw fall open a little.

"That was quite the entrance," she said. "Do you fight in the arena a lot?"

"Not really," said Charlie, walking towards her as he spoke.

"Mum says I've been falling off of things since I was a baby. I guess I just got good at it, is all."

"That makes a certain amount of sense, sure," said Kera, moving away from Charlie as quickly as he advanced. "Any ideas, Zephelous?"

"My name is Charles, actually. But, you can call me Charlie." The guard reached over his shoulder and drew a colossal sword that seemed to Kera like it was as long as she was tall. The weapon must have weighed in the dozens of pounds, but it seemed weightless in the guard's hands.

"It's nice to officially meet you, Charles," said Kera, "Say, here's an idea. How about instead of trying to kill each other, we just call it a tie?"

The question stopped Charles in his tracks. He seemed to consider Kera's offer, turning around to face the jailer.

"Sounds okay to me," he said. "What about you, Ombard?"

The gnome's face flushed red, then white, then purple.

"Cut. her. in. *Half.* "

Charles shrugged and turned back to face Kera.

"Sorry, Kera," he said. "No ties today."

Charlie whirled the huge sword around himself in a series of sweeping motions, crossing it this way and that in front of his body as he continued to advance towards Kera.

"It's a shame, really," Charlie continued. "You seem pretty nice when you aren't burning down libraries, bakeries, and taverns."

"That's what they say," Kera said, speaking quickly, her eyes watching every potentially deadly motion of the massive blade with growing unease.

Zephelous, now would be a great time to be talkative, she thought.

I REQUIRE A MOMENT, KERA, said Zephelous, I AM PREPARING.

Preparing for what? Kera responded.

YOU WILL SEE SHORTLY, said Zephelous. WE ARE NOT FULLY ATTUNED, THIS MAY NOT WORK AS ANTICIPATED. PLEASE TRY NOT TO RESIST.

Why don't I like the sound of this? Kera thought.

Suddenly, the world around her seemed to slow to a crawl. Kera felt detached, like another observer in the mostly empty arena.

Charlie leaned forward and charged like a bull, closing the distance between them at an alarming speed even in the slow time crawl. He swung his huge sword around in a vicious arc towards her midsection. Kera could hear the steel of the sword thrumming as the cleaving strike came closer to hitting home.

Holy gods, Kera thought, *he really is going to cut me in half.*

To her surprise, Kera watched herself throw her hips backwards, using the movement to evade the strike. Her hands brought Zephelous upwards at a sharp angle, the edge of the enchanted sword snapping into the back of Charlie's titanic sword. Charlie over-corrected and stumbled, staggering backwards slowly.

Are you doing this, Zephelous?

YES, I HAD THOUGHT IT WOULD BE OBVIOUS.

You didn't think to mention you could control time?

TIME IS BEYOND MY ABILITY TO CONTROL, said Zephelous. I AM MERELY ALTERING THE MANNER IN WHICH YOU PERCEIVE ITS PASSAGE.

Charlie corrected his posture and stomped toward her again, swinging his sword over his shoulders in a downward slash. Once again, Zephelous's edge slapped the sword away. With a grace she knew she didn't possess in her hungover state, Kera watched as she crouched low and spun, bringing Zephelous around in a sweeping arc towards the back of the guard's knees.

From her vantage point in slow time, Kera felt dread.

Don't cut his legs off, Zeph, she commanded mentally. *This far up north, that might not kill him outright, but it may as well.*

NEED I REMIND YOU THAT HE IS HERE TO KILL YOU? Zephelous asked. I SUSPECT IT IS NOT A PERSONAL AFFAIR FOR HIM EITHER. IN YOUR PRESENT STATE YOU DO NOT HAVE THE STAMINA FOR A LENGTHY DUEL. I HAVE NOTED THAT CREATURES WHO SUDDENLY LOSE TWO OR MORE LIMBS IN COMBAT ARE QUICK TO SURRENDER.

How often do they die afterwards?

FAIRLY OFTEN, I MUST ADMIT.

Can we win without killing him?

I UNDERSTOOD YOU TO BE AN UNSCRUPULOUS GRAVE ROBBER, Zephelous said. I AM PLEASED TO SEE THAT YOU DO INDEED POSSESS SOME SCRUPLES.

That can't possibly be the right way to say that, Kera said. *Listen, I want to walk away from this and I'd like it if he could be allowed to limp away.*

VERY WELL.

Hands more used to holding a shovel than a blade twisted the grip of the sword, bringing the flat of the blade to smack Charlie's legs rather than the edge.

I'm starting to like that move, Kera thought.

IT WOULD BE BETTER IF YOU STOPPED TALKING, said Zephelous.

Charles lost his balance and stumbled forward, the hulking guard moving several feet away in his effort to remain standing.

Charles recovered and paused to take a breath, giving Kera a moment of reprieve. The huge man adjusted his grip on his sword and thundered towards her once again. Kera sank low to the ground, holding Zephelous behind her in a reverse grip. In a move she wasn't sure she could have done while sober, Kera watched as she waited until Charlie was just a few feet from her before she sprang. She dove between the man's legs. Charlie tripped and dropped to one knee. She tumbled and rose, spinning her upper body to stab at Charlie, Zephelous's magically sharpened tip piercing clean through the guard's armour and into his shoulder.

Not too deep! Kera hissed. *You're going to kill him if you're not careful.*

THIS MAN SHOWS NO SIGNS OF RESTRAINT, KERA, Zephelous said. I APPRECIATE YOUR HESITATION TO END A LIFE, BUT THIS IS A TRIAL BY COMBAT AND IT MAY WELL BE HIM OR YOU.

Don't make it him, Kera said, *and don't let it be me.*

HOW VERY HELPFUL, KERA NO-CLAN.

If I don't die, remind me to commend you on being sarcastic, Kera thought.

IF YOU DO NOT DIE, I WILL COMMEND YOU FOR PROPER USE OF THE WORD 'COMMEND', said Zephelous. BRACE YOURSELF.

Kera watched as Charles adjusted his grip on the massive sword in his hands, moving the weight of the weapon away from his wounded shoulder. The massive guard still looked like an imposing threat, but Kera felt confident that they would win if the sword continued to guide her.

Brace myself for what? Kera thought.

YOU WILL SEE.

Charles whirled his sword around over his head like a rotor, making Kera duck low. He got back to his feet and brought the sword swinging downwards at her once more. Kera threw herself to the right, rolling in a short tumble that ended with her in a kneeling position, planting Zephelous on the ground to stabilize herself.

That wasn't so bad, Kera thought.

THAT WAS NOT IT, said Zephelous. THIS IS.

The moment Zephelous finished speaking, Kera felt a searing agony unlike any pain she had felt before. A heat stole the air from her lungs and filled her veins with fire, dimming her vision. Her every muscle strained from having been bent, stretched, and twisted in ways it hadn't been prepared to do. Her arms, unused to Zephelous's weight, felt numb and heavy, hanging limply at her sides.

Hungover as she was, this new wave of pain made Kera feel like she was dying.

Zephelous, she thought, *what the fuck?*

I AM SORRY, KERA NO-CLAN, Zephelous said. I HAD HOPED WE COULD RENDER HIM UNCONSCIOUS PRIOR TO THIS.

Kera fell forward and puked, discharging her stomach contents all over herself, Zephelous, and the ground around them.

You might be the worst magic sword of all time.

I HAVE BEEN TOLD THIS BEFORE, said Zephelous.

Struggling to breathe and fighting her own body on every breath, Kera managed to push herself up on to her feet, brushing the vomit off her hands. Through blurred vision, she watched Charles's head tilt inquisitively at her. The man's huge helmet made him look like a curious bear.

ARE YOU CERTAIN THAT I CANNOT KILL HIM?

Kera spat in an effort to get the taste out of her mouth, bringing a trembling hand up to her mouth to wipe the spittle and foam on her lips onto her sleeve. Charles was saying something to the gnome steward, but Kera's senses didn't register the words.

It sounds like a trombone having a conversation with an owl, she thought, *the little hooting kind from back home.* She felt delirious and would have laughed if she could but managed only a drooling smile instead.

The owl was hooting very quickly at the trombone now, hopping up and down on its little podium. Charlie the trombone rumbled something back, but this seemed to make the owl very angry. It knocked the podium over and hooted all the louder. The trombone made a defeated sound; Charles started lumbering towards her.

In Kera's eyes, Charlie was so big he blocked out the sun.

Don't cut down the tree, Kera struggled to think to the sword, *just trim the branches a little so the light shines through.*

BASED ON OUR PRESENT CIRCUMSTANCES, I BELIEVE I UNDERSTAND.

Kera's breathing suddenly steadied, her hands feeling a warmth radiating from Zephelous's handle.

More of this, she thought.

FALSE VITALITY, said Zephelous. IT WILL NOT LAST.

Charlie, still looming over her, hoisted his sword over Kera, the gargantuan weapon hanging like a guillotine blade.

Kera exhaled, firming up her grip on Zephelous as tight as she could. She hopped up onto her feet and leaped, a sideways tumble that had her springing to safety, Zephelous's blade trailing behind her. Charlie's swing came down as Zephelous went up, but Kera's sword snuck in behind the guardsman's and rose further still. Ancient dwarven starmetal cut through Charlie's bracers and wrists like a hot knife through butter. Kera landed in a cat-like stance, both feet and one hand on the ground while the other held Zephelous aloft and at the ready behind her.

Charlie fell to his knees screaming, pressing his bloody stumps together as they oozed with red, staining the sands beneath his feet.

She averted her eyes and tried to deafen herself to the man's piteous cries, turning her head to the stands as she rose to her feet.

"Come and get your champion," she said, visibly wobbling in place.

The little owl hooted and the other guard rushed to Charlie's aid. The temporary burst of adrenaline Zephelous gave her wore off, and exhaustion called to her.

"I think I'm gonna," she began, trailing off as she sat down and let herself lay flat on the sands. "I think I'm gonna take a nap, Zeph. Keep an eye on them."

KERA--

"I know, I know," Kera said dreamily, "you have no eyes."

Kera let her head roll to the side and came face to face with Charles' over-sized sword, his severed hands still clutching the handle. She grimaced and rolled her head the other way. The world around her became darker and a creeping numbness spread inward from her fingertips to the rest of her body.

Kera's grip on Zephelous loosened, then failed entirely. The sentient weapon dropped gently to the sand beside her. The world disappeared entirely; Kera fell into a deep slumber. She dreamt of dark forests filled with the scent of pine, the sound of hooting owls, of starry nights under open skies.

Like every night, she dreamt of fire.

Chapter Five

Kera woke with a start to the sound of a rooster crowing.

She sat up immediately and was surprised to find herself in a bed - a full sized one, with blankets and pillows.

"This doesn't look like jail," she said, "where are we, Zeph?"

There was no answer. Frowning, she looked around to see where the sword was. The sudden creak of a nearby floorboard made her heart skip; in a flash she reached for the dagger at her back. Drawing it instinctively, she brought it around to point at the source of the sound, her shoulders and arms radiating with pain in protest.

The small knife, a throwing dagger Kera had never bothered to learn how to throw, pointed squarely into the face of a young girl with long blonde hair holding what looked like an oversized muffin. The girl squeaked in alarm and froze in place, her face locked in an expression of extreme surprise.

Kera arched an eyebrow at the girl.

"You don't look like a jailer," said Kera.

She gave the room a quick once over; the bed occupied most of the room, the only other features seemed to be a small nightstand and a single large window on the wall opposite the bed. Other than the window, the only exit was a simple wooden door; the only thing between it and her was the girl.

Moving her gaze back to the girl in question, Kera smiled as she realized the girl hadn't moved yet and was still standing stock still.

"You don't need to be afraid," said Kera, holding her knife up into the air and wiggling it to get the girl's attention before putting it away. "There. Knife's gone, see?"

The girl's expression softened, but she was still silent. Kera noted her unusual clothing choices: a soot-stained apron that looked like it belonged to a blacksmith was tied over slacks and a shirt. Heavy leather gloves made for someone quite a bit larger than her were bound at her elbows to stay up. As Kera observed the girl, she felt the unsettling sensation of being examined; not seen, not observed, but examined. The girl's eyes, a shade of pale blue unheard of in these parts, crawled over her. The girl's eyes shone bright with curiosity and seemed to pick up every detail.

Is it just curiosity they're shining with? Kera thought, catching what looked like a faint glimmer of opalescence in the girl's brilliant blue eyes. The girl opened her mouth to say something but snapped it shut and dropped her gaze to the floor, looking sullen.

"Did I do something wrong?" Kera asked, confused.

The little girl shook her head from side to side, blonde hair swaying wildly. Kera considered for a moment, then smiled as realization dawned.

"You're not allowed to talk to me, are you?"

After a moment of sullen silence, the girl gave Kera a fast nod in response.

"Okay, that's fair," Kera said, "I'm a stranger. Talking to strangers is bad. That's a good rule to have. Is there an adult I can talk to?"

Moving slowly, Kera pulled the blanket away, finding it surprisingly heavy compared to what she was used to.

Fully dressed in my own clothes, Kera noted, *that's a good start.*

When Kera moved, the girl moved as well, stepping sideways to stay in exactly the same position in front of her. Kera frowned and gave the girl another look, eyes resting on the huge muffin in her right hand. Her left hand wasn't presented, Kera noticed, it was held tightly behind her back.

Kera's sense of alarm tingled, but she didn't let her concern show.

"Is that for me?" Kera asked, gesturing towards the muffin. "Is that what you were doing in here?"

The little girl nodded quickly.

Kera extended her hand out to the girl, keeping her eyes locked on the obscured hand. When her fingers touched the baked good, the girl snapped the muffin into her hand so quickly it made Kera recoil. Kera brought the muffin up to her mouth and gave it a sniff. The scent of blueberries wafted upwards.

Moving deliberately while still staring into the girl's eyes, Kera took a cautious bite.

To her relief, the muffin was delicious and still warm. She took another bite, her gaze never breaking from the little girl's hidden arm, and swallowed.

"This is really good, thank you," Kera said. "Can you show me what you have?"

The girl's pale cheeks flushed red. She shook her head.

"Is it meant for me?" Kera asked.

The girl considered for a moment and gave a non-committal head wag.

"Does that mean it *might* be for me?" Kera prodded.

The girl was still, then nodded the affirmative. Kera took another bite of the muffin, chewed, and swallowed. Her stomach felt as though she hadn't eaten for days.

Shit, when was the last time I ate? she thought.

"Well, how about this," Kera said to the girl, leaning back against the edge of the bed. "Since it *might* be for me, I think you should show it to me. You can keep it the whole time, I just want to know what it is. I'm just a very curious person, you know?"

Kera smiled warmly at the girl, wondering if she'd said the right thing.

The girl thought about this for a long time, then nodded and brought her arm around. Kera suddenly found herself staring down the barrel of what looked like a small cannon; a sturdy-looking silver tube that ended in a wooden handle - a handle which the girl's tiny hands were wrapped comfortably around. A vague aroma of sulfur and steel drifted out of the mouth of the weapon and Kera felt the need to back away.

I don't know what that is, she thought, *but I know a weapon when I see one.*

"That looks pretty dangerous," Kera said, concern seeping into her voice. "Are you allowed to have that?"

The girl nodded quickly, the weapon's aim not wavering in the slightest. Swallowing again, Kera decided to try a different approach.

"That's really interesting looking," she said, "can you show me how it works?"

The girl smiled brightly and moved closer to Kera, turning the weapon onto its side and holding it in both hands.

"*Morrillypallyke,*" a gruff voice barked from the door, startling the girl.

Surprised and relieved by what sounded like another adult, Kera looked to the door and saw a man who looked like he'd just emerged from a vat of oil. Wearing stained coveralls, leather boots, and a toolbelt filled to bursting, the man used a filthy oil-stained rag to wipe something tar-like from his hands and face. Less oil on his face made his features more visible. He looked to be in his forties, and had a hardset look on his face. Every crease in his skin and every hair of his trimmed beard seemed stained black with soot and oil.

"She's taken a liking to you for some reason," the man said as the girl moved to his side, offering the weapon to him. He held it out, checked it over, then holstered it on his toolbelt. "I'm hoping you're going to explain what you're doing in my house."

"Seems fair," said Kera, "how about we start with you explaining that jumble of sounds you just shouted at the poor kid?"

"Jumble of sounds?" the man repeated. "That's her name."

"What kind of name is *More-ally-pal-ike?*"

"Mo-rill-lee-pah-lee-kay," the man repeated, wiping his palm on his apron before lovingly placing it on the girl's head. "Yours is Kera, Kera *No-Clan*, apparently. Not the kind of name you hear around Zelwyr. Lot more common further south. Like the Wildlands, for instance."

"That is where it comes from, same as me," said Kera, making sure to keep eye contact with the man while discreetly reaching for her knife. "If this is your bed and your kid, I'm going to go out on a limb and assume this is your house?'"

"It is," the man said with a nod.

"You always let your kid play with weaponry?" Kera asked.

"I don't *let* her do anything," the man snorted. "She's her own person."

"Progressive," Kera quipped. "She still going to be her own person when she blows herself up with a hand-cannon?"

"This isn't some dwarven fire hazard, this thing is my pride and joy," the man said, running a loving finger along the weapon in its holster. "Besides, she's a better shot with it than I am."

The girl giggled happily and pressed herself into the man's leg in a crushing hug.

Kera pulled out her dagger and held it aloft, doing her best to hold it in a way that made it look like she knew how to throw it. The girl saw the knife first and squeaked, clinging to the man's leg. The man's gaze went first to the dagger point, then to Kera's eyes. He grimaced, moving Morri so that she was standing behind him.

"You know," he began, "just because it's not a name you normally hear in these parts, doesn't mean I don't know what *No-Clan* means."

"Oh yeah?" Kera asked rhetorically, keeping the knife in the air while she stepped around him and the girl to make her way towards the door. "Is that supposed to threaten me or impress me? Bit of both, maybe?"

"Oh, please," the man said with a scowl, rotating his body to keep himself between Kera and Morri as the graverobber moved across the room. "Don't flatter yourself. I thought you should know that I know what it means and that in spite of that fact, I still made arrangements to keep you hidden while you slept off your binge."

"So what?" asked Kera, eyeing the door. "I didn't ask you to do that. That's a choice you made on your own. I'm going to walk out this door and not come back. No one is going to follow me, call the guards, or anything. Or else there's going to be trouble, understand?"

The man's only response was to clear his throat, looking over Kera's shoulder.

"Like I'm going to fall for that," Kera scolded. "I basically invented that trick."

A hand suddenly planted itself on Kera's shoulder, its vice-like grip on her collarbone making her wince as it tightened painfully. Kera's immediate reaction was to bring the dagger around to stab at the arm, aiming to bury the blade as deep into the forearm the person holding her as she could. She expecting to hear a cry of pain, but instead heard the grating sound of steel scraping against steel.

Confused, Kera turned her head to find herself face to face with what looked like a woman made of metal; she stared into unblinking silver eyes set on an unmoving angelic face.

"Well, I invented that," said the man, a small smile breaking through his grim countenance. "I think that makes us at least equally accomplished."

The metal woman's face was framed with hanging lengths of wire cable, the copper strands standing out in stark contrast against her chrome skin. All her points of articulation - elbows, shoulders, wrists, knees, neck, feet, waist - had pliable sections of leather and black rubber to allow for movement.

She's beautiful, Kera thought, *that's a shame.*

Kera tossed the knife to her other hand and stabbed the silver woman in the eye. To her dismay, the dagger point scraped harmlessly up the construct's face, leaving a faint scratch on the bridge of her nose.

The mechanical woman stared at Kera for a moment. Still holding Kera by the shoulder, the construct took Kera's dagger in her free hand and began to close her fist around it, the sound of gears whirring and grinding accompanying motion she made. The silver fist closed harder, and the blade within it began to bend. She squeezed until the dagger was nothing but a twisted piece of scrap, then let it fall to the floor.

Gods, Kera thought, *I know when I'm beat.*

Kera raised her hands into the air in surrender.

"Maybe I'm not going anywhere," Kera said reluctantly, "what happens now? Quick trip to the Zelwyr slave markets followed by a family picnic in the park?"

The man glared at her, visibly bristling with anger.

"You wake up in a freshly made bed to the sound of my daughter delivering you breakfast - by *hand* no less - and you pull a knife the first chance you get?" he asked. The bright-eyed girl poked her head out from behind him, a contented smile on her face.

Kera looked to the girl, then back to the man.

Good thing you take after your mom, bright-eyes.

"Call it a bad habit," said Kera.

"You make a habit of pulling knives on kids?" the man asked.

"I get a little defensive when I wake up somewhere I didn't put myself," Kera said, her expression darkening. "Believe me when I say my first concern wasn't breakfast."

Morrillypallyke cocked her head confusion, looking up at the man as if expecting an explanation. The man pulled her closer, and returned Kera's steely gaze with his own thousand-yard stare. A tense silence filled the room as Kera and the man shared a long, hard look at each other. At last, the man broke the silence by clearing his throat.

"Let her go, Enaurl," he said. The metal woman, evidently named Enaurl, released her grip on Kera.

"Enaurl is a dumb name," Kera grumbled, putting pressure on the offended area, feeling a bruise developing. She turned around to get a better look at the steel-crafted woman. Interlocking plates of steel formed her armour-like skin, some of which were polished smooth while others were covered with rivets.

Noticing Kera studying her, Enaurl repositioned her head to get a better look at Kera. Her mirror-like eyes reflected the graverobber's stare back at her.

"It's kind of creepy," said Kera.

"How dare you!" shouted a tiny voice, every word tinged by a thick Akorsian accent. "Enaurl is not an *it*, she is a *she*. She's also beautiful and you're rather cruel to insult her like that. If anyone in this room is any sort of creep - or has a *dumb name* - it would be you, with your sharp knife and your mean words."

Kera turned her head back to face Morrillypallyke and her father and saw the girl standing in front of him, scowling at her.

Kera found herself torn between being impressed and being shocked.

"Sorry, kid," said Kera, a smile spreading across her face, "I take it all back."

Seeing the small girl's proud and defiant posture - small hands planted on tiny hips, eyes flashing with defiance and intelligence - Kera couldn't help but feel her edge soften a little.

Maybe we're not so different after all, she thought.

"As you should," the girl said, crossing her arms in front of her apron and looking very proud of herself. "Enaurl is a wonderful companion and an excellent assistant. She runs the forge whenever Father is occupied, helps keep the shop organized, and makes an excellent omelette. I appreciate your apology, but it's Enaurl to whom you should be apologizing. She can't say anything back but she'll *know* you've apologized, and that's what matters."

Morrillypallyke finished her reprimand with an expressive 'hmmph.' The light in her eyes swirled and danced, almost entrancing Kera.

Kera couldn't help but smile wider at the girl. She broke her gaze from the girl's eyes and looked up to the man. His only offered response was a slight shrug, his arms crossed in front of his chest as well.

Like father, like daughter, Kera thought. *I guess this means I'm safe here, at least as long as the Iron Lady isn't trying to kill me.*

"Fair's fair," Kera said, turning to face Enaurl. "Enaurl, I'm sorry I tried to stab you. I'm also sorry I tried to slice your arms open and for trying holding your family hostage. For what it's worth, I thought I was in danger and reacted poorly. I hope you can understand."

Enaurl readjusted her posture, standing less menacingly and more naturally, always to the tune of gears and pistons. Having finished, she turned back to Morrillypallyke. The girl smiled and nodded. For reasons Kera couldn't quite understand, she felt good earning the girl's approval.

A supremely confident expression on her face, the girl opened her mouth to speak again but the man interjected himself.

"Alright, Morri, she apologized," the man said, "why don't you go back downstairs and keep working on that project of yours?"

Morri? Kera thought, *thank the gods there's a short version.*

"The conductivity experiment or the heat treatment study?" Morri asked.

"Both," said the man. "Either. Doesn't matter. The grown-ups need to talk."

Morri gave her father a tight embrace and made to leave the room. She paused when she reached the door frame.

"I insist you have Enaurl stay with you," Morri said, putting a loving hand on the metal woman. "In the event you should suddenly require protection from harm."

The little girl furrowed her brow and narrowed her eyes at Kera.

"I'll be fine, Morri," said the man. "Kera's not going to hurt me. Are you, Kera?"

"Not unless I have to," said Kera.

"Really?" the man asked.

"Fine," said Kera. "I promise not to harm anyone who isn't harming me. Better?"

"Not by much, but it'll do," said the man. "Besides, I've got this."

He put a hand on his belt, reaching for the handle of his weapon. When his fingers touched only the leathers of his belt and apron, he scowled. Confused, he checked the other side of his belt, but still didn't find it. Frowning, he gave himself a pat down in search of where he'd put his weapon but to no avail.

"What is this, anyway?" Kera asked, holding the weapon up to the light. "I've moved a lot of things in my day, but I have never seen anything like this. It's a fancy hand-cannon, right? I thought these blew up on the user more often than not."

Morri made a loud and obviously intentional throat clearing sound that ended with a false cough that was clearly meant to convey the words *I told you so.*

The man scowled at Kera, then at Morri, then at Kera again.

"Be careful with that!" the man barked, seeing Kera hold the weapon up to look into the barrel. He crossed the room and snatched it from her hands, examining it carefully. He turned it over in his hands then flipped it back again, checking mechanisms Kera hadn't known existed to make sure they hadn't been tampered with.

Satisfied, he holstered it in his toolbelt again. He stared angrily at Kera, who met the man's gaze before flicking her eyes towards Morri and Enaurl.

To Kera's annoyance, he didn't catch on. Kera repeated the eye movement, including a tilt of her head and a slight rise of her eyebrows this time. The man looked confused, but followed her gaze. Comprehension dawned on him at last.

"Shouldn't you two be gone by now?" he grumbled.

With one final stare at Kera, Morri spun on her heel and began to leave the room.

"Come along, Enaurl," she called as she skipped away. "Let's leave Father and Kera alone. Why don't we try working on the armour stencils some more? I'm sure we can figure it out. It makes so much sense in theory..."

Enaurl's body turned to follow the girl out, but her head remained in the same position, letting the metal woman stare at Kera while leaving the room.

Well that's disturbing, Kera thought.

The girl and the construct left the room and walked out of sight, the sounds of Morri talking and Enaurl's gears fading.

Satisfied that they'd left, the man crossed the room and opened the window, leaning on the frame. They could both hear the sounds of Zelwyr: the noise of wagon wheels and horse shoes on cobblestone streets, the prattle of street vendors and their transactions, the backdrop of hammers and saws hard at work. Putting both hands on the window frame, the man leaned forward and took a deep breath.

Seeing his back turned on her, Kera took a quick look around the room to see if there was anything she could use as a weapon. There wasn't much.

There's a candlestick on the nightstand, what's left of my dagger, and a painting, she thought to herself. *I could probably make a rope out of the bedsheets and strangle him a bit, then use it as a rope and escape out the window. If I need to, of course.*

"So, what's the deal with the fancy silver thing?" Kera asked. "And while we're at it, what in all the various hells made you name your kid *Morrillypallyke?*"

"That 'silver thing' is Enaurl, and her deal is that she keeps Morri safe and happy," the man grumbled. "She gets a lot of shells in the omelettes, but she makes up for it by having a hell of a right hook. I didn't pick Morri's name - her mother did."

The man's surly attitude and angry tone shift made Kera regret that she hadn't followed through with her thought about strangling him. Remembering the way Morri's tiny body had all but collapsed into the man's when she hugged him made her decide she'd made the right choice.

"I wasn't asking about Enaurl, chief," Kera said, "I was asking about that thing on your belt. You didn't answer me earlier when I asked if it was a hand-cannon."

The man grimaced at Kera's question, drawing the weapon. His thumb pulled back a metal hammer on the back of the handle.

Ka-chick.

He raised the weapon, still facing Kera. She swallowed hard and made to raise her hands into the air again, but he moved the weapon away from her and pointed it out the window. He adjusted his aim so that the barrel was pointing upwards at the clouds, and pulled the trigger.

CRACK-*POW.*

The weapon thundered as the hammer snapped forward; a fist-sized plume of red fire shot out from the mouth of the weapon and rocketed towards the sky, leaving a trail of orange smoke behind it as it flew upwards and away.

"It shoots fireballs," said Kera, impressed. "That's kind of neat. Finding ways for folks not magically inclined to use magic is a pretty good way to make some co--"

BOOOOM.

A burning ball of flame exploded into being in the clouds above, casting a fierce red light over Zelwyr for a few seconds before fading away.

"Okay, what the *fuck?!*" Kera exclaimed. "You gave that thing to a *child?* She pointed it *right at me!*"

The man shrugged, his expression placid. Kera's eyes went wide.

"Seriously? A shrug? That's your response?"

"Like I said - she knows how to use it," he said, "and besides, that's not what it does when you shoot something at close range."

"Do I *want* to know what it does at close range?" Kera seethed. She'd spent a good portion of her life trying to avoid having weapons and dangerous magics pointed at her; the idea that a small child had been given something that was a mix of both in order to keep Kera in check did not sit well with her.

"Probably not," said the man, making a sucking sound and he pulled air in between his teeth and holstered the weapon. "Now that all that's out of the way--"

"Uh, no?" Kera interjected. "Nothing is *out of the way*. You still haven't told me how I got into your bed, for starters. And where's my sword? Where's Zephelous?"

"Hard for me to answer any of that, since I don't know the whole story myself," the man said, leaning on the windowsill behind him. "I found you in my bed two days ago and asked Morri about it, but all she says is that she 'found you' but won't tell me where, when, or how. She's been checking in on you every two minutes, keeps saying it's *the least she can do* but won't tell me what she means by that either."

He crossed his arms in front of his chest once more, leaning back against the window sill as he did. Every word out of his mouth felt gruff; his tone seemed perpetually irate. The combination of the two aspects about him made it easy for Kera to imagine again pushing him out the window to the cobblestones below.

But then Morri would be left with only Silverface taking care of her, Kera thought, surprised at her concern over the girl. She shook her head at herself. *I need to get Zephelous back and get the hell out of this town.*

"What about my sword?" Kera asked. "What about Zephelous?"

"I don't know who Zephelous is," he said. "As far as I know, you didn't have a sword with you. You'll have to ask Morri, maybe she knows."

"Let's do that, then," said Kera, "I'd like to be gone as soon as I can but I'm not leaving without my sword."

"Fine by me," said the man. "There is one other thing you should know; you're a wanted fugitive at the moment. At least, that's what all the posters of your face plastered outside my shop say."

Kera's heart skipped a beat.

Wanted posters? she thought, *that's a new development. Well, not new in general, but new for Zelwyr.*

"Is there a reward?" Kera asked, feeling her pulse quicken. Her fight or flight instinct kicked in, screaming at her to run. The door was plainly visible and she doubted the man would try to stop her. The urge to bolt through the door was almost overpowering, but she needed more information.

"There is," the man said, reaching into a pocket, "decently sized one, too."

He produced a folded up piece of paper and passed it to Kera, who took it eagerly. She went to unfold it but stopped as she noticed a dozen oil-stain fingerprints.

Decently sized enough that you keep opening this up, I take it, Kera thought.

She unfolded the paper and let out a low whistle.

"Surprised?" the man asked.

"Flattered," said Kera, "that's a lot of zeroes."

The poster featured a half-decent sketch of her along with a long list of crimes that she was being accused of; arson, vandalism, inciting a tavern brawl...

"How recent is this?" she asked, "this is the same list of crimes they tried to charge me with at the arena. Trial by combat. I got out of there free and clear."

"These started showing up the same day you did," the man said, turning around to close the window. "I heard about the trial at the arena. Cost Big Charlie both his hands. I didn't realize that was you."

"Not my best work," Kera admitted. "He was an obstacle between me and my freedom so I didn't have much of a choice."

"I'm going to have to assume that's a threat," said the man, latching the window shut. "Don't worry, I'm not going to turn you in. I thought about it for about a half a second before Morri turned those big blues on me and made me swear I wouldn't. You should probably thank her. She's probably checking on Charlie's hands downstairs."

Kera was stunned, frozen in place, staring at the depiction of herself on the wanted poster while she tried to process all the information that was being given to her.

"I don't understand," she said, "I already dealt with these crimes. That's what the stuff in the arena was all about."

She held the page tightly and waggled it towards the man for emphasis, as if that would somehow convey what she was saying more clearly.

"Well, seems that when you got your belongings back, you felt the need to celebrate. Hard," the man said, a hint of amusement in his voice. "You know what they say about barbarians and celebrating."

"Gods damned fae ash," Kera muttered to herself, tossing the poster onto the bed. She brought her hands up to the sides of her face and pressed on her temples, shutting her eyes and trying to wish away the outside world for a moment. When it didn't work, she opened eyes and looked at the man once more.

"You got a name?" she asked.

"Smith," the man answered.

A wry smile broke out on Kera's face and opened her mouth to speak but was interrupted by a raised hand from Smith.

"Don't," he said. "I've heard all the jokes. I'm a smith named Smith. I get it."

"What if I have an especially good one?" Kera asked.

"Nope," said Smith, shaking his head, "I've already heard it, guaranteed."

"Your loss, smithy Smith," Kera said with a shrug. She looked to the door, mulling over her options mentally. "I want my sword back."

"Well, I'm about finished up for the day," said Smith. "I can spare a few hours to help you find your friend or to help you find your sword, but I'm not doing both."

Kera didn't bother to suppress the smile that came to her face as Smith mistakenly associated Zephelous as being a separate entity from the sword.

At least this means he probably didn't steal it, she thought, *not that he seems like the thieving type.*

"The sword's more important," she said. "Shouldn't be hard to find. It's an old third age dwarven short-edge. It's a two-hander for me, but I bet Big Charlie could make a go of using it with one. Ancient, valuable, and sharp as fuck."

"You know your swords," said Smith. "That said, 'as fuck' is not a valid unit of measurement. The rest seems distinct enough. Haven't seen an old short-edge in gods know how long. Should be easy enough to find. Then again, you have been lying here for two days and have no idea where or how you lost it. Is there any chance your friend took off with it?"

"I doubt it," said Kera.

"That so?" Smith asked. "You keep especially good company, then?"

"The best," Kera said, "I'll explain more when you find the sword."

"*If* I find the sword," Smith corrected.

"I'm sure you'll do fine," Kera said, giving Smith a pat on the shoulder. "Which way to the kitchen? That muffin was great, but I haven't eaten in two days."

Smith let out a grunt that sounded very similar to Morri's 'hmmph.'

"It's downstairs," he said as he moved away from the window and towards the door, gesturing for Kera to follow. "If you get lost, ask Morri. Her and Enaurl do most of the cooking around this place."

Kera followed Smith out the door and down the narrow hallway beyond, a hallway that led to a set of stars that went straight down.

"Shouldn't that be your responsibility?" she asked. "You know, part of being the acting adult and all?"

"They won't let me cook anymore," he said, "not after last time."

"What happened last time?" Kera asked.

"I don't want to talk about it," said Smith.

The bottom of the stairs led to a single large room. Kera's mouth hung open in surprise as she stepped into it. It felt to Kera as if she'd just walked into an artificer's fever dream; the room seemed to be equal parts forge, foundry, kitchen, storefront, and scrapyard. High shelves filled with trinkets, gadgets, gizmos, and weapons ran along every wall. Pipes and tubing seemed to connect different parts of the room to other parts, but what function or purpose any of them served was a mystery. The middle of the room was dominated by a series of tables, each piled high with precariously placed scrap, discarded tools, and bits of weaponry and armor.

The far corner of the room was occupied by the forge and foundry implements. A pair of wall-mounted bellows, clockwork-driven and self-pumping, inflated and deflated rhythmically like mechanical lungs.

Enaurl and Morri were hard at work in front of the forge; Morri watched through a protective face shield as Enaurl, gleaming orange in the firelight, pulled something out from the heat and placed it on a huge anvil.

Rather than using a hammer, the automaton raised the flat of her hand up into the air and brought it swinging down onto the heated steel in front of her. If she had been human, the way she overextended her arm would have been painful at best or dislocated her shoulder at worst. Morrillypallyke hurried to one of the mountains of scrap, fished for something, then hurried back and passed it to Enaurl. The silver woman grasped the material and swung her arm back around into position – the wrong way around, Kera noted with a grimace – and pressed the object into the steel.

From where she stood, Kera couldn't see the details of what transpired next, only that Morri skipped over to beside Enaurl and whispered instructions to the automaton. Enaurl's silver fist stopped slapping the steel into shape and instead started using her fingers to roll up its edges. After a few moments, she held it up to Morri.

"Oh, Enaurl, that's perfect!" she said. "I believe we've done it this time. Go ahead and quench it. Once it cooled off, we can mark it to length for the cuts. Once the cutting is done, we can assemble it and poor Charles will have both hands back!"

Smith cleared his throat loudly to get the girl's attention.

"Oh!" Morri shouted, startled by Smith's sudden appearance. "Father, you surprised me. I hadn't realized you'd come in." The girl's bright smile flickered a shade duller for a moment when the girl saw Kera standing next to Smith.

"You've brought her along as well. Is she leaving now?"

To her surprise, Kera felt a little hurt at the girl's seeming impatience to kick her out. Kera was about to respond when Morrillypallyke began speaking excitedly, her sky blue eyes gleaming with excitement.

"You'll never guess what Enaurl and I have just completed!" she began, rolling onto the tips of her toes as she wiggled her fists in excitement.

"Once this segment cools, I'll have Enaurl cut it into a series of lengths equivalent to phalangeal digits," Morri said, waggling her fingers. "Paired with the skeletal base mechanism already installed, I firmly believe that not only will Charles the Large have full hand function once again - he may even have a stronger grip than before. Once this lattice is installed, he should also be pleased with how they look. I had Enaurl press a large letter 'C' into them. Oh, I hope he likes it!"

Morri's balled her fists in excitement and wiggled her hands through the air, her eyes flashing the blue of a clear and cloudless sky.

"He'll love it," Smith said. "You're doing a great job, Morri, I'm proud of you."

Morri made a squeal of excitement and rushed back to Enaurl's side.

"She's a witch, right?" Kera asked, eyes wide as she stared at Smith. Witches were known for having unusual abilities and strange, often magic-like powers.

"She's not a witch," Smith said quietly, watching Morri whisper something to Enaurl. "I've had the high priest look at her. Says she's just smart as a whip."

"But her eyes..." She said.

"I know," Smith said, "sometimes I come down here at night and find her sitting there with her eyes all lit up while she puts something together or takes something apart."

"And you don't think that's weird?"

"I was the same way at her age."

"Maybe, but I bet you needed light," Kera countered. "What does her mom have to say about this?"

Smith went quiet, visibly stiffening.

"That's not your business," he said, walking away.

He navigated his way around the heaps of scrap to make his way over to Morri. Rather than interrupt her work, he bent low and gave her a kiss on the top of the head. He whispered something to her and she nodded. He stood up and said something to Enaurl. The mechanical woman turned her head around to stare at Kera for a moment, then turned it back around.

That's probably not good, Kera thought. *It's definitely not great.*

A heavy knocking on the door made everything in the shop go quiet.

"Smith, you in there?" a voice called from through the door. "It's Treia. Just need to ask you some questions about a ball of fire in the sky a few minutes ago."

"Be right there, sheriff," Smith shouted, shooing Kera with a wave.

Kera's first thought was the number of zeroes there had been on the wanted poster. Her instinct was to run out the back door, but there wasn't one.

She might hear me running up the stairs, and that would be really suspicious, Kera thought. *I'm likely to knock these scrap piles over, so that's a no go. There are no windows to open and sneak out, and this is the only room in the house. I guess hiding in plain sight is the plan.*

Stepping as lightly as she could on the balls of her feet, she moved to stand behind the door. Smith tried to wave her upstairs but she shook her head and gestured towards the door. Smith repeated his waving, and Kera shook her head again.

"Everything okay, Smith?" the sheriff asked.

"Yeah, just a second," Smith called, making his way to the door. He opened it and stepped out, mostly closing the door behind himself. "Caught me on my way to come see you, sheriff."

"You were already on your way to come and file a report about a fireball in the sky?" Treia asked, speaking loud enough to be heard by Kera and Morri.

"Not exactly," said Smith, "and that was just a test."

"Uh-huh," said Treia, "normally I don't mind a few *tests* from you and Morri once in a while; you're both responsible, nobody ever gets hurt and that construct of yours always cleans up, but I can't have people causing explosions while there's a serial arsonist on the loose, Smith."

"I understand, Sheriff. Won't happen again," said Smith.

"Don't lie to me," said the sheriff, "just keep it contained for the next little while. That's what the arena's for anyhow. Come on - let's go get the paperwork done."

"Just one second, Sheriff," said Smith, "I have to tell Morri something."

"Be quick about it," said Treia.

"I will, Sheriff," Smith said, stepping back into the room and closing the door.

"I'm going to ask around about your sword while I'm there," Smith whispered to Kera. "If anyone else comes by, let Morri handle it. Enaurl won't let anyone in without permission."

"If that's true, how did I get in?" Kera whispered back. Smith heaved his shoulders in a shrug, a gesture Kera was quickly realizing might be the man's typical response to almost any question asked of him.

"Ask them," he whispered, pointing to Morri and Enaurl.

He opened the door.

"What is it you wanted to come down for, Smith?" Treia asked.

"I just finished inventory, and I hate to say it, but I think I might have been robbed," said Smith, stepping back outside and closing the door. "I've got a sword missing, an antique. Old dwarven greatsword--"

The door swung shut.

The very instant the door closed behind Smith, it seemed to Kera as if all sound in the smith shop abruptly stopped. Kera's gaze was still transfixed on the door, but she acutely felt the sensation of being watched. She turned her head to look back at Morri and Enaurl, finding them both staring at her. Caught in the act, the pair wordlessly returned to work as if nothing had happened.

"You know," said Kera, walking towards the girl and the machine, "you two are really going to have to decide whether or not you like me."

Enaurl turned her head to face Morrillypallyke. Morri's cheeks turned pink, but the girl said nothing and refused to look up from her work.

"The silent treatment doesn't work on me," said Kera, "and if your dad--"

"My *father*," Morri corrected, still refusing to make eye contact.

"If your *father* trusts me enough to leave me alone with you - that obviously means I'm not a stranger any more," said Kera, "which means you can talk to me now."

The girl chewed her lip, as if wanting to say something very badly but was uncertain as to whether or not she should. At last, the dam broke.

"It's not that Father trusts you, it's that he trusts Enaurl to stop you," she said, her Akorsian accent seeming to punctuate every word with an extra dollop of sass. "He knows that should you try anything untoward, Enaurl will simply crush the life out of you. She's quite good at it. Isn't that right, Enaurl?"

Morri smiled up at Enaurl, and while Enaurl's expressionless face showed no response the mechanical woman seemed to stand a little taller for a moment.

"And Smith was worried about my threats," Kera said under her breath, speaking mostly to herself. She gave Enaurl a closer look, eyeing the automaton with a mixture of curiosity and apprehension. Having just watched the creature slap heated steel into shape, she was intrigued and wondered how the mechanical woman would do in a fight.

I'd like to know how to take you down if I ever have to fight you, she thought to herself, *but I'd really rather not have to.*

Kera paid extra attention to the covered black sections at all Enaurl's articulation points, noticing that the area around her waist seemed to be the most flexible.

Everything has a soft spot, Kera thought. *I guess in your case, it's literal. Hopefully I have Zephelous back if we ever do have to fight.*

A twinge of anxiety struck her then, an accumulated anxious response to the events of the last few days. She hated feeling anxious. She gave the cluttered room a quick scan, wanting to deal with her anxiety in her usual way.

"I don't suppose your father keeps any wine around here, would he?"

Morri and Enaurl exchanged a wordless glance, making Kera feel suspicious.

There's something going on here, Kera thought as she scrutinized the pair, *something I'm not seeing… but what?*

"That's a yes," Kera deduced. "Is it nearby?"

Morri didn't respond, but Kera noticed her gloved fingers twitching. She had never been good with people, but she'd become great at reading them – an incredibly useful skill to have when you were often causing trouble.

"It's really close, isn't it?" Kera guessed, "closer to you than me."

"How do you do that?" Morri asked, her voice filled with wonder and surprise. Realizing what she'd done, she covered her mouth and looked away.

"Why are you shutting yourself up?" Kera asked. "Is there a reason you don't want to talk to me? Smith might be gone for a while. Paperwork takes time."

Morri flushed red once more but her gaze rose to meet Kera's at last. The girl's eyes were a soft pastel blue.

"There's something about you," Morri said dreamily, "something… unusual."

"That's a bit like the pot calling the kettle black, isn't it?"

"I'm afraid I don't know what you mean," Morri said.

"How about your eyes, for starters?"

"What's wrong with my eyes?" Morri asked, looking to Enaurl for reassurance. The machine woman tilted her head at Morri, and the two stared at each other silently for a moment. Morri nodded.

"Enaurl says they're lovely," she said to Kera.

"Enaurl doesn't talk."

"She thinks it, then."

"How do you know what she's thinking?"

"I know what she thinks because I can understand her."

Kera was hit by a sudden thought.

Can she talk to Enaurl the way Zephelous talks to me?

"When you… understand her," Kera began, trying to make her question seem as natural as possible, "does she have… a voice? One that talks to you in your mind?"

"A voice that talks to me in my mind?" Morri said, scrunching her nose at

Kera, "that's simply ridiculous. How would such a thing possibly work?"

Morri's accent and tone made the question feel downright condescending to Kera.

"Okay, fair enough," said Kera. "Just a hypothetical, really."

She paused for a moment, stepping to stand beside the girl and her silver-skinned companion. Rather than keeping her eyes on the pair, Kera spun slowly in place to see if she could spy the booze that was supposedly nearby. The bright glint of glass reflecting the light of the fire caught her eye and brought a smile to Kera's face.

A brown bottle was sitting on the corner of the table nearest Morri and Enaurl. It looked to be a whiskey of some kind - a little over half full.

A small victory is still a victory, she thought to herself, repeating a mantra she'd heard far too many times in her youth.

The memories that threatened to flood Kera's mind soured her smile.

With a renewed sense of need, Kera walked to the table's edge and snatched the bottle, uncorking it and lifting it to her lips. She realized then that Enaurl was staring at her and scowled at the metal woman.

"What's wrong, shiny?" Kera asked, "I'm just getting a drink."

She tilted the bottle upwards, letting the liquid spill its way its way to her mouth. The potency of the whiskey caught her off guard and she spat it out in a cloud of mist. The mist drifted towards the forge and ignited in a flash.

"Various fucking gods," Kera cursed, "what is this stuff?"

She held the bottle away from her face tried to read the label, but couldn't. Whatever it was, it was dwarven - a language she couldn't read but could recognize from the bold square characters aligned into a rectangle. She shrugged and took a smaller sip, swallowing loudly. The liquid burned her mouth and throat on its way down to her stomach, but left her feeling warm inside almost instantly.

"Thank the gods for dwarves," said Kera, smacking together lips that were already going numb.

"You shouldn't drink," said Morri. "It's not good for you."

"You're too young to say things like that," Kera said. "You're also way too young to be playing around in your dad's--"

"Father's," Morri corrected.

"Playing around in your *father's* workshop, sorry," Kera said, gently slapping her own face. Her cheeks felt warm. She took another sip from the bottle with satisfaction.

Thank the gods for dwarves.

"Really, though," she said to the girl, wiping her mouth with the back of her hand, "shouldn't you be out playing with other kids, or in school, or reading a book?"

"Children are boring and unproductive. I've already graduated and Father doesn't keep satisfactory literature," said Morri "I've asked for a membership to the library, but I was told I'd need to wait until summer. Now that it's been burnt down, I suppose I'll have to wait a while longer."

Kera was silent for a moment.

"You're fuckin' weird, kid."

"You shouldn't curse so much," said Morri, "it makes you seem uneducated."

"Maybe I am uneducated," Kera replied.

"I could have guessed that," Morri said. "It was fairly apparent and for several reasons besides your profanities."

Kera held her hands up in mock surrender, glancing at the bottle when it sloshed to make sure that none of its contents spilled out.

"Alright, you win, kid," she said.

Turning to face the table, Kera pushed some scrap aside, clearing herself a spot to sit. The clattering noise of the junk hitting the floor made Enaurl turn and stare at Kera, watching intently as the graverobber eased herself onto the table.

"How does she see me?" Kera asked, staring back into Enaurl's mirror-like eyes.

"Have you ever heard of prongfish?" Morri asked. Kera nodded.

"Of course. Big, dopey, eyeless fish with a bunch of wiggly bits on their faces. Mostly live in swamps. Taste great with some butter."

"Those 'wiggly bits' are called antennae, but you're correct. Prongfish have no eyes, but they are able to navigate the muddy rivers in which they live by using their antennae to detect obstacles and prey. Enaurl's visual detection system functions in a similar way."

"Visual. Detection. System," Kera said, repeating the alien sounding term slowly.

Does this girl know how insane she sounds? Kera thought.

She took another swig from the bottle then put it down and corked it, deciding she'd save the rest for later. When it sloshed louder than she had anticipated, she glanced at the bottle. It seemed she'd barely drank any.

"That is some strong stuff," she said. Seeing Enaurl still watching her, Kera offered her the bottle. "Did you want some, silverface?"

"You must stop calling her names," Morri said. "Her name is Enaurl."

"It's not like she can hear me calling her names," said Kera.

"As a matter of fact, she can," Morri began, beaming. "Are you familiar with the cave-dwelling variation of--"

"No, stop," Kera said, waving her hands through the air as if she were flapping away the girl's words. "Whatever you're about to say, I'm sure it's great, but I just don't care. She *can* hear, that's all I need to know. Actually, *need* is a strong word. I really don't need to know any of it. I just want Smith to hurry up and get my sword back so I can get out of here."

"If you're in such a hurry to leave, why don't you find your sword yourself?" Morri asked, hands planted firmly on her hips.

"I would if I could, Mo," Kera said with a sigh, "but your old man told me there are some bad people looking for me, so I have to lay low for a while. For some reason or another, he seems to be okay with letting me stay here."

"The people who are after you aren't *bad*. That's a terrible over simplification," said Morri. "They're legitimate officers of the law and they're searching for you because of the destruction you've caused."

"Yeah, well, I don't remember causing it and that basically means I didn't do it."

"I'm not so sure that's how the law works."

"I'm not so sure I care."

"You're very peculiar for an adult."

"Right back at you, bright eyes."

"I'm not an adult."

"You know what I meant," Kera said. "What's so peculiar about me?"

"Well, for starters - I've never been called 'Mo' before."

"What's so *peculiar* about that?"

"Nothing, I suppose," Morri said. "I actually like it. I don't fully understand why people insist on using shorter and shorter variations of my name, but 'Mo' does have a certain ring to it."

Enaurl decided then that Kera had ceased being a threat and returned to work. The silver woman rummaged through the scrap pile until she found several broken swords. She brought the collection to Morri, who started inspecting them.

"She seems really attached to you," Kera remarked.

"Enaurl? Yes, you could say that," said Morri. "She is my constant companion."

"Do you have any real friends?"

"Enaurl is very real and an excellent friend."

"I meant friends who aren't mechanical."

"I've never been terribly good with people who aren't mechanical."

"If you can't join 'em, build 'em. Makes sense."

"I hadn't thought of it like that," said Morri, "perhaps that did play a certain role."

"Smith doesn't seem like he gets along with most folks either."

"I'm afraid that's true."

"Maybe he should build himself an Enaurl."

"I suggested that," said Morri. "He took offense to it."

"He didn't want to admit that he was unlikeable?"

"Well, I had suggested it because he had seemed lonely to me. He said that I was wrong, and that myself and Enaurl were all he needed. That the effort and investment required to build another like Enaurl wasn't needed. I told him it would be worth the while, but he said there were other things I could be doing instead."

Kera felt unsettled by something, but couldn't put her finger on what it was that was bothering her. She drummed her fingers on the tabletop beside her. She replayed the conversation she'd just had with the girl in her mind. She understood what it was that had unsettled her.

"You mean other things *he* could be doing instead, right?" Kera asked.

She had a sense she knew what would happen next. Morri paused in her inspection of the bundle of swords. She gave Enaurl a pat on the shoulder and looked back at Kera, eyes and face rigidly set.

"Of course," Morri said, her tone flat. "I simply made a mistake is all."

You'd make a terrible gambler, kid, Kera thought.

"I'll pretend I believe you and won't press the issue," Kera said, "but in exchange, I'd like to ask you a different question and I'd like an honest answer this time."

"I'm sure I don't know what you mean," said Morri. "Ask your question if you'd like, I'll do my best to give you a satisfying answer."

Kera brought her hand up to her chin, resting her face in it. Something, or perhaps everything, about this unusual little girl was setting off alarm bells in her mind - the kind of bells that only rung around deep amounts of trouble. Still, she decided she'd go for broke.

"Your father told me to ask the two of you how I got into your room," said Kera, "he seems to think that Enaurl wouldn't have just let me get into the house - never mind all the way upstairs - unless I had permission. Since he didn't give it, my guess is that you did. Am I right?"

Morri flinched.

Oh yes, she thought, suppressing the urge to grin. *I've caught you now.*

"So what I'm getting at is this," Kera continued, "where did you really find me and why did you bring me into your house?"

For a moment, the only sound in the workshop was the dull roar of the flames at the forge. Enaurl added to the noise by putting the swords into a cutting press of some kind, using a handle to work a giant steel press that cut cleanly through the swords and spat slices of steel out onto the floor.

Once the swords had been rendered into sliced pieces of metal, Enaurl gathered them in a basket and brought them to Morri. She held up a fragment, inspected it, then put it back in the bucket with a nod. Enaurl put the basket down near the forge and went searching for something else.

"Well?" Kera prompted.

"Very well," Morri said. "Three days ago, Enaurl and I were at the market to purchase some materials for the shop. Rivets, coal, leather, a few items from the grocer - nothing unusual, of course."

"It's unusual that you feel the need to specify 'nothing unusual,'" said Kera.

"You're a rather suspicious person, aren't you?" asked Morri.

"I come by it honestly," said Kera. "By all means, I'd like to hear about the rest of your not-at-all unusual day."

"Well, you see, that's just it – it became unusual rather quickly," said Morri. "We'd just acquired the leathers from Holm, the tanner, and said good morning to his lovely wife Sienna. Enaurl was pulling the wagon, which was rather full, and we were about to head to the bakery for a cinnamon bun. I *love* cinnamon buns. They're my absolute *favorite* thing to eat."

"Cinnamon buns are great," said Kera. "What happened after you got it?"

"We didn't get one," said Morri. "It seems the bakery had been burned by an arsonist. Again. For the second time this week."

"Ah," Kera said quietly, "sorry about that."

"As you should be," said Morri. "I've not had a cinnamon roll in days thanks to your habitual pyromania. Sorely disappointed, we'd turned back to return home, only…"

"Only what?"

"I was startled to see a strange man standing on the road. He wasn't impeding our travel, or even particularly nearby, but he was simply *there* when I'm quite certain he hadn't been there a moment before. The marketplace is fairly busy in the mornings, there had to have been at least several dozen people there, all of them going about their business."

"Why does that matter?"

"This person wasn't going about any sort of business or even moving at all. He simply stood there and stared at me, leered rather, from under his cloak."

"He was wearing a cloak?"

"Yes, a rather distinctive one. Black with a thick red trim, with silver elvish whorl stitches all across it."

"What did the man look like?"

"I'm afraid I didn't notice much about him."

"You noticed the type of stitching used in the cloak he was wearing, but you didn't notice anything about the actual man wearing it?"

"There's nothing unusual about men being strange but stitching like that is quite distinctive." Morri said, completely satisfied with her explanation.

Kera was baffled, unsure how to respond.

"Truth be told," Morri continued, "I'm not entirely certain it was a man."

"What do you mean?"

"Well, it was a rather large cloak, you see, with a rather tall collar. All I could discern of the figure's face was a portion of their nose. The rest was hidden by either the cloak or the collar or else covered beneath the armor he was wearing."

"I don't suppose you can tell me anything about the armor?"

"It was steel, a dark blue and silver. I'd wager dwarven-made based on the epaulets, but the blue color implies it was likely cast at a private foundry at some expense. There is a fascinating technique of using heat to add color to the steel, one I've not yet fully mastered with the arrangements here at the shop. Did you know that the larger dwarven cities bind living creatures of fire and molten magma to their forges? It's simply fascinating. I should love to have something like that here in my workshop."

Kera was quiet for a moment.

"But you're not sure if it was a man or a woman."

"I'm afraid I didn't notice."

"Of course not," Kera said. "Who pays attention to that sort of thing?"

Chapter Six

A few hours and several probing questions in an effort to better understand this peculiar little girl later, the shop swung open and Smith walked back in. He closed the door behind himself, then quickly locked it and leaned backwards against it.

That's trouble, Kera thought.

"Father?" Morri asked. "Is something wrong?"

"Huh?" Smith asked, "no, of course not. Everything is fine."

"Should I be worried?" Kera asked. "Because this is what I would consider 'worrying behavior.'"

"What are you going to do?" Smith grunted. "Set the place on fire?"

"If it looks like it might be the best way out, I just might," said Kera, grabbing the bottle of spirits. "How about you tell me what's going on and I won't have to use this dwarven gold to burn the place down as a distraction and sneak out of town?"

Morri made a squeak sound and covered her mouth with her hands.

"That's simply ghastly!" said Morri. "You wouldn't really do that, would you?"

"If I have to," Kera answered with a shrug, "I'm hoping it won't come to that. I'm hoping your dad--"

"Father."

"Gods, kid, will you give it up already?" said Kera. "I'm hoping your dad will realize that if he tells me what's going on, I might be able to relax. I might be able to be useful. Unless he wants me to burn the place down, which I'm fine with."

"This is why I don't help people," Smith grumbled, scowling at Kera. "I should have expected as much from some wild barbarian."

"Listen," Kera said, her tone flat, "you called me that once, and I let it slide. Twice is as far as it goes, because the things get real messy on the third time. Got it?"

Smith screwed up his face in confusion.

"But your name is--"

"I know what my name is."   "

Which means you're from--"

"I know where I'm from."

"But that makes you a--"

"Say it," Kera said, hoisting the bottle, ready to hurl it at the blazing forge. "Say it and I will burn this place down. Go ahead."

A moment of awkward silence passed in the shop. Smith broke it with a cough and a noisy throat clearing sound.

"Enaurl, you can put that down," said Smith. "I don't think you'll need to use it."

Kera turned her head and found herself staring at the raised face of a blacksmith's hammer, Enaurl poised and ready to bring it hammering down.

She swallowed and put the bottle of spirits down. Enaurl did the same with the hammer.

"Is someone chasing you?" Morri asked.

"No, of course not," said Smith. "I got spooked is all."

"Spooked enough to lock the door behind you?" Kera asked. "It's the middle of the afternoon - what spooked you?"

Smith crossed the room and snatched the bottle of spirits, scowling at Kera all the while. He popped the cork, took a hearty swig and exhaled, wiping his mouth with the back of his hand.

"I found your sword," said Smith. "I'm pretty sure it's haunted."

"Haunted?" Kera said. "What are you talking about, Smith the smith?"

"Really?" Smith grumbled. "You're back on my name?"

"I might be a little drunk," Kera admitted. "That's not important. You found my sword – where is it?"

"You're not worried about it being haunted?" Smith asked.

"I'm a graverobber, Smith," said Kera. "To me, dealing with stuff that's haunted is like you dealing with stuff that's hot to the touch. It's just part of the job."   Smith took another swig of the spirits.

Kera extended her hand expectantly. Smith grimaced but passed her the bottle all the same. Kera took a drink from it as well then passed it back.

"Being an arsonist not enough character flaws for you?" Smith asked.

"After you burn down your third or fourth library, you just don't get that same feeling of accomplishment," Kera quipped. "Why do you think the sword is haunted?"

"Well," said Smith, rubbing the back of his neck as he chose his words. "Something talked to me when I touched it."

"Oh," said Kera, "That's normal."

"Normal?" said Smith. "How is that normal?"

"That's Zephelous," Kera said.

"Your friend?" Smith asked.

"I don't think I'm the one who used the word 'friend' to describe it, but sure, why not," Kera said with a shrug. "Zephelous is not a ghost which means it's not haunted. At least I don't think so. I haven't made up my mind."

"Your friend can make swords talk?"

"My friend *is* the sword."

"Right," Smith said disbelievingly, "explain that to me."

"Explain it how?" Kera asked. "It's a sword that can talk. Explanation over."

"I've made dozens of swords. Hundreds even," Smith said. "Not one of them, or any of the other weapons I've ever made, has ever talked."

"Maybe you're doing it wrong," said Kera.

"Cut the crap," Smith growled. "How does it talk?"

"Alright, well, according to Zephelous, some dead wizard from forever ago decided that giving a sword a mind would be a fun thing to do, so he did."

"Magic," Smith scoffed. "Magic is bullshit."

"Bullshit or not, that's the truth as far as I know," said Kera. "Where's Zeph? Did you drop it in your panicked run through the streets?"

"You pawned it," said Smith. "Seems like you weren't just celebrating your victory in the arena. You were celebrating it hard. Hornbuckle says your eyes were glowing so much he thought they might burst. I didn't take you for an ash-head."

"Yeah, well, who the hell is Hornbuckle?" hissed Kera. "And what business of his is it anyway?"

"Brenno Hornbuckle runs the pawnshop named Lucky Copper," said Smith. "He tries not to make a habit of caring what his clients get up to, but when someone sells him a magic sword and asks if he knows where they can buy some fae ash Brenno tends to keep track. Especially when the sword ends up being fake."

"What do you mean by 'ends up being fake?'" Kera asked.

"I guess you sold him on Zephelous being alive, but there hasn't heard so much as a peep," said Smith. "He's got it on display as an antique."

"Crankiest antique I've ever found," said Kera. "Let's go get it."

"Great plan if you want to get caught," said Smith. "They've doubled the guard patrols and have sent missives out to the neighbouring settlements looking for you. But by all means, feel free to leave any time."

"Well that's fucking great," Kera cursed. "Why are they taking it so personally? It was just a library and a bakery. I've been applauded for that kind of arson before."

"Who would applaud that?" Morri gasped.

"Rival bakeries and libraries," said Kera.

"Ah," said Morri, "I should have guessed."

"That's not why they're taking it personally," said Smith. "They're taking it personally because you burnt down the tavern."

"So?" Kera asked. "Zelwyr's got to have more than one tavern."

"It's not that you burnt down a tavern," said Smith. "It's that you burnt down the tavern, the Ass's Glasses."

"The tavern's name is the Ass's Glasses?" said Kera. "That's either the best or worst name for a tavern I've ever heard."

"The owner, Jim Cork, would agree with you," said Smith. "The thing is, Old Jimbo just so happens to be the former sheriff. Held his position for thirty years before he retired, at which point he opened up a tavern. Seeing as how he used to be the sheriff that tavern attracted clients who were mostly a certain type." Kera groaned.

"I burnt down a cop bar," she said.

"You sure did," said Smith. "They aren't happy."

"Great," said Kera. "Did Zephelous have anything useful to say?"

"It didn't really say anything," said Smith.

"If it didn't talk, what made you think it was haunted?"

"It was making a kind of moaning sound or maybe wailing," said Smith. "I heard it as soon as I put my hands on its grip. Must have damn near jumped out of my boots. Left the shop and got myself back here."

"It's weird having something talk into your mind, isn't it?" Kera asked.

"It's unsettling is what it is," Smith grumbled.

"A sword that speaks into your mind?" Morri asked. "Father, is she a witch?"

"Maybe," said Smith.

"I think I resent that," said Kera,

"You only think you do?" asked Smith.

"I'm not positive," Kera said. "I'll let you know when I've decided. Now, Mo--"

"'Mo'?" Smith repeated, looking down at Morri. The little girl shrugged and offered a bright smile in return. Smith shook his head, but gestured for Kera to continue.

"While I try to think of a way to get Zephelous back, why don't you tell me more about what happened at the marketplace?" Kera asked Morri.

"I can't remember much beyond what I've told you," said Morri. "Enaurl, will you fetch me a scrap of parchment and a quill? I'll try to make a quick sketch of the individual. We shall see if that helps our delinquent witch friend at all."

I should probably be offended, Kera thought, *but I've been called a lot of things that are objectively a lot worse, and it is pretty cute hearing it from her. Must be that damn accent.*

Enaurl obeyed Morri's request, navigating her way through the shop to find a stick of charcoal and some parchment from among its piles of scrap. Enaurl returned to Morri's side and offered the items to the girl.

Morri smiled wide and took them, but rather than finding a place to work on one of the tables the girl placed her parchment out on the floor and laid down in front of it. She started sketching, absently kicking her feet through the air while her face became locked in a mask of effort.

"It was sort of nondescript, really," said Morri, hastily sketching away. "It was almost as if the person was intentionally working to reveal very little about themselves."

"I don't understand," said Smith. "What happened at the marketplace?"

"Strange man in a cloak," said Kera. "Try to keep up."

"I would have liked to hear about this sooner, Morri," Smith rumbled.

"You're hearing about it now," said Kera. "If the cloak and armor are so distinctive, doesn't that alone reveal a lot about the person?"

Morri's feet quit kicking the air and the scratching of charcoal on parchment paused mid-stroke. After a moment of thought, both continued.

"This is going to sound quite peculiar," said Morri. "But I swear to the both of you it's the truth! While I saw this figure following me in the marketplace, I'm not certain that anyone else did. I'm certain that Enaurl couldn't."

"She couldn't see the person?" Kera asked. "What about her visible whatever whatever?"

"Visual detection system," Smith clarified with a grumble.

"Yeah, that," said Kera.

Morri blew onto the parchment, sending up a small cloud of black dust.

"I can't be certain, but I believe this person devised a way to avoid detection entirely," said Morri, eyeing her sketch. She added a few strokes with the bit of charcoal here and there, then nodded to herself satisfactorily. Picking herself up from the floor, she brought the drawing to Kera and handed it to her.

Looking at the drawing, Kera let out an impressed whistle; she didn't recognize the figure in the drawing but she doubted she would have any trouble doing so.

"Kid, I have seen a lot of drawings," said Kera, "this is one of the best I've ever seen." Morri's work with shading, lighting, detail, and blending were all impeccable.

"If this isn't magic, I'm a scaleless wyvern," said Kera. "You're far too kind," said Morri, "it's just a sketch."

The figure in the drawing was surrounded by a billowing cloak, which Morri had managed to draw so well that it seemed like it was moving on the page. Where the cloak parted, the armor Morri had described was depicted in extreme detail. As the girl had described, a low hanging hood paired with a high collar revealed only the smallest part of a nondescript nose – no blemishes, distinguishing marks, scars, or even so much as a freckle.

Kera frowned and passed the drawing to Smith.

"I still don't understand what this has to do with me," said Kera. "You've got an admirer that no one else can see, your silver-skinned bodyguard included. That's weird, no doubt about that, but it has nothing to do with me or how I got into your father's bed."

"That's just it," said Morri. "You could see him. You saw the person no one else could see."

"What do you mean?" Kera asked.

"Well, once it became clear that no one else could see this person following me, I grew frightened," said Morri. "I tried to hurry home directly, but the route was blocked. I opted for an alternate route through an alley which runs along the temple district before winding its way back here, but the one of the wagon wheels got caught on a bit of loose cobblestone. Enaurl managed to pull it out, but the mysterious stalker had gained on us quite a bit in that time. They came within feet of me and I became quite scared... No, it was worse than that. I grew terrified."

The girl's voice fell to a whisper as she continued.

"The figure extended a hand towards me, reaching for my neck or perhaps my throat. I tried to back away, but I found I couldn't move. In my head I was screaming '*run, run now!*', but it was as if my body wasn't my own and wouldn't obey."

Morri paused, looking out the window into the sunlight.

"I don't know how I knew, but I was certain this person had come to take me," the girl continued. "To where, I couldn't imagine, but I felt certain that once this person took me I would simply be gone. The fear was so intense it felt sharp and cold, as if a glacier was trying to erupt it's way out of me from within."

Kera realized at that moment that she had been clenching her fists so tightly that she'd dug her nails into her palm. She relaxed her hands, but noticed that Smith's knuckles had gone white. The gentle crackling of the flame in the forge as it died down hung heavy in the air and the room was still.

Morri broke her gaze away from the window at last, looking at Kera. Despite her harrowing recollection, the girl had a soft smile on her face as her otherworldly blue eyes shone at Kera.

"That's when you saved me."

I have absolutely no memory of this happening, Kera realized, *I need to quit doing fae ash - and actually quit this time.*

"Remind me exactly how I saved you?" Kera asked.   Smith grumbled something unintelligible under his breath, but Kera heard the word 'ash-head' in there somewhere. Being called an ash-head – the term used for people so strung out on fairy dust that they spent their lives chasing the high - stung a little.

"You began by tapping on the person's shoulder to get their attention. They froze in place, as if you'd caught them completely off guard. I would have liked to see the expression on their face, but it simply wasn't possible due to the cloak. They turned to face you, and that's when you, well..."

Kera guessed that the girl was about to describe some feat of athleticism and combat prowess that Zephelous had made possible.

Of course, they don't need to know that it was Zephelous's doing, Kera thought, *I can take some of the glory and earn some slack.*

"You mumbled something incoherent, and then just sort of... vomited on the person," said Morri, a disgusted expression on her face. "Quite explosively, I might add."

Smith hid his mouth with his hand, snickering into his palm. Kera glared at him, doing her best to use her eyes to bore holes through him.

Morri, oblivious to this exchange, carried on with her story.   "Truth be told, I'd never seen so much bile come out of one person. It was quite impressive. Utterly revolting, but impressive. You coated them about as thoroughly as my usual morning cinnamon bun gets coated with frosting."

Smith laughed aloud once - a single note of mirth - before catching himself.

"Then what?" Kera asked, still glaring at Smith.

"Well, the figure seemed revolted, as one should be in such a scenario," said Morri. "They pushed you down, slicking vomit and detritus off themselves while they did. They called you a load of awful things I'd never repeat in front of Father."

"Good choice," grumbled Smith.

"Once they'd realized that there was simply too much filth to wipe it, they grew quite cross with you," Morri continued. "Arcane sounding words were uttered and you were knocked aside with some sort of energy blast. I have to assume it was magic. It's fascinating stuff, really - magic, I mean. I've never quite understood how it works. The various properties I've seen displayed are all so tenuous, as if it's a force that exists in a constant state of flux, able to be manipulated at the whims of those who can wield it."

"As fascinating as all that is, I would appreciate it tremendously if you would finish the story before launching an investigation into how magic works,"said Kera.

"Oh, quite right," Morri apologized. "I have a tendency to prattle on about things from time to time. As I was saying, the figure caused some sort of force blast to displace you and you were sent hurtling through the air to land among some barrels and crates. I feared you would be badly injured as it made a tremendous racket. Smelling like a mixture of spoiled milk and raw fish, the figure turned back to face me. They loomed over me and I felt that same icy cold sensation of fear. Do you think the fear I felt was more magic? Some sort of sustained effect, perhaps? The fear dissolved the moment you interrupted them and only began anew once they'd disposed of you."

"Disposed of me?" Kera repeated. "I thought you said I saved you. So far in this story, I've puked on a stranger and got chucked into some barrels."

"Sounds like a typical night in the Wildlands to me," said Smith.

"But we aren't in the Wildlands," Kera responded through a clenched jaw.

"You know what they say," Smith chided, "you can take barbarians out of the Wildlands, but you can't take the Wildlands out of barbari--"

Kera exploded into movement then, closing the distance between herself and Smith in the blink of an eye. Not having her dagger, she made due with the sharpest looking piece of scrap she saw, snatching it and holding it to Smith's throat like a makeshift razor.

Smith's mirth died instantly and he stared into Kera's eyes. Kera's wild anger met Smith's cold fury and for a moment there was silence in the smithy.

Suddenly, Kera felt herself flying across the room. She realized midway through her short travel through the air that Enaurl had taken her by the collar and thrown her like a sack of potatoes. She managed to turn the arc through empty space into a graceful tumble, landing on to the far end of the smithy with her makeshift weapon still in her hands. She took a quick stock of the room: Enaurl was standing by Smith, hands at her side. Smith was standing with his arms crossed over his chest, his expression was one of unbridled anger.

"I should have known better," Smith said, shaking his head. "I let myself believe that if Morri saw something in you that it meant that you were someone I could potentially trust. That was clearly a mistake."

"The only mistake you've made is calling me a barbarian when I told you not to," said Kera. "Why don't you tell Enaurl to sit this one out and say it again?"

"Please," said Smith, drawing his weapon and pointing it at Kera. "You think I need Enaurl when I have this?"

"Think you can hit me before I'm on top of you?" Kera asked.

"You better hope I can't," Smith growled. "Otherwise Enaurl is going to be scraping pieces of you off the ceiling for a week."

"Is that a challenge?" Kera hissed.

"Stop it, the both of you!" Morri shouted, moving to stand in between the two adults, her arms out wide. "This is simply nonsensical. You're both arguing over rubbish and are acting quite childish. I suggest you apologize to each other."

Morri glanced from Smith to Kera with an expectant look on her face. Smith and Kera's eyes remained locked on one another, neither willing to be the first to back down.

Morri's look of earnest and expectation sank into one of disappointment.

"Father, I hope you realize that you're setting a terrible example for me."

Smith scoffed and growled something under his breath.

"You don't even sound like a person," Kera commented. "You're like a cranky bear covered in oil wearing people clothes."

Smith opened his mouth to say something back, but Morri interrupted by clearing her throat and planting her hands on her hips, giving Smith a stern look.

"Fine!" Smith grumbled, throwing his hands into the air. "I'm going back out. You three do whatever the hell you want, but stay inside unless you want to get arrested. Or don't. Believe me when I say it won't bother me either way."

"What about her apology?" Morri demanded.

"She's not getting one," said Smith. "She had a knife against my throat."

"You called her a word she didn't care for," Morri countered. "She was merely defending her honor against your verbal assault."

"Defending her honor?" Smith echoed incredulously. "Verbal assault?"

"Yeah, that's right." Kera said, slowly rising from her crouched position. "You assaulted the crap out of my honor, so I defended it with knives."

Morri turned around and lifted her head to face Kera.

"I believe you should apologize as well," said Morri. "Your non-conformance to societal norms is noted, but that's no reason to resort to such intemperate actions."

"My *what* is noted?" Kera asked. "Resort to what? Kid, when you talk, it's like we're not even speaking the same language."

"Welcome to my life," Smith grumbled, snatching up the bottle of dwarven spirits as he did. He uncorked it and drank a liberal amount of it before swallowing, wincing at the burn. He wiped his lips with the back of his sleeve and made his way to the door.

"Father, where are you going?" Morri asked.

"Yes, Father," teased Kera, "Pray, do tell."

"The Ass's Glasses or at least what's left of it," Smith grumbled, snatching up the bottle of dwarven spirits.

"What for?" Kera asked.

"To see what I can do about getting your bounty annulled so I can get you the hell out of my house," said Smith. "Enaurl, watch Morri."

Smith made his way to the door and left, letting the door bang shut behind him. A second later, he opened the door once more and poked his head back in.

"Nevermind watching Morri, watch Kera. Make sure she doesn't... I don't know, just watch her."

"What am I going to do?" Kera asked, lifting a piece of scrap. "Steal all this super valuable stuff?"

Smith glared at her from the barely opened door for a moment longer, then turned and left, letting the door bang shut once more.

Kera waited to see if Smith would pop back into the shop once again, but when it became apparent that he wasn't going to, she looked down at Morri.

"Your old man is a real grouch," she said.

"Yes, he can be rather short-tempered on occasion," said Morri.

"He doesn't... Hurt you when he gets angry, does he?" Kera asked in a monotone.

"Hurt me?" Morri repeated. "Father? No, never. He loves me far too much for that. Besides that, your comparison to a bear was quite correct. Only I like to think of him as a big grumpy bear that's been awakened from hibernation far too soon and is quite cross with everyone."

Kera gauged Morri's response and expression and decided that they were genuine. Sickly sweet to the point of being nearly nauseating, but genuine all the same.

"You should probably finish telling me about the attack in the alley," Kera said. Morri's smile slid off her face and disappeared entirely, leaving the girl tight lipped.

"I suppose you're right," said Morri. The girl heaved out a hefty sigh, one that seemed to carry the weight of the world with it. "After you'd been tossed away like a mere child's plaything--"

"Do you need to describe it like that?" Kera asked.

"Discarded like rubbish?" Morri offered. "Thrown away like a tattered old boot?"

"Forget I said anything," Kera said with a grimace. "Tell the story your way."

"Alright, I shall," said Morri. "Feeling that same unnatural icy fear once more made the hooded figure seem to grow larger in my mind's eye, making them tower over me at an impossible height. The shadow they cast seemed to swallow up every spot of light in the world, leaving me alone in a dark and frightening place."

Morri trailed off for a moment, looking distant and thoughtful as she fell into her memory of the event. Her little shoulders trembled, shuddering with the recollection. She shook it off and pressed on.

"That's about the moment when you interrupted him again, only this time..."

"Let me guess," Kera said. "I puked on myself. Or on his shoes. Or on your shoes."

"No, actually." said Morri. "You, well..."

Morri turned to look at the closed door as if concerned it would open. Satisfied, she tiptoed towards Kera with a look of wild satisfaction on her face.

"You kicked his ass," Morri said, giggling.

Kera smiled as Morri tittered with childish glee, reminding Kera very much of herself at that age.

"You kicked his *ass!*" Morri repeated, laughing once more. She heaved a sigh and wiped a tear from her eye as she smiled up at Kera. "Oh, how *fun*. Now, returning to the matter at hand--"

"Why do you do that?" Kera asked.

"Do what?" said Morri.

"Actively try not to be a kid," said Kerra.

"As I've said, children are fairly dull," said Morri. "The vast majority of them would be terrible engineers. I'm perfectly content with being myself the way I am, thank you."

"Ah," said Kera.

"If you could hold any further questions until after I've finished telling the story, I think that would be best," said Morri, stunning Kera into silence.

Wordlessly, Kera extended an open palm towards Morri and made a circular motion, gesturing for the girl to continue. Morri offered a short nod of appreciation.

"The fear was shattered when something hit the figure in the side of the head. Something metallic, a length of pipe I think, judging by the sound it made as it clattered on the cobblestones. You hit him quite hard, enough so that he stumbled to the side. That was enough to make the feeling of coldness break and to let my mind unfreeze. I know it wasn't a logical reaction to make but my first instinct was to make myself very small and hide behind Enaurl."

"Peeking out from behind her legs, I watched as the figure righted themselves and turned to reach for me again but a streak of something silver in color flew through the air and hit the back of his legs, causing him to tumble to the ground. I closed my eyes for a moment, but I heard shouting followed immediately by the sound of something making an impact against the ground. Someone grunted in pain and I heard the sound of swords clashing. I opened my eyes and saw you and the figure engaged in vigorous swordplay."

"If you'd asked me beforehand, I would have thought your sword was a touch too large for you, but the way you used it in combat was quite impressive. I swore several times that you were about to be stabbed or slashed or perhaps impaled on the end of the figure's claws--"

"I'm sorry, did you say claws?" Kera asked. Morri gave her a stern look and didn't answer. A moment of silence passed between the two.

"You still want me to hold my questions," said Kera. "Sorry, go ahead."

"As I was saying," Morri said, speaking slowly while staring intently at Kera.

Gods, kid, thought Kera. *Message received, get on with it.*

"There were several times I thought for sure you'd be killed but at the last moment you'd either swing that sword of yours into position or deflect a blow with the pipe, as if you knew when each attack was coming and knew to anticipate them. The speed at which you moved, paired with the precision... It barely seemed possible."

"The figure seemed to become frustrated as well and while it had been moving with a deadly precision initially, I watched as it began to slow. I should suspect this figure was not prepared for a lengthy combat. I could see the end of the struggle was coming, but even when it did I hadn't properly anticipated it. The figure lunged forward, bringing one clawed hand across and in front of itself in a slashing motion. You ducked backwards beneath the attack and spun on your heels and into a sort wind up swinging motion. The figure's arms were out wide to either side, opening them up completely. When they lunged, you swung upwards so forcefully that the pipe's arc brought it over your shoulders. I'll never forget the sound it made. *Plonk*."

"The figure stumbled backwards and seemed to struggle to stay upright. The whole world went silent for a moment and the silence seemed to go on forever. Finally, it was broken by someone shouting from behind the cart to ask what the holdup was and if we could hurry up and move along already.

"It seemed that the shouting shattered the effect. The hooded figure made an unusual sort of whimper of frustration and turned its head towards the rear of the cart. You followed suit and so did I. It was Mister Fogle, the woodcrafter, carting a bundle of lumber towards the Ass's Glasses--"

"Wait," said Kera, interrupting again. "You can say 'Ass's Glasses' perfectly fine, but the word 'ass' by itself is somehow so hilarious you forget you're not Professor Gloompants for two seconds?"

"For starters, 'Ass' in this context refers to the animal and I find nothing about animal husbandry amusing. Specifically, I find it uninteresting. Far too many variables," said Morri. "Second, while I'm not familiar with Professor Gloompants I do feel flattered at being compared to a scholar. I appreciate, thank you."

"What happened next?" asked Kera, rolling her eyes.

"When I looked away from Mister Fogle, the figure was gone. The space they'd occupied a moment before was simply empty as if they'd vanished using whatever impossible method they'd used to appear in the first place," said Morri. "I held Enaurl tight. I was afraid the figure would reappear and try to take me once more. You then began to blink rapidly and began having what I now strongly suspect was a whispered conversation with your sword. I have to assume the sword answered in your mind, as you put it, because the conversation seemed quite one-sided. I'm curious to know why you bother speaking out loud at all if the weapon truly can communicate with you directly. Can't you simply respond with it in the same manner or perhaps allow it to glean your thoughts rather than respond aloud?"

"It's..." Kera began, trailing off for a moment. "Complicated. What happened next?"

"Well, after you finished discussing something with the sword, you unsteadily made your way towards me and asked if I was alright. I said I was fine, asked you if there was anything I could do in return for saving me. You hopped into the back of my cart and asked me to take you to the nearest pawnbroker. Seeing as how we weren't far from the Lucky Copper, I asked Enaurl to take us there."

Kera winced and shut her eyes tightly as her stomach sank. She felt certain she could guess what had happened next.

"Once we'd arrived, you asked us to wait outside, saying you wouldn't be long – something I feel I should tell you was ultimately a lie. It took nearly a full hour for you to come back out. Once you did, you emerged with no sword and a radiant glow."

"Radiant glow?" Kera echoed dispassionately.

"Yes, it was actually quite beautiful" Morri said. "It was as if your eyes were burning with technicolor phosphorous, emitting dazzling light and sparks that shifted from color to color all across the spectrum. You laughed then, in a bizarre sort of detached way. You gave me a mock salute, thanked me for my service, then skipped down the street singing some sort of battle hymn."

"The last thing I saw you do before you turned around the corner was take a lit torch down from the side of the bakery. Enaurl and I made to return home, only to watch you sprint ahead of us from the opposite direction as a chorus of shouts rang out. I asked you where you were going and you hopped back into the wagon, saying 'wherever the winds take me!'"

"You'd fallen asleep by the time we got here, so I had Enaurl put you in father's bed. He rarely uses it and you're too large for mine. You spent the last two days making an awful racket with your snoring and you are no doubt familiar with the events of today. I believe that brings us back up to the present. Did you want to ask any questions now?"

"Nope," Kera said, a grim expression on her face. "I'm all caught up."

"You are?" Morri asked. "You're no longer curious about the claws? Not curious to know any specifics about combat?"

"The pawnbroker," Kera said. "What did your father say his name was? Something Hornbuckle?"

"Brenno Hornbuckle, yes," Morri said with a nod. "Unusual little fellow. Quite peculiar, though I'm told that's not a rare trait among halflings."

"We need to go pay him a visit," said Kera. "Do you have an empty crate laying around here? We're going to need a big one. We'll also need a tarp and a lid. Do you have those?"

"What do we need those for?" asked Morri.

"Well, Morri," Kera said with a smirk. "I'm going to need your help again."

"Doing what?" Morri asked.

"I need you and Enaurl to deliver something for me."

Chapter Seven

Brenno Hornbuckle was a halfling who had a few simple pleasures in life. He liked keeping the floors of his pawn shop, the Lucky Copper, clean and freshly swept. He liked to be able to see his reflection in the glass of the windows and on the display cases. The items in the display case had to be polished - the coins in his coffer neatly stacked. He was an organized man and had no patience for fingerprints, dust bunnies, errant pebbles, or trash. Unfortunately for Brenno, running a pawn shop this far north on Malzen meant that there was often trash in his store.

He called them clients.

Always clients, never customers. To Brenno, the word 'client' implied repeat business; repeat business meant more coin and 'more' was the best amount of coin.

Alone in his humble storefront – humble by his description only, as it contained a good number of valuable things - he scratched away a bit of gunk that had somehow stuck to the elaborate display case in which he kept his wares. Some of those items that would undoubtedly make the halfling very rich when he found the right buyer.

Custom-made and worth a small fortune itself, the display case had the strongest dwarven glass money could buy and its frame had been carved by the most renowned wood elf artisans Brenno had been able to lure out of the Glimmervale. A less than savory contact he had with a guild that preferred not to be named had been paid a handsome sum to install deadly traps on the locks - a secret he kept to himself.

Brenno was closer to middle age than not; he had no children or romantic entanglements to speak of - but he was perfectly content with his life. His routine in the shop was plenty fulfilling and the wares he'd collected and the coin he earned was all the family he needed.

He exhaled onto the side of the case, letting his breath fog up the glass before wiping it away with a cloth to reveal his own smiling reflection.

"Well, hello there," Brenno said to himself. "Someone is looking absolutely glorious today – and it's not just me."

He chuckled softly at his own joke. It didn't matter to him that he'd known the entire time that he was cleaning that he would make the joke or that he used the same joke on himself every morning.

It's knowing your audience that matters, he thought to himself, as he so often did. *If you can read a room, you can beat the room.*

Satisfied with the condition of his display, Brenno walked along its length. The case was taller than he was and so he'd had a wooden platform built along the back on which he could stand. Essentially a high stair, the platform served the dual purpose of helping him clean and letting him stand eye-level with the taller, non-halfling people of Zelwyr. He'd spent most of his life having to look up to those folks while speaking to them, and he hadn't once cared for it. The platform added a full two and a half feet to his height, letting him stand a little over six feet tall.

Of course, the fact that this meant he now towered over any other halflings who entered his shop was of no consequence – or so he said. In truth, the halfling man secretly cherished feeling tall and powerful; a feeling that was amplified when he could look down at the pleading faces of his kin and tell them 'no' with a smile on his face.

Just the thought of being able to do so was enough to bring a smile to his face presently and set his fingers wiggling with glee.

Maybe I'll get lucky and get to do exactly that at some point today, he thought.

His love for the art of haggling and bartering had led to his family joking that he was more dwarf than halfling. He had to assume they still did, but had no way to know for sure; he hadn't spoken with any of them in over a decade.

The bell mounted over his front door rang and Brenno felt a rush of excitement. Eager as he was to greet a new client, a deep scowl creased his face when the silver-skinned form of Enaurl walked through the doorway carrying a fairly sizable wooden crate in front of her with both hands.

That contraption is never more than a few feet away from its owner, he thought, crossing his arms in front of his chest as Enaurl moved through the store. When the automaton made to put the crate on top of his precious glass, Brenno practically squeaked in dismay.

"Don't put that there, you silver simpleton!" Brenno scolded. "Put it on the floor."

"You shouldn't refer to her as a simpleton, you know," Morri said, having walked in with Enaurl but remained hidden behind her. "She's quite brilliant and while she may not convey much, I'm certain that there is a depth to Enaurl that even you will come to appreciate one day, Mister Brenno."

The pawnbroker sighed. This was not a very auspicious start to his day.

"Hello, Morrillypallyke," Brenno exhaled. "What can I do for you?"

"I'd ask for you to apologize to Enaurl," Morri began, "but I've long since come to understand that you view her as a mere object rather than a person. It's quite callous of you, I must say."

"She *is* an object, Morrillypallyke," Brenno said with exasperation. "She is a physical item that your father constructed with scrap parts from failed projects and whatever other junk he had laying around his shop at the time. She could be taken apart, reassembled, or duplicated. As a matter of fact, 'she' isn't even a 'she'--"

"I believe you've quite made your point, Mister Brenno, thank you," Morri said, moving to stand beside Enaurl, close enough that she could put her small hands around the construct's arm. "Regardless of our differences in opinion, I'd been asked to ensure that the contents of this crate reach you in as direct a manner as possible. I've done so."

"Sent from your father, I assume?" Brenno asked, becoming curious. "I told him if he had something to sell me to have me come *there,* not bring it *here.*"

"Not from father, no. From one of his associates," said Morri. "As I said, I'd been tasked with ensuring it arrives here and now I have. Oh, before I go, I was also told this would be something you'd rather keep to yourself."

Brenno was long accustomed to the girl's unusual manner of speaking and didn't mind it in the slightest. It was a welcome reprieve from the mangled half-speak he often encountered from some of his less-civilized clients.

"Your father doesn't have many associates these days," Brenno said. "And what's more, those few that he has are still furious that he doesn't let them buy a machine like Enaurl or at least a copy of her plans. Hells, even I've offered him a small fortune to build me one to act as a guard."

"I think you mean to say 'enforcer'," Morri interjected.

"Potentially," Brenno said with a smile. "Regardless, your father's penchant for secrecy paired with his... shall we say *lack of diplomacy* have left him with very few associates, almost none of whom are Zelwyran. What in the world would someone be shipping him in a crate this size? What would possess him to have Enaurl bring it here if he didn't want it, rather than disassemble it for parts?"

The hair on the back of Brenno's neck was tingling; he liked to think this was his sixth sense. His experiences as a pawnbroker working together with his short-lived career as an adventurer to warn him about something suspicious.

"I'm afraid I couldn't say, Mister Brenno," Morri said. "All I was told was to deliver this to you and to assure you that you would desire privacy when you open it."

"That's twice you've mentioned that now," Brenno noted, arching an eyebrow. "Your father hasn't decided to send me some kind of trap, has he?"

"I sincerely doubt my father would have me deliver you something dangerous, Mister Brenno," Morri said with a smile. "I can stay with you while you open it if you would like."

Brenno mulled this over, glancing between the girl's face to the crate.

To hell with it, he thought, *the girl's right. Smith might be confusing, but he's certainly not reckless when it comes to his child.*

With a sigh of resignation, he stepped down from the platform behind the counter and walked around front. Morrillypallyke's eyes never left Brenno, setting him further on edge. He paused midway to the crate. He watched the girl's face carefully as he did, trying to see if he could spot any signs of unease.

If she's up to something, I want to know about it in advance, thought Brenno.

Morri's expression didn't change in the slightest, but the halfling swore he heard her breath catch. He smiled, feeling like a cat who had caught a mouse by its tail. Morri smiled back at him, seemingly innocent.

You're up to something, alright, Brenno thought. *I just don't know what.*

Smiling all the wider, he stepped away from the crate and back towards his display case and carefully undid the latch that held it shut. The second lock took him a few moments due to his caution around the mechanism; a misstep meant that the trap he'd had installed would fire a dart at him, one coated by a particularly effective paralyzing poison. Being clumsy here meant Brenno might find himself unable to move so much as his eyeballs for upwards of a week.

At last, the trap disarmed.

Ka-clunk, thunk.

Brenno swung the glass pane up and over his head to open it. Reaching in, he took an exquisite looking wooden crossbow with a paper sign in front of it. The sign read 'Magical! Reduced to clear! Un-BOW-lievable price!'

Next, he took a gilded silver arrow from off the top of a velvet pillow. The sign in front of it of it was just a skull Brenno had drawn.

Brenno loaded the arrow onto the crossbow and pulled it back.

Click.

"May I ask what you intend to use that for, Mister Brenno?" Morri asked.

Brenno swung the display case shut, letting the hinges swing closed without the faintest squeak. Once the glass pane closed, the trap rearmed.

Ka-clunk, thunk.

"May I ask first what's inside that crate?" Brenno countered.

"I'm afraid I couldn't tell you," said Morri.

"In that case," Brenno said, aiming the crossbow at the crate as he began to move towards it. "Perhaps you should think of it as insurance."

"Insurance against what exactly, Mister Brenno?" Morri asked.

"Well, my dear," said Brenno, "I have been a pawnbroker for many years. I've met all sorts of questionable persons with all manner of devious schemes--"

"Are you saying I'm up to something devious, Mister Brenno?"

"I'm saying that I feel unsure," said Brenno. "When I feel *unsure*, I like to take steps to *en*sure that I am *re*assured."

He tapped the side of the crossbow twice.

"This is that insurance."

"I shall have to take your word for it, Mister Brenno." Morri said, attention focused squarely on the crate. "Though I must admit, your assessment of me as being a questionable person is somewhat disheartening. I had thought us to be on good terms. Why, I've been so kind as to bring you cinnamon buns on occasion."

"Indeed you have," Brenno muttered, not paying any attention to Morri as he closed the gap between himself and the crate.

He was close now, barely three feet away. Moving cautiously, he stepped closer and reached a hand out to touch the side of the crate. He stood as still as he could manage, trying to see if he could detect any movement or activity in the crate.

"Cinnamon buns and generosity are well and good, but they don't put you beyond suspicion in what I believe is a highly unusual scenario."

"Atypical, perhaps," Morri admitted with a shrug. "Though I should hardly think someone delivering a crate to a pawnbroker would be considered unusual."

"Yes, well," Brenno said, releasing his held breath.

My senses aren't as sharp as they'd once been. I'm relatively certain that there isn't anything moving inside crate, he thought. *Still, I'm keeping the crossbow out.*

Keeping one hand on his crossbow, the halfling tried to use the other to open the lid of the crate but found it to be surprisingly heavy. To make matters worse, the lid was roughly shoulder level with himself, taking away any leverage he might have had.

"Can you open this for me, please?"

"Mister Brenno," said Morri, planting her hands on her hips. "Am I to believe that while this crate makes you fear for your own safety - enough so to arm yourself, I might add - you have no qualms asking a young girl to do what you're too afraid to do?"

She has a point, Brenno thought with a grimace.

"Fine," he said. "Can you have Enaurl open the lid for me?"

"If you'd like me to," said Morri.

"Please," said Brenno.

The tone of their conversation was civil, but Brenno couldn't help himself from feeling increasingly on edge all the while. A single bead of sweat formed at his temple. He wiped it away with the back of his sleeve.

Morri turned to Enaurl and gestured towards the crate, conveying a wordless instruction to the automaton the way she did. Brenno furrowed his brow.

It makes me deeply uncomfortable when she does that, he thought.

The synthetic humanoid bent low and leaned across the top of the box so that she could place a hand on either side of the lid. With effort noticeable only through the sudden increase in the volume of the mechanisms in her body, the construct lifted the lid up from the crate and held it aside.

From where he was standing, Brenno couldn't see all the way into the crate, so he tried to stand on his tiptoes to get a better look. Unfortunately, the height of the box made it so he could barely see half way down the back wall. With a cautious glance towards Morri and Enaurl, he inched his way closer to the box and made himself as tall as he could. Looking inside, he saw the glint of something metallic at the very bottom of the crate. He relaxed slightly and inched ever closer.

"I'm not sure I recognize that," he said, leaning over the edge to try to reach the object in the crate. "What is that?"

Suddenly, Brenno felt the unmistakable sensation of being kicked in the butt, hard enough that he tumbled over the lip of the crate and landed inside. The lid slammed down on him.

"In my line of work, we call it a distraction," said Kera, tapping the box from the outside. "How you doing in there?"

With a frustrated shout, Brenno righted himself and aimed his crossbow in the direction of Kera's tapping and squeezed the trigger. The arrow flew from the crossbow and pierced partway through the wood, the point emerging near Kera's hand.

"I'm going to take that as 'just fine'," Kera said with a smirk.

"Let me out of here at once!" Brenno shouted from inside the box, working to haul the arrow back out of the wood. "Morri, I'm going to have some stern words with your father when I get out of here! He's not going to be impressed with you, young lady!"

The halfling stood straight up in an attempt to push his way to freedom, but met such tremendous resistance that he was knocked back down.

Enaurl must be sitting on the top of the create, he thought.

"He might not be, but I am," Kera said, speaking into the box. "Besides, how do you think Smith is going to feel about you pointing a crossbow at his precious gem? Probably not too keenly, I would think. Besides that, I think it would be pretty understandable if Enaurl were to crush someone who aimed a loaded weapon at a little girl. What, with her being a lifeless simpleton and all."

Brenno howled in fury, shouting every curse word he knew at the graverobber.

"Gods, Brenno," said Kera, "there's a child present! Watch your mouth."

Brenno responded by stringing together an especially vulgar list of insults; the profanity made Morri's eyes and mouth go wide.

"Now that was just *foul*," said Kera, taking mental notes. "Since that's out of the way, I think it's time we started negotiating. What do you say?"

"What the *fuck* do you *want!?*" Brenno shouted.

"Easy," said Kera, "I just want my sword back."

"You sold it to me fair and square," Brenno protested. "You took a payment in exchange for relinquishing ownership of an item. That's how a selling something works. What makes you think you can just come back and steal it?"

"The thing is, I wasn't actually paid for it, was I?" Kera asked. "Seems I didn't leave here with a lick of coin on me."

"Payment in kind is still payment," Brenno grumbled. "You were paid and well."

"Oh that's right… you did pay me in incredibly illegal drugs, didn't you?" Kera asked rhetorically. "I must have forgotten about that. Thanks for reminding me."

"What's your point?" Brenno bristled. "You wanted coin to go out and find it on your own. I happened to have some inventory that needed to be liquidated so I helped you cut out the middleman. I did you a *favor*."

"Oh, I know and I appreciate it," Kera said. "It's just that I wonder how Sheriff Treia and Steward Ombard would feel about having a known ash dealer in town. A lot of official types don't take too kindly to that sort of thing."

"And why would they listen to you, eh?" Brenno hissed. "It would be my word - that of a respected and established professional, against yours – that of a thieving, drug-addled arsonist. How exactly do you intend to turn me in, eh? Through the bars of the jail cell you'll be thrown in the moment you're seen outside?"

"Well, not exactly," said Kera. "Seems there was a reliable witness who can verify everything. One that I could ask to go talk to the Sheriff for me – cutting out the middleman, like you put it."

"Convenient," Brenno scoffed, pulling the arrow free at last. "And just where would this mystery witness happen to be, eh? I've been blackmailed before, Kera No-Clan, and let me say this one of the weaker attempts."

"As a matter of fact," said Kera, "she's right here."

Brenno loaded the crossbow as silently as he could, thinking on Kera's words.

"Morrillypallyke," he realized grimly. "You're going to lie for this cretin, aren't you?"

"I'm afraid it wouldn't be a lie, Mister Brenno," said Morri. "I escorted Kera here that same morning and saw her immediately after she left. There was a very telltale glow about her eyes - a rather unmistakable instance of the reaction caused by ingesting a specific strain of luciferin present in fae ash, or 'fairy dust' as I'm being led to believe it is sometimes called."

"And how would you know that?" Brenno asked.

"I read a lot of books, Mister Brenno," said Morri.

"See?" said Kera, banging on the side of the crate. "Loosey ferrets."

"That's not at all what I said," Morri corrected. "It's luciferin. It's a biological compound that causes light. I've often wondered if it would be possible to replicate it in a non-magic means. You could bring light to the world. No fuel or mage required."

"Is now the best time to be thinking about that?" Kera asked.

"I suppose not," said Morri, failing to hide the disappointment in her voice.

"As I was saying," said Kera, speaking closely to the hole in the side of the crate. "I want my sword back. You give it up, I let you out, and we never have to see each other again."

"I hope you know," said Brenno, "that you made me the same promise the last time we spoke."

"I'm good at making promises," said Kera.

"Rubbish at keeping them, it would seem." Brenno grumbled.

"Only when it matters," said Kera.

"Are you trying to say you keep them when it matters or that you only break them when it matters?" asked Brenno.

"Both," said Kera. "Either. Depends on the day."

"Do you see the kind of woman she is, Morri?" Brenno shouted from inside the crate. "This is the type of person you want to associate yourself with? Do you really think your father would approve of trapping me in a crate and allowing this miscreant to treat me like this?"

"Truth be told, Mister Brenno, I'm not at all certain how Father would feel about this," said Morri. "But I know that Kera saved my life and so I owe her a debt that I cannot possibly repay. Regardless of the present situation, you did indeed break the law."

"And she is breaking it now!" Brenno protested.

"Yes, that's true," Morri admitted, "however, there are many instances in which one must deal with the original problem before moving on to the problems caused by it. I do hope you understand, Mister Brenno."

The halfling let out another barrage of expletives and didn't stop until Kera kicked the side of the crate.

"Show some class, Brenno," Kera said. "Remember, the sooner you tell me where my sword is, the sooner your alone time comes to an end."

"What's so special about this sword, eh?" Brenno spat. "You're a barbarian, after all. Can't you make do with a pointy stick and a large rock and just leave me alone?" Brenno's retort was met with a long moment of silence.

"Mister Brenno," said Morri, "I feel I should tell you Kera doesn't much care for being referred to in that way."

"Is that so?" Brenno asked, tone heavy with mock interest. "Do tell me why it is that I should care what a barbarian prefers to be called when they are acting positively barbaric?"

"I must admit, I am unclear on why nomenclature has such an effect on her," Morri said, her growing concern making her voice rise. "Unfortunately, I am very clear on the effects a lit torch has in a confined space."

"A lit torch in a…" Brenno said.

Realization hit him like a bolt of lighting.

"You're not going to let her put a torch in here, are you Morri?" Brenno asked, backing himself up to the far corner and raising the crossbow.

Instead of the lid being opened, the head of a torch burst in through the hole in the wall he'd made when he pulled the arrow free. The air in the crate became thick with smoke almost immediately, stinging his eyes and burning his lungs.

"Oh yes, this is quite civilized behaviour," shouted Brenno, sweating as the temperature in the crate began to rise already. "How could I possibly have been mistaken?"

"I don't believe Kera intends to harm you," said Morri, her concern now fully apparent. "I'm also fairly certain she wouldn't be upset if you were harmed accidentally."

"Oh, really?" Brenno asked sarcastically, practically frothing at the mouth with rage. "I hadn't realized that a barbarian in a foul mood might be dangerous to be around. It's almost as if I should have known better than to do business with a vile, degenerate, in-bred, savage like her from the moment she stepped her filthy boots into my store."

When resounding silence answered his taunt, Brenno felt quite satisfied with himself – or at least he did until he watched the torch get pushed through the hole to roll across the bottom of the crate, leaving a trail of burning oil behind it. The flame sputtered for a moment as it fell, leaking burning blubber in a puddle that covered nearly half the floor of the crate in flames.

"Let me out," Brenno shrieked, backing as far away from the crackling fire as he could. "Let me out of here this instant! Let me out!" He pounded his fists against the wall and the floor.

"You can't kill him," Morri told Kera. "You need to let him out."

"He made his choice," said Kera.

"I *will* die in here, Morri!" Brenno shouted, coughing. "You'll be letting her *murder* me. Do you understand that?!"

"Let him out," Morri said, panic creeping into her voice. "If you don't, I'll make Enaurl get him out. I don't want anyone to get hurt."

Kera said nothing.

Brenno braced himself and steadied his grip on the crossbow.

"Kera!" Morri pleaded. "Say something, please!"

Still, the graverobber said nothing.

"Enaurl, let him out!" Morri shouted.

Thank the gods I bet on that kid, Brenno thought, doing his best to figure where he thought Kera might be standing.

The pawnbroker readied his crossbow and prepared to fire.

This is going to be the first two-legged thing I've shot in decades, Brenno thought. *I'm going to enjoy this.*

Enaurl got off the crate, pushed Kera, and lifted the lid of the crate.

Several things happened at once; the first of which was the door to Brenno's shop opening.

"You busy, Hornbuckle?" Smith shouted. "Listen, about that sword--"

Morri whirled around to face Smith, a look of terror and shame on her face.

Brenno leapt up against the side of the crate and rode it down, landing in a kneeling position with his crossbow drawn, aiming at Kera.

He squeezed the trigger.

Click.

The arrow flew towards Kera, who threw herself to the ground.

The arrow skimmed over her, missing by inches, and struck the glass of Brenno's display case. It ricocheted back, flying over Kera and just missing the crate.

It flew through Morrillypallyke's back and erupted out through her front, the tip sticking out from just below her collarbone.

The girl's breath caught - a sound so faint it was almost inaudible - but seemed deafening to the adults in the room.

Morri, hands shaking, put her hands on the bolt. Confused by the texture, she brought her hands to her face. They were sticky and red with her own blood.

"Oh," said Morri, "I see."

The girl collapsed and would have fallen flat on the floor if it weren't for Enaurl rushing to catch her. Seeming unsure as to what to do, the construct looked around the room before lowering the girl to the floor, carefully resting her on her side.

For a moment, Brenno, Kera, and Smith stood frozen as they watched a dark stain spread slowly across the front of Morri's dress.

Enaurl carefully pulled her hands out from under Morri, leaning her face in close to examine the arrow in Morri's body. Enaurl's neck turned at a harsh angle as she snapped her head towards Brenno, unblinking gaze locked onto him.

"Oh, fuck," Brenno whispered, letting the crossbow drop to the floor with a clatter.

The machine was on him in an instant, closing the distance between them faster than Kera could register. She closed one metal hand around his throat, lifting him from his feet to slam him into the wall. She punched a hole into the wall beside his head with the other, plowing through the wood with so much force the bell above the door rattled.

Brenno's hands fought to try and loosen the automaton's choking grip, but couldn't find purchase on her polished silver skin. His legs kicked wildly as he fought for purchase.

Smith felt like he was moving in slow motion, rushing to Morri as fast as he could but never seeming to get there. The shallowness of her breath was deafening, the distance between them somehow enormous.

Kera stood slowly but stayed in place. Her every instinct screamed at her to run out the back door immediately - to keep running and never look back. For reasons she didn't fully comprehend, she ignored them and stayed frozen on the spot.

He scooped up the child – *his* child, his little girl – as delicately as if she were made of glass and stood. It seemed to Kera that it took him ages to stand again. In a space that seemed to exist between seconds, Kera looked into Smith's eyes.

He looked right through her. Kera saw pain, loss, and a heavy weariness.

Time came screaming back to full speed all at once. Brenno choking for air and the crackle of burning crate filled the air once more.

"Enaurl," Smith called, eyes watering as his hands wavered around the bolt protruding from Morri's chest.

Enaurl didn't move. She tightened her grip on Brenno's throat and bringing her face closer to the halfling's as he struggled for air.

"Enaurl!" Smith called again.

She looked at Smith.

"Let him go."

Enaurl's hand opened immediately, leaving Brenno to fall into a sputtering heap on the floor.

"Run her to the temple district. Find Speaker Gerhardt. If you can't find him, just find a healer, *any* healer. I don't care who. Do. *Not*. Jostle her. Do you understand? Don't do any more damage than what's already done"

The construct didn't respond, at least not in any way Kera could see. Enaurl turned and carefully took Morri into the crook of her arm before running full speed towards the door, flinging it open so forcefully Brenno's bell was knocked off. The bell's hammer clattered wildly as the ornament rolled across the floor.

"I'm calling the guards," Brenno said.

"To tell them you shot a little girl?" Smith snapped.

"That's not... There was more to it than that."

"Do you think that matters?" Smith asked. Brenno fell silent, holding his throat in his hands.

"Shouldn't you go after them?" Brenno asked. Smith unholstered his thunder cannon and pointed it at Brenno. The barrel was centered directly on the halfling but the weapon shook in Smith's quivering grasp. Brenno's shoulders slumped as he stared up at Smith through watery, bloodshot eyes.

"Well, go on with it then," Brenno said.

"Smith, I--" Kera said, stepping forward.

To her surprise, Smith brought the weapon to bear on her. She took a step back, slowly raising her hands as she did.

"Right back where we started, huh?"

"Almost," said Smith, "except this time, Morri might die. I was worried about letting her around you. She swore up and down that you protected her, that you kept her safe, and now..."

Smith's voice trailed off and the tip of the cannon began quivering all the more. The weapon started to rattle. Smith gripped it with two hands to try to stop the shaking entirely, but all he managed to do was reduce it somewhat.

Brenno made to move away from the wall, but Smith turned and pointed the barrel at him once more, stopping him dead in his tracks.

"We can't do this all day, Smith," said Brenno. "If you're going to shoot us, do it already. Otherwise, call the guards. I'll plead my case and our mutual problem over there ends up in irons and out of our lives."

Kera's insides felt cold.

"I'm not going to jail," she said, her voice like ice. "Like he said, if you're going to shoot, do it. I didn't hurt her. *He* did, but go ahead - I'd rather be dead than in a cage."

"Typical," Brenno said with a snort, "the barbarian wants to save her own skin."

"Call me that one. More. Time."

"Bar," said Brenno. "Bear. Ee. An."

Kera ran and jumped onto Brenno, flattening him with a flying knee that brought Kera down on top of his throat, cutting off his air supply. She raised a fist to punch his teeth in.

Crack-BOOM.

A sound like thunder rent the air.

Kera and Brenno turned to look as one to see Smith, weapon raised in the air above his head, glaring at them with unbridled fury. He lowered the weapon, a trail of smoke lazily crawling its way upward from the mouth of the barrel.

"Get up," growled Smith, pointing the thunder cannon at the entangled pair. The two rose awkwardly, standing side by side.

"Out," said Smith, swinging the barrel to the side to point towards the door.

Brenno and Kera spoke simultaneously.

"Smith, that crate is still burning and my floors are wooden. I need to--"

"Listen! I'm not kidding, I am *not* going back to jail, so why don't--"

"I said *out!*" Smith roared, eyes wild.

Click.

While neither Brenno nor Kera were familiar with the workings of the cannon, both knew enough to assess that the weapon was rearmed. Kera swallowed hard while Brenno put on a jaded grin.

"They'll arrest me on sight," Kera said.

"I won't let them," Smith growled.

"Because a tinkerer has *so much* authority," Brenno quipped.

"Out, both of you." Smith reiterated. Brenno made his way to the door first, a dour expression on his face. He spied the discarded bell on the ground and grimaced.

"I don't suppose you'll be paying to have that fixed," the halfling remarked. Smith's only response was stoic silence. "I didn't think so," Brenno said with a sigh. He opened the door wide and made a mock bow towards Kera.

"After you," he said. Kera looked to Smith once more, every bit of her wanting to run either out the door and away or directly at Smith to try to wrestle the weapon from his arms. The silent rage on Smith's face seemed to dare her to try either, the smoke still wafting from the mouth of the cannon, intermingling with the smoke from the burning crate. Resigned, Kera stepped out the door.

The first thing the pair saw outside was a small wagon with a tarp in the back.

"Get under the tarp," Smith ordered.

Chapter Eight

When the wagon came to a stop and Smith pulled back the tarp, Kera spied the unmistakable silver form of Enaurl standing outside the building in front of them. She spotted the temple markings on the building, a pair of crossed lines forming a wide black 'x' over a white background.

"The Lady in White," Kera murmured, recognizing the Crossed Roads of Perrus, the symbol of the goddess of healing, medicine, and botany. "Makes sense."

"What were you expecting?" said Brenno, "the Thunder-Bringer? The Fanged One? Some other savage god worshiped by the uncivilized?"

"Fuck the gods," Kera said quietly as she looked up at the temple looming before her. "They've never done anything for me. Why should I care about them?"

"And yet, you all but whispered," Brenno mocked. "Afraid someone on high might hear your curses? Maybe there's some sense in you after all."

"*Quiet*, both of you," Smith warned. Enaurl seemed to recognize Smith from a distance, her head turning at an unnatural angle to regard the trio as they approached.

"Unsettling as always," Brenno muttered.

Enaurl opened the door and stood to the side, letting the group enter the temple before she followed.

The temple reminded Kera of every other temple she'd been in, and she supposed that was intentional; a church was a church. Rows of wooden pews lined the walls, divided by a walkway filled with a carpet stretching from the entrance to the dais at the front. The carpet had elaborate patterns of interlocking circles, all monochrome, running down it, at the center of each was a stylized version of the White Lady's crossed roads.

Kera couldn't help but notice the droplets of blood that formed a trail all along the length of the carpet, leading towards the dais – atop which lay Morri, as still as before. An elderly man stood over Morri, hands raised above her. He was muttering something to himself, likely a prayer of healing. Smith brushed passed Kera and Brenno on his way to the pedestal. As an afterthought, he turned around and leered at the pair for a moment before returning his gaze to Enaurl.

"Keep them *here*," said Smith, hissing the words to the construct woman.

Enaurl's stance shifted, her gears grinding as she adjusted her posture, standing on the balls of her feet in a pose that showed she was equally ready to fight or give chase if the need for either arose. He crossed the temple quickly and arrived at the pedestal just as the old man finished his prayer.

As the last word his prayer hung in the air, the man lowered his hands towards Morri, a gentle yellow light shining down from them onto Morri. The light seemed to linger on Morri.

The man, evidently a healer, brought his hands together, each sweeping in towards the centre of her body from their respective sides. When they came together, the healer closed his fists except for each of his index fingers, one of which he crossed over the other to form the symbol of the crossroads directly over the open wound.

The bolt lay at her side, glistening red in the filtered light shining through a stained glass depiction of Perrus greeting the Broken God, Perroh - her divine brother and the god of death - at the intersection of life and death. The crossed fingers made the shadow of a wide 'x' over the center of the crimson stained tear in Morri's dress and flesh. A cloud inched its way in front of the sun, changing the light in the room. As the cloud moved across the sun, it seemed as though the shadow of the crossroads depicted on the pane of glass moved its way across the floor until it climbed up the dais and rested on Morri as well. Kera's breath caught and Brenno scoffed at her.

"So much for 'fuck the gods', eh?" Brenno whispered.

"Hating them doesn't make them not exist," Kera whispered back. "It just means I know they only give a shit when there's something in it for them. Besides, it was just a cloud."

"Clouds make you shake in your boots often?" Brenno asked, leaning in to speak softly as if they were children afraid of being caught. "If so, let me reassure you that they are perfectly natural phenomenon. I know your type doesn't get a lot of education about these sorts of things."

"What type is that, Brenno?" Kera asked, her veins flushing hot once more. Brenno seemed to be about to respond, but as he glanced back at Enaurl, he seemed to rethink the matter. He closed his mouth and looked away, pretending to be interested in something outside. "That's what I fucking thought."

Her cursing seemed to echo throughout the cathedral, garnering the attention of Smith and the healer. The old man had a gentle smile on his face, where Smith looked furious. Smith and the old man shared a quick conversation, too quiet for either Kera or Brenno to hear.

"Bring 'em here, Enaurl," Smith called out once they'd finished their exchange.

"Do try to be gentle, dear lady," the old man added. His voice was kind and filled with warmth. Though age had given it a bit of a warble, there was still a strength and tenor to it. Brenno yelped as Enaurl scooped him up over her shoulder like a sack of potatoes, which brought a smile to Kera's face until Enaurl did the same to her.

Kera tried to evade Enaurl's grip, but the automaton side-stepped into Kera's path and used her astounding strength to snatch Kera off her feet like she was weightless. It took Enaurl less than a dozen powerful strides to cross the temple, where she unceremoniously dropped the pawnbroker and the graverobber onto the small pedestal upon which the dais sat.

Kera and Brenno found themselves looking up to the mismatched faces of the serene old man and the contorted mask of rage that was Smith. Kera stood up and brushed herself off and Brenno did the same.

"You'll forgive me if I don't ask this correctly, it's just that I've never had to ask this question before," said the old man, still smiling warmly. "Would you be kind enough to explain to me which of you shot this small child?"

"He did it," Kera said immediately, hitching her thumb at Brenno.

The old man frowned, his wrinkled face crumpling in on itself as he looked down at Brenno.

"Is this true, Mister Brenno?" The old man asked.

"I'm afraid this lying, blackmailing, thieving arsonist is telling the truth, Speaker Gerhardt," Brenno admitted, bowing low before the old man – Speaker Gerhardt.

"Arsonist?" the Speaker echoed, bringing his eyes to rest on Kera.

She noted that they still contained a brightness, a certain vitality, that seemed to stand at odds with his age. Kera only shrugged in response.

"I've been called worse," said Kera, "I've also intentionally done worse, where as everything that's happened since I've gotten here as been pretty well an accident."

"There are no accidents with the divine," Gerhardt responded heartily. "As we are all but motes of divinity given form, we play a part in a greater plan."

"Oh, that's a relief," said Kera, her voice dripping with sarcasm. "Here I thought getting high out of my gourd on fae ash, going on a bender, burning half a city down, and accidentally getting a little girl shot might not be the right thing to do. Now that I know it's a part of the divine plan, I'm incredibly relieved. Thank you so much, Speaker Gerhardt." She mimed wiping sweat from her brow. "Whew, load off my mind."

"Show some respect, Kera!" Smith shouted at her.

"Now, now," Speaker Gerhardt said with a wave, "no need for shouting. I may be old, but the gods haven't seen fit to take my hearing away. Let's not give them any ideas, shall we?" He reached for something behind the dais.

Alarms started to sound in Kera's mind and kept going until she saw him step around the centerpiece with the help of a cane. She instantly relaxed. Speaker Gerhardt seemed to observe all this transpire and he halted his advance towards Kera. Resting both hands on the head of his cane, he regarded Kera and Brenno intensely, as if he were studying them. He maintained his silence for a long while, seemingly lost in thought. Finally he spoke again.

"I'm sure you'll both be relieved to know the girl is stable. The White Lady has seen fit to allow me to stay the hand of her dark twin."

Gerhardt smiled as he said this, but his smile seemed to slowly melt away once he'd finished. "However, for reasons I cannot fully understand - I find myself unable to fully mend the wound. It is healed enough that the girl yet lives, but not so much that she will awaken. I've asked Voldani to fetch a few relevant materials to search for answers."

Kera's eyes moved to Smith as the Speaker said those words, watching the man's face: his expression was an unstable mix of fear, stress, loss, and resolve. Kera, who did as much to ignore her emotions as she could, couldn't help but wonder how a person could feel so many different things all at once.

Probably something to do with being a parent, she thought. *Thank the gods that's not me. Want an obvious weakness? Have a kid.*

Speaker Gerhardt brought a shaking hand towards the pedestal. With great care, he brushed a few loose strands of Morri's hair away from her face. Once he'd finished, he gave the girl a pat on the forehead and carefully lifted the crossbow bolt off the dais. He held it by the shaft, careful not to touch the sharpened tip.

"Am I wrong, Mister Brenno, to believe there is an enchantment at work here in addition to the obvious poison? I have been by the tavern halls more than enough times to hear you rant about the traps, weaponry, magic, and poisons you have laying in wait around every corner of your shop."

"I wouldn't say *laying in wait* per say, Speaker."

"The glibness seems rather unnecessary," Speaker Gerhardt warned. "This is your arrow that I removed from poor Morri here, is it not?

"It is, Speaker."

"Fired from a crossbow that you shot?"

"Yes, Speaker," Brenno answered grimly.

"Then it seems to me you could stand to be less sharp-tongued and a bit more repentant, Mister Hornbuckle," said the Speaker. "You could start by elaborating as to what it is exactly that is ailing poor Morrillypallyke."

Brenno was quiet.

"Well?" Gerhardt prompted.

"Just trying to decide where to begin, Speaker," said Brenno said with a sigh. "The crossbow is enchanted. It rarely misses. When you shoot a target with it, you always seem to find that you hit it somewhere vital. I'm no mage, Speaker, I don't have a means to understand the enchantment exactly... I can only make my best guess."

"An enchantment such as that explains the placement of the shot, Mister Brenno, but does not explain why she will not wake. What of the bolt?"

Brenno splayed his hands wide, and his words faltered.

"Just tell him, Hornbuckle," Smith urged.

"I'm afraid I don't know," said Brenno.

"*You don't know?*" Smith echoed, incredulous and enraged.

"That's what I said," Brenno confirmed.

"You bought a magic arrow without knowing what it does?" Smith demanded.

"Not exactly," said Brenno. "An orc brought it in, told me it was poison. I asked him to prove it, so he stabbed his friend in the arm with it. His friend fell over dead, so I was convinced. In hindsight, they may not have been friends. Not good ones, at least."

"Orchestrate many murders to sample your wares, Mister Brenno?" the Speaker asked. "I can't help but find your story deeply troubling."

"I hardly orchestrated a murder, Speaker. I merely asked for proof," said Brenno. "I was given that proof, and so took the bolt into my store."

"But why?" the Speaker asked.

"Frankly, I don't see where your confusion stems from," Brenno said with outstretched palms, "I'm a *pawnbroker*. I provide a service to my clientele, and to all of Zelwyr proper, for that matter."

"Oh, piss off," said Smith. "Are you really trying to spin this into some public service you're providing? The fact that you take magic crap you don't understand?"

"I don't have to fully understand that bolt to know it's dangerous, much like many of the items that cross my threshold," Brenno said, looking from Smith to Gerhardt. "They come into Zelwyr in the hands of adventurers and campaigners, and if it weren't for me the streets of Zelwyr would see them put to far more nefarious uses."

"Ah," said Speaker Gerhardt, a wry tone in his voice. "Forgive me, Mister Brenno, I hadn't realized you'd been taking part in criminal transactions for the good of us all."

"It's as you said, Speaker," Brenno said, a sly grin spreading slowly across his face, "we all have our part to play."

Speaker Gerhardt furrowed his brow at the halfling, but couldn't suppress the small smile that turned the corners of his lips upwards.

"Very good, Mister Brenno," the Speaker said, pacing back around the pedestal to stand behind Morri once again. "Very good. It seems our hopes rest on what Voldani is able to uncover."

"What's a Voldani?" Kera asked.

"I am not a *what*," said a voice, clear and strong, speaking from the corner of the room. "I am a *who*."

All eyes turned towards the source of the voice and Kera's jaw fell open. Standing in the archway of a door she hadn't noticed before was the most beautiful woman she had ever seen.

She was tall and elegant, with deep black skin and tightly braided hair that hung in thin ropes. Kera couldn't decide if she was wearing a gown, a robe, or a suit of armor - it seemed to be all three at once.

Marching boots went part way up legs that disappeared beneath a white robe with gold trim that hung low between them, cut in such a way that allowed her freedom of movement and showed just enough of the statuesque woman's hips to drive Kera wild. Armor again appeared on the woman's chest, shoulders, and upper arms - arms which were cradling a large set of scrolls.

The final feature that caught Kera's attention was the woman's eyes, or lack thereof - instead, pools of soft yellow light shone out from the place where eyes should have been. It was impossible for Kera not to notice the similarity between this woman and the knights of Perrus depicted in the stained glass murals.

"Misters Smith and Brenno, I believe you have had the pleasure of meeting my newest associate, Lady--"

"Voldani will suffice," said the woman, "formalities are a waste of time."

She made her way to the folks gathered around the pedestal, passing the scrolls to the Speaker. As she walked passed Kera, the graverobber noted that her back was exposed from the base of her neck to midway down her back, exposing a shimmering tattoo of gleaming wings on her shoulder blades.

Holy shit, Kera thought, *she's a scion. A real, in the flesh, god-blooded scion.*

"Were you successful in your endeavor, Voldani?" the Speaker asked, hastily unrolling a scroll to scan its contents.

"As successful as an effort to locate dusty old scrolls can be," said Voldani. "You know, my previous Speaker had me come here in order to combat the machinations of a foul god. To date I have battled nothing but boredom, and unsuccessfully at that."

"I do apologize that clerical work is not to your liking, Voldani," the Speaker said, rolling a scroll back up before moving onto the next. "I did inform you that there was not much excitement to be had in these parts when you first arrived. In the meantime, perhaps you can find some solace knowing that your clerical work may yet help save the life of this young girl in front of us."

"I do find some joy in that, yes," said Voldani. "Have you any other tasks for me?"

"Not at the moment, I'm afraid."

"Then I shall return to my prayers," said Voldani.

"Good, yes," said the Speaker. "In meditation and inner reflection, the Lady in White reveals herself to us all."

"So I have been told," said Voldani, walking back towards the door. She paused, seeming to feel Kera's eyes on her as she walked. "Is there a problem with your neck?"

"Mine?" Kera asked. "Uh, no? Why?"

"Your head seems to follow me wherever I walk," said Voldani. "See that it stops immediately, least I be forced to remove it."

"My head or my neck?"

"First one, then the other," said Voldani.

Kera practically swooned on the spot.

"You got it," she said.

Voldani's luminous eyes seemed focused on Kera for a long moment, then the scion turned and left the room.

"You have a better chance of walking out of Zelwyr with all your crimes pardoned than you do bedding her," Brenno whispered.

"You keep acting like I'm not going to punch you in the throat," said Kera.

"So far, I've seen a lot of threats and very little action," said Brenno.

"I swear to every god in every temple in this whole district, I will shoot the both of you," said Smith, cocking the hammer of his firearm. "Give me an excuse, really."

"I've found it!" Speaker Gerhardt exclaimed, dropping all the scrolls he'd been handed but one. "There is an ancient Perrusian rite to cleanse all poisons, enchantments, curses, and other such ailments from a person."

"There is?" Smith asked, losing interest in Brenno and Kera entirely. "That's great. Let's get started. What do we have to do?"

"Well, according to this, we must simply recite a *very* old variation of the Crossway Prayer while praying over the victim at noon."

"It's almost noon now," said Smith.

"Just a moment, I'm reading about the requirements of the ritual," said the Speaker, clumsy hands struggling to move the parchment.

"Candles made with wax and ash, yes, an offering of nightshade and aloe, of course, an ointment of oil and... Oh."

Why don't I like the sound of that? Kera thought.

"Here it comes," Brenno muttered.

"An ointment of oil and what, Speaker?" Smith asked.

"Just a moment, Mister Smith, a moment if you please," said the Speaker, bringing the scroll closer to his face, head moving side to side as he scanned the text.

"Well?" Smith asked, jaw clenched.

"Oh," said Gerhardt. "I see."

Kera winced at the Speaker's unintentional repetition of Morri's final words. Smith seemed to be able to contain himself no longer.

"An ointment of oil and dragon blood," said the Speaker, lowering the scroll from his face. "It would seem that without the blood, the ritual is pointless."

The group was stunned into silence.

"Dragon blood," Smith said after a moment, voice low and filled with anger. "Should we get a unicorn's horn while we're at it? What about the eye teeth of a leviathan? While we're at it, how about a vampire's heart and a lich's phylactery?"

"Calm down, Smith," said Brenno.

"Don't," Smith seethed. "Don't you *dare* tell me to calm down, Hornbuckle."

"I'm just saying--"

"Saying what?" Smith interrupted. "You come across any dragon's blood while doing all that *civic duty* collecting magic doo-dads and mystic trinkets?"

"Well, no, but--"

"Didn't think so," said Smith. "How in the hells am I supposed to get *dragon blood,* Hornbuckle?"

"Not that anyone has asked me," said Kera, "but I'd be willing to bet there's plenty inside a dragon."

Smith and Brenno turned to face her.

"No shit," hissed Smith.

"Your genius astounds the mind," said Brenno.

"Oh, shove it, both of you," said Kera. "Unless either one of you has friends in Mian Dore, the only way you're getting your hands on dragon blood is by shooting one down with that fancy boomstick of yours, Smith. Shouldn't be a big deal."

"Shouldn't be a big..." Smith repeated, trailing off.

Veins began to bulge in his neck and forehead; Kera wondered if he wasn't going to explode.

"Have you ever even seen a dragon, Kera?" Smith asked.

"Yep," Kera answered. The casualness of her response seemed to catch the others off-guard and they all turned to face her.

"You have?" Brenno asked.

"Sure did."

"Whatever," said Smith. "Seeing one and fighting one are two different animals."

"I've done that too," said Kera. "Even killed one once."

"Bullshit," said Smith. "Horseshit. Drakeshit. Any kind of shit you can think of, all lumped together into one big pile of shit."

Speaker Gerhardt cleared his throat.

"Apologies, Speaker. I have a hard time believing anything that comes out of this woman's mouth."

"And why is that?" Kera asked.

"Where do I start?" Smith retorted with a snort. "There's the arson, the thieving, breaking and entering--"

"The blackmail," added Brenno.

"The blackmail, getting Morri shot, do I really need to continue?"

"Brenno shot her, not me." Kera corrected, pointing a finger at the halfling. "What does any of that have to do with whether or not I've killed a dragon?"

Brenno and Smith exchanged a look, then looked back to Kera.

"What color was it?" Brenno asked.

"Red," answered Kera.

"How did you encounter it?" asked Smith.

"It attacked the castle I was living in, and locked me in a tower," Kera quipped. "I stayed there, trapped outside space and time, waiting for a pair of thick headed idiots who could ask enough pointless questions for the dragon to set me free."

Speaker Gerhardt coughed as a cover to suppress a chuckle. Brenno made to

ask another question but didn't, while Smith's eyes seemed to glow with anger as
he glared at Kera.

"This isn't a fucking joke, Kera," Smith rumbled. "Morri is... Morri..."

The man took a deep breath, visibly fighting to stay on top of his emotions.
He brushed the back of a soot-stained glove across his face, and when he looked
at Kera again she could see tears welling up in the corners of his eyes.

"Morri is all I have," said Smith, fists trembling at his sides as he spoke. "If
you can do this – if you can actually do this – I need your help. I need her to be
okay, to be her happy, smiling, smarter-than-I'll-ever-be self again, do you
understand?"

Smith's voice quivered and threatened to break, which he tried to mask by
clearing his throat.

"She's my whole world. I lost her mom, I... I can't lose her too."

Speaker Gerhardt moved to stand beside Smith, putting his arm around the
other man's shoulders.

"There now, Mister Smith," the Speaker said, his voice calm and soothing.
"Be strong for Morri, that's what she would want. What's more, I'm certain that
lady Kera will do what she can do to undo the wrongs that have been wrought
since her arrival here in Zelwyr, isn't that right?"

Kera felt a tightness in her chest. The sensation only intensified when Smith
looked up at her, tears openly streaming down his face. He didn't sob, or have so
much as a catch in his breath, but Kera could feel the hurt and fear emanating
from the man, knew that he'd trade places with Morri in a heartbeat if he could.
She took a step backwards from the men, eyes already tracing the quickest route
off the platform, through the temple, and out the door. Speaker Gerhardt
followed the movement of Kera's eyes, seemed to see her intent on her face, and
sighed.

"Kera, I can see that you've had a hard life," the Speaker began.

Kera took another step backwards.

"What's that supposed to mean?" Kera asked, quickly taking stock of the four
other people in the room. Brenno was close enough to her that she expected he'd
try to stop her, and Smith likely would as well. Kera's eyes caught the intricate
etched iron barrel of Smith's thunder cannon on the pedestal beside the pale, still
form of Morri. She's just sleeping, Kera thought to herself, they'll find another
way to wake her up. She formed a plan. She would snatch the cannon, evade
Brenno's clumsy attempt to grapple her, side-step Smith, and then run out the
door before Enaurl could catch her. She winced, remembering how quickly
Enaurl had cleared the room at Brenno's shop, and how the automaton had

easily had several minutes lead on them when travelling from there to the temple.

"It means that I understand that look on your face," said the Speaker. "I realize you're looking for a way out of this responsibility that's being handed to you, even though it's one that needs to be done in order to undo your mistake."

"Brenno. Shot. Morri." Kera said, enunciating each word slowly. "None of this is my fault." Enaurl is too fast, she thought. Her eye went again to the thunder cannon. Maybe if I shoot her in the face I'll be able to get away, she thought, Smith can fix her, I'm sure.

"None?" Speaker Gerhardt echoed. "Not even the fact that she was following your instructions? That the entire situation only came about due to your own impatience? Smith came into the shop with the intent to purchase your sword – the one you sold so you could feed an addiction, and the very one you intended to steal. It would have been returned to you within an hour if you'd had the patience to wait. Instead, your recklessness and haste led to a dire fate befalling this small child, and you have the audacity to stand in the shadow of the Lady in White and say you are free of blame?"

"Well, when you put it that way..." said Kera, pausing slightly. "Yeah, pretty much."

She lunged for the thunder cannon, snatching it off the table. As she'd expected, Brenno and Enaurl both sprang at her. She dropped her shoulder and rolled between them, letting Brenno fall into a heap at the foot of the dais while Enaurl's powerful shoulder smashed into it so forcefully the stone cracked. Rolling to her feet, Kera immediately began sprinting down the center aisle of the temple.

The telltale sound of Enaurl's gear-grinding gait was all the warning Kera needed to turn back around. The construct had given chase, and a few powerful strides had already brought her frighteningly close to catching up. Kera brought the weapon to bear and fired. A thundercrack boomed through the temple, and Enaurl's chest seemed to cave inwards as if it had been pierced by a javelin with tremendous force. The construct stumbled and fell mid-stride, crashing into a heap among the wooden pews.

"Kera!" Smith howled after her. Twenty feet from the door, Kera turned back and offered Smith a sad smile and a wave, intending for this to be her farewell.

"Voldani!" Speaker Gerhardt shouted.

Kera suddenly found herself running directly into a brick wall, or at least that's how it felt.

"*Oof!*"

The impact knocked her to the ground hard enough to bash the back of her head against the floor. The carpet absorbed some of the impact, but it still caused a sharp burst of pain that radiated forward from the back of her skull. Her first instinct was to bring the thunder cannon up and point it at whatever it was that had stood in her way.

She did so, but was surprised to feel it torn from her hand and sent flying some distance away to clatter against the floor.

Kera opened her eyes to find herself looking into the pointed tip of a sword pointed directly at her face. She followed the point up to its wielder, and realized it was a sword being held by Voldani. The scion's blazing white eyes simmered as they glared down at Kera.

Oh great, Kera thought, *another obstacle, just what I wanted.*

"You really think you're going to stop me?" Kera asked.

"No," said Voldani, taking a step back and producing a second sword and holding it handle-first towards Kera. "I *know* I will stop you."

Kera stared up and Voldani for a moment.

"Stand," Voldani said. "Arm yourself."

Uncertain of what else she could do, Kera took the sword and got to her feet. She was dimly aware of Smith making his way towards Enaurl and of Speaker Gerhardt helping Brenno to his feet. Voldani kept the tip of her sword pointed at Kera, falling into a duelist stance.

Kera swung the sword back and forth, testing the weapon's weight and balance.

It's not Zephelous, she thought, *but it feels good.*

She studied Voldani as she did, the pair slowly circling one another; the armor the scion wore was as unblemished as the woman's complexion, and Kera hoped it was a sign the other fighter was out of practice.

"So what's the deal here," Kera asked as the two continued to circle around. "We duel, winner gets to leave?"

Voldani's face remained expressionless.

Great, thought Kera, *another Enaurl.*

"I have no intention of allowing you to leave," Voldani said. "Though should you defeat me in fair single combat, I am honor bound to allow it."

"That was a really fancy way of saying 'yes', I hope you know that," said Kera.

Voldani's stance lowered, which Kera interpreted as a sign that the armored woman was about to lunge. Kera brought the sword up in front of her at a diagonal and sunk down into a low stance, one arm behind her. Voldani struck first, bringing her sword in for two quick slashes as she pressed forward. Kera blocked the strikes easily with her own sword, falling back step for step with Voldani as the woman advanced.

Seeing an opportunity for a counter attack, Kera slashed a wide arc in front of her, forcing Voldani to leap backward out of the way. Not wanting to lose any more ground, Kera followed up the wide slash with a series of quick thrusts. She didn't expect any of them to land, but used them to keep Voldani on guard and moving backwards towards the door. As Kera thrust her sword outward once more, Voldani deftly stepped around the thrust and in towards Kera, bringing the pommel of her sword up to bash Kera on the forehead.

Kera grunted in pain and took two steps back as the world flashed white for a moment, using her free hand to apply pressure to her head. She would have a nasty bruise in a few minutes, and could already feel a welt blossoming. She pulled her hand away from her face and saw blood on her palm. Not wanting a slippery grip if she needed to change hands with the sword, she wiped the blood onto her pant leg.

"First blood is mine," Voldani said, an air of authority and confidence in her voice. "Now would be an ideal time for you to yield."

"Lady, I know you don't know me very well," said Kera as she adjusted her grip on the handle of her sword. "Believe me when I say 'yield' is the one thing I don't do."

With a battle cry that she hadn't meant to shout, Kera dropped her shoulder and charged into Voldani's midsection. Not expecting the savage tackle, Voldani seemed to fold around Kera, who thrust her head upwards in a vicious headbutt. The unmistakable crunch of a nose breaking told her she'd connected, but rather than relent she followed it up with a kick to the back of Voldani's knees, a move she hoped would lay the statuesque woman flat on her back.

Rather than be laid low, Voldani leaned into Kera's trip, arching her back far enough to place a hand on the ground above her head and spring her feet upwards and over – delivering a solid kick to Kera's chin on the way. Kera reeled as the steel greaves connected with her face, delivering a resounding blow that threatened to knock her unconscious.

Voldani's back handspring became a dangerous looking fighting stance, as the warrior woman kept her hand on the ground but brought her sword out wide, legs coiled under and ready to spring into a leap in Kera's direction at any moment. Kera shook away her reeling dizziness, and held her sword in front of her, both hands wrapped tightly around its hilt.

"Your technique lacks discipline," Voldani said, brilliant orbs staring upward into Kera's eyes. "You fight like a caged animal; all savagery, no skill." As she said this, Voldani brought her free hand up to her face and snapped her broken nose back into place without so much as a grunt.

"Yeah, well, you're stunningly beautiful," said Kera.

Voldani's expression changed at last, confusion creasing her otherwise perfectly serene face. Kera took a pair of quick steps towards Voldani and vaulted over her, bringing her sword around in an arcing slash directly over Voldani's head. Voldani rolled out of the way of the attack, using the edge of her own blade to slap Kera's sword aside for good measure, coming back into her low three-point combat stance. Kera completed her aerial somersault and landed on her feet, turning quickly to face Voldani once more.

"Does flattery work for you as a distraction?" Voldani asked, poised and ready to strike at any moment.

"Not typically, no," Kera said. "I just had to say that in case I killed you with that last move. Would have bothered me for a while."

"Which?" Voldani asked. "Killing me or not commenting on how my appearance is appealing to you?"

Kera swung her head from side to side, as if weighing out a decision.

"A bit of both, really." said Kera.

Reversing her grip on her sword, Kera brought it down beside her hip, blade facing forward. She swung it across in a low arc, fully expecting Voldani to spring backwards again the way she had previously. To her satisfaction, she watched the dark skinned woman arched her body backwards and begin to bring her legs upwards and over her head once more. Kera leapt forward in a flying front kick, her leather boot connecting with Voldani's spine midway down her back. The impact destabilized the the woman's otherwise graceful evasion, and sent Voldani sprawling into a heap. She tumbled and bounced along the patterned carpet for a few feet before correcting herself, rising to her feet, eyes gleaming with a righteous fury.

"You test my patience," Voldani said.

Kera noted with a certain degree of satisfaction that the other woman was now breathing heavily.

"If you've got better things to do, you could always let me leave," said Kera, trying to hide the fact that she was also breathing heavily.

She glanced behind her quickly. The door was no more than fifteen feet away.

All or nothing, she thought.

With a flourish that was equal parts distraction and necessary to readjust her grip on the sword, Kera flipped the handle of the sword around and threw it at

Voldani, the sword spinning through the air in a deadly blur of steel. Not bothering to watch how Voldani would react, Kera turned and bolted towards the door. She heard a high pitched ring of steel on steel, most likely Voldani deflecting the thrown sword, at the same time as her hands touched the latch of the door.

With as much haste as she could muster, Kera swung the door open wide and bolted outside. She sprinted down the smooth brick streets of the temple district as fast as she could, putting as much distance between her and the temple as possible.

Pushing her way through villagers and merchants, eliciting protests and complaints as she did, Kera raced through the streets of Zelwyr. A whoosh sound overhead brought a tingle of concern to the forefront of her mind.

Why don't I like the sound of that? Kera thought.

Still racing, she turned her head to look into the skies above her. To her dismay, Voldani was there, propelling her way through the air on a pair of shimmering wings the same gleaming color as her eyes. Kera watched as Voldani's eyes locked onto hers from above.

Oh fuck, Kera thought, *this is going to suck.*

Voldani folded her wings and, looking very much like a bird of prey, dove towards Kera. The winged woman fell through the air like a divine missile.

Kera tried to evade the blow she knew was coming, but Voldani corrected her flight and slammed into her with so much force it sent the pair of them hurtling into a nearby vendor's cart which shattered on impact.

I think a few of my bones might have shattered too, Kera thought.

She groaned long and loud, vocalizing the pain she felt across most of her body. To Kera's dismay, Voldani simply stood up and brushed herself off, staring at Kera all the while.

"Now," said Voldani, "Yield."

Kera wanted to say something witty in response, but words couldn't pierce the fog of pain that dulled her every sense. The best she could manage was a sly grin and an extremely rude hand gesture. Voldani shook her head in disgust. With a swift kick to the chin, she knocked Kera unconscious.

Kneeling down in the rubble of the cart, Voldani pushed aside broken boards and scattered fruit to clear as much rubble from Kera as she could. Once she'd finished doing so, she hoisted Kera off the ground and threw her over her shoulder, dispelling her wings as she did. The pedestrians on the street, one of which was presumably the merchant, watched in awe.

Sensing their concern, Voldani spun a slow circle, letting her gaze rest on each of their faces for a moment.

"This woman is a criminal," said Voldani, "I am apprehending her in the name of the church Perrus, and placing her under the divine sanction there of. Who owns this cart?"

One of the onlookers, a woman in a violet dress, sheepishly raised her hand. Voldani pointed her sword at the woman, and the crowd collectively gasped.

"Seek restitution at the temple of Perrus. Ask for Speaker Gerhardt."

The woman blanched, but nodded. Voldani sheathed her sword, and began walking back towards the temple, the crowd eager to part to allow the woman passage.

Kneeling beside Enaurl, Smith produced a small wrench and used it to hastily remove the plating on her chest. Essentially a breastplate, the section of steel came away once the bolts holding down were removed.

Grumbling and muttering to himself unintelligibly, he surveyed the damage; lucky for Enaurl, it wasn't too severe. The payload of his thunder cannon had been a simple lead ball, which had punched clear through Enaurl's outer layer of steel and lodged itself deep in the series of pumps, valves, and gyroscopic stabilizers that served as the automaton's internal organs.

Deft fingers maneuvered their way around hoses and wires, under valves and pistons, to rest on the smooth surface of the lead ball. Careful not to cause any further damage, Smith removed the lead ball just as cautiously as a surgeon might remove a cancerous growth. The only component that needed to be truly replaced was one that was responsible for Enaurl's sense of balance, which explained the construct's graceless tumble into the pews.

He disconnected the wires that ran from the small cylindrical tube, itself containing many smaller marvels of artifice, and pocketed it. Satisfied that he had done all he could without being in his shop, Smith reattached Enaurl's breastplate.

The internal grinding of gears resumed instantly, and Enaurl tried to sit up; lacking a proper sense of balance, the construct sat too far forward, flopping over like a drunkard. Smith helped right her, a difficult task given Enaurl's surprising weight. `

Ducking under the construct's arm, he strained himself to get the silver-skinned woman up off the ground and seated on the pew. He released his grip on her arm and stood up. Enaurl tried to stand with him, but promptly lilted sideways, threatening to collapse completely. Smith put his hands on her shoulders and pressed her back down onto the pew.

"Stay sitting," Smith said. "You're going to need some work done."

Enaurl's only response was to stare mutely into Smith's face before sitting down, coming to a perfectly still seated position that left her facing forward.

Satisfied, Smith trudged the few dozen steps towards the dais, painfully aware of the crack midway through the stone lectern. He checked Morri immediately, and was relieved to find no change in her condition; the girl continued to take slow, steady breaths.

Brenno sat on the edge of the raised platform around the dais, a dazed expression on his face, and Speaker Gerhardt stood next to him.

The Speaker recited a quiet prayer and light once again shone from the old man's palms, this time directed into the halfling's face.

Brenno seemed to shake off his stupor, offering a nod of appreciation at Gerhardt. Satisfied that the halfling would be fine, Gerhardt rose to his feet and moved to stand beside Smith as he stood over Morri.

"You've always had a penchant for keeping interesting company," Gerhardt said, kneeling to inspect the crack through the stone. "I'll have to have the mason's guild come and take a look at this. It seems stable enough, but perhaps we should find a better resting place for young Morrillypallyke, hm?"

Smith nodded, feeling as if he were hearing the Speaker from a great distance away. When he didn't answer the Speaker, Gerhardt leaned in closer to the man.

"Mister Smith?"

"Sorry, Speaker," said Smith. "It's been a long day."

"Yes, I should think so," said Gerhardt. "Having your daughter in a state such as this must be terribly taxing."

"It's more than that, Speaker," said Smith. "Morri said something about someone stalking her through the market a few days ago, someone no one else could see. She hadn't told me about it until today." Speaker Gerhardt raised a bushy brow.

"Being stalked by an invisible man?" the Speaker asked. "Seems rather implausible. How would she even know it was happening if that were the case?"

Smith shook his head and shrugged.

"She said she could see the person, but no one else could," said Smith. "Except Kera, apparently." Gerhardt's expression of surprise changed to one of dismay.

"A child's exaggerated version of the truth, I'm sure," said the Speaker. "I must admit to wanting to give lady Kera the benefit of the doubt, but after all of this... Suffice it to say that I have learned today."

"Here, here," said Brenno, gingerly stretching his shoulder.

The temple doors swung open, and in walked Voldani, Kera still slung over her shoulder. The mighty warrior woman casually strode her way up to the front of the temple, pausing only to remove the sword Kera had thrown at her previously from the pew it in it had lodged itself, and dropped Kera onto the pedestal at the foot of the dais as if she were a sack of potatoes.

Smith couldn't help but wince at the sound Kera's body made when it slumped down onto the stone floor.

"I have acquired your criminal, Speaker Gerhardt," Voldani said, bowing her head in reverence to Speaker Gerhardt without breaking eye contact. "What's more, I have made it known she is to be pressed into service of the church."

Gerhardt nodded and smiled affably.

"Well done, Voldani, well done indeed," the Speaker said. "Before you return to the communion hall, I would ask you to stay with us a moment until we have decided the fate of lady Kera."

Voldani offered a curt nod as she sheathed her sword.

"She does not fight like a lady," Voldani said. "She fights with the ferocity and intensity of a thunderstorm."

Brenno looked up at the impassive face of the armored woman.

"That sounded dangerously close to being complementary," the halfling remarked.

Voldani was silent for a moment, then nodded a single time.

"Perhaps it should be so," Voldani said. "She did not best me in single combat, but she came close. That is more than can be said for most."

The temple was silent for a long moment, except for the gentle sounds of Morri and Kera's unconscious breathing.

"Well," Brenno said, breaking the silence, "now what?" Speaker Gerhardt regarded Smith.

"Do you believe this woman is telling the truth about slaying a dragon?" Gerhardt asked.

"I'm honestly not sure," said Smith.

"I'm prone to be doubtful," Brenno added.

"Do you intend to obtain the blood of a dragon?" the Speaker asked.

"If that's what Morri needs, then yes," said Smith, grim with resolve.

The Speaker stretched his arms out wide, palms facing upwards.

"Then I'm afraid, Mister Smith, you don't have much choice," said the Speaker. "As it is, she can't remain in Zelwyr without threat of prosecution, though I can apply to have the charges standing against her dismissed via her service to the church of Perrus."

"So she can start clean all over again?" Brenno asked. "For what I believe would be the third time?" the Halfling shook his head vehemently. "No, Speaker, I'd advise against that. Press her into service if you must, but let her crimes against Zelwyr stand on their own. Clearly she has much to learn."

Speaker Gerhardt turned to regard Brenno with a curious expression on his face.

"And for yourself, Mister Brenno?" Gerhardt asked. "What have you learned from today?"

"Never make deals with barbarians," Brenno quipped with a smile.

He looked to see if either the Speaker or Smith found his joke funny, and was confused when their faces remained placid.

"Mister Brenno, I hereby press you into service of the church," the Speaker began. "You are hereby charged with assisting mister Smith and lady Kera in their efforts to retrieve however much dragon blood as you require to create the tincture which will revive young Morrillypallyke.

"What!?" Brenno erupted, jumping to his feet. "Speaker, you can't do this!"

"I'm afraid I can, mister Brenno, and I've just done so," Speaker Gerhardt said, his tone grim. "To reiterate the words of our... troubling associate who is currently unconscious on the floor, you did have a hand in all that has transpired here as well. After all, regardless of your intentions, it is your poison which even now threatens to stop the heart of this poor child." Brenno scoffed.

"And if I refuse?" The halfling asked, eyes hardened to dagger points as he glared up at the Speaker. Steel scraped against steel as Voldani unsheathed her swords behind the halfling. Brenno's face lost several shades of color as the blood drained out from it. He swallowed.

"I see," Brenno said. "How delightfully subtle."

Speaker Gerhardt smiled in earnest.

"Voldani has never had a mind for subtleties, I'm afraid," the Speaker said. "Fortunately, that is not the skill set which is required of her."

Brenno muttered something foul under his breath, but didn't vocalize it enough to have it be understood.

Speaker Gerhardt's smile never faltered, and he offered a simple shrug as to say his hands were tied in the matter. The Speaker turned to regard Smith, his gaze sliding to Enaurl still seated in the pew.

"Mister Smith, I believe it might be wisest if you and mister Brenno took Enaurl back to your shop," said the Speaker. "I should think you may need her assistance for the endeavor at hand. Voldani, please see that lady Kera is brought to the office of the town guard. Inform whatever captain is on guard that she has been pressed into the service, and that she is not to be harmed, transported, or otherwise disturbed until my arrival, which shall be forthwith."

Voldani replaced her swords, pommels clinking loudly against the sheaths. She offered the Speaker a nod which turned into a slight bow, then turned and hoisted Kera over her shoulder before striding back down the blood stained carpet and out the temple door. Smith's gaze lingered on Morri.

"Should I take her home?" Smith asked, voice filled with concern and softness.

The Speaker gave Smith a reassuring pat on the shoulder once more.

"I think it might be best if she remained here, under the watchful eye of Perrus." Speaker Gerhardt said. "I will clear a chamber for her, and you should of course feel free to remain with her as long as you like before you depart. Know that I, and perhaps Perrus herself, will keep a watchful eye over your child."

Smith drew a ragged breath, and gently stroked Morri's forehead, brushing back a few errant strands of hair. After a moment of heavy silence, he nodded.

"Brenno," he growled. "Help me get Enaurl back to the shop."

"How precisely would you like me to do that?" said Brenno. "She's easily twice my height, probably four times my weight."

"I didn't ask how, I just said help," Smith said. Still muttering under his breath, Brenno did as he was asked. The pair made their way towards Enaurl and did their best to help the automaton to her feet. Enaurl wobbled and teetered, but with Smith holding on to her arm and Brenno doing his best to steady her legs, the trio managed to leave the temple.

Alone with Morrillypallyke, Speaker Gerhardt let out a heavy sigh, and repeated Smith's gentle gesture of brushing hair away from her face.

"You poor, precious child," said the Speaker, speaking to no one but Morri.

Tenderly, he scooped her into his arms, and made his way off the dais and towards a door which led to the basement level; the basement was where all the residents of the church lived, and with most of his Listeners out on active assignment or making their annual pilgrimage to Mount Baesil, the place was empty.

Once he made it down the stone stairs, he walked past the doors which belonged to the living quarters of the Listeners until he reached the last door, the door to his own quarters. Turning around, he gently bumped the door open with his backside, careful not to bash Morri's head against the arch of the door. Once the door shut behind him, he surveyed his quarters.

As he had expected, nothing had been disturbed; the books which filled the shelves along the back wall remained undisturbed, and the small desk he used for reading and writing sat exactly as he'd left it. His bed, a large feather-stuffed mattress he'd been gifted some years ago, took up most of the relatively small chamber, sitting directly in the center.

He strode across the room and laid Morri down on top of it, covering the child with a blanket. Once more he brushed Morri's hair and sighed, an expression of grief and pain darkening his face. The Speaker shuffled the pillows around beneath Morri's head until he was satisfied she was comfortable, then nodded in affirmation.

Content with the girl's placement, the Speaker rose from the bed and made his way back towards the door. Hanging on the inside of it was an over-sized travel cloak.

It was black with a thick red trim, decorated with elvish whorl stitches.

Smiling to himself, the Speaker gave the cloak a pat and left the room.

Chapter Nine

Kera let her head drop forward, banging her forehead against the hard iron bars of her jail cell.

Bong.

She'd spent the better part of a week locked up, and hated every second. The first few days had been spent going through the agony of fae ash withdrawal. She'd been given a single bucket to use as a latrine, but the sheer volume of vomit she'd expelled during those days – coupled with the number of trips the guards had needed to make to empty it out - had led to three more buckets being placed in the already limited confines of the room. To refer to it as a room was a generous description; the place Kera found herself in was little more than a cage that built into a brick wall. Kera hated a lot of things, but cages were chief among them. She lifted her head up from the unyielding bars and let it drop heavily again.

Bong.

She winced a little, the pain being relatively minor compared to the uneasiness and anxiety she felt rising up from her stomach to fill her chest with tightness and pain.

Then again, she thought, *that might just be more vomit.*

Cautiously, she lifted her head off the bars, testing to see if her nausea was real or a construct of her anxiety; the bile that rushed up her throat and erupted out her mouth gave her all the proof she needed. Wiping her mouth the best she could with hands that were caked with dried puke from the previous few days, Kera took two steps to the side, wrapped each of her hands around an iron bar, and dropped her head onto the bars again.

Bong.

"Cease that immediately," Voldani commanded. "You will injure yourself, and I have been instructed to prevent any harm from coming to you."

Kera grimaced without opening her eyes. Voldani's constant presence as her jailer this last week had been less than pleasant. As far as Kera could tell, Voldani hadn't so much as moved from the post she'd taken up, standing some ten feet away from Kera's cell with her arms crossed over her chest, unblinking eyes surveying everything like a bird of prey. Kera forced a weak smile.

"What about psychological harm?" Kera asked. "Or emotional harm? Because I have to say, being locked up in here for a week has been really damaging to my psyche. I should probably be released as soon as possible."

When Voldani didn't answer immediately, Kera opened an eye to see if her self-appointed warden was actually considering releasing her. Voldani's cold stare was all the answer she needed. She let her eyelid slide shut. "It was worth a shot."

"I suppose feigning death by choking on vomit was also worth a shot?" Voldani asked.

"Absolutely," Kera answered.

"And attempting to flee when the guards rushed to your aid?" Voldani pressed.

"Well, yeah." Kera said.

"I suppose you also imagine your efforts to bribe me with coin, treasures, and sexual favors were 'worth a shot' as well?"

"Yes, yes, and the offer's on the table," Kera said, grinning wickedly.

The act of smiling brought on another round of vomiting.

"I shall try to resist," Voldani said coolly.

Hands trembling more than she'd like to let on, Kera wiped her mouth clean once more. She sent Voldani a sickly wink.

"I'll wear you down, just you watch," said Kera.

Voldani was about to respond when the door to the jail opened, and Smith walked in. He screwed his face up with disgust almost immediately.

"Various fucking gods," Smith cursed. "It smells like a distillery full of dead dwarves in here."

Voldani pointed her chin at Kera. Smith shook his head, covering his nose and mouth with his hand.

"I should have expected as much," he grumbled.

"Am I the distillery or a dead dwarf in this context?" Kera asked.

"Both," Voldani and Smith said simultaneously.

Smith handed Voldani an object wrapped in burlap. A long object, distinctly sword shaped.

"We finally dug it out of the ashes," said Smith. "Took a long while to burrow under Brenno's stupid cases to get to his basement, but once I got Enaurl up and walking again we were able to push through."

"Ashes?" Kera heard herself ask, attention locked completely onto the bundle.

Smith turned his head towards Kera, openly glaring at her.

"Brenno's shop burnt down," said Smith. "As in, down to the ground. The cases survived, but just about everything else is a complete write off."

"How did his shop burn down?" Kera asked.

Smith's jaw fell open, and he gaped at Kera for a moment before the acrid taste of her bile entered his mouth and he snapped it shut.

"You burned it down," Smith said.

"Not possible," said Kera. "I've been in here the whole time. Ask Voldani."

Kera looked to Voldani to see if the warrior woman would confirm what she 'd said, but was surprised to find Voldani and Smith both staring at her expectantly.

"What? I can't have burnt something down without being there to do it. I'm good, but I'm not that good."

"Do you happen to remember," Smith said, speaking at a deliberate slow pace, "what you did with the torch you used to try to smoke Brenno into giving you your sword afterwards?"

"The torch?" Kera repeated, her brow creasing with confusion. "Not really, I think I just kind of threw it away."

She was silent for a moment before realization dawned on her.

"Oh."

"Yeah," said Smith. "*Oh.*"

"Well, that's really not my fault," said Kera. "You were the one who forced us out of there under threat of being shot by your pocket cannon thing."

"It's a thunder cannon," said Smith.

"Dumb name, but whatever," said Kera. "If you hadn't shoved your thunder cannon in my face, I could have made sure that the fire didn't spread."

"If you hadn't gotten my daughter shot, I wouldn't have had to do anything," said Smith.

"Does no one care that it was Brenno who shot Morri and not me?" Shouted Kera. "I. Didn't. Shoot. Morrilly. Pally. Kay. It was Brenno, Brenno the halfling, Brenno shot your daughter. I didn't do a damn thing."

A low rumble started deep in Smith's stomach, and by the time it rose to his chest it was a roar.

"Gods damn it, Kera!" Smith shouted. "Will you take some responsibility for your actions? If not your actions, for yourself?"

Smith took the parcel back from Voldani and threw it at the bars of Kera's cell, filling the room with the clanging of steel on steel. Caught off guard by Smith's sudden burst of rage, Kera stepped back from the bars as he flung the object at her. She didn't feel threatened or intimidated by Smith's actions in the least.

She felt a righteous fury welling up inside her.

"Well then," Kera said, voice practically dripping with venom. "I thought *I* was supposed to be the savage one."

Smith's hardened stare, eyes filled with frustration and rage, was the only response he offered.

"You're at least supposed to be sorry, you gods damned barbarian."

Kera's face hardened and she glared back at Smith.

"I told you, I've been to the Wildlands," said Smith. "I know what No-Clan means. I don't know what you did you to earn that title, but I know what it means."

"Oh yeah?" Kera asked, voice hard as steel, here every muscle corded with anger and tension. "Let's hear it, then."

"It means you're an outcast," Smith spat. "More than that. It means you're a pariah, that you've been exiled. Not one clan of corpse-wearing savages in that whole mess of a place wants anything to do with you. Not one of them, not even your family, gives a damn about you."

"Believe me, the feeling is mutual," Kera said. "You think you know anything about Wildland culture? Why, because you've been there once? What are you, an idiot?"

Kera paused, but not long enough for Smith to speak.

"There's no concept of 'exile' in the blasted waste. When you never have a home, the concept of not being allowed to go back to one is meaningless. Life there is too dangerous to stay still, it's likely that you'll get eaten or crushed. That's why you have your clan. They protect you, they make sure you're safe when the lizards come down from the sky or when the earth quakes under your feet. The clan only works when everyone looks out for each other. If no one is looking out for you, you get killed."

Smith scoffed and rolled his eyes dramatically.

"Let me guess, you were supposed to be watching out for someone and you managed to do that wrong?"

Kera was quiet for a long time.

"Sure, let's go with that," she said, turning away from Smith, leaning her back against the bars.

Smith opened his mouth to say more, but the sound of the front door opening stopped him. Brenno walked in, wearing a deep green cloak over leather armor the color of pine trees.

"Smith, we found an ex-campaigner at the tavern who says he can help with the dragon, and... Gods above, below, and between," the halfling cursed, covering his mouth and nose. "It smells like a horse died in a river of excrement in here."

"Neigh," said Kera.

Brenno regarded her curiously.

"I'm somehow not surprised," the halfling said. When Kera didn't respond, Brenno turned his head to regard Smith. "There's a wizard at the tavern."

Smith frowned.

"A wizard?" He asked, breaking his stare away from Kera. "You couldn't find anyone else? No campaigners, no mercs, no ratcatchers, nothing?"

"It's been a week, Smith," Brenno said, speaking deliberately. "You already said no to the half-orc, and none of us have any experience with dragons besides Kera."

"Assuming that's not a load of shit," said Smith, looking to see if Kera reacted at all. When she didn't, he tightened his jaw. "Zelwyr is the only real stop between Stillwater and the coast."

"Between Stillwater and *this* coast," Brenno corrected. "I'm not saying there's a shortage of campaigners who travel through the area, but I am saying that it's not exactly every day that someone who has tangled with a dragon comes through Zelwyr. Hells, man. Half the people on the continent haven't so much as *seen* a dragon since the war."

Smith went quiet.

"There's always the old road, up and out towards Addalena's Keep," Smith said, thinly veiled hope in his words.

"No one uses that old road when they can take the highway through the Shimmervale," the halfling countered. "A fact you know full well, I might add. Face it, Smith. We have to take what we can get, and this wizard is what we can get."

Smith seemed to deflate as he submitted to the halfling's points.

"At least tell me he's not a crazy old man," Smith sighed.

Brenno made a face.

"Weeell," said the halfling, stretching the word out. "He's not old."

"I do not care for the company of wizards," said Voldani.

"That makes two of us," said Smith.

"I can't help but repeat myself in this instance," said Brenno. "We are out of options. Speaker Gerhardt says Morri's sleep is growing deeper, and it's safe to say that none of us are enjoying this makeshift partnership we all find ourselves in."

"I do not dislike this alliance," said Voldani. "However, I also do not care for it."

"A simple 'I agree' would have sufficed, I think," Brenno said.
"Do not demean me or my words, pawnbroker," Voldani responded. "I will not stand for it."

Brenno held his hands out defensively.

"Apologies, Voldani," said Brenno. "I did not mean to offend."

"Mind your words more carefully," said Voldani. "I have cut out tongues before, I assure you that I have become quite adept at it."

Brenno blanched slightly, but lowered his hands.

"All for the glory of Perrus, I'm sure," the halfling mumbled.

"Speak plainly, pawnbroker," Voldani said, sliding her swords out of their sheathes in a fluid motion that made the blades cross over one another in front of her.

"Voldani, this marks at least the tenth time you've drawn your swords at me this week," Brenno said, his tone grim. "It's beginning to lose significance. If you're going to kill me before I die on this suicide mission, go ahead and do it. It'll save me a good deal of travel if nothing else."

Voldani's gleaming eyes flared for a moment, but she sheathed her swords.

"I have adjusted my position on this alliance," Voldani announced. "I am dissatisfied with it." Brenno sighed wearily, looking at the floor. Spotting the bound parcel on the ground, laying within reach of the cell in which Kera stood, Brenno looked back to Smith.

"Did you not give it to her?" the halfling asked. "We dug through soot for hours to get into my cellar – Or rather, what remains of my cellar – because you said she wouldn't come along without that sword, regardless of the death penalty currently hanging over her head."

Kera feigned continued disinterest, but she absorbed every word.

Smith wanted me to have Zephelous back, she thought, *what am I supposed to think about that?*

"I gave it to her," the man said.

"Oh, you let me have it alright," Kera added.

Smith scowled, but kicked the bundle closer to the cell. It clamored against the bars. Kera willed herself to try to remain outwardly calm, to react as little as possible.

Slowly, almost leisurely, she turned back around and knelt, reaching for the bundle. Her fingers closed around it, and she could feel the familiar shape of Zephelous's hard edge beneath the burlap that covered it.

Zephelous? She thought, expecting to hear the booming voice of the sword at any moment.

When she didn't, she furrowed her brow and pulled the sack through the bars as hastily as she could. She unwound the burlap from around Zephelous – and it was indeed Zephelous – she couldn't stop the smile that came to her face. Gripping the hilt in both hands, she held the sword up in front of her.

Zeph? She thought at the weapon, trying to send her thoughts into the sentient sword the only way she knew how.

YOU SOLD ME, Zephelous responded, boisterous voice tinged with betrayal and hurt. YOU CONSUMED THE FAE ASH YOU POSSESSED, WHICH WAS A RELATIVELY LARGE AMOUNT, AND THEN SOLD ME TO ACQUIRE MORE.

"Well, there's a little more to it than that," Kera said out loud.

Voldani, Smith, and Brenno shared a look between them before collectively turning their heads to observe.

I DISAGREE, said Zephelous. WE HAD WON A SMALL VICTORY OVER THE FORCES OF DARKNESS, I HAD JUST BEGUN TO BELIEVE THERE MIGHT YET BE A HERO IN YOU, KERA NO-CLAN.

"I don't think a creep in an alley counts as 'the forces of darkness,'" said Kera. "And I'm pretty sure I told you from the minute I dug you up from that unmarked grave that I wasn't a fan of the 'h' word."

Zephelous sighed into Kera's mind, a sound that reminded her of the whale song she had sometimes heard off the southern coast of the Wildlands as a child.

I HAD FAITH IN YOU, KERA, Zephelous said. I AM CONCERNED THAT MY FAITH WAS MISPLACED.

Kera swallowed hard, and not from threat of bile this time. She shut her eyes, and slowly lowered herself into a seated position on the floor, boots dangerously close to a puddle of vomit.

Zeph, I... Thought Kera, struggling to keep her emotions in check. *I thought you'd be happy I got you back, happy to see me.*

KERA, I AM UNCERTAIN AS TO HOW I FEEL ABOUT BEING IN YOUR POSSESSION ONCE MORE, said Zephelous. IN ALL HONESTY, I HAD RESOLVED TO NEVER SEE YOU AGAIN. BEING SOLD TO A PAWNBROKER WILL DO THAT.

"Smith said," Kera said, not meaning to speak out loud. She sniffed.

Smith said you were wailing when he touched you, like you were in agony.

Zephelous didn't respond immediately, and when it did, its voice felt more monotone than it ever had before.

KERA, I WILL ADMIT THAT YOU CAUSED ME A GREAT DEAL OF

PAIN, said Zephelous. WHEN THE MAN LAID HIS HANDS ON ME, YOUR PSYCHIC IMPRINT ON HIM WAS GREAT. IT WAS, AS THEY SAY, SALT ON THE WOUND.

"Oh," Kera said quietly. "I thought maybe you were sad without me."

"Does she believe she is speaking to that sword?" Voldani asked, directing her question at Smith and Brenno.

"I believe she does," Brenno answered. Smith shushed them both.

SADDENED THAT YOU'D CHOSEN YOUR ADDICTION OVER ME, PERHAPS. Zephelous said. SADDENED THAT YOU CHOSE TO LET YOUR POTENTIAL GO TO WASTE, CHOOSING TO FLING YOURSELF INTO A FACE FULL OF FAIRY DUST OVER STANDING TALL AND FACING YOUR DESTINY.

"I don't believe in destiny, Zeph," said Kera. "I believe in shit. Shit happens. In fact, it happens to everyone all the time. Destiny doesn't."

I... I DO NOT WISH TO SPEAK WITH YOU AT THE MOMENT, KERA NO-CLAN, said Zephelous, before lapsing into silence.

"What, you're just going to give me the silent treatment?" Kera asked, staring intently at the sword.

She waited for a response that didn't come. Frustrated and angry, plus several emotions she didn't know how to describe let alone experience properly, Kera stared hard at the sentient sword.

"Fine," she said at last. "I don't need you. I got along just fine without you before, I can do it again."

Working hard to control her face, Kera let her hold on Zephelous's grip loosen until the sword fell from her hands and clattered against the stone.

"If she truly is speaking to the sword, I do not believe that the conversation is going well," said Voldani. Brenno made a face.

"You are a master of the understatement, Lady Voldani," the halfling mused.

"You are quick to make jokes, Mister Brenno," said Voldani.

"Thank you," said Brenno.

"It was not intended as a compliment, merely an observation," Voldani said. "To return to matters at hand, I believe we should have Kera cleaned off and brought to the tavern in order to assist in verifying the skill set of this wizard."

"And how do you propose we have her cleaned?" Brenno asked, eyeing Voldani curiously. "She's not a jacket to be left at the seamstress. If she were, she 'd be the first jacket in the history of clothing to rob a tailor and burn down his shop."

"I'm more concerned about her trying to get away," Smith said. "She knows we need her help, but that didn't stop her from trying to run before, and that was without her sword. She has it now, I don't know what's to stop her from bolting."

"I will prevent her from fleeing," Voldani said, adjusting her stance to stand even taller. "I prevented her escape once, I feel confident I could do so again."

Brenno and Smith looked towards one another, and nodded.

"You're likely the only one of us that could catch her," Brenno said. "Makes enough sense to me."

Smith nodded in agreement.

"Brenno and I will head to the tavern to meet with the wizard," said Smith. "See if you can do something about the way she smells, maybe splash some water on her face. Join us when you can."

"I do not appreciate the tone of command," Voldani began, "but given the circumstances I will assume you are merely pressed for time and feeling a great amount of concern over your small child. As such, I will forgive you for this accidental oversight."

Brenno opened his mouth to make a comment of some kind, but Smith silenced him with a look. The halfling shrugged and, after bowing low to Voldani, left the jailhouse.

Smith remained in place, staring at the sullen Kera for a moment longer before following after the halfling. Alone with Kera, Voldani approached the cell, careful to step around the pool of bile on the ground. Producing the key to the door from a small brown pouch at her waist, Voldani held the key up in front of her.

"I have learned much about you in this time we have spent together, Kera. I expect that when I open this cell, your first instinct will be to attempt to flee. I also expect you to be willing to fight me in order to gain your freedom if you must. I would like to advise you against this. You have not eaten, rested, or consumed an adequate amount of water this entire week. Under the circumstances, you would lose even easier than you did last time – especially given that there are no tricks for you to use this time; no sand to throw in my eyes, as it were. Knowing all of this, I ask that you give me your word that you will not attempt to attack me or flee. I would prefer not to have you bound and gagged while I wash you down, but I will if I must."

Kera smiled despite everything else.

"Is that a promise?" Kera quipped with a smirk.

Voldani scowled and approached the bars of the cell, vomit squelching under her boot. She eyed the barbarian girl solemnly for a moment, then reached for a loop of key rings at her belt.

"You are also quick to make jokes," said Voldani, locating the correct key and lifting it to the lock of the cell door. "I do not mean that in a--"

"Complementary manner, just observational," said Kera, repeating Voldani's words when she'd spoken them to Brenno a few moments before. "So I've heard."

"Consider what it implies," Voldani said, plunging the key into the iron lock and turning it.

Heavy tumblers clunked and moved away from the locking position. Voldani stood to the side and let the cell door swing open. Seeing the path to freedom in front of her, Kera lazily got to her feet, pausing to snatch Zephelous from the ground. She clutched its handle tightly, not allowing herself to think any thoughts at the sentient weapon who was evidently content not to speak to her.

"What would you say it implies?" Kera asked. "Not that I care, of course. Just curious."

"Of course," said Voldani. "I would never assume you would allow yourself emotional investment in something. That in itself is my point; it is clear to me that you are emotionally damaged, and as such you do not allow yourself to form emotional connections. For a woman who grew up a girl in one of the most socially involved cultures on the plane, I should imagine the adjustment has been difficult and has likely caused some level of psychological trauma as well."

"No offence, Dani, but you don't strike me as the healer type," said Kera. "And as... let's say 'nice' as this has been, I can't help but feel that the flying angel woman who tackled me into a fruit stand last week is the one I should be taking this kind of advice from."

"Followers of the Lady in White have devoted themselves to uncovering the remedies to all manner of ailments and hurt," Voldani explained. "We have learned that there are many sources of pain, sometimes great pain, that dwell in the mind."

Kera winced, clutching Zephelous with both hands.

"Got me all figured out then, huh?" Kera asked. "You and Smith both, trying to pick apart why I do things the way I do; because I'm an exile, because I'm damaged. Has it occurred to either of you that this might just be me?"

She held Zephelous in front of her horizontally.

"Has anyone stopped to consider," she said, voice raised as she spoke directly into Zephelous's guard. "That I've been honest about my intentions from the beginning, and that having all these extra responsibilities and expectations put on me by others isn't what I need right now?"

When Zephelous maintained its silence with her, Kera banged the flat of its blade against the bars of her cell. She didn't expect it would cause Zephelous any pain, but she hoped it would convey her frustration. She was surprised to feel Voldani's hands clasp down onto her shoulders. Confused, she looked at the angelic woman and was surprised to see a level of worry on the woman's face.

"I am concerned about your life choices," Voldani said. "I have been tasked with ensuring your safety to the best of my ability. My deductions have lead me to believe that the greatest threat of harm to you is presently yourself."

"Voldani, that's... not necessary," Kera said, surprised by the other woman's sudden display of warmth.

"I believe the second and third greatest sources of harm are your dangerous level of addiction and your tendency towards arson," Voldani added with an authoritative nod. "There is also a high probability that we die in glorious combat against a dragon in the near future."

Kera looked at Voldani with disbelief as the scion smiled wide.

"That's the thing that brings a smile to your face?" Kera asked, incredulous. "The very real threat of us being killed by a dragon?"

"Yes," said Voldani. "I expect it shall be a glorious struggle."

"And why is that a good thing to you?"

"In truth, I have not had many opportunities to leave the temple. When I first came to the temple of Perrus after learning of my divine ancestry, I was tasked with watching over Speaker Gerhardt. I have been performing that task to the best of my ability since it was assigned."

"Divine heritage?" Kera repeated. "Does that mean one of your parents was a god?"

"No," Voldani said simply, turning on her heel. "Come, I will escort you to the bathhouse, followed by the tailor, and then to the tavern."

"Are you going to join me at the bathhouse?"

"No."

"Will you tell me more about your parents on the way?"

"No."

Chapter Ten

The Ass's Glasses never emptied, and this day was no exception. The owner, old James Cork, lived upstairs with his wife, Hilda, and their eldest daughter, Gemma, whom they were grooming to take over the inn when the elder Corks inevitably popped off – a joke they made far too often for Gemma's comfort. Sitting in front of the fire in his favorite chair – a huge leather seat that resembled a throne – James Cork swirled the contents of his cup, gently mixing the morning's tea with the powdery, chalk-like substance he'd been told to start taking to ease the pain in his limbs.

In truth, he didn't mind the aches and pains; they reminded him of the nearly six decades he'd spent in defense of Zelwyr, and the battles he'd fought in order to do so. He'd begun his career as a member of the town militia, but developed a knack for swordplay early on. A few bandit raids and the odd monster attack later, James found himself a legitimate member of the town guard. His determined pragmatism – or pigheaded stubbornness, depending on who you asked – had led to him to earning the nickname *the ass*. The rest had become something of a local legend.

Rather than being stung by this innocuous moniker, James had made it his own, even going so far as to share his nickname with an enchanted shield he'd been gifted: the ass was too stubborn to let anything through.

While most of the occupied chairs and tables were filled with Zelwyrans he knew, or at least knew well enough to have a name readied to associate with their bar tabs, there were a few faces he didn't recognize. A bum laying face first on the table the back corner, a few campaigners, some young lads enjoying what might be their first pint of ale. Bums and youths were a non-issue for James, but one thing that rubbed him the wrong way was campaigners.

Of course, it wasn't just campaigners that bothered him; it was also the ratcatchers, the mercenaries, the thugs, the bloodthirsty vagrants, and the death-inviting glory seekers that got under his skin. As far as old James was concerned, taking up arms to defend what you loved was one thing; it was another entirely to take them up to go out and seek violence like these so-called 'adventurers' so famously chose to do as part of their profession.

A sloppy, untrained bunch for the most part. Old James knew he could probably teach the average campaigner a thing or two about swordplay, but at his age he was content to stand by the fire and nurse tea until the missus went out, when he'd switch to nursing ale while the missus did... well, whatever it was she did.

Last year she'd tried her hand at foraging with a group, this year she'd been having a great deal of fun with some sort of book appreciation group. Having often joked that he'd gone straight from the cradle to horseback, James had never had much appreciation for reading. He understood that it was a useful skill, but it was one he'd managed to do just fine without. He could make change when someone paid their tab in a currency he recognized, and could recognize names and signs he'd seen enough times to become familiar with. That was plenty.

With his distaste for campaigners regardless of what they called themselves, and his lack of use for reading, Jim was having a hard time coming to terms with a particular stranger in his bar that afternoon.

A tattooed wood elf was seated at the bar, wearing sleeveless robes that exposed his tribal tattoos; elaborate swirling markings that served as a personal history and family tree, an ancient tradition observed by all but an extremely rare few among the elves of the Shimmervale.

The bald-headed elf was hunched over a book that looked as though it weighed ten pounds. A staff of some sort, though it looked to Jim like little more than a gnarled branch, was tied to his back. The bald elf turned a page, and continued his reading. James shook his head.

Damn wizards, he thought to himself, *always bringing trouble around with them*.

The wizard paid the old man no heed, which was just as well. Comfortable silence between strangers was likely best; silence of any kind would do in a pinch.

Thank the gods for book enthusiast groups, he thought.

The door to the tavern swung outward, and Brenno walked in. James offered the halfling the barest nod, a gesture he reserved only for his staunchest and most loyal regulars. Brenno returned it, and scanned the room. Eyes landing on the tattooed bald elf, Brenno made a quick pointing affirmation towards the elf as if saying *that's the one*. Crossing in front of the hearth to make his way to the bar, Brenno pulled a stool back from the counter and climbed his way up to a seating position. The enigmatic figure glanced at Brenno for the briefest moment before turning back to his reading.

"Are you the pawnbroker?" the elf asked, voice melodic and light. Brenno nodded, fishing through his pocket for a silver coin. When he found one, he held it between two knuckles and knocked the hard edge of the coin against counter twice.

Tap tap.

Gemma made her way towards him after a moment.

"I am," said Brenno, speaking to the elf.

When Gemma arrived at the counter in front of him, Brenno made a quick pointing towards himself and then the wizard. Hilda held up a bottle of wine – a bottle of *top* shelf wine, no less. This was Hilda's way of informing a regular at her tavern that if he intended to buy, he should expect it to be expensive. Brenno put a second silver coin on the counter top, and Hilda poured a glass of wine for the elf and a pint of ale for Brenno.

"Word has it that you've got some experience fighting dragons."

"You *emalleon* have a knack for removing the poetry from words," said the elf, using the blanket term the wood elves of the Shimmervale often used to refer to non-elves.

He sipped a glass of wine in front of without the barest sound, his motions so fluid that the surface of the liquid seemed undisturbed throughout.

"To answer the question you did not properly ask, yes. I have indeed stood on the battlefield opposite *aznaur* and emerged victorious. Twice thus far, praises to Selbruinne."

Brenno sipped his ale, nodding.

"Did the dragon die either time?" The pawnbroker asked, paying the elf close attention as he did.

For a split second, Brenno watched the elf's eyes pause their scrolling digestion of the inscrutable material on the pages of his book.

"No, *aier,* they did not," the elf said, using his people's word for 'halfling'.

Brenno nodded. He hadn't expected that to be the case.

Dragons had become increasingly rare sights in the skies over Malzen in the days since the war, and seen near civilization even rarer; the few occasions otherwise were likened to natural disasters. It was as if the dragons who had survived that bloody ordeal were intent to fight like hell to ensure their continued survival. The elf pursed his lips and closed his book. He took another sip of his wine and regarded Brenno from the corner of his eyes.

"It should be worth noting that I did not die either," said the elf. "Given the scarcity of those who may say the same, I believe it is a statement that is worth some consideration."

Brenno nodded, making a steeple with his hands on the table.

"I suppose you'll be wanting that consideration to come in the form of gold," the pawnbroker said, his experience in bargaining and negotiating fees playing to his favor.

The elf smiled a tight lipped smile that showed no teeth, raising his glass to his lips once more.

"As before, you remove all that might be poetic from what you say," the elf began. "If you have a method to find a dragon, I will lend my experience to ensuring as many of your group survives the encounter. Once the dragon's hoard has been tallied, I ask for the first pick among its treasures."

"Fair enough," Brenno said with a nod.

The elf didn't know that the purpose of this venture wasn't gold or gains, but that didn't mean he needed to know. What's more, it wasn't as though they all stood to become considerably richer if they did succeed.

"I also require a forty percent stake in what remains," the elf added as if it were an afterthought. Brenno's entire being paused as if he were frozen mid-breath. His ability to perform mental mathematics was strong, and his ability to create a compromise was without parallel.

Enaurl won't need a share, he thought, *and it's not as if Smith or Voldani give two shits about anything but the dragon's blood. Kera, on the other hand...*

Still, he had himself to consider. And a store to rebuild.

"Twenty," Brenno countered. "Our group numbers six, present company included. Two of that number will share a stake between them, twenty percent is an even split." The elf made a steeple of his fingers on the book in front of him. He too seemed to pause in thought under Brenno's watchful eye.

"Thirty," the elf said after a pause. "An equal share implies each member is bringing an equally useful asset to the table. I bring the experience of having survived a dragon's wrath not once, but twice. What contribution do you and the others offer to this expedition that equates my own in value?"

"I'm providing the supplies and the means of travel," Brenno began, ticking off his fingers as he began his list. "Smith's gadget is what is helping us track the dragon. Enaurl is equal parts muscle and pack mule, Voldani offers aerial reconnaissance and doesn't require sleep from what I'm told, which means our camp will be guarded at night. I think you have to agree that these contributions are valid, and worthy of an equal share."

The wizard nodded slowly, contemplating.

"And the sixth?" The elf asked. Brenno scowled and drank deeply from his ale.

"The sixth claims to have killed a dragon," Brenno said, making little intent to hide his disbelief.

The elf smirked, mirth dancing in his eyes. He gestured broadly to the other patrons in the room around him.

"With enough ale and the promise of enough gold, how many of these would say the same?" The wizard's smile was one of glee and understanding, which Brenno felt combined into something of a condescending look. "You must have a very great level of trust for this person to put such faith in their words, to take claims of this level as fact."

Brenno's scowl deepened, his face darkening.

"Twenty five percent and first claim, final offer," Brenno said. "I'll balance it with the others."

He extended his hand to the elf, a handshake to seal the deal. The wizard looked down at his palm with an expression that Brenno couldn't discern as being pained or insulted. Smith walked into the tavern then, offering old man Cork a curt nod. James snored in response, having drifted off thanks to the warmth of the fire. Spotting Brenno and the wizard, Smith strode across the tavern. He offered his hand to the elf.

"You must be the wizard," Smith said.

The elf's eyes moved to Smith's hand, blackened by soot and stained with grease. The pained expression on his face intensified. Smith withdrew his offered hand and wiped it on the back of his trousers.

"I didn't mean to offend," Smith grumbled.

"And I don't believe you have, at least not intentionally," said Brenno. "I believe our friend simply isn't particularly fond of associating himself with our ilk."

"Our 'ilk?'" Smith repeated.

"*Emalleon*," Brenno said. "Non-elves."

"Huh," said Smith. "Are you helping us or not?"

"I have indeed been persuaded to lend you my assistance," the elf said, bowing his head and offering Smith the same toothless smile as before. "The good master Brenno and I have come to an arrangement that suits us both. We can leave as soon as the morning, if you would like."

"I'd prefer to leave now," said Smith.

The elf's smile spread wider, and Brenno couldn't help but feel as though there was a newfound element of arrogance and superiority in that tight lipped smile.

"Ah, but there is no sense hastening into a storm without being prepared," the elf said. "We have not even been properly introduced, though terms have been struck."

The elf readjusted his posture, sitting as tall as possible on his stool. He then offered Smith and Brenno a bow that was more a gentle dip of the head. "I am

Tanathar Vethni, wizard of the green circle. Well met, *emalleon*."

"Brenno Hornbuckle," said the halfling.

"Smith," said the man.

"Your surname?" the elf inquired.

"Not your damn business," grumbled Smith.

"Ah," said Tanathar. "I believe I've been acquainted with some of your relatives."

The door opened once more, and Kera and Voldani entered the tavern, Kera's hair still visibly damp. Both of them were dressed in travel gear, with Zephelous strapped to Kera's right hip. Brenno noted that the grave-robber's grip on the handle of the sword was tight enough to whiten the woman's knuckles.

Interesting, he thought, *perhaps there was a limit to how much snark and sass she had to offer after all.*

Seeing the previously unshakable Kera show a hint of apprehension, a hint of frailty, a hint of *humanity* was somehow both reassuring and deeply satisfying to Brenno. He slid down from his stool and beckoned for Kera and Voldani to join them.

"Mister Tanathar, might I introduce you to members four and five, Kera and Voldani."

Voldani offered the barest tilt of a head, so slight it could hardly be considered a nod, towards the wizard. Kera seemed to study the wizard, who returned her inquisitive gaze with his own scrutiny.

"I suspect you mean to say numbers five and six," said Tanathar.

"As you say," said Brenno. The elf glanced around the tavern, eyes resting on a table near the back. He nodded towards it with his chin.

"Perhaps we should move away from so open a place as this?" said Tanathar. The others followed his gaze to the empty table beyond the far side of the bar, towards the area of the tavern that sat furthest away from the doors and the other patrons.

"Seems reasonable enough," said Brenno, turning back to face Tanathar.

To his shock, the wizard was no longer seated at the bar table. The sound of a throat clearing loudly for dramatic effect on the other side of the table made Brenno grimace, as he knew full well what he'd see when he turned back around. Sure enough, when he looked towards the previously empty seat he saw Tanathar seated leisurely with his book open in front of him.

"Wizards," muttered Smith.

"Agreed," said Brenno.

"This appears to have been a relatively superfluous display of prowess in the mystic arts," said Voldani, striding forward to cross the tavern towards the elf.

"I actually agree," said Kera, falling into step behind Voldani. Smith caught Kera by the wrist as she walked past him.

"Why aren't you in chains?" He asked.

Kera's head turned to face Smith with a slowness that spoke volumes. Her eyes seemed to shine every bit as bright as Voldani's.

"Take. Your. Fucking. Hand. Off. Me."

Smith recoiled from Kera's intensity, releasing his grip on her wrist. His expression remained every bit as severe as he flexed his fingers apprehensively.

"Voldani let you out?" Smith asked.

Kera raised an arm and gestured towards Voldani, as if saying *well obviously* without using words.

"Fine." Smith rumbled.

Kera leaned in close to Smith for a moment.

"If I wanted to be gone, I'd be gone," said Kera, practically hissing. "I decided to stay and try to help Morri, but if you put your hands on me like that again not only will I be gone but I'll be taking an appendage or two with me. Understood?"

Smith made a sound in the back of his throat like stones grinding together deep beneath the earth, but he said nothing. Brenno intervened.

"I believe everyone in the room fully understands how we all feel about each other," said the halfling. "For the sake of Morri – if not for the sake of Zelwyr itself – perhaps it would be wise to refrain from murdering each other for a few weeks? Surely you can be content to dismember each other afterwards?"

Kera shot Brenno an icy stare before leaving to join Voldani and Tanathar at the table. Smith grumbled some more before turning on Brenno.

"Who made you the voice of reason? You're just as culpable as she is."

Brenno blinked slowly at Smith.

"Yes, Smith, I know that," said the halfling, tone flat. "We all know who is involved, and why. As I said, if we could stow the hostility at least temporarily, I'm sure this venture will be over all that much quicker."

Smith stared down at Brenno, crossing his arms over his chest.

"How do you figure?" the man said.

"For starters," Brenno began, "we're currently here having this conversation for what must be the hundredth time this week while the rest of our makeshift campaign group waits on us."

Smith looked to the table where Voldani, Kera, and Tanathar were now sitting. The three of them were all looking towards Smith and Brenno expectantly.

It took every ounce of his resolve and willpower, but Smith managed to push down the seething rage that even now threatened to boil over. He ground his teeth for a moment, then set off towards the table. Brenno sighed so heavily he felt as though he might melt into the ground, and followed after Smith.

Chapter Eleven

Zephelous had resigned itself to be patient and listen while the mortals prattled, waiting for a moment where it might be able to speak with Kera privately. Despite her flaws – her many, many flaws – Zephelous's every otherworldly sense told it that there was a potential for greatness within Kera.

It had felt the same way about Theus, and in all those who had come before him; Brigitte Lionsire, Praxus of Omari, the reviled Corlowaxis Asecti'Graz...

None had been born heroes, they had all earned that title one hack, slash, and thrust at a time while following the guidance of the sentient sword.

Kera, on the other hand, seemed to have a hard time obeying even simple instructions while bound and held at sword point. Or at cannon point. Or while in jail.

Zephelous sighed to itself, wishing it had hands and a face so it could use the hands to try to wring the stress out of its face.

AH WELL, it thought. *I SUPPOSE I COULD LISTEN TO THE PRATTLING.*

"So," Kera said, still resting Zephelous across her legs. "This is the wizard."

Zephelous didn't see, it perceived. It didn't hear, it understood. In the context of psychic power and psionic abilities, these distinctions meant that rather than looking around a table and seeing the faces of those sitting around it, Zephelous *felt* around the table with its mind; tendrils of invisible and intangible psionic power reached out from the sword to entangle around the fonts of thought and emotion and noise that surrounded it, separating the unique mental voices into individual bundles, then defining the bundles into the shapes they perceived themselves as – which is to say, people.

"It is indeed," said Brenno, his every thought and word bound with practiced patience. "Kera, Voldani, allow me to introduce Tanathar Vethni. He has survived encounters against dragons in the past, and is offering to lend his experience towards our venture."

"You say 'lend', but I can't help but feel you mean 'rent.'" said Kera.

If Zephelous had a mouth, it would have smiled then. Despite its misgivings about Kera, the woman constantly found a way to surprise it.

"He's a professional," said Smith.

Unlike Brenno, whose thoughts and words were like carefully wrapped packages, Smith felt like a stream of magma to Zephelous; his every thought seemed to brim with heat and pressure, his every word a spit of lava from the heart of a volcano which threatened to erupt catastrophically at any moment. Zephelous made itself a mental note to speak with this one in the future.

"Professionals understand that certain skill sets and talents are profitable."

"Don't talk to me like I'm an idiot, Smith," Kera said. "I once sold a nobleman the bones of his own grandmother for half the fortune she left him."

"And you're proud of that?" Smith asked.

"A little, yeah," answered Kera.

"That's beyond being mischievous, Kera," Smith rumbled. "That's being a lowlife, heartless criminal for the sake of being a lowlife, heartless criminal."

"By your own words, it's called being a professional," Kera said.

Smith said nothing, but Zephelous could feel the waves of anger radiating from him the way a creature with skin might feel waves of heat from a roaring fireplace.

"I grow tired of this banter," said Voldani. "Let us determine if the wizard can truly be of assistance. If so, we should leave this stinking tavern with haste."

Voldani was a breath of fresh air to Zephelous; her thoughts and emotions were powerful and direct, free of the doubts and worries and concerns most mortals had to work to suppress.

"And if not?" Kera asked.

"If not, we should leave this stinking tavern with haste," said Voldani.

Again, Zephelous wished it could smile. Everything Voldani said positively rang with certainty and confidence.

"The *autnosse* is most direct," a voice said, seemingly from nowhere.

Were Zephelous a creature of flesh, its blood would have ran cold as the ghostly voice spoke to those seated around the table. Instead, it did a quick psychic sweep of the table.

"We should settle the question of my skills and usefulness and begin our campaign at once." The voice wasn't coming from anyone at the table.

In fact, it seemed to be being broadcast directly at them in a manner similar to his own telepathic communications.

THIS IS MOST UNSETTLING.

"I don't usually care for wood elves," Kera said. "It's not a discrimination thing, I just usually can't handle the long winded conversations and the flowery poetic... Well, everything. Sharpening a sword doesn't need to be an art form, it just needs to be done."

"I'm certain there's a point following that tirade?" the voice asked.

It was conversing with Brenno, Smith, Kera, and Voldani, but none of them seemed disturbed by the fact that they were in talks with an ethereal voice without a source.

Zephelous was filled with frustration and concern.

WHAT IS GOING ON?

"Just that you're not like the wood elves I've met," Kera said, shrugging.

Zephelous caught snippets of old and painful memories in the woman's words, ghostly vestiges of sneering wood elves and uncaring facing turning away from someone looking up at them. Zephelous wanted to know more, to better understand, but this was hardly the time.

WHERE IS THIS VOICE ORIGINATING FROM?

Zephelous's psionic talent was practiced, but not without its limits; the tavern was nearly eighty feet across and something like sixty feet deep. It also had at least two floors above ground level, all of which contained gods only knew how many people. This would be difficult.

Zephelous concentrated on extending the radius its psychic tendrils could feel, slowly growing the circle of awareness that was centered on itself. The ephemeral ribbons that formed the intangible sphere of Zepheleous's senses pulsed and grew, catching more patrons in its wake as it swelled and ebbed ever outwards.

The vast majority of the patrons in the bar were human, with a few half-elves and half-orcs in attendance. This was not so rare, especially not in a town as far north as Zelwyr, where civilization existed nestled in the cradle of the wilderness around it.

"I assume I am meant to take this to be a good thing?" the voice asked.

"Don't know yet," said Kera. "In my experience, different doesn't mean good or bad. It just means different."

"This is an accurate statement," said Voldani.

"As was yours," said Kera.

"Indeed," Voldani said, nodding.

The ghostly voice laughed, a lilting giggle that felt deeply fake to Zephelous in way he couldn't define.

"This has been a most efficient test of my usefulness," said the voice.

"Apologies, Mister Tanathar," said Brenno. "Lady Kera is... unused to doing business in a formal capacity."

Zephelous's circle of awareness strained as it reached the edges of the tavern, pressing through the wood of the ceiling to reach up and encompass the second floor. There wasn't a single wood elf in his radius.

Something lurked at the edges of Zephelous's mind. Not an intruder or a presence of any kind but a faint shadow of a memory, something hinting at a yet unknown realization. It irked the sword greatly. Kera's mind flashed bright with a newfound spark of rebellion, sending a stream of mental pictures at Zephelous.

The pictures ran together and formed a scenario that involved her standing up on the table and kicking Brenno square in the mouth before knocking Voldani unconscious with a pommel blow to the head and running out the tavern door.

Zephelous didn't want to interfere with Kera's thought process, and it wanted to solve the mystery of the disembodied wood elf, but it had no choice; it flashed a mental image of Morrillypallyke into Kera's mind, showing the child locked deep in her poisoned slumber.

Kera's rebellion and rage flickered and went out, replaced with pragmatic thoughts of doing whatever was necessary to put an end to this forced arrangement once and for all. Kera's mind played the sound of an earth-shaking roar, a primal scream of challenge and pain.

To Zephelous, the sound of a dragon locked in battle – a sound it had heard far too many times over the centuries – was unmistakable.

When had Kera faced a dragon? How had she survived? So many questions that needed answering, and yet the most pressing of them all still went unsolved: *where was the wood elf?*

"How fortunate that you and I have already taken care of most of the business already," Tanathar said, speaking to Brenno. "Now pray tell *emalleon*, how exactly would you deign to evaluate my prowess?"

"What kind of dragons have you faced?" asked Smith.

"Are we willfully overlooking the part about the Hornbuckle and Vethni business partnership, or whatever arrangements have been made before we got here?" Kera asked, interjecting.

When no one responded, she rolled her eyes.

"I guess we are."

"White and red," said Tanathar.

Zephelous's tendrils of awareness reached their limits, covering the entire tavern and all its floors, spilling out onto the streets around it. There was no wood elf.

Something was amiss, the sword could feel it. It could also still feel the nagging stab of that free floating thought, teasing knowledge but not offering it freely. What was Zephelous missing?

"Was the battle glorious?" Voldani asked. Tanathar, or rather the voice that claimed to be Tanathar, paused for a moment.

"In the way an earthquake is glorious, perhaps," said the voice. "Have any of you been to sea?"

Zephelous caught flashes of thoughts from Smith, Brenno, and Voldani – memories of lazy voyages and months long expeditions. More things to explore. The only image that came from Kera's mind was a dazzling sunset seen from a high cliff overlooking a mirror-smooth ocean seascape.

"Have any of you sailed the orange sea?" The question was met with silence. "The orange sea is the place where the waters are in a constant battle against the earth; the earth spews molten rock into the sea, and the sea cools it to stone. Eventually some of that stone breaks through to the surface and erupts, giving violent birth to a new mountain. The earth roars loud enough to deafen while waves of searing heat and crushing wind explode outwards with enough force to crush galleons into scorched splinters. Sometimes it rains brimstone and soot, so much so that the air becomes toxic and the rain becomes acid. That... that is how I would describe battling a dragon."

"I do not see the glory in a natural disaster," said Voldani.

"Nor do I," said Tanathar. "Nor do I believe one should. However, that is how I would describe encountering a dragon in battle; you may as well be combating a mountain, or an ocean. They are older than any other race on Odellia, more powerful as well, and I suspect they will likely outlast all others."

More silence followed Tanathar's statement.

"I have seen a mountain felled," said Voldani. "I have seen wizards tame storms and clerics part seas. I will live to see a dragon destroyed, to watch the fire burn in its belly burn out as it breathes its last, broken body impaled on the ends of my blades. It will indeed be glorious."

"A bold statement, lady Voldani," said Tanathar.

"I am not a lady," said Voldani. "I am a warrior."

"Fucking eh, Dani," said Kera.

"My name is not 'Dani'," said Voldani. "I will not answer to a moniker I have not consented to."

"Are you saying I have to ask your permission to call you 'Dani?'" Kera asked.

"Yes," Voldani said with a nod.

"May I call you Dani?" asked Kera.

"No," Voldani said.

PERHAPS VOLDANI WOULD MAKE A MORE SUITABLE WIELDER, it thought, *SHE SEEMS VERY MUCH THE HERO.*

Kera's mind seeped a series of inappropriate and sexually suggestive nicknames she was considering proposing to the angelic woman. The harsh contrast between the two women gave Zephelous pause.

NO, Zephelous thought to itself, *THERE IS A GREATNESS IN KERA NO-CLAN, EVEN IF SHE REFUSES TO SEE IT. IT MAY BE BURIED DEEP WITHIN HER, BUT I MUST PERSIST, AS I PERSISTED WITH CORLOWAXIS, AS I PERSISTED WITH ORVOK THE TERRIBLE, AS I PERSISTED WITH LETHLIRIAN VETH--*

Zephelous practically squealed as realization dawned on it at last. It hadn't yet forgiven Kera for selling it, never mind that the transaction had been to fund her habit, but it couldn't keep this information to itself.

KERA, I HAVE INFORMATION FOR YOU.

Kera nearly toppled over backwards on her chair, but caught herself at the last moment, her chair slamming back down to the ground.

"Don't everyone look at me," Kera said. "Go back to spending all day talking about whether or not this guy can fight a dragon. It seems super productive so far, really just an incredible use of our time."

Smith grumbled, thoughts and emotions flaring angrily, but said nothing.

I was under the impression that you weren't speaking to me, Kera thought.

TRUTH BE TOLD I AM NOT ENTIRELY CONVINCED I WISH TO SPEAK WITH YOU NOW, Zephelous said. HOWEVER, I HAVE INFORMATION WHICH YOU MUST BE MADE AWARE OF.

Okay then, Kera thought. *Make me aware already.*

VETHNI IS NOT A WOOD ELF NAME, Zephelous said triumphantly.

So what? Kera asked.

THIS ELF IS NOT WHAT HE SAYS HE IS, Zephelous clarified. WHAT'S MORE, I CANNOT SENSE HIS PRESENCE.

I hate to sound like I'm repeating myself, Kera began, *but so what?*

Zephelous wished for teeth to grind, brows to furrow, and hair to pull.

LAY YOUR HANDS ON HIM, said Zephelous.

He doesn't seem like the touchy-feely type, said Kera, *and besides, he's not really my--*

ENOUGH, KERA, I BEG OF YOU, Zephelous said. THIS IS NOT THE TIME FOR YOUR INNUENDOS OR YOUR SUGGESTIVE COMMENTS, OR TO BE SPEAKING TO ME LIKE A PETULANT CHILD MIGHT SPEAK TO A PARENT. THERE IS SOMETHING UNNATURAL AT WORK HERE, SOMETHING EVEN I DO NOT FULLY COMPREHEND, AND I AM BEGGING YOU TO JUST DO AS I SAY.

Kera's mind rumbled in a very Smith-like fashion.

Fine, said Kera, after a moment of thought locked away from Zephelous's perception. *You get one minute of being the boss, but in return the silent treatment comes to an end.*

THESE TERMS ARE ACCEPTABLE, Zephelous answered.

Kera nodded, which earned her a curious look from Smith. Brenno and Voldani had been occupied speaking with Tanathar, though exactly what it had been Kera couldn't begin to guess.

"So we're agreed," Voldani said. "The wizard will cloak us with his sorcery, and we will ambush the dragon in its lair."

"Wow, I really should have been paying attention to this conversation," said Kera.

Brenno, Voldani, and Tanathar turned their heads to regard Kera.

"Yes," Brenno said. "You very much should have. Do you have any questions?"

"Actually, yeah, I do," Kera began. "For starters, how exactly are we going to be 'cloaked' from a bloodthirsty primordial killing machine slash genius? Spare me the wizardly fluff with the 'veils of moonlight' or 'concealing aura of mystical blah blah blah'. I'm serious, I want to know how we're actually going to be hidden."

IS THIS PART OF THE PLAN? Zephelous asked.

It's part of the other plan, Kera responded.

WHAT PLAN IS THAT? Asked Zephelous.

The plan to not die when we go to hunt a fucking dragon, said Kera. *Now shut up for a minute so I can concentrate.*

Brenno flashed with annoyance. The voice of Tanathar seemed amused, much to Zephelous's displeasure.

"Kera, the elf is a wizard," Brenno said. "I'm certain he knows what he's doing."

"Why?" Kera asked. "Because he said so? I said I've killed a dragon, and not one of you believed me. I'm pretty sure you still don't. This guy has a stick on his back and a big ass book, plus kind of a shitty attitude, and that's good enough? Bullshit. I want to know how he did it last time, how it worked, and why he thinks it'll work this time."

To Zephelous, Brenno and Smith did more than flash with annoyance - they burned with it.

"A peculiar choice of words," Brenno said, speaking slowly while vividly picturing the various poisons and toxins he kept in his shop. "Especially given that you haven't yet told us about your own encounter."

"If it ever happened," added Smith.

"I would also be delighted to be regaled by this tale," said Tanathar.

"I have grown deeply disinterested," Voldani said, sitting back in her chair.

"That's hurtful, Voldani," said Kera.

"I do not care," Voldani responded. "I came to test mettle, not exchange banter."

"That's not a bad idea," said Kera, speaking to Tanathar. "Why don't you and Voldani go a couple rounds? She's basically a dragon."

"In what ways am I like a dragon?" Voldani asked.

"You can fly, for starters," Kera said. "You've also got swords."

"Dragons do not use swords," said Voldani.

Zephelous's thought went once more to Corlowaxis Asecti'Graz, ancient green dragon and matriarch of the green dragon flight.

Some dragons did indeed use swords.

"What exactly are you proposing?" Brenno asked. "That we let our guide and our scout brawl it out in a tavern to establish whether or not we're ready for a dragon?"

"Not explicitly, but I mean… yeah, I think so," Kera said.

"That's a terrible idea," said Brenno.

"I'm having a hard time coming up with a reason why not," Smith said to Brenno. "Believe me when I say I'm trying hard not to agree with her."

"This hardly seems--" Brenno began, only to be interrupted by Voldani rising quickly from her chair, the wooden legs scraping loudly against the floor.

"Come, wizard," Voldani said, leaving the table to walk towards the door. "Today may yet be worth my while."

Zephelous's impatience was growing.

I FAIL TO SEE HOW THIS FOLLOWS ANY SORT OF PLAN, it said to Kera.

I'm on it, Kera responded, rising to stand. "Shall we, misters?"

"This is not happening," said Brenno.

"You must learn to relax, *aier,*" Tanathar said. "I have survived the wrath of dragons. If it will serve the double purpose of proving my worth and putting an end to this woefully drab conversation, I cannot help but see the merit."

Smith said nothing, but nodded.

Zephelous felt a hint of annoyance from Smith and Brenno – Smith's was annoyance that the group hadn't left yet, while Brenno's seemed to stem from being undermined.

KERA, I AM SO FAR DISAPPOINTED WITH YOUR SO CALLED 'PLAN', said Zephelous. EITHER REVEAL YOUR INTENTIONS OR LOWER YOUR PSYCHIC SHIELDING.

It's a distraction meets a bait and switch, basic stuff. Just watch and shut up, Kera said. *And I have no idea what you mean by psychic shielding.*

Kera's response stunned Zephelous into silence. How could Kera not know about psychic shielding given how secure her mind, even against the sword's own abilities?

"Well?" Kera said, speaking to Brenno, Smith, and Tanathar.

Smith didn't wait for further prompting, turning and following Voldani out of the Tavern. Brenno scowled, the careful packets that were his thoughts fluttering and reeling under the weight of his ire.

The halfling's scowl became a glowering stare at Kera, but he too followed Smith, leaving just Kera and Tanathar at the table. Tanathar sipped the remaining wine in his glass, finishing it off without so much as a sound.

He deposited the glass on the table, and slid his chair back to stand.

"Shall we, lady Kera?" Tanathar asked Kera, toothless smile spread wide.

"We could," Kera said, taking a few casual steps towards the elf. "Or we could stay here and you can convince me why I shouldn't tell them." Tanathar made a confused face.

"I'm afraid I do not understand what you mean, *merka*," Tanathar said.

Zephelous felt a pang of anger and irritation slip free from between the blocks of Kera's psychic wall.

"Don't call me that," Kera said, taking the now vacant seat that Brenno had occupied. "And I think you know exactly what I mean."

Tanathar's smile shrank almost, but not quite, unnoticeably.

Kera noticed.

KERA, WHAT ARE YOU SPEAKING ABOUT? Zephelous asked.

It's called a bluff, Zeph, I have no fucking idea what I'm talking about, Kera answered. *But he does, and that's what matters.*

"You are speaking nonsense," Tanathar said, moving to step around Kera.

"Am I?" Kera asked as the elf stood behind her. "Because I don't think I am. See, I wasn't lying when I said I had killed a dragon, you know. I never did get to explain how, because Smith and Brenno think I'm full of shit."

Kera took Brenno's half drank cup from the table, sniffed it contents, and shrugged. She emptied the contents into her mouth, dragging the conversation on intentionally in an effort to set Tanathar on edge.

"I have some special abilities, similar to your own, I think."

Tanathar scoffed and sneered at Kera.

"I am not interested in hearing about your barbarian magics, *merka*," the elf said. "I am a wizard of the green circle, I have very little concern about your so-called 'special abilities'."

"See, that's the thing," Kera said, placing Brenno's cup back on the table with a loud clunk before reaching for Smith's cup. She raised it off the table and found it to be empty, and so she put it back disappointed.

"You're not. On an equally important note, I'm pretty sure I've already asked you not to call me that."

"I beg your pardon?" Tanathar said, bristling under his collar. "I am not what?"

"A wizard," Kera said, grunting slightly and she stretched to reach across the table for Voldani's cup. She gave it a quick swirl to test to see if it was empty or not. Hearing the sloshing of liquids, she pulled it across the table and brought it to her mouth. Water. Kera scowled.

"Well, you might be a wizard – you've got the patented cliche mysterious wanderer look down, that's for sure – but you're not from the green circle. That's one lie, which makes me wonder what else might be a lie. For instance, did you really have those encounters with dragons?"

"What grounds could you – an uneducated girl from the blasted hell hole that is the Wildlands – possibly have to accuse me of not being who I say I am?"

"I've spent more time than I care to think about around wood elves," Kera said. "We're a long way from the Wildlands, in case you haven't noticed. Pretty much half a continent, if you think about it."

"I pray you have a point," Tanathar said.

"Just that while I might not feel the need to haul a giant book around to flaunt my superior intellect, I know that if you're going to run an elaborate con, you need to do your research first."

"And what makes you think a person of my station would stoop to performing a con?"

"Vethni is a high elf name, *parmaedhel*," Kera said, using the title wood elves gave their own kind.

It seemed as though all sound went out from the tavern, making the hairs on the back of Kera's neck stood on end. She felt as though lightning were running through her veins, and tightened her grip on Zephelous's handle in anticipation of a coming struggle.

"Well, shit," said Tanathar, in a voice completely different from the musical lilt he'd been using.

This new voice was less steady, but somehow warmer. It also sounded slightly drunk.

"I guess I have to knock you out and rewrite your memories."

WELL DONE, KERA, Zephelous said proudly.

Kera shook her head, though for whose benefit it was the sword couldn't tell.

"Won't work on me," Kera said. "I'll remember everything within an hour, a day at the longest. Though I have to say, I've dealt with more than my fair share of magical douchebags, and most don't bother to go to the trouble of memory erasing. Most would have just attacked by now."

"I've heard less clever lies before," said Tanathar. "Why should I believe you?"

Zephelous, if he does this now with no preparation, it will probably only wipe out the last couple minutes, Kera thought to the sword. *Tell me it's just like that time in Wreck Isle Mile.*

HOW DO YOU KNOW THAT? Zepehelous asked, AND WHY WILL THAT MAKE YOU BELIEVE ME?

I can't believe I'm saying this, Kera replied, *but trust me.*

"Give it a shot if you want," said Kera to Tanathar, adding a shrug for effect. "You won't be the first to try, and I have a feeling you won't be the last."

Tanathar's expression became serious and heavy, weighing on Kera as he studied her for any sign of weakness or mistruth.

For her part, Kera leaned backwards in her chair. Zephelous wished it could see through Kera's psychic shielding, to see how Kera felt in this moment. Whatever the woman was feeling, Zephelous admired her fortitude in that moment.

"Maybe I'm cynical," Tanathar began, "but I just don't believe you."

A mind in the tavern flared with effort, shining bright in Zephelous's sphere of perception, and there was a sound like overlapped horns playing a single vibrating note.

Kera blinked, having found herself suddenly leaning backwards on a chair at the Tavern she'd just been walking towards.

The chair threatened to kick out from under her, feet skidding on the tavern floor with a screech. She somersaulted backwards in the nick of time, landing on the floor in a low defensive crouch as the chair clattered to the floor. Hand on Zephelous's grip, she scanned the room quickly.

The barmaid behind the counter, a severe looking brunette, was scrutinizing Kera with the barest amount of interest. The head of an old man leered unsteadily at her from behind the side of a chair facing the fireplace. Rising quickly to her feet, Kera looked at the table and grabbed an expensive looking wine glass and held it up in the air, pointing at it and smiling.

"It's stronger than I thought," she said, loud enough for all to hear.

Diffusing the tension of a situation by placing the blame on herself was a trick she'd learned far too long ago, it came as easy as breathing now.

"Can I get one more of these, whatever this is?"

The barmaid crossed her arms over her chest, trying to size Kera up from across the room. After a moment, she walked away from the counter, to where Kera couldn't guess.

KERA, LOOK FOR A WOOD ELF, Zephelous shouted with urgency.

Kera scanned the room once more as she righted the chair. She brushed off her shirt and breeches, pretending to struggle with invisible dirt as she swept her eyes across the room more attentively.

I do not see a wood elf, Kera thought. *Hey, since when are we back on speaking terms?*

WE CAME TO AN AGREEMENT SEVERAL MINUTES AGO. Zephelous said. LOOK AGAIN, THE WIZARD IS TESTING YOU.

An elf and a wizard? Kera asked, *One of my least favorite combinations. Where's Voldani?*

VOLDANI IS OUTSIDE, said Zephelous. THE WIZARD IS ABOUT TO DUEL WITH HER, AND HAS JUST USED HIS MAGICS TO ERASE YOUR RECENT MEMORIES.

Guess I lost my duel, Kera said.

To her surprise, the barmaid arrived with a serving tray atop which sat a bottle of wine. Kera smiled appreciatively and took both in her hands.

"You're cut off after this," the barmaid said. "Speaker Gerhardt paid restitution on your behalf for the damages you did, but that doesn't mean I'm setting you up to launch another tavern brawl."

"I started a tavern brawl in the last few minutes?" Kera asked.

The barmaid's face darkened with concern, and she eyed the bottle and wine glass in Kera's hands with regret.

"I'm talking about the one from two weeks ago," the barmaid said.

"Ah," said Kera, uncorking the wine bottle with a pop. "I do not remember that."

"I'm not surprised," said barmaid. "You were even more out of your head than you'd been in the one the week before."

"I do not remember that either," Kera said, pouring herself a glass of wine and drinking it the moment the glass was filled.

"I suppose you also don't remember stumbling your way into my bedchamber the night prior, so drunk your legs barely worked?" the barmaid said, crossing her arms in front of her ample chest.

Kera poured another glass of wine, slower this time, as she looked thoughtfully at the barmaid. She was plain and beautiful all at once, and a wicked smile spread across her face.

"My legs worked fine the next day," Kera said with a wink at the barmaid. "I'm guessing yours didn't, otherwise you wouldn't have brought it up."

IS IT IMPOSSIBLE FOR YOU TO STAY ON TASK FOR EVEN A SINGLE MINUTE?

Gods, Zeph, Kera said. *I don't know if mind-deaf is a thing, but if you keep shouting like that I'm going to be the first ever example. Besides, what's wrong with laying a little groundwork with a lovely lass like this?*

YOU COULD BE IN DANGER, said Zephelous. VOLDANI MAY WELL BE IN DANGER. THE WIZARD IS DECEIVING YOU ALL, SMITH AND BRENNO INCLUDED.

I still don't see the problem, said Kera, watching Gemma walk away.

YOU TOLD ME TO TELL YOU SOMETHING THAT WOULD MAKE YOU REALIZE THE SERIOUSNESS OF THE SITUATION, said Zephelous.

Oh did I now? Kera replied.

THIS IS JUST LIKE THE TIME IN WRECK ISLE MILE.

Kera stood up from her seat so fast the chair clattered to the ground once more, eyes wide. Her insides knotted and squirmed with instant anxiety and concern, and she held Zephelous with two hands, at the ready in front of her.

Zephelous, unused to Kera being responsive or on guard at the best of times, was surprised by Kera's sudden change of pace.

"This is why nobody likes wizards. Where is he?" Kera asked, speaking out loud as she scanned the tavern.

She was being looked at once more, but paid neither the busty barmaid or the doddering old man any attention. She pivoted in place, facing away from the bar, Zephelous still held at the ready.

"I'm still not seeing any wizard-looking elves in this bar, Zeph."

I WAS ABLE TO DETECT HIM THE MOMENT HIS MAGICS WERE CAST UPON YOU, Zephelous said. HE IS INDEED WITHIN THE TAVERN. I SENSED THE FLEXINGS OF A MIND STRAINING TO COMMAND THE WEAVE SOMEWHERE NEAR THE FAR CORNER.

Kera looked at the corner tables. One of them had a small group of hulking, green-skinned half-orcs eating and drinking, speaking quietly to themselves. The other was empty, minus what appeared to be a burlap sack laying on the top of it. She frowned.

Is it the orcs? She asked Zephelous, uncertain what she would do if it was.

I DO NOT BELIEVE SO, said Zephelous. THE MIND I SAW WAS ALONE,

SEATED ACROSS FROM A GROUP OF PERSONS WHOSE ONLY
THOUGHTS WERE OF FOOD, BLOOD, AND VIOLENCE.

Kera watched one of the half-orcs eagerly tear into a quarter of meat, juices
spurting and bubbling around sharpened fangs that pierced cleanly through the
skin.

She winced, repressing a memory that tried to rise to the surface.

I think we can safely say that the bloody violent food lovers are present, she thought
to Zephelous.

She glanced once more to the table opposite the half-orcs, taking in their light
green skin and their thick black hair, their tattoos and their yellow eyes. One of
them caught her staring at them and offered her a smile, lips shining with grease
from the chicken. She smiled back and offered a wave, making her way to the
table.

Here goes nothing, Kera thought.

The half-orc who had spotted her, a tall male with his hair tied back in a top
knot, stood and offered her a hand.

"Well met, I am Oursh of the Thunderbringers," Kera took his extended hand
and shook it. Handshake completed, the hulking half-orc used his hand to gesture
to his companions in turn. "This is Vont, Gart, and Oula."

"Well met, Thunderbringers," Kera said, offering the group a slight bow.

It pained her even as she did it, to fall back to the customs of a clan that had
long ago abandoned her.

"What brings you to Zelwyr, wildling?" the one called Gart asked.

"I'm not a wildling," said Kera. "I'm my own person."

"Spoken like a true wildling," the one called Oula said, lips spreading into a
sinister looking smile. "We may be far from the Wildlands, but your blood still
hums with the song. I can hear it as surely as I can see you before me. Which
clan do you carry the banner of?"

"None," said Kera. "I am Kera No-Clan."

Gart and Vont gasped audibly, and Oula's smile seemed to freeze on her face.
Only Oursh seemed to be unaffected by this news. He held a commanding hand
up towards his companions, commanding them to silence their reactions.

"As Oula says, we are far from the Wildlands," Oursh began. "Are we so far
that we can overlook the laws of the Wild? I cannot say. You are clearly in need
of something, Kera No-Clan, I can see it painted on your face. Speak plainly, and
perhaps the Thunderbringers may be of assistance to you."

Oula began a protest of some kind, but Oursh silenced her at the first syllable
with a simple hand gesture. Seeing the power Oursh commanded over his

clansmen, the authority he possessed in his every gesture, threatened to open the floodgates for ever more painful memories.

Kera had known someone very much like Oursh once, a human who could urge a crowd of shouting people to silence themselves with nothing more than a raised hand. She pressed that memory down, deep down, and walled it away. This was not the time for such thoughts. She had work to do.

"I'm looking for a wizard," said Kera, actively ignoring the hateful looks she knew she was getting from the half-orcs who were still seated.

"Surely there are many of those to be found in the wide world," said Oursh. "Oula has some magic in her, a gift from Yrt herself. Perhaps she can be of assistance."

For her part, Oula sneered and made a snorting sound, disgusted at the possibility of helping Kera in any way. Kera has expected as much. Oursh's willingness to offer any form of assistance was the surprise.

"I'm looking for a specific wizard here, in the tavern," Kera clarified. "He took my memories and is now hiding somewhere, and I'm pretty sure it's right around here."

Oursh looked thoughtful for a moment.

"I cannot say if he is a wizard, but the drunk across from us seemed to be muttering many things while he fell into his cups," said Oursh, gesturing towards the table opposite them.

Kera looked across and saw nothing but the burlap sack. She furrowed her brow.

"Well, I guess he's gone now," she said. "Can I ask you something?"

"You may," Oursh said with a nod.

"Why are you helping me?" Kera asked.

Oursh took a long, slow breath, his chest swelling to an impressive size. He puffed it out from his mouth and seemed somehow defeated, shoulders hanging low.

"We are a long way from the Wildlands," said Oursh. "There are many here who view me and my kin as savages for our ancestry alone. Add to that our culture, and it becomes... difficult to coexist peacefully, and all but impossible to find work."

"I don't see what this has to do with me," said Kera.

Oursh offered her a pained smile.

"It is nice to see a friendly face," said the half-orc, "regardless of clan."

"Or lack thereof," Oula said with a sneer.

Oursh's head snapped towards Oula, glaring at the woman. Her sneer dissolved and she faced the table, sullenly reaching for a portion of the meat on the table before tearing into it. With an angry shake of his head, Oursh turned back to face Kera.

"I apologize for my clanmates," said Oursh.

"Don't bother," Kera answered. "It's what I expected. Thanks for the help."

Oursh bowed once more, maintaining eye contact all the while.

"Walk surely, Kera No-Clan," said Oursh.

"Step lightly, Oursh Thunderbringer," Kera said, offering a bow in return.

Well, That was a bust, she thought to Zephelous.

NOT ENTIRELY, said Zephelous. THERE IS INDEED A MAN SEATED ACROSS FROM YOU. HE WAS VERY INTERESTED TO EAVESDROP ON YOUR CONVERSATION.

Kera stared dead ahead at the table in front of her.

Zephelous, there's no one there, said Kera. *It's a goddamn sack.*

KERA, WE MADE AN AGREEMENT A FEW MOMENTS AGO, Zephelous said. THE TERMS OF THAT AGREEMENT WERE, AND I QUOTE, THAT I WAS TO BECOME THE BOSS, AS YOU PUT IT, FOR A TIME. AS THAT BOSS, I DEMAND YOU INVESTIGATE FURTHER.

Kera rolled her eyes, but sauntered her way up to the table nonetheless. She sat opposite the burlap sack and stared at it.

I can confirm that it is a burlap sack, Kera thought.

YOU ALSO BELIEVED YOU WERE SPEAKING TO AN ELF, said Zephelous.

You said I was speaking to an elf, Kera responded.

I DO NOT BELIEVE THERE WAS AN ELF, Zephelous answered.

"Okay, wait," Kera said out loud, face screwed up in confusion.

Seeing that Oula was glowering at her from the next table over, Kera made a mental note to try harder to keep her conversations with Zephelous in her head.

Was there an elf or wasn't there?

THERE APPEARED TO BE BUT THERE WAS NOT, Zephelous said.

Well, at least you're not giving me meaningless cryptic answers or anything, Kera thought in response.

She eyed the burlap sack once more. It was a dull brown, and seemed to contain something roughly the size of a pumpkin. Out of curiosity, she reached out with a finger and poked the seemingly discarded bag.

"Shit," said the burlap sack.

"*Holy shit,*" said Kera, jumping to her feat and bringing Zephelous to bear in front of her. "Zeph, the bag's alive, it's a talking bag."

The bag shimmered and rippled, as if it had been a reflection on a still pond and Kera had just thrown a rock through it. The image flickered and, after another few seconds of rippling and distortion, faded away entirely.

Kera found herself face to face with a grubby looking man wearing dingy red robes, with an unkempt beard and messy hair that were both the same shade of rusty red. A crooked smile spread across his face as he looked at Kera with eyes that were glassy and bloodshot.

"Busted," said the man, hunched forward on the table with an ale clutched in one hand and an amulet in the other.

BEHOLD, said Zephelous. THE WIZARD HAS BEEN REVEALED.

"You're not a bag," said Kera.

"You're not so bad looking yourself," said the man.

Kera scowled, standing while bringing Zephelous to bear on the man, the sword's wicked tip pointed squarely at his face. The man's only response was to blink slowly, almost unsteadily, and take a noisy sip from his ale.

"Now what?" the man asked.

"I'm not sure," Kera answered. "I guess that depends on what kind of magic bullshit you try to pull now that you know your little memory trick won't get you out of it."

The man snorted into his ale, plunking the tankard down onto the table. He wiped the foam off his lips, missing some that clung to his beard, wobbling like a jellyfish.

"I'm a little too preoccupied for my usual brand of bullshit," the man said wryly. "Your friend is actually pretty good, she might actually be able to go toe to toe with a dragon and not die."

"How would you know that?" Kera asked, still pointing Zephelous firmly at his face.

"I'm fighting with her right now," the man said, gesturing towards the window just behind Kera.

Not wanting to take her eyes off the wizard, Kera glanced quickly out the window to confirm what he was saying; she caught a glimpse of Voldani in the heat of battle, swords slashing and thrusting in a whirlwind of steel and technique.

To Kera's confusion, Voldani's opponent was none other than Tanathar, who brought his staff to up to block and deflect each of Voldani's strikes. Confused, Kera whipped her head back around to face the slouched wizard.

"I thought Tanathar wasn't real," said Kera.

"He's not," said the man. "Well, he was, he isn't any more. He died."

"You want to cut to the chase, or should I start cutting first?" said Kera.

"It's an illusion," the wizard said, pausing to hiccup into his hand. "It does what I want it to do, says what I make it say, and so on."

"So, when we were speaking to Tanathar…" Began Kera.

"You were actually talking to me," said the wizard. "Well, kind of. Illusions are tricky. Imagine a puppet without strings that both is and isn't real. Takes a lot of effort to conjure, and lots of concentration to maintain."

"But not so much that you can be drunk off your ass while you do it," said Kera, tapping Zephelous against the tankard on the table.

"Maybe I'm just that good," the man said, shrugging as he took another messy sip of ale. "I haven't lied, if that helps at all."

"You said you were an elf, so that's one lie," Kera said, noting from the corner of her eye that the Thunderbringers at the next table were now intently watching what was transpiring. "I'm guessing Tanathar isn't actually your name, that's probably two. Should I keep going?" The man nodded sullenly, frowning.

"Okay, fair," he said. "I'm not an elf, as you can see. Tanathar is not my name, it's William, William Decker. My friends call me Will… or at least they did before they died."

"*Ooh*, dark and edgy," Kera said, mockingly. "Everybody has dead people. That's life. It's not much of an excuse to go around pretending to be something you're not."

Will smiled up at her, hand tightening around the amulet.

"Isn't it, though?" Will asked. "I get the feeling you're no stranger to pretending, eh No-Clan?"

Kera winced involuntarily.

"What's that supposed to mean?" Kera asked.

Will lifted his ale once more, but frowned when he found the tankard to be empty.

"You tell me," said Will. "I've been to the Wildlands, I know what No-Clan means."

"I've been hearing that a lot lately," Kera responded. "And so far, everyone who has said it has been full of shit."

Will hiccuped once more, covering his mouth with his hand. His knuckles brushed against the wobbling foam still stuck in his beard, which made him glance down. Seeing the froth, he brought his hand to his mouth and sucked it off, slurping it loudly. He combed his fingers through his beard in a crude attempt to remove the remaining foam, succeeding only in spreading it through the wiry tangle.

"Just because I'm an illusionist doesn't mean I'm full of shit," said Will.

"So far I have to disagree," said Kera.

"No-Clan means you were abandoned by your tribe," Will began. "Worse than that, you're exiled. For what I can't say, but whatever it is it's bad enough that not only have you been ousted by your own clan, you've been declared damaged goods, persona non grata; so much so that not one clan, not one flea-ridden bunch of savages from the Wildlands, will take you in. That's kind of impressive in its own right."

Kera's face hardened into a mask of anger, her blood threatening to boil over and burst from her veins.

"Is it now?" She said, voice cool and sharp. "Care to elaborate?"

"Care to take that sword out of my face?" Will responded.

"Not particularly," Kera answered.

"Fair enough," Will said with a grimace. "What's impressive about it is that there are so few laws in the Wildlands, and almost none of them lead to exile. Even then, I honestly can't think of anything that would be so bad that you'd be denied from joining another clan besides whatever one that kicked you out in the first place. Then again, if the chatter I've been picking up over the last few days is at all accurate, you're basically a walking disaster."

Kera ground her teeth. She wanted nothing more than to swipe Zephelous through Will's head, to shave his stupid crooked smile off his face and take a good portion of his cheeks with it. Her knuckles went white as her grip on Zephelous tightened drastically.

Will saw this, and arched an eyebrow at her.

"Something I said?" he asked.

KERA, DO NOT KILL THIS MAN, said Zephelous.

"And why shouldn't I?" Kera answered, speaking out loud.

"Why shouldn't you what?" Asked Will.

HE IS NOT LYING ABOUT HAVING FACED DRAGONS BEFORE, said Zephelous. WHAT'S MORE, HIS PROWESS WITH ILLUSIOMANCY IS WHAT KEPT HIM ALIVE. I SUSPECT HE WILL BE A TREMENDOUSLY USEFUL ASSET.

"Or just a tremendous ass," Kera retorted.

Will pulled back from Kera, eyeing the woman with suspicion.

"What, ah… What's going on here?" asked Will. "Who are you talking to?"

TELL HIM NOTHING, said Zephelous.

"No shit," Kera said, speaking to Zephelous.

Sheathing it at her hip, she sat down opposite Will. Turning around to look for Gemma, Kera caught the bartender's eye and made a whirling gesture with the tip of her finger, signifying that she wanted another round of ale brought over. Will nodded appreciatively.

"Okay, well, that's a plus," said Will. "I take it you're not going to explain the whole 'talking to yourself' bit, huh?"

"Nope," said Kera.

"But you've decided not to kill me," Will stated.

"Yep," Kera answered.

"You barbarians sure have a way with words," said Will, grinning wide.

Kera lunged across the table, grabbing the illusionist by the front of his robes near his neck and hauling him towards her, bringing his face in close to her own.

"Call me a barbarian one more time," said Kera, her tone sharper than even Zephelous. "No, really, go ahead. I'm curious to see what happens to your little illusionary routine when I start punching your teeth out through the back of your skull."

Will smiled sheepishly, holding his hands up in surrender. Kera's eyes flickered briefly towards the amulet in his hands, now raised up to eye level; it was a medallion of some kind, made from silver. What caught her eye was the emerald in the center, cut into the shape of a sunburst.

"Okay, I get it," said Will. "You're not a fan of labels, that's cool. I'll make sure not to use them in the future."

INQUIRE ABOUT HIS INTENTIONS, said Zephelous.

Kera nodded slightly, but was silent.

Gemma approached the table, a tankard of ale in each hand, and deposited one in front of Kera and the other in front of Will. She eyed the pair suspiciously, but left them be. Kera sipped from her ale quietly, while Will slurped noisily from his.

"So, what's your deal?" Kera said, breaking the silence.

"I'm not sure what you mean," said Will.

"With Tanathar, and pretending to be a bag, and sitting here while you do whatever it is you're doing outside with Voldani," said Kera.

Will puffed air out between his lips, his breath making a squealing sound on its way out.

"It's a long story," said Will. "One that I'm not overly fond of telling."

"Give me the short version, then," said Kera.

"Fine," he said, taking a deep drink from his tankard, belching loudly as he did.

"You're kind of gross, you know that?" said Kera, noticing the many stains on

Will's red and black robes.

Tracing Kera's gaze to the stains that spotted his clothes, Will snapped the fingers of his free hand. Small swirls of silver sparks traced the stains in their entirety and then vanished, taking the stains with them.

"I thought you couldn't do your magic shit while you were doing that stuff outside," said Kera.

"That's barely magic," said Will. "It's basically a parlor trick, real beginner's stuff."

Something crashed outside loudly enough to be heard inside the tavern. Will winced, flushed face tightening with effort.

"Flying tackle?" Kera asked.

Will grunted and nodded in response.

"Yeah, she hit me with that one too. Painful, isn't it?"

"Tanathar doesn't feel pain," Will said, taking another noisy slurp of his ale.

"Must be nice," said Kera.

"It is," said Will, emptying the rest of his pint glass in one gulp.

"I think I'll join you," said Kera, doing the same with hers.

Chapter Twelve

Outside the Tavern, Voldani stood up from the splintered remains of a shattered cart, eyes burning like a pair of suns. Broken boards fell away from her as she rose, swords singing as she crossed them in front of her. She turned her unblinking eyes onto Tanathar, standing some thirty feet away from her, staff in hand and an impassive expression on his face.

"Impossible," Voldani said. "I have never failed to bring a target down with that method."

"You have today, *autnosse*," said Tanathar, smiling softly.

Voldani locked her jaw. She hated being smiled at; she was a divine warrior, not a cooing infant. Crouching low with her translucent wings outstretched, Voldani sprung forward with her legs while using her wings to propel herself into a spiraling lunge, blades shredding the air in front like a corkscrew towards the petulant elf.

Mere seconds before her blades bit into his flesh, Tanathar threw himself backwards to lie flat against the ground, looking up at Voldani as she passed overhead. As she spun, she caught him smiling at her still.

Splaying her wings out and tucking her neck, Voldani turned her lunge into a shoulder roll and came back up on her feet. Sliding her blades along each other once more, the ring of steel on steel calming her nerves and sharpening her focus, she allowed herself a growl of frustration. She was quickly learning to despise this wizard.

"Not possible," Voldani seethed. "I have used that very technique to slay dozens of fiends, often many at once. How did you evade it?"

"By laying flat on the ground, dear Voldani," Tanathar said, somehow already back on his feet.

He smiled at her again, and Voldani vowed to herself that she would live to see that smile punched out of his head this day. Gods willing, it would be her own fists that accomplished it.

"That is not what I meant and you are completely aware of it," Voldani said, glaring at the elf.

Some of her sisters had been graced with gifts of fire and light, the ability to sear the flesh from the bones of the unrighteous. While she wouldn't allow herself jealousy, Voldani found herself wishing she could trade her god given gift of wings for another – at least for the time being.

Brenno and Smith watched on from the sidelines, standing on the walkways that ran along the edges of the streets of Zelwyr. The halfling chuckled, slapping his hands together and rubbing them with glee. Voldani didn't care for the pawnbroker. Smith scowled and said nothing. He looked up to the sky, gauging the time of day by the position of the sun and the paired moons.

"We're wasting a lot of time with this," Smith grumbled.

Voldani nodded to herself. The man was right, and wasted few words. His company was tolerable to Voldani. More than that, she found his rumbling ire and directness a welcome break from the forced pleasantries and dull complaints most people she'd encountered seemed to offer.

"Can we agree that at the very least he's hard to kill and move on?"

"I concur," said Voldani. "I find myself having a very difficult time eviscerating him."

"You're only supposed to be testing him," said Brenno, voice filled with concern. "You weren't actually trying to kill him, were you?"

"If she was, she was failing quite spectacularly," Tanathar said with a laugh.

Voldani found her ability to stay in control of her emotions seemed to be failing her, as she noticed that her hands were straining to grip her swords ever tighter.

"I will draw blood from you this day, Tanathar Vethni," Voldani swore, pointing at the elf with the tip of her right sword.

"I'd really prefer you didn't," said a voice from behind Voldani.

Peering over her shoulder, Voldani found herself staring at the armored forms of a half dozen Zelwyran town guards. Their leader, a stocky human woman with red hair, had her hands on her belt. Voldani nodded at the figure.

"This does not concern you, Treia," Voldani turned back to face Tanathar, maintaining her combat ready stance.

"All due respect Vee, when I get reports of a brawl outside a tavern where that wild arsonist girl was seen, I get very concerned." Treia said as she walked over to stand between Voldani and Tanathar, her guards flanking her closely. "And when I'm on duty, I'd strongly prefer it if you called me 'Sheriff.'"

Voldani watched the armored woman carefully, eyes never straying from Tanathar. Treia made her way to the destroyed cart and kicked at the fragments.

"Another vendor's cart? Gods, Vee. This was someone's livelihood." Treia rubbed her hands across her face in exasperation. "What's the reason for today's brawl?"

"I am testing the mettle of this wizard," Voldani said, swords still at the ready.

Treia sighed, turning to face Tanathar.

"What do you have against Zelwyr?" Treia asked. "A personal grudge or some kind, or are you just not fond of entrepreneurial endeavours?" Tanathar blinked, but otherwise remained motionless.

"I'm afraid I don't understand," Tanathar said.

"Of course you don't," Treia said. She clasped her hands together behind her back and began pacing between the two, looking to Voldani like a mother scolding her children. "You ratcatchers are all the same. You don't spend so much as a single minute thinking about the world around you, you just start brawling. Doesn't matter if it's a city street, a tavern, or apparently even a church."

Treia shot a pointed expression towards Voldani as she said the word 'church'.

While I respect Treia, I find this obstinance and instistance on interfering bothersome and tedious, Voldani thought with a scowl.

"Are you finished?" Voldani asked, eyes still locked on Tanathar.

"I wasn't," said Treia. "But you are, both of you. Whatever this is, it's not happening on my streets anymore. Take it out of town, go kill each other in the forest or something."

"I have sworn to draw the blood of the elf on this day," Voldani refuted.

I will do all I can to uphold a vow I've made, she thought, *most of all one I have made to myself.*

Treia pointed eastward towards the nearest gate out of Zelwyr.

"So I heard. Sounds like a great time for everyone except the elf," said Treia. "Do it out there or I'll arrest you both. I don't give a damn what the Speaker says, the streets of Zelwyr are under my watch, not the Speaker's, and not Perrus's."

Tanathar continued to remain still, which irked Voldani for a reason she couldn't quite place. She scrutinized him intensely, studying his stance for any hint or signs of weariness. Seeing none, her scowl became deeper.

Perhaps I have already drawn his blood, she thought.

She studied Tanathar's unusual garb for any signs of nicks or scratches where the blade might have bit into the pale skin of the elf.

Finding none, she sheathed her swords in dismay. It seemed as though she hadn't so much as caused the elf's breath to quicken, which disappointed her even further.

Given the acrobatic nature of our duel, surely he should have been worn, Voldani thought, *yet somehow, he seems utterly unphased...*

"I propose we move on, *emalleon,*" Tanathar said. "Shall we consider my mettle tested, my worthiness proven?"

Treia nodded her approval, offering a mock bow of thanks in Tanathar's direction.

Even his words remain steady, Voldani thought to herself. *His pulse and breath remain as constant as the tides.*

She stared at Tanthar's chest as the elf turned to face Brenno and Smith, waiting to watch it swell with a new inhale so she could try to gauge the elf's stamina.

"Thank you, whatever your name is," said Treia.

"Tanathar Vethni at your service," Tanathar said with a bow.

Treia offered only a curt wave in response, visibly not interested in learning anything about the elf. Voldani ignored this exchange entirely, eyes still fixed on Tanathar's chest.

"Are we good Voldani?" Treia asked. "If I have to come back here, I swear to the Maker Gods I *will* arrest you."

Voldani didn't respond, still fixated on waiting for Tanathar to draw a breath. When several moments passed in silence, Treia scowled.

"Vee, are you listening to me?"

Voldani's eyes narrowed, and her response was to draw her sword from its sheath at lightning speed and hurl it at Tanathar.

"Gods damn it, Vee!" Treia shouted, drawing her mace and shield.

Voldani, meanwhile, stared in amazement as her sword passed clear *through* Tanathar, skipping and rolling across the cobblestone streets some feet behind him.

Brenno and Smith shared a gasp, while Treia turned slowly away from Voldani. Tanathar, still facing Brenno and Smith, furrowed his brow.

"Is there a problem, *emalleon?*" the elf asked, turning away from Smith and Brenno to face Treia and Voldani. He seemed confused, glancing from person to person before looking down at himself.

"Is there something amiss?"

"There is," said Voldani. "I did not miss."

Tanathar laughed.

"You misunderstand my words, Voldani," said Tanathar. "I meant *amiss* as in something wrong, not 'a miss' as in a projectile that has strayed from its target."

Treia's eyes seemed to darken, and she purposefully rehung her mace on the hook on her belt and slung her shield over her shoulder. She sucked air against her teeth before making a clicking sound with her tongue.

Voldani didn't understand what this reaction was meant to denote, but uncovering the meaning behind it was not her intention; uncovering the meaning behind the elf's treachery was.

Filled with a righteous fury at being cheated from the glory of a fair and noble combat, Voldani strode purposefully towards Tanathar. Treia did the same, the dark scowl still clinging to her face. Seeing the women approach him from either side, Tanthar's head swivelled back and forth between them as he smiled nervously.

"Is something the matter?" Tanathar asked, stepping backwards towards the tavern in an effort to put distance between the two women. "Surely we can discuss whatever it is that I have done to offend the pair of you."

Treia and Voldani made eye contact with each other. In another life, one not that far gone, the two had been companions, sisters in arms. They had taken very different paths with their lives since, there were some things which old friends simply never needed to say to the other out loud when a mere glance would suffice.

The women lunged at Tanathar simultaneously, Treia going for the elf's legs and Voldani going for his upper body. To Voldani's surprise and confusion, she felt absolutely *nothing* as she passed clean through Tanathar.

Landing in a heap atop Treia, Voldani quickly rolled to her feet and extended a hand to the armored guard and hauled her to her feet.

Voldani noted that Treia seemed to be quaking with rage.

"Something angers you greatly," Voldani said, probing for information in hopes of an explanation as to what had just transpired.

"William. Fucking. Decker." Treia seethed, stomping her way towards the tavern.

Uncertain as to what that meant, Voldani turned her head to face the pawnbroker and the blacksmith. When they offered only shrugs in return, Voldani turned and followed behind Treia.

The guard's stomping was so forceful Voldani wondered briefly if the woman might crack the cobblestone beneath her feet. She didn't know the cause for this righteous anger, but she approved of it nonetheless. Bringing her armored boot up, Treia kicked open the door of the Ass's Glasses and marched in, followed by Voldani who in turn was followed by the remaining guards.

"*William gods damned Decker, you show yourself right the fuck now!*"

"Busted," said Kera, drawing Voldani's attention to the back of the tavern. To her dismay, the grave-robber seemed deep in her cups once more, this time in the company of a teetering drunk with a beard.

"Yep," said the drunk.

"She looks mad," said Kera, cocking her head as she examined Treia and Voldani from a distance. "They both look pretty mad, actually. Think it's at you or me?"

"Probably me," Will said, hiccuping.

"You're in a whole mess of trouble now, aren't you?" Kera asked.

"Oh yes," said the wizard. "A very big mess. Hi Treia, you look great."

"You shut the fuck up, William." Treia hissed. "Get your shit together and get out of my town."

"What for?" The man, William it seemed, asked. "It's not like I've done anything wrong. I've been sitting here this whole time. How much trouble could I possibly get in sitting right here? I mean, I'm right here."

Will's words were slurred, and he offered Treia a dopey smile.

"A *lot*. More than a *lot*, a gods damned *fuckload*. Give me a dragon, give me ten dragons, give me anything but William Hinkles Decker."

Kera puffed out a discordant laugh, turning to face Will.

"Your middle name is Hinkles?"

She rocked back and forth as she laughed, swaying far enough to the side that Voldani wondered if she would fall off the bench. A huge part of her wanted it to happen, wanted to see Kera fall flat on her face. The girl had been sincere, or at least appeared to be sincere, when she and Voldani had spoken earlier.

"Kera, I expected a great deal better from you," said Voldani.

Behind her, one of the guards nudged the one standing beside him in the ribs, speaking to him in hushed tones.

"Hey Vaughn, that's the one that took out Big Charlie," said the first, pointing to Kera.

"That drunken sot?" said the second, Vaughn. "No way. Gregor said she was a Goliath. Ain't that right, Gregor?"

"Nah, I think Cliff's got it right," said Gregor. "I guess she just got bigger in the tales, always happens."

"I heard she cut his hands clean off," said Cliff. "It's her, I'm sure of it."

"Isn't she the one that started the fires?" asked Vaughn.

"Sure is," said Cliff.

"Not the one who started those tavern brawls?" asked Gregor.

"The very same," said Cliff. "As a matter of fact, I think she's also the one who--"

Treia silenced the chattering men with a raised hand, causing them to stand at attention. Curiously, she turned to face Voldani.

"Vee, you know she's a wanted criminal, right?" Treia asked.

Voldani could only nod in response, grimacing slightly as she did.

"Aw, she calls you Vee?" Kera shouted, smiling gleefully.

From the flush on both their faces, Voldani could see that both were well and truly drunk.

"That's really cute. Hey, how come she gets to call you Vee but I can't call you Dani? That doesn't seem very fair."

"There are a number of reasons," Voldani said, marching towards Kera. "Chief among them is that I trust her."

"What, and you don't trust me?" Kera asked, seemingly offended.

"No," said Voldani. "Nor do you seem to feel the need to give me a reason to begin doing so."

"That hurts, Dani," Kera said, feigning a wound to the heart.

"Do. Not," Voldani warned, looming over the pair of inebriated idiots.

"Uh oh," said Will. "I think you're in trouble."

"I think you might be right," Kera said, speaking in a drunken failed attempt to whisper. "She's so pretty when she's mad. Hells, look at her – she's pretty all the time."

Voldani slammed her fists on the table so forcefully that she smashed clear through the table, startling Kera and Will so much that they jumped in their seats and were stunned into silence.

"Get. Up." Voldani hissed, her eyes shining bright as the sun as she turned her blazing orbs to face Will and Kera in turn.

The pair stood, albeit clumsily, and stepped out from behind the bench.

"Out, the both of you, this instant." Voldani punctuated her statement by pointing towards the door.

"Yours is mean," Will mumbled to Kera.

"So is yours," Kera muttered back.

"Shut your mouths or I will remove them," Voldani growled.

"Remove them?" Kera repeated, aghast. *"How?"*

"Speak another word and I will show you," Voldani challenged.

Kera pressed her lips together and raised her hands in mock surrender.

"Wise choice."

Will and Kera made their way towards Treia and her guardsmen, who didn't part for them.

Without warning, Treia produced a small dart and used it to stab Will in the neck.

"Fucking *ow*," Will shouted, clamping his hand onto his neck around the dart. "Did you just stab me with a dart? What's wrong with you, you don't just stab people with darts! My fingers are numb. Why are my fingers numb? Was that a poisoned dart? It was, wasn't?"

"Yes it was," said Treia. Will plucked the dart out from his neck and held it out in front of eyes turned glassy.

"Is that... Is that my name scratched on there?"

"Yep."

"*Why?*"

"I think you know godsdamn well *why*," Treia said, staring the wizard down intensely.

Will held up a hand as if to bring up a counter, but staggered where he stood, staring off into the distance as if trying to remember something. He frowned and dropped his hand.

"Yeah, fair enough," he said, before crumbling to the floor.

"Did you just kill him?" Kera asked.

"Am I meant to be removing your mouth?" Voldani asked.

Kera raised her hands higher, taking an unsteady step back from Voldani.

"Well, no, but like... did she just kill him?" Kera asked. "And with the whole removing mouth thing, I just gotta ask; it's already a hole, so what would you be doing to take it away? Oh gods, I don't want to know, do I?"

Kera's eyes widened with fear and she glanced from Treia to Voldani.

"Zeph, save me from these hole stealers."

"Hole stealers?" Treia repeated. "Who have you been hanging out with, Vee?"

"Do you have more darts?" Voldani asked Treia.

The woman reached into her coat and produced a second feathered dart and passed it to Voldani, holding it carefully by the tip. Adjusting her grip on the weapon, Voldani advanced on Kera.

"Dani, come on, you don't need to do that," Kera said, eyes wide, hands raised into the air defensively as she backed away as quickly as her drunkenness allowed. "Zeph, c'mon, she's going to stab me with that thing. What do you mean I probably deserve it? Well fuck you too, you cantankerous old bastard."

Ignoring Kera's usual babble of nonsense, Voldani lunged and pricked Kera in the neck with the dart. The grave-robber winced in pain, clutching at the protruding bit of feathers.

"Dani, why?" Kera asked, looking forlorn.

"To paraphrase, I am certain you are fully aware as to why."

"I mean, I guess," said Kera.

She opened her mouth to say more, but her eyes rolled back into her head and her body went limp. It was only out of obligation that Voldani swept forward to catch Kera before she hit the floor.

Chapter Thirteen

Kera woke to the grinding sound of wagon wheels turning on axles that needed greasing. It grated against her senses and made her wince. As she became more aware, she realized that she was laying on her back against the rough wooden slab.

Eyes screwed shut in a futile effort to blot out the squeaking and thumping the caravan made as it rolled over pebbles and rocks, Kera sat up and tried to stand. To her dismay, she found herself bound and shackled. Opening her eyes to better assess the situation, she found herself wearing silver manacles that held her wrists together. The manacles were then attached to the floor of the wagon by a silver chain.

"There comes a time in life, alone in the night between dark rum and darker thoughts, where you start to think, you know?" Will said from somewhere outside Kera's field of vision, startling her.

She quickly turned around to see Will laying on the floor in the same position she'd been a few moments before, chained shackles and all. The wizard inhaled slowly, then exhaled a hearty sigh.

"You do that for too long, and the thoughts all turn into questions. 'Am I doing it all wrong?', 'Is this where I'm supposed to be', 'should I really be using illusions to seduce older women while I rob them?'. You know what I mean? The big questions."

Kera didn't make an attempt at answering, and it didn't seem to her as if Will was really waiting for an answer. She scanned the wagon once again, studying the interior – which took seconds. It seemed that they were in an empty section of the wagon, which Kera supposed might be used for cargo. She noted no apparent doors, no source of light besides a torch that flickered in between the boards that the wagon was built from.

She saw no signs of Zephelous, or any of her belongings. Seeing no other way out, Kera knelt to examine the chains and the anchor to which she was attached. Will's head rolled in her direction, and she briefly met the man's eyes. To her surprise, his eyes were still bloodshot and glassy.

"What do you think, Kera No-Clan-a-lan-a-lan?"

"Are you still drunk?" Kera asked.

"A little bit," Will said, holding up his manacled hands to measure out a tiny space between two fingers. "Like, this much if anything."

"That's pretty sad," said Kera. "I'm stone sober."

"Well yeah, *you* are," said Will. "I had a bit of a head start on you, but it's all good. I'm on top of it."

"Gemma looked about ready to cut you off before you did your magic bullshit on her," said Kera, realization dawning on her the moment the words were said out loud. "Oh shit, you've been zapping her brain all day, haven't you?"

"Three days, as a matter of fact," Will said, beaming at her through his scraggly beard. "I'm not a thief, I pay for them – I just make sure they keep coming."

"I can respect that," Kera said, slowly moving her arms in a circular motion to wind the chain around her wrists. "It's bullshit, by the way."

"I thought you said you respected it?" Will asked.

"Not the magic bullshit, I wish I could do that," said Kera. "I'm talking about your rant about your questions."

"What questions?"

"The big ones," said Kera. "The ones you think about between your *dark thoughts and darker rum*, as you put it."

Will laughed, a booming laugh that filled the caravan.

"I would say something like that," Will said, still chucking. "Gods, I'm an idiot."

"No argument here," said Kera.

"Hey, that's not fair," said Will. "You haven't even gotten to know me yet. Just wait until you do. I think you'll find out I'm not just any idiot, I'm a spectacular one."

"Again, no arguments," said Kera.

Will frowned for a moment.

"Hang on, that's not what I meant," he said. "What I meant was that while I'm an idiot, I'm also spectacular."

"I'm not saying I'm an expert in modesty here," Kera began, "but isn't spectacular an adjective you should probably let other people give you? It's like 'legendary', or 'generous', or 'good in bed'; It doesn't mean anything if you're the one saying it about yourself."

"My friends used to call me that all the time," said Will.

"Oh yeah?" Kera asked, feigning interest.

She wound the final length of chain around her shackles and turned away from the anchor, kneeling so that the chain ran over her shoulder and down her back.

"Why'd they stop calling you that?"

"Most of them died," Will answered, his voice flat.

Kera, knees coiled beneath her like a spring, launched herself forward. The chain went taught, and Kera growled with effort as she fought against the strength of the steel binding her in place.

"Oh, right. I think you might have mentioned that already," Kera grunted between breaths, muscles aching and straining to combat the unyielding steel of the chain.

With a determined grunt of effort, she surged forward with enough force that the bolts holding the anchor to the ground tore free from the floor, sending a small spray of splinters in the direction of Will's face. Feeling accomplished, Kera took breath.

"Sorry, you were saying something about your dead friends?"

"They said I was spectacular," Will said, blinking rapidly to dislodge a few small slivers of wood and bits of dust from around his eyes.

"I don't, ah, do this." Kera said, pointing between herself and Will back and forth.

"What? Oh, no, I'm not trying to hit on you," Will said. "Whatever your deal is, it feels like a lot more than what I'm willing to commit to. Besides, I saw you with Gemma, I kind of assumed that was your… y'know, your, ah, how do I say this…"

"Oh, for god's sake," said Kera.

"Hey, I've got nothing against it. I consider myself an ally to all sons and daughters of Tril. Definitely did not mean any kind of judgement, no judgement here." Will said, speaking with his still manacled hands.

As he did, the chain tether swung wildly and slapped him across the face, making him hiss in pain.

"Bet that hurt," said Kera.

"It did not tickle," said Will.

"Well, what I meant is that this whole sharing thing you're doing is not something I do," said Kera, standing on the balls of her feet to try and peer out through the small gaps between the wooden boards that made up the walls of the caravan. "Where do you think we're going?"

"Dragon hunting," Will said with a shrug, still laying flat on the ground.

"Yeah, but where?" Kera asked. "Where do you actually find a dragon these days? It's not like the old days and there's just laying around."

"Well, no, but you hear about them attacking settlements and towns all the time," said Will. "Burning down Dirtsville, flattening Hicktown, terrorizing Farmerton."

"I'm going to go out on a limb and assume none of those are real places," said Kera.

"Dirtsville was a real place," said Will.

"I have a really hard time believing that," said Kera.

"No, really," Will said, sitting up as he did. "Founded by a guy named Clementi Dirt."

"And how is it that you know this?" Kera asked.

"I was there when he founded it," said Will, smiling wanely. "I was also there when a dragon, scales red as blood, showed up and torched it to ashes and scorched stone."

"Sounds riveting," Kera said, moving down the wall to peer out through a different crack between the wooden boards.

"What's with the cold shoulder all the sudden?" Will asked. "Felt like we were getting along pretty well at the tavern, now you're all... edgy, and sharp."

"At the tavern we were drinking buddies, and that's just fine," Kera said, pulling back from the wall. "Now you're trying to be friends, and that's more than I'm willing to commit to."

"Nice, throwing it right back at me," Will said with a chuckle. "I probably deserve that."

"According to Treia you deserve a whole lot more," Kera said, trying to peer out through another slot. "I think we're going north. Do you have any idea why we'd be going north?"

"Like I said," Will said, letting his head fall back to thump against the wall. "Dragon hunting."

The pace of the wagon slowed and came to a halt.

"Guess we found one." Something howled in the distance, a single sustained note carried by the wind.

"I hope it's just a dragon," Kera said, her tone grim.

Chapter Fourteen

"What do you suppose that was?" Brenno asked Smith, seated beside the man at the front of the cart.

Voldani was seated cross legged on the roof, Kera's sword across her lap. She had taken to the skies to scout the road ahead several times that day, and had since retreated into a sort of meditative state, having insisted that she needed to 'assess the soul of the weapon'. It hadn't made a lick of sense to Brenno then, and it hadn't started to mean anything more since.

"Probably just a wolf," Smith said, sliding his way off the bench to land on the ground.

He unhooked a lantern from its perch on the front corner of the wagon and held it aloft, illuminating the murky roadside enough to show the immense depth of the woods in which they found themselves in.

"Probably won't come near us once we've got the fire going. We'll probably be fine."

"That's quite a few uses of the word 'probably', Mister Smith," Brenno said. "I believe I've just spotted your tell." As he spoke, Brenno examined Smith, noting that the man's spine was rod straight, his free hand hovering inches away from the holster of his thunder cannon, the slight tremble in the hand that held the torch. "Should we play some cards to pass the time?"

"Hard pass, Hornbuckle," said Smith. "Enaurl, find some wood. We'll camp here for the night."

Just outside the range of the torchlight, the sound of chains rattling and falling to the ground told Smith and Brenno that the construct had unhooked herself from the reins that allowed her to pull the wagon alongside the pair of horses.

The horses were used to pulling the caravan themselves, but the mechanical woman's strength had added to their own and hastened the progress of the travelling band. The fading sounds of gears whirring and grinding announced Enaurl's departure into the woods.

A soft thud, the sound of impact against the earth, made Smith draw his thunder cannon and whirl around, bringing the barrel up to point at the source of the noise. Voldani, looking unphased, glanced at the barrel and then to Smith, arching an eyebrow as she did.

"Are you typically this prone to panic?" Voldani asked. Smith growled and holstered the weapon, walking a few paces away from the wagon towards a small clearing just beside the road.

"You're lucky I didn't pull the trigger," Smith grumbled, kicking at some small shrubs in an effort to make room for a fire pit.

Still seated, Brenno chuckled.

His height required him to climb down from the carriage rather than hop down, but it only took him a moment to do so.

"I would wager that our friend Smith is uncomfortable in the woods," Brenno said, speaking to Voldani.

The halfling noted that the woman held Zephelous in her hand, and while she nodded slightly in response to his statement she seemed more detached than she typically was. He wondered what was going on between her and that sword, and eyed it greedily.

It would be worth several fortunes to the right buyer, the halfling thought. *Though I doubt I'm likely to possess it any time soon.*

As if she sensed Brenno's thoughts, Voldani plunged Zephelous into the ground, planting it like a flag.

"Alert me to trespassers, talking sword," Voldani said.

"You've spoken with it as well?" Brenno asked.

"Only briefly," said Voldani. "It does not trust you."

"How comforting to know," said Brenno. "How does it feel about you?"

"It has found comfort being in the hands of a warrior once more," said Voldani. "However, for reasons neither it nor I may never understand, it yearns to be returned to the graverobber." Voldani shrugged, her armor clanking with the rise and fall. "I disagree with it. It would better fulfill its destiny in my hands."

"Its destiny?" Brenno echoed. "What do you know of that?"

"It is a teacher, pawnbroker," Voldani said. "It senses those who are entangled with destiny, fated for greatness. To them and them alone it will impart its wisdom, that they might fight bravely against the darkness that threatens."

"How romantic," said Brenno. "I suppose the sword told you all this?"

"Yes," said Voldani.

"I can only surmise that it said that you were destined for greatness," Brenno said, sarcasm dripping from his voice. "And that you must follow its every lesson in order to succeed. Lesson one, let's rob this temple--"

"No," Voldani said. "My path is my own, I walk it with pride. I do not need guidance, nor have I asked for it. Should I feel the need to ask for directions, I would commune with the goddess to do so."

"Oh," said Brenno, taken aback by the warrior's statement. "Do you... Commune with the goddess often?"

Voldani said nothing and stood perfectly still for a moment.

"No," she said at last, walking away from Brenno, Smith, and Zephelous, leaving them in a lingering silence.

"Where are you going?" Brenno called out after Voldani.

"To find things that will burn," Voldani answered.

She punctuated her statement by bringing her shimmering wings into being. Brenno couldn't begin to understand the magics or the mechanics of how she did it, but he marveled at the glow of the wings nonetheless. Rather than use them for flight, Voldani spread her wings above and behind her, framing herself in a glowing halo of translucent feathers. The mystical glow of the wings was enough to illuminate Voldani and the area around her with a soft yellow light.

"You shouldn't be shouting like that," Smith said, speaking to Brenno without looking up from his current task.

Brenno turned to see what it was, and saw the man seated on a stone in front of what looked like a prepared fire pit with no wood. Smith's thunder cannon was out and laying on his lap, one hand caressing it while the other held the torch high over his head. The man's head spun in a slow circle, surveying the treeline.

Every time he completed a circuit, he snapped his head back around to its starting position and he began again. With a quick glance to ensure that Voldani was out of earshot, Brenno stifled a sigh of resignation and, against his better judgement, strode towards Smith.

"Mister Smith, I don't want to offend your sensibilities, but I'm afraid I have to ask you something," the halfling began.

"Let's drop the 'mister' shit, this isn't a city council meeting," Smith growled.

"Happily," said Brenno. "Smith, are you afraid of something? Is it the woods, perhaps? I've never known you to show fear."

"I'm not scared of shit," Smith said, not pausing in his treeline watch for even a moment.

"Suffice it to say I disagree," Brenno said, bringing his hands together behind his back.

"Suffice it to say fuck off," Smith grumbled.

Brenno pressed his fingers into his eyes in an effort to relieve the stress buildup he'd begun to accrue being around these people the last few days. As usual, it didn't help.

"Smith, I'm just trying to make conversation," said Brenno. "None of us wants to be on this campaign, and I'm sure we could all make long lists full of the names of the people we'd rather be on it with. Unfortunately for everyone involved, we are all in this together, at least until this thing is done."

"What's your point?" Smith grunted, still scanning the treeline.

"My point is that a little civility would make everyone's time together that much more bearable," said Brenno.

Several moments passed with only silence between the two of them, the only light on the moonless night coming from the dancing light of the torch in Smith's hand and the other affixed to the cart. Brenno's impatience overwhelmed him.

"Well?"

"Well what?" Smith said.

"What do you have to say about what I've just said?" Brenno asked.

"Seems not terrible," said Smith.

"Good, that's good," said Brenno, exhaling with relief.

He trudged closer to Smith and looked around for something to sit on. After a moment, he spotted a boulder that looked relatively comfortable.

"I'd like to ask you this question one more time, and I'm hoping you'll opt to be honest with me."

Brenno paused to gauge Smith's reaction to his words, but if the man was feeling anything there was no trace of it on his face that Brenno could spy.

"You're obviously afraid of something, Smith. Is it the woods? The dark?"

Smith's forehead creased into a frown of disdain, but he never stopped scanning the treeline.

"That's ridiculous," said Smith. "I'm a grown man, and I've seen a handful of campaigns from start to finish. Why the hells would I be afraid of the woods or the gods damn dark?"

As if to punctuate his sentence, a warbling howl echoed through the woods, filling the starless night with the lone cry of a pack dog somewhere in the distance.

The light danced and faltered as the torch in Smith's hand shook in his grasp. Without asking permission, Brenno strode over and took the light source from the man's hand, holding it aloft.

"Wolves, then?" Brenno asked, scanning the treeline as well.

"Not wolves, too big," Smith said, voice dropped to a near whisper. "Timbergnolls."

"This close to Zelwyr?" Brenno asked, feeling the involuntary shudder run down his spine.

Gnolls were dog-faced humanoid warriors, vicious and cruel, who lived in the prairies and plains in the southern places of the continent of Malzen, places like the Wildlands and the Blasted Fields.

The manic, constantly laughing creatures were as riddled with diseases as they were insanity, and worshiped gods of madness and war.

Timbergnolls, a breed of the wild dogmen that had long diverged from the primary gene pool and relocated to the cooler north, shared only one thing with their ancestral kin - their blood lust.

While traditional gnolls were wild and manic, timbergnolls were cool and calculated hunters, moving in packs to perform ruthlessly effective attacks and hunts on whatever prey they chose. Rumor had it that they had a special appetite for merchants travelling on the roads between the smaller settlements in the area.

A branch crunched behind the two men, who whirled around as quickly as they were able, Smith drawing his cannon as he did. The two found themselves face to face with Voldani, arms loaded with wood, wings still raised and glowing.

"I suggest you point your weapon elsewhere," Voldani said, striding towards the men and dropping the bundle of wood at Smith's feet and turned to face the treeline. "There may be wolves in the woods."

"Smith says it's timbergnolls," Brenno whispered, scurrying towards the discarded logs to hurriedly stack them into a makeshift bonfire pile.

"I have killed many gnolls in my lifetime," Voldani said. "Slathering, mindless creatures. Laughing even as they are run through, spouting feverish epitaphs to their mad god. Be that as it may, I have never heard anyone speak of timbergnolls."

"How long have you been this far north?" Smith said, slowly holstering his weapon as he did. "You've been at the temple four, five years now? Sent here from the capitol, right?"

"You are correct," Voldani said, nodding as she did. "Though I fail to see the relevance."

"Timbergnolls are a regular problem around these parts," Smith said. "Problem with all gnolls is they breed like dogs. Somewhere between six and ten pups a litter. Age a little like dogs, too. Takes about a year to go from newborn to juvenile, but most can use bows and arrows by the time they can walk which takes under a year. Let 'em get fully grown and they'll be trained killers by the age of three, and damned good at it too. Give them three generations and they've got an army, at which point they usually start getting really bold with their attacks. They turned half of Zelwyr into a bloodstained war zone last time that happened."

"How long ago was that?" Voldani asked.

Brenno completed piling the logs, and was now strategically placing sticks and bits of dried wood along the inside of the pile.

"About ten years ago," Smith uttered through a jaw clenched like a vice.

Brenno succeeded at lighting the fire, and the hungry flames grew within seconds, casting a dull orange light that was bright enough to illuminate the area comfortably while shedding light into the first several rows of trees along the road.

The trio shared a collective sigh of relief.

"Enaurl should be back soon," Smith said, breaking the silence that had settled on the group. "I suppose we should let the delinquents out of their cage."

"Wouldn't they be better off in their cage?" Brenno asked.

"More people means more shifts standing watch," Smith answered. "More shifts on watch means more sleep, more sleep means there's a better chance we don't die."

"There's something I haven't asked as of yet because I've been afraid of the answer," Brenno began. "But exactly how long do you expect this campaign to take?"

"However long it takes to find a dragon," Smith said.

A heavy foot fall snapped through several branches in the woods. The trio froze. Voldani drew her swords, Smith cocked his hammer. Another crunch in the woods, this time closer. Brenno cursed under his breath.

"I left my crossbow on the wagon," the halfling whispered.

"Quiet," Voldani commanded. "We are passed that moment."

"Easy for you to say," Brenno answered. "I'm unarmed."

"Quiet!" Smith urged as another heavy footfall sounded. Smith leveled his thunder cannon in the direction the sound had come from.

The howling beast in the night cried out once more, its dreadful cry echoing through the forest. Another crunch in the underbrush, then another. Brenno's eyes landed on Zephelous's hilt, the only available weapon in plausible reach.

He began tiptoeing towards the sword, inching his way to the weapon. The crunching grew louder and louder, until Enaurl stepped through the rows of trees and into sight. The fire light danced red and orange against her silver skin, except for what parts of her were hidden behind the massive load of wood she bore in her arms.

The automaton stomped her way to the fire and deposited the load of wood in a heap. Satisfied that her task was complete, Enaurl turned towards Smith and stared at him.

Smith puffed out another sigh of relief, brushing the sweat away from his brow with the hand that held the thunder cannon. He holstered it once more and scowled at the silver woman.

"Could you be any louder out there?" Smith asked. "Damn thing probably knows exactly where we are now."

"Are these creatures proficient hunters?" Voldani asked.

"Yes," said Smith, voice clipped.

"Then I suspect it has known where we are for some time," said Voldani. She broke away from Smith and the others and made her way towards the carriage. "No sense doing anything but being prepared, in as much as that is possible."

As she strode by Zephelous, Voldani grabbed it by the hilt and pulled it free from the earth. Brenno, who had been within reach of the sword, scowled slightly as he watched the woman pluck the weapon from the earth and walk away with it. She moved to the far side of the fire and replanted it there, sending a meaningful glance his way.

Brenno's eyes traced the outline of the sword, watching it gleam slightly in the light of the fire.

I wonder what that sword would have to say about a pawnbroker? Brenno wondered. *How it would judge my worth in terms of destiny. There are merchants as powerful as any king, and with twice the connections. I could become one of those.*

"How does releasing the drunk and the vandal help us prepare?" Brenno said, calling after Voldani.

Voldani arrived at the carriage and placed one hand on each of the handles of the double door at the back of the wagon. She took a breath to collect her thoughts.

"When I open this door, I fully expected to be greeted with a level of nonsense and prattling to which I am not yet accustomed," said Voldani. "The sooner it is over, the sooner we can impress upon them the seriousness of the situation in which we may find ourselves. The sooner that is done, the better things will be for all of us."

With that said, Voldani opened the double doors to the carriage and was nearly bowled flat by a still-manacled Kera, who had been leaning up against the door just moments before.

Voldani caught Kera by the collar of her shirt and held her aloft, stopping her from landing face first on the ground.

"Thanks Dani," Kera said ruefully.

"Stop calling me that," said Voldani. "I do you the service of not referring to you as a barbarian at your request, the least you could do is honor me enough to speak my full name when I request you do so."

"That's fair," Kera admitted. "In light of our newfound treaty of fairness, I don't suppose there's any chance you want to unshackle me?"

"No," Voldani said, depositing Kera on the ground. "How did you free yourself from the chains? They were well secured, I verified them myself."

"Chains and I don't get along very well," said Kera.

"That is a non-answer at best," said Voldani. "At worst it completely circumvents the question and acts as an unrelated statement."

"Yeah, I guess it does," said Kera, scanning the surroundings.

"What was all that howling we heard?" Will hollered from inside the caravan. Voldani leaned sideways to peer into the back of the carriage. Will was seated in the far corner, back against the wall. He raised his shackled hands and offered Voldani a wave.

"Still here, haven't gone anywhere. Would love to come outside, unless there's wolves everywhere."

"Smith believes we are in the company of timbergnolls," said Voldani.

"Timbergnolls, that makes sense," Will said, nodding. "In that case I'm happy to stay inside the caravan, thanks. Feel free to close and lock the door on your way out."

"A liar and a coward," said Voldani. "I should have suspected as much from an illusiomancer charlatan such as yourself."

"You probably should have," Will agreed, turning over to lay down on the floor. "See you in the morning, have a good sleep."

Voldani scoffed in disgust and stomped her way towards Will, who sat up in response to the thunder of the woman approaching him. He raised his hands in a feeble defensive gesture.

"Don't hurt me."

Without a single word, Voldani grabbed Will by the manacles and hoisted him to his feet. Chain links clinked noisily against one another as she did, making Will wince from the sudden sonic assault.

Without explanation, Voldani balled a fist and punched Will square in the shoulder.

"Ouch!" Will shouted, wincing in pain. "What in the hell was that for?"

"Mostly to ensure you hadn't some how created an illusion to take your place," Voldani answered, tapping Will's chest and face to test that he was really present.

"Only mostly?" Will asked.

"It was also partially because of your ruse two days ago," Voldani said, dropping Will back to the ground.

Reaching down to the ground, she undid the chains at the base of the anchor on the floor. With a jerk, he hauled Will behind her as she made her way out of the carriage.

"This seems a little unnecessary," Will protested, stumbling forward in an effort to keep pace with Voldani.

"On the contrary," Voldani said. "From what Treia has told me, you are best kept on a leash; a very short one if at all possible."

"She's not even here and she's hurting my feelings," Will whined.

Outside the caravan, Voldani found Kera staring at the treeline, frozen in place.

"Do you see something?" Voldani asked.

Moving as if in slow motion, Kera methodically raised her manacled hands and pointed them towards the north west. Voldani followed an invisible line between the tips of Kera's hands and the woods.

At the far end, standing no more than fifty feet from where Kera was standing, a pair of gleaming golden eyes stared back at Voldani. The eyes were large, far larger than those of a person, their pupils large black circles against eerie amber irises that shone outward in the night.

Without breaking eye contact with the beastly eyes, Voldani used her free hand to draw her sword. The steel rung out in the night, and the eyes made a slow blink in response.

Deep in the woods, something laughed - a deep, low laugh that sounded twisted and distorted. The eyes disappeared, and the creature howled deeply into the night once more.

The howl too took on a distorted quality, the single note fading and rising even as it echoed through the woods. Voldani found herself swallowing, felt her pulse quickening, her palms moisten.

Is this what fear feels like? She thought to herself. *I find it less than enjoyable.*

When the howl ended, the eyes were gone. A palpable silence hung over the group, broken only by the gentle clinking of chain links as Will shuddered.

"Gods, I hate those things," Will whispered.

"At least it's only one," Kera said, speaking softly. "Regular gnolls, the spotted laughing kind from the south, would be on us like a swarm right now."

"Haven't been north long, have you?" Will asked.

"Why is everyone is so concerned about the amount of time a person has spent in the north?" Voldani muttered.

"Because timbergnolls are a problem we have to live with here in the north," Will said. "A serious problem. Southern gnolls don't have any tact, any sense. Yeah they come at you like a swarm, but it's a swarm you can see and hear coming from leagues away. Timbergnolls don't do that. By the time you see one of them, you need to assume that there's a dozen you haven't seen waiting in the wings."

"Waiting for what?" Kera asked.

"The signal," Will said. Kera drew in a sharp breath and held it.

Voldani scanned the treeline, her nerves feeling like they were on fire. A minute of quiet passed, but to the group gathered there it felt like ages. When no signal came, the group moved as one towards the fire.

"What took so long?" Smith asked.

"Kera saw something in the trees," Voldani explained.

"Was it something real?" Brenno asked. "Or was it a distraction in an attempt to flee?"

"It was genuine," said Voldani. "I saw it as well. A pair of gleaming golden eyes."

"Fuck," said Smith. With a disappointed look on his face, he dug through his pockets for a coin and flipped it through the air towards Brenno, who caught it and pocketed it.

"Pleasure doing business with you," said the halfling.

"Get bent," Smith grumbled.

Voldani scowled at the pair.

"You placed a bet on whether or not we find ourselves surrounded by foes?" Voldani asked, facing each of them in turn.

"No, I'm afraid not," said Brenno. "Smith assumed we were already in peril. The coin was for a wager. I bet one silver piece that Kera would have come to her senses once she realized the peril she found herself in. Smith suspected she'd run for the hills and die screaming."

"Real nice," Kera scoffed.

"I didn't say anything about dying screaming," Smith said. "I only said you'd run."

"I admit that particular bit might have been my own embellishment," Brenno said, smiling widely as he did. "Wishful thinking, if you will."

Kera glowered at Brenno and advanced on him, manacled hands coming up chest high to be used as a makeshift weapon. Enaurl stepped into Kera's path, stopping the woman dead in her tracks.

"I'm not going to kill him," Kera said, looking up to speak to the automaton's face. "I'm just going to beat on him a little."

Enaurl's only response was to slightly adjust her position into a boxer's stance, gears whirring and grinding as she did. Kera frowned.

"I figured you'd say something like that."

Spying Zephelous planted in the ground, Kera's eyes went wide and she started towards the sword. Enaurl let her pass, watching her as she did. Cautiously, Kera extended her hands towards Zephelous's handle.

"It would prefer if you did not touch it," Voldani said.

Kera's outstretched hands lingered near the hilt, but her fingers didn't touch the sword.

"Oh yeah?" Kera said, speaking to Voldani while her eyes remained glued on Zephelous. "Did it have anything else to say?"

"That you were full of potential," said Voldani.

"Oh," Kera said, surprise evident in her tone. "I guess I expected--"

"It also said that you were a liar, a constant disappointment, and a probable addict," Voldani interrupted, crossing her arms in front of her chest.

Kera grimaced and let her arms fall slowly.

"That's... what I expected, yeah," Kera said.

After a brief pause, she walked away from the sword and towards the fire. Finding a flat enough spot opposite from Smith, she folded her legs beneath her to sit cross legged. The fire's glow danced wildly in the technicolor hues of her hazel eyes as she stared unblinking into its heart. Brenno tutted and broke away from the group.

"All out of clever retorts?" Brenno called to Kera as he made his way towards the carriage. "No more witty banter from that sharp tongue of yours?"

The halfling hoisted himself up onto the driver's seat of the carriage and located his crossbow, checking to see that it was drawn with a readied bolt.

"Fresh out," Kera called out to Brenno.

"Can we all stop shouting?" Smith hissed. "Or did the two of you want to get the rest of us killed?"

Will struggled with his manacles, trying in vain to rub his eyes with his wrists.

"You keep saying that," Will said, speaking to Smith. "But we keep not dying."

"Nor shall we," Voldani said. "Least not until we have faced the dragon."

"At which point we will likely all die," Brenno said, having joined the group around the fire. "That is, assuming we can even successfully locate one."

"We'll find one," Smith said.

"Will we?" Brenno asked. "Tell me, good blacksmith – where do you expect we will find a dragon? Hm? At the top of the highest mountains, perhaps? In the darkest places of the deepest woods? In deep dark caves a mile beneath the earth?"

"Wait, wait, wait," Will said, looking blearily from Brenno to Smith. "Is he serious? Do you not know where to even find the giant scaled war demon filled with hellfire and fangs that we're supposed to be killing?"

"A war demon?" Voldani asked. "I have slain a few demons during a war. Are those the same as a war demon? If so, I am prepared to slay it as well as the dragon."

"It's a figure of speech, lady," Will said. "The dragon *is* the war demon."

"Why refer to it as a demon?" Voldani asked.

"Wait until we find it," Will said. "You'll see."

Voldani nodded and was silent for a moment, looking out at the trees.

"Suppose we do not find one," said Voldani. "Or suppose we are murdered by these... What did you call them?"

"Timbergnolls," Smith and Brenno said simultaneously.

"Suppose we are murdered by timbergnolls this evening," Voldani continued, speaking softly. "How will I know of the glory of combat against a dragon?"

Will scratched at the side of his head with the edge of his manacles, pulling them away to reveal a smile.

"Voldani, are you... are you asking for a story?" Will asked, grinning broadly.

The warrior woman raised her shoulders in the slightest of shrugs.

"Perhaps," said Voldani. "Though I will not trade entertainment for mockery."

"I guess it's pretty much what you do when you're huddled together trying to ignore the fact that you might die at any minute," Will said, walking towards Voldani with his hands held upwards, bound wrists pointing skyward like a plea. "Would you mind?"

"I'll not unbind you, wizard," Voldani said. "Treia informed me of your penchant for treachery. Your mouth is uncovered, is that not all you need?"

"Only if you want the boring version of the story," said Will. "If you want me to tell it right, I need my illusions. To make my illusions, I need to move my hands."

"You're fully capable of moving your hands," Voldani said, pinching Will's index between two fingers and waving it from side to side.

"Oh, my mistake, you're right. I'm perfectly capable of doing this," Will said, wiggling his fingers back and forth. "But doing this," he said, wiggling them again for effect, "is not what magic is, despite what you might have heard. It's not all waggled fingers and arcane gibberish. There's more to it than that."

"I do not care," Voldani said. "Treia's specific words were 'Do not unchain him or you will never see him again'."

Will's smile never faltered, but it seemed to Voldani that for a moment the gleeful light that shone in his glassy eyes turned cold and sharp. Voldani recognized pain in that cold light, as well as the weight of a deep sadness.

She saw it often in the faces of those who visited the temple seeking forgiveness, saw it in the drunks and criminals she brought to justice. She saw it in Kera, who even now gazed as though lifeless into the crackling fire.

She saw it and recognized it for what it was, knowing why even as a quiet voice she kept tucked away in the back of her mind whispered that she knew what it was because she saw it in herself.

When Will opened his eyes, the warmth had returned to them. He smiled all the wider.

"I probably deserve that," He admitted, raising his shoulders and dropping them in defeat. "Chain my leg to something. It'll be worth it, I promise."

"Worth it in what way?" Voldani asked, eyeing Will suspiciously.

"Just trust me," said Will. "Chain my leg to a log or a rock or something, I'm not going anywhere."

"I have no reason to trust you," said Voldani.

"Do you have a specific reason not to trust me?" Will asked.

"Treia has given me several," Voldani said. "Let us not forget that you lied about the very nature of your existence on the first occasion we met."

"Tanathar didn't say anything untrue," said Will. "All he did was hide who he really was, which I think we can both agree is human instinct."

"I am not human," said Voldani. "Not entirely, at the least."

"Okay, fair," said Will. "Actually, no, not fair. Seems a little unfair, if you think about it."

"In what way is it unfair?" Voldani asked, crossing her arms.

"Kera got the privilege of disappointing you directly," Will said, nodding his head towards Kera. "I feel I should be granted the same privilege. Isn't that a tenement of Perrus's? 'Let all be treated equal – friend and foe, brother and sister, kin and not kin,'."

"Do not use the words of my lady against me, charlatan," Voldani said, hands lowering to rest on the pommels of her swords. "It is not something I will suffer. I will educate you, and while it will be painful it will also be quite thorough."

"Oh good, there's an upside," Will said mockingly. "Anyone want to just take a leap of faith and unchain my hands?"

Will's question was answered by utter silence.

"Smith?" Will asked, looking towards the man.

Smith smirked slightly, but said nothing as he continued to scan the treeline.

"Brenno?" The halfling shook his head no and he slid down and off of the stone he'd been sitting on, crossbow at the ready.

He began to pace a slow circuit around the fire, watching the forest at the edge of the light.

"Kera?" Will's voice raised slightly as he spoke the graverobber's name, indicative of his raised hopefulness.

Kera's eyes met Will's briefly, then broke away once more.

I've seen better thousand mile stares, but not many, Will thought. His gaze moved from Kera and settled on Zephelous for a moment. *Maybe she's just deep in conversation.*

Will's thoughts were cut short by the sudden unexpected sensation of a steel clamp snapping shut around his ankle. He looked down to see Voldani fastening the opposite end of his chain to his left leg.

Unsure of how to respond, he remained silent as the woman stood back up in front of him. She was tall, taller than him by several inches, and he found himself smiling up at her flawless features and radiant eyes.

"Well thank you, Voldani," said Will. "I really appreciate this."

Voldani's boot stomped down on top of the far end of the chain, and she took Will's manacles in her hand and began to unfasten them. With a series of clicks and a snap, the manacles popped open.

Will flexed his wrists and waggled his fingers to their full extent.

"Gods, that feels better. Now, I saw some pretty hefty logs in the pile--"

Will's speech was cut short by the sound of the manacles snapping shut once more. Will found himself speechless as he followed the clinking leash to its opposite end, the end now firmly locked around Voldani's right forearm. Flexing her hand experimentally, Voldani quickly snapped her arm to the side, wrapping her wrist around the length of chain to give herself as much leverage as possible as she hauled on it.

Forced to follow the chain, Will's feet went out from under him, and he found himself falling backwards towards the fire. Voldani hauled on the chain hard, stepping back as she did. Knocked off his feet and thrown forward by the strength of the woman, Will felt himself sail forward through the air before he thumped down onto the ground.

The sudden impact knocked the wind out of him and shook away the last of his inebriation, which he supposed was a fair trade for not getting horrible burns.

"Ouch," Will wheezed, his voice hoarse and airy as he tried to speak.

"I was proving a point," Voldani explained.

"Good job," Will said between coughs, lifting one hand off the floor just enough to make a circle with his thumb and index, making the hand gesture generally understood as 'well done' in this region. "Point thoroughly proven."

Wheezing and struggling to catch his breath, Will sat forward in the dirt and brushed himself off. He exhaled dramatically, coughing as he did.

"Whew. If I wasn't awake before, I am now."

"It's well into the evening and we are supposedly surrounded by bloodthirsty dogmen," Voldani said. "How could you not be alert already?"

"I've been surrounded lots of times, by all kinds of different bloodthirsty things," said Will. "I've made it out just fine every other time, and not once on any of those occasions did I have a warrior as mighty and fearsome as yourself to protect me."

"Flattery will get you nowhere," said Voldani. "Nevertheless, you are correct. I am mighty, and I will protect you."

Will smiled as he stood, bringing his hands together in a loud clap. He rubbed them together eagerly, excitement visibly building in him the way it might in a small child who was waiting for a piece of chocolate or a sugar candy.

"So," said Will, looking to each of the others in turn. "What do we want to hear? The story of the red dragon attack on Faltus? The time a white dragon ambushed a merchant caravan coming through the Frostpass?"

"Are those the only options?" Voldani asked.

Will's smile creased slightly.

"Well, I mean, yeah," said Will. "They're the only ones that I was in, at least."

"Is your involvement in the story mandatory?" Brenno asked as he circled around.

"Not strictly speaking," said Will. "But if you want it to be a good story, it's better if I get to tell one that I was actually involved in instead of just rehashing someone else's story. Tell the stories you know, that's what they say."

"Who is 'they'?" Voldani asked.

"I dunno," Will said, becoming slightly exasperated. "Just... 'They', okay? Look, do you want to hear the story or not?"

Voldani looked slightly conflicted.

"I suppose I do," she said after a brief pause.

"Your enthusiasm is staggering," said Will.

"Tell your story, bard," Voldani said.

"I'm not a bard, I'm an illusiomancer, but fine. It's... whatever, let's do this." Will closed his eyes for a moment and relaxed his shoulders, adjusting his posture as he took a series of slow and deep breaths.

When he snapped his eyes open, they were aglow with magical light, radiating a shimmering lime green that shifted into hues of yellows and oranges before returning to green once more. He smiled, a wide and genuine grin, and when he spoke his voice was magically amplified; the volume wasn't increased, but each word seemed heavier and more significant.

"I'll never forget the first time I ever saw a dragon face to face. Stories and descriptions from bards and scholars will paint you a picture of a gigantic lizard with rows of teeth, scales harder than steel, and deadly breath weapons of fire, ice, and poison."

As he spoke, Will's fingers danced through the air as if he were playing an invisible instrument or weaving an unseen tapestry. The tips of his fingers became blurred, fading and becoming lost in a faint orange mist that spread outwards from his palms and grew to become a sphere of gentle light roughly three feet in diameter.

Shapes and shadows danced and flickered through the sphere, intangible and formless at first, but gradually gaining context and definition. The silhouette of a dragon appeared, black against the orange of the mist, and spread its wings wide, mouth open in a silent roar.

Voldani leaned forward with interest, but neither Smith nor Brenno showed any signs of paying attention.

Kera's eyes flicked towards the image for the briefest second before moving back to rest on Zephelous. The showman in Will was disappointed, but he didn't let it show.

Focusing on his audience, he focused his attentions on Voldani as he began to weave his hands around in wider and wider circles around the edges of the gaseous orange sphere.

"These descriptions are not wrong," Will continued, as the illusory shadow of a dragon took to nonexistent skies with a single powerful stroke of its wings. "They say dragons were the first to walk the surface of this world, and that the gods favored their first-born--"

"Again with this 'they'," Voldani said quietly, speaking mostly to herself.

"As someone who has seen a dragon face to face," Will continued, speaking over Voldani. "I can confirm that this does indeed seem true; their iron-hard scales deflect all but the strongest blows, their razor sharp claws can cut a horse clean in two with one swipe, and their jaws are strong enough to chew up a warrior in full plate and spit them back out as nothing more than bits of mulched pulp and rent iron."

As Will described each of these happenings, the dragon shadow continued to fly forward. It spread its wings to their full extent before tucking one and then the other, sending it into a spiraling dive downward towards the bottom of the sphere.

It rotated faster and faster as it careened ever downward, unfurling its wings in a dramatic snap that sent it flying parallel to the ground once more. A mountain ridge appeared at the edge of the sphere, atop which stood a mighty looking fighter in deadly spiked armor.

The figure hoisted a sword into the air towards the dragon, and the dragon landed in front of it.

With deadly grace, the dragon reared back its head and opened its mouth before snapping forward. Its jaws snapped shut over the man, whose limbs – the only portion of his entire body that stuck out around the edge of the dragon's mouth – went limp almost immediately.

The dragon gave its head a quick shake to each side, and the limbs fell away from the rest of the body. The dragon lifted its snout to the sky and made a series of quick chewing motions before swallowing. It readjusted its pose on the cliff top, standing as if proclaiming to all that it had claimed this mountain as its own. The wings spread wide once more, and the dragon roared to the heavens.

Will added another layer to the illusion, using his mastery of illusiomancy to mimic the thunderous roar of the dragon's bellowing cry of challenge.

Voldani felt as though the roar came from all around her, and it caught her off guard. She unsheathed her swords and stood up immediately, realizing as she looked around that the sphere had grown to encompass the area in which she stood.

Deducing that the illusion was somehow contained by the orange mist, Voldani glanced towards Smith and Brenno in turn. Neither one of them seemed to have heard the sound, or if they had there weren't reacting to it. Voldani strongly suspected the former.

Kera, who sat at the very edge of the space which had been engulfed by the sphere, looked up towards Voldani at the sound of the roar. Feeling reassured, Voldani sheathed her swords with a snap and sat back down, noting as she did that the stone on which she sat now had the appearance of a fashionable leather chair that a noble lord or lady might own.

She smirked, finding such decadence both distasteful and unnecessary, but turned her focus back to Will only to find herself looking up at a full sized dragon looming over her. Easily forty feet tall in its current pose, the alabaster scaled white dragon – a shadowy silhouette no longer – gazed downward at Voldani the way a bird of prey might look down at a floundering fish.

Will had disappeared from view, but his voice seemed to ring out from all directions when he spoke.

"Masters of all they see, rulers of the land and the air, the very sight of a dragon can cause crippling fear in the unprepared," the dragon began to slither down the mountain towards Voldani, claws piercing clearly into the stone of the rock face with each footfall. The dragon growled, a bassy rattle deep in its throat. It reminded Voldani of the great hunting cats that stalked the prairies around her home city of Mistbreaker, magnified in every way. The dragon's fore paw slammed into the earth in front of her, and Voldani found herself rising to take a step backwards.

It's only an illusion, she thought. *To fear this would be the same as trembling at the sight of a child's drawing.*

The dragon lowered its face towards towards Voldani, giving the woman an up close view of the double row of dagger-long serrated teeth. Saliva dripped slowly from the tips of those fangs, and the dragon rattled another growl deep in its throat. Voldani swallowed despite herself.

A very convincing child's drawing. The dragon brought the tip of its snout level with Voldani's face. *This is not a real dragon.*

Looking up the dragon's snout and into its eyes, Voldani was filled with a sense of awe that bordered on fear.

This is not a real dragon.

The dragon puffed out a gout of air from its nostrils, sending a miniature flurry of chilled air tinged with snowflakes at Voldani's face. She stood her ground, but reached up to her face and wiped away a fine layer of frost from under her eyes. Lowering her hand away from her face, she inspected the snowflakes that she had collected on the tips of her fingers.

Just an illusion, Voldani reminded herself again, and again once more as a deep growl rumbled through the dragon's chest, so powerfully that Voldani felt the vibration in her eardrums.

The dragon lifted its head higher, letting its shadow fall over Voldani. She watched as its chest inflated as it took in a monstrous lungful of air. She knew what was coming, knew the dragon would unleash its fabled breath weapon on her, and felt the cold acid of fear begin to rise in her stomach.

It's not real, it's just an illusion.

The dragon squared its legs, bracing itself for its attack. With a roar it unleashed a torrent of icicles and snowflakes all over Voldani. The warrior closed her eyes and held her hands out in front of her, trying in vain to shield the skin of her face from the pelting ice and burning cold.

The next instant, the cold was gone. She opened her eyes to find herself surrounded by translucent butterflies in a variety of whitish blues that reminded her of ice. Standing among the floating creatures, smiling as wide as ever, was Will.

"The Frostpass is an awful, shitty way to get across Malzen," said Will, launching into his story as if he hadn't been interrupted. "Still, it's not the worst place to make a living if you're short on coin and don't mind listening to an endless litany of dwarven drinking songs."

Voldani, dark skin flashing with undertones of gold against the firelight, realized that she was holding her breath, and let herself exhale.

"I don't make it a habit to head up that way, but I was on the job. I was looking for someone, a merchant by the name of Pallux Faine. Turns out old Faine wasn't a merchant at all, but a hitman running a long con. His target was House Slagbreaker, a dwarven merchant clan operating out of Blackmouth. He earned his way into the good graces of Lady Slagbreaker over the course of a few years, even got himself invited to her son's wedding. He gave the boy a suit of armor as a wedding gift, said it was from the mainland. It wasn't. The whole suit was rigged to lock shut once it had been donned and there was some kind of contraption set up to spray acid into kid's face. He died screaming in front of his mom and about a hundred witnesses. Pallux hit the road in a hurry, leaving a trail a smell-blind dog could follow. Understandably upset--"

"'Upset' seems like an understatement," Voldani interrupted.

"Fine," said Will, furrowing his brow. "Understandably *distraught*--"

"Better," said Voldani.

"Can you please just let me tell the story?" Will asked.

"Do a better job telling it and I will not have to interrupt you," said Voldani. Will's shoulders sagged as he heaved out a sigh, but resumed his story once again.

"*Being super sad on account of her dead kid,* Lady Slagbreaker put out a bounty on Faine. A *big* one. The kind of bounty that lets people retire from bounty hunting and become grumbling innkeepers. Having run out of reasons to stick around Blackmouth, the thought of earning a few thousand gold pieces in exchange for a couple weeks worth of drinking with dwarves seemed like a pretty good idea."

Kera, sitting on a log near the bonfire with her manacles gleaming in the firelight, snorted. She brought both hands up to her face to scratch an itch.

"Get drunk and get paid," she said. "Sounds like a good plan."

"Do not interrupt," said Voldani. "I wish to hear the story."

"You *just* cut him off ten seconds ago," said Kera.

"Only in an effort to improve his miserable attempt at storytelling," said Voldani. "You are simply speaking for the sake of speaking – as usual."

"Ouch," said Kera.

"We couldn't have been more than a week and a half in when we saw the dragon for the first time," Will said, raising his voice to talk over Kera and Voldani. "It was big, *real* big. We didn't realize it was on top of us until we were in its shadow, until its wingspan blocked out the sun. I remember the darkness creeping up on us and thinking *I don't remember seeing any clouds this morning.* I looked up, but only managed to catch a glimpse of it as it flew over. It soared effortlessly and gracefully, flying lazy circles through the air like a giant kite. It spotted something – I don't know what, but I thank the gods it wasn't us – and dove. I'll never forget the sound, the way the air screamed around it as it fell from the heavens like a meteor--"

"Like what?" Voldani asked.

"A meteor," Will repeated, looking deflated.

"What is a meteor?"

"It's a big rock," said Kera. "Except it falls from the sky. Nobody knows where they come from, but they're always chock full of starmetal and precious stones. Worst case scenario, you're slightly richer. Best case scenario, you find a big hunk of starmetal and sell it to the nearest dwarf you can find for every last copper in their coffers. Ever see a shooting star?"

"Yes," said Voldani. "I used to count them at night with my instructor."

"Well, some shooting stars are meteors," Kera explained, rising to stand. "You don't want to be anywhere near the place they hit, though. I've seen them punch holes through castle walls and carve trenches big enough to bury a couple horses in." Kera stretched, or did her best to do so while still manacled, and made her way around the fire to sit next to Voldani. The graverobber's eyes moved to Zephelous, the sword plunged into the ground just in front of Voldani.

I wonder what you know about them, she thought, *probably more than I need – or care – to know.*

"Interesting," said Voldani. "Continue telling your tale, bard."

"I'm not a bard," Will said with a wince. "I'm a fully licensed wizard."

"You use cheap magics and spend most of your time talking," said Voldani.

"Call yourself what you wish, I will call you what you are – a bard."

"Comparing a bard to a wizard is like comparing a bonfire to an inferno!" Will protested. "They don't even get licensed – they just screw around!"

"I do not care," said Voldani. "Continue your story, bard."

Will sighed, but obliged.

"Whatever it was that caught the dragon's attention didn't stand a chance. Truth be told, I don't think it even saw the dragon coming." As he spoke, Will extended his hands in front of him, palms forward, and began to trace a large circle in front of himself. His hands began to leave a trail of light behind them as he weaved his magic, creating a shimmering window within the confines of the circle.

Looking through the window, Voldani and Kera saw a vast and frozen landscape boxed in by craggy hills and framed by mountains whose peaks were all frost and snow. The perspective of the window seemed to be a first person view, presumably showing the events Will was describing from the vantage point he had when they had occurred.

If they occurred at all, Voldani thought, *a man comfortable telling small lies becomes comfortable telling big ones.*

The window showed the dragon – huge, easily sixty feet long from snout to tail, scales as white as the snow all around it with just the barest hint of salmon pink – streaming downward through the air, moving so quickly it became a whistling ceramic blur against the cerulean backdrop of the sky. The dragon's dive took it beyond a ridge and the whistling ended with a *thump,* and a fountain of snow shot upwards into the air like a geyser, and something trumpeted piteously.

The dragon let out a deafening cry of triumph that drowned out the creature's wails of pain and echoed across the frozen hills. The full volume of its primal, terrifying roar inspired a newfound sense of awe and respect for dragons in Voldani; these were no mere beasts to be slain as a chore. These were scaled and winged *gods.*

Hands wearing ragged mittens and clutching a bottle of spirits appeared at the bottom of the window – Will's hands – and moved to cover his ears against the onslaught of sound. The view moved to the peaks and hills around it, watching as snow shook and rumbled, threatening to become an avalanche. When the last echo of the dragon's roar quieted, the snows settled. In the window, Will's shaking hands popped the cork off the bottle as he raised it to his mouth and drank heartily.

"Seems more believable now," said Kera.

"Shh," Voldani hissed.

"It was still daylight, but we figured the smartest thing to do was to set up camp and pray to all the various gods that the dragon was full and wouldn't come after us," said Will. "Maybe the gods were listening--"

"The gods are *always* listening," Voldani mumbled.

"*Shh*," Kera shushed, making an ugly face at Voldani, who sneered back.

"Or maybe whatever the dragon had found was a hearty enough meal that it didn't feel the need to have a merchant caravan for dessert. Only the gods can say for sure. Not one of us spoke a word that night. Most of us didn't sleep a wink."

The window faded to black and remained that way for a long moment. Will, ever the showman, remained silent as well.

"When dawn finally broke, it came with a welcome sight."

The window showed sunlight glittering across the ice, making it shine like so many diamonds. As the sun rose into the sky, so too did the dragon; its face and claws were stained red and its belly bulged visibly, so much so that it seemed to strain to pull itself into the sky. It roared again, making the mountains tremble and the snows rumble once more, then it flew up and out of sight.

"We felt like the immediate danger had passed, and resolved to get the hells out of there as quickly as we could. When we got to the ridge that it had ducked behind, we took a look to see what it had found. All that was left was an ocean of red snow and a pair of giant bloody tusks. A little halfling fellow named Vendel wanted to rappel down the side of the ridge and fetch them. He said mammoth ivory was worth its weight in gold and *then* some. Studdebaker, a salty old dwarf with a bad eye, took one look at those things and shook his head real slow."

"*Not a chance in all the hells,* he said, "*dragons love their treasure, ye be knowin' that*"

Will didn't speak Studdebaker's lines; a disembodied dwarven voice with a thick accent spoke them for him.

"*Aye, most of 'em prefer precious metals and gemstones, but not whites. A white dragon keeps kills for trophies like the hunters they are; they'd rather the skull of whatever they killed or the bodies of what failed to kill them, than any loot they might have had on 'em. Sure as the sun'll be up tomorrow, that white'll be back for those tusks, and it'll drag 'em up to its lair. Somewhere frosty, colder than this, and once it does it'll set them up just right. When it's satisfied, it'll breath its damned ice breath all over 'em until it's made a whole makeshift trophy case*"

"Something about the way Studdebaker whispered even though the dragon was out of sight told the rest of us that the old dwarf knew his stuff. We left the tusks alone and pressed on, eager to look out over snow that was any color but red."

The great patch of red snow became the central object in the window, the edges of which began to dissolve. The details of the landscape shown through the magic portrait faded until there was nothing but a crimson circle. The circle dissolved into red smoke which thickened into ribbons. The ribbons stretched themselves into lengths of cloth. The lengths of cloth whirled around Will like sheets on a clothesline blowing in a storm. One by one, they superimposed themselves on different portions of Will's robes and ceased to be, leaving the illusiomancer standing in front of the women with a satisfied smirk on his face and shining red robes.

"His robe was always that color red, wasn't it?" Kera whispered to Voldani.

"I believe you are correct," Voldani answered, not whispering at all.

"Correct about what?" Will asked, confused.

"Your clothes were always red," said Voldani. "Your illusion, while technically proficient, was utterly pointless. Explain to me once more what it is that makes you not a bard."

Will's face fell into a tight-lipped smile.

"The illusion wasn't pointless," said Will. "It was a distraction. I was buying time to try to count how many pairs of eyes have been watching us from the trees."

Kera and Voldani stiffened, beginning to turn around.

"No, no. Don't look! Stay where you are. Just pretend that I'm whispering something dramatic."

"You *are* whispering something dramatic," said Kera.

"I am inclined to agree," said Voldani.

"This is not helping," said Will. "It wasn't then the dragon attacked us," he said, speaking so loudly Kera wondered if he was magically amplifying his voice somehow. Smith, who had been tending to the horses, was startled by the sudden loudness and stomped his way towards Will, his gun drawn and at the ready. Brenno, seated on top of one of the horses, let out a small shout of surprise and turned his crossbow on the trio. Enaurl emerged from the shadows carrying a load of branches in her silver arms, dumping them by the fire, seemingly unphased. The construct looked up at them, the reflection of the fire dancing in her silver eyes, and cocked her head in confusion.

"Will you shut the hell up?" Smith hissed, veins bulging in his neck. "Do you have any idea what might be in these woods?"

"It was about a minute later the attack came," Will continued, voice still booming. Smith pulled back the hammer on his thunder cannon and leveled it at Will.

"I will happily shoot you to shut you up," Smith growled. "Between this shit and your little stunt back at the Ass's Glasses, I have half a mind to--"

"You don't understand," said Will, his eyes flashing with gentle violet light. His voice became distorted, layered on top of itself in a dozen different tones. *"You really want to hear this story, Smith. Come over here. Walk naturally."* Smith's pupils visibly dilated and the arm holding his weapon lowered. He trudged his way over to the fire.

"I can see them," said Voldani, looking into the woods over Will's shoulder. "We appear to be surrounded entirely from this side."

"There's more on this side too," Kera said quietly, anxiously clenching her fists. "Voldani, I'm going to need to get these manacles off. *Now,* if possible."

"I do not have the key," said Voldani. "The pawnbroker has them on his belt."

Will brought his palms close to one another in gesture like an open prayer, keeping them rigid as if he were holding an invisible box between them. He took a deep breath. When he exhaled, a shimmering silver mist poured out of his mouth and floated into the space between his hands. The mist thickened and became a sphere, which Will then raised over his head. The sphere bulged and trembled, stretching here and there until it gained the shape of a silver dragon. The dragon in his hands grew larger and larger.

"What exactly is going on?" Brenno asked, "And what have you done to Smith?"

"Nothing at all," said Will, the dragon growing to become the size of a dog, then a cow, then a horse. *"In fact, you should come over here too,"* he said, eyes violet once more. As Smith had done, Brenno lowered his crossbow and slid down from his horse, waddling his way to join the others around the fire. The instant pawnbroker and the artificer stepped into the circle of light that was the fire, the spell broke. The pair shook their heads to clear the daze of the spell.

"Now just what in the hells was that?" Smith barked, glaring at Will.

"The illusionist charmed us," Brenno said with a sneer. "Likely with a persuasion spell of some kind, I'd bet. That's dark magic. Cheap magic, but dark nonetheless."

"Hey, look at that," said Will, the shining illusory dragon nearly the same size as the actual creature it represented. "You know your spells."

"I've dealt with my share of patchwork wizards," said Brenno.

"Can we insult me later?" Will asked. "We're surrounded by what I'm guessing is a pretty big pack of timbergnolls and they're are going to attack any second."

"Fuck," Smith swore.

"Brenno, can you take Kera's manacles off?" Will asked.

"Y-yes," Brenno stammered. The bolt in his crossbow made a clicking sound as if it were bouncing up and down.

Why is it doing that? Brenno thought, looking down at the weapon in his hands. He realized then how badly his hands were shaking. *Ah, that explains it.* The pawnbroker swallowed hard and closed his eyes, willing himself to stop trembling. The tapping of the bolt slowed and eventually stopped. Brenno exhaled in relief. Voldani, moving deliberately and painfully slowly, rose to her feet and drew her swords, staring pointedly upwards at Will's gleaming dragon rather than at the dozens of eyes staring at her from just beyond the treeline.

"Does this illusion of yours have any practical use in combat?" Voldani asked, making a show of flourishing her swords and lowering herself into defensive stance, trying to make it seem as if she were mock fighting the dragon. One blade was held low with its tip angled towards the ground, the other held horizontally in front of her midsection. She slashed through the empty air in front of her and switched her stance.

"Depends on what you mean by practical," said Will.

"Will it cause any damage to our assailants?" Voldani asked.

"That's your definition of practical?" Will asked.

"Yes," said Voldani, shifting stances once again.

"Then no, not even a little bit," said Will. "I doubt it will hold their attention for much longer, either."

"Then what's the point of the damn thing?" Smith grumbled.

"I'm going to make it explode soon," said Will. "When I do, be ready."

"Explode?" Voldani asked. "Explode how?"

"A burst of light," said Will. "Should blind a bunch of them, temporarily at least."

"How about those keys, Brenno?" Kera interjected, her tone tense.

"R-right, c-coming," Brenno stammered, reaching down to his belt for his keyring. Too nervous to pay attention to his footing, he tripped on a stone and fell face first onto the ground, his crossbow clattering into the grass just out of arm's reach.

"I-I need that," Brenno whispered, rising panic evident in his voice. "I-I can't fight those things up close, a-all I have is a knife. They'll k-k-kill me."

"Stay calm, Brenno," said Smith, voice as strong as ever. "Enaurl's going to watch out for you. Aren't you, Enaurl?"

In response, Enaurl stood up and flexed her shoulders, seeming to make herself wider. The construct moved her head from side to side, a gesture that looked very much as though the metal woman was cracking her neck in anticipation.

"She won't let anything get to you. Now get up, get your keys, and unlock Kera. Kera, get your bullshit magic sword in your hands, and help fight. Bullshit magic sword, you... You do whatever bullshit thing it is that you do."

"I guess someone's taking command," said Will.

"You got a problem with that?" Smith asked, glancing sidelong at Will.

"What? No, not all," said Will. "Just the opposite. I just have a hard time managing my tone when I'm stressed out – like when I'm trying to time a split second blinding flash spell for the exact moment when an army of bloodthirsty timbergnolls breaks the treeline in an effort to eat me, for instance."

"Smart," said Smith.

"I thought so," said Will.

"Fall in love with each other later, uncuff me now," said Kera. "Brenno, get your shit together and get your ass over here with those keys."

"R-right," said Brenno, pushing himself up from the ground and back on to his feet. Trying to move deliberately, he began to walk towards Kera, fighting to put each foot in front of the other.

Run, damnit, run! he screamed internally. *You'll never make it out of this alive, just run. Get on a horse and go, leave the others. They can fend for themselves.*

His legs felt as if they'd been turned to stone and wouldn't let him move any faster than his slow shamble. His stomach heaved, anxious nausea threatening to bring the halfling to his knees. It took far, far longer than he would have liked, but one agonizing step after another, he made it. Hands quaking once more, he fumbled with the key ring, struggling to take it off his belt.

"Get it together, Hornbuckle," Smith said.

"I'm t-trying," Brenno said, succeeding at last at taking the keys off his belt. In his trembling grasp, the keys rattled and jingled on the iron ring like a wind chime.

"I am not certain I will be able to keep all of you alive," said Voldani.

"Oh," said Will. "Will you be okay, though?"

"I am certain that I will walk away from this battle," Voldani said definitively, missing Will's sarcastic tone entirely.

"Well, *I'm* dead *for sure* if these cuffs don't come off," Kera complained. "*Come on, come on, come on*, Brenno! No pressure. Aaany time. Right now would be a good time, though. So would now. And now. And--"

"If think you're being helpful, you're sorely mistaken," Brenno hissed to Kera. He steadied his grasp on the key ring and held it up to the firelight to get a better look at the keys there. A dozen different keys shone in the firelight.

"Oh, for *fuck's sake*," Kera cursed. "Why do you have so many keys on there?"

"It's a good sturdy key ring," Brenno spat back. "Keeping all of my keys on one ring is a practical thing to do."

"It sure as fuck isn't practical right now," said Kera, agonizing as Brenno flipped through one key after another in his search for the manacle key.

"You'll have to forgive me for not planning for this particular set of circumstances," Brenno hissed. "I don't have a lot of experience needing to hastily unlock the manacles of an arsonist before getting eaten by a pack of timbergnolls."

As he grumbled, the halfling held up another key to the light of the fire. "I think it's this one," he said, examining a bronze key. "Yes, it's definitely this one." Kera sighed in relief.

"Thank the fucking go--"

Before she could finish the sentence, a large ball of black and brown fur and leather slammed into Brenno from the side, sending him tumbling away and knocking the keys from his hands. With a grinding of gears, Enaurl launched herself onto the brown ball just as quickly as it had attacked Brenno. The trio tumbled away.

"Shit!" Will swore, bringing his hands together in a clap. The gleaming dragon erupted into a nova of harsh, white light that radiated outwards towards the tree line. Caught midway between the treeline and the companions, over a dozen timbergnolls stopped dead in their tracks, whimpering and using their hands to shield their eyes against the blinding burst of light. Fully illuminated, the companions counted their adversaries as quickly as they could.

"I count eighteen!" Voldani shouted, her eyes glowing yellow with divine fervor as they darted from one potential opponent to the next.

Much taller than the gnolls of the southern reaches, Voldani thought, *easily six feet tall apiece.*

Muscular physiques covered in thick black fur with spots of grey and chestnut brown, Voldani couldn't help but find them to be physically impressive creatures. Most wore motley ensembles of armor; leather here, plate there, chain mail everywhere else. Their weapons were just as eclectic, with no two timbergnolls armed the same.

Like their cousins to the south, they likely adopt whatever they can scavenge, Voldani thought.

She banged the flats of her swords together and adjusted her fighting stance.

They are welcome to try and claim these.

From over her shoulder, Smith's thunder cannon fired, sounding every bit as loud as its namesake. A timbergnoll yelped and dropped to the ground, a smoking hole in the place where its left eye had been.

"That makes seventeen," said Smith, snapping the firearm open to begin the reloading process. The nova of light began to fade, dimming to a glow before fading away completely. One of the timbergnolls snorted and shook its head, blinking rapidly to clear its vision. Sight restored, it narrowed its eyes at Voldani and snarled. With a savage growling bark, it pounced for her. Another member of the timbergnoll pack howled, the sound of which seemed to break Will's spell. The pack surged forward and the chaos of battle began in earnest.

Still grappling the timbergnoll that had leapt on Brenno, Enaurl's mechanically perfect sense of balance told her now was the ideal time to strike. Her iron grip locked onto the collarbones of the snarling beast beneath her and she rolled backwards, pulling hard with all her strength. Getting one of her feet onto the dogman's stomach to give her the leverage to launch it away, she rocked backwards and catapulted it into a nearby tree. The gnoll hit hard enough to rattle the tree's branches. As tall and bulky as she was, the timbergnoll was taller and bulkier. With an irritated growl, it leapt to its feet, drawing a sword from a sheath at its hip. It stepped back into the light of the fire, fur lustrous, its armor both modern and well-kept. An observer might have guessed that this was an alpha in the pack. Enaurl didn't care.

Enaurl wished the girl was here and that she hadn't stopped moving. She knew the dogman wasn't responsible, but she didn't care. Smith had given her a command, and while Smith wasn't the girl he cared for her. That made him acceptable. Perhaps more than acceptable. The gnoll barked at her, saliva dripping from its jaws at it snapped at her.

It lunged, leading with its sword arm. Enaurl sidestepped the strike, taking hold of the dogman's elbow and shoulder, her machine strength combined with the weight of her bulk letting her slam the dogman onto the ground while wrenching its arm painfully. The gnoll's neck was long enough for it to turn its head sideways, chomping down onto the leather and rubber of Enaurl's wrists. Sparks shot out from around the gnoll's teeth the way blood might have spurted out from a living creature. Enaurl's system registered pain.

She didn't like pain. Pain was unacceptable.

She balled her left hand into a fist and swung her arm around like a windmill to bring it hammering down onto the timbergnoll's skull. The pain from the bite became worse as the dogman bit down harder in response. She punched it again and the teeth loosened. The third punch made the dogman whimper loudly and break its hold, blood dripping down its face. It tried to snap at Enaurl's face, but she leaned backwards to evade the clumsy bite, raising her fist high above her shoulder in preparation of delivering a killing blow.

Before she could put the dog out of its misery, a second timbergnoll bounded into the fray, hurling its weight into Enaurl's chest and knocking her off her pinned opponent.

The two rolled sideways a few paces before separating, both combatants scrambling to their feet into hasty fighting stances. The gnoll with the bloodied face came for Enaurl from the side, lunging fang-first for Enaurl's face. The second gnoll, the newcomer, tackled her legs, using its teeth, claws, and daggers to slice and slash at the silver woman, looking to find purchase any place they could. Their brawl became a roiling heap of silver and brown.

Not ten feet away from Enaurl and her assailants, Brenno lay face down in the grass, using his hands to cover the back of his neck.

"I don't want to die like this," he whimpered, frozen in fear. "This is *exactly* why I gave up campaigning! It's always something, whether it's gnolls, or goblins, or kobolds." A gnoll flew over his head, trailing smoke and some kind of pink sparks, evidently Will's magic at work. "This is extremely far removed from my zone of comfort!" he squeaked.

All around him was the sounds of yipping, barking, and snarling, broken only by the occasional clash of weaponry and loads of grunting and cursing.

Damnit, Brenno, he swore to himself, *do something or die in the grass like a coward.*

Poking his head up, he tried to scan the skirmish as quickly as possible. He found himself face to face with the corpse of the timbergnoll whose eye Smith had shot out. He flopped backwards with a startled yelp and scrambled to pull himself away. As he did, his hands touched something sturdy, something made of wood with steel reinforcement. Something with a trigger and a loaded bolt.

My crossbow, he realized, *thank the various gods.*

Relief flooded through him as he snatched the weapon before rolling back onto his belly. Resting the butt of the crossbow on the ground in front of him, he scanned for targets from his new vantage point. The first thing he saw in his line of sight was Smith load a pair of small steel canisters into the back of his firearm. The second thing he noticed was a timbergnoll rushing towards Smith from behind. Drawing a bead as quickly as he could, Brenno followed the dogman's bounding strides towards Smith.

I haven't done this in a century, Brenno thought to himself, *here's hoping it's something you don't forget entirely.*

He pushed the air out of his lungs and held his breath, an old trick he knew to steady his aim. He imagined a target on the charging gnoll's center mass. His finger pulled the trigger.

Click.

The bolt sprang from the crossbow just as the timbergnoll leapt, lunging for Smith's back. The bolt hit first, and the dogman was knocked sideways through the air. It cried piteously as it fell away, drawing Smith's attention. Glancing over his shoulder, Smith watched the gnoll clutch at the bolt in its chest for a moment before it went still. Tracing a line backwards from the bolt to Brenno, Smith offered the halfling a quick nod before returning to the loading process.

With a flick of his wrist, Smith snapped the thunder cannon shut. Its payload – a steel tube filled with an chemical compound and a steel ball the size of a robin's egg – armed and ready, he leveled the weapon in front of him, seeing a timbergnoll bounding towards him on all fours.

"Come and get it, you hairy bastard!" Smith shouted at the gnoll, aiming his cannon at the dogman's face.

He fired, but the shot went wide as the timbergnoll closed the gap between them faster than Smith had anticipated, snarling as it knocked him onto his back. The dogman buried its teeth into the artificer's shoulder, and Smith roared in agony.

Gritting his teeth against the pain, he brought the butt of the thunder cannon up and slammed it against the back of timbergnoll's skull. The blunt weapon made a loud *crack* as it connected, and was louder on the second hit. The crack became a *crunch* on the fourth hit.

The timbergnoll released its grip and pulled back. Teeth red with Smith's blood, it opened its jaws wide and dove for Smith's neck. It stopped short as the unyielding steel of Smith's gun met the back of its throat. The gnoll looked at Smith, and Smith glared back at it before pulling the trigger. The gun fired and dogman felt nothing, even as its brains erupted out the back of the new hole in its head. Its body, now a corpse, sagged and fell forward onto Smith, pinning him to the ground.

Grunting with exertion, Smith shoved the corpse to the side and sat up, wincing at the pain in his shoulder. Snapping the firearm open to reload, he reached for his belt, fingers searching for another pair of steel canisters.

When his fingers felt only the leather of his belt, Smith frowned and looked down. The shells were gone. Scanning the ground around himself, he spotted the small bandoleer several feet away, lying in a heap close to where he had been standing just before he'd been attacked.

As he looked, the furred foot of a timbergnoll stepped onto the ground beside the shells. Smith's eyes followed the foot up to a leg, then a torso, and finally into a pair of gleaming golden eyes. The timbergnoll laughed at him, a deep throaty chuckle. Smith tested the range of motion in his wounded shoulder and snapped the firearm shut, holding it like a club.

"Alright, then. Let's go."

The man and the gnoll lunged, both howling in wild defiance.

From where she was standing, Voldani couldn't see Smith, but the sound of his thunder cannon and the fury of his battle cry told her he was alive.

For the moment, at least, she thought. *The Lady in White commands I protect those who cannot protect themselves.*

A pair of spear-wielding timbergnolls came rushing at her then.

It will have to wait.

They struck the moment they were in range, one stabbing high, the other coming in low. Voldani's warrior eye evaluated the attacks and found them amateurish, full of haste and aggression with no technique behind them. With astonishing dexterity earned over years of practice, the scion reversed her grip on her left-hand sword while thrusting both blades forward, sliding the flats of the weapons partway down the shafts of each spear before swinging her arms out wide.

The dogmen stumbled as their attacks went awry, staggering under the surprising effectiveness of Voldani's defense. Off-balance and exposed, Voldani saw an opportunity for a pair of clean killing blows. She surged forward to lop the heads off of both dogmen – only to stumble, caught short by the forgotten length of magical chain that bound her to Will. She landed hard on the ground, nearly knocking the wind out of herself.

"You hinder me, charlatan!" Voldani shouted to Will as she hauled on the chain. Will's foot went out under him and he fell face first onto the ground just as a sword whistled through the air where his stomach had been a moment before.

"You can unchain me any time, you know!" Will shouted back, rolling to the side to avoid a follow up strike.

"And allow you to turn invisible and disappear into the night?" Voldani called back, rolling backwards onto her feet.

Will tried to stand as well, but Voldani's roll pulled the length of chain backwards, forcing him to hop towards her or fall once again.

"Never."

"Hey, so, I don't know if you've ever fought with a wizard at your side before," Will called, making a hasty arcane hand gesture to send a stream of sparks into the face of a nearby timbergnoll. "But in case you're not familiar with it, we usually need to be able to concentrate. Getting tripped randomly is really not helpful towards that goal."

The dogman with the scorched face snarled and raised its weapon, a rusted two handed sword, and brought it around in a swing towards Will's middle. Voldani hauled on the chain once more, using her strength to yank Will out of the sword's reach.

"Okay, that was actually pretty helpful," Will remarked.

"I will not be able to fight if I must constantly keep you alive," Voldani shouted. She turned back to face the dogmen with the spears, realizing too late that one of them was already midway through a deadly leap, the tip of its spear aimed squarely for her heart.

She readied a defense, but knew it wouldn't work.

A sphere of blue light zipped over her shoulder and blasted into the airborne timbergnoll, exploding into deep green flames and blasting away skin and muscle on impact. The timbergnoll's attack became a midair flail, allowing Voldani to deftly stab the points of both swords into the gnoll's shoulders and used its own momentum to send it hurtling away.

Yipping, it rolled across the ground and lay still, oily smoke billowing up from its body.

"You know," said Will, grinning like an idiot. "I'm not going to be able to fight if I have to keep saving you. I'm just saying."

Splaying his fingers wide and putting his arms out to the side, Will conjured a glowing orb of light into the air above each fingertip.

"Perhaps you may have a use to me after all," said Voldani, stepping backwards to get closer to Will as she readied her swords.

Another timbergnoll had joined the remaining spear holder, this one brandishing a whirling length of chain. Facing down a trio of gnolls on his side, Will stepped backwards as well, positioning himself nearly back to back with the angelic warrior, letting the chain that bound them curl into a heap.

"You know, I think that might be the nicest thing you've ever said to me," said Will, watching as more of the dogmen bounded into position, advancing towards the group with weapons drawn. "Let's hope it's not the last."

"I'm hearing a lot of talking," Kera shouted, throwing herself to the ground to evade a lunging timbergnoll. "So far, *none* of it has been about uncuffing me so I don't fucking die and I'd like that to change!"

The timbergnoll she'd evade snarled and rolled through the dirt, rushing towards her with its sword slashing left and right. Kera let herself fall backwards and rolled into a reverse somersault, getting herself out of harm's way. Her bound hands threw off her balance and she staggered backwards. A timbergnoll howled and rushed at her from the side.

Kera let herself fall flat on her back, laying on the ground as the gnoll lunged over her. She brought her feet up and kicked out, using the momentum of the motion to bring herself back onto her feet.

"Don't everyone stop talking because I said something about it. Someone get these damn handcuffs off me! Will?"

Will, ducking beneath the swipe of a sword aimed at his neck, made a throwing gesture with his left hand. The orbs of light above his fingertips went upwards into the air behind him, took on the form of diamond-like points, and flew through the air like missiles. The timbergnoll was riddled with holes and blasted backwards, but one of its pack mates stepped into its place almost immediately.

Will's smile faltered, but he swirled his right hand up towards the face of the newest timbergnoll and made a crushing motion with his hands. The orbs of light surrounded the gnoll's head like a halo, then blew clear through it at different angles. The gnoll dropped dead.

"I'm a little busy!" Will shouted. "I'm also still chained to Voldani, and she's, ah, occupied."

Voldani grunted in response, using the sword in her left hand to block a swipe of a timbergnoll blade while using the sword in her right to deflect the thrust of a spear, twisting her body sideways as she did.

She straightened and whirled her swords around her in a practiced maneuver that looked not unlike an elegant twirl, droplets of blood spraying directions as she cut into the dogmen over and over. Two dropped dead, and were replaced just as quickly as the others had been.

"Exceedingly occupied," Voldani clarified. "I would perhaps be able to provide you with more help if this shoddy wizard could provide me with more assistance."

"Okay, *shoddy* is just uncalled for," said Will. "I blew through a lot of my reserves convincing Brenno and Smith to come closer, and that shining dragon spell wasn't exactly easy. That being said, I've got a personal favorite right up my sleeve that you might find useful."

Will's eyes flared blue and his fingers danced through the air as if he were playing an unseen instrument. He finished with a flourish.

"That should do it!"

"What did you do, wizard?" Voldani asked. "I see nothing."

"Look beside you," Will said, ducking beneath another sword swing.

Voldani glanced quickly to the left and right, amazed to see a pair of mirror-perfect copies of herself, each replicating her movements perfectly. The copies sidestepped towards Voldani and moved right through her, then repeated the motion once more.

"What are they doing?" Voldani asked, the copies miming the same.

"Three card monte!" Will yelled, shouting in pain as a dagger sliced through his shoulder. Voldani frowned.

"Am I meant to know what that means?"

"It means shuffle it up, Voldani!" Kera shouted, leaning backwards to avoid an arrow. "You never played a game of cards?"

"Gambling is unbecoming of a warrior of the Lady in White."

"For god's sake, just do it!" Will yelled, crying out as the tip of a spear slashed through his robes and grazed the side of his ribs.

With a nod, Voldani sidestepped and took the place of the right hand copy, then again to the left, and once more to the right. Confused but undaunted, the timbergnoll nearest Voldani advanced towards the centermost copy of Voldani, thrusting his spear clean through the copy. Seeing the gnoll off balance, Voldani wasted no time; she struck with both weapons, her right-hand sword coming downwards to cut the dogman's spear in half while her left-hand sword swiped cleanly through its stomach, dragging pink blood and grey entrails behind it as it emerged out the other side. The timbergnoll howled piteously as its organs spilled out onto its feet before it crumpled into a heap at Voldani's feet. The warrior silenced its death cries with a swift kick, her steel booted foot breaking the timbergnoll's neck.

"Good trick?" Will asked.

"It will suffice for the time being," said Voldani.

Blood curdling yelps paired with the sudden dimming of the light around her drew Voldani's attention to the fire pit.

Glancing over her shoulder, she saw Enaurl stomp a gnoll into the coals of the fire before leaping up in an explosive aerial kick to send another one sprawling. Still burning, the first gnoll scrambled to get itself out of the fire, only to drop to its knees and fall face forward onto the earth, a crossbow bolt sticking out of the back of its skull like a solitary flower.

"Show them no mercy, construct!"

Seizing the opportunity of Voldani's temporary distraction, a timbergnoll brought its sword whirling around to slash at Voldani, but she parried the blow. She wasn't able to parry the dagger that the gnoll stabbed into her hip.

"You'll die for that, dog," Voldani said, limping backwards a few paces to adjust her fighting stance.

The gnoll giggled madly, letting its tongue hang from its mouth.

Enaurl, elbows tucked and arms in front of her in a boxer's stance, ducked and weaved as the gnoll in front of her swung its swords. Each time she dodged a blow, she took a half-step closer towards the dogman. If the timbergnoll noticed, it didn't react. With a peal of manic laughter, the gnoll brought both swords together in an attempt to take Enaurl's head off at the neck. Instead, the swords bit through empty air as Enaurl ducked low into a kneeling crouch.

Dropping her shoulder and lowering her fist, Enaurl willed every spring, gear, and piston in her body to push upwards as they never had before, surging upwards to deliver a devastating uppercut. The construct's fist connected to the underside of the gnoll's jaw with every ounce of power her mechanical body could offer, and the steel of her body rang as if a gong had been struck. The timbergnoll's head went up and it fell backwards onto the dirt.

Not wasting any time, Enaurl hopped forward and landed on top of the gnoll's midsection, straddling its torso beneath her legs. She brought both fists up behind her head, and slammed them down onto the gnoll's chest. Hearing a crack, she repeated the motion. The crack was more of a squelch the second time.

Enaurl paused for a moment, sizing up her opponent. Sparks flashed out from behind the many holes and gashes she had acquired in her arms and torso. She could feel her energy levels dropping, but knew she couldn't stop until her command was complete. Her fists went up once more, arms seeming to expand and extend as she commanded synthetic muscle to shift in order to strengthen the next blow.

When her fists came down next, there was no crunching sound. In its place was meaty *splorch*. Her fists connected with the earth beneath her as she pounded clear through the dogman's chest cavity and into the earth below. Despite its condition, Enaurl raised her fists out of the pink and grey and brown puddle and held them at the ready. The concave timbergnoll made no signs of moving. Satisfied, Enaurl lowered her guard slightly and stood up to assess the battlefield.

Seeing Voldani and Will engaged with a half-dozen timbergnolls, Enaurl stepped over the mulched gnoll to head towards them. No sooner had she finished taking her first step towards them before an arrow slammed into her back, piercing through her tough outer plates and erupting out the front of her body.

More sparks, more synthetic agony.

Enaurl turned to face her new assailant just in time to have another arrow lodge itself into her body, breaking the silver plating of her cheek and lodging itself dangerously close to her automaton brain. The pain was artificial, but so was she – that made it as real as she was. The construct dropped to her knees as sparks crackled and hissed from behind the arrows. Lifting her head towards the enemy, she counted not one but two archers standing no more than forty feet away.

Enaurl could see that more arrows were being nocked, and that aim was being taken. Enaurl's mind performed a series of quick calculations to determine what the most viable course of action might be in this situation. The results came back dire.

Rising to stand once more, Enaurl carefully dislodged the arrow protruding from her face and dropped it to her feet, raising her hands into the boxer's stance once more. The timbergnolls began to laugh, evidently amused by Enaurl's show of defiance, enough so that they lowered their bows for a brief moment to cackle with laughter.

Something clicked, and the laughter of one of the gnolls was cut short. It choked and began pawing at its throat. Surprised, the other timbergnoll leaned towards its companion to inspect the object that was suddenly embedded in its pack mate's larynx; a crossbow bolt. Looking back over her shoulder, Enaurl almost didn't see the concealed form of Brenno laying on his belly in the grass, crossbow in hand.

Wasting no time, she snapped her head back around towards the other timbergnoll archer. Still giggling, the still unharmed archer eased its dying friend to the ground and turned to face Enaurl. The silver woman ripped the arrow out of her chest and dropped into a runner's stance, bolting at full speed towards the archer.

The dogman nocked an arrow and let fly, but Enaurl's silver hand swung out in front of her and slapped the arrow to the side, deflecting the attack as she leapt into the air in a flying punch. The gnoll dropped its bow and drew its sword, still cackling as the two fell into a violent heap of brown and silver.

The deflected arrow, flying wide, plunked into the ground inches from Brenno's face. The halfling flinched and reflexively shut his eyes in anticipation of a second arrow. When it didn't come, Brenno sighed with relief and dropped his head so low he could feel the cool dirt on his forehead.

"Why did I let this happen to me?" Brenno said, talking to himself. "I should never have let that damn woman step foot in my shop. I should have never sold her that fae ash. I should have said 'no' to Speaker Gerhardt when he pressed me into service."

Brenno loaded another bolt into his crossbow and drew it back.

"If I die here tonight, I'm going to strike a bargain with whichever demon necessary in order to come back to this plane and haunt you until your dying day, Kera No-Clan!"

"Yeah, well, my dying day is probably going to be today if no one unlocks these gods-damned manacles!" Kera shouted back, hissing in pain as a timbergnoll with a whip brought its unorthodox weapon snapping into her shoulder.

The iron manacles that bound her hands were heavy and well built – so much so that when Kera brought them across to swipe at the dogman's face, there was an audible crack as its jaw dislocated.

"That was supposed to be your cue to give me the damn keys, Brenno!"

Looking down, the halfling fumbled with his belt and frowned.

"I don't have them!" he shouted back. "I must have lost them in the grass!"

"You have *got* to be *fucking kidding me!*" Kera yelled.

The timbergnoll she'd struck shook off its stupor and reached up to snap its jaw back into place. It opened its mouth to laugh, but as it did its eyes rolled into the back of its head and it fell forward.

Standing just behind where the dogman had been, was a very battered and bleeding Smith. One eye swollen shut and breathing heavily, he wiped the gnoll blood off the handle of his firearm and advanced towards Kera.

"Gimme your hands," Smith rumbled.

"Did you find the keys?" Kera asked, extending the manacles towards him.

"Something like that," said Smith, lifting Kera's manacles skyward and placing the barrel of his cannon beneath them. "Look away."

They both looked down and Smith pulled the trigger. Kera winced, splinters and shrapnel went flying in every direction as her manacles were destroyed in a crack of thunder and wave of heat. Rubbing her wrists with her hands, Kera nodded in appreciation.

"That's a mighty fine lockpick you got there," said Kera.

"Does this really seem like the time for your smart-mouthed jokes?" Smith shouted, holding his arms out wide to gesture towards the battlefield. Kera grinned.

"It's always the right time for a good joke," she said, sprinting towards Zephelous.

Seeing what looked like easier prey, two of the timbergnolls engaged with Will and Voldani broke away from the chained pair and rushed for Kera, laughing deep and maniacally as they bounded towards her. Kera tumbled beneath the lash of a spiked chain swung by the first gnoll, but cried out as the tip of the second gnoll's spear scrawled a cursive letter down her back.

Her dive turned into a fall as she dropped into the grass, wincing as the pain blossomed anew from her back. She could tell the cut was shallow, but that didn't make it hurt any less. With a grunt of effort, she scrambled the rest of the way towards Zephelous on all fours, standing as she hauled the sword free from the earth, turning hastily to face her would-be attackers.

YOU ARE HURT, said Zephelous.

Now's not the time, Kera thought back.

AGREED, said Zephelous. LET IT BE KNOWN THAT I HAVE RESOLVED TO DISCUSS YOUR MANY FAILINGS WITH YOU. HOWEVER, YOU MUST BE ALIVE IN ORDER FOR ME TO DO SO.

Good idea, Kera thought. *Do you have a plan?*

YES, said Zephelous. WE PUT DOWN THESE DAMNED DOGS.

"That might be the best thing I've ever heard come out of your mouth," said Kera.

I DO NOT HAVE A MOUTH.

"Don't ruin the moment," said Kera. In her hands, Zephelous's grip grew warm to the touch. The dogmen bounding towards her began to slow, as did the sounds of battle all around her. The only sound Kera heard was her own ragged breathing, and all she could feel was the pain from her wounds and the thumping of her own heart in her chest. With each exhale, it seemed to Kera as if the world around her began to move slower and slower, until even the fire seemed to freeze in place.

Zephelous, are you doing this? She asked.

YES, said Zephelous.

"Why the hells didn't you tell me you could control *time?*"

THE ABILITY TO CONTROL TIME IS BEYOND ME, said Zephelous. HOWEVER, AS A BEING OF THOUGHT I HAVE LEARNED TO TEMPORARILY ALTER THE WAY IN WHICH MY WIELDER PERCEIVES ITS PASSAGE. THE WORLD SEEMS SLOWER BECAUSE I AM ALLOWING YOUR MIND TO MOVE FASTER, A MEASURE I EMPLOY ONLY WHEN I

MUST INSTRUCT SOMEONE HOW TO RESPOND TO MULTIPLE THREATS IN A MANNER THAT IS AS EFFICIENT AS POSSIBLE. IT DOES NOT LAST LONG.

How long is 'not long'? Kera asked. The timbergnoll with the whirling chain let loose, sending several feet of heavy metal laced with serrated points flying in her direction. To Kera's eyes, the chains seemed to move through the air like at a crawl rather than the whip-fast speed she knew it must be moving.

"Well, that's neat," said Kera.

A CHAIN IS A FOOLISH WEAPON, said Zephelous. USED BY FOOLS WITH MORE BRAVADO THAN TECHNIQUE. A SIMPLE OVER CORRECTION OF AN ATTACK SUCH AS THIS CAN RESULT IN A CRITICAL FAILURE.

Over correction you say, Kera said as she placed her left hand onto Zephelous's hilt as she held it in front of her. She ducked beneath the iron molasses chain and spun on her heels, swinging Zephelous in a high arc as she did. Zephelous's blade met the back of the swinging chains with force, too much for the seemingly slow moving timbergnoll to correct. The chain curled back towards the dogman with more momentum than the gnoll had planned for and began to wrap itself around its body, sharpened spikes piercing cleanly into fur and flesh beneath. The gnoll struggled in an attempt to free itself, succeeding only in helping the spikes dig themselves in further before it went down. *Something like that?*

PRECISELY, said Zephelous.

Kera's perception of time began to normalize, chugging forward as its speed seemed to struggle to return to normal. The gnoll with the spear stepped towards her, the tip of its weapon still glistening red with her blood. The dogman hefted his spear in her direction, and time snapped back to full speed as the point of the weapon was plunged towards her face. Kera pulled her head to the side and slapped the spear away Zephelous.

A little warning next time would be great, Kera said to Zephelous.

YOU WILL NOT GET ONE, said Zephelous. YOU MUST LEARN TO READY. A SPEAR IS A VERSATILE WEAPON WHEN ITS REACH CAN BE APPLIED. IT BECOMES CUMBERSOME AT CLOSE RANGE.

Kera nodded her understanding and stepped in towards the gnoll as he withdrew the spear.

IF YOU FOLLOW THE ARMS, YOU WILL SEE THE BLOW BEFORE IT IS MADE.

Kera watched the gnolls arms as instructed, watched as the spear was pulled straight back, watched as the arms extended straight forward with intent to impale Kera's midsection. Throwing her hips to the left while swinging Zephelous down towards the shaft of the spear, Kera knocked the spear almost wide enough to avoid being hurt. The razor sharp tip of the spear slashed a fine line of red across the right side of her body just beneath her ribs. Kera sucked air in through her teeth, hissing and cursing against the pain.

YOU ARE QUITE INJURED, said Zephelous.

"I'm quite pissed off, is what I am," Kera grumbled.

The timbergnoll seemed confused by Kera's sudden desire to speak, glancing quickly to each side for any signs of its pack mates coming to its aid. Kera followed suit as the two observed a brief unspoken pause.

All around them the battle raged; Voldani and Will continued to fight side by side, bursts of magic gleaming off the flashing steel of the warrior's swords. Smith's thunder cannon cracked from somewhere behind them, and a gnoll began to whine loud and piteously. The occasional click of Brenno's crossbow served as a dreadful metronome which underscored the cacophony of crunching, thumping, and squeals of mechanical effort and grinding gears that marked Enuarl's efforts to stop any further incursion into the fray by timbergnolls along the treeline.

Kera and the timbergnoll finished their surveying at the same time, their eyes meeting.

"Not looking good for you and your barky friends," Kera huffed.

"The flesh that fights feeds better for more nights," the timbergnoll said between pants, its voice deeper than Kera had anticipated.

She cringed in response to its rhymes.

"Really?" Kera said, whirling Zephelous into position with a flourish. "Rhyming? Fine, whatever. Tell me about the flesh that kills your furry ass."

The dogman smiled, or bared its teeth, or maybe both.

"The one that kills you takes all your ills, too," with a growl the timbergnoll struck, bringing his spear in for a series of quick and deadly pokes. Kera blocked each of them in turn, offering up her own counterattacks in the form of a pair of quick back and forth slashes near the dogman's throat. The first missed entirely, but the second drew blood and a yipe of pain from the gnoll.

"Got any fancy moves I can use to end this quickly?" Kera asked, glancing down to the blood pooling at her feet.

YES, said Zephelous. GO ON THE OFFENSIVE.

Kera widened the distance between her feet, lowered her stance, and tightened her grip on Zephelous.

"What's it called?"

IT IS CALLED 'GOING ON THE OFFENSIVE', said Zephelous. STRIKE, NOW.

"Well that's boring," said Kera, swinging Zephelous in an angled horizontal slash.

The dogman took a step towards the rear and threw his shoulder back, letting Zephelous whoosh through the air a finger-breadth in front of him.

DO YOU ALWAYS FIGHT WITH A SWORD? Zephelous shouted.

Not always, said Kera. *Usually it's whatever I have on me at the time.*

AND WHAT IS STOPPING YOU FROM DOING SO NOW? Zephelous asked.

Uh... Kera said, thinking. *I guess nothing.*

Following through with the horizontal slash, Kera threw her elbow into the gnolls face. It crunched into the dogman's nose, making him stagger backwards. Whirling her torso around, she spun from the waist up and delivered a follow up elbow to the back of the timbergnoll's head.

The gnoll stumbled forward. Kera spun a complete circle from the waist down before following through with her upper body, Zephelous whistling upwards once more in a ferocious vertical slash.

The edge of the impossibly sharpened sword cut into the timbergnoll's bottom jaw just before his throat before passing clear through its head and up through its skull. Blood erupted from the wound like a fountain, and the front half of the dogman's face slid away and fell to the ground. The rest of the gnoll, still standing, teetered for a moment before falling backwards into the dirt.

WELL DONE, said Zephelous.

Kera panted and waved away the compliment.

"It was nothing," she said between ragged breaths.

GOOD, said Zephelous. THEN YOU WILL HAVE NO TROUBLE DISPATCHING THE ONE BEHIND YOU. YOU SHOULD CONSIDER DUCKING.

Kera's eyes went wide and she crouched low, feeling the air above her head shudder as something large traveled through it at high speed. Her first thought was to tuck and roll away from whatever it was behind her, but the pain in her back and side was already beginning to blossom into agony. Instead, she scurried forward a few quick paces and turned around. Before her stood a hulking timbergnoll, fur solid black, wielding a monstrous great club that was easily the same size as Kera. The gargantuan dogman stood head and shoulders above its pack mates.

"Various. Fucking. Gods," Kera cursed.

The giant timbergnoll bellowed a demonic sounding laugh, heaving the great club into the air to tap it against its open palm as if the tremendous weapon weighed nothing.

"Leighlagh's blessed has come to fight," the dogman said, its voice so low and full of bass it seemed unnatural. "Your supple flesh I'll mark and bite."

"I think that was a compliment," said Kera, backpedaling away from the over-sized timbergnoll as it advanced towards her. "Supple is usually good, right?"

Spittle dripped from the mouth of the colossal timbergnoll.

"The god of fangs has blessed me so, I'll end you quick alluring foe," the gnoll rhymed.

"Okay, alluring is *for sure* complimentary, this guy might be into m--"

Kera was interrupted by the sudden and intense agony that exploded in her left side. Her legs gave out beneath her as she was sent flying through the air, knocked aside by the monstrous timbergnoll's gargantuan weapon the way a ball was sent flying by a stick. She landed in a heap, struggling to get her hands and legs beneath her.

Each breath sent new waves of pain lancing through her body, and she was certain she had at least two broken ribs. Struggling to catch her breath, she wheezed and coughed up a wad of blood. Wiping her lips with trembling hands, she looked up across the battlefield to see if the mutant timbergnoll was still advancing towards her, relieved to find that it was not. The relief faded when she looked ahead of where it was going, realizing it was stomping towards Brenno.

KERA, YOU ARE NOW SEVERELY WOUNDED, said Zephelous.

No shit, Kera responded, using the sword like a cane to stand back up.

Bracing her side with her spare hand, she took a step towards the monstrous dogman. Every step she took caused another wave of pain to pass through her.

KERA, YOU CANNOT FIGHT IT, said Zephelous.

"The fuck I can't," said Kera, spitting a wad of blood onto to ground.

YOUR INJURIES ARE--

"Are you going to help or are you going to nag?" The psychic sword was silent.

YOUR ANGER IS A GREAT FOIBLE OF YOURS, said Zephelous. IT CAN ALSO BE A TREMENDOUS ASSET, AS YOUR PEOPLE HAVE SHOWN REPEATEDLY THROUGHOUT HISTORY.

"Not really the time for a history lesson, Zeph." Kera said, bringing her hand away from her shattered ribs to hold Zephelous's hilt in both palms. She closed her eyes and took a deep, slow breath.

"Get to it quick."

RAGE, KERA, Zephelous said. UNLEASH YOUR RAGE.

"What rage?" Kera asked.

I HAVE LOOKED DEEPER INTO YOUR MIND THAN I HAVE ALLOWED YOU TO BELIEVE. I HAVE SEEN YOUR TRIALS, YOUR TRIBULATIONS, YOUR STRUGGLES. WITH THE CLANS OF THE PLAINS. WITH YOUR EXILE. WITH YOUR--

"Don't fucking say it," said Kera.

WITH YOUR FAMILY, Zephelous pressed on, ignoring Kera. WITH YOUR CLAN, WITH YOUR CHILDHOOD. WITH YOUR NIGHTMARES.

Kera shook her head slowly from side to side, reliving flashes of memory as Zephelous recounted the pains of her past.

I HAVE SEEN YOUR DREAMS OF FIRE AND BLOOD.

Kera's eyes snapped open, and her face hardened into a mask of rage. Her grip on Zephelous tightened so greatly that the leather on its handle creaked in protest. The battle cry that erupted from behind her blood stained lips was one of primal ferocity, of buried rage, of seething anger. The pain of her wounds left Kera and was replaced with rage.

It overwhelmed her, filled her completely with adrenaline and fire. It washed behind her eyes and left them seeing red, consuming Kera's psyche and leaving behind a different being – an avatar of berserker frenzy and unbridled anguish.

In her frenzy, Kera charged into battle against the over-sized dogman even as it raised its club to flatten Brenno. Her pain erased, at least for the time being, she sprinted forward and leapt into the air, bringing Zephelous around to hold before her like a stalactite of steel.

Landing on the creature's back, Kera plunged Zephelous into the monstrous gnoll's hide, the tip of the sword travelling between ribs and organs before bursting out its chest. The timbergnoll gasped and went still, letting out an extended mournful howl as it began to fall forward into a heap.

Kera rode the creature down to the ground, tearing Zephelous free before hoisting it towards the heavens while she bellowed her barbaric war scream. The dying howl of the timbergnoll giant paired with Kera's war scream demanded the attention of all those in the fray.

Silence fell across the skirmish for the briefest of moments. Many timbergnolls closest to the treeline turned and ran into the woods, leaving behind their dead and those still locked in combat.

WELL DONE, KERA, said Zephelous.

The sword's psychic message met a wall of resistance, and the sword's mind reeled as it made contact with the burning wall of rage and fury that was Kera's mind.

KERA?

Seeing an opportunity in her opponent's distraction, Voldani lunged towards the timbergnoll she'd been dueling just moments before. Her blades bit deep into the gnoll's belly, and when she spread them out wide to either side the dogman's entrails erupted from his body as if Voldani had upended a gory butcher bag.

Her reward was the sharp sting of a sword biting into her hip from the side, as another gnoll stepped into her circle of combat. Stepping backwards and away from her newest opponent, Voldani found herself limping and frowned. The illusory copies of herself that Will had conjured into being faltered and faded out of existence.

"Your tricks have failed, wizard," Voldani called to Will.

"They didn't fail, they ran out!" Will called back, conjuring a shield of shimmering air into existence in time to have a pair of arrows shatter to pieces as they impacted against it.

"I do not see the distinction," Voldani said, steadying her breath as she sized up her opponent.

The gnoll was slightly better armed than her previous opponents had been, with a pair of elegant curved swords. She wondered vaguely if they weren't Mian Dorean in design. The gnoll slid the edge of one blade against the other, letting the steel of each sword sing a single tortured note while it giggled senselessly to itself.

"You will ruin your blades if you continue to treat them in such a manner, mutt."

The dogman's giggle became a laugh.

"Your angel meat is such a treat," the gnoll said, whirling both blades around as if they were rotors before snapping them into readied reverse grip hold, one held out in front of and the other held off to the side. "To taste a god will please this dog."

Voldani took a double step forward, swords at the ready. The dogman raised its first sword to make a slash, but Voldani knocked it aside. The gnoll's second blade came around for a blow to the side, only to meet Voldani's waiting second sword which sent the strike skyward with such force the sword slipped free of the gnoll's grip.

Voldani's stuck her ironclad foot into the timbergnoll's face with such force that she broke most of its teeth. The dogman shook its head and backed away a few paces, keeping its sword at the ready.

"Your technique is sloppy and your poetry is vile," said Voldani. "Come. Let us end this."

"Blood of gods runs through your veins," the dogman snarled. "I'll gain your strength and ease your pains."

Voldani whipped her arm across her chest, throwing one of her blades like a missile aimed at the timbergnoll's heart. The gnoll deflected the improvised ranged attack with a clean swipe of its sword, only to find Voldani bearing down upon it.

Voldani hammered into the gnoll's guard with powerful and precise strikes, eyes scanning the dogman's stance and movements for a single moment of weakness, a momentary opportunity which would allow her to put an end to the foul creature. To her surprise and irritation, the gnoll seemed proficient with the sword in his hands.

Each time Voldani's sword came close to finding an opening in the gnoll's defenses, the curved blade seemed to reach just far enough to block her advances. Seeing that she was making no progress with this frontal assault, she stepped back and brought her blade into a readied guard.

"Is there no end to the frustration you will cause me this day?" said Voldani. In response, the gnoll lapped at the blood on its blade – Voldani's blood – and giggled.

"Your horse is high and tinged with violence," the gnoll barked, laughing maniacally. "The god of yours was rendered silent."

Voldani was stunned, and froze in place.

"What did you just say to me, cur?" Voldani asked.

"Leighlagh lives, no doubt at all," said the gnoll. "Did Perrus break after her fall?"

"Utter the name of my lady again, dogman." Voldani challenged, voice tense and wound tight with anger. "I swear on the crossroads of life and death that if you do so, it will be the last thing you do on this plane."

The gnoll threw his head back and cackled. Voldani could not keep her anger in check for a moment longer. Gossamer wings appeared to erupt from her back, flaring with the same intense light as her eyes. The timbergnoll's laughter tapered off into a small chuckle.

The dogman whirled his sword around and rushed at Voldani. The warrior woman hopped backwards and, with the aid of her wings, lifted herself ten feet into the air. When she had reached the maximum height the chain that connected her to Will would allow her, she hung in the air, pointing her the tip of her sword down towards the timbergnoll.

"Well?" Voldani called down to the gnoll. "Do you dare, man-hound?"

"The wrath of Perrus I do not fear," the gnoll said, licking its jaws. "The dead a cry for help can't hear."

The corner of Voldani's lips twitched upward for a brief moment, the woman allowing herself a brief moment of amusement.

"You've chosen poorly this day," said Voldani. "I have no pity for you."

Holding her sword aloft, she shouted the name of her god into the night as she plunged down from the skies, slashing at the gnoll with a powerful two-handed strike that was further strengthened by the momentum of her dive. The gnoll blocked the attack but was forced back by the might of Voldani, who even now attacked him in a frenzy.

To the gnoll, Voldani's sword seemed a blur of silver, seemed to be radiating its own light, seemed to be everywhere at once. Gone was the dogman's giggle and taunts, as he struggled to block on all sides seemingly at once as Voldani struck again, and again, and again.

Voldani's radiance surged from behind her eyes and flared in her wings, the luminosity of her divine heritage shining brighter and brighter as her ferocity increased. The glow encompassed her entire body, surrounding her in a chroma of brilliant yellow-white light. The light extended in to her sword, causing the ordinary weapon to shine with divine might.

Gripping her blade with both hands, Voldani flexed her powerful legs and flapped her wings, giving extraordinary might and strength to an overhand chop aimed squarely at the timbergnoll's face. The dogman brought that curved sword upwards to block, bracing the back of the sword with his hand. The ringing of steel on steel was cut short by the sound of something shattering, fragmenting into pieces like broken glass.

The gnoll's sword, unable to withstand the might of Voldani's blow, erupted into so many pieces of jagged steel that clattered to the ground around the dogman's feet. Voldani, breathing heavily, peered around the side of her sword. The edge of the weapon was buried firmly in the timbergnoll's skull, dark blood oozing up around the edges of the sword. Eyes and hands twitching wildly, the timbergnoll seemed unable to move.

Placing an armored boot on the timbergnoll's chest, Voldani pushed the dogman back while hauling on her sword, succeeding in freeing her weapon from the gnoll's cleaved skull. The sword came free with a *shlorp* sound, and the dogman fell to his knees before toppling over to the side.

Spying her discarded sword several feet away, Voldani made to recover the weapon and prepare herself for the next battle before she was caught short; she had reached the end of the chain that bound her to Will.

"I must recover my weapon, charlatan," said Voldani, tugging on the chain by stepping forward. Will, facing the other direction, took a series of hasty steps backwards.

"How's that?" Will called back.

Voldani took several paces closer towards her sword and recovered it, wiping the gnoll blood clean from each of them by rubbing them against the cloth that hung low around her waist.

"It will suffice," said Voldani. "Dispatch your pursuers that we might join the others."

"Oooh, I should be trying to *get rid* of the people attacking me," Will said sarcastically, bringing up his mystical shield once more to ward off an axe blow from a timbergnoll. "Any other advice? These suggestions of yours are simply brilliant."

"Avoid dying if at all possible," said Voldani, sizing up a nearby opponent.

"Warrior, scholar, tactical genius," said Will, grunting with exertion as he used the forcewall to push his attacker back. "How I made it this far without you in my life is an absolute mystery to me."

"I am in agreement," said Voldani, shouting over the din of her swords clashing against a timbergnoll's shield. "Enough of your prattle. Dispatch your foes."

"Is *that* what I should be doing?" Will shouted, stumbling as he stepped on the heavy chain that bound him to Voldani.

When the warrior woman's only response was a battle cry and the sound of steel on steel, Will figured that the time for banter had indeed passed. Puffing out a breath of air, he surveyed the forces aligned against him.

A trio of timbergnolls stood against him; the axe wielder at the forefront, a spearman standing to the side just behind him, and a swordsman opposite the spearman. Will took a moment to breathe deeply, feeling that his innate magical reserves were very near to being fully drained. He thought of his most powerful spells, spells which would seemingly warp reality around him, or conjure elemental beings, or render him temporarily invincible. All of those were out of his reach. He would have to make due with what he had left, and what he had left wasn't much.

Not the first time I've had to improvise, Will thought, *gods willing it's also not the last.*

Thoughts centered on how he could best turn the tide in his favor, he watched as the axe wielder growled and advanced on him, weapon raised for a killing blow. Instinct took over, and Will's hands waved through the air in an arcane pattern he had long since committed to memory.

The timbergnoll's face, inches away from Will's outstretched hands, was irradiated with a gentle pink light that shone from Will's hands. Its axe, raised and posed to take Will's head clean off not a moment before, slowly lowered.

The timbergnoll's eyes, pupils rung with rings of pink, met Will's. The dogman's tail began to wag.

"You're a good boy, aren't you?" Will said. The dogman barked excitedly, very much like a tame dog might do. "Who's a good boy?"

The gnoll barked again, more excitedly this time.

"You don't want to hurt poor old Will, do you boy?"

The gnoll shook its head from side to side, sending spittle and foam flying in all directions. Will grimaced as some of the drool splattered across his face, wiping it away from his mouth and eyes before flicking it to the ground.

"You know who does want to hurt me?" Will asked.

The timbergnoll cocked its head to the side in curiosity and concern. Smiling, Will pointed to the dogman with the spear.

"He does. He's a bad dog, a bad, bad dog."

The charmed timbergnoll growled, hackles on his monstrous shoulders raising. The dogmen with the spear and sword exchanged a confused glance, lowering themselves into a defensive stance. Will grinned.

"Sic 'em."

The axe wielder barked and pounced, lunging at his pack mate with the spear. Determining that Will was responsible for its pack mate's sudden change in loyalty, the timbergnoll with the sword advanced on Will, stabbing in with his sword. Will stepped back and tried to get out of the range of the weapon, but winced and hissed as the gnoll's weapon slashed into his shoulder. He felt the warmth of his own blood flowing down his arm, felt the burning pain of rent flesh. He tried to bring his hands up to conjure his force shield, but agony shot down his injured arm and he was forced to cradle it close to his chest.

"Okay, down to one hand. That's fine, I'm sure it's fine."

In his mind he ran through a list of spells he could cast using a single hand. It didn't take long.

With his good hand, he patted down his robes to see if he still had any spell components on him, items and ingredients he could use as a sort of mystical shortcut for tapping into the Weave, the ethereal and omnipresent force of latent power that connected all magic users. The first item he found beneath the folds of his robes was a small wooden box.

That won't do, he thought as he resumed his search.

He touched a small ball of something that squelched beneath his fingers, an iron needle, and a small book of spells that he'd hastily scrawled in a drunken haze.

None of those would help him now and he knew it. Continuing his frantic search, his eyes widened as he felt the outline of something long and soft with a semi-rigid core.

Smiling, he reached into his robes and withdrew a single feather, its plumage a bold orange with tinges of red, even as he ducked beneath a wild swing from the timbergnoll.

"You know, I was really hoping I'd get to use this for something more dramatic," Will said, speaking to the timbergnoll as much as himself. "Something really impressive and heroic looking, you know? The stuff that gets turned into a tavern tale. Oh well."

Pinching the feather between his index and middle finger, Will pointed the tip of the feather at the timbergnoll.

"Shada vista corta phaenix!"

No sooner had the arcane words passed his lips the feather began to glow a dull orange, gleaming like a coal plucked straight from the fireplace. The tip of the feather smoldered for an instant before bursting into flame, a wave of hungry fire surging outward from Will's extended hand. The flames screeched like a great predatory bird as the gout of fire took the form of a blazing phoenix that flew, claws extended, into the timbergnoll.

With a boom and a flash of red light so intense that Will was forced to look away, the bird disappeared in a concussive conflagration.

When Will looked back, all that remained of the timbergnoll was a smoking pair of legs and a circle of scorched earth.

"Did anybody see that?" Will called out, beaming as he inspected his handiwork.

When none of his companions responded he frowned.

"I really need a bard friend," he said glumly.

His reverie was interrupted by a sharp and piercing yipe of pain, pulling his attention back to the charmed gnoll and its opponent. To his relief, it seemed that his sway over the axe wielder had led to it burying its axe deep into the chest of the sword wielder.

Unfortunately, it also seemed that the dying cry of its packmate was enough to break the enchantment that had switched its allegiances. The timbergnoll shook the spell off and, seeing its packmate dying at the end of its weapon, growled low and deep.

Withdrawing the axe from the body of the other timbergnoll, the dogman's head whipped around to face Will once more.

"I was hoping that spell would last a little longer," Will said to himself.

His foot suddenly went out from under him as the chain that connected him to Voldani surged backwards, tripping him. He landed hard on his injured arm, crying out in pain.

The gnoll laughed and continued its advance as Will pulled himself up into a kneeling position. He saw the attack coming, saw the raised axe winging its way through the air, eager to separate his head from his shoulders.

Instinctively he splayed his hands outward and invoked his shield wall, closing his eyes as he braced himself for what would surely be the final blow. The blow never came.

Something made a wet splash.

Opening his eyes to peek out, Will's jaw fell open at the sight that greeted him. His shield had indeed been raised, but not as intended; rather than being conjured between himself and the timbergnoll, the shimmering wall of force had manifested beneath the timbergnoll and gone straight up – slicing into the dogman on the way.

Cut clean in half, the dogman had fallen into two matching and disgusting heaps of viscera and gore.

"Okay, that is something I have to remember to try again."

The axe the dogman had held moments ago glistened at his feet, close enough that its blade was practically touching the leather of his boots. Will winced at the realization of just how close he had come to death.

"On second thought, maybe not."

Somewhere behind Will the sound of Smith's thunder cannon surprised him, making him whirl around. The artificer looked to be in rough shape, but was holding his own nonetheless.

"You holding up okay over there, Smith?" Will shouted to Smith.

"I'm not dead yet," Smith growled back in response.

"Voldani says that's key," Will said. "Need a quick distraction?"

"Make it long enough for me to reload," said Smith, opening the chamber of his thunder cannon while tucking the weapon into the crook of his left arm. His right hand pulled out a silver cylinder which he held up to his eye to examine.

"You got it," said Will.

Raising his good hand palm first towards the air above Smith, Will swirled his hand back and forth as if he were struggling to open a door while his fingers traced shapes through the air.

A globe of green light shot up from Will's palm into the air over Smith, where it pulsed and flashed like an over-sized firefly.

"Not much of a distraction," Smith said, sliding the cylinder into the thunder cannon while he reached for a second round of ammunition.

"You said just to make it long enough to reload," Will said. "How long does it take you to do that? Ten years? Because it looks like ten years."

"Takes about six second," Smith said, sliding the second round into the weapon before snapping it shut with a flick of the wrist.

No sooner had he done so than a timbergnoll flattened him to the ground with a flying tackle. Smith tried to bring the thunder cannon up towards the dogman's face, but the gnoll pressed his hand back down against the ground and laughed into Smith's face.

"I'm getting really sick of this," Smith shouted into the face of the timbergnoll.

"The broken man who fixes things," the timbergnoll said. "I'll send you to where she still sings."

Smith's face, already a mask of anger and rage, hardened and smoothed over.

"What did you just say?" Smith demanded. "What the fuck did you just say to me!?"

"If sweet anguish is your battery, what will drive yo--"

The dogman's rhyme was interrupted by the crunch of Smith's forehead driving into the timbergnoll's snout.

The gnoll yipped and drew back, holding his snout in his hand – the hand that had been holding Smith's weapon to the ground. Smith brought the weapon up in an attempt to blow the gnoll's brains out, but the dogman recovered quicker than Smith had anticipated.

The dogman swatted the barrel away from its face just as Smith pulled the trigger. The cannon clicked and fire erupted from its muzzle, which was now pointed firmly at the timbergnoll's shoulder.

The dogman howled in agony and scrambled away from Smith, who noted a smoking severed arm lay on the ground beside him still clutching a crude looking sword.

Sitting up, Smith pointed his firearm at the maimed gnoll and pulled the trigger once more. The weapon clicked, but did not fire.

Without missing a beat, Smith pulled the trigger once again. As before, it clicked but did not fire, instead making a dull clunk sound inside its internal mechanisms.

"Son of a god damn, mother loving--" Smith said, launching into a string of profanities that ranged from insulting the timbergnolls parentage to making several hurtful comparisons to diseased goblin sex workers.

As he ranted, he stood up, holstered his thunder cannon, and struggled to pry the gnoll's sword from the locked grip of the severed arm at his feet. Succeeding at last, Smith rose to find himself facing another timbergnoll, this one armed with a leather whip and a shield.

Spitting onto the ground, Smith swung the sword in a set of lazy arcs, testing the weapon's weight and heft.

"Come on then," Smith said, hand tightening into a white knuckle grip on the ugly sword. "I said come on, you fuzz covered bastard!"

The gnoll obliged, stepping forward and sending his whip cracking towards Smith. The man winced as the weapon snapped into his side, sending a burst of pain rippling through his torso.

The gnoll giggled, and opened its mouth to utter more insane litanies. Smith didn't give it a chance. The moment the gnoll took the time to speak, Smith lunged forward. The gnoll stepped backwards and raised its shield, blocking Smith's attack. It tried to bring the whip around for another attack but Smith caught the tip of the weapon and pulled hard. His strength, already lowered by his previous injuries, was not enough to disarm the dogman, but that hadn't been his intention.

The gnoll lowered the shield and readjusted its stance in an effort to haul on the whip hard enough for Smith to release his grip on the whip.

Having predicted this, Smith released the whip instantly, staggering the gnoll and opening its defenses up even further.

Smith threw his fist forward in a straight jab, bashing the hilt of the sword into the gnoll's face. The gnoll reeled back, and Smith gripped his sword with both hands before slashing the blade across the gnoll's throat.

Blood streamed out from the gnoll's severed arteries like water falling off a cliff, and the timbergnoll fell to the ground gasping and choking as the life went out from him.

Each stride Smith took sent another wave of searing pain through his side, bringing another string of curses out of his mouth. His stride little more than a hobbled limp, Smith made his way towards the one-armed gnoll still cowering on the ground, trembling with shock.

"Got anything else you want to say?" Smith growled at the gnoll, pointing the tip of the sword at the gnoll's face. "Go on, let's hear it. I want to know what other insane bullshit your bonkers god has been filling your rotten brain with."

The gnoll laughed up at Smith, a feeble cackle that turned into a whimper.

"A mad god, a mean god, a new god, machine god," the timbergnoll said, rising to stand before Smith, still clutching the ghastly wound where its right arm had been. "Expend on me your tired hate, you've tied her life to a liar's fate."

"I changed my mind," Smith grumbled, plunging the sword into the timbergnoll's belly. "I don't want to hear any more of your bat shit nursery rhymes."

Bleeding profusely, the gnoll staggered to the floor and laughed quietly to himself for a few moments. After what felt like an eternity, the laughter stopped as the gnoll's eyes rolled into the back its head. Smith kicked it for good measure, watching as the timbergnoll rolled over and it's jaws went slack, tongue lolling to the side.

Satisfied, Smith looked around the fray, noting that many more of the dogmen seemed to have retreated into the woods. Those around the fringes of the treeline seemed uncertain, perhaps frightened of something. What that thing was he couldn't guess, but he suspected it had something to do with the screams of rage erupting from Kera, or perhaps the growing pile of bodies around her.

Impressed, he nodded and continued to survey the field of battle. When he didn't see what he was looking for, the silver tones of his automaton, he grew concerned.

"Enaurl?" He called, wiping the blood away from his face. When he still didn't see her, he called for her again. "Enaurl!"

A series of crashes and crunching sounds to his left drew his attention towards the treeline. Enaurl emerged from behind the trees, her shining chassis coated with gnoll blood and twigs, with bits of leaves and what Smith could only assume was brain matter slowly sliding down her body.

Relieved to see that she was still standing, still fighting, Smith nodded at the silver woman and pulled his firearm from its holster. Snapping it open, he was dismayed to see that the weapon had jammed.

Blood-slicked fingers went to work fixing the weapon. A snarl from behind him made Smith whirl around with his sword, only to see Enaurl sprint forward and deliver a flying punch at the jaw of the timbergnoll who had snuck up on him.

The gnoll, dazed, staggered like a drunk. Enaurl made short work of it; a straight left jab collapsed its windpipe, a right hook opened it up, and a devastating left uppercut snapped its head so far backward that its skull nearly touched its spine.

The gnoll fell to the ground dead. Enaurl turned to face Smith and stared at him with her unblinking chrome eyes. Smith grunted and resumed trying to fix his weapon as Enaurl chose another opponent.

Voldani plunged one of her blades into the ribcage of a gnoll, the steel of her weapon penetrating into its chest cavity and neatly slicing the heart within in two. The gnoll dropped dead.

Withdrawing her weapon, Voldani turned around and was forced to shield her eyes against a splatter of mulched meat. Lowering her hands, she watched as a compacted sphere of meat – meat which had clearly once been a gnoll – dropped to the ground and began to spread outward like a thick puddle.

Will, bent forward with palms against his knees to keep himself upright while he wheezed and gasped. He gasped as a gnoll advanced on him, spear raised and ready, only to fall back as the fletch of a crossbow bolt suddenly blossomed from its eye.

"Nice shot, Brenno," Will said between huffs, holding his hand into the air while making a circle with his thumb and forefinger. "A second later and I'd probably be dead right now."

"Pity," said Brenno. "Had I known I might have waited."

"You're a funny guy, Brenno," Will said, smiling.

"I do not believe he was intending to make a joke," said Voldani.

"What?" Will said. "That was totally a joke. Right, Brenno?"

"If that's what you'd like to believe," said Brenno.

"Is all this banter necessary?" Smith growled.

"I mean, I don't know about 'necessary'," said Will. "But it looks like we've won."

"Someone tell that to Kera," said Brenno, hitching his thumb towards the woman.

As one, Voldani, Will, Smith, and Brenno turned to watch as Kera, visibly seething with rage, buried Zephelous up to the hilt in a timbergnoll's chest.

The gnoll gasped and gaped, pawing at the wound. Kera punched him in the face and withdrew Zephelous, throwing the sword like a missile into the abdomen of the nearest timbergnoll before leaping onto it, audibly severing the dogman's spine as she crunched the sword deeper into its midsection before pulling it out with a roar of defiance – though what exactly she was in defiance of was not clear.

A gnoll sunk its teeth into her shoulder, but she paid it little mind. She balled her hand into a fist and punched it in the nose, forcing it to release its grip and back away from Kera.

Not sparing a single second, Kera hauled Zephelous out of the body of the gnoll at her feet and swung it around, loping the front portion of the timbergnoll's head clean off. Broken and battered timbergnolls lay on the ground in a grisly circle around where she stood, chest heaving with each ragged breath she took.

A wavering howl that ended in a series of quick yips filled the air, and the few gnolls that remained along the edges of the treeline abruptly disappeared into the woods, vanishing as quickly as they had appeared. For a few moments the sounds of a hasty retreat filled the clearing, a sound comprised of whines of pain and the snapping of twigs.

Another moment later and the only sounds that remained was the ragged breathing of those gathered therein and the gentle crackling of the fire.

The last gnoll in the clearing fell at Kera's feet, dead from a stab to the chest. Kera's entire body heaved with exertion, and she panted like a winded racehorse. Zephelous, still in Kera's grasp and still unable to communicate with her, hoping that Kera's rage had finally subsided.

I HAD EXPECTED A RAGE, the sword admitted to itself, *BUT I HAD NOT EXPECTED THIS.*

With an intangible psychic probe, the sword once again tried to reach into Kera's mind. As before, the white-hot rage that blotted out Kera's consciousness from the sword seared the edges of its consciousness. Zephelous recoiled, trying to glean what it could from the wall of fury.

The only images the sword could understand were less than flashes; glimpses of scenes and sensations played out discordantly in the sword's mind, each one leaving as quickly as it came.

A large gathering of disappointed people looking inward towards what was presumably the spot where Kera had stood, their faces heavy with varying degrees of resentment and dismay.

Anger that rose and swelled into rage and frenzy before falling away to guilt and confusion and shame and sadness.

Glimpses of a lone man in a simple loin cloth, body covered in scars and tattoos. The sticky wetness of hands slick and warm with spilled blood. A circle of people, faceless and blurred, surrounding someone and turning away as one, united in their disdain. More anger, red hot, white hot, burning hotter than the rivers of fire down below, hotter than the sun in the skies above...

Metaphor became reality on the psychic plane, as it often did, as Zephelous began to feel the scorching heat burning and blistering the edges of its own psyche the way flesh roiled and burnt when exposed to open flame. For the first time in a very long time, the sword found itself faced with a dilemma – did it leave Kera to face her memories and shield itself from the psychic flames of her berserker frenzy, or should it press through the pain in an attempt to reach the woman beneath the rage? Uncertain, it opted for a little of both.

YOU MUST NOT LET IT CONSUME YOU, KERA, Zephelous said, aiming a psychic shout at the wall of flames in an effort to pierce through it. THE BATTLE IS WON, YOU MUST TEMPER YOUR RAGE.

Buffeted by waves of mental heat, Zephelous brought up a wall of psionic force between its mind and the fires of Kera's fury, leaving itself open to communicate while blunting the brunt of the woman's psionic defenses. While all this transpired on the psionic level, nothing had changed on the physical; Kera stood where she had moments before, droplets of sweat flowing from her face while blood trickled out from her many wounds, panting with exhaustion as she held Zephelous held in her grip.

"Uh, Kera?" Will said, calling out to Kera. "Everything okay over there?"

When Kera still didn't respond, the weary wizard turned to face the others.

"Maybe she took a hit to the head?"

"Have you met many barbarians, William?" Brenno asked. "The last place you want to hit them on the head. That's where the bone grows the thickest."

Will chortled and Smith made a sniffing sound, but Voldani was silent.

"Good point. Let's ease up on the whole 'William' thing, though," said Will. "Just Will is fine, thanks."

Brenno shrugged. Voldani strode towards Kera with, a hand outstretched with intent to place it on the other woman's shoulder. Enaurl grabbed Voldani's wrist and held it back, making silent but meaningful eye contact with Voldani.

The two stared into each other's eyes for a moment, unblinking silver orbs meeting glowing radiant pools. Voldani nodded and stepped aside, making room for the silver construct to take her place behind Kera.

"Is she capable of speech?" Brenno asked Smith, nodding his chin towards Enaurl.

"She doesn't have a working mouth, Hornbuckle," said Smith.

"Well, not at the moment perhaps, but surely you could fashion one." Brenno said with a shrug. "She has the capacity to make independent decisions, I would wager that it wouldn't be a massive leap to allow independent speech from that point."

"Spend a lot of time working on cutting edge artifice in your pawnshop, Brenno?" Smith growled at the halfling. "Because it took me the better part of three days to repair a damaged stabilizer, how long do you think it would take to devise a mechanism capable of storing words for her to reference? How would you go about creating a synthetic voice that could say those words? Once you've figured all that out, how would you introduce the ability to use the logic patterns required to do any of it into her artificial brain?"

"Well, I'm sure I don't know," said Brenno.

"Me neither," said Smith. "Only difference is I'm not flapping my gums about it."

"She does not require speech to make her intentions known," Voldani added, watching as Enaurl reached a tentative hand out towards Kera. "That much is obvious."

"Exactly," said Smith, watching as Enaurl's hand came down to rest on Kera's shoulder. First rule of artifice, don't fix what ain't brok--"

Smith's words were cut short by the ear piercing shriek of metal being rent and torn. In response to the sensation of Enaurl's hand touching her, Kera had done a lightning quick turn about while swinging Zephelous in a deadly arc, the magically sharpened sword cutting clear through Enaurl's right arm midway through her artificial bicep.

Voldani, standing closest to Kera and Enaurl, looked from the severed arm that lay at her feet up to Kera's face; from the foamy froth of saliva around the woman's mouth to the wild and unfocused look in her eyes, all Voldani saw was blind rage paired with exhaustion.

Kera seemed ready to fall over any second, but clearly wasn't in control of her rage. Drawing her swords as quickly as she could manage it, Voldani brought the pommels of each up into the air in an effort to knock Kera unconscious.

Worn as she was, Kera deflected one of Voldani's swords by whirling Zephelous around in a semi circular block above her head. She was not fast enough to block both, and the pommel of Voldani's sword impacted the side of Kera's head with a *thump.*

Kera's eyes rolled into the back of her head as she collapsed, falling into an unconscious heap at Voldani's feet with all the grace of a rock being dropped into a puddle of mud.

Voldani puffed out a sigh of relief.

"Thank the gods for small mercies."

Chapter Fifteen

Kera woke to the sound of something popping over a fire and the rank smell of burnt meat. Her nose wrinkled in disgust and she groaned as a hundred points of ache and pain thrummed their way into existence across her body.

She felt as though she'd been thrown down a mountain and tumbled across every rock and crag on its surface on her way down. She felt earth beneath her back and legs, but something softer beneath her head.

She felt the weight of Zephelous laying on her chest before she registered what it was. She snatched at the sword and sat up, regretting the hastiness of her actions instantly as a tide of pain swept up and down her body.

MOVE SLOWLY KERA, Zephelous said.

"No shit," Kera wheezed.

"You're awake," Voldani said, startling Kera with her proximity.

"Looks like it," said Kera, looking around.

The small fire that had been started some hours ago had been dug out and made into a makeshift pyre atop which burned the bodies of a trio of timbergnolls. The pounding in Kera's head seemed to isolate itself to a wound on her forehead. Reaching up to inspect the area with her fingertips, Kera was surprised to find bandages.

"What hit me?" she asked.

"I did," said Voldani.

"Did you have to do it so hard?" asked Kera.

"If I hadn't you might have attacked me in retribution," said Voldani. "As you demonstrated with Enaurl."

"What happened to Enaurl?" Kera asked.

"You cut off her gods damned arm, is what!" Smith bellowed at her from the direction of the wagon.

Turning to look over her shoulder at Smith, Kera saw the man standing over a prone Enaurl laying on her back on an improvised wooden table made from what looked like the door from the back of the wagon.

"Do you have any idea how hard it is to fix this kind of shit at the shop, never mind on the road? Do you? Gods, first you shoot her, now this? No, that's not even right, the first thing you did was break into my house, then fill my daughter's head with all kinds of nonsense, then get her shot, *then* you shot Enaurl, and now look at her!"

Smith gestured towards Enaurl with both hands, one of which was holding a wrench. The construct's right arm was missing from just above the elbow, and the severed appendage lay next to where it belonged.

The arm itself looked as though it had been intentionally opened up to expose its internal mechanisms, a confusing looking tangle of wires and glass and pistons wrapped around a silver skeleton.

Enaurl's upper arm sparked intermittently at the place where it had been severed. Enaurl's head turned in the direction of Kera's voice and the silver woman tried to sit up, but Smith firmly pressed her back down by placing a hand on her chest and pushing her back.

"What in the shattered hells is wrong with you? She was checking to see if you were okay, godsdamnit!"

"Not exactly the first case of collateral damage you've suffered at her hands, eh Smith?" Brenno chimed in.

Kera turned to see where the halfling was, and watched as he struggled to turn the body of a timbergnoll face up. When the body at last rolled over onto its back, Brenno riffled through the dogman's pockets and the pouches at her - for it indeed seemed to be a female - belt.

He withdrew his hands to reveal smattering of coins, which he promptly threw over his shoulder. The tossed currency landed with a clinking sound as they joined in a small pile of mostly copper and silver coins behind the halfling. In another he found a small wooden totem which he inspected, eyeing it curiously.

"You stay out of this, Hornbuckle," Smith said, pointing his wrench at the halfling like it were a weapon. "You're just as culpable as she is."

"I've been saying since the onset that Kera was responsible," said Brenno, turning the trinket this way and that in his hands.

Intrigued, he tossed the pendant to Will, who caught it deftly.

"Perhaps now you'll begin to see that I was right."

Will crunched noisily into an apple, inspecting the pendant he held in his palm. He closed his hand over the necklace and closed his eyes and concentrated, still chewing loudly.

Blue light shone out from between his fingers for a moment, building to a gentle peak before winking out. He shook his head side to side in a quick negative.

"Nope," said Will, tossing the necklace back to Brenno.

The halfling caught it with both hands and smirked. Examining the necklace once more, the pawnbroker made a quick mental assessment of what he might be able to sell the trinket for as a cosmetic item.

His calculation complete, he frowned. He tossed the trinket into the burning pyre and continued searching.

Meanwhile, Smith was glowering at Brenno. The man muttered a series of threatening sounding syllables under his breath and returned his wrench to its place on his tool belt, withdrawing a screwdriver in the process and getting to work on Enaurl's severed arm.

"You have caused a disproportionate amount of trouble in comparison," Voldani said to Kera.

"Compared to Brenno? He's the one who actually shot Smith's kid, how does everyone keep forgetting that?"

"Compared to every other person I have ever met," said Voldani. "Rest assured, I have not forgotten whose crossbow felled the poor child."

"The same one that saved your life," Brenno rebutted, finger leveled accusingly at the scion.

The damning digit panned around to encompass the entire group.

"The one that saved each of you half dozen times, I might add."

"I did not require any of your assistance, though it was useful at times." said Voldani. "I have no doubt the others may have required your aid. Particularly William the Charlatan."

"Can we put this whole 'William' thing to rest already?" Will asked, biting into his apple once again. "And I'm really starting to take you constantly calling me 'charlatan' a little personally. Is it me specifically, or are you just not a fan of wizards in general?"

"You masqueraded as something you are not," said Voldani.

"So what?" said Will. "People do that all the time. Hell, some people do it every day."

"Most people do not use layers of illusion to deceive and manipulate the people around them," Voldani countered.

"They would if they could," said Will, smiling wide enough to let some juice from the apple dribble down his chin. "You can't even say that's not true." Will turned to face Kera. "Ask the talking sword, it'll back me up."

Reflexively, Kera held Zephelous tight against her body.

"Who said it could talk?" Kera asked, feigning ignorance.

As one, Brenno, Voldani, and Will all pointed at Smith, who seemed oblivious as he continued toiling away on Enaurl while muttering to himself.

"Somewhere between the fourth and fifth time he zapped himself," said Will. "But I can't remember where it landed on the insulting rant count. It was somewhere after 'self-centered humanoid raccoons with danger magnets shoved up their assess' and 'irresponsible children wearing the soiled skins of garbage adults as suits'. I dunno, I could be wrong about that. I know for sure that he has shouted the words 'drakeshit haunted talking sword' at least twice."

"Colorful," Kera said, wincing as she stood.

"You have no idea," said Brenno.

"I'm considering taking notes, if I'm being honest," said Will.

"I clarified that the sword is not haunted," said Voldani. "Alive, but not haunted."

"I see," said Kera. "And no one has a problem with this?"

"The sword seems focused on heroism," said Voldani. "I have no care for heroics. I exist to defend and to serve my lady."

"You defended the shit out of those gnolls," said Will. "I had a front row ticket, I watched you defend one almost in half."

"I was defending all of you from them," said Voldani. "I am clearly the most capable combatant among us, as such it is my responsibility to ensure you all survive."

"Hey, I'm not complaining," said Will. "But let's call a spade a spade, you were a monster out there, Dani."

"Do not call me Dani," said Voldani. "One person calls me that, you are not her."

"Right, sorry," Will said. "Treia can call you 'Vee' though. Hey, what's that about? Have the two of you known each other long?"

"I feel I should be asking the same, charlatan," Voldani said, glaring at Will through narrowed eyes.

"I'll tell you everything you want to know about me and Treia *and* stop calling you 'Vee', or 'Dani', or 'Olda' if you agree to stop calling me 'charlatan'," Will offered.

"I have never been called 'Olda' in my life," said Voldani.

"How do you feel about it?" Will asked.

"I despise it," Voldani answered.

"Okay, sure. Consider it part of the deal."

"Very well," said Voldani. "I accept your offer, mountebank."

"What's a mountebank?" Will asked.

"A person who deceives others, usually in an effort to separate them from their money," said Brenno, grunting with effort as he hauled the timbergnoll's body nearer to the pyre. "It's actually quite a bit more appropriate for you than charlatan was."

"What?" Will asked. "How is that better?"

"Charlatan implies you have no skills," said Brenno. "You clearly have some level of ability, as you've demonstrated here this evening. I suspect even Voldani might agree."

"Only reluctantly," Voldani added. "And only once."

Brenno pointed at Voldani as he made his way towards the next timbergnoll corpse, reinforcing the validation of his point by way of Voldani's confirmation.

"Speaking of which, we will of course need to revisit the agreement we made previously," said Brenno. "Or rather, the agreement made between Tanathar and myself."

"No way," said Will. "We shook on it."

"I shook on it," said Brenno. "However, I have to assume I was lifting a hand full of empty air while being fed the illusory sensation of a clasped hand?"

"You assume correctly," said Will.

"Then you admit yourself that there was no 'we' involved in the deal," said Brenno, straining with effort as he threw his shoulder against the prone timbergnoll. "As such, our arrangement is null and void."

"I didn't realize we were in a courtroom," Will said with a shrug.

"I don't need a courtroom to settle this," said Brenno. "Though I'm certain Voldani might object to any further intentional falsehoods. Surely the White Lady has a few things to say about that, doesn't she Voldani?"

"Indeed," said Voldani. "It is known that the church believes that intentional falsehoods at the expense of others is an offence against Perrus itself, and that the only salve for the wounds they cause is truth and reconciliation."

"There you have it," said Brenno, failing completely at his efforts to turn over the gnoll.

Walking somewhat unsteadily, Kera made her way towards Brenno and helped him flip the dogman over onto its back. Brenno eyed her suspiciously, and Kera shrugged.

"It's going to take you all night if you keep doing it by yourself," Kera explained. "And I'd like to know what my cut is sooner rather than later, thanks."

"Who said you were getting a cut of anything?" Brenno asked.

"I do," said Kera.

"You're pressed into service by the church," said Brenno.

"Last I checked, so were you," Kera countered.

"You burned down my shop," Brenno said, eyes narrowing into hard points.

"Take half my share," Kera said with a shrug. "I only need what I can carry, but I need to be able to buy food. Maybe some new clothes."

"Fair point," said Brenno, weighing out the possibility of how much coin he might stand to make. Satisfied with his mental mathematics, the halfling nodded. "I accept your offer. Equal shares for everyone else?"

"Works for me," said Will.

"I have no use for money," said Voldani. "I will use my portion to supply the Zelwyran soup kitchen, as well as the vagrant's refuge."

"I always thought those were the same thing," said Will.

"Hardly," said Brenno. "The soup kitchen is for native Zelwyrans having a hard go. The vagrant's refuge is a hostel for ratcatchers. I'm surprised you don't know that."

"I've never had to use either," said Will with a shrug, tossing his apple core into the fire. "I tend to go where I want to go, and where I want to go is usually a cheap bar with decent ale. I do some of my best work there."

"So we've seen," said Brenno, as he began to search through the pockets of the dogman at his feet. Another handful of coins joined the growing pile with a clatter. Kera assisted Brenno in rooting through the gnoll's goods, pulling out a glass small vial with a trio of abnormally large snowflakes suspended in a light blue compound of some sort.

"Got something here," said Kera.

"Toss it over," Will said, clapping his hands to indicate his readiness to catch the object. Kera made a careful underhand throw with the vial, allowing the item a gentle flight through the air before it plopped down into Will's hands. The wizard closed his palms over the item and closed his eyes. As before, a glowing light flickered out from between his fingers. Will smiled wide. "There we go, that's more like it."

"What is it?" Brenno asked, his eagerness apparent.

"It's an unresolved ice spell contained in some kind of suppression fluid," said Will, holding the small glass cylinder up to the firelight, the orange of the fire glinting off the hard edges of the egg-sized snowflakes. "Part spell craft, part alchemy, part time saver. Smash and dash kind of thing."

"I understand all of those words," said Voldani. "However, you seem to strip them of their conventional meanings when you use them, and that is something that irritates me."

"It's a spell in a jar, Voldani," said Kera. "I'm going to go ahead and guess something snow related."

"I'm pretty sure it's a runic ice trap," Will clarified. "A decent one, too.

Pouring this stuff onto a surface would transfer the rune onto that surface, and anything moving nearby would trigger the rune."

Will mimed an explosion with his hands, bringing his fingers together before splaying them out wide in all directions.

"Boom. Ice and pain for every one nearby. I'd guess a fifteen foot radius? Decent parlor trick. Well, if you want a bloody parlor full of ice."

"I have no use for a parlor," said Voldani, unsheathing her swords and laying them across her lap.

She produced a wet stone from somewhere and began sharpening the edges. "Bloodied or otherwise."

"Okay, Voldani doesn't want it," said Will. "If no one else objects, I'll take this for myself."

Will held the vial out towards Kera, who shook her head and raised a hand to ward off the offer.

He offered it to Brenno next, who examined it carefully but didn't touch it.

"Is it valuable?" Brenno asked.

"Not especially," said Will.

"How much would it cost you to attempt to buy one?" Brenno asked, eyes darting to the pile of coin and back to the vial.

Will shrugged.

"I dunno, somewhere in the neighborhood of a hundred gold, maybe a little more?" Will asked, eyeing the halfling suspiciously. "Why does it matter what it's worth?"

"Division of goods," said Brenno. "I'll pass, thank you."

"Smith, you want a bottle of ice?" Will shouted to Smith, not bothering to turn his head.

"Get bent," Smith shouted back.

Something zapped him and he cursed, returning to work.

"You could have just said no," Will said, turning the vial over in his hands. Satisfied, he tucked it into his robes. "What are the odds any of the rest of them have anything worthwhile on them?"

Kera and Brenno surveyed the killing field, quickly counting the dead. Over a dozen timbergnolls remained unlooted.

"At the very least there is coin to be had," said Brenno.

"I've never met a dead body whose pockets I didn't love," said Kera. "Comes with the territory of being a graverobber."

"Is that what you are?" Will asked. "I figured mercenary, maybe pirate. Burnt out campaigner with a terrible secret, maybe."

"I think you mean every campaigner," said Brenno.

"Look who's getting a sense of humor," Will said appreciatively.

"I've always had one," said Brenno. "The events of the last several weeks have been exceedingly trying, which should put a damper on any right minded person's mood."

"I try not to let this kind of stuff bother me," said Will.

"As I said," said Brenno. "Any right minded person."

Will chuckled at his own expense, and Kera managed a weak smile. Out of the corner of her eye she thought she might have seen the corners of Voldani's lips turn upward ever so slightly, but she couldn't be sure.

Kera and Brenno made their way across the clearing, searching the bodies of the timbergnolls one by one. By and large, they found little more than coins for the growing hoard.

KERA, Zephelous said as they neared the final group of downed gnolls, its voice soft and weak in Kera's mind.

Kera furrowed her brow. The sword had never sounded weak before.

"What's up?" Kera said. Brenno looked up at her in confusion, but Kera pointed at the sword.

Brenno scowled at her, but began searching the gnoll in front of him,

ONE OF YOUR FOES YET LIVES, said Zephelous. Kera stood up and drew Zephelous from its sheath, looking around in an effort to spot any sign of a live timbergnoll.

I don't see anything, Kera thought. *Where is it?*

ON THE GROUND, said Zephelous, its psychic voice strained and hoarse. IT IS UNABLE TO ESCAPE, SO IT WAITS.

You don't sound so good, Kera said. *Are you okay?*

I WILL BE FINE, Zephelous said weakly. I REQUIRE REST.

I didn't know swords needed rest, said Kera.

I WAS FORGED FROM THE FIRST METAL AT THE ANVIL OF CREATION, said Zephelous. MY BODY IS NEARLY INDESTRUCTIBLE. The sword lapsed into silence, leaving Kera waiting for a follow up.

But? Kera prompted.

HOWEVER, Zephelous corrected.

However is just a fancy but, Kera thought.

I AM NOT A GOD, said Zephelous. I HAVE MY LIMITS. ASSISTING YOU DURING COMBAT IS NO GREAT STRAIN.

Then what the hell happened to you? Asked Kera. *You sound like you're dying.*

SHIELDING MYSELF FROM THE BRUNT OF YOUR PSIONIC RAGE

WHILE I ATTEMPTED TO COMMUNICATE WITH YOU APPEARS TO
HAVE CAUSED A GOOD DEAL OF PSYCHIC DAMAGE, Zephelous
explained. I MUST SLEEP FOR A TIME.

Any chance I can get some clarification on the whole 'dying' thing? Kera asked.
Specifically a yes or no would be great.

I AM FINE, KERA NO-CLAN, Zephelous said. I SIMPLY MUST REST MY
MIND FOR A TIME. The sword's voice seemed to be moving away, as if it were
falling, dropping down into some deep pit in Kera's mind. BE WARY, the
sword's voice echoed. THE GNOLL JUST BEYOND THE HALFLING
INTENDS TO NEGOTIATE ITS RELEASE.

"What could it possibly have that we would want?" Kera said with a snort of
incredulity.

INFORMATION, Zephelous answered, its voice fading away as it spoke the
word.

"What could what have that we would want?" Brenno asked.

"What?" Kera said.

"Something has something we want," Brenno said. "What is it?"

"Information," said Kera.

"Information wants something from us?" Brenno asked, visibly confused.

"What? No, it has information," Kera said.

"What has information?" Brenno said, exasperated.

"It's just beyond you," Kera said, gesturing towards the gnolls behind the
halfling by nodding her chin in their general direction.

"This conversation is beyond me," Brenno grumbled, turning in place to
survey the area.

"Hey, I'm just saying what the sword said," Kera explained.

"What is it saying now?" Brenno asked.

"Nothing," said Kera. "It's tired."

"I wasn't aware a sword could get tired," Brenno said.

"Me neither," said Kera. "You learn something new everyday."

"I'd never suspected you were the learning type," said Brenno.

"Bite me, Hornbuckle," Kera said with a grimace.

She brushed past the halfling, holding Zephelous in front of her. The light
from the pyre illuminated the area well enough for her to see clearly without the
need of a torch. She wouldn't have needed a torch to find the gnoll; the flashing
red of the pyre light reflected in the golden eyes that stared up at her from the
ground was more than enough.

The timbergnoll blinked slowly, meaningfully, at Kera. It yawned, sliding its lengthy tongue out from between its jaws to lick at its muzzle as it did. The dogman spoke no words, but the message it was sending to Kera came in clear; *I am here, I see you, I am waiting...*

"I found it," she called to Brenno.

As the halfling scuttled his way towards her, Kera inspected the gnoll more closely; its arms appeared bound behind its back by way of a cruel looking spiked chain that had become wrapped around its torso and upper body. The spikes on the chain had buried themselves into the gnoll's fur and flesh, staining and matting its fur with blood.

Kera heard Brenno's breath catch when he spotted the gnoll, but she hadn't looked away from its eyes. Brenno walked a wide circle around the dogman, every deliberate step showcasing the halfling pawnbroker's cautious nature at work.

The timbergnoll's eyes followed Brenno's every step, watching the halfling the way a hawk watched a mouse. Brenno stopped dead in his tracks, unnerved by the glint of the fire against those haunting yellow orbs.

"Voldani," Brenno called, trying to mask the quiver in his voice. "Pass me my crossbow."

"No," said Kera, "Zephelous said it had information."

"What kind of information?" Brenno asked.

"It didn't say," Kera admitted. "Just that it would try to negotiate its release."

"Oh," Brenno said, relaxing considerably. Making pointed eye contact with the gnoll, Brenno sat down on top of the chest of the nearest gnoll corpse. Everything about the halfling, from his posture to his demeanor, seemed to transition from fearful and uncertain to confident and relaxed.

"I wasn't aware we were in civilized company. Kera, would you assist our new friend in the act of sitting up, please?"

Kera's eyes traced the spiked chain that wound its way around the gnoll's body. She grimaced and sucked air through her teeth.

"I'm not sure if I can without removing these chains from it," said Kera.

"Such poor manners," said Brenno, making a tut tut and a finger wag. "Never refer to someone as an 'it' when you can simply ask them what their name is."

"It was just trying to kill us," Kera said.

"That's true," said Brenno. "But now the gentlegnoll is trying to do business with us, and there is a certain etiquette that goes along with doing business. I'm sure our captive would agree, would you not?"

Fully in his element, Brenno smiled at the gnoll and leaned back.

The gnoll giggled softly to itself, but nodded. The movement caused the chains to shift, moving the spikes along with it, and the gnoll's chuckle ended in a gentle whine like a struck puppy. Brenno scowled.

"This simply won't do. Voldani, could you please assist us?"

Pausing in the act of sharpening her swords, Voldani glanced towards Kera and Brenno. Sheathing her swords, she stood and strode towards the pair and the gnoll.

"Am I to execute it?" Voldani asked, eyeing the gnoll.

"No, I think not," said Brenno. "Could you assist us in getting our new friend over towards the fire?"

"I am not friends with this dog," said Voldani. "I find myself struggling to tolerate the present company as it is."

"It's merely a figure of speech, my good Voldani," said Brenno.

"I am not yours," said Voldani.

"Another figure of speech," Brenno clarified.

"I am not enjoying these figures," Voldani said as she stepped closer to the gnoll. Inspecting the timbergnoll's state for a moment, Voldani turned to face Brenno.

"Moving it while it is bound by this chain on will be quite painful."

"I can try to unwrap it," Kera suggested. "Or maybe we could--"

Voldani knelt and threw the timbergnoll over her shoulders before Kera could finish. The dogman yipped in pain as the chains shifted once more, the spikes pressing into its flesh.

"I was merely making an observation," said Voldani, adjusting the weight on her shoulders to the dogman's increased pain.

Brenno winced on the gnoll's behalf, watching as the chains cut into the outer layers of his flesh like a saw through wood.

"Do try to be gentle," said Brenno.

"I shall be as gentle as this one's kin were during the fray," Voldani said, making her way back to the funeral pyre before depositing the bound timbergnoll.

The gnoll dropped with a thump and yipped again, louder this time. Brenno scurried over to the timbergnoll's side.

"Gentle, Voldani! Surely you've had at least one parlay before?" The halfling scolded. Turning to face the timbergnoll, he offered a look of sincere remorse. "I am sorry for that... unpleasantness, truly. I understand you wish to negotiate, and am told you have information to offer; information that might prove to be of some use to us on our quest. Am I correct in this?"

"A path of blood with no set end," the gnoll said. "For guidance you must make amends."

"Anyone else getting sick of the rhymes?" Kera asked. Will, looking exhausted, eyed the timbergnoll and smirked.

"Right," said Will. "You and your pack attacked us, but we're the ones who need to make amends. Makes about as much sense as anything else I've ever heard come out of a gnoll's mouth."

For a moment no one spoke. Voldani strode towards the gnoll and unwound the first several lengths of its chain. She did so with all the finesse of a lumberjack, hauling the chain free much to the gnoll's increased agony.

"Daughter of healers, descendant of the light," the timbergnoll said, its voice tinged with whimpers. "Yet not one Perrusean thought of mercy this night."

Voldani's swords appeared in her hands, so quickly did she draw them. She pressed the tip of one against the throat of the gnoll.

"Your kin spoke the name of Perrus after I advised them not to," Voldani said, glaring at the gnoll. "They now lie in pieces scattered across the floor. Consider this your warning against the same fate and circumstances."

"Voldani, please," Brenno said, scowling at the divine warrior. "The gentlegnoll is looking to do business. Is that not so, my good dogman?" Brenno offered the timbergnoll his flashiest salesman smile.

"My wounds are fresh and blood flows freely," the gnoll said, making a show of trying to lick at a gash on its chest but failing. "This would not be so to deal, ideally."

"We've no healing potions to offer you," said Brenno to the gnoll. The halfling glanced towards Will. "Are you learned in the school of restoration magic perchance?"

"I can make it *look* like he's not bleeding," Will said with a shrug. "He will absolutely still be bleeding, though. I'm an illusiomancer, not a cleric."

"I see," said Brenno. He turned towards Kera next. "I don't suppose you'd have any herbology or survival skills that would help ease the pain our furred friend is experiencing?"

"The only herb I care about that eases pain is a certain green one smoked heavily by the elves," said Kera. "Believe me when I say if I had some, I'd already be smoking it."

"I should have known fae ash wouldn't be your only substance of choice," Brenno grumbled. Looking back towards the wagon at Smith, Brenno's brow creased with preemptive disappointment. "Smith, I don't suppose you've got any means of assisting this timbergnoll with his wounds?"

"I do," Smith said, removing his revolver from its holster. "It's called a bullet."

"Not quite what I meant," said Brenno. Voldani slammed her swords into their sheaths and harrumphed, removing her armored gauntlets with an expression of distaste on her face

"I am seeing a pattern forming," said Voldani. "One which paints you all as being in dire need of my abilities least you fail completely and utterly at all you do."

"What are you going to do?" Kera asked.

"Solving one problem while potentially creating another," Voldani grumbled. Reaching out, Voldani took the gnoll's face in her hands and stared into its eyes. Looking up into the face of the angelic woman, the gnoll laughed quietly.

"You beg a god for the power to heal me," the gnoll said. "When Leighlagh speaks she does so clearly. The church of Perrus has emptied, nearly. Does she speak to you, one loved so dearly?"

Kera groaned.

"You're killing me with the rhyming," she said to the gnoll. "Is it absolutely necessary?"

"The god of fangs blessed my kin first, to honor her we speak in verse."

"Okay, but what if we put it on hold for like five minutes?" Kera asked.

"I will not risk the red god's curse because you are averse to verse," the gnoll answered, its eyes flitting towards Kera as it did.

Bringing them back to look at Voldani, the gnoll opened its jaws slightly in what might have been its version of a grin.

"If your aim is to converse, be terse. Dispense your magics, nurse."

Voldani's grip on the sides of the gnoll's face tightened, as did her jaw. She brought her face in close to maw of the timbergnoll, unafraid.

"It would be incredibly easy for me to end your life," Voldani said to the gnoll, slowly forcing the dogman's head to the left while still holding it in her hands. "A mere fraction more of my strength applied in this manner and your neck would snap. Who would utter inane poetry to your blood soaked deity in your place?"

Voldani continued turning the gnoll's neck as she spoke, bringing it far enough that Kera cringed in anticipation of a dry crack that would announce the dogman's neck breaking.

The gnoll's eyes never broke from Voldani's.

"With all you've gained from your ancestral godhead, you should know I cannot help if dead," said the gnoll. "If dragon's blood is what must be shed, Leighlagh knows where you must tread."

Voldani stopped turning the gnoll's head.

"How do you know what we seek?" Voldani asked.

"The gods see much, this truth is known. Have you not thought to ask your own?"

Will rubbed his eyes and face with both hands, leaning forward to rest his elbows on his knees as he did. He shook his head.

"I don't like this, whatever it is," said Will. "All this god stuff makes my skin crawl. Voldani, either kill him or heal him, let's get this over with already."

"Do not kill him," said Brenno. "We have to negotiate. Heal him."

"Why are you so eager to bargain with this thing?" Will asked. "We're pretty far from the ashes of your pawnshop, I don't see why this is so exciting for you."

"You'd be surprised at how much information can be gained from one good conversation," said Brenno.

Kera slapped her hand against her face and dragged it downwards across her features.

"Oh gods, he's rhyming now too," Kera said with a groan. "Just kill me now. I quit."

"I can guide you towards your dragon, and ward my kin off you and your wagon," said the gnoll to Voldani.

"We dispatched your kin just fine this evening," said Voldani. "What would make you believe we could not do so again?"

The gnoll laughed, low and terrible.

"These were but scouts to gauge your strength," the gnoll said. "The pack will come for louts at length."

The howls of dozens of timbergnolls filled the night air in answer to the timbergnoll's threat, long and warbling and punctuated with sinister laughter.

Voldani grimaced and brought the gnoll's head back to face her directly.

"I will heal your wounds, mutt man." Voldani said to the gnoll, speaking low and deliberately. "But know this; I swear to Perrrus and every god of light who stands with her that if you do not honor your arrangement, I will personally see to it that you and your kind are eradicated from these woods. Have I made myself clear?"

"Cure me with your holy light and you will survive the night."

Voldani tightened her jaw so forcefully she could feel the strain in her teeth. She closed her eyes and began to pray.

I find myself at a cross in the roads, my lady. Guide me that I might choose the correct path.

Voldani waited for a moment, though for what she couldn't say.

She would not, could not admit to herself that it had been so long since Perrus had spoken to her that she almost couldn't remember what the voice of Perrus sounded like.

Her warrior soul told her that perhaps this was an answer; if the lady was not demanding the death of this vile savage, then she was quietly showing Voldani the path to take.

She chose to believe this was true. Opening her eyes again, she found the timbergnoll smiling up at her, it's body wracked with silent laughter.

"My aim is not to encourage violence," said the gnoll. "Leighlagh laughs at Perrus's silence."

Voldani ground her teeth together, but maintained her composure.

"Be silent or I will change my mind and kill you," said Voldani.

Taking a deep breath, Voldani reached inside herself for the light and warmth of Perrus, the inner glow of divinity that shone from her eyes and burned in her heart.

The light grew within her, filled her chest with strength and resolve. She commanded the light to move from her heart to her hands, which began to glow as if surrounded by a pair of shining halos.

The rings of luminosity flared yellow, flashing brighter than the campfire, brighter than the stars, and surged into the timbergnoll. The dogman arched his back as Voldani's divine power poured into its body, ribbons of yellow-white light extending outward from its eyes and open wounds. The influence of Voldani's divine magic made open wounds knit themselves shut, leaving reddish scars where moments before blood had flowed from rent flesh.

The gleam of light faded from around Voldani's hands, and she withdrew them from the timbergnoll's face. The light lingered in the dogman's eyes for a moment longer before it too faded, letting them return to their natural golden state.

"Brenno, have you any bandages on your person?" Voldani asked the pawnbroker.

"I have a good supply in the wagon, yes," the halfling said.

"Fetch them," said Voldani, as she unraveled the chain from around the timbergnoll. "You may begin your bargaining as you bandage our captive."

"How kind of you," Brenno grumbled.

The halfling made his way to the caravan and returned with a roll of tan-colored cloth just as Voldani began to coil the spiked chain into a neat pile.

"What do you suppose that might be worth?" the halfling asked.

"It is worth keeping," said Voldani, "I do not care beyond that."

"I'll assign it an appropriate value," said Brenno, approaching the timbergnoll who now sat unbound before the fire.

The eyes of all the companions save Smith and Enaurl were firmly rooted on it, waiting for any sign that the dogman might try to escape.

For its part, the gnoll seemed calm. It's eyes moved from person to person before settling on Brenno, who held up the bandages.

"Shall we begin negotiations, my good dogman?" The timbergnoll snickered. "Good. Let us begin with the most pressing issues; namely, we have your word that we will not be attacked by your kin this evening, is that correct?"

"I will send word unto the pack," said the gnoll. "To advise that they should not attack."

"Very well," said Brenno, reaching for the gnoll's arm to begin bandaging it. "I imagine you don't require any traditional means of doing so, am I correct?"

The dogman nodded, and took in a full lungful of air before letting out an ear piercing howl that ululated across the forest.

A chorus of howls and barks answered from somewhere beyond the trees, sounding far closer this time.

Kera and Will tensed and scanned the trees. Kera noted that Smith seemed to freeze in place while working on Enaurl. The construct tried to sit up, but once again Smith pressed her back down.

The timbergnoll by the fire sent out another howl, and this time the cry went unanswered and the forest lay silent.

"Excellent," said Brenno. "Am I wrong to assume that had you not spoken with your kin just now, they would have assaulted us momentarily?"

"The air is thick with gnollkin blood," said the dogman. "They would have crushed you like a flood."

"I suspected as much," said Brenno. "I'll consider that a deposit towards sparing your life. I believe the next item on the agenda should be the matter of the information you have. I take it your previous offer to act as a guide was more metaphorical than literal, am I correct?"

"Leighlagh knows where dragons sleep; that I would go there is a leap."

"I feel like a simple 'no I will not go' would have been plenty," Will said, leaning backwards to lie against the stone he was sitting on, staring up into the stars above. "But what do I know? I'm not the one worshiping a freaky chimera god lady who wants me to speak in rhyme."

"Indeed, nor are you the one negotiating at the moment," said Brenno.

Tying off the bandage, he moved to stand behind the gnoll in order to begin covering more of the new pink flesh that marked where his previous wounds had been.

"I believe our bargaining might go a touch faster if we were introduced properly. What's more, I like to know the names of the people I do business with. It's a guild thing, you understand. What are you called?"

The gnoll was quiet, eyes moving from Will to Voldani to Kera and back. Brenno tapped on the gnoll's shoulder to make him look back, then gestured that the gnoll lift his arm so that Brenno could wrap the bandage across his chest. The gnoll obliged.

"It is Ratbite you meet this night," said the gnoll.

"Well met, Mister Ratbite. I am Mister Brenno Hornbuckle, certified pawnbroker and member in good standing of the Merchant's guild, and as such my word is my bond. Still, I could write up a contract if you'd like."

Brenno tied off the final bandage and walked back around to sit in front of the gnoll.

"You've got to be kidding me," Kera said as he walked. "Just ask him the questions and let him go, for the love of every god."

"I'm with her," Will said, yawning wide as he spoke. "We have no idea if anything you're doing right now is worth a damn. I don't care either way, I'm going to sleep."

"Right now?" Kera asked.

"I am drained," Will said, crossing his arms into a makeshift pillow under his head. "I'm all out of tricks. I mean, I'm never completely out, but the best I can probably do for you right now is make a tiny dancing girl illusion and some sparks. Can't even promise the sparks would hurt that much. Trust me, if we do end up getting attacked at three bells you're going to be damn glad I took a nap."

Will yawned again, readjusting his head to get more comfortable as he did.

"You kids have fun. Moon gods watch you."

"I have no idea what that means," said Kera.

"It means I'm sleeping now, leave me alone," Will answered.

"Leighlagh is a god of laws, else I'd have that one in my jaws." Ratbite snarled, licking his snout once more. "To barter I have sheathed my claws, and have since been wrapped and bound in gauze. I will not attack without just cause, I fear no wrath besides Leighlagh's."

"Excellent," said Brenno. "We are in agreement. The standing offer is your life in exchange for a ceasefire between your people and our caravan, in addition to any and all information you have about this dragon your god has told you about."

"I would like to know what else the mad god has to say about us," Voldani added.

"Lonesome for a new godly voice?" Ratbite said with a sneer. "Leighlagh would reward your choice."

Voldani stared hard at the timbergnoll.

"Hardly," she said. "My understanding of the gods is such that I am troubled to know that the Fanged One has deigned to take note of this feckless band."

"I say fuck all the time," Kera interjected.

"My point exactly," said Voldani.

"I take the proper offense to being called feckless," said Brenno. "Though I concede your point. Mister Ratbite, in addition to our peace treaty of sorts and any and all knowledge about this dragon you may have, we hereby include requesting all you know as to what your god has told you in regards to anything to do with us."

"The deal is struck in Leiglagh's name," said Ratbite. "Though I'd have told you just the same." Brenno nodded appreciatively.

"Leighlagh knows of what you do, knows motives false from intentions true. She wagered you could not hold true 'gainst the odds splayed against you. Had you been unable to subdue a motley band of twenty two, 'gainst drakes and more what could you do?"

"I don't like that he put the 's' on there," said Kera. "Singular is fine for me, one is good." Voldani crossed her arms.

"I care not how many dragons I must slay," said Voldani. "I am curious to know what could be considered 'more' beyond them."

Ratbite laughed, a high pitched manic laugh that was met by a chorus of equally mad laughter from the woods around the clearing.

"She gives us glimpses and commands, we are not required to understand," the gnoll said, still giggling to himself madly.

"You were all aware your own god might have been sending you to your deaths?" Brenno asked, his fingers steepled in front of his face.

"A swordsman she bade wield a chain," Ratbite said with a shrug and an eerie chuckle. "I did not ask; I merely came."

"What sort of god would throw her own people into the fire?" Kera asked.

Ratbite's eyes went to the crackling gnoll corpses in the pyre and he began to laugh, rolling backward with his grim mirth.

Kera blanched and shook her head.

"That's not what I meant, and is incredibly dark."

"Above all she knows survival, and sought to test what tests a rival," said

Ratbite. "Through my eyes she's seen an eyeful, might and magic and furies primal. You've all ascended nature's spiral, and lived to pass through Leighlagh's trial. We'll not harangue you all the while."

"As per our arrangement, of course," Brenno said with a nod.

"All the while of what?" Kera asked.

Confused, Brenno looked towards Kera.

"Excuse me?" Brenno asked.

"He said 'They'll not harangue us all the while', right?" Kera said, looking from Brenno to Ratbite. "Right, that's what you said? What does that mean? 'All the while' what, while we look for a dragon to kill? While we're on the road?"

"I know not and can't assume," said Ratbite. "She sings of steel and certain doom, of scales and veils and forge-lit fumes. Her song speaks of maws that seek to consume, of temples with a thousand rooms, of keys that lie in pilfered tombs where shadows breed and darkness looms."

Kera's breath caught in her throat.

Zephelous, are you hearing any of this? She sent to the sword. As before, the sword was silent and did not respond. *Of course not. Looming darkness actually comes up, and you're busy taking a power nap.*

"What of the dragon?" Voldani asked.

"Make your way north and there you'll find a prime example of their kind." Ratbite broke into a monstrous cackle as he finished his rhyme, and his mirth was once again echoed by the dozens of other voices in the woods.

Smith growled and threw down his wrench, pulling out his weapon. Wild eyed and veins bulging, he turned to face Ratbite.

"Tell your friends that I'm about to start shooting," Smith shouted, face red with exertion. "I've dealt with your bitch god and your insane kind before. Did she happen to mention that at all?"

Smith cocked the weapon, and the laughter from the forests fell silent. Dozens of gleaming golden eyes appeared all around the caravan,

"Only contract holds them back," Ratbite chuckled. "Though yours would be the first attack, know in good faith the pack reacts."

"And we appreciate the show of faith your kind has shown us by not already attacking, Mister Ratbite," said Brenno, hastily injecting himself into the exchange. "We also appreciate your candor, though we intend to abide by our ceasefire. Isn't that right, Mister Smith?"

Smith only answer was to spit on the ground, never breaking eye contact with Ratbite. The gnoll giggled to itself and stood, stretching to test its mobility while bandaged.

"We've done our duty here this day," Ratbite's maw began to drip saliva, and he shook his head from side to side as if he were a wet dog drying itself off. "Leighlagh's content with this fray, and we've told all she bade convey. Unless you intend to broker melee, pack your things, be on your way."

"We had hoped to set up camp for the night," Brenno said, furrowing his brow.

"If resting here had been your mission, you should have made it a condition," Ratbite laughed. "To tarry here is to give permission to succumb to a war of attrition."

"I understand," said Brenno. "Very well, we will move on."

Brenno marched towards the gnoll and looked up, far up, into the dogman's gleaming eyes. With hardly a quiver, the pawnbroker offered his hand towards the timbergnoll.

"Deal well struck, Mister Ratbite."

The timbergnoll seemed awestruck that the halfling was offering him a handshake. Moving slowly, as if dazed, the dogman accepted the handshake, eyes locked with Brenno's.

"And now this is a night of firsts," Ratbite said quietly, without so much as a chuckle. "Leave now, while your lives hold worth."

"I do not need to be told twice," said Kera, elbowing Will in the ribs.

The wizard woke with a start, sitting forward and bringing his hands in front of him.

"Are we being attacked?" Will asked.

"No, we're hitting the road," said Kera.

Brenno quickly gathered up his things, ferrying the piles of coins and the trinkets they'd deemed valuable enough to attempt to sell into the back of the wagon.

Smith snatched Enaurl's still severed arm off the makeshift table with a snort of disdain, helping Enaurl to her feet. The makeshift camp was hastily taken down, the wagon door reattached, and the companions piled in. In short order, the group was on the road again, their path illuminated only by the pair of torches at the front of the wagon.

Smith and Will chose to ride inside the wagon, along with Enuarl who Smith continued to work on. Voldani opted to ride on the roof of the caravan while Brenno and Kera sat up front. Hours passed in silence, with only the creak of the wheels and the occasional whine of the horses as they caught the scent of timbergnoll on the wind.

Golden eyes revealed themselves to Kera and Brenno from the treeline, as if reminding the group that they were still within the territory of the pack. The pair passed the time in silence, with Brenno holding the reins so tightly the leather nearly cut into his palms and Kera clutching Zephelous as if her life depended on it.

As time passed the number of eyes in the woods diminished, along with the frequency in which they appeared. The sky began to brighten as morning approached and the sun crawled its way across the horizon towards them.

At last, the first of its rays broke through the gloom, bringing with it a clear night and the gentle trill of early morning birdsong. Kera heaved a sigh of relief, letting herself rest back against the bench. From the corner of her eye, she watches as Brenno began to shake silently.

"Brenno, what's wrong?" Kera asked.

The halfling shook all the harder.

"Did you get bitten, or shot, or something?"

Kera sat forward and moved to inspect the halfling, only to be caught off guard as a peal of laughter erupted from the pawnbroker.

Kera arched an eyebrow.

"Uh, Brenno? Everything okay?"

"I shook his hand," said Brenno, wiping tears away from his face. "I, Brenno Hornbuckle, marched up to a timbergnoll and shook his hand. I even offered to write up a contract!"

The halfling laughed and laughed, and Kera found she couldn't suppress a smile.

The pawnbroker's mirth was contagious, and soon she found herself laughing as well.

Chapter Sixteen

As the sun rose over Zelwyr, it shone down against the prolific stained glass windows of the temple of Perrus. Bathed in the gentle rose-colored light of the morning sun through the windows of the Speaker's chambers, Morrillypallyke Smith stirred and stretched.

Her eyelids felt heavy as they fluttered open, exposing the opalescent eyes to the world. Sitting up, she found that the bed she was in was not her own, and grew afraid.

Nervous, she clutched at the luxurious silken blankets that covered her. The scent of warm cinnamon and freshly baked pastries wafted in to the room from somewhere beyond the door, and Morri felt her stomach growl hungrily in response.

She frowned, confused at the intensity of her morning hunger, and thought back to the last time she'd eaten. All at once, the memories of the incident with Kera and Brenno returned.

Her hands automatically moved to the place on her chest she'd seen the arrow break through, and was relieved to see an expertly wrapped bandage. It looked clean, as if the wound had been redressed recently.

Feeling as though this meant she was somewhere relatively safe, Morri relaxed and lowered the blanket. Spinning on her bottom, she swung her legs over the side of the bed and hopped down and out.

The brick floors were warm under her feet, and soft from wear and age. Curious, she took a slow walk around the bed and examined the room she was in. Besides an extensive row of bookshelves, there appeared to be little else in the room. She noticed a hook for hanging cloaks on the back of the door, but saw that it was currently unused. Besides a desk with dozens of books in various states of being read, there wasn't much else in the room.

Morri noticed then that the light in the place seemed to have an odd color to it, as if it were being filtered. She looked to the windows and instantly recognized the black and grey stained glass.

I'm in the temple of Perrus then, she thought. *Where are father and Enaurl? For that matter, where is Speaker Gerhardt?*

Her stomach rumbled its displeasure once again, and the aroma of cinnamon seemed stronger than ever.

I suppose it couldn't hurt to find out where that divine scent is coming from.

Seeing only one door to exit or enter the room, the large oak affair with a rounded top, Morri tiptoed her way to the heavy door. Just as she placed her hands on the iron handle, the door swung inward with a creak.

Startled, Morri let out a small shout and hopped backwards. Speaker Gerhardt, startled by Morri's squeak of shock, stumbled and nearly dropped the tray of food he was carrying.

"Good heavens!" Speaker Gerhardt shouted, nearly falling on his face as he staggered forward in an effort to prevent the food from sliding off of the tray. "Gods above! You nearly frightened the life out of me, child."

"I'm terribly sorry, Speaker Gerhardt," Morri gasped, rushing to help the Speaker by taking the tray from him and placing it onto the bed. "I had no idea you'd be coming in just then, I meant only to take a peek to see where you were."

"It's quite alright, young lady, quite alright," the Speaker said, smiling at Morri as he placed a hand on his heart. "Gave me quite a start, is all. I'm at no risk of dozing off during this morning's recollections, that's for certain."

The Speaker smiled warmly at Morri, catching his breath and moving to sit on the bed beside the food tray as he did.

"Whew!"

"As I said, I'm terribly sorry, Speaker," Morri apologized, moving to sit by the opposite end of the tray.

Her stomach growled in response to the proximity of the delicious smelling pastries. She eyed the plump cinnamon bun, marveling at the succulent spiral shape and still-molten sugar frosting.

Her mouth watered.

"Would it be terribly rude of me to assume one of these is meant for me?"

"Of course, how silly of me!" Speaker Gerhardt exclaimed. "Please, eat child, you must be famished. You've been asleep for the better part of a week I'm afraid."

Morri hastily tore into the cinnamon bun, its warmth and sweetened goodness filling her belly.

"A week?" Morri said, covering her mouth as she continued to chew. "Why was I unconscious for so long? Where are father and Enaurl?"

The Speaker's smile froze for a moment, and the elderly man looked away for a moment.

"I'm afraid it's a rather complicated story," said the speaker, rising to stand.

"Please, continue to eat, I'll do my best to recount it."

Reaching down to take a portion of the cinnamon bun on his side of the tray, the Speaker held it towards Morri the way a teacher might point with a pen as he began to speak.

"For starters, I'm sorry to say that you had been poisoned by Mister Hornbuckle. Quite inadvertently, from what I understand, but poisoned nonetheless. Your father was incensed, of course, and after he had Enaurl rush you here to me for medical aid he brought Kera and Brenno to the guard's office to see Warden Treia. I won't bore you with the details, mostly because I'm afraid I don't fully understand them, but it would seem that there is some legal action required in order to clear Mister Hornbuckle from responsibility, lest he face the death penalty for needlessly endangering the life of a child. Lady No-Clan too must face the courts, and it would seem that a witness was required. To that end, your father and Enaurl have taken it upon themselves to escort the pair of them to the high courts in Linreigh."

"I see," said Morri, speaking between bites. "It certainly makes sense. Though, I'm surprised to learn that father would opt to leave me behind without Enaurl."

"Lady Enaurl was required in order to prevent Lady No-Clan from fleeing," said the Speaker. "As was Lady Voldani, if you can believe that. You've made a very unusual friend, young Miss Smith. A rather dangerous one, at that."

Morri sighed, pausing to take a drink from the small cup of milk that had been laid out alongside her bun.

"Father did not seem fond of her either," said Morri. "And given the way in which recent events transpired, I'm prone to agree that it seems a continued friendship with her is unlikely at best. Still, I can't help it."

The Speaker dipped his chin closer to his chest, curious.

"Can't help what, child?" the Speaker asked, taking a deliberate sip of his own milk.

"It's hard to explain, Speaker," said Morri, shaking her head. "The reason father lets me help in the shop is that I can somehow... see things, sometimes. Not things exactly, but rather the connection between things, can understand the purpose for a component at a glance."

"I've marveled at your talent, truly," said the Speaker. "As does your father, of course."

"Thank you Speaker, only I don't bring it up to boast," Morri said, swallowing another piece of her breakfast. "What I mean is that while I've no idea why or for what purpose, when I see Kera I get the same sort of sensation I do as when I'm working on a gyroscopic stabilizer and find a coiled spring that's precisely the right size. I suppose that must sound like a load of gibberish to you, I do apologize."

"My dear, I have been a Speaker in this temple for nearly sixty years," Speaker Gerhardt said with a warm smile, reaching across the breakfast tray to pat the girl on the shoulder. "Believe me when I say that if there is anyone who should be apologizing for blathering nonsense in these halls, I would be the first in line to do so."

The Speaker laughed heartily at his own joke, and Morri joined him out of politeness. By the time the shared chuckle ended, Morri had finished the entirety of her breakfast. Still smiling, Speaker Gerhardt shoveled the uneaten half of his bun onto Morri's plate.

The girl's eyes widened like saucers.

"Speaker, I couldn't possibly," Morri began, only to have her protests waved away.

"Nonsense," said the Speaker. "Eat, eat. I insist. There is only so much sweetness I can stomach at my age, I'm afraid. Now, as I was explaining, or rather attempting to explain, your father has left you here with me in his absence, and promised to return as soon as possible."

"Did he provide a timeline for when I should expect his return?" Morri asked.

"Hard to say, unfortunately," said the Speaker. "Once a matter reaches the High Courts it can take some time to resolve."

Morri frowned. That was unusual of her father, the man whose daily routine could typically be predicted to the minute.

"Did he leave a note or any instructions for me to run the storefront?" The Speaker's smile again seemed to fade for a moment, which felt unusual to Morri.

"I believe he left a letter, yes," said the Speaker. "Only, I'll be damned to the shattered hells if I can remember what I've done with it. I'm sure it will turn up. As for instructions on running the shop, I was to inform you that you are to rest and relax, in order to ensure that you have fully recovered from the effects of the poison."

"I see," said Morri, feeling a small pang of anxiety at the pit of her stomach.

In all her life, she'd never spent as much time away from her father as she already had, and was now looking at three times that amount of time if not more.

"I don't suppose you might require any assistance or aid during my time here, Speaker Gerhardt?"

The speaker seemed to mull this over, stroking his beard for a moment as he thought on the idea.

"Well," he said at last, "I'm due to take make my rounds at the shared infirmary this morning. There's a young man there who very recently lost his leg, a wagon accident from what I understand. I was planning on using a portion of the church's goodwill reserves to purchase the young man a pair of crutches from the carpenter's guild. That's quite a walk for someone my age, I don't suppose I could convince you to go in my place?"

The Speaker beamed at Morri, all teeth and wrinkles.

"Certainly, Speaker," said Morri with nod, gulping down the last of the remaining cinnamon bun. "That poor young man."

"Yes, it's quite tragic," said the Speaker, sighing as he looked out through the nearest stained glass window. "I'm told he was something of a dancer, or he was when he wasn't working to support his mother and sisters. Still, he's alive, thank the gods."

Morri's eyes darkened as she fell deep in thought, noisily drinking the last of the milk in her cup. As she finished, her eyes went wide and shone with opalescence.

"I believe I may be able to offer him something better than a pair of crutches, Speaker," the young girl said, smiling bright as heaps of ideas piled into her brilliant young mind.

"I must admit, I was hopeful you might say something like that," the Speaker said, smiling softly as he stood and looked down at the small girl.

"Rather hopeful indeed."

Chapter Seventeen

Dawn stretched into early morning, and the skies remained glorious and clear throughout. The forest around the caravan seemed to change, becoming less dense and more hospitable, going from a place of constant danger to idyllic wooded copse.

The birdsong persisted and became a chorus as more woodland creatures woke and joined in the joyful song. In the hours since the pair had shared an adrenaline fueled laugh, Kera and Brenno had lapsed into a comfortable silence. They watched as the path the wagon traveled became more defined, widening enough that two wagons might pass side by side while becoming more worn and better maintained; less a path and more of a road.

As the daylight shone down on the road, the night's fear seemed to wash away. Zephelous still remained silent in Kera's hands, but the woman wasn't worried. Though it was silent, the sword felt as if it had a presence in her hands, and that was assurance enough.

Legs going numb from sitting for too long, Kera readjusted her posture and moved Zephelous close to her chest, a movement that Brenno caught out of the corner of his eye. The halfling mused for a moment, weighing out whether or not he wanted to break the silence that had settled in and speak with Kera.

"You know," said Brenno, having decided to start talking after all. "It never spoke with me, not a word."

"What's that?" Kera asked.

"The sword," Brenno clarified. "I had it in my store for two days, must have held it a dozen times. Polished it twice. Never bothered to speak with me."

"Oh," said Kera, unsure how to answer. She glanced at Zephelous.

"It spoke with Voldani," Brenno continued. "Smith seems terrified of it. I'd wager he still believes it's either evil or haunted. Knowing him, I suspect he believes it's a bit of both."

"You think?" Kera asked, smiling.

"Absolutely," said Brenno, turning back to watch the road. "For all his pragmatism, he's quite superstitious."

"I've never understood superstitious people," Kera said. "What's the point of worrying about spilling the salt in a world where the undead rising from their graves is a very real problem?" Brenno eyed Kera with a mixture of curiosity and doubt.

"I take it you've seen your fair share of reanimated corpses?" Brenno asked.

"Oh, sure," said Kera. "Probably more than my fair share, if I'm being honest. Skeletons, zombies, ghouls. I'm pretty sure I met a vampire once, but it might have just been some weirdo. You run a pawnshop, I'm sure you know how it is."

"I ran a pawnshop," Brenno corrected. "Hard to run anything after it's been incinerated."

"Fair," said Kera. "Would it help if I blamed it on the drugs?"

"No," said Brenno. "We are judged by our actions, not our intentions."

"Says who?" Kera asked.

"The courts, for one," said Brenno. "Laws are fairly straight forward. There are only so many ways 'do not burn down someone else's property' can be interpreted."

"Laws are stupid," Kera said. "They don't allow for context."

"I don't understand," said Brenno.

"Of course you wouldn't," said Kera.

"No, you misunderstand," said Brenno. "What I mean to say is that I understand what you mean. Please, elaborate." Kera was caught off guard by the halfling's lack of animosity towards her, or rather towards her topic of discussion.

"Do you actually care or are you just making conversation?" Kera asked.

"I suppose I could ask you the same," said Brenno. "I've not known someone with your... shall we say 'cultural heritage'? Do you have even the slightest interest in laws of any kind."

"There aren't many laws in the Wildlands," Kera admitted.

"So I've heard," said Brenno. "Among other things, of course."

"Look," Kera said, frustration evident in her tone. "I get that my people are basically a big joke to all you northerners because we're just *so* different, but if this is just going to turn into you making a bunch of quips about being uneducated and savage, I don't want to talk any more."

Brenno paused for a minute, choosing his words carefully.

"I meant no offense," said Brenno. "While I'm happy to say that I squarely place the blame for this entire misadventure on your shoulders, last night has made me reconsider my stance in regards to how I've treated you so far."

"Near death experiences will do that," Kera said. "But that's usually not real, that's just the adrenaline talking. You'll be right back to hating me by sundown."

"For someone so set against being prejudiced, you seem to make an awful lot of judgments," Brenno said with a scowl. "My campaigning days may be behind me, but they aren't so far gone that I remember how much easier it is to sleep when the band isn't at each other's throats throughout the entire way."

"I didn't realize you were actually a campaigner before all this," Kera said.

"Do I not strike you as the adventurous sort?" Brenno asked.

"Honestly?" Kera began, letting the question hang. "Not even a little bit." Brenno chuckled, offering the reins to Kera. The woman took the leather straps, and watched as the halfling produced a small pipe and a rolled ball of tobacco.

"That's good," said Brenno, pulling hard on the pipe.

"You didn't light it," Kera remarked, only to watch as Brenno exhaled a puff of smoke.

"Self lighting," Brenno explained. "Bought it from a wizard who was particularly down on his luck. Needed coin to get out of Zelwyr and back to the capital. I was happy to assist."

"So long as you came out on top," Kera added.

"Well of course," Brenno said, pausing to take another lungful of smoke. "I'm a businessman, not a charity. If you want selflessness and sacrifice, talk to Voldani or that addled old man, Speaker Gerhardt."

`"Who wishes to speak with me?" Voldani asked, her sudden injection into the conversation startling Brenno enough that he fumbled with his pipe. Kera leaned backwards and looked straight up towards the lip of the caravan's ceiling. Sitting there, leaning slightly over the edge in order to peer down at Kera and Brenno, was Voldani.

"Morning, pretty lady," Kera said with a smile.

"Flattery is a waste of words," Voldani said.

"'And a pleasant morning to you as well, Kera the Magnificent'," Kera said, doing her best impression of Voldani's rigid manner of speaking.

"I do not speak in that manner," Voldani said crossly.

"'That is correct'," Kera said, continuing her impression. "*Truly, this is the manner in which I speak. How was morning watch, Kera the Illustrious?*' Oh, it was fine. Few eyes in the woods, something snarling and laughing in the darkness, no big deal. *'It sounds as though you must have shown a great amount of courage and fortitude to keep watch and remain sane.'* You know, I *do* feel pretty brave, so thank you for saying that."

Voldani glared at Kera.

"I would not say any of those things," said Voldani, retreating away from the lip of the caravan. "What's more, you have not earned one of those titles. Assigning them to yourself removes all meaning from them."

"Ouch," Kera said, clutching at her heart in mock pain. "Voldani, that's cold."

When Voldani didn't respond, Kera shook her head and looked back towards the halfling, catching the pawnbroker heaving in silent laughter. Still chuckling to himself, the pawnbroker turned back to face the road. Suddenly Voldani shouted.

"There is someone on the path!" the scion yelled.

Brenno's head snapped forward, his eyes going wide with fear. Sure enough, he saw a woman, an adult human wearing a fine floral dress, standing just in front of the wagon, arms crossed expectantly. She seemed unafraid, glaring towards Brenno while staring near enough that she was about to be run over.

Quick as he could Brenno jumped to his feet and snatched the reins from Kera, hauling on them with all his strength in an effort to bring the horses into a skidding halt.

The animals, startled by the sudden flurry of activity, snapped to attention in an effort to follow through their rider's commands, their hooves coming to a thundering halt mere inches in front of the woman.

Kera was thrown to the floor of the wagon as it lurched to a stop, and rolled off the seat and onto the ground.

Voldani staggered forward and nearly toppled over the ledge, stopping herself just short of falling over. A series of dull thumps sounded inside the carriage, followed by a muffled train of curses from Smith.

Kera winced as she rubbed the back of her head, the part of her body she'd had the great fortune of landing on first as she fell, throbbed with pain. Snatching up Zephelous and snapping it into its improvised sheath, and feeling more annoyed than hurt, Kera stomped her way around the over-sized horses to confront the stranger.

"Shattered hells, lady," Kera called to the woman, still rubbing the back of her head. "What's your problem? Are you trying to get yourself killed?" The woman's gaze didn't move from staring straight towards the Caravan.

"Goddamnit, Will Decker," the woman said. Kera stared at the woman.

"You know Will?" Kera asked. The woman didn't answer, and her gaze didn't move. Kera took the moment of silence as an opportunity to better scrutinize the stranger who seemed to know Will. The woman looked to be about Kera's age, perhaps a little older. Her hair was a shade of auburn that seemed to be at once either reddish-brown or brownish-red, depending on how the light hit it. Her eyes were hard and hazel, glaring forward with focus and what looked like serious intent to cause damage. Kera instantly recognized the expression from personal experience, and found herself struggling to decide whether or not she should find this situation amusing or not.

"Oh yeah, you know him alright," Kera said. "Should I go get him for you, or?"

"I know you can hear this, William," the woman said, still glaring hatefully towards the carriage. "Just like I know you read the letter."

"Okay then," said Kera, "Do you maybe want to just go talk to him, or are you going to stick with the shouting?"

"How many times do we have to go over this?" the woman continued. "This is it, I have to move on. You need to start doing better."

"This seems like it's getting really personal," said Kera. "Maybe you guys should just, like, go somewhere and talk like normal people who are not wizards do?"

"I don't know who put that void in your heart, Will Decker," the woman shouted. "All I know is that it wasn't me, and you need to stop shaping that hole to look like me in hopes that I'll be able to fill it." Kera threw her hands in the air and turned to walk away.

"Fine, do it your way," Kera said, grimacing as she shook her head and stomped off ahead of the caravan. "I'll just go to where I can't hear you, which is the exact opposite of what would make sense, but that's what I'm going to do because wizards are fucking weird. You keep talking through walls or whatever."

Brenno, still gathering himself up from the floor of the caravan, took the rein and held them, climbing to stand on top of the chair in an effort to look over the horses at the shouting woman.

"Madam, I hope you realize that had you been injured the fault would be wholly on yourself!" the pawnbroker shouted, visibly agitated as he dusted himself off and smoothed his cloak. "Surely you could have found a more appropriate means to resolve this quarrel?"

"I agree," said Voldani, rising to stand on the roof of the caravan. "While I would never wish ill-fortune on an individual, I would be hard pressed to sympathize with any wounds you may have acquired."

"I second the thought," Brenno said, glowering at the woman.
She ignored Brenno and Voldani, scowling at the caravan with a sudden increase in ferocity.

"There's nothing left of who I was back then, Will," the woman called. "I'm not the person you remember. I took the knife that is the memory of you and used it to carve my soul into a new shape. This is what I am now, a marionette. It's your fault, and you know it is."

"If you're intent on having this conversation through walls, would you mind stepping a few feet to the side to have it?" Brenno said, sighing with exasperation. "Even just a few paces?"

The woman didn't move, and continued to stare.

Brenno sighed once again, heavier this time.

"My lady, you seem very determined, and determination is a quality I value highly. With that being said, could I please entice you to step off the path just for a moment? I'm happy to offer you a few silver pieces convince you to step aside?"

The woman scoffed.

"How could you say that to me?" The woman on the road asked.

"Madam, there is no offense in accepting a payment for services rendered," said Brenno, scowling. "It's not as if I'm trying to bribe you."

"It seems very much like bribery," said Voldani.

"I'm not asking her to do anything illegal," Brenno said. "I'm simply asking her to accept coin in exchange for doing something for me."

"You are not convincing me," said Voldani.

She stood tall and drew one of her swords, using it to point down at the woman from the top of the caravan.

"Sister, I ask that you step aside. Whatever quarrel you have with the mountebank is between you and he, there is no need for you to be impeding our progress."

The woman shook her head, locks of auburn swaying from side to side as she did.

"You're a coward," she said.

"I beg your pardon?" Voldani asked, drawing her second sword so quickly it seemed to leap into her hands.

"A godsdamned coward," the woman said.

"Say that to me a third time," Voldani said, her golden wings flickering into existence. The rear door of the caravan flung themselves wide as Smith booted it open from the inside.

"What's with the driving, Hornbuckle?" Smith hollered. "I almost had the bicep reattached, then you slammed on the breaks and sent Enaurl rolling across the floor like a damn log down a hillside."

"Apologies, Smith," Brenno shouted back. "It would seem our illusiomancer friend has something of a visitor, and that said visitor is determined to speak her peace while standing in the middle of the road. Would you care to send him forward?"

"I'll wake him up," Smith grumbled, disappearing into the back of the caravan.

"I need to move along," the woman on the road shouted.

"Yes, precisely!" Brenno agreed.

"I can't keep waiting on you like this," the woman said.

"Now I'm afraid you've lost me," said Brenno.

"What's everyone shouting about?" Will said, emerging from the back of the caravan, rubbing the sleep from his eyes.

"Ah, there you are," said Brenno. "You have a guest."

"A guest?" Will asked, looking as though he were still half asleep.

"Of sorts," said Brenno. "If you could come and speak with her, that would be great. If you could convince her to move from standing directly in front of the horses, that would be even better."

Will nodded, stretching his arms out to the side as he made his way down the ramp at the back of the caravan. He waggled each of his fingers individually, flexing them and tensing them in a series of warm ups. Seeing Kera off to the side of the road, Will offered her a wave.

"Hey Kera," he called. "Whatcha doing over there?"

"Trying to keep out of your personal problems," Kera shouted back.

"What personal problems?" Will asked, rounding in front of the horses as he did.

Seeing the auburn-haired woman standing there, Will stopped dead in his tracks, eyes going wide as his jaw fell open for a moment. He recovered quickly, snapping his jaw shut with a clack.

"Ah."

"I need to put my energies elsewhere," the woman yelled, still facing towards the caravan. "Frankly, you should too."

Will's expression sank into a deep grimace.

"Yeah, you said it," Will said, raising his hands up in front of him.

Bringing the tips of his fingers together into a cluster, he then twisted his palms outward from each other while splaying his fingers out as wide as they would go.

The woman exploded, bursting into a thousand blue and red sparks. Brenno and Kera gasped. Voldani leapt into the air, using her wings to let herself glide into a flying tackle that brought Will to the ground.

"A mountebank and a murderer," Voldani seethed, pointing the tip of her sword at Will's throat. "I should execute you here and now."

"Easy, Voldani, easy!" Will said, hands raised in surrender as he looked up into the vengeful radiance that was Voldani. "She isn't real, I didn't murder anyone."

"She is nothing now, that much is clear," Voldani said, gesturing to the place where the woman stood just moments before.

"She was always nothing," Will exclaimed. "Well, no, that's not true. She was everything. The only thing. But that… that wasn't her, that was just a memory."

"So many words out of your mouth," Voldani said, "and none of them a satisfactory explanation."

The sword tip pressed harder against Will's throat.

"She's just a memory," Will said, gulping against the cold steel of Voldani's sword against his skin. "An apparition, and illusion of something that was probably never real in the first place but won't go away."

"Explain yourself," said Voldani, scowling at Will.

"I am!" Will shouted.

"Do a better job of it," Voldani hissed, leaning closer towards Will.

"Okay, okay!" Will shouted, bringing his hands closer. "I'm going to bring her back, just don't stab me when you see me doing magic, okay?"

"This had better not be a trick," Voldani threatened, applying more pressure to Will's throat with the blade.

"It's not, gods," Will said, gasping as the blade pressed in, just at the point of threatening to pierce into his skin. "Just look, okay? Watch."

Will's eyes shone with a gentle teal-colored light, and he waved his hands through the air in front of him. His range of motion was hampered by the sword, and he gently tapped on it twice with his thumb to convey this to Voldani. The woman growled and moved the sword a few inches away, allowing Will to finish his spell weaving. With a pop, the woman reappeared in the spot she'd been standing just moments before. She was smiling this time, strumming a wooden guitar.

"See?"

Voldani looked from Will to the woman and back, slowly sheathing her sword. Making her way towards the guitar playing woman, Voldani slowly reached a hand out towards her shoulder. Instead of coming down to rest on it, the hand passed through the woman entirely. Swiping her hand from side to side through the woman's shoulders to test the illusion further, Voldani turned back to face Will.

"Why did you conjure her onto the road?" Voldani asked.

"I didn't," said Will.

"I mean no offense," said Brenno. "But clearly, you did."

"Okay, yes," said Will. "I did technically conjure her, but I didn't mean to."

"The amount of words you speak compared to the amount of information you disperse continues to infuriate me," Voldani said.

"I'm beginning to agree with Voldani," said Brenno, watching the guitar player. "She is rather beautiful."

"She is," said Will. "That's besides the point. The point is, she's not real." Will repeated his twisting finger cluster explosion motion, and the woman laughed and burst into sparks once more. Her laughter, light hearted and daring, lingered after her image was dispelled. Will grimaced and sat up. Kera shouted at him from the roadside.

"Are we done exploding people now?" Kera yelled, cupping her hands in front of her mouth. Will offered a rude hand gesture in her direction. "I can't see that, I'm too far away." Shaking his head in dismay, Will waved his hands and fingers through the air, and a moment later a giant illusory hand formed above his head. Partly transparent and glowing, the hand was easily twice the size of Will. It curled into a fist and raised its middle finger, aimed at Kera's direction. "Real classy," Kera shouted, making her way back towards the wagon. Answering Will's unspoken command, the giant hand rolled over in the air and plucked the wizard off the ground the way a child might pick up a marble. Lifting Will into the air, the hand deposited him on his feet. Brenno furrowed his brow.

"How is it an illusion can be tangible?" Brenno asked.

"I don't know what you mean," said Will.

"The hand touched you, lifted you from the ground," Brenno explained. "But Voldani's arm was able to pass clear through that woman just a moment before."

"That's the difference between a wizard who does illusion magic and a dedicated illusiomancer," said Will with a shrug, dusting himself off. "I can weave spell effects into the illusions. Try not to overthink it."

"I will not think about it at all if I can help it," said Voldani, making her way back to the caravan as she did. "I have learned that attempting to converse with you is all but impossible, and will strive to avoid doing so in the future."

"Ouch," said Will. "For some reason, that's really hurtful."

"It was not my intention to harm you," said Voldani.

"Is that an apology?" Will asked.

"No," said Voldani. With a powerful flap of her wings, the divine warrior lifted herself up into the air and flew her way back to the roof of the carriage. Brenno cleared his throat.

"If I may," said the halfling, "You have yet to explain this mishap."

"Yeah," Will admitted. "I was kind of hoping we could collectively just forget it and move on. It's not too late, if we all commit we can still do it."

"I'm afraid I'll have to pass on your generous offer," Brenno said. "I'd like an explanation, or at least a warning as to whether or not I should expect phantoms to be appearing on a regular basis."

"Illusions aren't phantoms," said Will. "They're nothing, just shaped fragments of memory filled with magic."

"An important distinction, I'm sure," said Brenno, somewhat haughtily. "Now, should I be expecting this to be a regular occurrence or not?" Will dismissed the illusory hand with a snap of his fingers. Looking tired and rueful, he shook his head.

"No?" He said, rubbing his eyes and making his way back to the caravan.

"That seemed more like a question than a statement," Brenno said.

"Maybe it was," said Will.

"Do you see?" Voldani said. "He is incapable of providing an answer to any query."

"I agree," Brenno said with a nod. "It is exceedingly frustrating."

"What's frustrating?" Kera asked, rejoining the group around the caravan.

"Trying to get an illusionist to give a straight answer," said Brenno.

"Ah," said Kera, looking from Brenno to Will. "So, what was up with the ghost filled with your emotional baggage?"

Will scowled.

"She wasn't a ghost, she was--"

"An illusion, yes. That much we know," said Brenno.

"Isn't that enough of an answer?" Will asked.

"No," said Kera, Brenno, and Voldani answered simultaneously.

"Fine," said Will, stopping just short of entering the caravan. "I maybe sort of might have a little bit of a control problem." Will's explanation was met with silence.

"Which means… what, exactly?" Kera asked.

"It means that sometimes illusions just… happen," Will said.

"Unintentionally?" Brenno asked.

"Sometimes," said Will. "Unintentionally, or subconsciously, or unconsciously."

"Unconscious as in when you're sleeping," Kera said, nodding. "That explains a lot."

"No," said Brenno, disagreeing. "It doesn't. It explains what just happened, but it doesn't explain why it happened. Furthermore, it doesn't answer the question of whether or not it might happen again in the future."

"It is as I've said," said Voldani. "Many words spent, yet very little information given."

"I actually agree with Voldani," said Kera.

"Why are you surprised that what I have to say is correct?" Voldani asked.

"I'm not," said Kera. "I just mean that I agree with you."

"Do so without shock next time," said Voldani. "I am often correct."

"Noted," said Kera, firing a mock salute in Voldani's direction. "So, what's the deal, Will? Is that going to happen more or what?" Will's shoulders slumped, and he let his forehead bang against the wall of the caravan.

"I don't know," he said. "Probably?"

"I can work with probably," Kera said with a shrug. "Let's get going."

"You don't want to know why it happens?" Will asked. "Or why I can't control it?"

"Do you want to tell me those things?" Kera asked. Will shook his head.

"Not particularly," the wizard mumbled.

"There you go then," said Kera. "Let's get back on the road."

"That's all you require as an explanation?" Brenno asked, raising an eyebrow at Kera. "By all accounts, it seems the man accidentally conjured an illusion of a woman who stopped us on the road to berate him for failing as a lover."

"I did not fail as a lover," said Will. "I failed her at being everything else."

"Is it really worth making the distinction?" Brenno asked. Will was silent, thumping his head against the caravan once more. "I'll take that as a 'no'," the pawnbroker said.

"Listen," said Kera, pulling herself up into the bench. "We've all got shit."

"I do not possess excrement," Voldani interjected.

"You know what I meant, Voldani," Kera said. "Just because our ghosts don't show up on the street to yell at us doesn't mean they don't exist."

"I am not afraid of ghosts," said Voldani.

"What about silence?" Will asked.

"I beg your pardon?" said Voldani.

"I spent most of last night chained to you," said Will. "I heard every weird ass rhyme those dogmen had to say to you about your god. Or should I say your apparently dead god?"

"I didn't know gods could die," said Kera.

"They can indeed," said Brenno. "Gods died in droves during the War of the Black Flight." Kera furrowed her brow.

"I thought they just became the new gods," said Kera. "Perrus is one of the new gods, isn't she Voldani?"

"Yes," Voldani answered with a nod. "She and her brother, Perroh, have only graced this plane with their presence for a handful of centuries."

"Was she an old god before she was Perrus?" Kera asked. "Or was she just not a thing?"

"In truth, I do not know," said Voldani. "We are taught in the temple that endings foster beginnings, and that were it not for the calamity of the War, the so-called new gods would not have come to our plane. I am not a Speaker, I am merely a disciple."

"Okay, but, like…" Kera said, pausing to choose her words. "You're an angel. Doesn't that mean you can just ask the gods?"

"I am not an angel," Voldani said.

"But what about the wings?" Kera said, using her hands to mime a wingspan. "And the glowing eyes and the flying?"

"They are gifts from my divine heritage," said Voldani. "They denote that my ancestors have been blessed in the past."

"Blessed how?" Kera asked.

"I cannot say," said Voldani. "While I may grasp the power within me, and recognize from where it comes, I am but a mortal. I claim no knowledge of what the gods portend."

"Can't you just ask, though?" Kera asked. Voldani was silent for a moment.

"I have," said the warrior woman.

"And?" Kera asked.

"Perrus has not seen fit to answer," said Voldani.

"Oh," said Kera.

"Does this surprise you?" Voldani asked.

"A little," said Kera. "I would think that if I were a god, I'd be pretty keen on answering the questions my little demigod children might have."

"I am not a demigod," said Voldani.

"Then what exactly are you?" Kera asked.

"There are many words for people like me," said Voldani. "Many in the church call us divinekin. Many call my people the god-blooded. In the capital, I recall being referred to as a scion." Kera nodded.

"What do you prefer to be called?" Kera asked.

"Voldani is fine," said Voldani.

"Fair enough," said Kera.

"Are there not god-blooded among your kind?" Brenno asked.

"Supposedly," said Kera. "When I was a child I heard rumors that the chieftain of the Fire Carrier tribe became a scion after earning the blessing of Forgg, but it was only ever a rumor." Brenno scratched at his chin thoughtfully.

"Forgg," Brenno began. "Remind me, is that the orc god of war, or the god of the forge?"

"All orc gods are gods of war," Kera said. "Some are just into stuff besides conquering."

"Well yes," Brenno said with a smirk. "But specifically, which is Forgg?"

"I have no idea," said Kera.

"Forgg, the Tyrant King," Voldani said. "God of piracy, pillaging, and spoils."

"There you have it," said Kera.

"Forgg is native to your homeland, is he not?" Brenno asked. "How is it a northerner knows more about your own regional deities than you do?"

"Do I seem to you like someone who gives a damn about the gods?" Kera asked. Brenno shrugged.

"You seem to know a good amount about the past, specifically in regards to what value various items might have," said Brenno. "I would think theology would go hand in hand with archaeology." Kera shook her head.

"We don't exactly have a lot of temples in the Wildlands," she said. "Markets and vendors aren't even that common."

"Then where did you acquire your knowledge from?"

"What knowledge are you even talking about?" Kera asked quizzically. "I go to places where dead people buried other dead people, and check to see if anything valuable was buried alongside them. I have no idea what knowledge you're talking about."

"Well," Brenno said, caught off-guard. "You have to locate these tombs and graves, do you not?"

Kera shrugged.

"I guess so," the woman admitted. "Mostly I just go to shithole taverns and do a lot of listening. It doesn't take a genius to rob graves."

"Clearly," Brenno said, seemingly dismayed. "Can we get on the road already? We're wasting a lot of daylight, and I would like to put as much distance between myself and that forest as possible."

"No objections here," Will said, slapping the side of the wagon twice. "How long until we swap roles?"

"Another two hours," said Brenno, looking up at the wayward moon, already part way to its zenith.

Will nodded.

"I'll tell Smith."

"Yes, do that," said Brenno. "Try not to nod off if you can avoid it. I would hate to have to deal with more of your… problems."

Will grimaced.

"Right," said the wizard, ducking into the carriage and closing the door behind him.

Kera gave Brenno a sidelong glance, watching as the halfling effected a self-satisfied smirk. Deciding it was better to say nothing, Kera puffed air out from between her lips and got comfortable, resting her boots on the front of the wagon while using her arms as a makeshift headrest.

I fucking hate campaigning, she thought. *Fighting I can deal with, but all this crap in the middle is just the worst.*

Chapter Eighteen

The infirmary, a colossal wooden building that had once been a noble estate long ago in Zelwyr's history, loomed over the small girl like a mountain. The wind blew a fair smell like rotting meat towards her, and she wrinkled her nose in disgust. The shadow of the building felt heavy, weighted with the suffering within.

"Are you prepared, Miss Smith?" Speaker Gerhardt asked, startling the girl.

"Speaker, you surprised me," Morrillypallyke said, clutching at her chest to slow her thumping heart. "I believe so. Though I must admit I feel a touch apprehensive."

"Yes, I would imagine so," said the Speaker, nodding his head slowly. "To my knowledge, you've not spent any time in the infirmary due to illness thus far in your young life, isn't that so?" Morri nodded.

"I'm afraid that's not entirely correct, Speaker," the girl said. "From what I understand, I spent a very brief period of time here during my infancy after my mother… Or rather, just before my mother… Perhaps I should say 'while my mother'…"

The Speaker gently placed his hands on the girl's shoulders from behind.

"Ah, yes," said the Speaker, patting the poor girl's shoulders twice. "How could I have forgotten your mother's death? Such a tragedy. Your poor father, a wreck physically and emotionally. You, barely old enough to walk. Your mother, fighting to the very last. What a proud and formidable woman she was. I remember that day well."

"You were there, Speaker?" Morri asked, tilting her head to look the Speaker in the face.

"Briefly," Speaker Gerhardt said with a nod. "And only at the very end."

"What was she like?" Morri asked.

"Does your father not speak of her?" the Speaker asked.

"He does, yes," said Morri. "But scarcely, and only when pressed. Her memory pains him, that much is plain. I only wish I had a memory of her to cling to whatsoever, for all the respect and admiration she seems to have earned." The Speaker nodded solemnly for a moment.

"I've often felt that the word 'hero' has become overused," said the old man.

"As such, I would not use it for your mother. Rather, I would call her a champion."

"The term champion implies victory," said Morri. "Victory implies a struggle." The Speaker smiled and nodded.

"What I wouldn't give for a dozen disciples as astute as you, young lady Smith," said the Speaker. "Yes, there was much struggle in your mother's life, most of which she triumphed over. She was one of Zelwry's finest guards during the Unearthing Siege."

"Unearthing?" Morri repeated. "As in, to uncover from the earth?"

"You are correct, yes," said the Speaker. "Are you familiar with the War of the Black Flight?" Morri nodded.

"I've done my fair share of reading on the subject," said the young girl. "Some refer to it as the birthplace of modern artifice."

The Speaker stroked his beard.

"Is that so?" Gerhardt asked. "I wasn't aware of that."

"Oh, yes, Speaker," Morri said, smiling with enthusiasm. "Some of the machines produced by dwarven artificers in Blackmouth during the war still function today, albeit this is largely due to extensive maintenance and upkeep efforts - not to mention complete retrofitting of various bits of the machinery."

"Yes, I've heard quite a few interesting tidbits about the dwarves and their machines," the Speaker said with a nod.

Morri gave the Speaker a curious look.

"You've never struck me as being particularly interested in artifice," said Morri.

"Oh my dear," the Speaker began, smiling earnestly. "You don't get to be my age without hearing a thing or two about most everything under the sun and both moons."

"A fair point," the girl said, turning back to face the infirmary. "I sometimes forget that I am so young. Such an odd thing to forget, isn't it?"

"Not at all," said the Speaker, giving the girl another reassuring pat. "Especially not when your extraordinary talents are taken into consideration."

"I merely dabble in artifice at my father's shop, Speaker," the young girl said, shivering slightly as the wind picked up once more. "I will admit that my vocabulary is rather extensive, and my ability to comprehend and retain is rather impressive. However, given that there are men and women in this world who can conjure living beings of fire into existence using nothing but sheer will power, I would hardly call myself gifted."

The Speaker chuckled softly.

"Let us agree to disagree," said the old man, stepping out from behind the girl and making his way to the entrance of the infirmary. "Shall we press on?" The girl looked over the infirmary once more. She nodded, feeling daunted but resolved.

"I don't suppose there's any point in prolonging it," said the girl.

"I hope you understand that your presence here is not mandatory," the Speaker said, turning back to face the girl, his expression one of deep concern.

"No, of course not," said the girl. "But there is a young man in there who I may be able to help, as I helped with Charles."

"Without your father present, are you certain you can still aid him?" the Speaker asked.

"Yes, Speaker," said the girl. "There are some elements of artifice that can be mastered in a short amount of time, even one as short as my own young life."

"Good, good," said the Speaker, gesturing for the girl to take the lead.

Morri did as she was bade, climbing the stairs up to the massive door made of black oak with bronze trimming. Carved into the wood was a mural of Perroh and Perrus, twin gods of death and medicine, meeting at the fabled crossroads between life and death. Perroh, a sickly and broken young man, offering his sister a patchwork soul in one hand while accepting a meager and frail looking one in the other.

"When we step inside, we will be greeted by the black priests. Do not be alarmed at their unusual garb."

The girl nodded, and approached the doors with some hesitation. Arriving at the top of the stairs, she paused. Reaching for the brass knocker, feeling its weight in her hand, she exhaled.

Her nerves and emotions were running rampant at the thought of entering this place, this awful dark place full of suffering and pain, this terrible building that had taken her mother from her. She felt the Speaker's eyes on her without the old man needing to say a word.

Redoubling her resolve, she lifted the heavy knocker and let it fall. The thump of the bronze against the oak echoed, reminding Morri of her father and his thunder cannon. She hoped he would not be gone much longer. The double doors opened inward, and the Speaker stepped in. Realizing she should follow, Morri stepped in as well.

The heavy doors swung shut, closing with another echoing thud. She found herself in a small and dimly lit room, no larger than fifteen feet in either direction. A second set of double doors awaited at the other end of the room.

"Just the two of you?" A distorted voice asked, speaking from somewhere beside the doors.

Morri turned to see who it was and gasped. Standing behind her and to the side of the door was what appeared to be a human - or at least humanoid - man dressed in a mix between armor and the carcass of an enormous insect.

The face mask featured a pair of bulbous red orbs that covered much of the face. The arms and legs had jagged protrusions on the backs of them, very much organic by design. Morri recognized the base material as being chitin, fitted in places with steel rivets and sections of leather which connected the armor and formed a sealed suit.

"Yes, just the two of us for now," the Speaker said. "Though I suspect the young lady will be needing some of her tools and supplies brought over in the immediate future. Would someone available to acquire a few things? A cart load at the most, I should think."

The person inside the insect suit nodded.

"Isn't that Smith's girl?" the black priest asked. "Surprised she's down here."

"Yes, I am," said Morri. "I should also like to make a note of saying that I prefer being addressed directly when I am being spoken to."

The man chuckled, the noise sounded weird and bottled inside the insect helmet.

"Yep, you're Smith's girl alright," said the priest. "Alright, if you want in, I need to cleanse you first."

"Cleanse me?" Morri asked, surprised. "Cleanse me from what exactly?"

"Whatever you might bring in accidentally," the man in the suit said. "It's harmless, really. The only thing that's going to happen is that this room will get foggy for a few seconds. Don't be alarmed. Oh, and the fog is going to be a sort of bright yellow. It's sort of like soap, but for your whole body."

Morri gave the man in the suit a hard look.

"I beg your pardon, sir priest," said Morri. "But an air-soluble antibacterial is hardly the same as 'soap for your whole body'."

The man turned his bug-eyed helmet towards Morri and said nothing for a moment. He fixed the ruby orbs on the Speaker once more.

"Definitely Smith's kid," said the priest, tinny laughter echoing inside the helmet.

"She is indeed," said the Speaker. "And very much her mother's daughter."

"Never knew her," said the priest, pulling down on a chain that ran upwards before disappearing into a box-like contraption on the ceiling. "Heard she was something else."

"*Something else* hardly covers it," said the Speaker. "She was a fighter, a crusader. There is a very real chance Zelwyr still stands thanks to her."

"Ah, a crusader," the priest said. Something behind the wall hissed and squeaked, and a thick yellow mist billowed down from somewhere up above. "I didn't realize she was one of yours. Well, one of the church's, I should say."

"No, I'm afraid she was not under Perrus's banner," said the Speaker.

"Too bad," said the priest. "Can't win 'em all, eh?"

The yellow mist filled the room completely, so thick it obscured Morri's view of the priest and Speaker Gerhardt. The mist had a distinctly sterile smell to it, an odor that reminded Morri of rubber and ozone and dust.

The priest pulled on the chain once more, the sound of its links rattling the only indicator that he had done so.

The mist dissipated and eventually cleared, leaving the three of them standing in the small room as before. With a nod of his bulbous helmet, the death priest knocked an elaborate pattern on the inner door of the infirmary. The pattern was met with a double-tap knock in response, and the inner door opened.

Unsure of what to do, Morri looked from the Speaker to the priest and back, waiting for a sign of confirmation from one or the other. The priest ducked through the inner door first. Speaker Gerhardt, catching Morri's gaze, gestured for the girl to lead the way.

Morri obliged and followed the black priest into the inner sanctum of the infirmary.

The Speaker followed, and the doors once again clanged shut.

Morri was startled as a sudden hiss-pop noise sounded. Looking for the source of the sound, she saw that the priest had removed his insect helmet. The face beneath it made her wish he hadn't.

The man's face was so hideously burnt it looked as though his face had melted away. Morri gasped, causing the priest to look at her.

"Oh, right," the black priest said, moving to replace his helmet. "Sorry, kid."

"No, no. It's fine, there's no need for that," Morri said, gesturing for the priest to stop replacing his helmet. "I'm the one who should apologize, for being so rude in regards to your disfigurement. Leave the helmet off, I insist. It must be terribly hot inside."

The black priest smiled an uncomfortable looking smile, teeth visible through most of his face regardless. He snapped the helmet down and twisted it into place. The suit made a faint hissing sound as it sealed up.

"Kid, you're an absolute sweetheart," said the priest, setting off down the corridor in front of him. "Just don't take up gambling."

Morri's face went flush and her ears burned with embarrassment. She followed behind the black priest, looking everywhere except where he stood. The corridor was wide, thirty feet across from side to side.

Each side of the corridor was lined with makeshift beds, sacs of fabric filled with straw atop a wooden table, most of which were occupied by the various sick folk of Zelwyr.

Here, a fisherman recovered from surgery to remove a deadly parasite acquired during a coastal voyage. There, a man bound in bandages lay still next to a pile of rent and battered armor. Some were very sickly, hacking and spewing and wheezing. Others slumbered in sleeps far too deep to be natural.

"He's just a little further, Speaker," the black priest apologized, voice buzzing slightly through the mouthpiece of the helmet. "Sorry about the walk. We were going to move him closer to the entrance, but things took a turn for the worse."

"A turn for the worse how, Pephe?" the Speaker asked.

"For starters, we weren't able to save the leg," said Pephe, stopping just before a large white sheet that had been erected to act as a makeshift wall.

Morri couldn't help but notice that much of the sheet was covered in what looked like fresh blood stains. Pephe pulled the sheet aside, revealing a bed with a young man on top of it.

The man was dressed only in a simple loincloth, his left leg amputated just above the knee, wrapped neatly in tightly bound bandages. His other limbs were entirely wrapped in bandages as well, but while the bandages on the amputated limb were white and fresh these were stained yellow and black. A black ooze visibly dripped from the underside of the bandages, droplets of a substance that looked more like tar than blood beading up and dropping onto the floor with a plop.

"Gods of Light," the Speaker gasped. "What manner of infection is this?"

Pephe shook his head.

"It's not just an infection," the black priest said. "There's a magical element at work here. We've had sages, scholars, and seers take a look at that stuff coming out of him, and whatever it is, it isn't blood. The fluid he was carrying in the wagon spilled on him when it crashed, and it ate away at his leg. Now it seems like it's trying to do the same to the rest of his limbs. Once those are gone, I suspect it'll go for the organs. He won't last long once that starts."

Pephe opened a pouch on the front of his suit and withdrew a cloth. He shook it out and offered it to the Speaker, who took it with a nod.

Covering his mouth, Gerhardt moved closer to inspect the body. The substance was reflective and dark, leaving tiny yellow stains on the floor around the places it splattered.

"What of the amputated leg?" the Speaker asked.

"Burnt it," said Pephe. "Went up like a greased pig stuffed with black powder."

"And what remains of the leg is otherwise uninfected?" the Speaker asked.

"So far, it seems," said Pephe. "No telling how long until it spreads from where it is."

Turning to face Morri, the Speaker heaved a tremendous sigh of exasperation, still hiding his face behind the cloth.

"I am sorry you had to see this, Morri," the Speaker said, shaking his head ruefully. "My intention today was to ask for your assistance, not to subject you to such horrors as this."

Morri, face drained almost entirely of blood, swallowed her nausea. She shook her head from side to side, stopping when it threatened to cause her to throw up.

"I understood what entering this place might entail, Speaker," Morri said, forcing herself to look at the Speaker and not at the young man's decaying limbs. "You brought me here to assist in replacing this young man's leg, and I intend to do so. What's more, if priest Pephe--"

"Just Pephe is fine," said Pephe. "Not a fan of mandatory honorifics, no offense."

"Very well. If Pephe says this man's limbs need to be amputated to save his life, I suggest doing so immediately. If my supplies can be delivered, I believe I can create sufficient replacement limbs. He may not dance again, but he'll walk."

"Are you really up for that, kid?" Pephe asked.

Morri took a deep breath and thought of her Father, putting on the bravest face she could muster as she did.

"I am," said Morri. "And my name is Morrillypallyke Smith. I answer to it, not 'kid'."

Reaching behind her head, the girl began to tie back her long locks into a ponytail.

"I should like to be present during the surgery. With your assistance, Pephe, and the assistance of your associates, I believe I may be able to anchor the prosthetic directly to the bone. What's more, I should like to see what remains of the muscular system once the limbs have been removed. I admit I'm not as adept with my anatomy as I would like, but I suppose this will make an excellent education."

The Speaker, his face still covered by the cloth, looked to Morri and Pephe.

"Morrillypallyke Smith," Pephe said slowly, nodding his head inside his helmet. "I'll remember it now, believe me. I'll get my team prepped and have someone get your supplies. I don't suppose you have a list?"

"I'm afraid I don't," said Morri. "I could scrawl one up quickly."

"Great," said Pephe. "Do that and I'll have an initiate run and get the items from your shop."

Speaker Gerhardt raised a hand.

"Nonsense," said the Speaker. "Allow an old man the opportunity to do something useful while you talented young folk save a life. Morri, if you'd be so kind as to write the list, I'll see to it that the items are delivered."

Morri nodded, looking around for a parchment. With his spare hand, the Speaker reached into his robes and withdrew a small bound tome, a quill and small inkpot tucked away into an embossed pocket on the cover.

"I always keep this handy," the Speaker said. "I've found that inspiration often strikes at the most unexpected times."

Morri smiled and nodded, taking the offered book. Pulling the quill free from its holder, Morri flipped to the first page.

Finding it blank, she gave the Speaker a confused look.

"On the first page?" Morri asked. "Bound paper is expensive."

The Speaker nodded.

"I have droves of them at the temple," said the Speaker. "Go on, really. It's no trouble."

With a nod, Morri started writing. Once she'd finished, she blew on the ink to set it on the paper. Satisfied, she nodded and smiled at the Speaker.

"That ought to do it," said Morri.

"Yes," said the Speaker, snapping the book shut.

His face was still covered, but his eyes seemed to dance with the light of a smile hidden beneath the cloth.

"I believe it should."

Leaving Morri and Pephe to their task, the Speaker made his way out of the makeshift room and back down the corridor.

The look of pure and utter elation never left his eyes.

Chapter Nineteen

The caravan continued on its path, heading ever further west and north along the trade road out of Zelwyr. The sun shone down on them during the day, and the nights were clear and starry. Two days passed without incident, the group stopping only occasionally in order to rest the horses, make camp, or take turns driving the carriage.

The morning of the third day began with Smith, Brenno, and Enaurl at the front of the carriage. Enaurl held the reins firmly in her lone hand while Smith worked tirelessly on reattaching her left arm. The repair was now mostly complete, with most of the inner components having been re-calibrated, re-wired, or re-connected.

The silver 'skin' of the appendage was still opened wide, as if it had been unzipped at the seam, allowing Smith a clear view of the various components within. The man's hands were using a minute screwdriver and pry bar to readjust something.

Every few minutes, sparks hissed out at Smith, who cursed as the dancing bits of electricity stung at his hands and face. Invariably, Brenno would chuckle softly. For his part, the halfling was occupied with his task.

Sitting on the floor of the driver's area and using the bench as a makeshift desk, the pawnbroker was hard at work writing out a lengthy document on a sheet of paper.

A small rock he had found on the side of the road sat on top of a pile of five previously completed versions of the same manuscript, preventing them from blowing away in the gentle spring breeze. With a satisfied jab of his quill, Brenno scrawled his signature on the bottom of the page and held it up to his face to review.

Satisfied, Brenno nodded.

"There we have it," said Brenno. "Official form contracts for each of us to sign. No more of this verbal agreement nonsense, it never ends well. Doesn't hold up well in the courts, either."

"You really think anyone gives a damn?" Smith asked, popping the tiny screwdriver between his teeth to get a better look something in Enaurl's arm. "Find a dragon, get its blood, go home, be done with all this shit. Simple as that."

Brenno parsed his lips.

"In my experience, nothing is ever as simple as that," said the halfling, frowning as he read the contract line by line. "A simple ride through the woods becomes a life or death struggle. A simple attempt to dispose of unwanted merchandise becomes a campaign to slay a dragon."

Smith's fingers brushed the wrong component, and a surge of electricity ran through his hands and up his arm.

Smith grunted in pain as the arc of electricity forcibly contracted his muscles and locked his jaw. With effort, he withdrew his hand and shook away the pain, ignoring the fact that his fingertips had blackened and were smoking slightly. Brenno raised an eyebrow at Smith.

"A simple repair becomes a painstaking three day ordeal."

"Fuck you, Hornbuckle," said Smith. "What makes you think reattaching an arm is simple? Want to get in here and give it a try?"

"I'll pass, thank you," said Brenno, holding the contract up so the light of the sun shone through it. "I guess I'm just confused as to how it is you could construct a thing such as Enaurl in the first place, but are struggling so much to repair her. Needing a week to repair the gryoskepticwhatsit in town after Kera shot her in town makes enough sense to me, but this seems excruciating."

"Gyroscopic stabilizer," Smith said, still shaking his hand.

"If you say so," said Brenno, nodding his approval of the contract.

After quickly blowing on the page to ensure the ink was dry, he presented the contract to Smith.

"What am I supposed to do with that?" Smith growled, staring at the piece of paper with open disdain. "I don't even have anywhere to put it."

"I'll take care of the contracts," said Brenno, furrowing his brow at Smith's resistance. "Just sign your name along the bottom next to my signature, and it will be dealt with."

"What's the point?" Smith asked.

"Signing it makes it binding," said Brenno.

"I know how a contract works," Smith said. "I mean, what's the point of the contract."

"It ensures we all get an equal share," said Brenno.

"An equal share of what?" Smith asked, turning away to focus on Enaurl once more. "An equal share of dying on the road? Don't need to sign up for that. Did you make sure to include the part about me murdering anyone who tries to run out on this shitty campaign and leave me and Morri high and dry?"

"I felt it was implied," Brenno said dryly. "Add to your own threat the fact that we've been pressed into service by the church of Perrus, and as such face the threat of being blacklisted from any town with a temple to the White Lady, and I think you can put your fears of us abandoning you to rest, Mister Smith. If anyone would have done so, I believe the night of the timbergnolls would have been the time to do so. Even the illusionist is still present."

"For all the good sparkles and ghosts will do against a dragon," Smith grumbled. "Assuming we can even find one."

Smith took the screwdriver from between his lips and stuck it into Enaurl's open arm at a sharp angle. He turned it carefully, using only his fingertips, and something inside Enaurl clicked

"C'mon," Smith muttered, pulling the driver out and staring intently. "C'mon, c'mon, c'mon."

As if obeying Smith's pleas, gears and mechanisms in Enaurl's formerly severed arm began to whir and spin. The silver panels swung themselves closed and snapped shut with a click.

The automaton turned her head away from the road to look at her newly repaired limb, raising her arm tentatively. The limb moved up and down as the construct flapped her arm like a bird, bending and extending the elbow repeatedly.

Satisfied, Enaurl rolled her wrist and flexed her fingers. Finding her functionality restored, Enaurl nodded and Smith and offered the artificer a single silver thumbs up before turning back to face the road.

"Yes!" Smith shouted, punching the air triumphantly. Brenno applauded.

"Well done, Mister Smith," Brenno said dryly. "You've successfully done something for the second time."

"What do you mean the second time?" Smith asked, snatching the contract from Brenno's hands.

"Well, you built her arms in the first place," Brenno said. "Now you've built them again."

"Right," said Smith, scanning the contract. "Give me your quill."

"Haven't you got one of your own?" Brenno asked, holding his quill tight to his chest. "You managed to produce a set of extremely specialized tools from nowhere, surely you thought to pack a quill?"

Smith lowered the contract to scowl at the pawnbroker.

"I'm an artificer, Hornbuckle, not a damn scribe," Smith said, snatching at the white feathered quill the pawnbroker was holding.

Brenno threw his shoulder into Smith's path, shielding the quill with his body.

"First you must promise to be careful with it," said Brenno. "This is my favorite quill. This plume once belonged to an albino greatowl."

"What makes you think I won't be careful with it?" Smith said with a scowl.

"Our entire history together," Brenno said, scowling back in return.

"I'm not going to break your damn own quill, Hornbuckle," Smith said. "Do you want me to sign it or not?"

Brenno looked down at his quill, seeming conflicted. With a frown, he sighed and offered the quill to Smith. The artificer pressed the contract against the wall of the caravan behind him and hastily scrawled out his signature, offering it and the quill back to Brenno. The pawnbroker beamed and accepted both, inspecting Smith's contract.

"You know, I don't think I've ever learned your first name," said Brenno. "I've always just known you as 'Smith'."

"That's how I prefer it," said Smith, replacing his tools in his tool belt.

Enaurl perked up, and the construct rose to stand in place.

Smith turned his head first to face the construct and then towards the road ahead.

"What are you seeing?"

"How exactly *does* she see?" Brenno asked. "As far as I can tell her eyes appear to be solid orbs of metal. She also doesn't blink, which I must confess is more than a tad unnerving."

The halfling's free hand absently moved to his neck, remembering the time not so long ago when the silver woman had pinned him to the wall with his feet dangling beneath him.

"None of your--" Smith began.

"*Damn business*, yes," Brenno finished. "I had figured it would be another instance of that. Gods forbid a simple question be answered. Honestly, between yourself, the illusionist, the graverobber, and the scion, I might as well not try to converse with anyone."

"You do that," Smith said absently, still trying to peer ahead and see whatever it was that Enaurl was seeing. "Does it look like a fight?"

The construct shook her head from side to side, and balled her newly reattached fist. Reaching behind herself, she banged the wall of the caravan twice before bringing her arm back around to point ahead.

"What does that mean?" Brenno asked, climbing to stand on the bench in an effort to look into the distance.

"Caravan like this one," said Smith. "Heading this way."

"Oh," said Brenno. "That's fine then. This is a merchant's wagon, and I purchased through the Merchant's Guild. If the wagon approaching us really is like this one, it's likely to be vendors of some kind."

"Cheap bastard," Smith muttered.

"I'm not so rich that I'll ignore a substantial discount," said Brenno. "Though if I live to see the end of this campaign, that may change. Regardless, the point is that if Enaurl says the wagon is indeed the same type as this one, we can be sure that it's oncoming merchants."

"Or bandits disguised as merchants," said Smith.

"Are you always this suspicious?" Brenno said with a snort.

Smith took a deep breath.

"In the last two weeks, a stranger broke into my house while high on the drugs you sold her. Seemed harmless enough, at least right up until she convinced my daughter to break about *seven different laws* all at once, only to have her get *shot* - by *you* - and poisoned, *and cursed*. Because for whatever reason, you couldn't *just* shoot someone, could you? No. You had to shoot *and* poison them for whatever *drakeshit* reason. So now, shot, poisoned, and cursed, she's lying *unconscious* in a temple being *kept alive* by the constant work of priests to a god *I don't give two shits about*. In order to clean up after all you *dimwitted fuckwits*, I have to *hunt a godsdamn dragon* for its *blood*. Of course, there is a bit good news on that front. We hired ourselves a campaigner, a *dragon fighting wizard* no less. Except no, we didn't, did we? What we got was an opportunity to get *duped* by some *drunk bullshitter* and his *equally bullshit hocus pocus*. That same bullshitter is still tagging along and is probably going to get us killed somehow, but the upside to that is that he and the serial arsonist *are really starting to get along*."

Smith paused to take a second deep breath of air, his complexion reddening with as much oxygen deprivation as emotion as he opened up the exhaust vent on his pent up rage.

"All of this despite the fact that we don't even *know* where to find a dragon, so we're heading to Faltus on *blind fucking hope* that some fucking how I can buy some fucking dragon blood, which is probably going to cost me *everything* I own assuming we do manage *find* a bat shit crazy alchemist willing to sell us dragon blood. I'm *pretty sure* I'm going to have to give them Enuarl for it, never mind the fact that I just spent the last three days reverse engineering a godsdamn *arm*. Best case scenario, we'll find some godsdamn *campaign poster* asking for us to slay some godsdamned dragon that's been tormenting the people of *Whogivesafuck Village*. But hey, we know that as long as we keep heading northwest, we'll find a *prime specimen* - we know that, because that's what we were told by an *ass sniffing, rhyme shitting, foam faced dogman."*

Smith took several ragged breaths, veins throbbing in his neck, saying nothing more.

Stunned into silence by Smith's sudden outburst, Brenno said nothing.

Smith, feeling a wetness on his face, used the back of his hand to wipe away the spittle he'd accidentally expectorated onto his chin during his rant. Closing his eyes, the artificer puffed out a sigh, taking a series of controlled breaths.

Opening his eyes again, he turned to face the halfling.

"Look, I'm sorry about that, Hornbuckle," Smith said, the man's weariness evident in the way his voice cracked and his shoulders slumped.

It seemed to Brenno as if the man had aged ten years in front of his eyes over the span of the last ten breaths.

"I shouldn't have unloaded on you like that. It's been a long couple weeks, I'm tired, and I'm anxious for this to be over so I can get home to Morri. If I lose her, I..."

Smith's voice cracked again and trailed off. After a brief pause, he cleared his throat.

"I don't want to lose her."

"You won't, Smith," Brenno said, feeling a hefty weight of guilt and responsibility press down on his chest like a vice. "I swear I'll help you make this right, help undo this terrible comedy of errors. If I could give any of my possessions to help undo this entire series of events, I would do so in a heartbeat. Morri is far too sweet a girl to deserve this, even despite the fact that she held me at gunpoint."

Smith chortled.

"She held you up at gunpoint?" Smith asked.

"Yes," said Brenno. "Quite expertly, I might add. She's an exceptional child."

A small smile crept across Smith's face. He sighed and shook his head.

"She's so much like her mother, in all the ways that count," said Smith, peering forward at the spot in the distance slowly become a caravan as it approached.

"I'd say she has quite a bit in common with you as well, Mister Smith," Brenno added, smiling as he gathered up the remaining contracts.

"How's that?" asked Smith.

"Well, for starters, the both of you have brought me uncomfortably close to soiling myself using only your words," Brenno said, offering Smith an impish grin.

Smith froze for a moment, not having expected a quip from the pawnbroker. All at once his composure broke, and the man erupted into a barking chain of laughter, guffawing noisily and wholeheartedly.

Brenno's cheerful laughter joined him, and the two shared a much needed moment of brevity. The back door of the caravan swung open, and Kera popped out.

"Did we just run over a timbergnoll?" Will asked, fully serious. "It sounds like it's in a *lot* of pain."

Smith and Brenno were silent for a moment, then burst out laughing all the louder. Realizing the source of the sound, Will grinned wide and ducked back into the carriage and hurried to the bench where a sleeping Kera was currently curled up.

"Kera, wake up," Will said, shaking the woman's shoulders. "Smith is laughing, and it's *terrible*."

When Kera didn't respond, Will shook her a little harder.

"Kera, I'm serious. Wake up, you need to hear this."

The graverobber was limp under Will's hand, rolling like a rag doll at the wizard's touch.

The smile on Will's face faded, and his brow creased with concern.

"Kera?"

The woman's head rolled to the side, bringing her face around to look up into the illusionist's. Looking into her vacant eyes, wide open with their pupils rolled up into the back of her head, and seeing her mouth move in a feverish litany took the smile off his face completely.

"Oooh-kay," said Will, taking several backward steps away from Kera. "That's, uh… That's probably not ideal."

Chapter Twenty

When Zephelous awoke, it was onto the psychic plane, a place just beyond the real that was little more than a void filled the shattered fragments of thoughts and ideas.

Creatures and landscapes that existed only in dreams and nightmares peppered the endless abyss. It was a place where the horrible creatures from children's worst nightmares lurked in the shadows of fairytale castles, where hordes of fears made real roamed between one pocket of fertile imagination to the next, feeding on stray thoughts and weak minds. Metaphor was as strong a weapon as a sword in this realm, willpower the greatest strength, creativity a mighty asset.

Constraints and limitations such as physics and bodies were less than afterthoughts, as they were attributes and aspects that could be altered at the barest whim of those denizens and visitors who possessed the mental fortitude to do so.

As Zephelous's awareness grew, its form solidified into being. Subconscious habit shaped that form; a sturdy and imposing dwarven greatsword, a masterpiece of form and function from centuries long gone. It probed its immediate surroundings, finding itself floating mid air, upright with the hard angled tip pointing straight down at a sea composed of a green and red liquid that refused to mix fully, forming an endless and seamless collage of puddles and rivers and lakes.

"Why have I returned to this place?" Zephelous wondered, thinking aloud as the nature of the plane shaped internal thoughts into audible speech.

The sword's voice - as deep and loud and strong as the earth shaking rumble of the rock slide that had buried it - caused visible ripples in the air around to radiate outward from itself. The rings distorted the world it passed through, causing the air they passed through to ripple as if the world itself was nothing but a great pond and Zephelous's thoughts a thrown stone.

Imagery was as powerful as any enchantment in this place, emotion mightier than evocation. Zephelous's experience was its power in this place. Here, Zephelous's millennia-long life made it a veritable juggernaut.

Zephelous imagined itself a great steel dragon, and a great steel dragon it became. Its wings were an array of blades, its claws razors the size of men. Scales shaped like overlapping tower shields covered every inch of a body the size of a barn, a double row of spikes like farmer's scythes running down its spine. Its whole body shone the same shade of baleful white light as a full summer moon on a starless night. Its eyes were the burning incandescent orange of heated steel.

Zephelous believed that this form would be nearly unstoppable, and its belief made it so. Bulges like steel barrels pressed themselves outward from between the scales on its back, positioning themselves on either side of the place where wing pinion met spine. The back ends of the barrels opened and roared with flames, propelling Zephelous through space so quickly the air around it screeched and tore.

Zephelous surveyed the mindscape around it, a giant sphere of comprehension and awareness extending around its body. The sea of fluorescent red and green was a persistent feature beneath it, as were the miniature clumps of stone either breaking through the liquid's surface or floating above it. Some clusters were little more than groupings of stones and boulders, while others were floating mountains or the beaches of islands jutting out from the shining sea.

Zephelous corkscrewed between ruins and flew helixes over fortifications occupied with all manner of being, humanoid and otherwise, searching for the reason it had been pulled to this plane. Reality itself shook and trembled as a terrible scream of hurt and pain echoed through its entirety, shaking loose bricks from the walls of decrepit castles and sending them splashing into the waters below. The voice screaming was unmistakably Kera's.

"I suppose I should not be surprised," Zephelous said, performing half an aerial somersault while rolling like a barrel, righting itself to fly back in the direction it had come.

In the distance it saw a wall of fire that stretched from the sea to the sky, extending as far as the horizon on either side. It had not existed before, but it did now, roaring with deadly heat and infernal hunger. Zephelous felt as though it were flying into the sun. It also felt confident it would do so successfully.

The bottoms of the barrels thrusting it through the air reconfigured themselves, and the jets they created intensified. Zephelous's speed increased dramatically, and it angled its flight upward and towards the wall. Higher and higher the steel dragon climbed, its chrome body reflecting the reddish orange light of the flames before it.

The higher it flew, the less frequent the masses of imagination, clusters of thoughts becoming more and more scarce as Zephelous's flight became ever loftier.

When it had flown so high that it could no longer see the greens and reds of the sea below it, Zephelous decided it had flown high enough to accomplish what it suspected it would need to do.

In the psychic realm, suspicion led to possibility, and so by believing the task before it would be difficult Zephelous increased the likelihood that it would be.

Having experienced the searing strength of Kera's psychic shielding on the prime material plane, Zephelous could not help but believe they would be all the stronger here. Prepared, the steel dragon tucked its wings tight to its body and let itself plummet, rocketing downwards towards the earth like the falling star that had carried the metals from which it was forged to the earth. Zephelous spiraled as it dove, a helix of smoke trailing behind it as it flew towards the blazing barrier.

Zephelous dove into the wall of flame, engulfing itself in the sweltering sun-like heat of the barrier, a magma spray erupting out behind it, lava coiling around the gleaming tail of the dragon weapon as it plunged into the inferno. Zephelous felt a crushing pressure bearing down on it from all sides, adding pulverizing friction and unrelenting force to the unbearable heat. The dragon's corkscrew motion slowed but did not cease.

The propulsion jets on its back howled like a wild wind whipping through the naked branches of bare winter trees, the constant droning noise they made growing louder by the second. The dragon's outermost scales began to soften, yielding to the heat and the pressure, melting around their edges.

Form and mind were one on this place, damage to the form represented damage to the mind and vice versa. Zephelous cried out against the searing pain, a tortured draconic roar louder that made itself heard above the whine of the jets and the raging of the flames. Steel edges began to round and melt, metal running and sloughing off the dragon like sweat from a runner's brow.

"How can this be?" Zephelous roared, pushing through the pain as it plunged ever forward. "A will such as this, a mind such as this, in a graverobber from the Wildlands?"

From somewhere beyond the flames Kera screamed again, and the wall of fire shuddered against the force of the psychic onslaught. Caught in their path, Zephelous's vision darkened and its senses dulled, the scream bringing with it sensations of dizziness and sleepiness that threatened to render the dragon unconscious.

The flames were affected as well, rippling and peeling back, loosening their grip on Zephelous as they quivered and recoiled. Knowing that this was its chance, silently dreading that it might be the only one it would get, Zephelous redoubled the power of its thrusters. The noise from the engines pitched upwards until they were deafening, and Zephelous barreled through the forcefield.

The burning continued, and Zephelous vision continued to darken, growing dimmer and dimmer until even the blaze of the fires around it was dulled into nothing more than a dark brown veil that hid the world. Scales hissed as they dissolved into nothingness, swords sizzled as they melted and disappeared into clouds of metallic vapor.

Zephelous roared in torment, determined to persevere through its suffering out of sheer determination. Its vision darkened from brown to black, and Zephelous felt its engines sputter and falter.

Gathering all the strength it could muster, gathering all of its power it could collect through the hellish pain, Zephelous screamed and thrust forward once more.

At last, the dragon broke through to the other side, the metal of its body glowing white hot as if it had just been pulled from a colossal forge. There was water beneath it, not the typical greens and reds of the mindscape beyond the barrier but actual water.

Relieved beyond words, Zephelous lazily spun its way down into them, crashing into the cool depths. The water hissed and steamed, boiling around the metal dragon as the former only gradually cooled the latter.

Because it was logical to Zephelous that being quenched would both temper it and undo the damage from the inferno, it was so. The sword made dragon emerged from the lake triumphant, the dark steel of its body glistening and lustrous once more.

The landscape around it was a prairie that stretched for miles, mountains looming in the distance. Gone was the wall of flames and the floating isles of the mindscape. Zephelous now found itself in a fragment of the Wildlands, a bubble of land that was a perfect copy of the original, created from memory.

"From Kera's memory, no doubt," said the dragon, plodding its way to the shore of the lake.

Its wings reached upwards and curled around its face and body, and when they unfurled the dragon was gone. A humanoid dragon with silver scales the size of a man stood in its place, a towering shield in one hand and Zephelous's sword form in the other.

The dragon's wings unfurled themselves out of existence, becoming a flowing and tattered cloak the color of blackened wrought iron on the back of the silver dragonman. In its new form, Zephelous stepped onto the sands of the beach and gazed around in all directions, searching for any sign of Kera.

"Perhaps I should be looking for trouble," Zephelous mused, "the two so often seem to go hand in hand."

The plains appeared empty as Zephelous scanned them, but another scream from Kera drew the attention of the dragonman. Kera appeared, occupying a space that had previously been vacant just a moment before. The woman was running full tilt, eyes wide with fear.

She tripped over something buried in the tall grass of the plains. Rather than take the time to get up, the clearly frantic and terrified Kera began to crawl as fast as she could towards Zephelous.

Seeing nothing pursuing her, but knowing that sight alone was nothing to rely on in this place, Zephelous hurried towards Kera. He reached the graverobber as she fell once more, clothes and skin catching on the barbs of cruel briers that had sprung up beneath her.

"Please!" Kera yelled, eyes wide with terror. "Please, you have to help me! I thought they were scraw eggs, I didn't know what they were!"

Nodding, Zephelous hacked the briers to pieces, extending a clawed hand to the downed woman.

"I am here, Kera No-Clan," Zephelous said. "It is I, Zephelous. I know not how we arrived at this place, but I will assist you in battle."

"I can't fight it, what do I do?" Kera asked, tears welling up in her eyes. "It's bigger than me. It's bigger than everyone, It's killing everyone."

Unused to any sign of weakness from the otherwise stubborn and resolute woman, Zephelous was taken aback by this sudden show of vulnerability.

"Kera, I do not understand," said Zephelous. "Of course you can fight, you are a capable warrior and a formidable woman."

Taking the still prone Kera's outstretched hand, Zephelous's staggered as the earth suddenly trembled beneath the claws of its feet.

"It's coming," Kera whispered, blood draining from her face. "It's mad about the eggs. I didn't mean to, I didn't know!"

Zephelous scanned the horizon and saw nothing, the earth trembling rhythmically as if a tremendous creature were striding towards the pair. Gripping Kera's hand tighter, Zephelous pulled in an effort to drag the woman to her feet. Kera felt as though she was mired in quicksand, moored to the earth.

Zephelous grunted with unexpected strain and effort. In the distance, the skies had suddenly taken on a ruby red hue.

"Kera, what is that creature?" Zephelous yelled, taking Kera's hand into both of its scale-covered paws.

The dragonman pulled with all its might, but the woman remained stuck, barely peeling away from the ground.

"It's coming," Kera whispered, "it's coming, it's coming, it's coming."

The ruby red of the sky deepened, then spread to the ground. Everything around Zephelous had suddenly caught fire, filling the air with thick black smoke. The stomping continued, and was followed by a roar - one Zephelous recognized as being distinctly draconic.

"I do not understand what is happening, Kera No-Clan. You said you slew a dragon in your past, is this that instance?" Zephelous grunted, eyes locked on the horizon.

The side of a hill trembled and burst open from within, broken rock and liquid magma spilling out from the inside. The air was rent with the roar of a dragon once again, but the creature that emerged from the hillside did not look like any kind of dragon Zephelous recognized; it seemed to the sword more like a walking nightmare.

Scales as red as blood were broken up by patches of mold and rot, some of which were severe enough to cause openings that showed the thing's insides - as rotten in there as it was on the outside. Kera thought of it as a titan, and so a titan it was - it blocked out the sun, it moved like a shambling horror, it loomed over them with a halo of ash and flies.

The environment around them had changed again, now into a tight cluster of small tents and caravans. They were burning, everything was burning, and the creature was getting closer.

"I trust you will provide an explanation at a further time when we are not in danger of having our mental faculties destroyed."

Looking down at Kera, Zephelous's mouth fell open. Gone was the fierce warrior woman he knew; in her place was a scared child, looking perhaps a little younger than Morrillypallyke.

"It's coming," young Kera whispered, tears running down her cheeks. "There's nowhere for me to hide."

Stunned, Zephelous's gaze moved slowly from the girl to the approaching terror, when suddenly a human man appeared before it. His skin was the same sun-kissed tone as Kera's, his hair the same shade of chestnut brown. His physique was broad and muscular, tattoos of animal paw prints on nearly every part of his otherwise naked upper body.

"Kera?" the man called, shielding his eyes against the smoke and ash that were steadily filling the air. "Where are you, Kera?"

Fires blossomed all around them, but the man ignored them even as they burned him. He looked around, either seeing clear through Zephelous or ignoring the dragonman entirely.

"Kera?" He shouted. "Ke--"

The twisted red dragon's sharpened tail burst through the man's chest, sending blood and bits of bone spilling out around it. It reminded Zephelous too clearly of the way the hills had broken to let the thing out. The man gasped, unable to make a noise that wasn't a tortured wheeze. Still, mangled though he was, he struggled to free himself - struggled even as the dragon hoisted him towards its mouth, and even more after it had bit off one of his legs. The struggle stopped only when the dragon popped all that was left of him into its mouth. Kera made herself very small, cowering into a smoke-filled corner of a hut that was burning fast.

"Sssuch sssweet meat," the horror said, sniffing the air. "I can sssmell them on you, my sssweet. There'sss nowhere to hide."

The nightmare hissed, its voice the threatening rattle of a thousand desert snakes, its tongue flitting out of its mouth to run along its jaws before dipping into the empty hole of its eye socket.

"I'm not going to eat you," the dragon called out. "No, not you. I'm going to make you sssuffer, make you hurt for ssso long, and ssso badly that you'll wish I had, you filthy little *egg thief.*"

The roof above Zephelous creaked as the dragon forced its head into the building. Zephelous's jaw snapped shut, and the dragonman's eyes once again blazed orange. Gone was the brier patch, young Kera was now cowering beneath a bed. Seeing this enraged Zephelous further.

"No," said Zephelous, succeeding at last in pulling the girl free, placing her on the ground outside of the reach of the grasping vines. Kneeling to look the horrified girl in the eyes, Zephelous took both of her tiny hands and held them, squeezing them reassuringly.

"*No.*"

Rising to a stand, Zephelous drew its sword and shield. So intense was the dragonman's anger that the steel of its eyes began to puff out a trail of glowing smoke. The nightmare dragon continued to swing his head from side to side, his features slowly distorting as Zephelous approached.

"Come on out now, egg thief," the nightmare said. "Aren't you going to run? Aren't you going to show me your deliciousss fear? I've taken everyone elssse, you are all that remainsss... Jussst waiting for me to find you and crush you like you did to my eggsss."

Zephelous's anger flared, the mindscape turning emotion tangible, making an expression into fact, cloaking the dragonman in an aura of flame. With a challenging roar, the dragonman grew, expanding outward to match the fiend in height and returning to his steel dragon form

"No," Zephelous repeated, raking steel claws across the fiend's chest, making it recoil. *Now* it saw Zephelous, *now* it struck.

It lashed out with rotten claws, bit at Zephelous with a maw that was missing teeth, slashed at it with a tail that showed bone in more places than not.

"Back!" Zephelous bellowed, whirling its bulk around to smash the nightmare in the face with its iron tail. Black bile oozed out from out of the thing's mouth, but the demon seemed unphased. Zephelous lunged at it, and the two rolled and bit and slashed and scraped and battled for a time that felt like an eternity, two titans battling in Kera's mindscape.

"Let'ssss get thisss over with, egg thief," the nightmare said, words garbled as they stumbled out from a mangled mouth. "Your sssong doesssn't make you sssafe from me. I will hunt you, haunt you, until your very lasst daysss... Which will be very, very sssoon."

"You will not harm her," Zephelous bellowed. "You are a memory, a twisted imagining of a young girl who made you into a nightmare."

"Asss long asss I live, you will have no ressst, will know no sssafety, will gain no sssecurity... I will ssstalk you for asss long asss I exissst."

"An acceptable condition," Zephelous roared, opening its mouth wide.

A steel barrel moved upwards from somewhere inside its chest and locked into position at the back Zephelous's throat. The gleaming silver dragon took a great breath of air; an instant later, a river of blue flame jetted out from its mouth.

Fueled by the dragonman's fury, the fire sheared clean through the nightmare dragon's arm as if Zephelous were a colossal dwarven cutting torch and the arm a wayward bit of slag.

At this the fiend recoiled, but Zephelous gave it no ground. Burying its claws into the side of the monster's head, Zephelous grappled the demon and pulled its face into the torrent of flame. Flesh roiled and melted from muscle, muscle blackened and peeled away from bone, bone burnt and crumbled to ash, ash blew away and was obliterated.

Zephelous angled its mouth towards the upper body of the creature, blasting a cyan-colored conflagration down the thing's neck and into its throat and beyond.

The entire middle portion of the body dissolved in seconds, leaving Zephelous holding on to a pair of severed half-nightmares.

Still not satisfied, Zephelous smashed the remaining pieces together, bludgeoning meat against meat over and over again until all that remained was paste.

Panting with effort, grey gore dripping from its elbows down to its hands, the dragon that was Zephelous turned and walked back towards Kera, shrinking with each step it took.

By the time it returned to Kera's side and knelt down, Zephelous had returned to its dragonman form.

"There, there," Zephelous whispered. "You are safe now, child."

"It's not coming back?" Young Kera asked, sniffling.

"No," Zephelous said softly, hugging the girl.

"Where do I go now?" the girl asked. "What do I do?"

Zephelous didn't have an answer, didn't know if giving an answer to this version of Kera would matter, didn't know if *anything* that had happened here would matter. Uncertain about everything that was happening in this place, the dragonman did all it could think of doing.

It held young Kera closer, squeezing her.

Chapter Twenty-One

Back on the prime material plane, Kera drew a sharp breath and sat upright. Her hands immediately went to either side of her, and she found Zephelous there. Instantly relaxing, she sighed with relief.

"Oh, you're awake," said Will. "I was worried about you for a minute there, with the whole crazy eyes and the muttering gibberish. Thought maybe you had caught a fever from one of the timbergnoll bites or something. Glad you're not dead."

"Same here," said Kera, hardly paying any attention to the wizard.

Zephelous?

I AM HERE, KERA NO-CLAN, Zephelous responded. MAY WE DISCUSS WHAT JUST TRANSPIRED?

"Fuck no," said Kera.

"Fuck no what?" Will asked.

"Not you," said Kera, holding Zephelous up in one hand and pointing to it with the other. "Talking to the sword."

"Oh, the stabby ghost is back, that's good," Will said jokingly, opening the caravan door just wide enough to poke his head through the opening. "Nevermind, she's awake, everything is perfectly normal here. The sword is talking again too, so that's a plus."

"You say these things as if any of us were concerned," Voldani called back, loud enough that her voice carried clear into the caravan.

Will leaned back into the caravan and closed the door behind him, smiling at Kera.

"Well, Voldani's thrilled to hear you're okay," said Will.

"So I heard," said Kera.

I LEARNED MUCH ABOUT YOU DURING OUR TIME TOGETHER IN THE MINDSCAPE, said Zephelous, the sword's comments making Kera furrowed her brow. THAT BEING SAID, I WOULD LIKE SOME CLARIFICATION.

"Yeah, well, I would have liked for you not to have seen that shit," said Kera. "But here we are, neither one of us getting what we want."

"Still talking to the sword, huh?" Will asked.

I CAN UNDERSTAND YOUR HESITATION TO SPEAK OF THE DEMONS OF YOUR PAST, KERA, said Zephelous. I CAN EVEN RELATE TO A CERTAIN EXTENT.

"The fuck you can," said Kera, scowling.

"Yep, still talking to the sword," said Will, frowning. "While ignoring me completely."

KERA, YOU AND I HAVE ONLY KNOWN EACH OTHER A SHORT TIME, said Zephelous. IN THAT TIME I HAVE LEARNED THAT YOUR ABILITY TO MAKE POOR CHOICES IS SECOND TO NONE.

"The fuck's that suppose to mean?" Kera asked.

"You know, I bet you could include me in the conversation if you wanted to," Will complained. "Unless this is some sword and sword-wielder relationship stuff, that would make sense why I wouldn't need to be included. Is that what's going on?"

IT MEANS NOTHING, IT IS MERELY ONE ASPECT OF WHO YOU ARE, said Zephelous. THERE IS MUCH MORE TO YOU, A GREATNESS, A POWER, A--

"If you say the word *potential* I will sell you to Brenno," Kera warned. "For real this time, no breaking in to get you back."

"I'm going to choose to believe I'm right," Will said with a nod, taking a seat on the bench beside Kera. "Feel free to include me at any time, it's not like I feel left out or anything."

VERY WELL, said Zephelous. THEN ALLOW ME TO SAY THAT IN ALL MY YEARS, I HAVE NEVER SEEN DENIAL AS STRONG AS YOURS.

"And what is that supposed to mean?" Kera asked, her tone growing defensive.

WHEN YOU FIRST UNEARTHED ME, I BELIEVED YOUR MIND WAS SHIELDED, Zephelous explained. NOW I KNOW THAT THIS WAS NOT THE CASE; THE TRUTH IS THAT YOU CREATED THE BARRIERS YOURSELF, AND NOW I UNDERSTAND WHY.

"Shut up," said Kera, standing up from the bench, leaving Zephelous resting on its surface. "You poked your pointy head into one nightmare, you don't know shit."

YOU MISUNDERSTAND, said Zephelous. I AM IN AWE.

"Wait," said Kera, raising a hand to make a stop gesture at Zephelous. "Are you saying you're impressed with me right now?"

I AM CURRENTLY EXPERIENCING AN EQUAL MIXTURE OF FEAR AND WONDER IN REGARDS TO YOUR MIND, said Zephelous. THAT

YOUR TRAUMA HAS SOMEHOW AFFECTED YOUR MIND SO GREATLY THAT YOU DEVELOPED LATENT PSIONIC ABILITIES, ONLY TO USE THEM TO CONSTANTLY HELP YOURSELF FORGET...

"Yeah, I don't think so," said Kera. "The booze and ash help me forget."

"Respect," Will said with a knowing expression on his face as he raised his hand into the air, palm towards Kera, offering her a congratulatory slap as was the regional custom.

I HAVE NOT EVEN BEGUN TO ADDRESS YOUR ALCOHOLISM, Zephelous said, sounding surprised to the point of incredulous at Kera's statement. THE EFFORT REQUIRED TO MANIFEST THAT SORT OF DEFENSE ON THE PSYCHIC PLANE IS EXTREMELY TAXING ON THE MIND. NORMALLY THIS WOULD BE QUITE HARMFUL, BUT FOR WHATEVER REASON YOU SPEND EXTENDED PERIODS OF TIME UNCONSCIOUS.

"Booze and fae ash are pretty straight forward reasons, actually," said Kera.

BE THAT AS IT MAY, IT SEEMS THAT YOUR UNCONSCIOUS IS DRAWN TO TRAVEL TO THE PSYCHIC PLANE. EXTENDED TIME THERE ALLOWS YOU TO RECHARGE, ALL WHILE YOUR UNCONSCIOUS MIND LIES DREAMING IN THE MINDSCAPE. THE VERY NOTION FILLS ME WITH AWE.

"You're really just going to leave me hanging like this?" Will said, a frown on his face as he waved his unslapped hand at Kera.

"Believe me, Zeph, if I could read people's thoughts or some shit, I'd know about it by now," Kera said, shaking her head at the sword. "It's like I said earlier, everyone's got shit. Whatever you think you saw in there, all you were actually seeing was my shit."

"Yeah, this is getting weird even for me, so," said Will, raising his hands into the air. "I'm going to go hang out with the guys if that's cool, say literally anything to me if you want me to stay."

HAVE I MENTIONED LATELY THAT YOU ARE NEEDLESSLY CRUDE? Zephelous chastised. THERE IS NO REASON FOR IT.

Will stood and made his way towards the caravan door.

"Have I mentioned lately that I don't give a shit what you think?" Kera asked. "I don't remember inviting you to poke around inside my head, Zeph."

IN TRUTH, I DID NOT INTEND TO DO SO, Zephelous said. WHEN I AWOKE, AS IT WERE, I FOUND MYSELF IN THE MINDSCAPE. I HEARD YOUR CRIES, AND I CAME TO YOU. FROM THERE--

"I know what happened from there," Kera interrupted, "I don't remember asking you to fight my battles for me."

BUT KERA, Zephelous said, making a noise like a psychic gasp inside Kera's mind as it spoke. THAT HORROR CAME FOR YOU, SLAUGHTERED YOUR CLAN, LEAVING YOU ALONE--

"Yeah," said Kera, tone cold. "I know."

I... I DO NOT UNDERSTAND, said Zephelous.

"You left before the ending," Kera said, striding towards the bench with a grim expression on her face. She lifted Zephelous off the bench and inspected its blade, wiping off a spot of dried gnoll blood.

I WOULD NEVER WITNESS SUCH A THING AND STAND IDLE NEARBY--

"I'm talking at the very end, Zeph," Kera said, flipping Zephelous over in her hands before sheathing it at her hip. "At the very end, I kill him."

The wagon lurched to a stop, but Kera stood firm as the carriage swayed beneath her.

DO YOU ALWAYS DREAM THAT WAY? Zephelous asked, sympathy ringing its voice.

"Not always," said Kera, making her way towards the caravan door. "But I kill him every time."

Chapter Twenty-Two

"What exactly is this contract for?" Will asked, his eyebrows furrowed with concern as he scrutinized the parchment, crumpling the bottom corner in the process.

Standing opposite from Will, Brenno snatched the contract from the wizard's hands with an irritated grumble.

"I may not have campaigned for some time, Mister Decker," Brenno grumbled, slapping the page against the back wall of the carriage, running his hand up and down the back side of the contract in an effort to smooth out the wrinkles.

Satisfied, he held the contract at arm's length and made a flicking motion with his wrists, causing the paper snap into shape with an audible pop.

"But I assure you, the terms of this contract are fairly standard. Didn't you say you'd been contracted for work in the past?"

"Well yeah," said Will, "but I meant the past as in the last few years, not the past as in last century. That thing is oldschool. *'Should the aftersigned perish during the efforts of the campaign, in the event that they leave no heirs, they yield any and all unclaimed titles, holdings, belongings, and investments - including those in the persistent campaign - to whichever active member of the campaign first makes a legitimate and valid claim of ownership'*. Gods, man. Are you a pawnbroker or an advocate? Everyone knows you call dibs on the dead guy's stuff."

"Precisely," Brenno said, offering the contract back to the illusionist. "By signing, all you're consenting to is to abide by that rule in such a manner that prevents possible legal scandal or discord among those who survive you."

"I guess that seems reasonable," Will admitted, an apprehensive look on his face as he accepted the contract and began to read it once more. "Okay, what about this part: *'the undersigned hereby agrees that one representative of the campaign, the duly designated Brenno Figtree Hornbuckle'*, Figtree's a great middle name by the way, *'to act as lead treasurer and head mathematician'*."

"What part about this confuses you?" Brenno asked, planting his hands on his hips.

"Where are the other treasurers and mathematicians?" Will asked, grinning. Brenno's eyes narrowed as pawnbroker glared at the wizard with every ounce of ire in his body.

"Oh, come on, it was funny."

"What was funny?" Kera asked, approaching the pair from the back of the wagon.

"My totally awesome joke," said Will. "Brenno wants to be the lead treasurer."

"Makes sense," said Kera, "What's the joke?"

"Where are the other treasurers?" Will asked, smiling at his joke once again.

"There aren't any," said Kera.

"What?" Will said, confused. "I think you're missing the joke."

"I think you're missing a joke entirely," Kera countered. "Why are we stopped?"

"Caravan coming up," Smith shouted down from the roof of the wagon. "Hornbuckle says it's a merchant, but we can't know that for certain."

"Good thinking," said Kera. "Where's Enaurl?"

"Under the wagon," said Smith.

"What's Enaurl doing under the wagon, Smith?" Kera asked.

"Waiting until their wagon gets here," said Smith, snapping his thunder cannon open to load shells into its body before snapping it shut. "If things go south, she's going to take out their wheels, maybe a horse or two if she has to."

"Let's hope it's merchants, then," said Kera, looking off towards the approaching caravan, shielding her eyes against the sun. "If not, free horse meat is free horse meat."

"Your people eat horses?" Brenno asked.

"My people eat a lot of things," said Kera. "Do I get a contract or what?"

"Yes, of course," said Brenno, rifling through the pile for Kera's. Finding it, he offered it towards the graverobber. "You'll notice proviso that we previously agreed on, of course."

"You get most of my stuff, got it, don't care," Kera said, making a snapping motion with one hand while holding the contract in the other. "Gimme a quill."

"You're just going to sign it?" Will asked, incredulous at the notion.

He held his contract closer to his face, furiously scanning each line of the diminutive halfling's handwriting.

"Aren't you worried it's going to have some kind of legal crap hidden in there that makes you have to do something you don't want to do?"

"Will, look real hard at the situation I'm already in, then ask yourself if it could possibly get any worse than it already is." Kera asked rhetorically, frowning at the shoddy-looking, half-broken quill Brenno offered her. "Oh come on, there is no way you wrote these contracts with that quill."

The halfling scowled, looking down at the mangled writing implement.

"It's perfectly serviceable," said Brenno.

"If you want them to sign it, give them the quill," Smith shouted from up top.

"I offered them a quill," Brenno said.

"You know what I'm talking about, Hornbuckle," Smith said. "Let them use the damn owl quill."

The halfling looked miserable.

"I'd rather not," Brenno grumbled.

"What makes it an owl quill?" asked Kera. " Is it made from owls?"

"If that's what you'd like to believe," Brenno said, producing the quill from a pocket on the inside of his travelling cloak. "It also happens to be my personal favorite, so please be careful. The feather once belonged to an albino great owl."

"No it didn't," said Kera, holding the quill up to the light. "That's a muckscraw feather."

"I beg your pardon?" Brenno said, aghast.

"Musckscraws. Don't you guys get those up here?" Kera said, fanning the quill from side to side. "Nasty things, about seven feet tall. They can't fly, but they're crazy fast runners."

"Ridiculous," said Brenno.

"Ridiculously dangerous," said Kera. "I once watched a muckscraw horse-kick an antelope, killed it instantly." Kera signed her name on the contract, offering Will the feather.

"Now I know you're joking," said Brenno, watching anxiously as the quill changed hands from Kera to Will.

"You pay a lot for this quill?" Will asked, looking closely at the feather.

"A fair amount, yes" Brenno admitted, parsing his lips.

"How much?" Will asked, signing the contract as he did.

"Three gold pieces," said Brenno. Kera made a high pitched whistle.

"That's a lot of gold for a feather," said Kera.

"You're telling me," said Will. "Hey Brenno, can I ask you another question?"

"I suppose," said the pawnbroker.

"Have you ever seen an albino great owl?" Will asked.

"Well," said Brenno, seeming apprehensive to answer the question. "No, not exactly."

"Kera, how many muckscraws would you say you've seen?" Will asked Kera, handing the quill back her as he did.

Kera took it and put on pensive expression.

"In total, I'd say probably a few hundred," said Kera. "Every single one of them had feathers just like this."

Smiling impishly, Kera offered the quill back to Brenno.

Scowling, the halfling took the writing implement with both hands, treating it as tenderly as ever.

"So it might be a muckscraw feather," said Brenno, scrutinizing his beloved quill. "What of it? Still worth every copper."

Kera nodded.

"Sure, yeah," said Kera. "Hey Will, you ever campaign much down south?"

"A couple times," Will said with a nod. "Trade routes and all that."

"Did you ever eat roast muckscraw on the road?" Kera asked.

"Absolutely," said Will. "Seems like there's a muckscraw vendor every few hundred paces. Roast muckscraw, fried muckscraw, muckscraw strips."

"Who doesn't love a good strip of scraw jerky?" Kera asked.

"Mmm, mmm," Will answered, rubbing his belly in delight.

"What is going on here?" Brenno asked, eyes moving from Kera to Will. "Is this some sort of private joke?"

"Say, William?" Kera asked.

"Yes, Keratherine?" Will answered.

"*Keratherine?*" Kera repeated, arching an eyebrow at Will.

"Just go with it," said Will.

"Fine," said Kera. "How much do you remember paying for a hearty muckscraw meal?"

"Well, I only ever bought whole roasted muckscraw," Will said, scratching his chin. "But if I remember correctly… two? No… three, three coppers."

"Sounds about right," said Kera.

Brenno's expression moved from suspicion, to dismay, to being utterly crestfallen. He looked down at the quill in his hands.

"Three coppers?" Brenno repeated quietly. "For the whole bird?"

"In all fairness, I have no idea what a feather goes for," said Will. "Then again, I had no idea they were so valuable."

"Me neither," said Kera, laughing.

Brenno merely growled his displeasure.

"Do the lot of you have an aversion to silence?" Voldani asked. "I feel as though you feel the need to speak simply in an effort to make noise."

"You know if you think about it, speaking is just making fancy noise," said Kera.

"Cease your prattling," said Voldani. "We are now within earshot of the approaching wagon."

Kera peered up at Voldani before up the road, seeing that the caravan in the distance was now only a few hundred meters away.

"How can you tell that we're in earshot?" Will asked.

"If you would close your mouth for longer than a few seconds at a time you might realize the sound of their wheels can be heard," Voldani said, voice quiet and irate.

Will cupped his hand behind his ear, tiling the side of his head towards the approaching carriage. The sound of wheels turning and an axle in need of grease made their way down the road, reaching Will gradually.

"Hey, I can hear it now," said Will. "You were right Vol--"

"Silence," said Voldani.

"I'm just trying to say you wer--"

"Silence," Voldani repeated, radiant eyes beaming down at Will, who closed his mouth. In the silence that followed, the faintest creak of wagon wheels and the clip-clopping of hooves could be heard in the distance.

"Now what?" Kera whispered.

"We wait," said Smith, cocking the hammer on this firearm with a click. The wagon in the distance appeared to swell as it approached, gaining feature and definition. While it did appear to be very similar to Brenno's wagon, this one was significantly longer and slightly taller. As the wagon rounded a gentle bend in the road, it became apparent that it had four sets of wheels and appeared to be segmented in the middle, in reality two conjoined wagons with a pliable gasket in the middle.

"Seems a bit excessive," Brenno muttered.

"Envy will gain you nothing," said Voldani. The wagon continued its approach, its horses and riders becoming more defined. The driver, a black-bearded dwarf with a single strip of hair running down the middle of his skull, pulled on his reins to bid the horses to stop. The larger caravan slowed to a halt a little under a hundred paces from Brenno's wagon. The dwarf with the mohawk stood up.

"Hail," said the dwarf. "I see from yer wagon that ye be merchants, or would like me to think ye be merchants. If ye're thinkin' of tryin' to waylay me, I strongly suggest ye reconsider unless ye like dyin'."

"My good dwarf," said Brenno, offering a low bow in the direction of the merchant. "We are merely travelers, campaigners, on the road to Faltus. We've come through the old route from Zelwyr, and wished only to ensure you meant us no harm. What's more, as a certified member of the Merchant's Guild, it is my solemn duty to inform you that the trade road on which you travel is unsafe. We ourselves were attacked by a throng of timbergnolls."

The dwarf nodded thoughtfully.

"A throng o' timbergnolls," the dwarf said, sitting back in his chair. "Not quite a horde, then?"

"I beg your pardon?" Brenno asked, confused.

"Ye sure it wasn't more of a drove?" The dwarf continued. "Could have even been multiple droves, but of course one drove too many and ye've got a swarm. Are ye certain it was a throng and not a swarm?"

"I'm afraid I'm not certain," said Brenno, furrowing his brow. "Does it matter?"

"Bah," said the dwarf, waving his hand through the air in Brenno's direction. "Of course it matters. If ye can't differentiate a throng from a swarm, how are ye supposed to know the difference between a squadron and a unit?"

"I'm not sure I understand what's happening here," said Brenno.

"Don't mind Torgil," said another voice, clear and strong and feminine.

The speaker to whom the voice belonged, a mature woman with flaming red hair wearing an emerald green dress with gold and copper stitching, emerged from a door just behind the dwarf.

"He does *so* love his words."

"Love is a bit strong," said Torgil. "Comes with awkward romantic implications."

"Treasure, then," said the redheaded woman offered, which Torgil accepted with a nod.

Addressing Brenno and the others once more, the woman returned Brenno's bow.

"My sincerest apologies, my fellow merchants. I am Marie Valshaw, alchemist of some renown and wizard of none. The expert on elocution you see before you is Torgil Ashfist. Our caravan includes a number of others, all of who I can introduce once pleasantries have finished being exchanged. What might I call you, good Misters and Ladies?"

"Brenno Hornbuckle," Brenno said, offering another low bow.

"Well met, Mister Hornbuckle," said Marie.

"William Decker," said Will, eyes wide as they drank in every detail of the woman's alluring frame.

"Well met, Mister Decker," Marie said, smiling warmly.

"Just Will is fine," said the illusionist, clearing his throat in an effort to hide the fact that he was blushing. "I'm not a merchant, just a wizard."

"Oh, come now, William," said Marie. "I've known a fair share of wizards in my life, and not one of them was 'just' anything. I strongly suspect the same is true of you. Are you a specialist or a general practitioner of the arcane arts?"

"Specialist," said Will.

"Oh?" Marie asked, inquiring with nothing more than a raised brow.

"Illusiomancy," Will said, clicking the fingers of one hand while performing a flourish with the other.

A bouquet of flowers appeared in his hand, the snapped fingers now clutching the stems of exotic looking plants that blossomed into blue and red petals. He tossed the bouquet to Marie, passing them to her with an underhand throw. Before she could catch it, the bouquet became a flock of brightly colored birds which scattered in all directions, flying into the trees and sky before dissipating into nothingness.

Marie watched them leave.

"A bit of a showman as well?" Marie asked.

"Maybe a bit," Will admitted sheepishly.

"He is a mountebank and former charlatan," Voldani said, leaping down from the carriage roof. "Do not trust a word he speaks."

"I'll remember that, dear scion," said Marie. "And your name as well, once you've given it to me, of course."

"Voldani," said Voldani.

"No family name?" Marie asked.

"Solreki," said Voldani.

"You have a last name?" Kera asked. "Why didn't you tell me?"

"I did not care to do so," said Voldani.

"And you are?" Marie asked.

"Kera is fine," said Kera.

"A visitor from the wild south," Marie remarked. "From what clan do you hail, fair lady Kera?"

Kera opened her mouth to answer, but Voldani spoke for her.

"She is Kera No-Clan," said Voldani. "She is in exile."

"Hey!" Kera said. "That's kind of personal, Dani."

"Do not call me Dani," said Voldani.

"Too bad," said Kera. "You owe me now, I get to use it."

"I do not agree," said Voldani.

"Yeah, well, I do," said Kera. Speaking to Marie next, she waved. "I'm also not a merchant, but feel free to keep calling me *fair* and stuff, I'm into it."

"I can tell," said Marie. "I'll do my best to gently pry the tale of your exile from out between your lovely lips."

"Ooh," Kera said, dreamily. "Yeah, you should do that. Do you have booze?"

"Keep it in your pants," said Smith with a scowl.

Marie's eyebrows went up in response to Smith's gruffness, eyes moving to the man.

"And you are?" Marie asked.

"Smith," said Smith. "Just Smith."

"He too is a certified merchant," Brenno said, interjecting himself back into the conversation in hopes of commandeering it before Smith could say anything rude. "Might I ask what brought an alchemist and a wordsmith to journey to Zelwyr?"

"Of course, you're correct in bringing us back to business, good Mister Hornbuckle," Marie said, bowing low once more, Will and Kera's eyes glued to the neck of her low-cut dress. "We too are travellers, merchants and surveyors, agents of the Merchant's Guild on contract in order to establish whether or not the guild should be dedicating any of its resources towards improving the safety of this route. It would seem you've answered that question for us, at least to a certain degree, and for that we should thank you. Might I offer you allow us to do so in a manner more fitting for victors who have triumphed in battle? What say you to a shared camp? We've plenty of wine and spirits, and I'm certain good Mister Ashfist can spare a keg of his precious ale. Isn't that right, Torgil?"

The dwarf chuffed.

"One less won't hurt," said Torgil. "Breaks up the dozen, but I suppose that's tolerable enough. Not sure if that leaves me with several or many. I'll figure it out."

"Excellent," said Marie. "Torgil, be a dear and wake the twins, have them break out the plates and cutlery. Shall I have them prepare five additional portions or six?"

"I'm sorry?" Brenno asked.

"The armored one under your wagon," Marie said, pointing to Enaurl through the wood and paneling of Brenno's carriage. "Will she be dining with us, or does she intend to skulk there for the entirety?"

When no one spoke for a moment, the redheaded woman scanned the gathering of people, all frozen in uncertainty on and around the halfling's wagon.

"Have I said something wrong?"

Brenno unfroze first.

"No, of course not, not in the slightest," said the pawnbroker. "Enaurl is, ah, well, you see, it's difficult to explain. You see--"

"She doesn't have a mouth," Smith said, stepping down from the roof onto the driver's seat, wedging himself between Will and Brenno to step down onto the ground.

"Doesn't have a mouth?" Marie repeated. "How does she eat?"

"She doesn't," said Smith, walking over to the side of the carriage. Kneeling down, he offered a hand to Enaurl.

The automaton took it and pulled herself out from the caravan, rising to stand as her gears ground an earthy symphony of noise inside her chassis.

"Oh my," said the woman. "Oh my, my, *my*."

The woman fingered her lip, scrutinizing Enaurl from a distance. A noise like a thousand bubbles popping all at once was heard, and suddenly she was gone from where she stood.

The noise happened again, and she appeared behind Enaurl, walking a slow circle around the construct.

"Fascinating," she said, reaching down into the plunge of her low cut dress to fish out a pair of glasses, which she perched delicately on the end of her nose. "Where did you find this wonderful thing?"

"Well *that* was cool," said Will.

"She's not a thing," Smith grumbled, watching the woman intently. "And I didn't find her anywhere. I'm an artificer."

"Aah, of course," said the woman. "I should have known. Fingers blackened from oil stains and electrical burns, soot and ash in the folds of your boots, the lingering scents of steel and angst... As plain as the road before me, but I let it slip by unnoticed. Happens to the best of us, I suppose. How much?"

"How much what?" Smith asked.

"Don't be coy," said the woman, smiling playfully at Smith, her eyes moving from the man's face to his hands and back again. "Or do. Certainly your choice to make, and I shouldn't discourage that. What I meant, of course, is how much to buy her?"

"You couldn't afford her," Smith said, crossing his hands in front of his chest.

"My dear boy," said the woman, playful smile spreading ever wider as she peered at Smith from under the crook of Enaurl's arm. "You've no idea what I can afford."

"Not her," said Smith, "and I'm nobody's *boy*."

"Pity," said the woman, straightening her posture.

She ran her thumb across Enaurl's polished cheek, wetting it on her tongue to wipe away a smudge, glancing sidelong at Smith as she did.

"On both counts, of course."

Smith shook his head and stormed off, stomping his way towards the back of the carriage while muttering unintelligible nonsense. The woman watched him walk away, smiling absently.

"What is it about the prospect of a new project that seems so alluring even when you know full well how much work would go into it?"

"Beats me," said Will. "But if you figure it out, please tell me."

"I'd be a way better project," said Kera. "I mean... Yeah, no, I stand by it."

"You'll have to excuse these two," Brenno said, speaking over Kera and Will. "Besides not being merchants, I'm afraid they are little more than criminals and hired muscle."

"That's not entirely true," said Kera.

"Not entirely?" Marie asked, fixing her emerald eyes onto Kera's earthy brown ones.

"Okay so maybe a little," Kera said, going flush.

"Sounds interesting," Marie said, stepping towards Kera.

"Hey Kera, remember that thing you and I were talking about earlier?" Will asked, putting a hand on Kera's shoulder.

"What? What thing?"

"You know, the super important thing?" Will said. "The thing about you were worried you looked like an overeager goof that one time and didn't come across as cool as you wanted to?"

Kera said nothing, still staring dreamily at Marie. Comprehension dawned on her at once, and she shook free of her lurid daydreams.

"Right, right," said Kera. "That time with the beautiful lady alchem--"

"Wizard," Will finished, nodding.

"Right," said Kera. "The beautiful alchemizzard with hair like silky fire and skin like milk-colored silk dappled with droplets of the sun."

"Right, yep, that's the one," Will said, gently pulling Kera off to the side. "Definitely a different time, not at all from today. Let's go talk about it over here, out of earshot."

"Yeah, sure," said Kera, following Will as he lead her towards the back of the wagon.

The two began to whisper back and forth excitedly, just out of earshot. Brenno winced, agonizing as his professionalism was put in question by the actions of the others in his company.

"I must apologize once again," said Brenno, visibly flustered. "Were they employees, I would dismiss them for incompetence. As it is, I don't have much choice."

"I wouldn't worry about them, Mister Hornbuckle," Marie said with a smile, returning to her inspection of Enaurl, slowly pacing a circle around the automaton. Enaurl's head turned to watch her all the while.

"It's not the first time I've left someone struck with awe, and gods above and below I hope it won't be the last."

"Nonetheless," said Brenno. "If I had my choice of travelling companions, it would certainly not be these people."

"I feel the same way about someone who speaks as if I am not present," Voldani said, scowling at Brenno.

"Not you, Voldani," said Brenno. "Not Smith either. Just... those two." Brenno finished by waving his hand in the general direction Kera and Will had walked off in.

"I'm afraid I find myself confused," said Marie. "Did you not describe them as sellswords just a moment ago? Surely that means you purchased them."

"Well, no," said Brenno, fingers hooking and unhooking nervously behind his back, an anxious tick from his youth he had never fully been able to leave behind. "Not exactly. It's... quite a tale, I'm afraid, and I'm certainly not the right person to tell it."

When Brenno looked up, Marie was suddenly in front of him, her hands coming down to rest on his shoulders. She smiled down at him, eyes filled with the sparkle of amusement.

"Now, now, Mister Hornbuckle," said Marie, walking around the halfling as she'd done the construct, her fingers trailing across the back of Brenno's neck, making the hairs there stand on edge. "You mustn't sell yourself short. You never know what you are capable of until you try."

A high window on Marie's wagon opened up, rolling like a shutter. Torgil's mohawk emerged first, followed by the rest of him.

"Soup's on," said Torgil. "On the verge of simmering presently, but it'll be gently boiling soon. After that, should be ready in about fifteen minutes."

"Thank you, Torgil," said Marie. "Why don't you set up shop while we're waiting?"

Torgil nodded, the rear of his mohawk brushing against the frame of the window as he pulled his head back into the darkness beyond. Marie stood behind Brenno, hands on his shoulders.

"You may enjoy watching this, my good halfling. I know I always do."

Not understanding, Brenno watched the caravan. From inside, a series of thumps, thuds, and cranking sounds were heard.

All at once, the exterior of the double-sized caravan unfolded and extended, portions of it springing outward or sliding forward like a child's mechanical toy.

Sections and panels swung open like the doors on a wardrobe, while what looked like counter tops slid into place like mine carts on unseen tracks. A pole strung with tarps emerged from the top corner of the front-most wagon and traveled to the rear, while a pole from the back of the rear wagon moved in the opposite direction towards the front.

The two poles met at the midpoint of the caravan where they locked in place, tarps fully extended into a tent-like roof that covered the other sections. With a singular tremendous click, all the portions snapped into position and stopped moving, revealing an entire storefront complete with shelves, a front counter, and rows of vertical display cases complete with glass panes.

It reminded Brenno of his own shop, only far superior... And far less burnt down. His shoulders slumped, a feeling of dejection washing over him like a crashing wave.

"Something wrong, Mister Hornbuckle?" Marie asked, gently massaging his shoulders. "You seem terribly tense all of the sudden."

The halflings ears burned, and he couldn't help but hear Voldani's words echoing in his mind.

Envy will gain you nothing.

Chapter Twenty-Three

"You gotta be cool," Will said, speaking to Kera to the side of the wagon.

"What is that supposed to mean?" Kera asked.

"Well, for one, you're on the verge of openly drooling," said Will.

"What, like you've never gone gaga over an older woman?" Kera said accusingly, crossing her arms over her chest. Will raised his hands in mock surrender.

"Oh, believe me, I have made a tremendous fool of myself in front of many women," Will said.

"Would you say you were a spectacular fool?" Kera quipped.

"Ouch," Will said, lowering his hands. "That was just mean."

"Oh, come on," said Kera. "Your words, not mine."

"I know they're my words, that's why it hurts so much when they're used against me," said Will. "Listen, the point is, what I'm trying to say is that because I've made such a fool of myself in front of so many women, I can tell when someone else is doing it. Like you are just now, for instance. 'I would be a better project?' What does that even mean?"

"I'm just saying that I'll volunteer if she's looking for a short-term project," said Kera. "She's a damn fox, admit it."

"That is so not in question," said Will. "What's in question is why you've turned into a schoolboy ogling a busty milkmaid with a half-laced top bent over on her stool."

"That's a really specific example," said Kera. "What was her name?"

"Whose name?" Will asked.

"The milkmaid," said Kera.

"It was Evangeline, and she was a gift from the gods," said Will. "But again, that's not important. You weren't even like this at the bar. What's gotten into you?"

Kera mused for a moment, standing on the tips of her toes to peer at Marie from over Will's shoulders.

"Honestly?" Kera asked.

"No, I want you to lie to me some more," said Will.

"Bold choice of words coming from an illusiomancer," said Kera.

"Shut it," said Will. "Seriously, what's going on with you?"

Kera chewed on the inside of her cheek for a moment, peering over Will's shoulder at Marie once more.

"Honestly, I have no idea," said Kera. "Just looking at her makes me feel drunk and giddy."

Will turned his head to look at Marie, who was talking to Brenno about something, the details of which he couldn't hear.

"I mean, she's a looker, there's no doubt about it," said Will. "But she can't be the first attractive older lady you've seen."

"Well, no, she's not," said Kera, wagging her head from side to side as if she were weighing out her thoughts, trying to sieve out the correct choice of words from the sea of nonsense that seemed to be filling her mind. "Something about her makes me feel... hot."

"Are we crossing into a weird new place in our friendship here?" Will asked, eyebrows raised. "Because I mean, I'm fine with it, but I was not prepared for this."

"Not like that, you tremendous pervert," said Kera, punching the wizard in the shoulder, hard. Will winced and rubbed the area, certain that a bruise was forming. "I mean, a little in that way, but mostly not. It feels like my blood is on fire, and my heart is beating like a war drum."

"I have no frame of reference for what that sounds like," said Will. "I'm assuming that means beating fast?"

"Yes, it means beating very fast," said Kera, scowling at Will. "I feel flush, and energized, and weirdly excited. I honestly have no idea why."

"Ask the sword," Will said with a shrug. "Maybe it knows something we don't?"

"It probably knows a lot of things we don't," Kera said, eyes moving to Zephelous's hilt. "I kind of prefer it that way, to be honest. Things are starting to get really personal between me and it, and I'm not sure I like that."

"What do you mean?" Will asked.

"It's been spending more time inside my head than I'm comfortable with," said Kera, flicking Zephelous's pommel. She knew the gesture was utterly harmless to the sword, but the symbolic victory felt worthwhile, even as a twinge of pain ran through her finger.

"Can't, uh," Will asked, pausing to collect his thoughts. "Can't it hear all this?"

"Probably," said Kera

"And you're okay just kind of talking about it like this?" Will asked.

"Absolutely," said Kera. "I told it that if it does it again, I'll bury it where no one else would ever dig it up again."

"Okay, yeah, sure," said Will, eyes also going to the sword. "Call me old-fashioned, but I'm a little wary of talking swords."

"Yeah, me too," said Kera, unsheathing Zephelous and dropping its blade into her palm, holding the weapon flat between herself and Will. "I'm pretty sure it's harmless, though."

"That's what they all say, right before the thing takes over their minds and turns them into demented murder puppets," said Will, eyes still locked on the sword.

"I don't think Zeph would do that," Kera said, running a hand up and down the length of Zephelous's blade. "I think in its own dumb, boring, grumpy, nagging, insistent way, it's trying to help me. I don't know if I trust it, but I think I'm starting to understand it."

"Okay," said Will, nodding. "So why are you telling me this stuff? Shouldn't you be telling it to the sword?" Kera shook her head.

"I think I needed to say it to myself first," said Kera.

"Oh," said Will. "Do that, then."

"I just did," said Kera, giving Will a confused look. Will held Kera's gaze for a moment, then scoffed and threw his hands into the air, turning to storm back towards the gathered caravans. "Where are you going?" Kera called.

"Away," said Will.

"Why?" Kera asked.

"Because nobody actually talks to me," Will called, his voice growing louder as the distance between the two grew further. "I might as well just sit here to look pretty."

"You're not even that pretty," Kera shouted back. "You're all scraggly, and you're pretty much constantly a mess." Will's only response was to raise both his hands into the air with both middle fingers extended and aimed at Kera as he continued to storm off. Kera smiled to herself as she watched the surly wizard stomp away. She remembered her present task and sighed, her gaze falling to rest on the handle of the sword resting on her hip.

"Alright, Zeph," said Kera. "Let's hear it."

HEAR WHAT? Zephelous said.

"Whatever it is you're going to say," said Kera.

I DO NOT UNDERSTAND, said Zephelous.

"Drakeshit," Kera cursed, flicking the sword's hilt once again. "You heard every word I just said, so open up already."

I AM SORRY TO DISAPPOINT YOU, KERA, said Zephelous, BUT I DO NOT EXIST MERELY TO SERVE AS A RECEPTACLE OF KNOWLEDGE TO BE DIVULGED AT YOUR INCONSTANT WHIMS.

"Hang on," said Kera, "are you mad at me for something?"

NO, said Zephelous.

"Then what's up?" said Kera. "Because I don't know what's going on with you, and there's something weird going on with me, and I was actually kind of hoping you'd have something to say about it. For once."

WHILE I UNDERSTAND REPRESSING MOMENTS WHICH ARE UNCOMFORTABLE IS IN YOUR NATURE, KERA--

"I really don't see how that's rele--" Kera protested.

KNOW THAT IT IS NOT IN MINE, Zephelous said, talking over her. THE IMPLICATIONS OF WHAT I LEARNED IN YOUR MIND ARE WEIGHING ON ME. I AM PONDERING THE SIGNIFICANCE OF IT ALL, TRYING TO UNDERSTAND JUST HOW IT IS THAT YOU FIT INTO THE GRAND DESIGN, TO SEE HOW YOUR STRAND OF FATE IS WOVEN INTO THE TAPESTRY.

"You keep talking about that," said Kera. "And all that keeps happening is one disaster after another. There's nothing fateful here, Zeph, none of this is part of some grand design."

WHO IS IT THAT HAS CAUSED EACH OF THESE DISASTERS YOU SPEAK OF?

"Well, Brenno caused at least one of th--"

KERA, Zephelous shouted, its voice so loud in Kera's mind that she winced. PLEASE. FOR ONCE, BE HONEST WITH ME. IF NOT WITH ME, THAN WITH YOURSELF.

"Fine," Kera said, taking Zephelous's hilt in both hands and plunging the sword into the dirt. She crossed her legs and sat in front of it, staring into a distorted version of her own reflection as she spoke to the sword. "Okay, so maybe I caused some issues, and maybe I have some issues. So what? Everybody's got sh--"

DO NOT FINISH THAT SENTENCE, KERA NO-CLAN, Zephelous said. DO YOU REALIZE THAT YOU SIMPLIFY AND TRIVIALIZE EVERYTHING WE HAVE COME ACROSS? FROM YOUR OWN TRAUMA TO THE SERIES OF CRIME SPREES-

"It's wasn't technically a spree, more like a string," said Kera.

FINE, YOUR STRING OF CRIMES, AS WELL AS YOUR ADDICTIONS TO ALCOHOL AND FAE ASH, ALL FOR WHAT? Said Zephelous, its hanging question ringing like an echo in Kera's mind. She broke her eyes away from Zephelous, moving her gaze to stare into the dirt where it was plunged.

"Who says it has to be for something?" Kera said at last, still not bringing herself to look at the sword. "Can't something just be what it is, and have that be enough?"

NO, said Zephelous.

"Why not?" Kera said, "Who died and made you the lord and master of all things wise wisdomous? You're not even a person, what would you know about what it's like to be one?"

BRIGITTE LIONSIRE, said Zephelous.

"What?" Kera asked.

BRIGITTE LIONSIRE, ORVAK THE TERRIBLE, CORLOWAXIS ASECTI'GRAZ, ALYSSA OF THE INKLESS, THEUS VRAN, DASTION LEGACETO, HAZAHD THE MAD, LETHLIRIAN VETH-

"Zeph, stop! What is this, what are you saying?"

YOU ASKED HOW I COULD KNOW ABOUT WHAT IT IS TO BE A PERSON, said Zephelous. THESE ARE THE NAMES OF BUT A FEW OF THE HEROES I HAVE GUIDED IN THE PAST. I INSTRUCT THEM IN THE ART OF COMBAT, AND JOURNEYED WITH EACH OF THEM FOR A TIME, BRIEF COMPARED TO ALL THAT I HAVE KNOWN, BUT NOT SO FOR MANY OF THEM.

"I don't understand," said Kera.

THEUS VRAUN WAS BLUDGEONED BY A STONE AND SWALLOWED BY THE EARTH WITH ME ON HIS SHOULDER. ALYSSA DIED FROM AN AGONIZING AFFLICTION THAT ROTTED HER BODY AND SOUL WHILE I LAY ON A TABLE BESIDE HER. HAZAHD THE MAD WAS MAULED BY A WYVERN, HAD ONE OF HIS LEGS TORN FREE, BUT MANAGED TO CRAWL IN BETWEEN TWO BOULDERS WHERE THE BEAST COULD NOT GET TO HIM. HE BLED OUT OVER THE COURSE OF THREE DAYS, ASKING ONLY THAT I TELL HIM STORIES OF GREAT BATTLES WHILE HE GREW MORE AND MORE TIRED.

"Gods," Kera said, softly. "That's some intense shit, Zeph."

DO NOT DARE TO TRIVIALIZE THE DEATHS OF MY FRIENDS WITH YOUR CHILDISH VULGARITIES, Zephelous boomed, the grass near where it stood trembling as if a wind were blowing across it. THEY WERE HEROES ALL, THEY EARNED THEIR PLACES IN THE TAPESTRY OF FATE. THAT I THOUGHT FOR EVEN THE BRIEFEST MOMENT THAT YOU MIGHT BELONG BESIDE THEM IN THAT MOST AUSPICIOUS PLACE WAS

CLEARLY FOOLISHNESS, PERHAPS A SIDE EFFECT OF MY PROLONGED ISOLATION. The hurt Kera felt at Zephelous's words surprised her, left her eyes stinging and her chest feeling as if she'd just been punched.

"Zeph, I..." said Kera, voice soft and cracking. "I'm sorry. I didn't know about any of that, I had no idea."

ALL YOU HAD TO DO WAS ASK, said Zephelous. TO INQUIRE ABOUT THE MEANING BEHIND MY WORDS RATHER THAN DISMISS THEM AS YOU DO EVERYTHING ELSE IN YOUR LIFE THAT DOES NOT ANSWER AN IMMEDIATE NEED. A SIMPLE ENOUGH TASK, I WOULD HAVE THOUGHT.

"Zephelous," Kera said, tears welling up in her eyes. "I'm sorry, I didn't mean to--"

OF COURSE NOW IS WHEN YOU ARE SORRY, said Zephelous. AFTER YOU HAVE ALREADY DONE WHAT YOU--

"Stop," Kera said, leaning forward to place her hands on Zephelous's hilt, tears streaming down her face and dripping from her chin. "Please, just... Stop." She let her head hang, banging her forehead against Zephelous's guard.

The two remained there for a time, sitting in silence.

"I want you to keep believing in me," Kera whispered to the sword.

WHY? Zephelous asked, its tone rough as sanding paper.

"Because if you keep doing it, maybe I'll start too," said Kera.

DO YOU HONESTLY WANT THAT, KERA NO-CLAN? Zephelous asked. DO YOU TRULY WISH FOR ME TO CONTINUE TO BELIEVE THAT THERE IS GREATNESS IN YOU, THAT YOU HAVE UNBRIDLED POTENTIAL, THAT YOU COULD BE A HERO?

"Yes," Kera admitted, nodding as she wiped away her tears. "I really do."

THEN START FUCKING ACTING LIKE IT, said Zephelous. Kera nodded, standing hastily and pulling Zephelous out of the ground. Making her way back towards the group, Kera nearly made it all the way to the caravan before she stopped.

"Did you just say f--"

DO NOT SAY ANOTHER WORD.

"Yep, sure, that's fine."

Chapter Twenty-Four

"So much for the advice of timbergnolls," Brenno mused, speaking to Marie. "Though I suppose we should have known better than to put much stock in improvised lyrical prophecies."

"Advice from timbergnolls?" Marie asked, suddenly standing beside Brenno. "Is that what you said? What sort of improvised prophecies did that bitch god of theirs have them spew?"

"A valid assessment of Leighlagh," Voldani said, hoisting a circular shield up from the racks. Spokes ran from the center of the shield out to its edge, looking somewhat like flattened metallic wagon wheel. Torgil nodded as she inspected it.

"That's a good one," said Torgil. "Returns when thrown. Not by magic, by physics. Bounces like a rubber ball, but is plenty hard enough to block a sword."

"Shields are a waste of time," said Voldani. "I protect myself with swords."

"It's nothing," said Brenno, speaking to Marie. "While we battled the dogmen, they prattled on with their rhyming lines, taunting us and goading us."

"That is the way of the dogmen," Marie said, running a finger along her chin thoughtfully. "Though for them to tell a prophecy in battle is unheard of."

"It was after the battle was won," Brenno explained. "All the timbergnolls who engaged us had died or fled, leaving only Ratbite behind."

"Ratbite?" Marie echoed.

"Yes, Ratbite," Brenno clarified. "The name of the timbergnoll."

"It gave you its name?" Marie asked, intrigued.

"Well, yes," said Brenno. "I had introduced myself properly, as one should when negotiating the terms of a bargain or contract."

"Contract?" Marie asked, intrigue growing to incredulity. "Negotiate? I wasn't aware those words were in the timbergnoll vocabulary."

"Nor was I," Brenno admitted, smiling with pride. "I've since learned better."

"So it would seem," Marie said, amusement visible on her every feature. "Please, go on. Tell me of these negotiations."

"It was rather straightforward," said Brenno. "We bartered Ratbite's life in exchange for safe passage out of the woods and any information it might have about dragons."

"Dragons?" Marie asked, her tone falling from amused to serious. "What on all the earths would you need information about dragons for? And from a timbergnoll, no less."

"Well," Brenno admitted, embarrassment threatening to color his ears red. "When one has no idea where to find something, it is sometimes best to check everywhere. As for why, well... Suffice it to say it is relevant to our campaign."

"Your quest," Marie corrected. "Though I suppose the term campaign is more modernized, more fitting, and I suppose technically more accurate."

"Aye," Torgil added.

"Still, a quest is timeless," said Marie. "A quest to find a dragon especially so. Pray, do tell, what is the reason for this quest? Do you find yourself in need of gold, good Mister Hornbuckle? Is this a quest for revenge, perhaps? Was one of your parents murdered by one of the old ones and now you seek revenge?"

"Nothing so grand, I'm afraid," Brenno said with a smirk. "We find ourselves in need of dragon's blood. Not a great quantity, I shouldn't think, but some all the same."

"I see," said Marie. "A quest for power, then. Magics dark and terrible, to be used for whatever mysterious reason you have that has given you a hunger to taste arcane power."

"No, not at all," said Brenno. Marie blinked, appearing confused.

"Then what?" Marie asked.

"We require its blood to make a healing tonic," said Brenno. "In order to counteract the effects of a cursed poisoned arrow."

"Which is it?" Marie asked. "Cursed or poisoned?"

"Both," Brenno said flatly, posture slumping again.

"How egregious," said Marie, smiling playfully. "And who is it that had the terrible misfortune to be both cursed and poisoned?"

Brenno felt ill, wishing he could disappear. He looked to see if Smith was still engaged inspecting the various wares on Torgil's shop.

Seeing that he was, he sighed.

"Smith's daughter, Morrillypallyke," Brenno said, hoping and praying the woman wouldn't press the issue.

"Aaah, that name is like music to my ears," said Marie, head swaying as if she were hearing an unseen melody that accompanied the use of Morri's name. "I've always found the first tongue had an incomparable sense of of *music* to it, don't you agree? Ah, but I'm going off track, I apologize. What happened to the girl?"

Brenno swallowed hard, or tried to. His mouth had dried completely, and so in trying to swallow he nearly choked.

"She was shot," Brenno whispered.

"Shot, poisoned, and cursed," Marie said, making a tut-tut sound with her tongue against the roof of her mouth as she shook her head. "What an unfortunately unlikely fate."

"Yes," said Brenno, his tongue feeling like a beached whale. "Unfortunate and unlikely."

Marie's gaze moved to Smith, and her index finger moved to rest between her teeth.

"That does explain how the man wears anguish like a cologne," Marie said, eyes actively bathing in the pools of Smith. "Talented and miserable. If I had the energy I had a few decades ago, the gods themselves couldn't keep that man out of my grasp."

"Not too many decades ago, I should think," said Brenno.

"And I'll thank you to go on thinking that," said Marie. "Alchemy is a wonder."

The two lapsed into a moment of silence, with Brenno desperately hoping saliva would return to his mouth and Marie seemingly having the opposite problem.

"Did they have anything useful to say?" Marie asked after a moment.

"The timbergnolls?" Brenno clarified, to which Marie nodded. "In a manner, I suppose. You'll forgive me if the exact wording escapes me, but I believe what Ratbite said was 'continue north and there you'll find a prime specimen of their kind', or something very similar. Smith was content with hearing the words 'go north, find dragon', and so here we are."

"Hmm," said Marie, deep in thought. "I suppose that's meant to be flattering to a gnoll."

"I beg your pardon?" Brenno asked.

"Prime specimen," Marie repeated, shaking her head, peeling her eyes off of Smith to point her emerald gaze in Brenno's direction once more. "Not much of a descriptor, no inherently useful information associated with it, just that it will be prime. Prime in what sense? Large, strong, smart? No idea. You don't even know what *color* this specimen is that you should be looking for."

"Well," Brenno said, parsing his lips. "I suppose you're right on those counts."

"I'm certain that I'm right," said Marie. "How far north are you meant to travel?"

"Until we find a dragon, I suppose," Brenno said, shrugging.

Marie threw her head back and laughed gleefully for a long while. Wiping a tear from her eye, she patted Brenno on the shoulder and sighed.

"Oh, my dear pawnbroker," said Marie. "Is this your first quest?"

"Not entirely," said Brenno, embarrassed once more. "I was a campaigner once."

"Oh?" Marie asked. "You say that as if it were a lifetime ago."

"In a manner of speaking, I suppose it was," Brenno said with a grimace. "I'm nearing my hundred and thirtieth year. My campaigning days took place during my adolescence."

"A hundred years since your last adventure," Marie said, nodding. "I suppose in that time, you forgot how to read maps?"

"No, of course not," said Brenno, brow furrowed.

"You've forgotten how to converse with folks of the non-dogmen variety, then," Marie posited, counting her points on the tips of her fingers.

"Certainly not," said Brenno. "We're conversing now, are we not?"

"We are, we most certainly are," said Marie. "And in all this time, you've yet to ask if I have any information about dragon sightings. Of course, you could simply continue north without bothering to do so, but I might be able to save you some time."

"What, no, certainly, I," Brenno stammered, his ears feeling very hot. He took a measured breath, forcing himself to calm down. "I would deeply appreciate that information."

"What information?" Marie asked coyly.

"The information you may have in regards to dragon sightings," said Brenno. "I'm certain we can come to an affable arrangement. We have coin and services to offer, and I could write up a contract--"

Marie laughed once more, this time more impish than mirthful.

"My dear halfling," said Marie, shaking her head. "None of that will be necessary, I assure you. You and your band have provided us with information in regards to the state of the road ahead free of charge, the least I can do is return the favor. I have no doubt that continuing north will eventually lead you to discover a dragon in the same way that you'll eventually find the frozen peaks of the Crown of the World. That being said, we've come this way after leaving Sundial Vale and the town which shares its name."

"Sundial Vale?" Brenno repeated. "The settlement?"

"A settlement once," said Marie. "It has grown tremendously in the last handful of years."

"Settlements this far north are typically sacked and razed to the ground within a matter of months," Brenno said. "How is it that Sundial Vale still stands?"

"How is it that any place stands against the hardships of the world, its many horrors, and the ravages of time?" Marie asked, arching an eyebrow while smiling, amusement painted on every inch of her flawless face. "Brave folks rose up to protect it. A band of campaigners found the town in a sorry state, and took it upon themselves to become its guardians. They've been mostly successful at doing so."

"Mostly?" Brenno asked.

"There is a bit of a problem, one they have yet to overcome," Marie said, walking around Brenno as she spoke. "The farms and vineyards on the outskirts of the Vale are regularly pillaged and plundered, the farmers and their cattle carried off for food."

"Carried off by whom?" Brenno asked.

"Isn't it obvious?" Marie said, letting the question hang.

"A dragon," Brenno whispered, feeling a wave of anxiety and fear roll through him.

"Exactly," said Marie. "A white, by all accounts. The denizens of the Vale have begun calling it Frostshadow, a name that it most likely has no idea is being used for it."

"The Vale has not been able to press it back?" Brenno asked. "Or bring it down?"

"From what I understand, the Vale is regularly beset by timbergnolls, orc bands, trolls, and all manner of giants. Keeping a town standing is no easy task, like holding water in cupped hands. Try as you might, a few drops will be lost."

"I don't know that I would liken a dragon to a few drops of water," Brenno said, rubbing the back of his head with his palm.

"No," said Marie, nodding. "But in the grand design, losing a few cows here and the odd farmhand there seems like a small price to pay in exchange for keeping the creature at bay. At least, so the residents of Sundial Vale seem to believe."

Will rounded the corner of the nearest wall of the mobile ship, holding a pair of vials in hand.

"Surely a dragon could raze their town to the ground if it wanted to," Brenno said, frowning. "To use your own words, of course."

"Oh, surely," said Marie, speaking slowly. "*If it wanted to* being the key. Dragons are far fewer in the days since the war. Most are content to hide themselves from the world, slumbering away in their gold lined hidey holes until they feel the world is ready for them once more. Some aren't contented to slumber. Some prefer to make nests in remote locations and live very much as they have before, keeping a low profile. Well, as low a profile as is possible for a dragon, is what I suppose I should be saying."

"How low of a profile could a dragon possibly maintain?" Brenno asked with a scoff.

Marie smiled at him, looking down at him the way a mother watched over a small child, blinking her dazzling emerald eyes at him so slowly he could almost watch her lashes curl and uncurl.

"You would be surprised, Mister Hornbuckle," Marie said. For the briefest moment, Brenno thought he saw speckles of red in the green of her eyes, thought he saw her pupil elongate and narrow...

Then the moment passed.

"Question for you Marie," Will said, injecting himself into the conversation as he rounded the corner of the shop, a pair of glass vials filled with a gleaming liquid of some kind in his hands.

He held them up to the light, scrutinizing them and their glowing contents.

"These just say 'motes' on them, but the type of mote isn't specified."

"Right you are, Will," Marie said, long legs turning a stride towards the illusionist into more of a glide. "In actuality, if you note the color of the hook from which the vials hang, you'll see what they are. Here, allow me to show you--"

Placing a hand on Will's back, Marie gently guided him towards the section of the storefront in question.

The two fell into an animated discussion about the different practical uses to having a concentrated mote of raw magic, but Brenno wasn't listening. All he could hear was a distant roaring that he was only mostly certain he was imagining, visions of scales and teeth floating through his mind.

Chapter Twenty-Five

When Speaker Gerhardt returned to the infirmary, he was trailed by two hooded acolytes working in tandem to pull a wagon behind them. Morri had tied her long locks of hair back into a neat braid, which promised to keep flowing strands of hair away from her face.

She had donned a diminutive suit of armor similar to that worn by the other black priests, one Pephe told her had once belonged to a dwarven member of Perroh's chosen.

The helmet, when donned, obscured her vision entirely, the bulbous red orbs sitting too high on the helm's face to align with Morri's eyes.

"Speaker, you've returned," Morri said, releasing the rope of hair, letting it swing freely behind her.

She offered the elder a bleak smile, one that betrayed just how fearful she felt about her current endeavor. The Speaker smiled and nodded in return, gesturing to the cart and the silent acolytes pulling it.

"I have indeed, Miss Smith," said the Speaker. "And I've brought every item from your list. You'll forgive me for the time it took to gather the various odds and ends, I'm afraid none of us are half as adept with the terminology as we would like to admit. Nevertheless, I'm confident that everything you requested is present."

Morri rounded the table on which the unconscious man sat, careful to give the infected and dripping limbs a wide berth as she did. Peering over the edge of the cart, she sifted through the various mechanical bits and pieces that had been gathered in a heap on the back of the wagon.

Finding every coil, every length of steel, every piston and component she had listed, she nodded.

"You've done an excellent job, Speaker," said Morri, scanning the contents of the cart once more. "Not a single item appears to be amiss. I must commend you on your efficiency, and would humbly suggest you have more knowledge than you let on."

The Speaker chuckled and waved off the compliment, leaning heavily on his cane.

"You're too kind, miss Smith," said the Speaker, dismissing the acolytes with a wave of his hand. "I am merely an old man doing his best to keep up. If anyone should be commended, it is you, for your more than admirable efforts here today."

"I would save the accolades for after the operation, Speaker," Morri said grimly, her gaze moving from the cart to the man strapped to the operating table. "It's certainly far too soon for commendations of any sort."

She swallowed, feeling her stomach acids roil as anxiety threatened to overwhelm her. The Speaker seemed to sense all of this, and wordlessly moved to place a reassuring hand on Morri's shoulder.

"Young lady," said the Speaker, his voice strained. "Know that even if you fail here today, you'll have taught an invaluable thing or two to an old priest."

"And a half dozen extremely useful things to a not so old one," said Pephe, stepping into the makeshift surgical arena.

The black priest was carrying a load of sheets in his arms, which he deposited on the floor. He picked one up and spread it out on the floor, a black-green stain slowly spreading as the fabric soaked up the spilled fluid from the man's grisly infection. Pephe repeated this process until he had covered the floor entirely before moving on to doing the same to the walls, using what looked like clothespins to create a rigid curtain of fabric around the patient.

Sensing the eyes of Morri and the Speaker on him, Pephe turned and offered a shrug, his insectile suit rising and falling with the motion.

"It's to try to prevent the spread of contagion," said Pephe. "We don't know anything about this stuff except that it came from whatever he was carrying in that wagon. We don't know how it spreads, how it got into him, nothing. I'm just covering my bases."

"I'll not fault you for being prudent," Morri said. "I'm grateful for your efforts, Pephe."

"No problem, kid," said Pephe. "Likewise."

Another black priest stepped into the room, this one carrying what looked like a massive cleaver. Morri blanched and gasped, and Speaker Gerhardt groaned softly.

"Surely that's not what I think it is," said the Speaker.

"I'm afraid so," said Pephe, hoisting the monstrous cleaver with both hands.

The blade sparkled in the light of the infirmary, its pristine surface reflecting and distorting the scene around it.

Morri gulped audibly.

Pephe glanced in her direction, setting the huge blade down on the table.

"It's either this or the saw, and believe me when I say you don't want to use the saw."

"Dare I ask why?" Morri asked, her tiny voice faltering and threatening to quit altogether.

"Well for one, it's real messy," said Pephe. "For two, it takes longer."
"I see," said Morri, nodding grimly. "I should think we'd prefer to avoid any spattering of the infected fluids onto ourselves."

"Exactly," said Pephe, nodding. "You know, you've got a knack for this, Morrillypallyke. If artifice ever bores you, I'd be happy to write you a recommendation to come work here."

"I appreciate the offer, Pephe," Morri said. "Though I doubt father would approve. What's more, I suspect I far prefer working on Enaurl to what I'm about to experience. For one, Enaurl is far less…"

When Morri's sentence trailed off, Pephe jumped in.

"Squishy?" the priest offered.

"I suppose that sums it up rather nicely," Morri said.

The nameless priest who had brought the massive cutting implement returned once more, this time bearing a wooden stool.

Without a word, the chitin-armored individual strode across the room and placed the stool beside the table. Not entirely satisfied with its positioning, the figure used their foot to slide one corner of the bench slightly closer, then nodded.

The figure offered a quick bow to Pephe, Morri, and Speaker Gerhardt in turn, then left the room. Morri took a slow breath and walked over towards the bench, stepping up onto it.

She hadn't been this close to the young man before, and her newfound proximity only served to hammer home the fact that what she was about to do was completely and utterly alien to her in every way conceivable.

This was not an engine that needed tuning, a gadget whose workings had come undone. This was a living, breathing, flesh and blood man who was about to have an extensive amount of that flesh removed by way of a colossal butcher's knife, which was likely to cause potentially catastrophic amounts of fluid to spill out from inside the man, pouring like a floodgate to stain the floors.

Stain the floors? She thought to herself. *Funny that that's what I should think of, of all things.*

Morri did her best to silence her thoughts, worried that even the slightest errant thought would stop her from being able to look at what was laid out in front of her and see him as nothing but the anatomical marvel that he was. It was far better to think of him as a series of connective tissues, fluid containers, and internal mechanisms than it was to think of him as the same sort of creature she was.

Far, far better.

Pephe hoisted the blade in both hands once more, letting the monstrous cutting surface come to rest against the man's shoulder. Glancing at the girl, Pephe paused.

"Are you ready for this, kid?" Pephe asked.

"Morrillypallyke," Morri corrected.

"I know," said Pephe. "But that's a real long name, and we're going to have to move quickly once this gets started. Real quickly."

"Morri, then," Morri offered.

"Works for me," said Pephe. "Speaker, can I get you to take a few steps back?"

"Yes, certainly," said the Speaker, backing up until he was pressed against the sheet that was the makeshift wall of the operating theater. "Is this adequate?"

"I certainly hope so," said Pephe, raising the cleaver up and into the air. He paused, letting the blade hang like an unwieldy guillotine. A moment of tense silence passed.

"Well?" Asked Morri, looking to Pephe.

"Just making sure you were ready," said Pephe. "On three. One, two--"

If the black priest said the number 'three' out loud, the sound was lost between the whistling of the cleaver and the thump the blade made as it chopped through the meat and thumped against the table on which he lay.

The thump was followed immediately by a second, then a third, then a fourth as Pephe expertly adjusted his positioning around the table to deftly remove the limbs.

Morri had expected red fluid to pump and spatter in all directions, and was startled to see that the only fluid that exited the grisly wounds was a thicker, more sludge-like version of the blackish-greenish ooze that had dripped from the man's limbs previously.

She felt the blood drain from her face, watched as if removed from her own body as she ran to the cart and prepared the necessary pieces of artifice she would need immediately: wires, pistons, and a small hand torch that was normally used for cutting through thin sheets of steel but would be used to cauterize wounds this day.

Without conscious effort, she watched her own hands hastily place iron clamps and spin them to the proper adjustment, feeling as though she were watching someone else do the grisly work, as though someone else's gloved hands were wiping a mass of congealed goo away from an open wound that exposed the grisly and sticky inner workings of human anatomy. It wasn't her who torched pink flesh to black, it was whoever was controlling her diminutive hands. That same controller used an extensive knowledge of artifice to blend nerves with wires, muscle with piston, and bone with steel to create the base point from which an entire limb could later be attached.

She watched in a daze, sick to her stomach all the while, as that same controller repeated the same process on both legs and the other arm. The implements she'd attached were a far, far cry from the final limbs she intended to create for the man, but they were the base from which the final products would spring; a foundation where steel and iron would mark girl's best attempt at artificial organic life.

The clamps squelched into flesh in the manner Morri had hoped they would, settling nicely. The body would try to reject the metal, seeing it as a foreign and hostile invader, but with the right regimen of roots and herbs, that involuntary response could be suppressed all together. It would take time, and it would not be easy, but Morri was confident that the man would walk again.

The surgery was over before Morri realized it, her hands wiping themselves clean on a cloth offered by Pephe. The girl glanced at the discarded limbs, laying in a slowly growing pool of brackish liquid. Nausea reared its ugly head, but Morri forced it down by taking a quick series of breaths.

"We're done," said Pephe, wiping his hands and suit clean of the sickly spatter.

"So quickly?" Morri heard herself ask, still feeling detached from her own being.

"I don't know about quickly," said Pephe. "Took the better part of four hours."

"Four hours?" Morri repeated, incredulous. "That can't be. We only just started."

"I believe the good priest Pephe is correct in this matter, Miss Smith," Speaker Gerhardt said, his voice muffled as he spoke through a cloth that once again covered much of his face. "Though I must admit the weariness in my old bones makes it seem as if it were twice that amount of time, if not more."

The Speaker chuckled lightly as he spoke, slowly making his way toward the unconscious man.

The old man poked at the brackets that marked the place where flesh met metal, where tissue met artifice, lifting the stub of a limb to get a better view of the open connections that waited for their matching pieces.

"Is this all it takes?" the Speaker asked.

"*All it takes?*" Pephe repeated, laughing sarcastically. "Speaker, I've been a member of Perroh's chosen since I was a boy, and a black priest from the moment I was eligible. I've studied tomes and scrolls the way men far less mangled than I study women and tavern wenches. Believe me when I say that what Morri did here today is unprecedented. More than that, it's revolutionary. I'm going to file a report with the black bishop, see if we can't implement procedures like this across Malzen. Hells, I bet the churches on the mainland would be more than a little interested to learn about stuff like this."

As Pephe spoke, he walked around the table, gathering the severed limbs as if they were discarded logs, piling them up in his arms.

"What happened here today is just short of a miracle, Speaker. I'm sure I don't need to tell you that."

Speaker Gerhardt nodded solemnly, leaning heavily on his cane once more.

"Surely we should monitor the patient first and foremost, no?" the Speaker asked, brow creasing with concern. "I should think making certain that the procedure is successful is paramount to spreading the news of it being attempted to every corner of the wide world."

"Says you," said Pephe, reaching over the collection of severed limbs to unseal his helmet and remove it. "This is revolutionary, Speaker. You and I just witnessed history in the making. What this girl just did is worth carving into the pages of the old tomes. Everyone needs to hear about this, every priest and healer, every temple to every god both above and below."

"You're absolutely right," said Speaker Gerhardt, coughing into his hand. "It's nothing short of miraculous. I'll trust you to make those arrangements, as I couldn't even begin to make them myself. The temple of Perrus is far emptier these days than it once was, as you well know."

"No disrespect speaker, but that hardly seems relevant," said Pephe, the scarred flesh on his face heaving with every word he spoke. "This man was as good as dead earlier today, from something we couldn't even identify let alone diagnose. Thanks to Morri there's a very good chance he'll walk out of here - on metal legs, no less."

"Please," said Morri, stepping away from the surgical field to brace herself against the stone wall that stood opposite the makeshift sheet. "Your praise is far too gracious, Pephe. I've merely done what I could, what anyone would do in my place. My father would have done a far more exact job, and with much more confidence I've no doubt."

"Yeah, because Smith would give a shit," Pephe said with a snort. "I mean, no offense. He's your dad, I get that, but he's not exactly known for his caring attitude."

"Father," said Morri, voice trembling as she fought the shakes.

"Eh?" Pephe asked, readjusting the pile of severed limbs in his arms.

"Terminology is all," Morri explained. "I far prefer 'father' to 'dad'."

"Whatever floats your boat, kid," said Pephe. "I mean, Morri, not kid."

Morri offered Pephe a weak smile, one that relayed just how exhausted and drained the poor girl felt after what she'd just seen and done. Her smile left her face immediately, replaced with a mask of horror. Her eyes went wide, and her mouth fell open. Trembling hands raised to point at Pephe.

"What?" said the priest, smiling through the holes in his face. "I'm just too pretty, aren't I?"

An extended slurping sound caught Pephe's attention, causing him to look down at the bundle of limbs in his hands. The sickly fluid, the brackish green-black ooze, that had been dripping freely from the limbs a moment before had ceased falling - had ceased being a liquid all together.

A squirming, fluid, snake-sized maggot made entirely from that unnatural substance writhed among the limbs in Pephe's hands, rearing up like a royal cobra in front of the black priest's scorched visage.

"Aw, fuck," Pephe whispered.

The ooze struck, the extended tendril splashing into Pephe's face. The priest screamed and clutched at his face, his muffled cries barely escaping from under the tar-like coating of ooze that covered his head.

Morri screamed, and Speaker Gerhardt sputtered and started.

Shambling towards the black priest with all the speed he could muster, the Speaker held a hand over the now prone black priest's body and began muttering under his breath. The old man's eyes flickered and shone with silver light, his fingertips emitting piercing beams of the same color. The beams plunged into the ooze, and it cried out as if it were a living creature. The slime peeled itself away from Pephe's face and pooled nearby, its surface bubbling and smoking as if it were boiling and burning. The pool simmered itself away to nothingness, leaving only stained fabric in its wake.

Morri hurried to Pephe's side, rolling the priest onto his back. The man still held his face in his hands, moaning softly. Gently but determined, Morri pulled his hands away from his face. Her breath caught in her throat, and she gasped despite her best efforts.

"Be honest, kid," Pephe asked, sounding weary and pained. "How bad is it?"

"I..." Morri started, unsure how to respond as she looked down at the priest.

Before, his face had been burnt horribly, bits of mutilated flesh stretched over openings that showed clear into muscular tissue beneath. The girl wished that were what she was staring at now, wished for awful strips of pink and red flesh, for any color other than the porcelain white of exposed bone and the haunting blackness of empty orbital sockets.

"That bad, huh?" Pephe asked, coughing. "Can you get it off of my eyes at least?"

"I..." Morri said, all the blood draining from her face.

She felt dizzy and weak, once again no longer in control of her own body. She heaved, her stomach threatening to expel its contents all over the downed priest. She was only dimly aware of Speaker Gerhardt's arms around her waist, lifting her away from Pephe and towards the far corner of the room. She retched forcefully, feeling as if her stomach were trying to escape through her mouth.

Pephe coughed weakly, but managed a meager sputter that was unmistakably a terrible laugh.

"Worse than I thought, eh?" Pephe asked, weak laughter dying into a sputtering cough. "That's bad. That's real bad."

The priest's voice was a shallow shadow of what it once was, sounding airy and lofty.

"Hey Speaker," said Pephe, pausing only to for a wetter and wetter sounding coughing fit to wrack his body. "I don't suppose you've got the strength in you to lift that cleaver, eh? I'm starting to feel the pain now. It hurts real bad. I'd like that to stop."

Morri's vision swam at the priest's words, and she retched again. The Speaker was silent, looking from the priest to the table. Wordlessly, the old man moved towards the table and gripped the handle of the terrible cutting implement. With a grunt and a visible struggle, he slid it off the table. Staggering under the weight of the steel blade, the Speaker stumbled his way towards Pephe.

With a grunt and groan of effort, elderly body threatening to crumple beneath the now black-stained blade, the Speaker lifted the edge of the sharpened weapon over Pephe's neck.

"I am sorry beyond words that it came to this, Pephe," Speaker Gerhardt wheezed, straining to keep the blade aloft.

Pephe coughed, a thick wad of blood and mucus spattering the front of his exposed skull.

"That makes two of us, Speaker," Pephe wheezed.

The Speaker grimaced, tightening his grip on the blade. With all the strength he could muster, he raised the weapon higher, intending to use the weapon's own weight to assist him in his grisly task.

The old man's knuckles tightened around the handle, his face set itself into a mask of grim resolution.

"May Perrus guide you to a place without pain," the Speaker said.

"May Perroh swallow my suffering," Pephe responded.

With a sigh, the Speaker inhaled a slow breath, readying himself to act as executioner.

"Wait," Morri said, wiping the sick from her chin. "Speaker, please, a moment."

Shaking and trembling still, Morri rose. The Speaker looked at her from over his shoulder, arms threatening to give out at any moment under the weight of the blade. With a groan, he lowered it, letting its tip rest against the sheet covered floor.

"What is it, Morri?" the Speaker huffed, breathing heavily as he stared at the girl. "Be quick about it, I implore you."

"Yeah," croaked Pephe. "Let's not waste any time. It's starting to feel worse."

"I understand, Pephe, truly," said Morri, fighting to control the quiver in her voice.

"No," Pephe said, hacking up another wad of blood. "You don't."

Morri felt the dizziness and impending nausea return, threatening to overwhelm her once more. Resolved, Morri clenched her fists and her jaw and swallowed her bile.

"Be that as it may," Morri said, "So long as you are not resolved to death, and provided there is no trace of the sludge still within you, I may be able to construct for you--"

"Kid," Pephe interrupted. "I'm dying. Spare me the gold plated words, just get to it."

"I believe I can save you," said Morri.

"From a state such as this?" Gerhardt asked, astonished. "How?"

"Using similar methods to what father and I used for Enaurl," said Morri, kneeling to examine Pephe's flayed face. "Enaurl has no eyes, but she sees just fine. With what I've learned today working with nerve endings, I suspect I could combine that information with the methods used to give Enaurl sight and do the same for you, Pephe."

"Will wonders never cease?" Speaker Gerhardt said, clasping his hands together in a sign of thanks, holding them to the heavens. "Thank you, Perrus, thank you, thank you, *thank you.*"

"It is a little soon to be thanking anyone, Speaker," Morri said grimly. "I've no idea if this will work, and only the barest idea how to go about performing it. Worse still, I would need for Pephe to remain awake throughout, to tell me when his vision is restored."

"Oh good," Pephe said, gasping. "I'd hate for it to be too easy."

"Do you have all that you require?" Gerhardt asked.

"No," said Morri. "There are a few items I require from father's shop."

The Speaker snapped his fingers, and from behind the sheet the two hooded acolytes appeared, walking as one. The Speaker withdrew the notebook from the inside of his robes, flipped it open, and looked expectantly up at Morri.

"When you're ready."

Without saying a word, Morri walked over to the Speaker and gently took the book from his hands, hastily scrawling out a list of several items. Smiling ruefully, she handed the book back.

"Apologies, Speaker," said Morri. "Some of these items have quite elaborate names, I felt it was just quicker to do it myself. Will your acolytes recognize these items, or shall I draw them out as well?"

The Speaker's eyes roamed up and down the list Morri had written, and he nodded to himself as if it all made perfect sense. Without so much as a glance in their direction, he passed the book to his acolytes, who took it and left.

"They'll be perfectly fine," said the Speaker. "Do you truly believe you can do this?"

"I believe it is my duty to try," said Morri.

"Spoken like a black priest," Pephe said, his voice becoming steadily more hoarse.

"You mustn't talk, Pephe," Morri said, kneeling just behind the black priest's head, lifting it gingerly to let it rest on her knees. "The acolytes won't be long, I promise."

"Sure," said Pephe, voice wavering so much it was a strain for Morri to understand it. "I'll just wait here if that's okay. I'm tired, it's been a long day."

"Of course," said Morri, tears welling up in her eyes. "I wouldn't have it any other way." The acolytes returned in a few minutes, but it felt to Morri as if it had taken days.

Strange, she thought, *a procedure that takes hours passes in moments, and mere moments feel as if they take ages. I suppose it goes to show that the passage of time is relative.*

The creaking of wooden wagon wheels on the decrepit stone of the infirmary signaled the return of the acolytes, the pair of silent hooded monks approaching much in the way they had before; unspeaking, moving in a stilted manner as if the grimness of the scene before them had made them reluctant to approach.

Rather than being stocked full of mechanical odds and ends, the wagon contained only a single woven basket filled with a small assortment of gleaming mechanical oddities. The Speaker approached the wagon first, lifting the basket out from it as if its contents were as delicate as a newborn child. A wrinkled hand with spindly fingers reached into the basket and removed a sphere of seamless metal that resembled a ball bearing.

"Do be careful with that please, Speaker," Morri said, wincing slightly as the old man held the orb close to the torch on the wall to better examine it. "I'm afraid it's rather delicate until it's been installed into its housing."

"Certainly, my dear," said the old man. "Where should I place it?"

"Back in the basket would be ideal," said Morri, wiping the beads of sweat from her brow. "At least until I've had time to prepare the receptacle." The Speaker nodded solemnly and carefully placed the orb back into the basket. Noting that there were very few contents besides the orb and its twin, the Speaker frowned and turned to look at Morri.

"There are dreadful few elements in here," said the Speaker, passing the basket to Morri as if he were handing the girl a tray filled with balanced eggs. "Perhaps I'm simply uneducated on the subject, but I see nothing that resembles a housing or a receptacle."

Morri blanched as she accepted the basket from the Speaker, swallowing hard once more as the bile in her stomach threatened to rise into her throat.

"Neither of those components are in the basket, Speaker," said Morri.

The old man's bushy brows knitted together into a single line of concern across his brow.

"Oh?" The Speaker said. "Was something left behind? Shall I send them back?"

"That won't be necessary, Speaker," said Morri, stepping up onto the stool beside the surgical table. "I've everything I need here."

"But the receptacle," said the Speaker. "And the housing?"

"I'm afraid it's Pephe who will be providing both of those elements," said Morri, gently depositing the basket beside the horrible faceless visage of the black priest.

Pephe sputtered, a weak and sickly cough wracking his chest and throat.

"I knew you were going to say that," said Pephe.

"Hush, Pephe," Morri said, her small hands gripping the armored glove of the priest, squeezing tightly. "You must save your strength."

"You're probably right," said Pephe, another miserable coughing fit punctuating his sentence. "I just want you to tell me one thing, kid, and swear to me by the endless tomes of the Black Warden that you'll be honest."

"Anything, Pephe," said Morri. "So long as you promise you'll stop talking after."

"Sure, sure," Pephe said with a lazy nod, the bleached skull of his face rocking back and forth, the orange glow of the torch shining through the glaring holes in the skull and into the slick wetness beyond.

"Is it going to hurt?"

Not knowing what to say, Morri said nothing.

She squeezed Pephe's hand all the harder, squeezed until her arms hurt from the strain. She felt a wetness on her chin, and removed one hand from the wounded priest's to wipe it away.

Holding the offending liquid up to the flickering light of the torch, she found drops of water clinging to her fingertips. Pressing those fingertips against her face, she realized she'd been crying.

She sniffled and wiped away the tears, and for the hundredth time in the last few days wished and prayed to every god that might be listening that her father would come home.

"You don't have to say it, Kid," Pephe rasped. "Message received. It's okay. Do what you have to do."

The weakness in the priest's words brought Morri back to the present and out of her wishful reverie. She gave the back of the priest's hand the most reassuring pat she could muster, and swallowed hard.

"Save your strength," she reminded him, pulling her hands away entirely and reaching into the basket.

From within, she pulled out a delicate looking pair of pliers and a small scalpel, and placed them on the table.

"I'm dreadfully sorry to say that you will need it."

The Speaker clapped his hands twice in quick succession, garnering the attention of the acolytes. When the hoods turned and face his direction, the Speaker gestured towards the exit with a nod of his head.

Without a word, the acolytes departed once again, leaving only Morri, the Speaker, and Pephe in the room.

The Speaker cleared his throat, stepping closer to the stained wood of the surgical table, once again producing the white cloth from the inside of his robes to cover his nose and mouth.

"Can I be of assistance to you in any way, young lady?" the Speaker asked, voice muffled by the sheet of cloth in his hand.

"I'm afraid I rather doubt it," said Morri, tying her hair back into a tight ponytail. Midway through the action, she stopped, freezing in place. "On second thought, it might be prudent of you to hold Pephe's head still."

Nodding grimly, the Speaker flapped the cloth like a flag, extending it out to its full size. Reaching around to the back of his head, the old man tied a quick knot so as to keep the rag in place.

Moving with a slowness that Morri wasn't sure was meant to be attributed to his age or to his apprehension of the task at hand, the Speaker moved to stand at the head of the table. Aged hands reached for exposed bone, gently holding the head of the mangled priest still, thumbs and forefingers encircling the ears.

Meanwhile, Morri reached into the basket once more and produced another set of implements – a small rod with a claw on one end and a plunger on the other, what looked to be a loose strand of serrated metal, a small hammer, and a varied set of screwdrivers. Placing the final implement on the table, Morri paused to collect herself, taking as deep a breath as her juvenile lungs would allow her to.

"Whenever you are ready, my dear," said the Speaker.

"Take your time," rasped Pephe. "No need to hurry on my account."

Blowing all the air out from her lungs, Morri chewed her bottom lip for a moment, picturing in her mind the steps she would need to follow in order to hope to succeed in the operation she was about to undertake – quite possibly the single most important and ambitious task she had attempted in her entire young life.

With a slow breath of resolve, she leaned in close to the gaping skull that was Pephe's face, looking deeply into the empty eye sockets, searching for nerve endings and examining the condition of the musculature that still remained.

It was not as bad as she had feared. It was utterly grisly and unimaginably gory, but still not as bad as she had feared.

Nodding to herself, Morri backed away from the skull.

She decided then that she would not see Pephe as a man, not see him as the friendly infirmary worker with dark humor and an undoubtedly rough and painful past, not see him as the man who had only a few hours ago been openly admiring both her and her mother. That was too difficult, too painful a series of thoughts to bear.

No, it was far better if she saw Pephe as a broken object, a mangled bit of artifice in need of repair. She did not see herself as a healer, or a physician of any sort – but a mender of broken things, an artificer, working to repair damage that had been done... That she could do.

Confidence somewhat restored, she nodded to herself. Puffing out another lungful of air, she took up the scalpel and the hooked apparatus with a plunger.

"I'd not answered your question earlier, Pephe," Morri said, seriousness hanging from her every syllable. "I feel I should do so. I'm afraid the answer is that yes, chances are good that what I am about to do will be exceedingly painful. For that, I apologize."

Pephe moved to speak, but Morri silenced him by gently using her thumb to press his jaw shut, teeth clacking against each other noisily.

"I'm going to begin now."

Pephe said nothing and made no move to respond. Looking up at the Speaker, she saw the man's eyes wide open and fixed on the tools in her hands.

"Are you ready, Speaker?"

The old man's eyes went from the tools in her hands to her face. He nodded eagerly, staring at her intently. She returned the nod, and brought the tools into the open sockets of the black priest.

For a long time after, the infirmary was filled with the sound of Pephe's tortured screams.

Chapter Twenty-Six

"Why's it called Sundial Vale, anyway?" Kera asked, sitting on the roof of the caravan beside Voldani, legs hanging over the driver portion, swaying freely as she idly kicked at the air.

"You'll see in a moment," said Brenno, glancing up at Kera's boots over his head, scowling as bits of dirt and dust showered him with a fine particle spray.

"Or you could just tell me," said Kera. "That's a valid option that's just sitting right there, you know. It would probably take you seconds, and would stop me from pestering you."

"I highly doubt your incessant chatter could be silenced so easily," said Brenno, shifting further down on the bench to get out from under Kera's swinging boots while brushing the dust out of his hair with the other. "Besides, you have a history of asking pointless follow up questions."

"Pointless questions?" Kera asked. "Since when?"

"Precisely," said Brenno.

Kera grimaced but said nothing, contending herself to enjoying the view around them. The woods around the road were becoming more dense, the air cooler and more crisp the longer they traveled. In the distance, the snow-capped peaks of mountains loomed, their frosted heights glittering hues of orange and gold under the bright afternoon sun. The breeze blew by, bringing with it a hint of the cold from the frozen mountaintops. Kera shivered as the chilled air brushed against her skin.

"What is the problem?" Voldani asked, giving Kera a sidelong glance.

"Huh?" Kera said. "What do you mean? I don't have a problem."

"There are those who would beg to differ," Brenno called up.

"Shut it," said Kera. "Really though, I don't know what you mean, Voldani."

"You shuddered just now," said Voldani. "As if in revulsion."

"I didn't shudder, I shivered," Kera explained. "I've never been this far north before. The wind is a bit chilly, is all."

"I see," said Voldani.

"Aren't you cold?" Kera said, eyes moving to the dark brown skin of the warrior woman's exposed thighs. "You're not exactly dressed for it."

"Are you implying impropriety in my dress?" Voldani asked, turning to face

Kera. "My wardrobe is entirely up to my discretion, I'll not stand for disparaging remarks."

"What? No," said Kera, shaking her head. "I actually really like the way you dress," Kera said, her eyes once again flickering to the woman's muscular thighs. "Like, a lot. I just... I don't know, don't you get cold?" Voldani raised her chin proudly, facing forward once more.

"In truth, I do not feel the cold," said Voldani.

"Like at all?" Kera asked.

"I sense the shift in temperature, and can feel the change in the air," said Voldani. "However, exposure to the elements is not a concern I possess."

"Are you winter proof?" Kera asked. "What about in the summer? You must get all hot and sweaty under all that armor."

"Your comments have a sexual connotation that I do not care for," said Voldani.

"Hey, they do not!" Kera said. "Not this time, anyway..."

"If you are truly curious and inquiring for the sake of expanding your knowledge of me and my kind, then I will tell you," Voldani said. "The answer is no, I do not feel affected by the heat or the cold. In extremes, I imagine I would be tested by the elements, but under typical circumstances my heritage has blessed me with great fortitude against such inconveniences."

The wind blew once more, bringing with it the crisp scent of fresh snow. Kera shivered again, crossing her arms over her chest and using her hands to rub the skin of her arms, using friction to create warmth.

"Must be nice," said Kera.

"It is an enjoyable enough advantage to possess, yes," said Voldani.

The carriage rounded the bend, the horses nickering as Brenno bade them to slow down and take the corner at an easier pace. As the group came around the turn, the woods opened, exposing a great valley at the foot of a lone, severe-looking mountain.

The sun, shining from behind the spire of stone, caused the mountain to cast a shadow like an outstretched single digit, a shadowy finger that stretched clear across the valley and the town it contained, forming a narrow wedge of shadow.

"Oooh," said Kera. "Sundial Vale. I get it. That's neat."

"Honestly, what did you expect?" Brenno said, looking up at Kera's boots. "The place is called 'Sundial Vale'. What else could it have meant?"

"Well I don't know," said Kera. "Lots of towns have dumb names."

"Places named after certain features tend to be the exception," said Brenno.

"Mistbreaker is the single mistiest, foggiest place I've ever been," said Kera.

"Well, the capital got its name because of how it was discovered, not what it does," said Brenno. "It's more of a historical anecdote than a description."

"Blackmouth is neither black nor a mouth," said Kera.

"When the dwarves first arrived on Malzen, the ore pits and harbors you know today were nothing but a gaping hole on the side of a cliff face. That's common knowledge," said Brenno. "What's more, the onyx and black quartz found there are exclusively, well, black."

"Fine," said Kera. "What about Fire Lake?"

"The magma from the nearby volcanoes."

"Glassdust Ridge?"

"The trees of the Glass Forest excrete bits of silica, which collects there."

"Whoreknuckle?"

"Founded by a union of escorts."

"Bonetown?"

"Bonetown?" Brenno repeated, uncertain. "I've never been to bonetown."

"Hmm," said Kera, beaming. "You know, I think I could tell."

"Why are you smiling like that?" Voldani asked.

"I don't know what you mean," said Kera.

"You are grinning like a child committing mischief," said Voldani.

"Am I?" Kera asked. "How strange."

Voldani stared at Kera for a time, then broke away her gaze, looking ahead and into the valley. Rising to stand, she brought her glowing wings into existence.

"I will scout ahead," said Voldani. "I know nothing of this Sundial Vale, and aim to be more informed before we walk boldly into it."

"Sounds good," said Kera. "Let us know what you--"

Voldani knelt and launched herself into the air before Kera could finish her sentence.

"...See."

Kera and Brenno watched as Voldani climbed ever higher into the air before making a beeline into the valley, presumably to scout the bustling looking town at its center.

"Well, I guess I'll wake the others," said Kera, easing herself down onto the driver's seat from the roof.

With a hop, she let herself fall from there to the ground, jogging to keep up with the wagon as she made her way towards the rear door and pulled herself up and onto it. Without bothering to knock, she opened the door and made her way in, leaving Brenno alone outside.

"I've never even heard of Bonetown," the halfling muttered to himself.

Chapter Twenty-Seven

From her vantage point high in the sky above Sundial Vale, Voldani's powerful vision allowed her to see details others might have missed - provided they found a means of flight to be in her position. Wings of light batted through the air effortlessly, keeping her aloft with only minimal effort on Voldani's part.

Perhaps the most powerful gift she had inherited, her ability to fly was controlled by her determination. When she required the wings exist, they did. When she needed to fly higher, she could. When she wanted to dive, she did.

She couldn't explain the mechanics behind it, nor did she feel the need to - this was simply how things were, and that was all she needed to say.

Spreading her wings wide, Voldani soared and spun a great circle over the town below.

The outlying sections of the vale seemed to consist of dozens of interconnected pools and platforms, in and on which various types of grain and other foodstuffs were growing.

Larger platforms contained paddocks, inside which plump grazing beasts and furry cattle of all sorts roamed, seeming content to munch at whatever grain they could reach by sticking their heads and tongues out between the posts of their paddocks.

Farmers, or what Voldani assumed were farmers, stood here and there among the creatures, wearing over-sized fur cloaks and large hats to keep the cold and sun at bay. A few of them saw her, noticed a streaking shadow pass over them and their fields and hastily looked up, shielding their eyes with their hands to get a better view at what it was they had seen.

Some scattered, some stood their ground, others simply returned to work. If what Marie Distrol had told them was the truth, she suspected that most were simply trying to make sure she wasn't the dragon returning for another meal.

With a mighty beat of her powerful wings, Voldani propelled herself through the air, moving ever faster towards the village at the heart of the valley. Collared creatures and shanties surrounded by crops gave way to shacks and cottages, the homes of farmers and those citizens who couldn't afford to live within the boundaries of the town.

That boundary, from what Voldani could see, was a stone wall that ran around the edges of Sundial Vale proper. No taller than eight feet at its highest point, the wall made the place seem more like a loosely-fortified settlement than an established town.

I am surprised they have not yet been flattened by a band of giants, Voldani thought as she gazed at the wall. *Timbergnolls and foot soldiers might have difficulty overcoming such an obstacle, but surely giants would not.*

The glint of something metallic just above the wall caught her eye, the afternoon sun shining up at her from the tip of the wall's defenses; a series of ballista made into seated turrets, barbed javelins that could skewer an ox loaded on each one, poised and ready to fire.

Each ballista station was manned by a pair of guards, many of whom were looking up at her as she flew, some pointing inward towards the city.

Where do they attempt to steer me? Voldani wondered, using the outstretched arms of the men and women below as a series of compass points.

The largest buildings in the town were clustered tightly together at its core, stone and timber lodges four and five stories high, some connected by covered bridges that spanned the gap between them, high over the streets below. It was towards the tallest of these that the many arms pointed, directing her towards a long and squat building nearly the size of the temple of Perrus back in Zelwyr.

Flying high in the air above, a great set of red-speckled eagle wings bat at the air. The being at the center of the wings was an armed and armored woman with a shock of red hair that protruded from beneath her helmet.

She hovered in place, wings impassively beating the air as she waited with a sword in her hand. At the sight of the wings - those wings, *her* wings - Voldani's heart stopped.

Her lungs felt suddenly empty, her breath wouldn't come.

It isn't you, Voldani thought, even as her eyes traced the raised lion crest on the front of that too-familiar armor. *It cannot be you.*

Her wings faltered by half a beat, and that briefest moment of uncontrolled flight shook away the shock that had momentarily held her. The woman's eyes went to the hilt of the angular sword whose every curve she had memorized, saw the rounded shape at the end of the pommel that she knew had a crest on it, a crest it shouldn't be - a crest it *could not* be - and her hands moved to her swords.

Her eyes went back to the armor; armor she would never mistake, the armor she had seen every day of her life until the dreary afternoon where she'd watched it get covered by dirt, one shovel full at a time, as it was buried with the body of Protector Keilara Haddonfield, seeming every bit as noble and proud in death as she had in life. Voldani noticed then that there was something more than just shock assailing her senses, something that stung her lungs with each breath she took and made her feel as though a migraine was coming on.

The skin of her arms felt clammy, the air tasted more and more like earth with every breath. The smell of rot filled her nose, and the buzzing of insects began to drone louder and louder in her ears. She recognized this collection of events and sensations for what they were - her literal god-given gift of recognizing the presence of the undead.

The sensory overload only served to confirm what she already knew; this woman, Keilara Haddonfield, had been dead for just over a decade.

Voldani's swords were in her hands before she realized she'd drawn them, the gap between her and what her senses were telling her was the animated corpse of her beloved mentor.

"I know what you're thinking," said a voice, coming from the thing in Keilara's armor, the voice sounding exactly the way Voldani remembered it, the way it couldn't possibly sound.

The mimicry was perfect, too perfect, and it made Voldani furious.

Her grip tightened on her sword, her fists shook. She vowed silently to herself and to Perrus that she would bring an end to this as soon as she was able to. Her lessons at the church, many of which had come from Protector Haddonfield, had taught her much about the nature of the undead and the signs of dealing with the vile magics of necromancy, its evils long decried by the church.

She knew the burning rage of righteous fury needed to be tempered until she could better assess the situation, and slowed her approach. The swords remained in her hands.

"You've never beaten me in your life," said the undead. "Despite what it may seem, not much has changed since we last saw each other."

The taunt wasn't meant to be cruel, it was spoken with endearment, a loving jab. Voldani's stomach turned, and she arrived to hover just before Keilara.

"You cannot know anything," Voldani said, words sharp and cruel, the current outlet for her range. "Explain to me the nature of your presence here, that I might end your existence as soon as possible, *abomination*."

The hand that wasn't holding a sword came up to her helmet and pulled it off, revealing the smiling face that appeared in so many of Voldani's most treasured memories, from her first flight to her first day in battle. Though the woman appeared young, Voldani knew she was ancient; the godblooded did not age the way most mortals did, yet another benefit of their godly ancestry.

Keilara had lived to see four hundred years before she'd died, and she always had the appearance of a woman roughly the same age Voldani was now.

"I missed you too, Solreki," the woman said, speaking with the authority of a military official - which she was, or had been.

"Do I at least get a hello?"

"Do not speak to me as if you were her," Voldani said, raising a sword to point its tip at the face of the undead. "I will cut you from the skies and remove pieces of you until you answer my question. What is the nature of your existence?"

Keilara snorted, sheathing her sword.

"Glad to see you haven't changed," said Keilara. "I'd advise you to lower your weapon. That is, unless your plan here is to die before we get a chance to talk."

As she spoke, Keilara gestured towards the city below them. Glancing in the direction the other woman had pointed out, Voldani saw that for every two turrets that manned the wall around the central city, one of them was now pointing up at her, the guards manning the station watching for a reason to fire. Seeing the tips of more than a dozen over-sized javelin pointing up at her, noting for the first time that many of the turrets had great reels of chain attached to them, Voldani grimaced.

"What manner of trap is this?" Voldani said through clenched teeth, fighting against her every instinct to will her sword arm return the weapon to its holster instead of pointing it at the undead creature that stood in front of her.

It's not a creature, Voldani thought, *it's an abomination. Every moment it exists is an insult to the memory of a proud and noble woman.*

"It's not a trap, Solreki," said Keilara, arms spread wide to encompass the city itself in a gesture. "It's a retirement plan. Come on down, I'll explain."

"Willingly enter your unholy citadel?" Voldani scoffed. "I think not."

"It's the town hall, actually," said Keilara.

"The secret headquarters for your unholy cult of dark zealots, then," Voldani said, narrowing her eyes. Keilara rolled her eyes and shook her head.

"The ground floor is a tavern," said Keilara. "Pretty typical of a settlement town, but it was the most defensible structure still standing when we got here. Improved on it some, as you can see, but still a tavern at the end of the day. The only nuts you'll find in there are the kind that get served with beer. You can come and see for yourself, or you can stay here and become a kabob. Your choice, Solreki."

Voldani was silent for a moment, staring after Keilara as she descended. Her gaze once again traveled to the colossal batteries pointed up at her. She felt the warmth of blood on her fingers, which made her realize she'd been clenching her fists so tightly she'd dug her nails into her skin.

Waving them through the air to send the blood flying away, Voldani grimaced and began her descent.

"How long have you existed in this state, creature?" Voldani demanded reluctantly

"Voldani, I'm going to ask you something," Keilara said, looking up at Voldani. "And if you ever cared for me in your life, I want you to think long and hard about your answer before you open your mouth and let all that fire burning in your belly spill out some more."

"I cannot prevent you from asking questions," Voldani muttered angrily.

"Be furious, be appalled, be whatever you want to be," said Keilara. "But whatever you do, I am asking that if you ever loved me before, to stop with the 'creature' and 'abomination' stuff. If you valued me in life even the slightest, I need you to do this for me. At least until you leave this building, and I swear to you that you will leave this building, I need you to say absolutely nothing about what it is you're sensing right now. It might be nice if you could even consider having a conversation with me, or hells, how about a hug? I've missed you, Dani."

Voldani's breath caught entirely, her wings skipped a beat, their light flickering.

"Do *not*," Voldani gasped, staggering slightly as she touched down on the roof of the building below. That name, spoken from that person, with that voice… She heard it in her ears since she was a girl, since before she'd ascended and became a scion.

It hurt to hear it again, made her feel raw and sick on the inside. For a moment it felt as though her lungs wouldn't fill with air, and she struggled to steady her breath.

"Do *not* call me Dani."

Chapter Twenty-Eight

"Yeah, I don't think she's coming back," Kera said, staring in the direction of the building Voldani had landed on, using her hands to shield her eyes from the setting sun. "Guess that means we go in? How's she going to find us?"

"I'm sure she'll find us," said Will, sitting on top of the caravan in the place Voldani usually sat. "I mean, how many travelling bands are going around with a mechanical woman?"

"That's true," Kera admitted. "And you could always set off some kind of beacon, right?"

"I'm great at beacons," said Will. "I can do a half-decent floating trail, and if you gave me a couple days to work on it, I'd have an illusionary maze like you wouldn't believe."

"If it's an illusion couldn't I just walk through the wall?" Kera asked.

"Illusiomancy isn't the same as illusion," Will said. "I said this earlier, but I guess you weren't paying attention. It's totally separate, two very different schools of magic."

"It doesn't seem that different," said Kera.

"Illusion is tricking the mind into believing something is there," said Will. "Illusiomancy is convincing the mind that it is."

"Oh, of course. It's so obvious to me now, how didn't I see that before?" Kera said with fake interest, voice heavy with sarcasm. "It's not just a *trick*, it's a *trick*. I've been such a fool."

"Fuck off," Will said. "It's a lot more complicated than throwing fireballs at stuff."

"So why don't you just do that?" Kera asked. "I mean, it's gotta be more efficient."

"I'm not a great evoker," said Will.

"I thought you were a wizard?" Kera asked.

"What, no, an evoker is… Wait, do you really not know this?" Will asked.

"I don't, and I honestly don't think I care," said Kera.

"Ouch," said Will. "You are really are bad at being friends with someone, I feel I should tell you."

Kera leaned her head back against the chair to look up at Will.

"Who said we were friends?" she asked.

"You know, if you don't start being nicer to me, you are going to lose me," said Will.

Kera made an exaggerated gasp and clutched at her heart.

"Oh no," said Kera. "How ever will I live the rest of my life without the shining light of Will... What was your last name again?"

"Fuck off," Will said again, sliding backwards and away from Kera.

"No, really, it's on the tip of my tongue," Kera said. "For some reason the words 'Spectacular idiot' keep coming to mind. That's not your last name, is it? Are you Willy Spectacular Idiot, by any chance? I'll be honest, you kind of look like a Willy Spectacular Idiot."

"Mean," said Will, "Mean and uncalled for."

The carriage spent the next hour rolling down and into the basin, winding its way through farmland and fields. Curious cattle turned their heads to watch the passing merchant wagon. The farmers, uninterested, paid them no attention. The wheels of the carriage spun on, rolling in and out of muddy puddles as the wagon pressed on. Farmlands and grazing fields gave way to shacks and shanties, the overall construction and general state of the buildings below slowly improving the closer they were to Sundial Vale proper.

A stone wall perhaps ten feet high appeared before them, with colossal doors installed at regular intervals. Each door was heavily reinforced, and had a pair of spear-launching turrets on each side of it, the turrets manned by a pair of guards. The turrets above the nearest door oriented themselves towards the wagon, the deadly-looking points of the tree-sized lances aimed squarely towards the horses and the driver's seat.

Standing directly above the midpoint of the door with a single hand raised into the air was a lone guard, her chainmail and scale armor partly covered by a bright red jacket. The carriage slowed, lurching to a halt in front of the door.

"Who goes there?" the guard called.

"Pawnbroker Brenno Hornbuckle and Artificer Smith," Called Brenno. "Certified members of the Guild of Merchants."

"A pawnbroker, eh?" The guard asked, spitting downwards off the wall, throwing a long braid of blonde hair over her shoulder as she did. "Don't see many travelling pawnbrokers, never mind ones who are artificers and smiths."

"You're somewhat mistaken," said Brenno. "I'm simply a pawnbroker."

"Alright. Who's the artificer?" The guard asked.

"I am," said Smith.

"And the smith?"

"What's that now?" Smith asked.

"The smith," the guard asked, speaking slower. "Where is the smith?"

"We don't have a smith," said Smith.

"Why'd you say you had an artificer and a smith?" The guard asked, tone becoming guarded.

"I didn't," said Brenno. "I merely introduced you to my companion, the artificer Smith."

"So your name is Smith?" the guard asked.

"Yep," said Smith.

"But you're an artificer," the guard clarified.

"That'd be about the sum of it," Smith said with a nod, an awkward forced smile on his face.

Brenno saw the ugly attempt at smiling Smith was making and cringed.

Gods, Smith, Brenno thought as he looked at the strained face of his friend. *You look like you're in pain.*

"Well isn't that a funny little anecdote," said the guard. "Hey, as an artificer do you have to smith things?"

"On occasion," Smith grunted, face twitching.

"So you're not Smith the smith, but you're a Smith who smiths," the guard said, savoring every twisted syllable in the loose wordplay. "That's fun to say. Anyone ever make that joke to you before?"

"Nope," said Smith, corner of his eye twitching. "You're the first."

"Well how about that, isn't that something?" said the guard, becoming more chipper. "Anyone else in the wagon with you coming in?"

"Three other occupants and one construct," said Brenno.

"Okay," said the guard, lifting up a wooden plaque on which a sheet of parchment had been transferred.

The text contained on the piece of parchment was small, forcing the guard to lift it near to her face and use her finger to look to locate a particular passage.

"Ah, there we go," she said, locating it. "Does the function of the construct fall within the confines of Ferrigan's Laws?"

"Yep," said Smith.

"Because this is official business, I'm gonna need you to say 'yes' instead of 'yep', ok hon?" The guard said to Smith, offering him a sickly sweet smile as she did.

"Sure, sorry," said Smith. "Yes."

"Does the construct require being bound or attuned with in order to take commands?"

"Yes."

"Does the construct possess sentience?"

"No."

"That's a relief, that stuff never ends well. Does the construct possess any weaponry?"

"No."

"Has the construct recently, or ever before, been exposed to magics, spells, or enchantments from a spellcaster you don't know?"

Smith's forced smile creased with the increased effort to contain his building irritation.

"Not that I'm aware of," Smith said through gritted teeth.

"Gotta be that yes or no, hon."

"No."

"That's good, also not a great thing to have happen. Trust me on that one, whew. Okay, almost done here. Let's see. Does the construct possess a kinite battery, power cell, receptacle, or any component which performs in a similar function to those previously listed?"

"Yes."

"Well that's too bad," said the guard, pulling the board away from her face. "I was hoping I could just wave you folks straight through to the market square, but you're going to have to get the mayor regent to sign off on that construct of yours first. Find him in the town hall, straight ahead. If you haven't gotten a permit by sundown, I'll have to haul you out. I don't want to have to do that, so make sure you get that permit taken care of, okie dokie?"

"Sure thing."

"That's not a yes, but I'll let you have a pass on that one, hon. Alright, open the doors, let 'em in, folks."

The guard made a circular motion in the air above her head, spinning her finger in small loop. With a groan, the doors shuddered and began to open inward on their massive hinges, opening up like a great oak maw.

"Have a great time in Sundial Vale, y'all!"

With a flick of the reins, Brenno commanded the horses to walk through the doors and into the city proper. The only immediate differences that Brenno could see were the gas lamps on the street corners of the now cobblestone streets.

"The city appears to be laid out on a grid," Brenno remarked, noting the ninety degree turns spaced out evenly across the perfectly-aligned buildings. "I have to imagine it makes it much easier to find your way through town, at least in comparison to trying to do so back home in Zelwyr, with our damnable spiral layout."

"If you say so," said Smith, massaging his jaw with his fingers.

"Gods, man," said Brenno. "Is it really that difficult for you to look happy?"

"I just had to smile for a full minute, Hornbuckle," said Smith. "That's unnatural."

Within minutes, the carriage arrived at the town hall and slowed to a stop. Its history - and present - as a tavern was evident; empty casks and kegs lined the walls along the outside of the building, on top of which a few disheveled folks who stank of ale and whiskey were sound asleep.

"Charming," said Brenno, holding his nose as the wagon wheels rolled through a puddle of vomit that had accumulated around the unconscious form of a particularly burly half-orc.

Spying a row of hitches for tying trailers and horses on the side of the road opposite the tavern, Brenno tugged on the reins to gently guide the horses across the street. The wheels of the wagon rolled to a stop, and Brenno and Smith disembarked from the caravan.

"I'll tie us off," Smith said.

"Very well," Brenno nodded. "I'll inform the others that we've arrived."

The halfling made his way around the caravan towards the rear door. The instant his hand touched the handle for the door, it burst open from the inside, staggering him and sending him reeling backwards. From inside emerged Kera and Enaurl.

"Are we there yet?" Kera asked. Brenno sighed.

"Yes, we've arrived at the town hall," said Brenno.

Kera sniffed at the air.

"Smells like booze and puke," said Kera.

"Does that offend your delicate sensibilities?" Brenno quipped.

"Hardly," said Kera. "If anything it excites them."

Kera strode out from the back of the wagon and stretched.

"That wagon is not big enough for three people."

"It's a merchant wagon," said Brenno. "It was designed primarily with storage and transportation in mind, not comfort."

"Yeah," said Kera, arching her back, the joints in her neck and shoulders popping audibly. "I could tell."

Enaurl seemed unconcerned by all this, and merely stepped out of the wagon, the chorus of gears and pistons accompanying her every movement. From behind them, a disgruntled Will emerged, hands on the back of his neck, leaning his head this way and that.

"Gods, man," Will groaned. "Halfling-sized beds are basically torture."

"Could have slept on the floor," said Kera.

"And risk getting flattened by Enaurl again?" Will asked, wincing at the memory. "No thanks, I'll pass. Is this the market district?"

"I'm afraid not," said Brenno. "We need to have Enaurl inspected and approved by a city official before we can be allowed to roam the city. Evidently this is the place to do that."

"This looks like the building Voldani swooped down on to," said Kera.

"I suspect that as well," said Brenno.

"Can't you just say 'yes' once in your life?" Kera asked. "In case the gently wafting scent of stale vomit and yesterday's ale didn't cue you in, this isn't a college or anything."

"For someone who has so much to say about the way others address you, it ought not be a problem the way those same others compose themselves," said Brenno. "It's almost as if you forget that the reason any of us are here is because of your delinquency."

"Whatever you say, shortstack," Kera said, rolling her eyes. "Let's get some drinks."

Chapter Twenty-Nine

The group of five filed their way into the tavern as a group, with Smith and Enaurl leading while Brenno, Kera, and Will followed. Inside, the tavern was well lit and smelled like fresh meat and stale beer. Rows of tables filled a vast floor space, at the centre of which was a raised platform on top which rested musical instruments.

"Looks like more of a performance hall than a town hall," said Kera.

"I was just thinking that," said Will. The tavern was roughly three quarters full, the chairs around the rectangular tables filled with humans, half-orcs, elves, half-elves, halflings, dwarves, and more. Will nodded appreciatively.

"Surprisingly diverse crowd," said Will.

"What's that supposed to mean?" Kera asked.

"Nothing much," said Will. "Except I'm about eighty percent sure that's a minotaur from the Ashen Herd seated across a dwarf from Silverbulge."

"So?"

"The fact that they aren't trying to kill each other means there must be some pretty strict consequences preventing them from doing so."

"You always this observant?" Smith rumbled.

"Well, I don't know about always," said Will. "But I try."

"Perhaps you could lend your skills of observation to finding someone who can direct us towards the regent mayor?" Brenno suggested.

"That guy," Will said, pointing to the man behind the counter, a surly looking man with brown hair and a pushbroom moustache.

"How could you possibly know that?" Brenno asked.

"We're at a bar and he's behind the counter," Will said. "That basically makes him a god."

"Amen," said Kera. "Let us worship at his feet."

"You're both idiots with drinking problems," Smith grumbled, making his way towards the bartender as he did. Catching the bartender's attention with a wave, he beckoned the mustached man to come nearer.

"Looking for the regent mayor," said Smith.

"Can't miss him," said the man. "He goes on in half an hour."

"On stage?" Smith asked. "He making some kind of speech?"

"Hardly," said the man, smiling jovially. "He's a bit of a showman, and a heck of a performer. He's here at least once a week performing for the people."

"And that day just happened to be today," Smith said, eyeing the bartender suspiciously.

"I don't know why you say it like that," said the bartender. "He's here every Gowsday, nothing suspicious about that. Though I have to say, your sudden suspicion is in itself a little suspicious. Then again, the band you walked in with looks awful weary and your horses hard travelled, so I imagine you've earned your suspicion and won't fault you for it." Smith stared at the man for a long time, saying nothing.

"You talk too much for a bartender," Smith said at last. "There any way to see the mayor before he goes on stage? I need to approve my construct." The bartender nodded.

"See Bortch at the base of the stairs there and he'll show you through," the bartender pointed to a wide wooden staircase tucked against the far wall that spanned the 30 foot height between the floor of the tavern and whatever lay beyond its high ceiling. Smith noted that there was no one currently at the base of the stairs.

"Who's Bortch?" Smith asked.

"Lemme get him for you," said the bartender.

Turning in place, the man pushed open the window nearest to him, poking his head out the side.

"Bortch, time to work!"

A bassy grunt was heard through the open window.

"He'll be with you in just a moment. If you don't mind, I'm going to tend to some other customers. It's not that I'm being rude, but I'm running a business and I hope you understand," the man said, smiling warmly at Smith before moving down the bar to pour ale for a trio of heavily-tattooed dwarves.

The doors to the inn swung open, and the scent of puke and ale crawled into the tavern air, accompanied by the tremendous shadow of an even larger figure behind it.

Standing at an easy seven feet tall was the same orc who had been passed out on the barrels outside the tavern a few minutes earlier.

Eyes red and bleary, dressed in white and blue robes with a plethora of dark green and yellow stains on the front of them, the orc yawned loudly and stretched. Satisfied, he scratched at his butt and stomped his way over to the staircase, pushing his way through the crowd.

Smith groaned internally and rubbed his hand on his face.

How many godsdamned drunks am I going to have to deal with?

Already feeling the first sparks of anger burning in his chest, Smith followed the orc at a distance as the drunken sod made his way towards the stairs. The others fell in step with him, their physical closeness only serving to irritate him further.

"What is the plan?" Brenno asked.

"We talk to Bortch," said Smith.

"Who's Bortch?" Kera asked.

Smith felt another pang of anger build. He felt pretty certain it was obvious who Bortch was, but reminded himself that Kera probably wasn't paying the slightest amount of attention to anything happening around her at the moment.

"That's Bortch," Smith said, pointing at the orc.

Bortch yawned, stretched, and sat down on the lower steps of the staircase, using the first four as a makeshift chair.

"I figured," said Kera.

The sparks of anger Smith felt threatened to turn into a fire. He kept his mouth shut and made it the rest of the way to Bortch, tapping the orc on the shoulder to get his attention. Bortch stood up to his full height, looking down at Smith and the others.

"Whatcha need?" Bortch asked, the foulness of his breath turning every syllable out of his mouth into an assault against Smith. "The rules say I need to ask."

"I need to see the regent mayor," said Smith.

"What for?" Bortch asked, scratching at his belly over his robes. "Gotta ask. It's in the rules. You can ask what I'm here for if you'd like."

"I'd rather not," Smith said.

"I will!" Kera shouted gleefully. "Whatcha here for, Bortch?"

"I'm here to work until I can start drinking," said the orc. "Then I drink until I start working. It's a vicious cycle, I'll admit, but it's what I need to numb the hurt inside."

"Not what I expected to hear," said Kera. "Good for you for being honest with yourself."

"Can we get back on track?" Smith growled. "I need to get my construct approved."

"Alright," said Bortch. "Got your papers? Can't let you by without your papers, it's in the rules."

Smith turned to look at Brenno. The halfling was using one hand to pinch his nose shut while the other was offered the papers in question out to Smith.

Taking the pages from the halfling, the artificer unfolded the bundle and passed it to Bortch. The orc's bloodshot eyes peered at the pages for a moment, then nodded and offered them back.

"Seems to be in order," said Bortch. "I can let the two of you and the construct in, but sellswords stay out here. It's in the rules."

"I'm noticing a lot things seem to be in the rules around here," said Brenno. "And yet, the rules themselves aren't posted anywhere for the public to view. Why is that?"

"Can't let strangers know all the rules," said Borth.

"And why not?" Brenno asked.

"It's in the rules."

"Oh, for the sake of every heaven and all the shattered hells," Brenno cursed, turning to face Smith with a wild look in his eyes. "If Voldani is already in here somewhere, I don't see the harm in leaving Will and Kera alone for a little while."

Smith snorted.

"Have you met them?"

"Unfortunately, I've had the pleasure."

"You know we can hear this, right?" Will asked. "We're standing directly behind you."

"Haven't you gotten used to be ignored yet?" Kera asked.

"No, not at all," said Will. "Honestly, it's pretty hurtful."

"Aw, poor wizard," said Kera. "Wanna drink about it?"

"Yes," said Will. "A lot."

"There you go," said Kera. "We'll be at the bar stuffing out faces with ale. We'll wait here for Voldani, you three go get your permit or whatever and then meet us here."

"How do I know you'll still be here when I get back?" Smith asked, eyeing Kera with suspicion. Kera shrugged.

"I guess you don't," said Kera. "But if you leave behind a couple pieces silver for a bar tab, I can guarantee neither of us is going to go anywhere until we've drank every last copper worth of ale we can afford."

Smith glowered at Kera. Brenno reached towards a pouch hanging from his belt and produced a pair of gold coins, flicking them into Will's hands.

"I think this should be enough to keep the both of you occupied for a while," said Brenno. "At least I should hope so. I would like the change back."

"There won't be any," said Kera, putting her arm around Will and pulling him towards the bar. "We'll be over there, but maybe check the floor around the stools just in case."

"You're far too proud of your excessive consumption," Brenno scolded, watching as the barbarian eyed another tankard of ale.

"Big words coming from a halfling," Kera said, sneering at Brenno from over shoulder. "Shouldn't you be getting starting on your third breakfast by now? Or it is fourth lunch?"

"As a matter of fact," Brenno began, raising a finger at Kera as if he were a teacher scolding a way ward student.

Kera waved him off, putting more distance between them.

"Don't care, can't hear you," Kera said. "Too busy staying put."

Brenno frowned, an expression he was growing far too familiar with making, and shook his head.

"I suppose that's one problem resolved," said Brenno.

"And about fifty more waiting to happen," Smith rumbled, looking back to the hulking half-orc with crossed arms in front of him. "Satisfied?"

"That you've met the requirements of the rules? Yes," said Bortch. "With my emotional health and general state of being? No, but I'm getting there."

Smith's every muscle tightened with anticipation of an angry outburst, but he refused to let the anger control him.

"You talk too much for a bouncer," Smith said. Bortch nodded, standing aside.

"That's true," said Bortch. "I think it's because being at work is my comfort zone, and it gives me the social confidence I lack otherwise. Go on up, second last door. If you hit the wall you've gone too far, if you don't get to the second last door you haven't gone too far enough."

Smith muttered sub-tonal grievances as he stomped his way up the stairs, heavy boots pounding on each wooden plank.

Enaurl followed, her mechanisms making repeating pounding and whirring noises that made her sound like a dwarven assembly line.

Brenno did his best to keep pace, but fell behind after the first dozens stairs. Having reached the top of the staircase, Smith peered down the hall in which he now found himself.

Besides the patterned carpet, this floor of the building resembled the tavern in many ways; the wood paneling, lamps, and windows were all the same. Puffing, Brenno caught up to them.

"Whew," said the halfling. "Had I known stairs were in order, I wouldn't have worn my armor."

The halfling took a deep breath.

"Though I suppose a little exercise will do my heart good. Shall we?"

Smith nodded, striding down the corridor, forming the point of a wedge completed by Enaurl and Brenno. As they neared the second last door, Smith noticed that it was ajar, and that voices could be heard from the other side of it.

"--there's just no way we can afford to lower our rates," said a sniveling, plaintiff voice.

"I'm afraid ye've got no other choice," said a second voice, bombastic and bold, with a thick dwarven accent. "Less ye think ye can negotiate better with the timbergnolls. Pretty far from Dogtown, but ye're welcome to give it a try."

"Mister Barrelbinder, please understand--"

"That's regent mayor Barrelbinder, I'll remind ye."

"My most *sincere* apologies, regent mayor Barrelbinder," said the voice.

The way in which the whinier voice of the two emphasized the word sincere made Smith instinctively want to punch whoever it belonged to.

"But our rates are placed where they are to cater to our exclusive clientele--"

"Hogwash," said Barrelbinder. "Ye're sellin' magic trinkets, same as five or six other merchants are doin'. What makes ye think yer lot is better than them, eh Germwald?"

"It's actually pronounced *gurmwald*, regent mayor Barrelbinder--"

"Is that really how it's actually pronounced, or is that how ye're sellin' it to yer *exclusive clientele?*" asked the mayor, eliciting a peel of laughter from a third voice, a woman somewhere out of sight.

"He's got you dead to rights, Germwald," said the woman.

"There ye have it," said Barrelbinder. "Now, as for yer rates, either lower 'em by thirty percent, else get yerself on the road elsewhere."

"Thirty percent?" Germwald wailed. "My lord, are you aiming to put me in the poorhouse? I'm simply trying to make an honest living."

"Bah," said Barrelbinder. "Ye're simply tryin' to make a quick bunch of coin on yer way through town, and ye don't give two silver shits about what ye'd do to the local economy in the process. Local merchants see you movin' the same magic crap as them for twice the price and they'll up their prices. The weapon and armor smiths'll follow suit, then the leatherworkers, then everybody else, and suddenly the cost o' livin' in Sundial Vale is twice what is was all because some merchant named *Germwald* tried to make a quick extra coin off the ignorance of what he assumed was witless northern folks. Sound about right?"

"Well, I don't know about *all that*," Germwald muttered. "And I certainly object to my expertly-crafted wares being called *magic crap...*"

"Is it magic?" Barrelbinder asked.

"Yes," said Germwald.

"Is it strictly speakin' necessary for everyday life?"

"Well... No, I suppose not," Germwald admitted.

"Magic crap," Barrelbinder said once again, affirmatively. "Ye gonna lower yer rates?"

"Upon further consideration, and based on your insightful wisdom--"

"Easy, Germwald, a *yes* will do. Keep blowin' hot smoke around me hairy bunghole and ye're likely to start a fire," Barrelbinder said. "Get goin', and don't let me so much as hear the whisper of a rumour that ye're pricier'n the locals, or I'll have Sir Tethys stop by an' say hello. Course, he's not the biggest talker. Tends to be more of the *smash first an' smash later* persuasion, if ye catch my meanin'.."

"Yes, regent mayor," said Germwald. "Of course, regent mayor."

"Use the other door, it'll take ye to the street directly," Barrelbinder said.

"Right away, regent mayor, thank you regen--"

"Enough, Germwald, just get," said Barrelbinder.

The sound of a door opening and closing was heard, followed by a profound sigh.

"Can't stand that lot. Shouldn't even let 'em in town, but they pay the tariffs squarely. I'll never tell 'em to their faces, but some of those trinkets they sell aren't half bad. Self lighting lantern, comes on when ye clap. Fantastic."

"Truly this is an age of wonders," said the woman's voice. "The miracles never cease."

"Alright, Elli, what d'ye want?" Barrelbinder said, a tacit weariness in his voice.

"The same thing I always want when I come to see the illustrious regent mayor," said Elli. "To discuss the importance of the zoning bylaws regulating the farms, specifically all cattle and annual crops along the west rim. I know that irrigation doesn't rank high on your list of things to worry about, but this time of year it's on the top of mine. I'd stop worrying about it if only that meant someone else would do a decent job of making sure there wasn't cattle poop in the whole town's drinking water, but you and I both know that's not going to happen."

"Make it quick, Elli, what d'ye need?"

"A team of surveyors, credit with the guild of masons and the guild of carpenters, a team of labourers, and six hundred gold pieces," said Elli, going through her list at high speed.

"How much credit with the guilds?"

"Five hundred with the masons, three hundred with the carpenters."

"What's the six hundred gold for?"

"Food and wages for the laborers, surveyors, and myself?"

"Five oughta cover it then. Come tell me ye've solved the runoff and I'll personally count out an extra two hundred gold pieces from me coffer. Hundred fer ye, hundred fer the laborers."

"What about the surveyors?"

"They get paid too much to stand around as it is."

"Well said, regent mayor. I'll take my leave."

"Ye could take the back stairs."

"No thanks, I have new contract money to drink away."

"Shoulda said four hundred," Barrelbinder muttered.

"Shoulda," agreed Elli.

The sound of boots on wooden floors told Smith and Brenno that Elli was heading their way.

Uncertain what to do, the two men stood still and waited. Sure enough, Elli - who was revealed to be a pale-skinned woman with a shaved head and pointed ears that gave away her elvish ancestry - opened the door.

Startled to see Smith, Brenno, and Enaurl, Elli started and clutched at her chest for a moment, the flowing green dress she was wearing moving like liquid trailing after her every gesture.

"Oh!" Elli said. "Gods, you startled me."

The elf woman's eyes moved from Brenno to Smith to Enaurl, and there they lingered.

"Oh my. You're something."

Moving slowly, as if she were afraid she might spook Enaurl, Elli stepped towards Enaurl and placed her fingers on the smoothness of the construct woman's face.

"Amazing. Did you build this?" She asked the men.

"I did," said Smith.

"Ellimonrea Arvinleigh," said Elli, offering a delicate hand to Smith, who shook it.

"Smith," said the man.

"Just Smith?" Elli asked, arching an eyebrow.

"Just Smith," the man nodded. Elli withdrew her hand, eyes lingering on Enaurl, and turned her head closer towards the open door.

"Two more to see you, regent mayor," Elli called. "Make that three."

"Tell 'em to be quick, I go on in ten minutes," Barrelbinder called back. Elli nodded absently, still enraptured by Enaurl.

"It's beautiful," said Elli.

"She," Smith corrected.

"My apologies," said Elli. "I didn't want to assume."

The elven woman shook herself from her fascination with Enaurl.

"If you two will excuse me, I've got a party for one to attend."

Smith and Brenno moved to either side of the hallway to make way for Elli to be able to pass. She smiled at them appreciatively and left.

"Now or never, folks," the mayor called out to them, prompting the pair to walk into the mayor's chambers.

The room was lavish but not excessively so, with fine linens on the bed, and what appeared to be a statue of a dwarven god carved from stone standing on a pedestal in the far corner. A regal looking oak desk sat against one wall - a stack of parchments, scrolls, and loose papers piled high on its surface.

Regent mayor Barrelbinder was seated in front of a makeup table with a large mirror in front of it. It was through this mirror that he, a sturdy looking dwarf with a thick black mustache and beard, looked at the men as he applied a layer of starch white stage makeup onto his face.

"Thank you for seeing us, your grace," said Brenno

"Yer grace?" Barrelbinder repeated. "There a crown atop me head I don't see?"

"Well, no," Brenno said.

"'Cause I ain't no king," said Barrelbinder, chuckling. "Hence the 'regent' bit in that whole 'regent mayor' title. The folks o' Sundial Vale asked me to help out, and I'm doin' that until someone more qualified comes along. Ye got about three minutes o' me time before I go on stage, so be quick about it. What d'ye need?"

"Apologies, regent mayor," Brenno said, producing the papers that had been given to him by the guard at the wall. "We were told to have our construct friend approved before we could be allowed to browse the market district."

The regent mayor nodded, turning in his chair to take the pages and review them briefly.

"Standard procedure *now*," Barrelbinder said. "Had a couple o' loons from Gregoir come through with what they claimed was a self-propelled wagon. Somebody rear ended the damn thing, so it *stood up* on two legs like a steel giant and started wreckin' the place. Took a month to get the market district back in shape, and believe me when I tell ye I was no a happy mayor that day."

The dwarf finished perusing the bundle, folded them neatly and handed them back to Brenno.

"Seems to be in order. This is her, I can't help but assume?"

"Yep," said Smith.

"Make her yerself?" Barrelbinder asked.

"Yep," Smith said again.

Barrelbinder gave Smith a look, then shifted his gaze to Brenno.

"He always this talkative?" Barrelbinder asked, hitching his thumb in Smith's direction

"I'm afraid so, lord mayor," Brenno said with a nod.

"Yer grace, lord mayor... Ye're awfully serious for a halfling," said Barrelbinder, clapping his hands together to brush off the excess makeup on them as he rose to stand. "Most of your kin that I've met have been fairly relaxed. Course, the Addelena's Keep crowd are a special lot."

Barrelbinder walked up to Enaurl and examined her, tapping on her plating in places as he slowly circled around her.

"She runnin' on kinite or magitech?"

"Bit of both," said Smith.

Barrelbinder let out a low shrill whistle.

"Artificers. Not just content to be playin' with fire, are ye?" Barrelbinder said, glancing at Smith as he continued to inspect Enaurl. "Gotta be the ones playin' with fire while balancin' on a highwire - one ye built yerselves that's also on fire, no less."

"I'm not worried," Smith grunted. "She's well built."

"I can see that," said Barrelbinder. "I'm no expert, but I've seen more than me fair share o' constructs, mechanized whatsits, an' automated thingamajigs. This is one o' the nicest I've seen to date."

The mayor rubbed his hands together.

"Last thing I gotta do before I can sign ye in is a quick spell to make sure ye're not smugglin' anything in ye shouldn't. Do ye consent?"

"You don't look like a wizard," Smith said.

Brenno looked appalled.

"What my associate means to say is yes, you are certainly welcome to perform your spell, regent mayor," Brenno said, speaking quickly, his nervousness apparent.

Barrelbinder chuckled.

"Wound up right tight, aren't ye?" The mayor said to Brenno.

The dwarf's eyes rolled upwards, his pupils disappearing into the back of his head. The grubby dwarf's hands began to emit a gentle yellow light, as if there were lit candles glowing just behind the skin of his palms.

Reaching out towards Enaurl, Barrelbinder placed his hands on her wrists and began to mutter under his breath, syllables that sounded foreign and muddled. Roughly thirty seconds later, the mayor's eyes returned to normal and the glow in his palms ceased. He offered a smile to both men, holding his hands out towards Brenno once again.

"Beautiful piece of work. 'Course, I don't really understand half of it, but ye don't need to be a painter to recognize a masterpiece or a writer to recognize a good book."

Brenno fumbled the papers, but produced them. Barrelbinder took them and strode towards his desk, clearing a space to lay them flat with one hand while reaching into the top drawer to produce a quill and ink pot with the other.

Dipping the quill into the inkpot, the mayor scribbled a quick signature along the bottom of the pages, blew on the ink, and handed it back to Brenno.

"That's pronounced 'Rag-Dane', before ye ask."

"Ragdain Barrelbinder, elected regent mayor of Sundial Vale," Brenno read, nodding. "Thank you for your time, regent mayor."

"Bah, it's nothin'," said Ragdain. "It's literally me job. Runnin' this place by the skin o' me pants and every last bit o' wit and scrap o' bardic magics I got in me. If ye gents wouldn't mind, I got a show to do. If ye're aimin' to head to the market 'fore it shuts down for the night, ye'd best be goin' now. That door'll get ye on yer way."

Ragdain hitched a thumb over his shoulder at the door opposite them in his room. Brenno and Smith nodded, and made their way towards the door.

"Oh, and one last thing," Ragdain called after them.

The men turned around to face the mayor, whose mustache bristled as he smiled at them from under his makeup.

"Welcome to Sundial Vale."

Chapter Thirty

Back in the tavern below, the sound of a pair of empty glasses clanging onto the bartop sounded as Kera and Will finished downing a glass of ale. The mustached barkeep cheerfully took the glasses and looked to the pair.

"Another round?" He asked from behind.

Kera belched loudly in response, making Will snicker like a school child. The barkeep seemed unphased.

"That's her way of saying yes," said Will.

"You got it," said the barkeep, disappearing with the empty cups.

"Smith and Brenno have been gone for a while," said Kera, turning in her stool to lean her back up against the counter, her elbows propped up on its surface.

"Worried they won't come back?" Will asked.

"Not particularly," said Kera. "I know they'll be back sooner or later, I'm just saying it out loud as a reminder to myself."

"Reminder for what?" Will asked, nodding appreciatively at the barkeep as the man placed a pair of frothing beers in front of the duo.

He tapped Kera on the elbow to get her attention, nodding towards the drinks that had just arrived. She spun back around on her stool and caressed the glass eagerly, bringing it up to her lips for a satisfying gulp. The beer was ice cold and crisp, smooth on her tongue with a hint of citrus. She drank deeply, and sighed heavily. The glass was half empty when she put it back on the counter.

"A reminder that I shouldn't just cut and run," said Kera, watching as Will drank from his own glass, nodding as he did. "Knowing that Voldani would flatten me into the nearest rock or tree is a pretty good incentive to stay put."

Will chuckled, sputtering in his drink. Pulling his beer away from his face and wiping his chin with his sleeve, the wizard gasped and grinned.

"And then you'd hear about it at length from Smith," said Will.

"I'm less worried about him yelling at me than I am that vein on his forehead just popping and spurting blood all over me, like a raging blood geyser," said Kera, miming an explosion using her hand.

Will threw his head back and laughed, slapping the table. They were four ales in, and his face had begun to grow flush.

"Poor Brenno would pass out on the spot," said Will.

"Yeah right," said Kera. "He'd start wringing his hands and fretting about the paperwork. *I must say, William and Kera, the pair of you will be required to sign an abundant amount of legal waivers in regards to this matter.*"

Kera's Brenno impression was not especially accurate, but it was close enough to leave no question as to who it was she was impersonating.

"*Furthermore,*" Will added, "*I'll be filing a report in triplicate in regards to this matter with Speaker Gerhardt. I want no part in these shenanigans.*"

Kera laughed heartily.

"Do you think the word *shenanigans* is even in his vocabulary?"

"I'm going to say yes," said Will.

"You think so?" Kera asked, finishing the last of her ale.

"Oh, absolutely," said Will, doing the same with his glass. "*I, Brenno Hornbuckle, here to swear that I am not responsible for the shenanigans, antics, ploys, plots, tricks, or general actions of one Will Decker and one Kera No-Clan.*"

The barkeep returned and took the empty glasses, holding them up towards the pair while arching an eyebrow.

Kera nodded, and the barkeep disappeared down the line once again.

"What do you want to bet he has something that says almost exactly that somewhere in all those pouches and pockets of his?" Kera asked.

"Oh, I'm not taking that bet," said Will.

"Afraid you'll lose?" Kera plied.

"Oh, I know I'd lose," said Will. "I've known law keepers less prepared than he is."

"Do you think maybe that's what he wanted to be?" Kera asked. "It would explain why he always talks like he's in court."

"You know, I was wondering about that too," said Will. "I know he was a campaigner."

"A hundred years ago," said Kera. "And that's literal, not figurative."

"Halflings and their lifespans," Will said with a sigh. "Doesn't seem fair."

"It's not just halflings," said Kera. "Dwarves, gnomes, elves--"

"Elves," Will scoffed. "Can you imagine living a thousand years and spending the whole time studying poetry and planting gardens?"

"I can't imagine spending *one day* doing those things," said Kera.

"Right?" Will said, framing the question rhetorically.

The lights in the tavern dimmed, and heavy curtains were drawn over the windows, creating near-perfect darkness in the tavern.

"How am I supposed to see my drink?" Will complained.

"Do a magic," Kera suggested.

"I will do a magic," Will agreed. "That is an excellent suggestion."

Will brought his palms together and rubbed them back and forth as if he were warming them, his eyes glowing a gentle teal color. Holding his hands together, he brought them close to his mouth and blew air into the space between them, the teal light leaving his eyes and coming out as a gentle glowing vapor.

He rotated his hands in opposite directions and shook them as if he were about to roll dice. Satisfied, he placed his hands on the counter and unfurled them as if they were petals on a flower, revealing a scantily-clad teal dancing girl roughly the same size as his cup. The softly glowing illusory dancer twirled and spun, using Will's glass as a prop for a routine.

"I want one," said Kera.

"You got it," said Will.

Holding his hands palms towards the dancer and thumbs touching, Will framed the dancer in the space between his index fingers and slid them towards Kera's glass. A copy of the illusion appeared beside her ale as well, dancing provocatively.

"You're the first wizard I've ever met who does magic the right way," said Kera.

"Because I can make illusionary dancers?" Will asked.

"Because you can make tiny dancers," said Kera, planting her chin on the counter to stare at the dancing girl. "She reminds me of a doll I had as a kid."

"Pretty provocative doll," said Will.

Kera slugged him in the shoulder. A spotlight clanged into being, drawing the tavern's attention to the center stage. Standing under the glaringly bright white light was the mustached bartender.

"Ladies, gentlemen, and others," the man began, speaking to the crowd as if he were the ringmaster of a circus. "It is with great pleasure that I get to introduce tonight's opening performer. To call him a bard of great ability would be an understatement, to say he is the heart and soul of this town would be nothing less than the absolute truth."

"Don't set up unreasonable expectations or anything," Will muttered.

"Right?" Kera said, reaching for her ale. "How good can one bard possibly be?"

"I hope you're excited, folks, because I know I am!" The bartender continued.

"Wait, you're excited?" Will mockingly asked, whispering to Kera.

"Haven't you heard?" Kera asked, bringing her glass up to her mouth. "He's not just a bard, he's the heart and soul of this town."

"The one, the only… Ragdain Barrelbinder!"

Kera's eyes went wide and she gasped in surprise, which made her choke on her ale, setting her coughing and sputtering.

Will thumped her on the back a few times, trying to ease her efforts at breathing. The spotlight on the barkeep cut out, and the sound of an accordion being drawn and a hurdy gurdy being wound as a drum roll began filled the tavern, the collective noise drowning out Kera's coughing fit.

"You okay?" Will asked, leaning in close to Kera to be heard.

"Yeah, I'm fine," said Kera. "I just thought he said… Nothing, it's fine."

The spotlight returned, shining onto the face of a dour looking dwarf with a bristling black beard and an angular mustache, a thick layer of makeup making his face look like a painted clown. A purple and gold harlequin costume completed the ensemble, the bard looking to be a perfect fool.

"Gods above and below," Kera whispered.

The instruments twilled in unison, and the performance began, the musicians newly appeared on stage playing a pomp-filled ballad that had the makings of a perfect dwarven drinking song.

True to dwarven fashion, the song detailed the heroics of Ragdain and his band of travelling adventurers, and featured a constantly repeated chorus about how they worked tirelessly to keep Sundial Vale safe by repelling invaders and monsters. The communal cheering and hollering from the crowd was deafening, most every patron joining in to sing along at the chorus.

Will leaned towards Kera.

"Must be a pretty popular song," Will said, shouting to be heard over the music. "Everyone seems to know the words."

When Kera didn't respond, Will looked to Kera's face and saw her expression; her stunned look of confusion and bewilderment.

"Something wrong?"

Kera was silent, eyes locked on the dwarven bard.

"I'm not crazy about clowns either, if that's what this is about."

The tempo doubled and the folks in the tavern cheered, beginning a rhythmic clap to the beat dictated by the dwarven jester.

"Crowd seems to love it," Will shouted, head moving on a slow swivel as he looked around the tavern. He sipped his drink. "Holy shit, Kera, look at the size of that guy! What a great distraction from the clown!"

Not waiting for an answer, Will put his hand on the back of Kera's neck and turned her face to the left. The table he showed her was removed from the others by platform that was high enough to require a set of stairs, creating a balcony that overlooked the entirety of the pub.

"Must be the VIPs."

Kera saw the table in question, but didn't register it or the people sitting around it.

Is that who I think it is, Zephelous? She asked the sword.

HMM? Zephelous questioned, a nonverbal question that sounded like an oversized cat purring in Kera's mind. ALLOW ME TO INVESTIGATE.

The sword sent out its sphere of senses, its mind reaching outwards to gain a better understanding of the world around it and the persons who filled it. The globe of understanding grew, allowing Zephelous to see more. The sword's mind took in regular patrons and drunks alike, learned which were workers blowing off some much needed steam and who was merely a parent using the pub as a temporary reprieve from their children.

The sword's mind touched on a tortured artist looking to turn his experience into communicable art, on envious musicians who wished they could command a crowd as well as this dwarf, and the heartbroken souls of those fools on the hook of unrequited love.

The outer edge of Zephelous's radius of telepathic power encompassed the elevated table. The sword's mind was seized with a sensation very much like fear as it felt a combination of shock and surprise.

Through Kera's impression, Zephelous recognized a one-of-a-kind set of armor. Reaching through it for the mind inside it, the sword sensed only the barest wisp of a mind. Ignoring the other persons in its sphere, Zephelous focused the entirety of its cognitive abilities on the fragments of thought it felt emanating from the man who should not - who *could not* - be here to wear it, but somehow was.

IT CANNOT BE, said Zephelous.

"It's really Ragdain?" Kera asked, sharing Zephelous's state of shock. "How can that be?"

I DO NOT KNOW OF WHOM YOU SPEAK, said Zephelous.

"I asked you if that was who I thought it was," said Kera. "You said 'let me check'."

AND YOU BELIEVED I WOULD KNOW WHO THIS RAGDAIN CHARACTER WAS SIGHT UNSEEN? Zephelous asked.

"Well I don't know," Kera hissed. "I honestly can't figure out half the shit you do. It seems to vary when it suits you, and that pisses me off."

ANOTHER ITEM IN THE EVER-GROWING LIST OF THINGS THAT

ENRAGE KERA NO-CLAN, Zephelous said dismissively, its focus still on the armored knight. HOW IS IT YOU ARE HERE, TETHYS HASKENVALT?

"Who is Tethys Haskenvalt?" Kera asked.

As if on cue, a verse about Sir Haskenvalt began, detailing the colossal knight as being the son of a human lumberjack and a dainty giant, who found himself rather inadvertently pulled through time to fight alongside Ragdain and his crew by way of magics unknown.

"I guess that answers my question," said Kera.

THIS ORIGIN STORY SEEMS TO BE OMITTING A KEY FACT, Zephelous said, anger building in its psychic voice. SIR HASKENVALT GAVE HIS LIFE IN A BATTLE SOME FOUR HUNDRED YEARS AGO.

"Maybe he survived and you didn't know it," said Kera.

DOUBTFUL, said Zephelous, AS I WATCHED HIM DIE.

"Whoa!" Will said, a look of boyish happiness spreading across his face as the projected image of the heroes riding into battle thundered across the open air.

Beaming excitedly, he turned to face Kera.

"See the details on them? This is some top quality illusion work. You don't normally see this kind of stuff from a bard, I'm honestly impressed!"

The phantom adventuring band separated into the far corners of the room and charged into one another, colliding and creating a spectacular burst of colorful sparks and ribbons of light that rained down onto the patrons of the tavern. The music hit a crescendo and fell away, and the crowd roared and stood for a standing ovation.

The dwarf modestly waved down the applause, but beamed wide and took several bows, waving and blowing kisses towards the patrons in the various points in the tavern.

Will and Kera watched as he beckoned for Bortch to come to his side. The orc strode through the crowd as if it were a cornfield, pushing and brushing his way through the gathered patrons without so much as a second thought for all the patrons he stepped on, knocked over, or shoved into others.

As Bortch approached the bard, the dwarf shielded his mouth with his hand and spoke something into Bortch's ear, pointing to Kera and Will as he did.

"Uh oh," said Will. "That's probably not good. What do we do, Kera?"

What do we do, Zeph? Kera asked the sword.

I SENSE RESENTMENT, RAGE, AND IRE, said Zephelous. I DO NOT SENSE ESPECIALLY MURDEROUS INTENT.

"What the hells does 'especially murderous' mean?" Kera asked.

"Do I even want to know what you're talking about?" Will asked.

When he looked back towards Bortch, the orc was already on them, standing directly in front of the pair.

"Oh, uh. Hey, Bortch. How's it going?"

"My perpetual ennui is renewed with every unenthusiastic breath I take," said Bortch. "What's more immediately pressing is that you've been asked to join the regent mayor and his companions at their private table."

"And if we refuse?" Kera asked.

"Are you planning on refusing?" Bortch asked, the already-tall orc becoming a veritable mountain as he stood to his full height, adjusting his posture in anticipation of a brawl that might come. "It would be good for me to express some of my pent up emotions through my fists."

"Then it's a good thing we're not refusing," Will said, offering Bortch a nervous smile. "Lead the way, oh mighty Bortch."

Rather than lead, Bortch merely stood aside and pointed towards the elevated platform on which the table sat.

"It's that way," said Bortch. "And I appreciate the compliment. I like to feel mighty."

Will nodded, rising from his stool, bidding Kera do the same.

"Alright, Kera, let's go have a talk with a clown," Will said, laughing nervously.

"He's not a clown, he's a jester," said Bortch.

"I know a dwarf you'd get along really well with," said Will.

Kera slid down from her stool and looked up at the table, looked into the glint of light she assumed were Ragdain's eyes. Her hands and feet felt like they were itching, her every muscle wanted her to stay seated, to leave the tavern, to go as far away from this place and that dwarf as she could.

As if self-directed, she watched her feet move the rest of her body across the tavern, watched them climb the stairs to the balcony one step at a time. By the time she got to the top of the stairs, the dwarf was facing away from her, looking down towards the rest of tavern. A thick haze of smoke surrounded him, rising steadily from the cigar stub held between his fingers and the meat smoker he stood beside.

A cacophonous noise like music warbled out from the platform below as another musical act began warming up to go on. The dwarf looked at Kera and Will from over his shoulders, dark eyes that peered out, glittering like polished rocks against the contrast of the stark white stage makeup. The dwarf pointed at the two vacant chairs at the foot of the table.

Kera felt herself sit down, didn't notice Will doing the same.

Her eyes were still locked on the dwarf.

"Ragdain Barrelbinder," said Kera, half speaking and half whispering the name. "I never thought I'd see you again." The dwarf grinned, a black cigar stub rolling between yellowed teeth.

"Oh aye," said Ragdain with a nod, bits of dried grease paint makeup flaking away from his face and falling on to his chest. "I can believe that with nary a doubt. Given that the last time I saw ye, ye were leavin' me for dead inside a half-flooded crypt."

Ragdain exhaled a thick plume of chalky grey smoke, knocking the accumulated ash loose with a tap from his stubby fingers as he spoke. He smiled wide at Kera, his moustache bristling, his missing teeth standing in stark contrast to those that remained. Kera's nostrils flared as the tendrils of smoke made their way towards her, filling her nose with not just the smell of smoke but something earthier and muskier beneath.

"Aye, nary a doubt at all."

Chapter Thirty-One

"Come on, Rags, I didn't leave you for dead," Kera said, leaning back against the bench while resting her arms on the table, cracking her fingers one by one. She knew the smell of what was lingering in the air, barely masked by the stink of cigar and stale beer, knew it as well as a baker knew the smell of bread or a florist knew the scent of a rose. Her years robbing graves had all but inundated her with that scent, that sickly sweet scent, the unmistakable smell that was the aroma of dead and decayed flesh.

"You were dead, so I left you. There's a difference."

"Aye," the dark dwarf said, laughing grimly. "Aye, I suppose there is."

"Wait…" Will said, worry and confusion knitting his brows. "What?"

"Ye heard the lass," Ragdain said, beaming wide, tendrils of smoke crawling their way up over the dwarf's beard to dance across the dried and crusty stage paint, lingering for far too long on the surface of the dwarf's unblinking eyes. Will shuddered.

"Ah," said the wizard, looking uncomfortable as he reached for his ale. "I guess that explains all the illusioplasm in the air, I just assumed it was from your stage performance."

"Illusio-what?" Kera asked, looking to Will.

"Illusioplasm," said Will. "It's sort of like a residual charge from too much magic being used in one spot. It's what motes are made of. This place is caked with layers of illusion magic."

"Ye're not wrong," said Ragdain, chomping on the cigar once more. "And ye're also right about some of it bein' for the performance. It's a pain to keep 'em all up, but it keeps that lot entertained."

Ragdain raised his glass towards the nearest table of patrons, who saw and raised theirs in return for an impromptu cheers. After a deep drink, Ragdain placed the cup down on the table.

"As for usin' it to mask a few others things, well…" Ragdain paused, pulling from the cigar once more, the cherry glow of the lit stub casting a sinister reflection in the dwarf's unblinking eyes. "Ye may be right about that too. I'll ask you to keep quiet about that particular school of magic around these parts. Most folks don't take too kindly to the undead, ye see."

"Right," said Kera. "You used to feel that way too, didn't you Rags? I remember an awful lot of hate for the zombies and wights we'd bump into while we were running the deep tombs."

"S'funny, so do I," said Ragdain. "Only I suppose it slipped my mind, on account of me being busy thinking about how ye turned tail and fled back in Othbvein, leaving me for dead."

"I feel really weird having to repeat this," said Kera. "But you were dead."

"Except I wasn't," Ragdain corrected, waving his hand through the air, the smoke from the cigar tracing a whirl of smoke through the air. "Not for a long while, at least."

"Fifty tons worth of stone ceiling crashed down on top of us the minute we peeled off that seal," Kera countered. "What did you want me to do, Rags? Use my shovel to dig through a hundred yards of stone? Let's not forget there was only one entrance to begin with."

"Except there wasn't, was there?" Ragdain asked, rising to stand.

Kera and Will rose as well, but one of the massive hands of Sir Haskenvalt dropped on to each of their shoulders, gently but firmly guiding them back down and into their seats. Will glanced up at the imposing armored figure of Sir Haskenvalt and nodded, sitting back down. Kera's eyes remained fixed on Ragdain the whole while.

"What are you talking about?" Kera asked. "Every other tunnel was flooded, there was no other way in to that viewing chamber."

"That's right, ain't it?" Ragdain said, speaking with an exaggerated casual tone. "No other tunnels in or out of Othbvein. Not one way in or out of that chamber. Remind me again, me memory bein' spotty and all, of what kind of chamber it was that we happened to be lootin'?"

"The observatory," Kera said blankly.

Ragdain raised his eyebrows, saying nothing as he exhaled a thick cloud of smoke between Will and Kera's faces. The mass of grey lingered and had begun to accumulate in the air around them, building into a stinging cloud. Realization dawned on Kera.

"You're not talking about the starport, are you? A big rat couldn't fit down that tube, and that's assuming the collapse didn't take that part of the ceiling down with it."

"Ye know what?" Ragdain said, his slow circuit around the table bringing him to the food trolley. He snatched a piece of smoked meat and held it aloft, the juiced dripping down from his fingertips onto the plate. He smiled, popping the portion into his mouth and chewing heartily.

"It's the damnedest thing, and ye'd never believe unless you'd been there to see it - like I was - but that damn star-finding hole made it through the cave-in just fine. Not so much as one pebble rolled down that hole in the ceiling, an' I'd wager it's still there now. Of course, ye wouldn't know that though, would ye? After all, it's not like ye bothered to check."

"Gods above and below," Will whispered, aghast. "You really are a terrible person. If you knew there was a chance, why didn't you check?"

"Do you even know what a starport is?" Kera snapped to Will.

"Well, no," said Will. "I assume it involves the stars."

"No shit," said Kera.

"A starport, iffin' I may," said Ragdain, interjecting himself into the aside between Will and Kera. "Is a tunnel through rock, 'bout the size of an apple. Old dwarven citadels, ones that were built closer to the surface than they are nowadays, had plenty o' holes in 'em. Those holes were made in just such a place so that they lined up with different constellations in the night sky, so long as they stayed in the same place."

Ragdain scarfed down another bit of dripping meat, then another. The juices spattered onto his lips and into his mustache, leaving reddish brown dots on his cheeks as it splashed onto his makeup.

"Thing about dwarven engineering, 'specially from them days, is that everythin' was built to last… The builders had more patience back then, y'see, more foresight. They knew it'd be easier to reinforce a starport so that it'd survive a trap bein' triggered that it would be to dig out a new one afterwards. Ye'd know that, of course, if ye'd bother to check."

"Even if I had checked, what would you have expected me to do?" Kera asked.

"Y'know, I thought a lot about that," said Ragdain. "As ye can imagine, weren't much else to be thinkin' about at first. At first I hoped ye'd come along and bring food, that maybe ye were on yer way to drop a few jerky rashers fer yer ol' pal Rags. A few days after that, I started hopin' ye'd bring a bit of whiskey and a good, sharp knife. Didn't have to be big, s'long as it was real sharp."

Ragdain paused to grind the stub of his cigar into the ashtray at the center of the table, imposing himself between Kera and Will to do so.

"Weren't long after that I started hopin' fer just the knife."

Sir Haskenvalt thundered away from behind the pair, pulling out a chair at the foot of the table to sit. Every movement made by the tower of armor that was once a great knight seemed rigid and stiff, making his gait seem as mechanized as Enuarl's. The armored gauntlets thumped on to the table hard enough to set the ashtray rattling.

"He's a big fella," said Will. "What have you been feeding him?"

"I can't believe I'm about to say this," said Kera. "But this is not the time for jokes."

"I wasn't joking," Will said with a nervous laugh. "I know how animated corpses work. Most of them, anyway. Serious question, what have you been feeding him?"

Ragdain leisurely made his way back to the head of the table and pulled out his chair. The legs creaked as the chair dragged across the floor, and groaned as the undead dwarf lowered his weight onto it. Coal black whiskers spread wide to the sides of his face as the dwarf beamed at them.

"Sundial Vale is a safe town," said Ragdain. "Me and my little band o' merry adventurers have been keepin' it that way fer two years now. In fact, the town's been gettin' to be safer an' safer."

"Oh gods," Will whispered. "They've been eating all the criminals, and now that we know their secret we're next on the menu."

"Bit of a leap, an' dramatic at that," said Ragdain, busy brows raised. "Where'd ye get that from?"

"What?" Will asked. "I mean, isn't that where you were going with your little speech? *The town's gettan ta be sayfur an sayfur* feels like it means 'we have been eating people' in undead."

"And that's supposed to be yer impression of me?" Ragdain asked.

"Not if you're going to eat me because of it," said Will.

"Terrible, just terrible," said Ragdain.

"What do you want, Rags?" Kera asked. "Dead or not, you seem to be pretty much your sore old self, give or take an extra grudge."

"A grudge?" Ragdain repeated, chuckling to himself. "Wouldn't call it a grudge, m'self."

The dwarf snapped his fingers in the air until he got Sir Haskenvalt's attention. Once the knight responded, creaking as he sat up to denote alertness, Ragdain pointed at the scraps of meat. The armored goliath awkwardly leaned forward over the table, using his incredibly long arms to reach to where the tray of sliced meats was being kept.

Pinching the platter between thumb and forefinger, Sir Haskenvalt deposited the meat plate onto the table in front of Ragdain. The dwarf nodded and waved the knight away. Sir Haskenvalt sat back in his chair while Ragdain began shoveling portions into his mouth.

Kera felt Zephelous's anger build before she heard its words in her mind, the sword's outrage building like a physical heat at the edge of her senses.

TETHYS HASKENVALT WAS A COURAGEOUS KNIGHT AND A HEROIC CHAMPION FOR GOOD, said Zephelous. TO SEE HIM REDUCED TO LITTLE MORE THAN A TRAINED PET SERVER AND MINDLESS BRUTE IN DEATH IS SACRILEGE.

What do you want me to do about it, Zeph? Kera asked. *The man inside that armor died a long time ago, whatever is left of him was left to rot under the earth. It belongs to Ragdain now.*

YOU COULD CONDONE SUCH BEHAVIOR? Zephelous asked, furious.

Remember how I introduced myself to you back when I found you? Kera said to the sword. *Kera, who robs unmarked graves. Necromancy is just a more literal version of grave robbing.*

Ragdain seemed to take note of Kera's silence, not realizing she was in conversation with Zephelous. The dwarf paused from eating for a moment.

"Ye were never been the quiet sort," said Ragdain.

"Classic Kera, am I right?" Will said, radiating nervous energy. "Won't shut up when you want to be quiet, quiet when you want to her talk. Drives everybody crazy, you know how it is, I'm sure. Now, if I may - and I don't want to sound like I'm repeating myself or anything - but I'd like to go back to the part where we were talking about what you're feeding this guy, because I'll be honest; watching you eat strips of juicy meat over there is making me queasy. That's not pieces of someone who disobeyed you or anything, is it?"

"Beef tataki," said Ragdain. "I like it with an au jus."

"Oh," said Will, visibly relaxing. "Can I have some?"

"No," said Ragdain, licking the juices from his fingertips before clapping them to clean any bits of food that might still be stuck on them. "An' to answer yer question, I feed 'em anythin' dumb enough to keep attackin' the city. If I kenna find any fresh meat from what's attacked us, sometimes we go on patrol to push back against the doggies an' the giants. If that still don't lead to any meat, an' only rarely has it ever not, then we've got ourselves a boomin' beef market here in Sundial Vale."

Ragdain smacked his lips together, sucking at his moustache to ensure that he hadn't missed any of the juice from the sloppy food.

"Turns out it's a lot easier to be a successful farmer iffin ye're not gettin' sacked by timbergnolls every other week. Successful farmers can pay taxes, taxes can build fortifications, and next thing ye know ye've got a town - not just a bunch o' makeshift lodges and cabins, but an actual town - on yer hands."

"So naturally, you set yourself up as its dictator," Will said accusingly.

"I was elected as regent mayor," said Ragdain. "Twice now. Of course, it's only on account of bein' the mouthpiece for the heroes o' Sundial Vale."

"Titles don't mean as much if you give them to yourself," said Will. "Right Kera?"

"I didn't pick that flashy bit of words," Ragdain corrected. "The folks that live here gave it to me. Well, I suppose I should be sayin' us."

WHO ELSE HAS THIS FIEND DEFILED? Zephelous roared into Kera's mind. WHAT OTHER HEROES IN THE SLEEP ETERNAL HAS HE STOLEN FROM?

The sound of footsteps on wooden stairs came from the rear of the room, drawing the attention of those present. First down the stairs was an eagle winged scion with a shock of red hair, pale skin, and freckles.

"Feeding time already, Rags?" said the woman.

"Just about," said Ragdain. "Lemme finish this beef and I'll juice ye up."

"Sounds good to me," said the woman.

Looking to Will and Kera, the pale woman smiled.

"I think these belong to you, Dani."

"Did you say *Dani?*" Kera asked, watching as Voldani stepped out from behind the furled wings of the redheaded woman. "What's going on here, Voldani? Who's this?"

"Kera, William," Voldani said, addressing each of them in turn.

The god-blooded woman had an expression on her face neither of them had seen previously - something dangerously close to despair.

"While I never imagined I would need to do so again, allow me to introduce Keilara Haddonfield. She was the warden of the church of Perrus when I was a girl, the one who took me in and oversaw my education."

Do you know anything about this one, Zeph? Kera asked.

I AM NOT FAMILIAR WITH THE NAME, Zephelous answered.

"Just Voldani's baggage, then," Kera muttered out loud. "It's nice to meet you, Keilara. Been dead long?"

Voldani looked aghast, and Will seemed to freeze in place. Ragdain ignored the comment if he heard it, content to noisily enjoy his barely-cooked meat.

Keilara, for her part, said nothing, merely scrutinizing Kera.

"So this is the one?" Keilara said to Voldani, who nodded.

"Why don't I like that?" said Kera. "I'm the one who what?"

"Got Voldani out of the church, for one thing," said Keilara, walking to stand beside Ragdain, hands planted on her hips as she studied Kera and Will. "For two, evidently committed a number of crimes while carrying a talking sword from the first age. Have I missed anything?"

"She won't let me call her Dani," said Kera. "Are you the reason why?"

"Hardly what I meant," said Keilara. "And hardly important."

"I'll give you that," said Kera. "So. Where'd Rags dig you up?"

"Kera," Voldani said, scolding her.

"It's fine, Dani," Keilara said, waving down the other scion's irritation. "Once you've been to the sea of stars and back, you get a sense of perspective. It'll take a lot more than an uppity girl from the Wildlands with an untamed mouth to get under my skin."

"But not much I bet," said Kera. "What, on account of it threatening to fall off your bones if you go long enough without eating something. Or, y'know, someone."

"Classy," said Keilara.

"That's me," said Kera, grip tightening on Zephelous's handle. "All class."

Ragdain scarfed down the final scrap of meat on the plate, sighing in satisfaction.

"What a feast, mm," said the Dwarf.

"All set?" Keilara asked.

"You bet," said Ragdain.

Keilara lowered herself down to her knees, bowing in front of the undead dwarf. Voldani seemed stunned and shocked, her mouth hanging open as she watched on. Unsure what was happening, Kera stayed in her chair, her every muscle wound tight like a spring and ready to snap into action at a moment's notice.

Ragdain wiped his hands off on the front of his shirt and lifted his butt out of his chair, just enough to rotate it ninety degrees so that he was facing Keilara, hands held out over the back of her head.

"Keilara, what…" Voldani asked.

Her question was answered a moment later when sickly green light began to radiate from around Ragdain's hands, shining out from behind his eyes and from the blackness between his missing teeth. The green light cast a pallid glow on all those present, making Kera feel nauseous just by looking at it. Will's face went pale, and he began to sweat.

Voldani took a few steps back, stumbling as she did.

"What manner of wickedness is this?"

"Not wickedness," Will answered. "Well, not technically. It's necromancy."

"Right ye are," said Ragdain.

"Since when are you a corpse jockey?" Kera asked.

"What in the hells is a *corpse jockey*?" Will asked.

"Have you never campaigned?" Kera asked Will, irritation visible on her face and audible in her question. "Corpse jockey is slang for someone who raises the dead. Y'know, like bone dancer, or flesh puppeteer."

"Yeah, I'm an actual wizard," said Will. "We don't use your janky slang, we use the correct terminology."

Will pointed at Ragdain.

"That's necromancy, and I'd bet that what he's doing right now is dumping a bunch of negative energy into Voldani's dead friend to keep her going. I'm guessing that's what he meant by 'juicing her up'."

"This is vile," Voldani whispered. "Unnatural. Unbecoming. Unholy."

"Accordin' to who?" Ragdain asked, flashing Voldani a sinister grin made all the more imposing by the vibrant green light radiating from his hands and from his pupils.

"According to the gods," said Voldani, standing defiantly.

"A few of 'em, I suppose," Ragdain nodded.

"The Lady in White would never stand for such an abomination."

Ragdain chuckled.

"Ye run into any problems with yer god since ye came back, Key?"

"Can't say I have," said Keilara. "Of course, she knew I was bored to tears out there."

Kera's bile rose in her stomach and her skin began to crawl, goosebumps breaking out all over her body as her living flesh recoiled in response to the proximity of so much necromantic magic. She wanted to puke, or run, or both.

"I think that's probably why she let me leave," said Keilara.

"Perrus allowed you to leave the place beyond?" Voldani gasped. "Knowing that you would return to this plane as an abomination?"

"Seems a bit harsh fer an old friend," Ragdain said with a chuckle.

"Dani doesn't mince words," said Keilara. "It's an admirable quality she possesses, one of many I might add. Did you make Protector yet, Dani? I made a bet with Speaker Trost that you would have by now. Not like I can collect, but I'll settle for the satisfaction of knowing I won."

"I have not," Voldani answered. "I have been assigned to be a watcher for Speaker Gerhardt for some time."

"Gerhardt, eh?" Keilara said, looking up at Voldani from her kneeling position, her eyes brimming with green energy that pooled like tears. "Seems like a waste of your talents to put you so far up north. What do you do with your days, break up bar brawls and enforce city bylaws?"

"I defend the city of Zelwyr," said Voldani. "And the Zelwyran temple."

"Defend it from what?" Keilara said. "Drunks and the odd gnoll pack?"

Voldani's grimace was answer enough for Keilara, who chuckled.

"So much for Malzen being the 'last frontier for adventure', eh?" Keilara said. "Still, I always thought there was something off about Speaker Gerhardt. He plays at being a doddering old man, but I've never been convinced."

The light pouring out from Ragdain's hands faded away, and Keilara stood tall once more. She stretched, tilting her head to the side until her neck cracked with a *pop* that made the still-living folks in the room flinch.

"That's the stuff," said Keilara. "Makes me feel alive again. Always leaves me feeling hungry afterwards though."

"There's a reason for that," Will said grimly.

"I bet," said Keilara, eyes shining darkly as she smiled at the wizard.

"As fun as this has been, I have patrols to fly, and Rags has a city to pretend to run. Dani, it was great to see you. Let's not wait until one of us dies before we see each other again, okay?"

"I should never have seen you again," said Voldani.

"And yet you get to," said Keilara. "How lucky is that? Don't be a stranger, Dani. Come find me in the skies next time you're out this way."

Voldani mumbled something Kera couldn't understand.

"What was that?" Keilara asked.

"I shall consider returning," Voldani repeated.

"Good, I hope you do," said Keilara, making her way to Voldani and pulling the other woman into an embrace.

Kera saw Voldani tense up, watched her fists tighten as she was pulled into the embrace, saw the scion's spine go straight as the undead woman pulled her close. Something like a shudder moved through her before Keilara finally dropped the hug.

"I really hope we can catch up once you've had some time to think," said Keilara, backing away from Voldani and making her way towards the stairs they'd come down. "I knew this wasn't going to be easy on you, but I guess I was hoping it wouldn't be this hard. Take care, Dani."

Keilara hesitated for a moment before leaving, and it seemed to Kera as if she was waiting for Voldani to say something. When the scion's lips stayed sealed, Keilara parsed her lips and nodded, then made her way up the stairs. Voldani's eyes followed her every step until she was out of sight. A weighted silence hung in the room for a long time after.

"Right then," said Ragdain, "now that everyone has had a bit o' nostalgia, I suppose it's about time I asked what it is ye were doin' in my city in the first place."

"We need to kill a dragon," said Will.

"What for?" asked Ragdain.

"We need its blood," said Kera.

"At the risk o' repeatin' meself, what for?"

"Some kind of magic thing," said Kera.

"Gettin' into necromancy, are ye?"

"Fuck no," said Kera.

"Divine magic," said Will. "It's a crucial component to some kind of holy rite of Perrus meant to break curses and cure poison."

"I heard o' many a spell that uses dragon blood, an' I can't say I know o' many that're used for healin'," said Ragdain. "Then again, I ain't exactly a priest, is I? Tell ye what; if ye can make it happen, bring me some o' that blood and I'll make it worth yer while."

"How worth our while?" Kera asked.

"Fer starter's, I'll bury our little grudge," said Ragdain.

"I thought you said you wouldn't call it a grudge."

"Vendetta, then."

"I like grudge better."

"Thought ye might," said Ragdain. "Besides that, I can pay. Handsomely. What's more, I'll set ye up in the luxury suite for as long as yer in the Vale, an' I'll see to it that yer well-provisioned before ye head out. Seem fair?"

"Might I also suggest--" Will started.

"An' I'll take care of yer bar tab," Ragdain finished.

"Excellent," said Will, looking around for a server. "Most good."

"We're in agreement, then?" Ragdain asked, extending his hand. Will shook it happily, then Kera. Ragdain turned to Voldani, but the scion was still staring up the stairs Keilara had gone. The dwarf shrugged and dropped his hand.

"Right," said Ragdain. "Iffin ye don't mind, I really do have a city to run, so I'll be on me way. I'm sure ye know where the door is."

"We do," said Kera.

"It's near the bar with the free beer, I think," said Will.

Without a word, Voldani turned and walked down the balcony stairs towards the ground floor. Kera and Will exchanged a glance, and hastily followed after her. Voldani brushed her way past the burly orc, walked by the bar, and pushed her way out the door.

"Do we follow her?" Kera asked.

"I don't think so," said Will. "All the free beer is in here."

"Yeah..." Kera said pensively. "I can't believe I'm saying this, but I feel like we need to follow her."

"Why would we do that?" Will asked. "What's she going to do, lecture someone for an hour?"

"I feel like she's not in a talking mood so much as a sword-swinging mood," said Kera.

"And you want to go *closer* to her while she's like that?"

"If only to make sure she doesn't swing those swords in such a way that we get screwed out of free hooch."

"Yeah, that would suck," Will said, wistfully staring at the bottles behind the counter. "Alright, let's go. Quickly, before I change my mind."

Chapter Thirty-Two

"This place must be razed to the ground," Voldani said, speaking quietly with a distant look on her face. "The ashes should be sifted through to find the remains of Ragdain and his undead minions, and those should be cremated once again."

"We can't just burn the place down, Voldani," said Kera, shaking her head. "And believe me, the irony of that statement is not lost on me. There are a lot of innocent people in there, and even more who rely on Ragdain and Keilara and the others to keep them safe."

"They are monsters." spat Voldani. "Horrors in the guise of people guarding citizens who are unaware of the nature of those they believe to be on their side."

"They *are* on their side, Voldani," Will interjected, scratching at his beard. "As much of a contradiction as it might seem, Ragdain and his zombies are Sundial Vale's best hope."

"Keilara is not a zombie," Voldani said, glaring at Will.

The illusionist shrugged and raised his arms.

"Okay, Ragdain and his zombies and your uncategorized undead friend," Will said. "Is that what you want to hear? I don't know what to tell you."

"Tell me there is a way to end the dwarf's hold on her," said Voldani. "Or a way to restore her to true life. Truly, tell me you know of any way to revive her or reinstate her vitality or rid her of her undead status."

Will winced, sucking at his teeth.

"That's pretty much four different ways to say the same thing," said Will. "And unfortunately, that's way out of my depth. I do illusions, not undead. You'd have to talk to either another necromancer--"

"Out of the question," said Voldani.

"Okay, then you'd need to ask a high priest of some kind," Will said with a shrug. "You work in a temple, doesn't this kind of stuff come up from time to time?"

"No," said Voldani. "The undead have not troubled Zelwyr in decades."

"At least not that you know of," said Kera. "Given what we just saw."

"Indeed," said Voldani, holding her chin in her hand. "Indeed. I must alert Speaker Gerhardt and have arrangements made to mobilize a squadron of Deadbane Guards to come and cleanse the city. Perhaps the temples here have some number of clerics capable of destroying or undoing the undead and their necromantic magics."

"Voldani, you can't do any of that," said Kera.

"And why not?" Voldani glowered.

"Because if you do, you'll start a panic," said Kera. "You'll terrify the citizens."

"They should be terrified," said Voldani. "They have unknowingly placed their trust in a revenant and a necromancer, one who uses the flesh of fallen foes to keep the dark hunger of his monstrosities sated."

"They aren't monstrosities to them," said Will. "As far as the common folk are concerned, Ragdain's gang are heroes. There wouldn't be a Sundial Vale without them."

"Then perhaps there should not be a Sundial Vale," said Voldani, marching away.

Will and Kera exchanged a concerned look, then hurried after the armored warrior.

"Voldani," Kera began.

"You can't be serious," said Will.

"I almost always am," said Voldani.

"Got me there," said Will.

"Dani, come on--" Kera's sentence came to an abrupt halt as Voldani drew both of her swords and whirled to face Kera, holding the point of one of the weapons dangerously close to Kera's face.

Kera froze in place, eyes wide and focused on the weapon.

"Do. Not," Voldani said, speaking deliberately. "Call me that."

"Is it because that's what Keilara used to call you?" Will asked.

"Mind your business, mountebank," said Voldani.

"Seeing as how you're threatening to completely sidetrack a quest that I'm supposed to get paid for, handsomely so I might add, I'd say I am minding my business," said Will.

"Your concerns about coin are noted," said Voldani. "Assist me in destroying Ragdain Barrelbinder and his ilk, in putting Keilara to rest, and I will ensure that you are rewarded."

"Voldani, she was at rest," Kera said, eyes still on the sword in her face. "And by all accounts, she hated it. What kind of warrior wants an eternity of peace?"

"The valiant kind," said Voldani. "The kind who know that war and struggle are merely the precursors to peace and tranquility."

"Okay, sure," said Kera. "Quick question, probably unrelated. Was Keilara valiant?"

"Yes," said Voldani. "Her courage in battle knew no bounds, her determination to better the world around her was unequaled. She was not my mother, though she may well have been. To see her in this way turns my stomach and boils my blood."

"Isn't that what she's doing now?" Kera asked. "Protecting the innocent people in this town, letting them grow crops, raise livestock, and whatever else in peace? This is a pretty remote settlement, Voldani, we're days away from the nearest town, weeks away from the nearest city with any kind of standing army. If it weren't for Ragdain and Keilara, this whole town would probably get flattened by giants within a month."

"You cannot know that," said Voldani.

"It's not that much of a stretch," said Will. "We were ambushed by timbergnolls three days out from Zelwyr. Three days! A place like this, without Ragdain and the others--"

"Would be far better off," Voldani interrupted.

"You can't know that," Kera said, shaking her head.

"I can," Voldani said through locked teeth and a clenched jaw.

"How?" Will asked. "The capital uses constructs and golems to protect some of the outlying towns. This isn't all that different, if you think about it."

"Machines do not require a steady diet of flesh and dark energy," Voldani countered. "Constructs must be built, not reanimated from corpses."

"Constructs can't make decisions," said Will. "A machine can't run a town."

"Enaurl is perfectly capable of making decisions," said Voldani.

"Enaurl is… Enaurl," said Kera. "She's different. Besides, all her decisions revolve around what to punch and how to punch it. That's a far cry from negotiating trade contracts and keeping the guilds from taxing the townsfolk into the ground and you know it."

"Be that as it may, this cannot stand," said Voldani. "The city must be cleansed."

"Voldani, what's the word for when an outside force comes in and destabilizes the standing government?" Will asked, crossing his arms.

"A coup," Voldani answered.

"That's what you're talking about," said Will. "You're not talking about making the town any more 'pure' or 'righteous' by your actions, you're talking about staging a violent uprising against the regent mayor because of your prejudice."

"It is not prejudice to destroy the undead," Voldani sneered.

"If the undead in question are busy protecting a few hundred people right up until you destroy them, I feel like it might be," said Will. "Help me out here, Kera."

"I'm trying to," said Kera.

"Try harder," said Will.

"Real helpful."

"That's about as much help as you're being."

"Fine," Kera said, puffing out a breath. "Voldani, what is Ragdain doing wrong?"

"Excuse me?" Voldani asked. "How could you even have the audacity to ask such a question?"

"I think I've proven myself plenty audacitatious by now," said Kera.

"Audacious," Will quietly corrected.

"Whatever," said Kera. "I've proven myself plenty audacious by now, just like you've proven yourself to be plenty righteous and lawful and whatever. So, really, tell me what Ragdain and Keilara are doing that's wrong?"

"They masquerade as something they are not," said Voldani.

"Hi there, Will Decker," Will said, offering a mock handshake to Voldani. "I make a living out of masquerading as things I'm not, and occasionally making other people or the world around me do the same."

"Hardly comparable," said Voldani.

"Isn't it?" Kera asked. Voldani's furious glare was the only answer she received. "What else are they doing that's so terrible?"

"They sustain themselves on flesh," said Voldani.

"Gnoll meat and chunks of giant," said Kera.

"Flesh is flesh," said Voldani.

"I eat flesh all the time," Kera countered. "Pig flesh, cow flesh, fish flesh…"

"Why do you insist on twisting words and meaning to suit your argument?" Voldani demanded, shouting into Kera's face.

"Why do you?" Kera answered, speaking softly.

"What words have I twisted?" Voldani asked.

"I don't want to get technical," said Will. "But necromancy isn't inherently infernal. Some necromancy uses infernal magics, some don't. As far as I can tell, Kera's buddy Rags is using good old-fashioned necromantic magics - emphasis on the 'old-fashioned'. Whatever magics he found in that tomb are from the oldest of old schools, predating half the gods. The new ones like Perrus, at least."

"You think the amount of time she has spent on this realm signifies weakness?" Voldani demanded. "Do you think her a weak god, that her words and followers are insignificant?"

"I didn't say any of that," Will said. "Seems like a bit of a reach."

"Say another word that implies Perrus is weak," said Voldani. "I will demonstrate my reach, and the reach of my blades, with a pointed argument."

Will gulped.

"He's not saying your god is weak, Voldani," Kera said, still speaking softly to the enraged warrior. "He's saying your argument is."

"You have no qualms with an undead secretly taking control of a town?" Voldani asked.

"They elected him," Kera said. "Twice."

"Because they do not know any better," said Voldani. "I aim to educate them."

"No you don't," said Will. "You want to convince them they should be afraid, and for what reason? Some archaic rule your brand new god has against the reanimated?"

"They should be afraid," said Voldani.

"Why?" Kera asked. "Because they're being kept safe? Because they can sleep soundly at night knowing Rags and Keilara will defend them against whatever monsters might come out of the woods to smash their homes and eat their children?"

"They should know that there are monsters already inside their town," said Voldani.

"What makes a monster, Voldani?" Kera asked. "What separates a monster from a person? Because I've known people far more vile than any timbergnoll, and while Ragdain might not be the friendliest guy on the plane, he's doing a lot more good for a lot more people than I ever have. Hells, I'd be willing to bet you haven't even--"

"Finish that sentence and I will end you," Voldani threatened, pressing the sword closer to Kera's face, the tip of the weapon wavering inches away from her skin.

"You'd kill me over a factual statement you disagree with?" Kera asked, arching an eyebrow at Voldani. "That makes me feel real safe."

"You think it a fact that I have done less good than a band of horrors?" Voldani leered.

"Keilara said it first and I don't know if she was wrong," said Kera. "Do you do much defending of the innocent in Zelwyr, or is it mostly drunks and the odd timbergnoll?"

"Let us not forget handling vagrant arsonists," Voldani said, narrowing her eyes at Kera.

"I'm actually glad you brought that up," said Kera, staring back into Voldani's face. "Because if I remember right, the first time you 'handled' me, you did it by smashing me through a vendor's cart. Did you ever go back to make sure that the vendor was able to rebuild?"

Voldani's silence was her only response, and it spoke volumes to Kera. Feeling confident, Kera pressed her luck.

"Ragdain is making sure hundreds of merchants can operate, feed their families, and sleep soundly at night. Tell me *one* thing evil about that."

"He is a revenant," Voldani said, the sword lowering as her resolve faltered.

"And I'm a grave robbing arsonist with mild impulse control problem," Kera said.

"Is it just mild, though?" Will asked.

"Not helpful," Kera said to Will. "The point is, if you start judging people based on what they are and what they aren't, you'll find yourself on a slippery slope towards becoming one of the monsters you're so worried about."

"He reanimated her corpse," Voldani said. "Filled her with false life."
"Which she seems grateful for," Kera countered. "And from what she says, Perrus herself allowed it. How can you argue against the word of the god you're so adamant on using as justification for destroying this town?"

"Keilara must be mistaken," Voldani said, her sword fully lowered at this point. "Perrus would never allow… would never tolerate…"

"You're the god-blooded one," said Kera. "Why don't you ask her?"

"I…," Voldani began, her words failing. "I cannot at this time."

"Then ask her later," suggested Will. "Right now, the only thing you need to decide on is whether or not you want to use fear to cause this city to self destruct."

"And whether or not that's what your god would want," Kera added.

Sighing in resignation, Voldani sheathed her swords.

"Perhaps I am…"

"Mistaken?" Kera suggested.

"Acting hastily?" Will prompted.

"Not informed enough to make a proper decision," Voldani finished. "The Speaker will know best how to proceed. We do not possess the numbers nor the capacity to reinstate a functional government in this place, and I suppose that alone should be reason enough to stay my hand."

Voldani turned away from Will and Kera and began walking towards her chambers.

"Nevermind the morals and ethics conversation," Will mumbled.

"Let's just take the win," Kera sighed. "I think that's enough for now."

Chapter Thirty-Three

Having made their way across town, which in Sundial Vale was little more than a dozen city blocks, Smith, Brenno, and Enaurl made their way towards the market district. The buildings around them began to become more closely clustered, with merchant stalls and vendor carts appearing more and more frequently. Instead of the same oil lamp posts present in the other parts of town, the ones here were gas powered and appeared poorly made; their posts were made from uneven bits of rusted steel held together by crude welding, the metal littered with bulges and slag.

Shoddy work, Smith thought. *Could explode and kill somebody at any minute.*

"Reminds me of Faltus," said Smith to Brenno, looking up at the gas powered lamps installed along the streets of the market district. "Lotta artificers busy doing things because they can, nobody doing things the way they should."

"Sounds terribly elitist of you," said Brenno.

Enaurl, as always, said nothing. Foot traffic in the area became steadily heavier as the trio neared the heart of the market. The air around them began to become filled with snippets of conversations about products and services from shouting merchants mixed with bits and pieces of exchanges between enthusiastic hagglers. A group of musicians could be heard playing from somewhere nearby.

"Sword sharpening, get your swords sharpened while you shop! We'll get your blade so sharp you could shave a dwarven baby's bottom with it!"

"Refurbished armor here, discounted for quick sale! All the dents have been removed, there are very few stains, only one previous owner!"

"Bottomless pockets, folks! Pockets so deep they might as well be pants!"

The trio were pressed closer and closer together as the market thickened, stalls and vendors taking up more and more space on either side of streets filled with more and more pedestrians.

Closing ranks, the two men watched for signs of an alchemist or some other vendor that might happen to be stocking dragon's blood, a scenario that was so unlikely that Smith couldn't think about it.

The impossible hope that he might have a chance encounter with a wealthy Mian Dorean merchant, that he might be able to just use money to put an end to this ridiculous quest, might be able to go home to Morri, might be able to just make things go back to normal life before some half-naked woman had broke into his house and gotten his daughter shot.

And not just shot, thought Smith, *but shot with a cursed arrow from a godsdamned enchanted crossbow, because for whatever unimaginable reason she - with her brain more powerful than an academy of artificers - decided it was a reasonable thing to blackmail Hornbuckle over some GODSDAMN VAGRANT ARSONIST and her HAUNTED FUCKING SWORD...*

A pain in the side of Smith's cheek made him realize he'd been clenching his jaw, had been letting himself get caught up in the swell of his anger. Again.

He took a slow breath, reminded himself to gradually unclench his fists and jaw. Morri's mother would have laughed at him if she'd been there, would have reminded him to unclench his butt cheeks while she kissed him on the forehead and made everything make sense before bringing out those wings and charging headfirst into battle...

Smith exhaled forcefully, pushing aside the thoughts of her. They wouldn't help him get through this, she wasn't here to swing her sword at the problem, or tell him to calm down when he was winding himself up too far, or to sing that beautiful damn song whose words he couldn't remember to the daughter who was growing up without her, or any one of the other thousand things he was certain hadn't been done right without her. This train of thought brought on a fleeting sense of despair, which brought his anger thundering back.

The target of his ire this time was himself, his own pathetic lack of resolve against letting himself get sucked in to that dark place in his head. He inhaled slowly, controlling the swell of his lungs; his anger burned in his chest, ever present but controlled. It was easier to be angry. The boiling in his blood kept him more focused on what he needed to do, which was ending this bullshit as quickly as possible.

That meant checking here.

"Everything alright, Smith?" Brenno asked.

"What do you think?" Smith asked, not bothering to face Brenno.

"I mean besides all that," said Brenno.

"That's about all I've got going on right now, Hornbuckle," said Smith.

From the mass of people and vaguely people-shaped creatures around them, a robed man approached them.

"Interesting," said the figure, peering into Enaurl's face with keen interest. "May I inquire as to your method?"

"Proprietary," Smith grunted, making to move past the man.

"Of course, of course," said the man, nodding passively. He reached towards Enaurl's face, fingertips moving towards her silver eyes. "How does she see?"

Enaurl's silver fingers curled around the man's wrist, forcing the arm down and away from her face.

"Just fine," Smith said. "Let's go."

"Wait, please," said the man, hurrying after the trio and they brushed by. "I represent a wealthy prince, we would pay you any price you name to purchase a hundred such soldiers! Our people are attacked every night by eyeless beasts with glistening teeth--"

"Can't help you," Smith interrupted, offering the barest of shrugs.

"Why not?" the man asked, deflating.

"She's not a soldier," Smith said.

Brenno turned his head as he walked, watching the man in the robes deflate further, practically wilting before shuffling back into the mass of people browsing the market. The halfling couldn't help but feel guilty, though why he couldn't imagine.

"You ought to think about it some time," Brenno said, turning back to resume reading the makeshift banners and improvised signage of many of the vendors.

"Odds are that whole story is drakeshit," said Smith. "There's always a prince somewhere who needs help with something."

"Not that," said Brenno, looking over into his distorted reflection in Enaurl's profile as he spoke. "Don't tell me you haven't thought about how useful a second Enaurl could be."

"Of course I have," said Smith.

"And?"

"It's not going to happen," said Smith. "Besides, she gets too much attention as it is."

"How so?" Brenno asked.

From the side of the street, a debonair middle aged man with an expertly coiffed mustache and goatee called towards the trio, shouting at them from behind the shelf of a vending tent.

"You there, with the silver golem!" The man called.

Smith stopped, giving Brenno a quick stare, as if this were all the explanation needed to answer his previous questions.

"What do you want?" Smith shouted to the man.

"Only to ask a few questions about your mechanical companion," the man called back.

"Do you happen to know where I can buy a vial of dragon blood?"

"In Sundial Vale?" the man asked, stroking his goatee. "No."

"Know anything about the white that's been attacking these parts?" Smith asked.

"Well," the merchant said, thinking for a moment. "No, I don't."

"Too bad," said Smith, proceeding to carry on with his walk. "Come talk to me when you know either of those two things and I'll tell you everything I know."

The merchant's sculpted moustache rose like wings on either side of his face, and he nodded, turning to bark orders at a pair of hooded apprentices.

"If it's attention you're seeking to avoid, why not sell the patent?" Brenno asked. "It's only a matter of time before another artificer creates something similar and does the same. It's a fortune waiting to be had, one big enough to buy any amount of privacy you could ask for."

"That's not what I meant, Hornbuckle," said Brenno. "And not what I want, either."

"You don't want to be wealthy?" Brenno asked, flabbergasted.

"Not like that," said Smith. "Not by turning Enaurl into a mold for grubby kings and rich assholes to pour armies out of. She'd never be okay with that."

"What does it matter what Enaurl thinks of it?" Brenno asked.

"I wasn't talking about Enaurl," said Smith.

A trio of dwarves appeared in the path in front of them, standing out from the crowd by virtue of their stillness.

One held a staff that looked like it was meant to double as a jackhammer, another wore armor that belched black smoke out from exhaust ports on its back, and the third was completely encased in the glass shell atop what looked like a motorized minecart.

"The Blackmouth engineerin' guild would like a word with ye," said Hammerstaff.

"Ideally in private," said Minecart, voice echoing inside the glass bubble.

"Just a quick and highly lucrative conversation," said Smoke Armor.

"Bring any dragon blood with you?" Smith asked.

The three looked towards each other for a moment, sharing a silent conversation.

"Not exactly a walkin' around trinket, is it?" asked Hammerstaff.

"Not to mention fairly unstable," said Minecart.

"We could possibly requisition some. Why d'ye want to know?" asked Smoke Armor.

"Need it for something," said Smith. "If you haven't got any, I'm not interested in speaking with you or any other guild."

"I'm sure we can come to an arrangement," said Hammerstaff.

"There are some reserves in the mages guild," said Minecart.

"If we could offer you what ye need, would ye talk with us?" Smoke Armor asked.

"Depends," said Smith. "How soon can you get it?"

The dwarven trio shared another silent conversation, each taking pensive expressions.

"Well, that's just it, ye see," hammer staff began.

"There would be a lot of paperwork to file, favors to call in," Minecart added.

"Shouldn't be longer than a few months," Smoke Armor finished.

"Too long," Smith said with a shake of his head. "Not interested."

"Now, let's be reasonable folks," said Hammerstaff.

"Established merchants as we are," said Minecart.

"We'd be willin' to give ye a sizeable payment for yer patience on the matter," said Smoke Armor.

Smith shook his head and sidestepped around the trio, Enaurl and Brenno in tow.

"We'll just figure it out on our own, then," called Hammerstaff.

"We've the weight of an entire guild behind us," said Minecart.

"Coulda been rich," said Smoke Armor.

"Been hearing that a lot today," Smith called back. "But not one person has been able to give me what I actually want. You want to talk about Enaurl? I want dragon blood. End of story."

"Dragon blood?" said a voice, high pitched and warbling. "Expensive, pricey. Too much for gaudy mech. Needs cleaning, can tell from here."

Looking around and not seeing the source of the voice, Smith continued walking.

"And where is 'here', exactly?" Smith demanded.

He felt a tapping on his leg. Looking down, he saw what appeared to be a goblin wearing an oil stained bathrobe as a cloak. Greasy black hair sticking out from under the hood, hanging low around huge yellow eyes.

A variety of crude tools, many of which looked improvised and poorly made, were tucked into the tied knot around the goblin's waistband. The goblin extended a filthy hand towards Smith.

"Bucket, goblin breakfixer," said the creature.

The goblin's eyes, large and yellow, were fixed on Enaurl as it spoke. Unlike the previous merchants, they weren't wide with awe - quite the opposite.

"Balance is off. Gyro is wrong."

"Not a chance," said Smith. "Put that in myself."

"Put it in wrong yourself," said Bucket.

"How could you possibly know that?" Brenno asked, examining Enaurl and finding nothing unusual. "She's standing perfectly still."

"Still, yes," said Bucket. "Perfect? No. Leaning to the left, arm drags too. Loose connection, no problem. Easy break to fix."

"What's that now?" Smith repeated.

"Happened from a break," Bucket said with a shrug. "I can fix, it's what I do. Something breaks, I take the broken thing. Make something fixed instead."

"That's great," said Smith, releasing the goblin's handshake. "Not interested."

Smith passed the goblin in an effort to continue his search, but the breakfixer called after him.

"Interested in dragon's blood, yes?" Bucket said. "Bucket knows where it sleeps."

Smith stopped mid-stride, planting his foot and turning to scrutinize the goblin from over his shoulder.

"Know where what sleeps?" Smith asked.

"The sheep-stealer, the farmer-eater," said Bucket. "The white dragon."

"Horseshit," Smith cursed. "How would you know that?"

"Am a breakfixer," said Bucket. "I build things. Things like your silver lady, only better."

"Yeah, right," Smith said, not believing the goblin for a second. "I've seen goblin artifice before. Explodes half the time it gets used."

"Not Bucket's," said the goblin, pointed ears sticking out from his hood as he shook his head from side to side. "Bucket's a rogue, because Bucket's a breakfixer. Boommakers don't like breakfixers."

Smith scowled at the goblin.

"Am I supposed to know what that means?" Smith asked. "Because it sounds like gibberish."

Bucket shook his head.

"Not gibberish," said the goblin. "Gobbledegook. Close, not the same."

"Of course," said Brenno, rolling his eyes. "What a foolish mistake to make."

"You make jokes, I no help," said Bucket, throwing his hands into the air, causing the sleeves on his bathrobe to flail wildly. "Bucket's a serious breakfixer. Joke at somebody else, see if they tell you how to find the white. They don't know, only Bucket knows."

"And how does being a breakfixer tell you where to find a dragon?" Smith scoffed

"Like I said, I make things," said Bucket. "Crawling things, flying things. Seeing things, spying things."

Smith winced.

"If you start rhyming, I'm out of here," said the man. "Dealt with enough of that shit already this week, I don't need any more of it."

"I wasn't rhyming," said Bucket, with a confused look up at Smith. "Just a trick of the timing."

Brenno snorted, and Smith groaned.

"Must have been," said the halfling, chuckling softly. "Now, these crawling, flying, spying things you speak of... Am I to assume that those are the devices with which you've found the lair of the white dragon?"

"You betcha," said Bucket, nodding the affirmative. "Made a scrap falcon, sent it to follow the dragon back to its hidey hole."

"Did it work?" Brenno asked.

"Bleh," said Bucket, letting his tongue flop out of his mouth in a gesture of disgust. "Already told you I built it, of course it worked. Scrap falcon watched it go up towards the frostpass, then swoop back towards the Vale and into its hidey hole. Only a few kilometers from here, but some of those is vertical."

"Some kilometers are vertical?" Brenno asked. "How far is that in miles?"

"Don't know, don't care, miles are stupid," said Bucket. "Some of the meters in those kilometers is vertical."

Brenno and Smith exchanged a glance. Brenno raised his eyebrows, as if to say *can we really take the word of a goblin on anything?*

Smith's shoulders rose and fell, and he shook his head from side to side, conveying the response of *it's not like we have any other choices, and I just want to be done with all this.*

Brenno nodded, the exchange clear as day to him. Gesturing with his arm for Bucket to take the lead, Brenno smiled at the goblin.

"Lead on, good breakfixer," said Brenno.

With a nod, Bucket began walking off, with Smith, Brenno, and Enaurl trailing after him. The goblin led them through increasingly shady areas of the market, where less merchants openly asked about Enaurl and more than a few seemed to stare greedily at the construct, some pausing to whisper hastily to each other.

"I'm beginning to grow concerned about our company," Brenno whispered to Smith, moving to stand closer to Enaurl and her strength.

"If you're bringing us down here to get jumped, I will shoot you first," said Smith, hand moving to rest on the holster of his firearm.

Bucket shook his head, pointing up to the rooftops above as he did.

"No need to worry," said Bucket. "Make more than scrap falcons. Nobody looks close at pigeons. You safe, I safe, we all safe."

Brenno and Smith's eyes moved up the dirty buildings to see the gutters and stoops atop them, which were littered with birds. While most seemed to shuffle about idly, cooing at each other and pecking at the tiles beneath them, every fifth bird stood stock still, peering into the alley below with beady black eyes, copper and brass bands poking out from between grey and white feathers.

"Concerning," said Brenno.

"Not bad," said Smith.

Several more twists and turns took the group to a narrow alley, the end of which appeared to be blocked up with fallen crates and an overturned wagon.

"What's this?" Brenno asked.

"The shop," said Bucket, clapping his hands twice.

The ends of several of the crates opened up, revealing pneumatic arms and pistons made from all sorts of springs and gears. A large crate swung open, revealing its true nature as a man-sized door. Bucket walked through the door and disappeared into the darkness beyond.

When the breakfixer realized he hadn't been followed, he poked his green head with oversized yellow eyes back out towards the artificer and the pawnbroker.

"Well? You coming or not?"

"Yep," said Smith, making his way towards the makeshift shop.

Brenno puffed out a sigh. Pausing, Smith turned to face the halfling.

"Something the matter, Hornbuckle?"

The halfling muttered something under his breath in response.

"Speak up, I didn't understand a lick of that."

"Even the goblin has a nicer shop than I do," Brenno said, exasperation evident on his face. "Sure, it's a stack of crates and barrels, but they're automated and not burnt to ash."

The artificer nodded, and clapped a hand on the halfling's back.

"Hard to feel bad for you on account of you shooting my kid," said Smith. "But yeah, lots of real nice shops, all of 'em better than yours."

"The affirmation feels wonderful," Brenno grumbled, falling in step with the artificer as they stepped into the goblin's domain.

The inside appeared to be formed from the empty space created by the strategic stacking of the wooden containers, reinforced here and there with metal slats and bits of scrap.

Gaslight torches were installed in each corner, illuminating the workshop. Their light glittered off the chaotic mess of scrap piled up on the floor of the goblin's house.

"The city know you're running those in here?" Smith asked, pointing towards the torches.

"They should, but they don't," said Bucket. "My contract to light the district. Underpaid, thinking Bucket doesn't know better. Fine by me, get the difference back in free utilities."

"Overcharge on the maintenance fees?" Smith asked.

"Of course," said Bucket. "Not Bucket's first day."

Smith chuckled to himself for a moment before realizing that Brenno was shooting a dirty look in his direction.

"What?" Smith asked.

"You've done maintenance on my shop," said Brenno.

"Sure have," said Smith.

"Have you overcharged me?" Brenno asked.

"You?" Smith asked, smiling wide. "Never."

"I see," said Brenno, glowering at the artificers. "Good to know."

Bucket, meanwhile, was rifling through the piles of scrap on the floor, humming an off-key tune to himself.

At last, he held up an object that looked as though someone had affixed skeletal wings to a tin milk bottle.

"Found it," said Bucket.

"Doesn't look like much of a falcon," said Smith.

"Repurposed the falcon," said Bucket. "Improved the design, scaled up. Always wanted to fly. Not as enjoyable as expected. Still, handy to have."

"If you say so," said Brenno, not following with what the goblin was saying.

The halfling scrutinized the oblong object, small enough to be held comfortably in one of the goblin's hands.

"And what exactly is it that you're holding?"

"Nothing exact," said Bucket. "Bird core. Has the stuff in it. Needs the thing."

"Of course," said Brenno. "It was obvious, really."

"I thought so," said Bucket. "Didn't want to embarrass you."

"Kind of you," said Brenno.

"Welcome," said Bucket, still rooting around the pile. "Ha, found you."

The goblin held up what looked like the head of a falcon made from a bit of scrap decorated with weld beads. The goblin held the head in one hand and the top portion of the tin bottle in the other, aligning them in a particular orientation.

With a nod, the goblin pressed the pieces together, then twisted the falcon head into position. It snapped into place, and its eyes began to glow a faint yellow as the mechanical falcon whirred to life.

Kicking away some junk to clear an empty space on the floor, Bucket set the mechanical contraption down so that it stood upright facing the wall opposite the door. Tiny goblin thumbs slid into holes where a bird's ears might be, and made something click.

The scrap falcon whirred louder, and its eyes began to pulse with light.

"What's it doing now?" Brenno asked.

"You'll see," said Bucket. "Turn the gas down."

Smith obliged, turning the knob on the base of the gas pipes to the left to lower the flow of fuel to the fires. The light in the workshop grew dim while the eyes of the bird gadget continued to glow brighter.

Reaching their peak, the eyes suddenly shone twice as bright, projecting a moving picture onto the wall.

"Fascinating," said Brenno, watching enraptured as the moving picture sharpened into focus, becoming an aerial view of Sundial Vale.

Tiny figures milled about here and there, looking like ants from the literal bird's eye perspective of the capture.

"Could Enaurl do something like this?" Brenno asked Smith.

The man shrugged.

"Probably," said Smith.

"Probably?" Bucket echoed.

"You got a problem with what I said?" Smith asked.

"No, no problem," said Bucket. "Just funny answer is all."

"Just show us the damn dragon already," said Smith.

"Check check," said Bucket, moving his thumbs inside the head of the artificial bird.

The scene below sped up, the tiny ants moving at breakneck speed from place to place inside the confines of the town. The scene grew darker as the shadow of the thin spire crossed over Sundial Vale, demonstrating at full speed why and how the town had earned its name. The scene suddenly shook madly, and Bucket removed his fingers; the speed of the scene slowed and returned to normal pace. Rather than peering down at Sundial Vale, the falcon was scanning the clouds, slowly moving its head from side to side to watch its perimeter.

A dark shape moved through the clouds to the right of the falcon, little more than a blur of motion. The only evidence of its passing was the swirl of the clouds in its wake. The falcon moved in that direction, intent on locating the source of the disturbance in the air. Flying through thick greyish wisps, the mechanical bird broke through the cloud cover and at last spotted its prey - a porcelain-scaled white dragon, its body easily thirty feet long from snout to the tip of its tail.

Salmon and teal accents dotted its snowy white scales, the soft colors running high up the webbing of wings that spanned at least forty feet across. Brenno gasped at the sight of the giant winged reptile, talons the size of long swords extending from the toes of its powerful rear legs, claws like daggers on the ends of each of the fingers of its forepaws.

Most terrifying was the teeth, many of which looked to be about as large as Brenno. The halfling swallowed nervously.

And that's the creature we're meant to assail, thought Brenno. *That colossal pile of armor and claws and teeth. We're all going to die.*

"It's just an image," Smith said, his voice missing much of its signature gruffness as the man looked at the pallid monstrosity projected in front of him. "Just an image, Hornbuckle."

The dragon made a few lazy circles around the area the falcon flew, then folded its wings and dove like a missile towards the outer edge of Sundial Vale. The falcon did its best to dive and follow, but its speed was no match for that of the plummeting dragon. Even as the ground came rushing up towards the bird, the streak of white that was the terrible flying lizard had already leveled off and begun rising.

The falcon adjusted its flight path to follow, bringing the image of a full grown cow - still alive and mooing with terror - impaled by the dragons talons, being carted off to become the its next meal.

With powerful strokes of its wings, the dragon moved through the air, turning north and away from Sundial Vale. The falcon followed, maintaining an even amount of distance behind the chalk and salmon beast.

"Takes a long time," said Bucket, fiddling inside the bird's head once more. "Wait please."

Something clicked, and the recording once again sped up. The dragon's wings pumped up and down furiously, an overfed and color-drained hummingbird moving through the air at breakneck speed. The mountains of the Frostpass appeared on the horizon and began to swell, growing into view at impossible speed. Bucket nodded to himself and clicked something inside the head of the falcon, making the recording pause.

"Why'd you stop it?" Smith asked.

Bucket withdrew his thumbs from the birds head and cracked them in turn. Standing up, he turned and faced Smith and Brenno before looking up at Enaurl.

"I stop because now we talk," said Bucket, still staring up at Enuarl.

The construct seemed to sense the intensity of his gaze, and she peered back down into the goblin's face.

"I have what yous need, you gots to give me what I need for it."

"You're not getting her," Smith said, the gruffness returning to his voice instantly.

"Why would Bucket need her?" Bucket asked with a sneer, still examining Enaurl all the while. "Pretty, yes - flashy, yes - but all form, no function."

"If you'll allow me to interject," said Brenno, becoming defensive on behalf of both Smith and Enaurl. "I've seen Enaurl in combat firsthand. I can assure you, she has a great deal of 'function' in addition to her form."

"I bet, sure," said Bucket. "But not enough. Too much work to make a punchbot, far too much. Why was she built this way? War machines don't need soft faces, they need spikes and teeth."

Brenno scowled down at the goblin.

"She's not a war machine," Smith said.

"Oh no?" Bucket asked. "How many she killed in that fight, small one?"

"I presume that question was directed at me?" Brenno asked.

"You small?" Bucket asked.

"In comparison to these other two, I suppose you could say that," said Brenno. "Though by halfling standards I'm actually quite tall."

"Don't care, small one," said Bucket. "Asked if you small, not for life story."

"Right," said Brenno, tone becoming terse. "Well, in that case, I'd wager she killed at least a half dozen timbergnolls. Maybe more, I couldn't say for sure."

"Soft face construct kills six people at once," Bucket said, nodding. "War machine."

"They weren't people, they were timbergnolls," said Brenno.

"They talk at you?" Bucket asked.

"Well, yes," said Brenno.

"Like I do?" Bucket pressed.

"Not in the same manner of speech, but yes, the way you are speaking to us now."

"Bucket not people?" The goblin asked pointedly.

Brenno opened his mouth, but no words came out. The halfling was stunned into silence.

"You softkins all the same. Think you decide who be people and who be monster. What the difference between an orc and an elf?"

"I'm sure I don't know, or at least can't be certain," Brenno said, ears burning, feeling as if he'd been caught in some sort of trap. "There's the teeth, for one--"

"Four shades of green and a hundred pounds of muscle," Bucket said, grinning wide at the halfling.

Brenno, doing his absolute best not to wring his hands with anxiety, looked at the goblin for a moment, trying to gauge the breakfixer's comment.

"I'm afraid I don't understand," said Brenno.

"It's a joke," said Bucket. "Suppose to laugh."

"Oh," said Brenno, feeling somewhat relieved. "My apologies."

"You wanna just cut to the point already?" Smith grumbled. "What do you want, Bucket?"

The goblin's smile faded to a smirk, pointed teeth making the expression still seem sinister in the dimly lit interior of the goblin's workshop.

"Bucket needs a shop," said the goblin. "Council won't give one to Bucket because Bucket isn't people. Funny thing, council has dwarves, humans, elves, and scions. Guess they all people and goblins not. Don't know who decided that. Maybe the gods. Maybe the people."

"What makes you think we can give you a shop?" Smith asked.

"Her," said Bucket, pointing at Enaurl. "Folded steel plates, gyroscopic stabilizer, pistons and gears and custom rubber fittings."

"I don't see what you're getting at," said Smith.

"Whoever can build one of her needs a lot of tools," said Bucket. "Lot of tools takes a lot of space. Lot of space means a big shop. Good news is, Bucket's not a big goblin. Don't need much space to set up. Builds small things, won't need to use tools for long times."

Smith was silent, as was Brenno. Enaurl moved her head to face each of the two men in turn before turning her attention to the frozen picture of the white dragon projected on the wall. The automaton stepped towards it, examining the image of the draconian as closely as she could.

"That's all you want?" Smith asked. "To be able to work out of my shop?"

"You betcha," said Bucket, nodding affirmatively, the hood to his bathrobe falling off. "Bucket needs a space. You got lotsa space, I bet. Give some to

Bucket, and you get that."

The goblin hitched a thumb at the parked scrap falcon.

"Keeps it in case you get lost. Bucket'll wait here for yous to come back, then we go to your shop. Is where, by the way?"

"Zelwyr," Smith said numbly, feeling removed from his body. "What makes you so sure we'll be coming back down?"

Bucket's grin blossomed wide, the needle sharp points of his teeth glistening in the light from the scrap falcon.

"I can smell the power core burning," said Bucket. "Charged kinite coiled around a godseye core, yes? Dangerous stuff, very dangerous. Makes a big hole when it blows."

"And how would you know that?" Smith asked, brow furrowed.

"Bucket didn't always need a place," said the goblin. "Had one once. Tried a kinite-godseye engine. Kabooooom!"

The goblin mimed an explosion with his grubby hands.

"Bucket learned his lesson. Leave that stuff to experts. You should too."

"I am an expert," said Smith. "You saw the people clamoring to buy her today."

"Saw, yes," said Bucket, walking up to Smith.

The goblin lifted Smith's firearm up part way from its holster before letting the weapon fall back into place.

"Saw this, too. Good design, very clever. This makes sense to me from your hands." Leaving his statement hanging, Bucket turned to face Enaurl once more. "She is different. She is more. More than you, maybe."

"Get to the damn point already," Smith growled.

"Point is, if things go bad, use the core," Bucket said with a shrug. "Not hard to add a trigger. Course, dragon bites the bot, bot blows up, no trigger needed. Easy peasy."

"Easy peasy," Smith repeated with disdain. "Just like that."

"You betcha," said Bucket.

"And if I don't want to sacrifice Enaurl to take it down?" Smith asked.

"Not sacrifice," said Bucket. "Temporarily remove the core. You built it once, build a new one after. Not so hard for an expert, like you."

"Right," said Smith. "An expert like me."

"Exactly," said Bucket. "So, we have a deal?"

"If I may," Brenno interrupted, producing his quill and a piece of parchment from the pouch on his cloak. "A deal such as this requires a contract. After all, we're all professional people here, are we not?"

Smith grunted and gave a curt nod, while Bucket's enthusiastic head waving sent his hair splaying in all directions.

"Professional people," said Bucket. "Experts."

"Agreed," said Brenno. "Now, shall we iron out the specifics?"

"Sure," said Smith, feeling distant and hazy, as if he might fall over.

He thought he could hear himself screaming in his own head, but pushed the thought away.

"Why not?"

Chapter Thirty-Four

A half-hour later, Brenno, Smith, and Enaurl emerged from Bucket's lair. Brenno held a rolled contract in his hands, which he carefully tucked into a tube that hung from the strap of his cloak. Enaurl held the scrap falcon, the device looking very much like a primitive mechanical totem in the hands of the silver construct. Smith's hands were empty, clenched into fists to hide the fact that they were shaking ever so gently.

"I must say," said Brenno. "While I've never negotiated with a goblin breakfixer before today, I would do it again. That Bucket has a sound head on his shoulders. Assuming everything goes well and he does move in to your shop, I bet I could refer him to the merchant's guild."

"That's a big assumption," Smith heard himself say as the trio began to walk back across town towards the inn.

"Not as big as you might think," said Brenno. "There's an entire merchant's league in Dogtown. Dogtown, of all places! If gnoll fur traders can become recognized, I'm certain Bucket can as well. After all, artificers are known to be an eccentric lot as it is. No offense."

"That's not what I meant, Hornbuckle," said Smith. "I meant that it's a big assumption to already be thinking about if everything goes well."

"Well," said Brenno, mulling his cheeks. "I admit there's a bit of a rough patch ahead--"

"Bit of a rough patch?" Smith repeated, incredulous. "We have to bring down a *dragon*, Hornbuckle. Did you see that thing? Did you see the size of the teeth on it? Lifted a damn cow off the ground the way a hawk picks up a field mouse."

"Well, yes, but--"

"But what?" Smith demanded. "Somehow the six of us are going to bring it down? How, exactly? Will's tricks? What happens once it realizes it was duped?"

"Well, I'm sure I don't--"

"I'll tell you what happens," Smith interrupted. "We get eaten, hopefully not alive. Voldani might be able to hold her own for a minute or two, especially if the wizard helps her out, but then what? We hope Kera and her haunted sword can pull through and do something? In the meantime, what are you and I suppose to do? Shoot the hell out of it and hope we don't get killed first for annoying it with bullets and arrows? Do you even know if your crossbow can punch through a dragon's scales? I bet I can with a good shot, but how many of those do you think I'm likely to get, Hornbuckle? Two, maybe three? Now, how many do you think it's going to take to actually bring down an armored man-eater like that?"

"I don't suppose I'm meant to be answering these questions, am I?"

"Too fucking many, that's how much," Smith continued, either oblivious to Brenno's statement or ignoring him entirely.

"Too fucking many," Smith repeated, his voice cracking.

Seeing Smith, the man Brenno considered to be quite possibly the single most resolute and stubborn being on the entire plane, faltering this way made Brenno feel cold on the inside, made his tongue swell and his mouth dry up. The trio continued walking in silence for a time, ignoring the world around them.

"You know," Brenno began, clearing his throat when his voice failed him. "Out of all of us, I'm fairly certain I'm the one most likely to die."

"What are you on about?" Smith grumbled.

"Well, Voldani is a seasoned warrior, and she can fly. I figure she's the most likely to survive. Next most likely would be our illusionist friend, William. If he can convince the five of us that he's actually an elf while being piss drunk, I imagine he could find some way to deceive a dragon long enough to escape if things take a turn for the worse."

"Hornbuckle," Smith began.

"I'm not finished," said Brenno, dismissing Smith's interjection and continuing his list. "Next is a tie between yourself and Kera, because I'm honestly not sure which of the two of you is the more stubborn. You have Enaurl to protect you, she has Zephelous. Beneath the two of you would go Enaurl, who only holds this position now due to the newfound possibility of her becoming some sort of explosive device, if I understood Bucket correctly."

"Brenno," Smith said, trying once more to interrupt.

"Nearly finished," said Brenno, waving Smith down. "Of course, with everyone else eliminated - or should I say determined to be unlikely to be eliminated - that leaves me at the bottom of the list. For good reason, too. I've got no mystical powers, no warrior's skillset. I'm not half bad with a crossbow, but it's as you said; how many shots will I be likely to get? Will my bolts pierce dragon scales? I strongly suspect this will not be the case, and truthfully I'd been planning to serve myself up as a distraction."

Smith stopped walking then and took the halfling by the shoulders.

"That's enough," said Smith, looking into the pawnbroker's eyes. "You were a campaigner, for god's sakes."

"A century ago, Smith," Brenno said. "A literal lifetime ago, I fired a few bolts at goblins from behind the safety of a half dozen heavily armed and armored men and women. There is a very real chance that I don't make it out of this, and I've accepted that. It's why I drafted those contracts to be so inclusive."

"What are you talking about?" Smith asked.

"Well, as you know, I have no children," said Brenno. "And I'm the last of the Hornbuckle line in Zelwyr, so if I die--"

"Which you won't," Smith added.

"If I die, I have no heir for my shop - or rather the charred lumber piled on the ground where my shop once stood - or any of my other worldly possessions. I drafted up the contracts so that if I don't make it, my things will go to you and Morri. Hopefully it will help erase this, all of this, that we've had to go through since I shot your girl. And I know I've said it before, but Smith I need you to know that I am *sorry*, that I am so, *so* sorry that all of this has happened. If I had any foresight, I would have at least used a standard bolt and not, well..." Brenno trailed off.

"And not one that's both cursed and poisoned?" Smith finished.

"Well... yes," said Brenno, wiping at his eyes. "Just... promise me one thing, Smith."

"Depends what it is," said Smith.

"If I do die--"

"You won't,"

"If it happens... Would you keep the name of my shop the same? I like the idea of knowing that there would still be a Hornbuckle in Zelwyr, even if it was just a building."

Smith was stunned into silence and said nothing. Brenno was quiet as well, making only a sniffle as he wiped at his nose. Smith knelt down and pulled the halfling into a tight embrace.

"You're a good friend, Hornbuckle," said Smith. "I don't think I've ever told you that."

"I don't think you've ever said anything outright nice to me before in general," said Brenno. "A few quips and some banter, but nothing nearing a compliment."

"You're ruining the moment," said Smith. "Just shut it."

"Very well," said Brenno. "I suppose I could--"

"Damnit, Hornbuckle," Smith interrupted. "I said shut it."

Chapter Thirty-Five

The suite Ragdain had moved the party to featured multiple private rooms and a common room with oversized cushions and chaise lounges strewn around a fireplace. It was there that Kera, Will, and Voldani sat - all staring mutely into the fire as they absorbed the events of the evening.

"Wow," said Will. "Just… wow. Today was a day."

"Your commentary is not required," said Voldani. "Nor is it appreciated."

The door to the suite opened inward, and in walked a tower of bundles piled high. The legs beneath the bundle walked into the room, and the bundle dropped to the floor, revealing Brenno.

"One of you could have offered to help," the halfling remarked.

"That's true, we could have," said Kera, sitting on a wood bench beneath a window, looking out at the pair of glowing moons, the large First Moon and the smaller Wayward Moon, hanging low in the sky above. Smith walked in next, also carrying a pile of brown sacs in his arms, and dropped them beside Brenno's stack. Enaurl entered last, wearing half a dozen stuffed and loaded backpacks on her shoulders, the iron bird from the goblin breakfixer still held carefully in her hands.

"Hey Enaurl," said Kera, looking at Enaurl and the scrap falcon in her hands. "That's a nice little bird friend you've got there. Did you give it a name?"

Enaurl held the bird up to her face and looked at it for a moment, as if contemplating.

"It's not a bird," said Smith, taking the scrap falcon from Enaurl's hands. "It's a map,"

"I can't say this for sure, but that's almost definitely a metal bird and not at all like any map I have ever seen, and that's a lot of maps," Kera countered. "Also, it's clearly a bird."

"Stop being a smartass," Smith said, setting the falcon down in the center of the room, its beak pointing to the wall just above the fireplace.

The artificer reached for a small instrument on his belt and slid it into the hole on the side of the falcon's head. The clicking of something snapping into place sounded, and the eyes began to flicker with scenes of white and grey.

"Can your illusions make it darker in here?"

"A 'please' would be great for next time," said Will, already weaving his hands through the air as they traced the outline of an imaginary sphere.

The space the sphere darkened and became opaque. Will used his fingers to pinch at the air around the sphere as if he were picking up a cloth, then pulled it wide apart. The sphere grew and swallowed the lights in the room from everything but the eyes of the scrap falcon. The scene of the falcon spiraling up into the air before it had spotted the dragon again played out, starting from the beginning.

"Well holy shit," said Kera. "Why don't you have any cool inventions like this?"

"You think this hunk of scrap is cool?" Smith rumbled.

"Uh, hells yeah," said Kera, enraptured by the moving scene. "This is amazing."

"You've not seen the best part yet," said Brenno. "Or should I say the worst? I suppose it's a matter of perspective." In the projected recording the dark shape moved through the clouds, and the falcon moved to follow it.

"What was that?" Will asked. "I thought I saw something."

"You did," Brenno said gloomily. "Keep watching."

The dragon broke free from the cloud cover, porcelain scales spotted with salmon and teal, sword-sized teeth, sickle-sized claws, colossal bulk of armor and muscle. Brenno felt faint seeing it again, and couldn't help but remember the long, long list of reasons why he was most likely to die on this campaign.

"Wow," said Will. "It's majestic."

"Indeed," said Voldani. "A mighty creature such as this will be a glorious opponent."

"*Glorious opponent* seems over-confidant at best," Brenno said.

"Do you doubt my abilities with the blade?" Voldani asked.

"No, of course not," said Brenno. "I merely doubt there will be much glory to be found waltzing into battle against what amounts to an armored slaughterhouse that eagerly awaits the chance to eviscerate us."

"Your lack of confidence will be the death of you," said Voldani.

"I'll add that to the list," Brenno muttered.

The dragon dove and plucked the cow from the farm, the animal bleating wildly in fear and terror. Brenno couldn't help but feel a kinship with the cow in that moment.

I wouldn't even be enough of a morsel to pick up like that, the pawnbroker thought. *Claws that big would just cut me in two.*

The dragon winged its way north from Sundial Vale, following the lazy curves of the Low Frostpass far beneath it. The dragon banked and wheeled about in the sky, spiraling closer and closer to the ground below.

A small mountain, little more than a large hill when compared to the great mountains on the horizon whose peaks stretched miles into the air, came into focus. The top of it was flat, more plateau than peak, with a winding path that connected it to the Frostpass below. The plateau looked like a frozen plain from the perspective of the scrap falcon, an icy flat littered with glittering ice formations that reached skyward.

The dragon landed between some of these icy pillars and deposited the cow, the wounded animal crying out frantically as it bolted. The dragon inhaled, its chest and throat swelling as it drew in a breath of air.

With a roar like the crashing of a waterfall, the dragon exhaled a violent spray of white mist and ice shards, snowflakes scattering away from the edges of the stream of power erupting from the dragon's maw.

The cow cried out once and was obscured by the whiteness. When it cleared, the poor animal was seen to be half encased in ice, it's rear legs and most of it's back half trapped in a block of ice. The animal whined. The dragon's long neck brought its jaws into reach of the cow.

There was a moo, a crunch, and a blossom of red in the snow.

With a twist of its neck, the dragon ripped the cow in half and began chewing, its jaws crunching down, into, and through large pieces of bovine bone. The dragon swallowed, licked its lips, and shuffled into the mouth of a cavern at the far end of the plateau. The projection went dark for a moment, then began to start again from the beginning.

Smith inserted the thin rod into the ear of the falcon once again, and clicked the mechanism off. The projection faltered and disappeared.

"You can bring the lights back," said Smith.

"Any thought about that word we talked about using?" Will asked.

"Now, wizard," Smith grumbled.

"I can't win with any of you," Will muttered, snapping his fingers. The globe of darkness was dispelled, and the light of the fireplace once again illuminated the room.

"We should leave first thing." said Smith.

"First thing?" Kera asked. "In the morning? Don't you want to spend a few days in case someone shows up to sell dragon's blood?"

"You got any Mian Dorean friends running around with the stuff that you haven't mentioned before?" Smith asked.

"No," said Kera.

"Then we do this," said Smith. "The Speaker said the longer Morri sleeps, the worse she'll be when she wakes up, I don't want to waste any time."

"Being prepared isn't the same as wasting time," said Kera.

"Like you'd know about being prepared," said Smith.

"I don't," Kera admitted. "But I know an awful lot about rushing into something with a half-baked plan, and that's exactly what I'm seeing here."

"What choice do I have?" Smith shouted. "What other option is there for me to save Morri? If you can think of something, you let me know, because short of going after that thing, I have no other ideas or suggestions. The Speaker said we need dragon's blood, so I intend to get some godsdamned dragon's blood. Unless you have a better plan, we leave in the morning. Hornbuckle, make a list of all the provisions and the equipment we might need, and we'll get it in the morning, then it's straight north towards the Frostpass."

Smith snatched the scrap falcon up from the floor and tucked it under his arm, then stomped his way towards one of the private chambers in the suite, slamming the door behind him, leaving the others in a stunned silence.

"Well then," said Brenno. "I guess that's that."

Chapter Thirty-Six

The wagon was packed and ready before dawn, the cabin and stuffed with all the goods and supplies that had been made to fit while still leaving just enough room for the group of six.

They took the road north out of Sundial Vale, a path that wound its way through the farm paddys and paddocks. The road had a distinct angle to it, an incline that kept the caravan on a gradual climb for the entirety of the first day and night worth of travelling.

The morning brought with it the smell of frost and snow, carried southwards on a steady cool wind from the north. The scenery around them was a thick forest of oak and pine, the tips and branches of which became more and more frosted as the wagon carried on.

The group spoke very little, the image of the white dragon still fresh in their minds each time they stopped to eat, rest the horses, or review the recording from the scrap falcon. On the morning of the fourth day, they came to a place where the road ended and met a bridge of sculpted ice and rock, an ancient highway that was all that remained from a kingdom.

"That's our access to the Frostpass," said Brenno. "From there, it's only another two days to the cavern in which the dragon seems to be roosting."

"Roosting is such a misleading word," said Will. "It makes it seem like we'll just find it curled up in a nest of twigs and sticks, when in reality it'll be bone and blood."

"How delightful," said Brenno, bidding the horses begin their climb up and onto the elevated wall of stone and ice. The Frostpass was a well established route that served as a trade route for merchants in the north, as well as travelers looking to cut across the northern half of Malzen.

It was on this route they'd need to travel for another few days before reaching the lair of the dragon.

Chapter Thirty-Seven

A common misconception about the Frostpass was that it cut a straight line across the continent, when in reality it curved across the upper reaches of Malzen like the bend of a horseshoe. The further along the pass a band traveled, the further north they invariably went. The temperature steadily dropped degree by degree, until everyone but Enaurl had no choice but to don the heavy coats and hats Smith and Brenno had purchased. Kera, unused to the frigid air of the north, sat in the driver's bench beside Smith and Voldani, wearing not only her coat, but the spare, as well as one of the blankets typically used by the horses.

"Gods, it's c-c-cold," she shivered.

"It's not that bad," said Smith. "Sun's out. It's nice."

"The sun being out d-doesn't automatically make it nice," Kera said, bringing her legs up onto the bench to help her better preserve what scant warmth she had. "I've n-never been so c-cold in my life." Smith frowned and shot the woman a sidelong glance.

"Never been this far north before?" he asked.

"Isn't it obvious?" Kera said, drawing the blanket around her more closely.

"Here," Smith said, reaching into his coat. He produced a flask, unscrewed the lid, and passed it over. "It'll warm you up. On the inside, at least."

Kera snatched the flask from Smith's hand and drank deeply, exhaling a sigh of relief.

"What's that?" she asked.

"Gnomish vodka," said Smith. "Stuff'll make a dwarf have second thoughts."

"Not this," Kera said, swishing the flask. "That."

Smith looked ahead and saw what it was that had caught the graverobber's attention; scattered pieces of wood, fiber, and metal, along with a few intact wagon wheels and several large red stains in the snow. The scattered rubble looked like an upended puzzle, its many pieces having once been a wagon not too different from their own. Smith reached for the flask, which Kera obligingly put back in his hand.

"That means we're close," said Smith. "Won't be long now."

"Oh, g-good," said Kera. "If we d-die, I hope I get sent to one of the w-warm hells."

"Do not blaspheme," said Voldani. "If you die in glorious combat, you will be sent to a place of warriors and champions."

"How about we plan for nobody to die?" Smith said.

"Agreed," said Voldani.

"Seems a little optimistic c-coming from you," said Kera. "But sure, why not?"

As the wagon rounded a lazy bend, they were greeted with the sight of the very same cavern they had seen in the scrap falcon's projections.

"At least it won't be long either way."

The cavern was off the main pass, connected to it by a bridge of ice that lead to a plateau. The mouth of the cave was dark and ominous, icicles hanging down from its ceiling like so many frozen, pointed teeth.

A great roar sounded from deep inside the cave, and was carried across the distance by a sudden warm wind that battered caravan.

The roaring was mightier than that of any savanna lion Kera had ever heard, more fearsome than any jungle dwelling beast. There was no mistaking the sound for anything but what it was: the roar of a dragon. Voldani stood, while Smith and Kera tensed and froze in place. The wind began to blow harder, carrying more unseasonable warmth with it. The air began to thicken with mist and vapor, obscuring the cavern from sight. Voldani drew her swords, holding them before her.

"Get the others," Smith said.

"Are you talking to me or Voldani?" Kera asked.

"I really don't care," said Smith, checking that his thunder cannon was loaded and primed. "Someone get the others." Kera fumbled with the blankets and coats that shrouded her for a moment before Voldani hopped off the side of the carriage.

"I will alert them," the scion said, swords still in hand. Smith commanded the horses to slow their pace, the swirling mists making it difficult to see further than a few feet ahead. Voldani waited for the wagon's back end to near her, then stepped onto the platform that led to the rear door. She kicked it open.

"We appear to have arrived."

"We heard the roaring," said Will, snapping shut the book in his hands.

"Indeed," said Brenno, examining his crossbow. "I believe we should formulate a plan."

"Mine is 'try not to die,'", said Will, as Enaurl stepped past Voldani to exit the caravan. "Sure is foggy out. Is it fog or mist this high up?" The wind blew again, rustling his robes. "That's not normal."

"The wind is not normal?" Brenno asked, walking beside the wizard.

"Wind is normal, but a *warm* wind on the Frostpass is not," said Will. "And this misty fog stuff is kind of... warm, almost like it's steam."

"What are you saying?" Brenno asked.

"That weird stuff is happening," said Will.

"Useful," said Brenno.

Through the mist, a large rectangular shadow loomed. As they neared it, the object broke through the clinging mists and revealed itself as a forty foot tall pillar of ice.

Ensconced in that pillar, frozen in place with an arm raised in what might have been a battle stance, was the gargantuan humanoid form of a giant. The arm ended with a jagged stump at the elbow, a small piece of bone sticking out from the edge of its icy tomb.

Easily twenty feet tall, wearing furs and leather armor, the giant looked as if it had been midway through making a battle cry when it had been trapped inside the block of ice.

"You don't see that every day," said Kera.

"You do when you're near a white dragon lair," said Will. "They like to keep trophies."

"We should tie the horses to it," said Smith. "Leave them out here."

"I agree," said Brenno. "And we should come up with a plan."

"What kind of plan?" Will asked. "*Go in* and *not die* are my two suggestions."

"I second Will's plan," said Kera.

"It's hardly a plan," Brenno said with a scowl.

"Though I am loathe to admit it," said Voldani. "I too agree with the wizard's plan."

"That's two votes for the Will Maneuver," said the wizard.

"There is no maneuver, and it's not even a plan," Brenno bristled.

"What maneuver are we doing?" Smith asked.

"The Will Maneuver," said Kera and Will simultaneously.

"What's that?" Smith asked.

"It's nothing!" Brenno shouted. "It's just more nonsense that these two have banded together in order to annoy me, when all I'm trying to do is keep us alive if at all possible!"

"No need to shout," said Will.

"Yeah, Brenno," said Kera. "Keep making that kind of noise and you're going to get the dragon's attention before we have a plan, and that'll get us all killed."

"Is getting us all killed the Brenno Maneuver?" Will asked.

"I think it might be," said Kera.

"If you two can be serious for one solitary moment, I would very much like to try to make sure that no such 'Brenno Maneuver' occurs," said the halfling, leading the horses towards the pillar of ice with the giant entombed inside it. He produced a length of rope from his belt and tied it to the animals, walking around the pillar entirely before knotting the rope together. "That should do the trick. Now, do we have any thoughts?"

"The mouth of the cavern was not especially large," said Voldani.

"Good note," said Brenno. "Why does that matter?"

"I may not be able to fly while inside," said Voldani.

"I see. Does your ability to fight rely on you being able to do so?"

"No," said Voldani. "Though my plan was to fly into its face and cut out its eyes."

"Why didn't we talk about any of this on the way here?" Will asked.

"Because we were basking in the gloominess of our impending demise," said Kera.

"Ah," said Will. "That makes sense."

"You've dealt with a white before, right?" Smith asked, speaking to Will.

"I've survived one before, I wouldn't say I *dealt* with it," said Will. "Why, what do you want to know?"

The ground beneath their feet shook as another roar emanated from the direction of the cave, this time followed up with a thud so forceful it rattled loose bits of ice and stone.

"Any idea what that was?" Smith asked.

"Not a clue," said Will.

"Are we making a plan or not?" Kera asked.

"Right," said Smith. "Will, what can you do for us?"

"Uh," Will began, "I can make us invisible, or I can make more of us--"

"I enjoyed having multiples of myself in combat," said Voldani.

"Duly noted," said Will. "I can mess with the terrain, I can mess with the lighting--"

"Can you hurt it?" Smith asked.

"Some, sure," Will said, wincing. "Nothing major, mostly the stuff you saw against the timbergnolls. Magic force darts, walls, barriers, stuff like that."

"Right," said Smith. "So nothing especially useful."

"Well, that's not entirely true," said Will. "But it seems like you're specifically looking for things in the 'make stuff go boom' category, and that's not my forte."

"Right," said Smith. "All tricks."

"I wouldn't simplify illusiomancy as being 'all tricks', but I mean... I guess?" Will said.

"Can your tricks keep us alive?" Brenno asked.

"I'll do my damndest," said Will with a shrug. "Not that anyone asked, but whites have a frozen breath weapon. I don't know dragon biology worth a damn, so I can't explain how it works, but I know that if it suddenly takes a deep breath, you want to get away from its mouth or else you'll end up looking like this guy here."

Will hitched a thumb at the frozen giant in the colossal block of ice.

"That's pretty hard to come back from."

"So what do I do?" Kera asked.

"You said you fought a dragon before, right?" Smith asked.

"A long ass time ago," said Kera. "But yeah."

"What did you do that time?" Will asked.

"Got close to it while it was distracted, slit its throat and ran away." Kera said.

"Good," said Smith. "Do that. Your haunted sword should be able to help."

"What are the odds we can simply bargain with this beast?" Brenno asked. "I've heard many tales of dragons being persuaded to part with their treasures in exchange for other goods or services rendered."

"I am not servicing a dragon," said Kera.

"Must you always be so crass?" Brenno asked.

"You should honestly be used to it by now," said Kera.

"Point taken," Brenno admitted. "Still, why not approach diplomatically?"

"Can't bargain with a white," said Will. "All they want to do is eat and fight."

"How can you be certain?" Brenno asked.

"Mages guild training, dragon basics. Fight with whites, pay dues to blues, no greens to be seen, blacks will attack, if it's red you're dead."

"Charming," said Brenno. "Anything else to contribute from your time as a scholar?"

"Not really, no," said Will. "I only remembered that part because of the rhyme."

"Of course," said Brenno. "Smith, do you have a plan?"

"I'm going to shoot it in the face," said Smith.

"I like the simplicity," said Kera. "What's Enaurl going to do?"

"Whatever she thinks is best," said Smith. "Probably bust it up some." Another roar, this time followed more thrashing and thumping, the sound of stones falling and ice breaking following the reptilian bellow. "Does it sound to anyone else like there's a fight going on?"

"A little," said Kera. "Maybe we got lucky?"

"I have no use for luck," said Voldani, striding forward through the mists. "Though I have plenty of use for a valuable distraction."

"I said I could do a distraction," said Will.

"And I specified 'valuable,'" said Voldani. Will frowned, but began following after Voldani. Kera and Smith did the same, leaving only Brenno and Enaurl standing with the wagon.

"I don't suppose you'd like to make a plan, would you?" Brenno asked Enaurl. The construct turned her face to look towards the pawnbroker, then looked to Smith. She followed after the group.

"I didn't think so," Brenno said with a sigh, trudging along after her.

Marching in silence towards the mouth of the cavern, the group passed by more frozen trophies: one contained a band of reptilian hounds that looked poised for battle, another contained what looked to be a group of armored knights, while a third large one contained a bloodied dragon.

"Is that another white?" Kera whispered, fearful under the frozen gaze of the colossal creature. Will brushed off the outer layer of frost and pressed his hands and face against the pillar of ice.

"Doesn't look like it," said Will. "I think it's a blue."

"I didn't know dragons killed each other," said Kera.

"Almost as much as people," said Will. "Historically, at least."

"Depressing," said Kera.

"What part?" Asked Will.

"All of it, obviously," said Kera.

"Yeah, fair," said Will.

The mists and vapors thickened around them, swirling and dancing like a dense liquid failing to properly mix into a base. It reminded Brenno a little of adding cream to coffee, except everything was varying shades of white. At last the cavern mouth loomed in front of them, breaking through the mists like a wave of stone over an ocean of ice.

From inside, the dragon's roar echoed and rang out, so loud the sheer noise of it parted the mists temporarily before they knit themselves back together like a great spider's web.

"If everybody dies, it's been good to know you," said Will.

"I cannot say the same," said Voldani.

"Agreed," said Smith.

"Can we maybe have one moment of solidarity before we charge into a dragon's lair?" Will asked, fingers twitching at his sides.

The ground beneath their feet trembled once more, this time rhythmically rather than a single occurrence.

"I... I think it's coming this way."

"Shit," said Kera, drawing Zephelous from its sheath. "Are you ready for this?"

"As ready as I'm going to be," said Will.

"I was talking to the sword," said Kera.

"Right," said Will. "What did it say?"

"The same thing you did," said Kera.

"Oh good," said Will. "There's that moment of solidarity I wanted."

Chapter Thirty-Eight

"Can all of you shut your mouths for one godsdamned minute?" Smith hissed at the others, unholstering his weapon and cocking the hammer. "You're going to bring the damn thing right out on top of us with all that racket."

"Right, because us talking is just going to make a drag--"

Kera's words were cut short by the rhythmic hammering of the earth, as if a great drummer were pounding on the planet itself. From out of the mouth of the cavern, breaking through the mists like the prow of a great ship, came the dragon. The creature towered over them, head rising twenty feet into the air. Standing at the mouth of the cavern, it seemed to bob its head slightly, as if it were woozy.

"Something's wrong," Will whispered.

"How so?" Kera whispered back.

"Look at it," Will said. "It looks half dead."

"Great," said Smith. "That's half the work done for us."

"Aren't you even a little bit concerned by what might have done that first half of the work?" Will whispered, voice rising with his frantic energy.

The dragon opened its mouth, displaying row after row of vicious jagged teeth, and made to roar. Instead, it's eyes rolled into the back of its head and it fell forward, jaw slamming down onto the ground.

"You should have bargained with my envoy, Chelreigamanth," said a voice, deep as the earth and heavy as a mountain. "Instead, you slaughtered one of my favorite hatchlings. Even a creature as impulsive as you had to have known there would be consequences to your actions."

The white dragon sputtered, blood seeping out from between its jaws. It rose to its feet and turned, staggered, to face the mouth of the cave.

"Style yourself after the Az all you wish, Orionatsaron," the white hissed. "You're not one. You merely play at flightlord, and when Signax Corva'laaz learns of your hostilities, it will be you who will have to face the consequences of rash actions."

"Perhaps," said the first voice, still speaking from deep within the cavern. "Though I'm left to wonder - once you are dead, who is it that will inform the Teeth of Winter about my hostilities?"

"You wouldn't dare," said the white.

"Wouldn't I?" answered the voice.

The speaker revealed itself, breaking through the vapors with even more majesty than the white dragon had; a colossal blue dragon, looking regal with cerulean scales and and a crown of horns that morphed into a double-row of jagged spikes that ran down its neck and back.

"When you reach the hereafter, if you find yourself in the eye of the storm rather than the endless ice, remember who it was that sent you there."

Chelreigamanth roared in defiance into the face of the blue, who lunged forward, head snapping down and around like a great serpent. The fangs of the blue pierced into the scales of the white, tearing into its throat. The white dragon's roar was punctured, the noise from its mouth falling away from a roar to a gurgle.

Its wavering neck fell limp once again, the jaws of the blue still clamped firmly around it. The blue chomped down harder and snapped the neck of the white with a sudden jerk of its head, abruptly ending its piteous cry.

"*What the fuck,*" Kera whispered.

"*Shhhh!*" Will hissed, eyes wide.

"It's a blue," said Brenno. "What was the rhyme? Pay dues to blues?"

"Really doesn't seem like the time to be going over that," said Will.

"I disagree," said Brenno, stepping out from behind the rocks.

"Hornbuckle, you're going to get us all killed!" Smith seethed.

"Pardon me, lord dragon," Brenno shouted to the towering mound of azure scales and bone-white spikes. "Orionatsaron, was it? Pardon the interruption, but--"

"Who has the gall to speak to me in my lair?" The dragon thundered, turning its head towards the halfling.

Catching sight of Brenno, the titanic lizard stomped over towards the halfling, each step sending rattling the halfling's bones. The dragon rose up before him, a predatory mountain looming like a specter of death, and waited.

"Well?"

"B-Brenno Hornbuckle, Lord Orionatsaron," said the halfling, stammering and stuttering.

The pounding of his own heart in his ears was deafening, the moisture in his palms and brow uncomfortable. "I am a simple merchant, come from Zelwyr to make trade."

The dragon snorted, sparks crackling out from its nostrils as it did.

"You know your station, there is that much to be said. What use do you hope to offer one such as myself?" Orionatsaron asked. "Your hands are too soft for a blacksmith. Do you lead your field in gemcraft? A purveyor of ancient secrets and lost knowledge, perhaps?"

"I regret to inform you that I am neither of those things, your..." Brenno's words failed him, and his stomach leapt into his chest.

Say something, damnit! Anything!

"...Your greatness."

"Hmm..." Said the dragon, curling over itself, dragging the body of the white dragon deeper into the heart of the cavern as it did. "Out with it, then. What are you?"

"A pawnbroker, your... mightiness," said Brenno, hearing his own voice crack.

"A pawnbroker?" Orionatsaron repeated, with something close to mirth in his tone. "What use did you think you could offer me, pawnbroker Hornbuckle? I've no tawdry wares here, no heirlooms in need of converting to currency. Quite the opposite, as you can see."

The dragon gazed around the cavern.

"Coins frozen into the walls and floors. For vanity, I must assume. As it is, I have no use for them, so they shall remain where they lie. You and your band of poorly hidden companions have no purpose here. Begone."

Brenno's mind reeled with panic.

What do I say to that? Brenno thought, scuffing the floor with the toe of his boot, seeing more gold coins sparkling up at him. *Smith won't leave without the blood, and if it won't bargain, I'll bet my hat it will come to blows, and if it comes to blows I bet my corpse I won't survive, and gods above and below do I want to survive...*

"I believe you misunderstand, Lord Orionat--"

"Out with it," the dragon interjected.

The halfling's body shook like a leaf on the wind, sorely wishing he'd had the precious few seconds of stalling time he'd been denied.

He has no use for coins, what can I offer? Brenno thought, mind in full panic. He looked around the room as the dragon had a moment before, and indeed spotted the faces of hundreds if not thousands of coins frozen into the walls.

"Well?" The dragon prompted.

He has no use for coins... He has no use for coins...

"I tire of your presence, pawnbroker. I find when I tire, I hunger." The dragon's words rattled low in his chest, sounding like the rumbling of a giant stomach.

He has no use for coins...

All at once, clarity struck. Brenno felt himself stand taller.

"Good dragon, if I may," the pawnbroker began. "You have no use for coins."

The dragon lapsed into silence for a moment before a low rattle began in the base of his throat.

"Repeating my own words back to me?" The dragon questioned. "I've seen less impressive, but not by much. Leave, before boredom is replaced with wrath."

"I'm afraid you misunderstand, Lord Orionatsaron," Brenno said, feeling his lungs threatening to give out with every syllable. "As a pawnbroker, I encounter all sorts of items, sometimes of great magic and greater worth, and often they sit in my display case for decades. I myself am not an adventurer or a campaigner, and so I have no use for items such as those. Someone such as yourself, however..."

Brenno let the implication hang. His heart felt like it was pounding through his chest, ready to explode out of his rib cage and splatter an anxious stain all over the frozen cavern floor.

The dragon was silent, though if this meant the creature was considering, Brenno had no way to know. All he knew was that it felt like an eternity had passed, and nothing had happened except his blood pressure had surely risen.

"What sort of items?" Orionatsaron asked at last.

Brenno didn't know whether to be elated that he had piqued the dragon's interest or terrified that he didn't know what to say next.

"A-all sorts of items, mighty Orionats--"

"Enough with the honorifics. What sort of items?"

"Gems and jewels, for one," Brenno said, hastily remembering that the dragon's first inquiry had been if he was a gemcrafter. "Large and small, of all varieties imaginable."

"Hmm..." The dragon rattled, sounding like a colossal crocodile.

The noise made Brenno feel like he was nothing but a mouse being played with by a gigantic cat, as if he were being toyed with for amusement before the dragon lost interest and devoured him.

"What else, pawnbroker?"

"Magic items," said Brenno, the words coming out of his mouth before he realized he'd even thought them. "Weapons, trinkets, enchantments, tomes..."

"What use do you think I would have for some second-rate human enchanter's moderately enhanced cudgel?" the dragon boomed.

"You underestimate me, good dragon," Brenno heard himself say, the words coming out over the constant scream of terror and anxiety in his mind.

"Do I?" the dragon asked, a hint of coyness in its tone as it raised a deadly clawed hand to its face and licked away a spot of the white dragon's blood that lingered there. "Illuminate me."

"Well, for example..." Brenno's thought trail faltered.

For example what? I acquired a cursed crossbow you could never use? I often acquire enchanted dwarven knicknacks and gnomish doodads that would serve very little purpose to you? That the most recent item worth mentioning led to my shop being burnt down?

Brenno glanced towards Zephelous, the sword's hilt shimmering in Kera's sheath.

"As an example, just a few weeks ago I acquired a relic from ages past, a living sword that calls itself Zephelous. A first, but surely not the last."

This seemed to give the dragon pause, which let Brenno dare to have a trace of hope.

"Are items such as this the norm?" Orionatsaron asked.

Brenno gulped despite himself.

"Not the norm per say," said the halfling. "Though once word gets out that the coffers of Brenno Hornbuckle are open to acquire more of their like, I have no doubt this would quickly become the case."

The dragon turned its head to Brenno, its maw so large it could snap a horse clean in half, its eyes yellow orbs the size of large pumpkins.

"The coffers of Orionatsaron," the dragon corrected.

"Of course," said Brenno, offering a slight bow.

Gods above and below, is this working?

"Though the general public would be unaware, of course."

"The general public is typically unaware of the machinations of their superiors," said the dragon. "As they have been since my ancestors scorched away the shadows that hunted them when recorded history began."

"It is as you say, Lord Orionatsaron," Brenno offered, bowing once more.

The dragon rumbled, an earthy bass note that vibrated in the back of Brenno's ears.

"Perhaps there is a use for you," said the dragon. "What of the others?"

Brenno shot a quick glance over his shoulder towards Smith, Kera, Voldani, Enaurl, and Will. Will looked as if he were ready to pull every hair out of his head, while the others seemed ready for combat to begin any second. *Well, it's worked before...*

"Sellswords, your greatness," said Brenno, turning back to face the dragon. "As I said, I am no adventurer. I required assistance to ensure my safe passage here to see you--"

"To see Chelreigamanth," the dragon corrected.

"Of course," said Brenno, feeling his ears burning with the white hot intensity of the sun. "In truth, we knew not to expect one such as yourself, and came prepared to barter with the previous owner of the cavern."

Orionatsaron snorted once more, a band of electricity crawling its way out of his nostrils and up his face before buzzing away into nothingness.

"And what did you plan to leave with?" the dragon asked. "There are dwarves with coffers as deep as this," the dragon gestured with a clawed limb towards the frozen gold all around them. "And deeper still: elves with patience for investment, humans with greed aplenty, gnomes with heads full of schemes. For what purpose did you seek a dragon?"

"In truth..." Brenno began, unsure how to address the real reason they'd come. "In truth, we hoped to leave with but a small portion of dragon's blood, an item which you now seem to possess a surplus of, given the fate of Lord Chelreigamanth."

"Chelreigamanth was no lord," said Orionatsaron. "Nothing but a brute, a grunt. A solitary hunter who knew not when to pay tribute. His end was well deserved."

"Once again, it is as you say, Lord Orionatsaron," Brenno said, bowing low. "Being the foolish creature that he was, surely you can consent to allowing us to rid you of his remains?"

"No," the dragon said immediately, the quickness and seriousness of the response giving Brenno pause, leaving him visibly taken back.

"Surely we can--"

"*No.*" the dragon bellowed, voice raised to the point of nearly being a full blown roar, slamming its forepaw into the ground.

The frozen surface beneath the dragon's claw cracked and splintered, sending coins and shards of ice skittering across the ground. Loose icicles on the ceiling clinked together like wind chimes, knocking each other free to rain down like a volley of shards towards the halfling.

Brenno shrieked and cowered from the rain of ice, turning away and making himself as small he could.

This is it, he thought, *this is how I die.*

Bracing himself to feel the sensation of a dozen skewers of ice impaling him and pinning him to the ground, Brenno was surprised to hear the sound of ice shattering and feel bits of frost spit up at his face from the ground instead.

Opening only one eye and peeking upwards, he saw a pink shield of light floating above his head, a shield that had evidently just saved his life.

"Magic," said Orionatsaron, eyes flaring blue-white, electricity crackling and spitting out from their surface. "I suspected you to be another band of wizards looking to become blood mages. It is gratifying to be correct."

"There must be some mistake!" Brenno squealed. "Blood mage? What is that?"

"Silence," said the dragon, inflating his chest and lungs with a massive inhale, the air in the cavern beginning to taste like copper and smell like ozone. "To the hereafter with you."

Lightning crackled out from between the dragon's teeth, flashing white and blue and bright as the sun. The hairs on Brenno's arms and neck stood on end.

It's from the electricity in the air, he thought to himself, *I was wrong before. This is how I die.*

Smith's thunder cannon interrupted Brenno's train of thought, firing with a crack and boom just behind him, making Brenno flinch.

The weapon's payload punched into the side of the dragon, forcing a roar of pain from it as a fist sized crater of blood and flesh appeared in the dragon's scales midway down its snout.

The dragon's head was knocked sideways, the charged lightning behind his teeth let loose across the ceiling. Ice evaporated and stone was scorched stone as tendrils of raw power skittered and arced out from the dragon's mouth.

"Everybody scatter!" Smith screamed, and everything seemed to happen all at once, so frenzied was the activity in the cavern.

"To glory!" Voldani yelled, gleaming wings sprouting from her back.

She leapt at the dragon then, blades drawn, jaw set with determination. Orionatsaron hadn't the time to recover from Smith's attack before Enaurl was on him, slashing and stabbing at his exposed underbelly. Her blades bit into the dragon's scales, but not deep enough to cause serious wounds.

Orionatsaron roared with pain, and brought a forepaw through the air, batting Voldani away with the back of his claw. Voldani tumbled through the air but recovered, turning the fall into a swooping arc to come in from a new angle of attack. Orionatsaron's eyes followed the motion, his serpentine neck allowing him to intercept Voldani's flight path, jaws dripping with saliva, ready to crunch the flying scion in half.

Smith's cannon roared again and another pit of blood appeared near the base of the dragon's neck, a ball of hot lead lodging itself deep into his flesh. Orionatsaron howled in pain, setting his sights on the artificer.

With a low growl reminiscent of a great jungle cat, the dragon lunged towards Smith. Instead, he found himself held back, the momentum of his lunge stolen from him by a an impossibly strong figure hauling on his tail in the opposite direction.

The dragon's bulk slammed into the ground, and it twisted its neck to looked behind itself, watching as Enaurl - feet planted squarely, arms wrapped around the spiked end of the dragon's tail - bent her body in a way that would have been impossible for a living creature: legs up and over her head, dropping the tail to begin running up the dragon's spine.

When she reached the place where the dragon's wing pinions joined the rest of his body, Enaurl leapt into the air, using her forward momentum to rocket towards the front of the creature. Both iron fists came together and smashed down on to the top of Orionatsaron's skull, driving the dragon's head to the ground with a crunch.

Before the dragon could recover, a searing hot line of pain tore down his left side, an enchanted dwarven sword slashing through the scales near its ribs. Kera was there, dragging Zephelous's edge through the dragon's flesh as she ran past, leaving a garish red line of gore behind her.

Orionatsaron tried to raise his head, but Enaurl sprung from her perch onto the wall, using her powerful legs to launch herself back towards the dragon, delivering a piston-driven haymaker to the dragon's jaw, making the world around him spin.

The dragon slashed its claws at Enaurl, only to have the deadly appendages pass through empty air, the vision of the construct dissipating. The world stopped wobbling in the dragon's view, but where there had been one silver construct there were now three, each poised and ready to strike.

The dragon scanned the battlefield, searching for the source of the spell, looking for the wizard responsible. Spotting Will standing in the distance, muttering arcane words, eyes gleaming with soft turquoise light, the dragon snarled. His great wings unfurled, and he snapped them upwards and downwards in quick succession, creating a sizable gust of wind that knocked Kera across the floor and Voldani hurtling through the air. Enaurl stood her ground, leaning against the wind, fists curled and eager to deliver another punishing blow.

"Enough!" Orionatsaron screamed. *"Enough!"*

Another forceful flap of his wings set Enaurl tumbling backwards, dispelling the illusory copies. Orionatsaron, great and terrible blue dragon of the north, stood tall and proud over his would-be assailants. In a single bound he leapt across the thirty feet between himself and Will, bringing his tail slamming down on top of the wizard as he landed. Will saluted the dragon and winked out of existence, leaving behind sparkles and luminescent butterflies.

"What is this?" Orionatsaron bellowed. "More deception?"

"Right," said Will, revealing himself to be standing in the far corner of the room, conjuring a bubble shaped barrier around himself as he spoke. "Because you being a dragon makes this a totally fair fight otherwise."

"Fairness?" the dragon snorted, colossal head swiveling as he sized up his targets. "Since when has equity of any kind been a concern among blood mages?"

A crack - followed by a shrill whistling - sounded as a red ball of fire arced upwards towards Orionatsaron, leaving a glowing stream of smoke trailing behind it, all the way to the barrel of Smith's smoking gun.

The dragon ducked beneath the glowing orb, only for it to explode above him, bursting into a fireball reminiscent of a small star. The heat scorched the scales along his back and wings, while the concussive blast shook loose a shower of debris from the ceiling.

Together, these developments infuriated Orionatsaron. He locked his eyes onto the artificer, orbs narrowing into slits of unadulterated rage.

Orionatsaron opened wide his terrible maw and roared, the sound nearly deafening as it echoed in the cavern. He charged towards Smith mouth first, a great shark ready to rend flesh and tear meat from bone.

Kera lunged at him, but was backhanded away.

Voldani dove at his face, but was swatted away by the dragon's tail.

Enaurl leapt into the dragon's path, silver hands grappling with fangs as long as her arms, wrestling the dragon's face sideways in an effort to drag the great serpent's face along the floor of the cavern.

She tried to plant herself, to stop the advance, but the dragon's full strength proved too much for her, and she slid backwards across the frozen surface and bumped into Smith, accidentally knocking the ammunition he'd been loading out of his hands. The shells spun across the ice, sliding across the floor and out of reach. Smith felt the wetness and heat of the dragons breath, could smell the rot and death with every exhale that gusted out past Enaurl as the two battled.

Smith searched his pockets for spare shells, but found none. Feeling frantic, he looked around to find the rounds that he'd dropped. A dozen paces away a small pile of ammunition sat haphazardly around Brenno's feet. Brenno hadn't moved so much as an inch.

"Throw those over, Hornbuckle!" Smith shouted to the halfling, reaching out expectantly.

Brenno didn't move, and stood where he was, eyes locked squarely on the titanic form of the dragon, his entire body trembling with fear.

"Hornbuckle!" Smith's words carried to the halfling over the din of combat, but had no effect.

The halfling was frozen with fear.

"On it!" Kera yelled, slashing at Orionatsaron's leg with Zephelous, rolling over the dragon's tail as it lashed at her in response, tumbling her way to Brenno. "Brenno, snap out of it!"

HE WILL NOT, said Zephelous, HE IS PARALYZED WITH DRAGONFEAR.

"What's that?" Kera asked, snatching a fistful of shells from the ground.

YOUR HERITAGE CAUSES YOU TO EXPERIENCE A SENSATION OF MIRTH AND SLIGHT DELIRIUM AROUND DRAGONS, said Zephelous, FOR OTHERS, THE SHEER POWER OF A DRAGON ASSAULTS THE MINDS AND ASSAILS REASON, TRIGGERING A FEAR MECHANISM OLDER THAN TIME ITSELF.

"Standing still and doing nothing seems like a shitty fear mechanism!" Kera shouted, throwing herself flat on the ground as Orionatsaron attempted to eviscerate her with a swipe of his claws.

The swipe cut through the air where she'd been standing a moment before, and she rolled to her feet. She sprinted towards Smith, the shells held in her hand, reaching towards Smith's outstretched fingers.

Kera could hear the strain in Enaurl's mechanical frame as the construct struggled to keep the dragon's killing jaws occupied. The dragon's labored breathing as it tried to free itself from the mechanical woman enduring hold filled the cavern.

"C'mon, c'mon, c'mon!" Smith shouted.

"I'm running as fast as I can!" Kera shouted back, watching as the dragon's eye moved to watch her.

The pupil narrowed into a razor straight slit of black on yellow. The dragon growled, another reptilian rattle deep in its throat.

Kera's hand was inches away from Smith's when she found herself caught in the dragon's clutches, his free arm reaching to clutch her and stop her from delivering the ammo.

Voldani called out a war cry and dove at Orionatsaron, blades extended together for a killing blow aimed at the base of his skull. The dragon's body rolled like the tide, its neck twisting to allow its head to stay in place.

Orionatsaron swung its claw, the one holding Kera, at Voldani, hurling Kera at the winged woman as if she were nothing more than an improvised weapon.

The two connected solidly, Kera's head smashing into Voldani's chest plate, the pair becoming a tangled heap midair before falling, plummeting towards the stone below.

Will's bubble of force appeared beneath them, the pair falling through the top but bouncing harmlessly off its interior. The dragon whipped around and struck the bubble with his tail, batting the bubble towards Will, sending the sphere careening towards the wizard.

"Well that's not good," Will said as the forcefield that enveloped them slammed up against the wall, dissipating on impact, leaving the three in a groaning pile on the ground.

The dragon stood on its rear legs and raised its head; Enaurl was still standing in his mouth, her feet planted on his lower jaw and her arms pushing up against the upper jaw, preventing him from opening or closing his mouth. The dragon inhaled, and an electric humming noise began deep in his chest.

Wounwounwounwounwoun...

"Enaurl, get out of there!" Smith yelled, but it was too late.

The dragon's mouth erupted with bolts of lightning, power surging through Enaurl's body. Her silver chassis blackened, her rubber joints began to melt, filling the cavern with an acrid and acidic stench. She convulsed and shook, parts of her frame bursting at the seams, oily smoke trailing up from her body in multiple places.

Straining even as her body smoldered, Enaurl held firm.

With a growl of impatience, Orionatsaron reached towards his mouth and took hold of Enaurl, prying her from his jaws. Enaurl snapped one of the dragon's teeth off and plunged it into Orionatsaron's hand.

The dragon roared in pain.

"I SAID ENOUGH!" The dragon howled, tightening his grip on her.

The dragon pulled his hands apart, savagely tearing Enaurl's body in half. Bits and pieces of interior components rained down onto the floor as Enaurl convulsed in the dragon's hands.

"You *bastard!*" Smith howled, *"You big blue bastard!"*

He ran for the nearest discarded shells, snatched them off the ground, and slammed them into his thunder cannon. He aimed the weapon at the dragon's heart, or at least where he thought it might be, and let off two shots. The bullets whizzed through the air and buried themselves deep into the dragon's chest, causing Orionatsaron to scream in pain.

Letting Enaurl's lower half fall to the ground, the dragon whipped the construct's torso at Smith. The artificer tried to duck out of the way, but the body of his fallen companion struck him square in the chest and flattened him to the ground, knocking the wind out of him.

"Enaurl!" Smith wheezed, cradling the ruined construct in his lap.

Enaurl twitched, her back arching as spasms shook what was left of her body. Silver eyes looked up into Smith's face, and a ruined hand trembled as it reached up for Smith, fingers caressing the side of the artificer's face. Something sparked inside her, and Enaurl shuddered. Her hand stayed on Smith's face, unblinking eyes looking up into the face of her maker for a moment longer, until something crackled and she went still.

Her arm dropped, and the smoke billowing out of her thickened. Smith held Enaurl tightly, bringing her in for an embrace. Breathing heavily, Orionatsaron loomed over the artificer and his downed construct.

"So much emotion wasted on a golem," said the dragon.

Smith held Enaurl tighter.

"You're going to die today," the man whispered to the dragon.

"Once more," the dragon taunted, *"with feeling."*

"I said you're going to *fucking die today*, you *son of a bitch!*" Smith screamed at the dragon, spittle flying from his mouth as he shouted.

His eyes were wide and wild.

The dragon sneered, a throaty growl beginning.

"Much better," said Orionatsaron. "Your death will be infinitely satisfying."

The dragon rose up, positioning himself to strike the final blow on Smith, only to shriek in pain as Voldani's blades buried themselves into his back.

"How many times do I have to-- *AUGH!*"

His words were cut short by the agony of Zephelous cleaving into his underbelly. Spinning in place, the dragon struck at Kera with his tail and shook Voldani from his back, the women landing on their feet with their backs towards the cavern entrance.

Will shimmered into existence between them, hands weaving an intricate pattern through the air. Growling, the dragon stalked towards the trio, who hastily backed away.

In the shadow of the dragon, Smith searched for a weapon, a dropped shell, *anything* he could use to hurt the dragon. His hands touched something unfamiliar, making him look down. Seeing the discarded core of the scrap falcon, his eyes hardened. His body trembled with rage. With one hand he snapped open his firearm and disconnected the firing mechanism from the barrel.

With the other, he reached up and into Enaurl's core, fingers searching for her kinite-godseye heart. Finding it, he tore it out.

His vision went red and his hands went to work.

"Anyone have any ideas?" Will asked Kera and Voldani, hastily conjuring a barrier around them as the dragon swiped at them with its claws, still advancing towards the trio.

The barrier shattered, and Will conjured another just as the dragon to took a second swipe.

"I can't do this forever, you know!"

"Zephelous, what do we do?" Kera asked.

USE YOUR RAGE, the sword answered, GIVE IN TO THE SONG AND ACCEPT THE POWER IT HAS TO OFFER.

"What did it say?" Voldani asked.

"To give in to my rage," said Kera.

"Sage advice," Orionatsaron thundered. "Go on then, barbarian. Fly into your dragon-killing rage. Let us see what you are made of."

Will and Voldani looked at Kera expectantly.

"Well?" Voldani asked.

"I don't even know what that means," Kera said.

The dragon laughed.

"A savage so uneducated she knows not her own birthright," Orionatsaron gloated. "How unexpectedly precious."

Will looked over his shoulder, seeing the exit.

"We could run," he suggested. "I mean, uh, tactically retreat."

"And leave the others behind?" Kera asked.

Orionatsaron swiped at them, and this time there was no barrier to protect them. Will jumped back while Kera and Voldani guarded themselves with their swords.

Kera cried out in pain as the dragon's claws raked her side and leg, and Voldani grunted in pain as the razors cut into arms and neck.

"What ever will you do?" Orionatsaron asked, lowering his bulk to the ground, a colossal cerulean panther ready to pounce. "Would you care for a suggestion?"

"I've got a suggestion for you," shouted Smith. *"Shove this up your ass and die, you big scaly motherfucker!"*

The artificer lobbed polyhedron of gleaming stone, coils of smoking metal bound around it, towards the dragon. It landed on the ice just beneath Orionatsaron's belly and slid forward, emitting a soft hum. The trigger and hammer from Smith's gun had been hastily fused with the core, and cocked.

All eyes in the cavern settled on Enaurl's core.

The hammer went off with a click, and Orionatsaron scrambled to bat it away, but moved too slowly.

The rigged core exploded with more noise and fury than anything the dragon had unleashed, detonating mid-air near the dragon's face.

Orionatsaron screamed, recoiling from the blast and trying to use his wings to shield himself from the destructive nova.

Kera, Voldani, and Will were launched away and sent sprawling.

The cavern groaned and crumbled, huge sections of the roof falling away and collapsing, boulders and sheets of ice raining down to form a makeshift wall of rubble just in front of where the trio had landed, burying the dragon and blocking access to the rest of the cavern.

Chapter Thirty-Nine

Kera gasped and wheezed as the dust settled around her, finding herself laying flat on her back, eyes closed and body aching all over.

"Is it too late to retreat?" she groaned.

Something above her cracked and shifted, making Kera open her eyes. Directly above her, a massive pillar of stone broke free from the ceiling and began to plummet towards her. Frozen in place, she drew in her breath and held it, waiting for the end. Voldani tackled her, hurling her aside and sending her rolling away. The stone slammed onto the ground.

"Dani, no!" Kera screamed, scrambling to get back to her feet.

Voldani was pinned, buried beneath stone from the waist up, face looking skyward with a serene expression on her face.

"No!" Kera shouted again, running to Voldani's side.

She dropped Zephelous and threw herself against the boulder, straining her every muscle in an attempt to move the hunk of rock.

The stone wouldn't move.

"Will!" Kera yelled, grunting with effort as she forced her body to work even harder to try and free Voldani from the rubble. "Will, get over here and help me!"

The stone weighed hundreds of pounds, and Kera couldn't find any purchase. Voldani coughed, bright red blood spraying out of her lips.

"Hold on, Dani, *just hold on.*"

Kera grunted and groaned with effort, digging her boots into the ground and straining every muscle in her body to try and move the stone. The boulder shifted the slightest amount before resettling, causing Voldani to cry out in pain as the crushing weight pressed down on her once more.

"Gods, I'm so sorry, Dani. For fuck's sake, Will, get over here and help me lift these rocks!"

"I can't," said Will, his tone heavy with defeat.

Breathing heavy and sweating with effort, she struggled against the impossible weight. She made no headway, and in just a few moments Kera felt her arms tire and threaten to give out on her.

"Fine," she said, grunting. "I'll wedge Zephelous in and push them up, you pull her out."

"I... I can't do that either," said Will.

Unable to keep the effort up for a moment longer, Kera's arms gave out and she fell forward. Voldani wheezed in pain, coughing more blood. Kera looked over her shoulder at Will, eyes stinging with sweat and tears, face caked with dirt and dried blood.

"Why the *fuck*... won't you... at least *try*... to help me?" Kera said, spitting her words out between gasping breaths.

Will's expression was one of absolute sorrow and remorse.

"It's not that I don't want to," said Will, taking a step back. "It's just..."

"Just... what?" Kera puffed out, still fighting to catch her breath. "Afraid of... a little blood? Gods, man, she's... she's *dying*. Get over here... and *help*."

Will shook his head, tears welling up in his eyes.

"I can't," he repeated.

"*Get* over here... *Now*," said Kera, eyes narrowing at the wizard, blood boiling.

"I'm sorry, Kera." said Will.

Tears dropped from Will's face, but before they reached the ground they twinkled and faded out of existence.

Having watched them fall, Kera noticed that Will's feet from the ankle down had disappeared as well.

"Are you seriously... Running away?" Kera wheezed.

Will shook his head, wiping his eyes. When he pulled his hand away from his face, he was smiling the saddest smile Kera had ever seen.

"Worse," said Will, fading from existence. "I was never here."

His torso began to fade, as did his hands and wrists. When all that was left was his head, he stared hard into Kera's eyes.

"I'm sorry, Kera, I'm so, *so* sorr--"

Words unfinished, he ceased to be.

Kera found herself alone with Voldani in the collapsed tunnel.

"You son of a bitch," said Kera, speaking to the empty space where Will had stood a moment before. "*You son of a bitch!*"

Her words echoed in the tunnel.

"Kera..." Voldani whispered, voice faltering.

Kera immediately turned to face the downed warrior, tears streaming down her face.

"What is it, Voldani?" Kera asked.

"I... I had..." Voldani said, a thick trail of blood running down the side of her mouth.

"Easy, Dani," Kera said, cradling the woman's head in her hands. "Don't try to talk, just stay with me okay."

"I had…" Voldani said again, "I had hoped…"

"Hoped what, Voldani?" Kera asked, her vision blurred with tears.

"I had hoped… it would… be glorious," said Voldani, smiling up at Kera. She coughed, shook for a moment as she seized, then lay still in Kera's hands.

"Dani?" Kera whispered.

The scion's only response was a long and slow exhale, the sound of life rattling out of her lungs. The ethereal wings pinned beneath her flickered, faltered, then faded away.

Kera's vision crystallized and blurred as she stared into Voldani's face - her unblinking white eyes, her mouth hanging slightly open - It wasn't until droplets of water began splashing onto Voldani's face that Kera realized she had started crying.

She gently brought a trembling hand up to Voldani's face and closed the woman's eyelids using the tips of her fingers.

Her lungs burned, but her chest was too tight to let her breathe. Her body shuddered as a single, sharp inhale wracked her body, paired with a tortured sob.

Her shoulders hurt, her arms hurt, her chest hurt, her everything hurt. It hurt to breathe, hurt to think, hurt to do anything.

With all the grace she could manage, she delicately moved Voldani's head off of her leg, tucking a flat rock against the back of her head as a makeshift pillow. She loosed another singular lilting sob as she drew in a lungful of air and slid herself sideways, leaning her back up against a fallen boulder as she drew her legs into her chest.

The heel of her boot bounced against Zephelous's guard, the sword scraping against the stone as it slid a few inches away.

She knew she should probably pick up the sword, and that Zephelous would have something to say.

Zephelous always has something to say, she thought, her own inner voice sounding weak and hollow in her mind.

She forced herself to grab the sword, bringing it to rest between her knees, letting her forehead rest against the flat of the blade.

KERA, WE MUST--

"No," said Kera. "No, we mustn't… we must not do anything. Everyone is dead, Zeph. Enaurl is dead. Brenno and Smith are either already dead or will be soon enough. Will is gone. Voldani is…"

Kera's voice faltered, a new wave of tears coming to her eyes. Fighting to control a hand that would not stop quaking, Kera pet the side of Voldani's cheek.

"Voldani is dead. The only thing I *must* do is get out of here and pray to the gods that it doesn't hunt me down. I can leave you here if you feel you must do something, but I am not doing anything that isn't getting the hell out of here."

OH? Zephelous said, its sarcasm evident. AND WHERE WOULD YOU GO?

"South, back on to the low Frostpass," said Kera. "The wagon's probably still there, unless Will ran off with it. Even if it's not, it's only a few days walk from here. We could make it, Zeph, you and me. We'd get there no problem if we wanted to."

IS THAT WHAT YOU WANT TO DO? Zephelous asked. RUN, AND LEAVE WITHOUT KNOWING THE FATE OF YOUR FRIENDS?

"It's that or join them in what is most likely their deaths," said Kera.

YOU ARE A FOOL, said Zephelous. A SELFISH FOOL.

"The fuck I am!" Kera shouted at the sword, her words echoing in the tunnel, tears still streaming down her face. "I'm not a sword made from star metal, Zephelous. If I go back in there, that dragon will kill me. You saw what he did to Enaurl, for fuck's sake. She might as well have been a stuffed animal in the hands of the neighborhood bully the way he ripped her in half."

SHE MUST BE AVENGED, said Zephelous.

"At the cost of my life?" Kera asked. "No. Nuh-uh. Not happening."

THEY WERE YOUR COMPANIONS, said Zephelous.

"Sure," said Kera. "For all of a month, and not even by choice."

THEY WERE YOUR FRIENDS, Zephelous countered.

"Haven't you heard, Zephelous?" Kera said, her voice full of anger and hurt. "I'm bad at being friends, which is why I don't bother with having them."

YOU CAN LIE TO YOURSELF, KERA, said Zephelous, OH, HOW YOU CAN LIE TO YOURSELF. HAVING SEEN THE PSYCHIC EMBODIMENT OF YOUR DENIAL, I KNOW HOW ADEPT AT IT YOU'VE BECOME.

"Fuck you!" Kera spat, voice strained. "I didn't ask for you to go into my head, Zeph, you did that all on your own and you did it without bothering to ask. What kind of messed up shit is that? Are you some kind of evil psychic thing, is that what you do?"

KERA--

"Is that why you always wanting to take control of me?" Kera pressed, voice rising with her accusations. "You start taking control of my body and going into my head, then what? Do I start being your puppet while I'm asleep, is that what's next?"

KERA, YOU ARE BEING HYSTERICAL--

"Actually, I'm being logical, Zeph," Kera said, shaking her head defiantly at the sword. "Things always go bad with a talking sword."

HAVE I ONCE STEERED YOU WRONG? Zephelous asked.

"Seems like that's what you're doing right now," said Kera.

KERA...

"I mean, really, what you're asking me to do is basically suicide."

KERA CINDERPINE, Zephelous hollered, booming the name into Kera's mind.

"Don't call me that," Kera whispered, holding her head against the pain of Zephelous's psychic shout that rang in her mind like a gong. "That's not who I am any more."

I WILL CALL YOU THAT BECAUSE THAT IS HOW YOU WILL BE REMEMBERED IN HISTORY, said Zephelous. THERE IS A GREATNESS IN YOU, KERA.

"Zeph, please. Not now," Kera whimpered, bringing her knees back to her chest. "I've heard enough of this shit. Please, not now."

THE TIME FOR YOU TO AVOID YOUR RESPONSIBILITIES IS OVER, KERA, Zephelous shouted. NO MORE RUNNING FROM PAST DECISIONS, NO MORE HIDING FROM FUTURE CONSEQUENCES. I SPEAK OFTEN OF THE TAPESTRY OF FATE--

"I'll leave you here, I swear," Kera threatened, her tone pleading.

DO IT THEN, said Zephelous. ENOUGH THREATS. ENOUGH FEAR. ENOUGH DENIAL. EITHER STAND UP AND RESOLVE TO FIGHT, TO ACCEPT YOUR DESTINY AND REACH GREATNESS... OR SLINK AWAY A COWARD. MAKE YOUR CHOICE.

"Zephelous, I--"

MAKE. YOUR. CHOICE.

Kera was quiet for a long time afterwards. Zephelous was too.

"It would be so easy to run," said Kera, voice soft and quiet.

IT WOULD, Zephelous agreed.

"To just say 'fuck this, I'm out of here!'. Head down the mountain, get back to Sundial Vale. Get Ragdain to rustle up some work for me, or maybe hitch a ride to Faltus or Linreigh. Anywhere along the coast, you know?" Kera paused and took a slow breath. "I've always wanted to see the mainland. They say it's boring, but I'd still give it a shot. What do you say, Zeph? We could go to Falconaire and see the floating city. Let's go check out Brasswelt, the dwarves in

Blackmouth never shut up about the city-forge."

Kera had a small laugh, unenthusiastic but not forced.

"Actually, dwarves anywhere won't shut up about it."

KERA, said Zephelous, its voice soft and apologetic in Kera's mind. I WOULD LIKE TO TELL YOU SOMETHING I SHOULD HAVE BACK ON THE ROAD.

"Is it that you were wrong about me this whole time, and that I don't need to own up to any kind of bullshit heroic destiny?" Kera said, fighting to suppress a sniffle. "Because that would be great."

I AM AFRAID IT MAY BE JUST THE OPPOSITE, said Zephelous. HAVING BEEN FORGED BY GODS ONLY TO OUTLIVE THEM, I HAVE GAINED TREMENDOUS PERSPECTIVE, NOT JUST ON THE TAPESTRY OF FATE BUT ON LIFE ITSELF. I DO NOT CLAIM TO BE A MASTER OF ITS MANY WHORLS AND WEAVES, BUT I HAVE LIVED LONG ENOUGH TO SEE THE SIGNS OF GREATNESS TIME AND TIME AGAIN. I HAVE NURTURED THE SPARK OF POTENTIAL INTO A FIRE OF GLORY COUNTLESS TIMES BEFORE YOU WERE BORN, AND I WILL DO SO UNTIL THE SUN BURNS OUT FOR LACK OF MY DEVISING A WAY TO KEEP IT LIT.

"Gods, Zeph," Kera said, accidentally snorting as she laughed unexpectedly, her face covered in tears and mucous. "A little dramatic, don't you think? Maybe you've been right about a lot of things, but you're wrong about this. My fate isn't to go back in there and die at the foot of a dragon just because you say so. That's not destiny, that's suicide."

SO YOU CONTINUE TO SAY, said Zephelous. I WOULD LIKE TO TELL YOU ANOTHER THING, KERA.

"Is it that you'll be the anvil of creation for the universe after this one?" Kera quipped. "Because short of making me the same kind of super immortal thing you are, there is nothing you can say that's going to get me to go back in there."

DO YOU REMEMBER THE WAY YOUR BLOOD SANG AS WE APPROACHED? Zephelous asked. THE WAY IT SANG AROUND THE ALCHEMIST ON THE ROAD?

"Marie?" Kera asked.

IF THAT IS WHAT SHE CALLED HERSELF IN THAT FORM, said Zephelous. KERA, YOU ARE CALLED NO-CLAN. DO YOU KNOW WHAT THAT MEANS?

"That I'm an exile," said Kera. "And what do you mean 'in that form'?"

AN EXILE, YES, said Zephelous. AN EXILE FROM THE WILDLANDS. HAVE YOU EVER WONDERED WHY THERE ARE SO FEW DRAGONS IN

THAT REGION?

"Because we used to hunt them," said Kera.

PRECISELY, said Zephelous. A DRAGON HAS NO NATURAL ENEMIES IN THE WILD, SAVE FOR OTHER DRAGONS. CENTURIES AGO, NECESSITY CAUSED THE CREATION OF UNNATURAL PREDATOR. WHEN THE BLACK DRAGON ROSE UP AND DECLARED THE AGE OF GODS TO BE OVER, SOMETHING THAT MIGHT PREY UPON A DRAGON WAS REQUIRED. THAT ENEMY WAS YOU, KERA, YOU AND YOUR PEOPLE.

"Right," said Kera, sniffing. "I rob graves, Zephelous, I don't kill dragons. I can apparently get my ass kicked by them just fine."

WOULD YOU LIKE TO KNOW WHY YOUR BLOOD SANG THE WAY IT DID? Zephelous asked. WOULD YOU LIKE TO KNOW WHAT THE SONG MEANS?

Kera was quiet. Her curiosity clashed with her desire to flee.

"Yes," she whispered at last.

IT STEMS FROM AN ANCIENT WIZARD NAMED LAAVIMINNERAX GORN'ULAZ, Zephelous began. A GREAT GOLDEN DRAGON WHO, UNLIKE THE REST OF HIS FLIGHT WHO REMAINED ALOOF, FOUGHT ON THE SIDE OF THE ALLIED FREE PEOPLES AGAINST THE DARK DRAGON AND HIS ARMIES. THE CULMINATION OF HIS WORK WAS A POWERFUL BLOOD MAGIC RITE, ONE THAT LED TO THE CREATION OF POWERFUL BLOODLINES WHOSE VERY EXISTENCE WAS TIED TO THE THREADS OF FATE UPON WHICH THE WORLD IS WOUND. IT IS CALLED THE LAST WORLDSPELL, AND IT IS WHY YOUR BLOOD HUMS IN YOUR VEINS WHEN YOU ARE NEAR DRAGONS. LIKE RECOGNIZES LIKE.

"My blood sings because of a dragon wizard," Kera repeated. "So glad you could clear that up for me. It all makes so much sense now. Can we please leave now?"

LAAVIMINNERAX GAVE HIS OWN POWER TO THOSE BLOODLINES, said Zephelous. HE GAVE THEM THE POWER OF IMMUNITY TO DRAGONFEAR, AND CREATED WITHIN THEM A SORT OF POWER BATTERY WHICH PROVIDES STRENGTH AND STAMINA IN THE FACE OF OVERWHELMING ODDS.

"There aren't odds much more overwhelming than one on one with a dragon." said Kera, shaking her head. "I'm not seeing how this is better than running away."

IF YOU WILL LISTEN TO ME, AND IF YOU WILL LISTEN TO THE SONG, I CAN SHOW YOU HOW TO ACCESS THAT STRENGTH, said Zephelous. WITH IT, YOU CAN BOLSTER YOURSELF USING YOUR OWN DEFENSES.

"What defenses?" Kera asked.

THE GREAT BARRIERS IN YOUR MIND.

"Denial is going to kill a dragon?"

NO, said Zephelous, BUT WITH MY HELP, YOU COULD USE THE BLOODSONG TO REACH INSIDE YOURSELF, INTO THE PLACE WHERE YOUR PSIONIC ABILITY RESIDES. ONCE YOU UNDERSTAND HOW TO WIELD IT, YOU CAN TAKE THE WALLS YOU HAVE ERECTED AROUND YOUR PAIN AND YOU WILL LEARN TO USE THEM AS YOUR ARMOR AGAINST THE WORLD.

"Even if I believed you, Zeph, I..." Kera took a breath. "Feelings don't stop claws."

THEY DO IF YOU ARE PSIONIC, Zephelous countered.

Kera was quiet.

"Let's say I believe you," she said. "And that I think maybe you can show me how to make walls of pain or whatever. What's the point of going back in there and doing it? If I'm some kind of psychic badass, why don't I just go make a name for myself somewhere?"

BECAUSE, said Zephelous, ALREADY YOUR PAIN AND GUILT AND SELF-LOATHING THREATEN TO OVERWHELM YOU, WHICH IS WHY YOU KEEP IT LOCKED AWAY. LEAVING NOW, CREATING MORE UNCERTAINTY, MORE DOUBT, AND MORE ANXIETY WITHIN YOURSELF WILL ONLY MAKE YOU WEAKER. BY ACCEPTING YOUR DESTINY TODAY, YOU MAKE YOURSELF IMMEASURABLY STRONGER FOR EVERY BATTLE THAT COMES AFTER THIS ONE.

Kera's shoulders sagged, but she found she was able to take an easier breath. She saw Voldani's face again, laying still as if she were deep in sleep, and closed her eyes as another wave of grief watched over her. When she opened them again, there were no tears. She brushed Voldani's hair away from her face, and gave her lips a gentle pat with the tips of her fingers. She took a ragged breath which threatened to become a sob, but controlled it. She took another breath.

She rose, sheathed Zephelous, and walked out the cavern, eyes blazing with anger and murderous intent.

Chapter Forty

The roar of the collapse had been enough to shake Brenno from his dragonfear, and the halfling had hidden away while loose bits of stone and ice rained down and continued to entomb Orionatsaron.

Brenno coughed against the dust in the air as it threatened to choke him and render him sightless in the gloom. He cautiously stumbled his way through the cavern, arms stretched out in front of him.

"Smith?" The halfling called. "Smith, where are you?"

The only sound he heard was the settling of the rubble, and a great and palpable silence.

"Smith, say something!"

"Here, Hornbuckle," Smith answered, voice low and hoarse. "I'm right here."

Rubbing at his eyes, Brenno navigated himself towards the sound of Smith's voice, finding the man sitting up against the wall of the cavern, Enaurl's lifeless remains still cradled in his lap.

"That explosion… what did you do?"

"Took the goblin's advice," Smith said, gently swaying from the waist up, as if he were rocking Enaurl to sleep. "Used the core. Made a bomb. Killed a dragon."

"Yes, I saw," said Brenno, still rubbing at his eyes. "It was something."

"Yeah, it was something," said Smith. "Which is the exact opposite of what you did."

"What?" Brenno said, taking his hands away from his eyes. "I tried to negotiate with that thing and nearly succeeded, that's something."

"You talked. Right," said Smith, snorting derisively. "And when the fight broke out, you stood there like a statue." The man resumed his rocking, then shook his head and stopped. "No, a statute would have stood. You cowered."

"Well, I…" Brenno began, words failing him. "I didn't mean to, I was afraid."

"Sure," said Smith. "Like how you didn't mean to shoot Morri, but did anyway because you were afraid. Or how you took drugs instead of dumping them, also out of fear. Or was that from greed? I'm having a hard time keeping your failings straight right now."

"Smith, I…" Brenno took a half step back, stung by the artificer's words. "You don't mean that, you can't. You know that I… that I would never--"

"I don't want to talk, Hornbuckle," Smith said, using the back of his palm to brush an accumulated layer of dust away from Enaurl's face. "I don't want to talk." Brenno nodded dejectedly, wiping at his eyes to clear them from the remaining dust and the newly formed tears. "I'll leave you to gather yourself," said Brenno.

"I don't need to gather anything," said Smith. "I need to be left alone."

"Right," said Brenno, turning away. "Of course."

The halfling pressed his palms into his eyes, wishing that the pressure would help clear up the anxiety and self-loathing he felt welling up inside himself.

What a coward, he thought to himself. *What an absolute coward I am.*

Putting some distance between himself and Smith, Brenno basked in the anger and disappointment he felt for himself. The sentiments festered quickly and grew to become loathing, and Brenno found himself in need of breaking something.

He looked for a piece of ice, or a loose stone, or anything that he could destroy in an effort to vent some of the unbearable emotions rising up and threatening to overwhelm him, filling his chest with what felt like a thousand white-hot knives. He spotted a loose looking chunk, a dozen gold coins shining inside it. He stared at the coins, and the coins stared back.

With an angry shout, he ran up and kicked as hard as he could, sending the piece of debris hurtling towards the pile of rubble. The ice exploded against the rock, sending the coins spraying in all directions, clanging off stone and spiraling down to lay flat on the frosty floor below.

He found another piece and kicked it again, harder this time. A few smaller stones in the pile shifted and clattered, and gold coins sprayed out in all directions before noisily scattering across the cavern.

Feeling a little better about himself thanks to his destructive outlet, Brenno found a third piece and kicked it as hard as he could manage, sending the ice chunk skipping across the cavern floor before it exploded against the rubble. More small stones shifted, and again coins clattered noisily about.

When the stones and coins settled, a large stone heaved and fell over. Then another, and another. The rubble pile heaved as if it were breathing, and Brenno's breath caught in his throat.

"Smith?" Brenno called timidly.

The rubble pile rose, great boulders of stone rolling away, coins and ice and rocks falling in all directions.

"Smith!"

Out from under the tomb of stones and ice and gold emerged Orionatsaron, bruised and bloodied but not beaten. The dragon roared in pain and frustration as it freed itself entirely, pulling one limb after another out from the pile. A clawed foot planted itself down on the cavern floor just before Brenno, and the halfling looked up to see the dragon's eyes focused squarely on him.

"*Smith!*" the halfling squeaked.

"*You,*" said the dragon, stomping his way towards the halfling. "I thought you the barbarian, or the scion. Perhaps even the wizard. But to find you is unexpected."

Brenno turned and tried to run towards Smith, who he saw hadn't moved from his place or even stopped rocking. The dragon reached out and plucked the halfling off the ground as if he were an overripe grape being torn from the vine.

Rising to stand on his rear legs, the dragon held Brenno aloft, the halfling squirming and wiggling with all the energy he could muster. The dragon squeezed harder, forcing the air from Brenno's lungs. Brenno could see nothing but blue scales.

"And you, tinkerer," Orionatsaron growled, speaking to Smith. "All out of tricks now that your toy soldier has been broken apart?"

"Guess so," Smith muttered.

Orionatsaron made his way to Smith and snatched him up with his free hand. The artificer didn't struggle, and his only movement was to hold Enaurl close to himself as the dragon limped his way across the cavern, the thunderous footfalls staggered from his sustained injuries.

Reaching the opposite side, Orionatsaron dropped the pair into what looked to be a makeshift prison, a bare spot on the floor that butted against the wall, spikes of ice and bone affixed to stalagmites all around it. Brenno hit hard and wheezed as the wind was knocked out of him, while Smith fell limp and sat up to cradle Enaurl once more.

Rolling over onto his hands and knees as he struggled to breathe, Brenno looked up at the battered dragon. Orionatsaron was licking at his wounds, lapping up the blood that seeped out from the many cuts, slashes, and gashes that dotted his hide.

"What…" He struggled to say, making a sound like bagpipes as he fought to catch his breath. "What happens to us now?"

The dragon stopped licking at his wounds and bared his teeth at Brenno, revealing fangs stained red.

"I eat you," said the dragon. "For all the trouble you've been, I should gain something."

"Is sustenance..." Brenno gasped, still wheezing. "So valuable... You'd give up... the riches... we discussed?"

"Do you think me a fool?" Orionatsaron bellowed. "That I would fall for the self same ploy twice, blood mage?"

"I am... no blood mage..." Brenno said. "Nor are any of... the others."

"*Were*," the dragon corrected.

"It is... as you... say," said Brenno. "*Were* we... blood mages... wouldn't we... have used... blood magic... against you?"

Brenno had no idea where the words were coming from, but they wouldn't stop spooling out from his mouth, like a ball of yarn being pulled by a cat. Orionatsaron paused for a moment and regarded Brenno, giving the halfling the distinct impression that the dragon was deciding whether or not to simply eat him on the spot.

"Fair point," said the dragon at last.

Feeling suddenly revitalized, Brenno caught his breath and took a moment to steady himself, waiting to see if the dragon had more to say.

"Explain your interest in dragon's blood, pawnbroker." Orionatsaron demanded.

"There is a girl," Brenno began. "A child. I... She is terribly wounded."

"And so you sought the blood mages," said the dragon.

"No!" Brenno said. "We sought a healer, a priest. He told us the only curative strong enough to restore her required dragon's blood to be made."

"And you believed this priest?" the dragon asked.

"Of course," said Brenno. "He is trustworthy."

The dragon snorted.

"You have been fools," said the dragon. "Naive, ignorant fools."

"Perhaps," said Brenno. "We lacked the guidance of one as learned as yourself."

"You'll not flatter your way to freedom," Orionatsaron boomed.

"Nor was that my intention," said Brenno. "I was merely stating facts."

"Good," said the dragon, looking away from the halfling to resume his licking.

"Of course, I can't help but note..." Brenno forced himself to say, feeling his stomach fall away inside himself.

Shut up! He thought to himself, *shut up, shut up, shut up!*

"If I am eaten, you will have no choice but to contend with all these useless coins. As you say, it seems only right that you should gain something from today.

Merely an observation, of course."

The dragon's eyes narrowed and moved to rest on Brenno once more, the dragon's ire evident by the rattling low in his throat.

The dragon glared at the halfling.

"*Of course,*" the dragon repeated. "And I suppose you would have a proposal to remedy this observed situation? You'll give me your word to obey my commands and flitter down the hills, no doubt to flee into some hole deep in the earth in an effort to hide yourself."

Yes! Brenno thought. *A thousand times yes!*

"Of course not," he said. "I am a reputable merchant, and a certified member of the merchant's guild. We could draft up a contract--"

"A contract?" the dragon said, his tone shifting to something that Brenno couldn't identify. "And I'm to believe you would abide by words on parchment?"

"Of course," said Brenno. "A contract is a contract."

Orionatsaron was silent for a long moment, and Brenno heard nothing but the pounding of his own heart in his ears.

"Indeed," said the dragon, breaking the silence at last, stomping away from the ice prison.

Brenno wasn't sure whether to feel relieved or terrified at the events transpiring. Before he could make up his mind, Orionatsaron pounded his way back, a massive roll of parchment held in his claws.

Without ceremony or explanation, the dragon dropped the parchment at Brenno's feet, the paper unrolling and revealing dozens of smaller pages held on as if stuck with glue, plus several large format portions of writing.

"What is this?" Brenno asked.

"A contract," said Orionatsaron. "*My* contract, the one Chelreigamanth was meant to sign. It pledges subservience to myself."

"You would have me sign in the dragon's place?" Brenno asked, awed.

"Hardly," said Orionatsaron. "I'd sooner have a mouse stand in for a lion. However, I'd prefer to gain a pawn than leave the field without acquiring another piece."

"As you say," said Brenno, reading through the contract. "May I have a few moments to review?"

The dragon's only response was a dip of the head, as the cerulean terror again returned to licking his wounds. Brenno's mind swam as he read the contract, struggling to comprehend certain portions of the agreement in front of him.

The signee, hereafter referred to as... does solemnly pledge complete and utter obedience... to serve as if unto a king, placing before any gods...

To call the contract dense was an understatement, and only Brenno's familiarity with the nature of such agreements helped him navigate the document. Several minutes passed as the halfling scrutinized the contract in front of him.

Finding what he believed to be a problem, Brenno furrowed his brow, scratching at his chin. He hesitated, feeling the eyes of the azure dragon watching his every move.

"If I may," said Brenno, working up the courage to speak. "There seems to be a mistake--"

"Unlikely," rumbled Orionatsaron.

"There is a section here which lists a number of tasks to be fulfilled under *extraordinary measures*," Brenno said, pointing to a small section of the floor-sized contract in front of him. "While I see several enumerated lists, there are several line items that appear to be missing."

"Those are not line items, they are provisos," Orionatsaron corrected. "By signing, you agree to abide by them and, under extraordinary measures, will strive to carry them out least you find yourself in violation of the contract."

"The consequence of which is?"

Brenno asked, pulling his glasses away from his face to peek up and the towering blue dragon. An expression that closely resembled a smirk of satisfaction spread across the dragon's scaly features.

"I suggest you keep reading," Orionatsaron said.

"I will," said Brenno, "it's just that..."

"Just what, pawnbroker?" the dragon asked.

"How am I expected to agree to conditions which I cannot see?" Brenno asked. "How can I be expected to abide by the terms and provisos which aren't apparent, and may not become apparent until it's too late for me to realize that they are beyond my ability?"

"When you hock your tawdry wares, do you keep them under lock and key or leave them out in the streets, where peasants and criminals and the otherwise unintended might collect them?" Orionatsaron asked, voice echoing in the cave. "I should think the former, as I thought you a man worth doing business with. Do correct me if I am wrong on either count."

"No, of course," said Brenno. "I am just unfamiliar with the act of bargaining with a dragon."

Orionatsaron threw back his head and laughed, a deep and rolling laugh that threatened to deafen Brenno even as it set the hairs on the back of his neck on edge.

"Dragons do not bargain with lesser being," said Orionatsaron, once his laughter had subsided. "Dragons decree, and lesser beings submit. That is the true nature of the relationship between our races; to my kind falls the duty of leadership, to yours the responsibilities of subservience. Sign where indicated, and be quick about it. My patience with this arrangement is already wearing thin."

The dragon's speech became a low reptilian growl, an unsettling reminder of the raw primordial power the apex predator before him had.

A part of him wanted to laugh at the fact that he was using paperwork to defend himself from what amounted to a dinosaur wizard, while the rest of him wanted to run as far away from the titanic cerulean beast that towered over him as he could.

Instead, he feigned a renewed interest in the contract held in his shaking hands, painfully aware of the sound of gore dripping from jaws still slick with the blood of his friends.

Brenno scanned through the page in his hand, and the next, and the one after it: he saw no place for such indications.

Reptilian eyes the size of his head flashed shut for a moment in front of him, the alien blink unsettling Brenno as he felt their weight on him, the dragon watching his every move without missing a beat.

The halfling's heart thundered in his ears, drumming so loudly he was certain Orionatsaron was able hear it.

How could he not? The halfling thought, *it's so loud I can't hear myself think. Why don't I see any indications to sign? It should be plain and noticeable, something I'm not seeing.*

"I don't suppose a portion of this contract would happen to be invisible?" Brenno asked. "Cloaked, hidden, or otherwise shielded from the naked eye in some manner?"

"You are capable of learning." the blue dragon said with a snort. "So much the better for you and your life expectancy. Sign it, and they will be made visible."

His entire body shaking, Brenno shakily brought the quill up to the dotted line and signed his name, every letter a struggle.

"Good," said the dragon. "Now you may see."

A rippling wave of cerulean and violet light shone from the dragon's eyes, and the pages of the contract flickered, bringing into existence several layers of writing that had not been visible before.

New conditions, responsibilities, and tasks unveiled themselves, and Brenno strained to absorb them all, sweating under the stress.

"You know, I've heard a lot of stories about dragons," Kera shouted, drawing attention to herself. "Never heard one where they used paperwork to bore someone to death,"

"K-Kera?" Brenno stammered, shocked. "How?"

"Yes," Orionatsaron thundered. "How indeed?"

"You know how it is with us barbarians, big blue," said Kera, unsheathing Zephelous. "We're a hard bunch to keep down."

"So I am learning," said the dragon. "You would make a useful pawn."

"I wish I could, but I've got other obligations."

"Oh?"

"Yeah. See, first I have to fight you, then I have to haul a bunch of your blood back to Zelwyr." Kera began walking towards Orionatsaron, pacing along the outside edge of the rocky cavern, throwing aside her coat as she did. "We tried asking nicely, you refused, then you tried to kill me. I'm going to have to make you bleed now."

"What reason have you to declare war against one such as myself?" the dragon bellowed. "Are the past atrocities committed against my kind by yours not enough? Are you not satisfied with a decimation of my kin? Must you strive for extinction?"

"Shut up and *bleed*," Kera growled through clenched teeth, springing off the stalagmite and into the air.

Zephelous slashed through the air, weaving a deadly 'x' as Kera neared the dragon's face.

Anticipating Kera's lunge, the dragon flattened its wings against its back and threw itself low to the ground, rolling across the stone floor of the cavern to get beneath Kera's attack.

"A literal blood lust," the dragon rumbled as it righted itself. "How uninspired. Though I suppose should not have expected anything more from a human, let alone a mindless berserker from the southern lands."

DO NOT LET IT GOAD YOU, Zephelous warned.

I don't feel goaded, Kera answered. *I'm feeling a lot of emotions right now, but goaded is not one of them.*

IS ONE OF THEM ANGER? Zephelous asked.

Fear, dread, terror, self-loathing, Kera listed, ducking low to avoid a swipe of the dragon's tail as it came whipping through the air.

The powerful appendage plowed clear through several stalagmites, peppering

Kera with sharpened bits of stone that cut her skin in several places,.

There's definitely some anger in there.

EMBRACE IT, said Zephelous. IT MAY BE WHAT SAVES YOU.

A ghostly whine sounded from somewhere distant, a haunting horse cry from outside the cavern. The clip clopping of hooves echoed throughout the cavern, announcing the arrival of the creature before it leapt into Kera's view; a horse, ash grey and mostly translucent, thundered up to her, a twisted horn atop its head. Behind it trailed a fog of ghostly trail of distortion and blackness following its body like a living shadow.

The creature, a spectral unicorn, stampeded towards Kera, ducking its head low to scoop her up onto its back. Orionatsaron bellowed a roar of anger.

"What trickery is this?" the dragon demanded, coiling its body like a great blue snake in order to lash at Kera and the spectral steed.

His tail smashed into the ice and stone where Kera had been just a moment before, pelting her with a rain of debris. The steed skipped away and divided into two, then four, then eight versions of Kera mounted on horseback, each apparition adding the din of its hooves and wail of its mournful whinnies it made to the overall clamor.

The dragon reached out and made a twisting motion, weaving a minor spell in the direction of a pair of Keras; ice shards the size of javelins erupted from the ground, skewering a pair of spectral horses and riders.

The ghostly unicorns cried out in pain, as did the Kera riding each of them, and dissolved into small columns of black smoke. The remaining horses and their riders crossed in front of each other, weaving a trail of confusion as they neared the dragon. Orionatsaron inhaled deeply, muscles straining to accommodate the massive influx of air.

With a roar, the blue dragon spat a conic blast of electricity at the floor in front of the riders. Bolts of lightning evaporated ice and burnt the stone beneath as a veritable storm of power streamed out from the dragon's mouth. Another spectral unicorn fell to the barrage, bolts blasting the ground around it until one found its mark. As the others had done, the horse and rider evaporated.

The remaining figures advanced on the dragon, moving wide to either side of the surging breath weapon. Rallying, the charging figures charged towards the cerulean terror, riding up the sides of the walls and onto the ceiling to gain access to normally impossible angles of attack. Within seconds, they closed the distance between themselves and the dragon.

As one, they leapt at Orionatsaron, pointed horns and slashing swords aiming to cut into the dragon's hide.

The dragon lunged towards one of the riders and caught the horse between its jaws. Feeling substance there, he crunched down with his jaws. The horse exploded into a blast of fire, scorching the inside of his mouth and blackening the scales of its muzzle.

Orionatsaron howled in anger and pain. Agony blossomed from its neck as Kera, what he could only assume was the *real* Kera, rode down his back, the tip of the dwarven sword in her hands slicing a long gash down the side of his throat.

The dragon pounced towards the assailant in question, paws outreached, the entirety of the dragon's bulk slamming onto its target as it struck. Claws the size of sabers pierced through another spectral unicorn, the Kera riding it was sent hurtling through the air towards the dragon's face. The steed billowed away as a puff smoke.

The woman let out a scream of war, flying through the air with Zephelous poised for a powerful slash.

Orionatsaron retreated from the blow, but not quickly enough - Zephelous's edge sliced clean across his muzzle and his face before cutting through his right eye, rupturing it.

An uncontrolled bellow of agony tore its way out of Orionatsaron as the dwarven-forged steel opened him up and darkened his world, so loud in the enclosed space it nearly deafened even himself.

Instinct took over, and the dragon reared up onto its hind legs, wings working furiously to send a gust of wind outward all around it.

The illusions dissipated, battered into oblivion by the winds. Kera flew sideways through the air, sailing ten feet through the air before slipping across the ground like a stone on a pond. She rolled to a stop, hastening to her feet, bringing Zephelous out in front of her as she panted.

"You *worm*," Orionatsaron growled, "you *insignificant, short-lived, inconsequential WORM!*"

The insult came out as a roar, spittle and blood flying in Kera's direction as the dragon screamed at her.

"Where is your trickster mage? Your petty illusionist?"

A flash of blue and pink sparks whirled like a pinwheel atop an ice column near the dragon's remaining eye. The pinwheel widened to a hoop, and split into a pair which went in opposite directions.

The image of a bruised and bloodied Will appeared, one eye swollen and blackened, dried blood running down his nose and into his facial hair.

"It's illusio*mancy*, actually," said the apparition. "There's a difference. And why would I show myself? That would be the single dumbest thing I could do. I'm far more content to stay invisible, thank you very much. Nice eye, by the way. Hey, we match."

The dragon snarled and lifted its head away from the apparition, scanning the room.

"Your arrogance will be your undoing," Orionatsaron swore, whipping his tail towards Kera's midsection.

The woman threw herself flat against the floor and tumbled under the blow, using the roll to bring herself closer to her quarry. The ground beneath her feet sloped upwards, becoming a ramp leading up to the dragon's stomach. Kera charged, but was swatted away like a gnat as Orionatsaron lashed out with his forepaw.

Her world exploded into a daze of pain and stars as she slammed into the cavern wall.

"Away from me, worm! Without the trickster mage you are beneath my notice, nothing but a slobbering barbarian girl."

Kera reeled and wheezed, scrambling to crawl behind a large boulder, feeling certain that she had at least one broken rib. She rose to her knees and planted Zephelous's tip into the ground like a cane, resting wearily against the blade, a creature of blood and sweat and dirt and ice.

I think I'm all out of anger, Zeph, Kera thought to the sword.

ANGER, PERHAPS, said Zephelous. BUT THERE IS PLENTY OF *RAGE*. LISTEN TO THE SONG IN YOUR BLOOD, KERA. EMBRACE THE RAGE, ACCEPT THE PRIMAL POWER IT OFFERS. Kera tried to scoff, but it came out as a labored breath.

Oh, is that all? She asked.

YES, said Zephelous, YOU MUST STOP USING YOUR ABILITIES TO SHIELD YOURSELF FROM PAIN, AND INSTEAD USE THEM TO MAKE YOUR PAIN INTO A SHIELD.

"Defend myself with a shitty metaphor, got it," Kera wheezed. "Anything else?"

"I have you now!" Orionatsaron shouted.

The air hummed and smelled of ozone as the dragon belched lighting bolts at a collection of stones less than a dozen feet away from her.

"Oops! Not real," Will's image taunted.

"*Silence!*" The dragon shouted at it.

I think a fake me just died, Kera thought to Zephelous. *I'm starting to think the real one isn't going to be far behind. I'm willing to bet Will's running out of tricks, and I don't think I have anything else left in me. How did you talk me into this again?*

YOU ARE RIGHT, KERA, THERE IS NOTHING ELSE, Zephelous agreed heartily.

That's not as helpful as you make it sound, Kera thought.

THERE IS ONLY THE RAGE, THE POWER, AND THE SONG.

"What?" Kera said.

THERE IS ONLY THE RAGE, THE POWER, AND THE SONG. SAY IT.

"There is only the rage," said Kera, steadying her breathing. "There is only the rage, the power, and the song."

AGAIN.

"There is only the rage, the power, and the song."

LOUDER.

"There is only the rage, the power, and the song!"

"What trivial thing are you fussing about, barbarian?" The dragon called out, head swiveling around to face Kera.

"Should you be worried about her when you can't even find me?" Will's image quipped. "I'm not an expert at being a dragon, but based on the shape of your face I'm going to say you aren't either."

"ENOUGH!" Orionatsaron howled.

The dragon inhaled once, and then again, over-inflating itself.

Electricity danced and crackled all along the spines on his back, blue-white light blazing from his good eye. Lines of current ran up the dragon's horns, filling the air with a buzzing like a thousand bees. The fine hairs on Kera's body stood on end, compelled by the electricity in the air. A humming tone built and began to rise in pitch.

*wounwounwoun*WOUNWOUNWOUN**WOUNWOUNWOUN**...

"This is going to be bad, isn't it?" Kera asked.

LIKELY, said Zephelous.

The humming tone peaked and dropped, becoming a chaotic concert of high intensity buzzes, each streak of lightning among the myriad bolts singing an electrified note of raw energy.

Anything in the path of the river of power that was the dragon's breath was demolished; stones were obliterated, snow evaporated, ice disintegrated. Will's voice, magically amplified, was heard over the droning of the beam.

"Nope," Will taunted. "Nope. You're wrong. Not this time. A total fabrication. Nope. Wrong again."

The beam continued its onslaught of destruction, swinging towards Kera.

MOVE, Zephelous urged. *NOW.*

There is only the rage, the power, and the song, Kera repeated, scrambling to get clear of the dragon's stream of power, wishing she better understood what the mantra the sword had given her was supposed to mean.

There is only the rage, the power, and the song.

A fist-sized chunk of stone came flying across the room, smashing into her skull. The pain was incredible, setting off a ringing in her head so loud it drowned out every other sound in the cavern.

She felt dizzy, felt the thumping of her pulse and the warmth of her own blood trailing down from a welt on her forehead. The world around her fractured and wavered, two dizzying versions of reality failing to sync up into one.

The droning sound of Orionatsaron's breath weapon faded and was lost beneath the ringing in her ears. She staggered and fell, using Zephelous like a crutch. The ringing grew louder, accompanied by a deep and completely incoherent warbling, like a distorted tuba playing somewhere in the distance.

The cacophony continued to grow louder and louder, drowning out the singsong tuba and the buzzing of the dragon's breath. The singular note she heard in her ears pitched and wavered, and became several notes. The notes distinguished themselves and became a chorus, and the chorus became a song - a wordless song, a primitive one that begged to be howled to the moon.

The song grew louder in her ears, steadying her breath and slowing her heart rate. She exhaled, felt strength return to her arms, saw the wavering world around her stabilize and become one solid environment once again. Everything was quiet, there was nothing but the song.

She took a slow breath, and tightened her grip around Zephelous.

NOW, KERA! Zephelous shouted.

Her feet started moving without her bidding them to do so, racing her way towards the dragon, who was facing away from her.

The lightning stopped pouring out from between its fangs, and it was snarling at Will's image.

"Is this your first time fighting off adventurers?" Will asked. "Because if it is, that would really explain a lot."

"I will *end you*, trickster," Orionatsaron threatened.

"Please, you can't even *find* me," Will taunted. "How are you going to *end* me?"

The dragon was silent for a moment, then lunged upwards towards the projection of Will, grabbing at the wizard with its arms.

Kera dimly noted that the illusion didn't disintegrate, that the wizard winced in pain as the dragon's fingers curled around him ever tighter.

"Took you... long enough."

The dragon tightened its grip, squeezing the man in its grasp as if he were a toy. Kera heard the cracking and popping that she was certain was the breaking of Will's ribs.

"What did you think you would accomplish here, charlatan?" The dragon demanded, bringing Will close to his remaining eye. "Are you so vested in this fabled curative that you'd *die* for it?"

"Why does... everyone... keep... calling me that?" Will gasped.

"Because that is what you *are*, wizard," the dragon boomed. "Illusion is hardly worth calling a school of magic. Parlor tricks to entertain children and tavern wenches, nothing more."

"It does... a few things... really well..." Will wheezed, a crimson line trickling down from the corner of his mouth.

The crushing grip was unyielding and offered no quarter.

"Go on then," Orionatsaron taunted. "Educate me."

"It makes... a really good... distraction," Will said, his voice hardly more than a whisper.

"A distraction requires a follow up," the dragon leered. "Your friends are dead or captured, your escape route is buried beneath the same rubble that undoubtedly brought an end to your god-blooded friend. So much for the divine."

Kera was only a few dozen feet from the dragon now, heart pounding, feet racing, the song in her ears. Her blood danced and burned along with the chorus, pounding in her ears, heating her from within.

"I'm counting... on someone... who isn't a friend," Will said.

A platform appeared in front of Kera, a floating ledge that acted like a stair. Another appeared beyond it, and another still, creating a makeshift stairway. She leapt from ledge to ledge, the burning in her blood growing ever louder. Her vision turned red, either from the blood flowing down her face or the fury in her veins, perhaps a combination of the two.

She leapt from the final platform, and could not contain the rage any longer. She opened her mouth and let loose a war scream that held every ounce of rage and pain in her soul.

The dragon turned its head slowly, too slowly, and Kera realized that Zephelous was once again altering her perception of time. She flew towards the behemoth's head, saw it raise its free arm to swat at her.

She tucked and rolled over the strike, Zephelous raised so far over her head as to be parallel with her spine.

The screaming, the rage, the song, the fury… it was all she knew.

She channeled all of her strength, pain, and anguish into her strike, letting every ounce of struggle, agony, and hurt guide her blade.

Zephelous struck true, cutting a jagged line through the scales behind the dragon's head and into its skull. As Zephelous's edge pierced through the dragon's scales and into softer flesh beneath, the sword gathered every ounce of psychic power contained with in it and compressed it into a singular point of psionic energy.

Using that energy like a drill, Zephelous telepathically blasted its way past the dragon's mental defenses and into the deepest recesses of its mind. The dragon roared in agony.

Zephelous felt pain wash over it, but pressed on, digging its way ever deeper into the dragon's mind.

There the sword found what it had been looking for.

ORIONATSARON, Zephelous began, its voice a deafening psychic roar in the mind of the dragon. YOUR TRUE NAME IS SHIVOOR AK TSEM, AND WITH IT I CLAIM POWER OVER YOU.

"How is this possible?" Orionatsaron bellowed. "Name yourself, phantom!"

I AM NO PHANTOM, Zephelous shouted. I AM ZEPHELOUS OF THE FIRST AGE. MY TRUE NAME HAS BEEN SPOKEN BUT ONCE IN ALL OF TIME, WHEN IT WHISPERED UNTO ME DIRECT FROM THE MOUTH OF COL.

"What fear should I hold for the dead god you name?" Orionastaron sneered, straining against Zephelous's hold over him.

PERHAPS NONE, said Zephelous. THOUGH YOU WILL LEARN TO FEAR MINE. IF YOU WILL NOT FEAR IT, YOU WILL RESPECT IT, AND YOU WILL UNDERSTAND THAT I AM NOT TO BE TRIFLED WITH.

"You would threaten me, you soulless piece of steel?"

I WAS NOT FORGED TO MAKE THREATS, said Zephelous. I WAS FORGED TO EDUCATE. ALLOW ME TO BEGIN DOING SO.

The pinpoint of psionic energy erupted into a pincushion of psychic spikes within the dragon's mind. Although intangible in most senses, the spikes pierced the dragon's psyche and slashed into its mind.

For the first time in centuries, Orionatsaron shrieked in pain.

Blood welled out from behind his good eye and dripped down from his ears, serving as the only physical indicators of the tremendous psychic damage delivered by Zephelous.

"Why are you doing this?" Orionatsaron cried.

YOU ARE AWARE OF THE REASON, said Zephelous.

"My blood?" The dragon roared. "Truly? Then come and get it."

In a blind rage, he lashed out, whipping his tail towards Kera.

Kera ducked, rolling across the dragon's scales before sliding back on to her feet. When she stood, she found herself holding something foreign in the hand that wasn't on Zephelous - a small vial filled with snowflakes, suspended in a light blue liquid.

"Will?" She asked, looking around.

Orionatsaron shook itself free from the pain caused by Zephelous's psychic attack, and the dragon lunged for Kera, aiming to pin the graverobber and the sword against the wall.

"This better work!" Kera shouted, smashing the vial on the frozen wall. The dragon's head came for her, mouth wide like the gates of hell.

Ice sprang into existence, forming cruel spikes and jagged lances of frozen water that reached out from the wall to meet the dragon. Where the two met, blood and ice erupted.

With a roar of anguish and defiance, Orionatsaron was skewered, pierced through the mouth, neck, and throat like a great pincushion. With a titanic amount of effort, the dragon broke free from the icy skewers and pulled them free from his body.

Orionatsaron, blood running from his neck and mouth like water from a spring, faltered and collapsed into a heap. Blood pooled around him, steaming on the ice as it spread slowly outward.

"May whatever evils... the dark ritual... you attempt to perform... consume you... Zephelous of the First Age."

THERE IS NO EVIL IN REDEMPTION, Zephelous said. THERE IS NO DARKNESS IN SAVING A LIFE.

"Necromancy, then" Orionatsaron coughed, spewing a gout of blood, "You must know... that life... cannot be restored... by the rites... of undeath."

"It's to save my daughter's life!" Smith shouted.

"How, exactly?" the dragon asked, color visibly fading from his cobalt scales.

"There's a ritual, one that needs dragon blood--" Smith began.

"You'll find no restorative in my lifeblood, human," Orionatsaron wheezed, blood beginning to pool around his head. "Magic, yes. Power, yes. Restorative? No."

"There's no point lying now," said Kera.

"Even now, what makes you believe I would waste the effort required to lie on your kind?" The dragon's voice faltered, but remained proud.

"We know the truth, Orionatsaron," said Brenno. "The Speaker himself consulted the scrolls, he told us about the ritual."

The dragon was silent.

After a long moment, a pause so long Kera briefly wondered if the beast had died beneath her, the dragon's body began to heave.

It must be in its death throes, she thought.

She was deeply confused when the dragon started laughing.

"A priest looked at a book and told you you had to kill a dragon for its blood in order to work a miracle," said the dragon, pausing several times to cough up more blood. "And you, *naive idiots* that you are, simply took this man at his word and stormed your way to the nearest dragon's lair without so much as a single question asked or resource consulted."

The dragon laughed once more, but its amusement was cut short by a surge of blood in its throat that caused it to choke and sputter.

"I suppose you should consider yourselves lucky."

"How so?" Brenno asked.

Orionatsaron curled its blood stained lips upwards, forming the draconic equivalent of a grim smile.

"Imagine the trials you might have faced had you been instructed to kill a god instead of a dragon," Orionatsaron laughed once more, his mirth collapsing once more into a series of wet, sputtering coughs.

Feeling the strength leave his limbs, seeing his vision fading to black, Orionatsaron summoned the last reserves of his strength to drag his head across the cavern floor, sliding his neck through the slickness of his own blood. He locked eyes with the halfling.

"Remember, pawnbroker" said the dragon, even as the light faded from his eyes. "A deal is a deal."

With that, the dragon went limp, eyes rolling into the back of his head and tongue falling out from between crooked jaws.

A palpable silence fell over the cavern.

"Zeph, is he… Is he dead?" Kera asked between ragged breaths.

YES, Zephelous answered.

"Was he lying?" Kera asked.

HE DID NOT BELIEVE SO, said Zephelous.

"Fuck," said Kera.

INDEED, said Zephelous.

The song in Kera's ears faded as the adrenaline left her system, the rage that had fueled her cooled into a weariness unlike any she had ever known before.

Her every muscle felt as if it would give out at any moment, her entire body alternating between a state of tingling numbness and throbbing ache. She wanted to drop Zephelous to the ground if only to be free of the sword's weight, but her fingers wouldn't release their vice-like grip on the sword.

She heard a garbled droning, formless noise so meaningless it was several breaths before Kera realized it was the sound of Zephelous attempting to speak to her.

She tried to say something, but her mouth wouldn't work the way she wanted it to. She tried to think a response towards the sword, but found herself incapable of forming the words.

She didn't realize she had been walking until she found herself standing in front of the prison of ice and bone. Zephelous spoke to her again, as incomprehensible as the first time. Kera's labored breathing was the only thing she heard, in both her ears and echoing in her mind.

She wanted to let herself drop to the ground and sleep for a hundred years. It surprised her to see her arm, her sword arm, bring Zephelous crashing back and forth through the ice spikes and makeshift bars of the cage holding Brenno and Smith.

Zephelous babbled something more, speaking at length. Whatever the sword was saying, the droning noise began to feel soothing, somehow taking on a relaxing and peaceful quality.

Kera wondered briefly what the sword was saying, but felt the numbness win out over the pain in her body. The sensation of absolute nothingness spread inward from the tips of her fingers and toes. She also wondered briefly what it was that Smith was cradling in his arms, rocking back and forth like a baby.

The oblivion took her arms and legs, and began working its way through her core and up her neck. The last thought she had before everything went black was the realization that it was pieces of Enaurl that Smith was rocking back and forth.

Chapter Forty-One

Brenno's gaze was locked on to the mountain of bloodied scales and akimbo limbs that had once been the terrifying bulk of the blue dragon Orionatsaron. The dragon hadn't stirred, hadn't moved, hadn't so much as twitched since its collapse. If it was breathing, there was no sign of it.

The sudden noise of shattering ice and bones clattering as they skittered across the cavern floor made him wince, but still he kept his gaze locked on the fallen dragon.

I have to know, Brenno thought, *I have to know for certain.*

Kera mumbled something incoherent and unintelligible, opened her mouth to make a single 'ha' sound, then collapsed into a heap on the floor.

The dragon didn't react.

Tearing his eyes off the dragon for a moment, Brenno examined Kera.

Unlike the corpse of Orionatsaron the woman was still breathing: the sword that was resting on her chest rising and falling visibly.

"Smith, I think Kera will need to be carried out of here," Brenno said, speaking to Smith.

The words out of his mouth seemed unbearably loud, and for the hundredth time Brenno feared that the dragon would awaken and snap them up in its jaws.

"Smith?"

Brenno turned to look at the artificer, still clutching the burnt and blackened remains of Enaurl, rocking back and forth as if he were trying to lull an infant to sleep.

The man looked more haggard and worn than Brenno had ever seen him, his clothes scorched and singed, his face looking as though he'd aged fifty years over the course of the day's events.

"Smith?"

"Did you see the way she reached for me?" Smith asked, his voice soft and empty. "The way she put her hand on my face and just looked at me... It was the same way when... How do you think she knew to do that? Why would she do that? She's just a pile of parts, she's not... she's..."

Smith stopped his rocking stared into Enaurl's face, her unblinking silver eyes, her immovable lips. The artificer ran his hand down the braided cords of wire and rubber that sprouted from the construct's skull.

"It was like she was sad... like she was hurting... like she was another broken woman in my arms, dying full of hope that I'd be able to save her."

"Smith, you... you can't know if Enaurl was thinking any of that," said Brenno, eyes darting cautiously to Orionatsaron, his anxiety and fear getting the best of him.

"I can and I do," Smith intoned, resuming his rocking.

"Okay, sure, you would know better than I," said Brenno, realizing that this battle was not the one that needed to be fought at this particular moment. "Can you help me with Kera?"

Smith shook his head, holding Enaurl's remains closer to himself.

"I'm not leaving her here," said Smith. "I'm carrying her."

"But Kera is still alive, and needs to be--"

"I'm not leaving her here, Hornbuckle," Smith said, looking up to the halfling, eyes bloodshot. "Ask her damn sword to help."

Without another word, Smith rose to his feet, careful not to disturb Enaurl. He gave the halfling a harrowed look - a look of palpable, unfiltered anguish - and stepped over Kera to begin walking towards the entrance to the cavern. Brenno felt his ears burning before he realized he was angry.

"You can just fix her!" Brenno shouted out to Smith. "Or use her parts to build a new one! Kera is a living, breathing human being, Smith, and yes, this is all her fault, but you can't just leave her here to die while you bemoan a construct you could just repair at home."

Smith stopped walking, but did not turn back to face the halfling. He shook his head, letting it hang.

"Except I can't, Brenno," said Smith.

"You can't what?" the halfling demanded.

"Build her, fix her, repair her," Smith listed. "Any of it."

"You fixed her arm before we got to Sundial Vale."

"Poorly, according to a damn *goblin*, and it took me three days to do it."

"So what? It got done, didn't it? Just like the gyromatic whatever."

"Took me a *week* to fix that gyroscopic stabilizer."

"I don't see the problem, that's two major repairs you've managed to do just fine."

"*Major repairs?*" Smith scoffed. "*Done just fine?* Brenno, it took me three days to reconnect a limb that was cut off, and a week to properly reinstall a replacement part that was already laying around."

"Find more replacement parts, then. I'm sure Bucket will have what you need."

"I'd have to know what I needed before I could ask."

"I don't understand. Surely you remember how you built her the first time?"

Smith's shoulders sank at Brenno's question.

Realization dawned on the halfling.

"*Reverse* engineer. Back in the market district you didn't say you *engineered* her, you said had to *reverse* engineer her arm."

Smith sank even further into himself.

The halfling's tongue felt swollen in his mouth, and he forced himself to swallow.

"Smith, who built Enaurl?"

The artificer shook his head, and slowly trudged towards the exit.

"Morrillypallyke built her, didn't she?"

Brenno shouted, his words reverberating off the cavern walls. Smith didn't respond, but he stopped walking.

"Yeah," Smith admitted, speaking quietly. "She did."

"Why have you been taking the credit for building her all this time?"

"I didn't take the credit, I took the responsibility," Smith said, whirling around to face Brenno once more. "Do you remember what I said about her back in the market? What about before we left town, or before the gnolls hit us?"

"Not the precise words per say, but--"

"It's a dangerous thing being known as the artificer who built a thinking machine," said Smith. "I can deal with it. Morri can't. She's... She's not..."

Smith closed his eyes, screwing them up tight in an effort to contain the tears that welled up at the corners of his eyes. He failed. As the beads of moisture ran down his face, he brushed them off with his tattered sleeve.

"Just get the blood, Hornbuckle. Get the blood and we can all go home, and this nightmare ends."

Brenno offered Smith only the slightest nod, which was enough for the artificer to continue his march towards the mouth of the cavern and the wagon beyond. The silence that followed Smith's revelation hung heavily in the dragon's lair, Brenno watching the back of the artificer as he limped his way to safety. Brenno shook his head.

Of course she built Enaurl, he thought. *All this time, all of Smith's worry, all his ire and his griping... I suppose it all makes sense now.*

The halfling pressed his palms into his eyes, feeling overwhelmed by the day's events.

"One thing at a time," he said to himself, "Start with the blood, then deal with Kera."

He looked again to Orionatsaron and the dark puddle beneath the dragon's body. In his mind, he imagined the dragon's eye - the one that remained - opening, the fearsome orb beneath hidden the heavy lid focusing itself onto him. He swallowed.

Maybe I'll start with Kera.

Task chosen, Brenno took the few steps to where Kera was laying and reached down to lift the woman up from under her arms. The dead weight of the graverobber made the task difficult, and Brenno struggled with propping the woman up enough that she was sitting.

Once that was done, the halfling wrapped his arms around Kera's waist and hauled, walking backwards as he dragged her like a sack of potatoes. When he could go no further, he stopped. Breathing hard, he looked up to see how much progress he'd made. He was dismayed to see that he had barely dragged the woman four feet away from where he'd started.

"Doing it like this will take forever," Brenno said to himself. "Surely there's an easier method..."

Brenno looked around the cave, intentionally avoiding the dragon's corpse, in an effort to find something that he might be able to use as a sled or a wagon to help ferry the graverobber out of the cavern. Seeing nothing, he frowned and looked back down at Kera.

"I don't suppose you have any ideas?"

Kera didn't stir, laying flat on her back, Zephelous still clutched tightly in her hands. Seeing the sword made Brenno think.

"I wonder..." He said, contemplating.

Moving cautiously, afraid that too sudden a movement would make the sword snap at him like a dog, Brenno reached a hand out towards Zephelous. With his other hand, he fought Kera's surprisingly strong grip on the sword.

Finally succeeding in prying her fingers off the sword, Brenno stumbled and tripped, landing squarely on his bottom with the dwarven sword held in his hands. For a moment, he sat in silence, expecting the sword to speak to him in his mind the way Kera and Voldani had explained. He waited, but heard nothing.

Perhaps there's an attunement time required, Brenno thought, *maybe I simply need to be patient.*

Resolved to wait, Brenno sat on the cavern floor staring at Zephelous until the cold of the floor began to bite at his skin through his pants.

Grumbling, Brenno stood.

"Is there a reason you won't speak with me?" Brenno asked the sword. "Is it because I'm not a warrior like Voldani? Or a fighter like Kera? Is it because I'm nothing but a pawnbroker, lucky to be alive and somehow unworthy of your time?"

The words reverberated throughout the cavern, but did not seem to coerce Zephelous into talking. Brenno sighed.

"Is this how insignificant I am? Not worth a dragon's effort to kill, not worth a sword's attention to speak to. What is to become of poor old Brenno Hornbuckle?"

WHAT INDEED, said Zephelous, startling Brenno.

"My apologies, Mister Zephelous," said Brenno. "I wasn't aware you were listening."

THERE IS OFTEN LITTLE ELSE FOR ME TO DO BUT LISTEN, said Zephelous, BECAUSE I LISTEN NOT ONLY TO WORDS BUT STRAY THOUGHTS, I HEAR FAR MORE THAN MOST. IN FACT, I HEAR FAR MORE THAN MOST REALIZE.

Does that mean it knows my thoughts? Brenno wondered.

WHILE I AM IN YOUR GRASP, YES, said Zephelous, startling Brenno once more. THERE IS NO NEED TO SPEAK ALOUD TO COMMUNICATE WITH ME, THOUGH IT SEEMS TO BE KERA'S PREFERRED MANNER TO DO SO.

Speaking of Kera, Brenno thought, glancing towards the downed graverobber. *Is she...?*

SHE WILL BE FINE, said Zephelous. SHE HAS TAXED HERSELF IN MANY WAYS ON THIS DAY, AND WILL REQUIRE A GREAT DEAL OF REST.

"Good, good..." said Brenno, nodding.

He tried to stop himself from thinking, knowing that the sword would hear his every thought, but his efforts only made it that much harder.

Why wouldn't you speak to me while I had you in my possession? Why is it that you spoke with Voldani, and Kera, and apparently the dragon, but are only now doing so with myself?

I WAS FORGED BY THE GODS, BRENNO HORNBUCKLE, Zephelous began, AND WHEN I WAS AWAKENED, I WAS GIVEN A SINGULAR TASK - TO SEEK THOSE WHOSE DESTINIES WERE BOUND TO THE TAPESTRY OF FATE, AND TO INSTRUCT AND ASSIST THEM IN THEIR EFFORTS AGAINST THE DARKNESS THAT LOOMS.

Yes, I believe Kera has mentioned that, Brenno thought, albeit somewhat mockingly.

SUCH IS THE NORM FOR KERA NO-CLAN, Zephelous said with a sigh.

"Indeed," said Brenno, sighing as well. "You're certain she is meant to wield you?"

FOR BETTER OR WORSE, THE FATE OF KERA NO-CLAN IS GREATNESS, said Zephelous, SHE IS DESTINED FOR GRANDEUR, DESPITE HER MANY PROTESTS.

"How can you know?" Brenno asked.

THE SIMPLEST MANNER TO EXPLAIN IT WOULD BE TO LIKEN IT TO DIVINATION MAGIC, said Zephelous. IMAGINE A SORT OF RESIDUAL AURA ATTACHED TO CERTAIN BEINGS, AURAS WHICH ARE INVISIBLE TO ALL SAVE MYSELF AND A FEW OTHERS. THESE HELP GAUGE THE IMPACT A PERSON WILL HAVE ON THE WORLD AROUND THEM AND HISTORY AFTER THEM.

"And Kera's aura, as you call it, is large? Powerful?"

YES, said Zephelous. THOUGH IT IS NOT AS SIMPLE AS THAT.

"I wouldn't think so," said Brenno, lapsing into silence.

Once again, he dared not think the thoughts he wished to ask. As before, he failed to stop himself.

And what of mine? What of Brenno Hornbuckle, the shopless pawnbroker from Zelwyr?

DO YOU TRULY WISH TO KNOW? Zephelous asked. THERE ARE SOME THINGS BEST KEPT TO SECRETS AND WONDERING.

"Perhaps," Brenno said, doing his best to control his thoughts in an effort to prevent them from saying *tell me, tell me, tell me, TELL ME.*

Zephelous sighed, making him assume he had failed.

I WILL DO SO ON ONE CONDITION, said Zephelous.

"Anything," said Brenno, clutching the sword as hard as he could.

YOU MUST RETURN ME TO KERA'S HANDS, AND MUST NEVER SPEAK OF WHAT HAPPENS BETWEEN NOW AND WHEN WE RETURN TO THE CARRIAGE.

"Between now and the carriage?" Brenno asked, furrowing his brow. "Won't that be a matter of minutes?"

YES, said Zephelous, GIVE ME YOUR WORD, BRENNO HORNBUCKLE, AND I WILL ANSWER YOUR QUESTION. WHAT'S MORE, WHEN I AM RETURNED TO KERA'S HANDS, I WILL ASSIST YOU IN LEAVING THIS PLACE.

"How?" Brenno asked.

YOU WILL SEE, said Zephelous, BUT YOU WILL NEVER SPEAK OF IT. ARE WE IN AGREEMENT?

Brenno nodded vigorously.

"You have my word," said Brenno.

Zephelous sighed again.

THE DESTINY OF BRENNO HORNBUCKLE IS A GREAT ONE, said Zephelous. INDELIBLY INTERTWINED WITH THE TAPESTRY OF FATE, YOUR TALE IS ONE THAT WILL NO DOUBT BE SEEN AS GREAT IN SO MANY WAYS...

Brenno was stunned.

AND TERRIBLE IN SO MANY OTHERS...

"Great... and terrible?" Brenno repeated, shocked.

TERRIBLE IS NOT TO BE TAKEN IN THE CONTEXT OF QUALITY, said Zephelous. INSTEAD, IT SHOULD BE TAKEN IN THE CONTEXT OF DIRE GRIMNESS.

"*Well obviously,* based on the context, but..." said Brenno, dazed but still speaking. "How can you know? How can you be so certain?"

I KNOW ONLY THAT I AM CERTAIN OF THIS, said Zephelous. IT IS SAID THAT MEMBERS OF THE BLUE DRAGONFLIGHT ALSO POSSESS A CERTAIN ATTUNEMENT TO FATE, AND AS SUCH WORK TO SURROUND THEMSELVES WITH PERSONS OF NOTE AND EXCEPTIONAL TALENT.

"That didn't seem to be the case," said Brenno, remembering his conversation with the dragon. "Quite the opposite, in fact."

BELIEVE WHAT YOU WILL, BRENNO HORNBUCKLE, said Zephelous. I HAVE UPHELD MY END OF THE BARGAIN, I ASK THAT YOU NOW DO THE SAME.

"Yes, of course," said Brenno, scrambling to his feet. "A deal's a deal."

Careful not to cut himself on the sharpened edge of the living sword, Brenno replaced Zephelous in Kera hands.

To Brenno's surprise, Kera stood up, eyes still closed.

"Zephelous?" Brenno asked, floored.

"Indeed," said Kera, "I will trust you to honor our arrangement."

"You can... control her body?"

"Yes, temporarily at least," said Kera. "It is not always in my power to do so, and it is something that Kera would never allow. Hence the required silence."

"I understand," said Brenno. "Would you be so kind as to assist me collecting some of this blood before it all freezes? I bought some vials from Marie, I think they'll do to hold the blood."

"I believe that is acceptable," said Kera.

Chapter Forty-Two

Sitting comfortably in the driver's seat of the wagon, Brenno took a moment to gather himself. His mind worked on overtime as he struggled to comprehend all that had transpired this day. He felt cold, sick, sweaty, and nauseous all at once.

The carriage creaked suddenly, rocking slightly to the side.

Brenno's eyes snapped open, certain that the sound had been the dragon crawling out of the rubble to loom over him, snap him up and throw him into his mouth, or lift him into the air and tear him in half like it had done to poor Enaurl.

Looking around frantically, he saw nothing.

Sighing, he rubbed his hands with his face for several seconds, then got the horses going with a quick flick of his wrists.

Brenno spent the next several hours lost in thought, wary of every creak and groan the carriage made as it wound its way back down the mountain. His distraction was so great was that he almost missed the soft chiming sound coming from somewhere on his person.

Confused, the halfling patted himself down in an effort to find the source. His fingers touched solid. He withdrew it, finding a black oak tube with a stopper on the end. He uncorked it, and the contents slid out.

He found himself starting at he dragon's contract.

Brenno's heart stopped, and so did the chiming.

Hands trembling and his chin quivering, Brenno clumsily leafed through the papers. He could see the glow of illuminated text beneath layers of paper, and he felt a terrible need to know what it said. Anxiety and fear made his hands clumsy and stupid, but at last he turned to the page in question. There, beneath his own signature, shining as if written in glowing ink, shone the words:

In the unlikely case of the untimely death of the great and powerful Orionatsaron, the one bound to the dragon's contract agrees to perform the following tasks…

Chapter Forty-Three

The sun rose peacefully over Zelwyr the next morning, its gentle rays softly breaking through the window above Morrillypallyke's bed. It wasn't the sun that woke her, nor the dawning of the new day, but the gentle rapping on the door to her room.

"Miss Smith?" Speaker Gerhardt called. "Are you awake?"

Morri stretched and yawned, drawing her blankets around herself as she sat up in bed.

"Only as of now, Speaker," said Morri, stretching once more. The previous day's work in the infirmary had been taxing and had left her feeling sore all over.

"I'm sorry to have woken you," said the Speaker. "I had hoped you might accompany me to the temple this morning, but I can return at a later time."

"No need, Speaker," said Morri, sliding out of bed. "If you can wait just a few minutes, I'll be ready. Under an hour, I swear it."

"No need to rush on an old man's account," Gerhardt said with a chuckle. "Shall I fetch us a pair of glazed cinnamon buns for breakfast in the meantime?"

"Oh, please do!" Said Morri, instantly feeling more chipper and awake with the promise of sweet pastries in the near future.

The Speaker chuckled and shuffled away, the sound of his cane becoming more faint as he left the house. Morri washed and dressed herself in record time, going as far as setting plates and glasses of water for herself and Speaker Gerhardt. The old man returned at length, carrying a pair of cinnamon buns wrapped in paper, wearing a heavy travelling cloak and a sturdy pair of boots.

"Are you going somewhere, Speaker?" Morri asked.

"What's that, dear?" Gerhardt asked, offering Morri her cinnamon bun. The girl took it and began to eat with gusto, covering her mouth to speak as she devoured the delicious pastry.

"Your boots and cloak," said Morri. "Are you going somewhere?"

"Ah, I see," said the Speaker, smiling warmly. "No, no, I'm afraid not. Spring is upon us, and with spring comes spring rains. I'm afraid my old bones can barely stand up to regular rain, much less the more enthusiastic downpours we get this time of year. Shall we walk and eat at the same time? Would that be alright?"

Morri nodded enthusiastically, sliding down from her chair. Speaker Gerhardt held the door open for the girl, letting her go first. Morri finished her breakfast before they'd made it halfway to the temple of Perrus. Seeing this, Gerhardt offered the girl his. Morri smiled politely at the old man but waved it away.

"I couldn't, Speaker, but thank you," said Morri.

"I insist," said Gerhardt, putting the cinnamon bun in the girl's hands directly. "My appetite isn't what it used to be I'm afraid, and it does my heart good to watch you enjoy them."

Sheepishly, Morri took the second cinnamon bun and eagerly began devouring it. She finished it long before they arrived at the temple.

"What duties are we performing today, Speaker?" Morri asked.

"Mostly ritualistic today," said the Speaker. "Would you be so kind as to help me carry a few things up from my chambers?"

"Of course, Speaker," said Morri. "I wouldn't mind at all."

"Excellent, excellent," said Gerhardt, a gentle smile on his wrinkled face. "Do lead on, you certainly know the way after all."

Morri nodded and obliged, practically skipping through the deserted halls of the temple of Perrus. In no time, she found herself at the door to the Speaker's chambers, which she opened when the Speaker waved her through. The inside of the quarters appeared much as they ever had, books and bookshelves taking up most of the space.

"Would you be a dear and locate a volume titled *The Sleeping Dog Who Gaurds The World?*" Morri nodded happily and made her way to the bookshelf, scanning for the title.

"What is it about?" Morri asked.

"You wouldn't be interested," said Gerhardt.

"You'd be awfully surprised at what catches my interest," said Morri.

"A fair point!" Said Gerhardt. "With a mind like yours, I imagine a steady diet of information is required to keep everything running sharp."

"You could certainly say that," Morri said proudly.

"Very well," the Speaker said with a soft chuckle. "*The Sleeping Dog* is a bit of a theological document, a study on the god Kine. Are you familiar?"

"I can't say I am, Speaker," said Morri.

"A pity," said Gerhardt. "Given that he is a god of artifice, I had hoped you'd know."

"You'd *hoped* I knew, Speaker?" Morri repeated, stressing the unusual word choice.

"I believe 'assumed' is the correct word here," said Gerhardt, correcting himself. "My dearest apologies, Miss Smith."

"No apologies necessary," said Morri, scanning the volumes.

"Try the second shelf," said Gerhardt. "Perhaps closer to the middle?"

Morri nodded and followed the Speaker's instructions. At last she found the book in question.

"It's here, Speaker," said Morri, "just where you said it would be."

"Excellent!" said Gerhardt. "Pull it from the shelf, but mind the bindings."

Morri pulled the book, but was surprised when it suddenly pulled back when she'd only removed it halfway. She let out a startled cry as the entire bookshelf suddenly sank forward into the wall and slid away, revealing a dimly lit hallway. Peering in, Morri saw a hallway that ran thirty feet ahead before making a turn to the left.

"Speaker," said Morri, shocked. "There's a whole room in there."

Speaker Gerhardt chuckled, stepping past Morri and into the hallway.

"Yes, it's one of my better kept secrets," said the Speaker. "A place just for myself, to get away from it all. So long as you don't mind the ticking and grinding, it makes for an excellent place to sit and think, or read, or what have you."

"Ticking and grinding?" Morri repeated.

"Don't you hear it?" The Speaker asked, turning back to smile at the girl. "Listen."

Morri went quiet, listening intently. Gradually, she became aware of a steady, solid ticking, accompanied by grinding and whirring sounds that made her think of Enaurl.

"What is it, Speaker?" asked Morri. "It sounds like a great clock."

"More or less, yes!"

The Speaker smiled, nodding at the girl before turning to continue shambling his way towards the door at the far end of the hallway. "It's called the clockwork corridor, and it was built as a sort of celestial timepiece, you might say. I can explain it all to you another time, but suffice it to know that every inch of this hall, every cog and every gear, denotes the positioning of one constellation or another, one astral body or the next. A sort of cosmic calendar, if you will."

Morri stepped into the hallway and looked around, marveling at what she saw; as the Speaker had said, nearly every inch of the corridor was gears, or had gears, or opened up to reveal gears beyond. Most of them had markings in a language that she didn't recognize, etched into the mechanical contraptions in what she surmised must be intensely precise locations.

So amazed with the corridor was she that she barely registered walking through it and arriving at the far end, where the Speaker awaited. He offered a warm smile down at her, and opened the door, gesturing for her to lead the way.

The room inside was brightly lit by torches, and while it too seemed to be composed of clockwork, the room was smaller and dominated by a single element - an intricate metal sculpture of an beautiful angelic figure. The beauty and intricacy of the piece - her every feather a single piece of wrought steel, her bones a gleaming silver, her strands of hair golden wire - left Morri feeling awestruck. She walked around it several times, studying each element as intensely as she could.

"It's beautiful, Speaker," Morri whispered. "What is it?"

"She's not a 'it'," said the Speaker. "She is a 'she'."

"Apologies, Speaker," Morri said with a smile. "What is she?"

The speaker sighed.

"Little more than a relic, I'm afraid," said Gerhardt, walking over to stand close to her, fingers tracing her metallic feathers. "Though not so long ago, she was much more."

"Oh?" Morri asked, intrigued. "How so?"

"She played a very important role," said Gerhardt.

"In the church?" Morri asked. The Speaker nodded.

"In the church, in the community... She was certainly something," said the Speaker. "Though what she saw in your father, I'll never know."

Morri didn't register the comment.

"Speaker?" she prompted, only half-realizing the implications.

"I had thought you'd simply *know* when you saw her, but I suppose that's not the case," said the Speaker. "Morri, I'd like you to meet your mother. Properly this time."

Morri gasped and pulled her hand away from the mechanical angel.

"W-what?" Morri asked. "That can't be, that's not possible."

"I'm afraid it is, on both counts. Isn't she marvelous?" Gerhardt asked, running a loving hand over metallic sinew and steel bones. "A scion with the blood of the machine god running through her veins, improving and rebuilding her every fiber with each beat of her mechanical heart. Imagine what she might have become if she'd been able to complete her transformation, to ascend beyond the trappings of flesh and its inherent mortality, instead of dying defending your simpleton of a father against a pack of fevered dogmen. Do you know what she would have become?"

Terrified, Morri backed away from the Speaker, pressing herself flat against the wall. She wished she could walk through it, wished for the hundredth time that her father or Enaurl were here. The Speaker's mad gaze turned to her, as if he expected her to answer. She opened her mouth but found she couldn't talk, so she simply shook her head.

"No?" said the Speaker. "Care to wager a guess?"

Morri shook her head again, her hair swaying wildly. The speaker's lips spread wide in a smile unlike any she had seen; there was no warmth in his expression, only a sinister mania. The old man threw down his cane, letting it roll away on the floor.

"I think I know. I've seen the *Codex Mechanicus*. I've studied the plans. I believe your mother was on the path to attaining godhood by way of becoming one with Kine, her essence fusing with the machine god."

The Speaker removed his hood, and began unlacing his boots. He kicked them off one at a time, the heavy boots flopping out from under his cloak and onto the ground.

"What...", Morri began, swallowing her fear. "What are you doing?"

"I was hoping you might critique my work," said the Speaker. "I'm certainly not as gifted as you, my dear, and I'm far too old to be a prodigy... but what I lack in natural talent, I believe I've more than made up in devotion."

The Speaker unbuttoned his heavy cloak and let it fall to the floor, unveiling himself to Morri. The girl gasped and covered her mouth, her eyes going wide at the sight before her; the man's arms and legs had been removed, replaced with bulkier, more powerful versions of the limbs she'd installed onto the young man at the infirmary. The Speaker's chest and abdomen appeared to have been replaced; in place of his own body was a sturdy steel chassis with winding gears and glass windows that showed a mixture of mechanical contraptions and pallid organs beyond.

"Well?" Speaker Gerhardt asked her, gesturing to his monstrous new body. "Quite the improvement, don't you think? I don't think I'll have to worry about the spring rains and my old bones any more, eh?"

Gerhardt's manic grin spread wider until he was beaming a horrible, deranged smile at the girl.

I want to be with father, Morri thought, *I want to be back in bed, I want to be in the infirmary, I want to be anywhere but here!*

Seeing the fear on her face, Gerhardt stood back, his legs visibly extending, letting him stand taller than ever before.

He turned his attention back to the metallic corpse, the mechanized remains of her mother. He ran an iron finger down the side of her mother's silver skull, laughing to himself all the while.

"You're not like her, of course. Not yet at least. You're not a scion, but her blood runs in your veins. I'm certain that once I've brought you to his temple - and provided the correct stressors, of course - I can prompt your latent potential to become a scion. It won't be an exact science, I'm afraid, and there are bound to be a few mishaps... Fortunately, with your father gone and likely dead on a fool's errand, there's no one to come looking for you. You're all mine at last, Miss Smith, all mine!"

Gerhardt cackled like a madman, staring into his own reflection as seen in the polished silver bones in front of him.

Run! Morri heard herself think. *Run now, run as far as you can.*

She bolted, her legs working overtime to drive her out of that room. She ducked beneath Gerhardt, stepping between his mechanical legs, and ran down the clockwork corridor.

"Do you really think there's anywhere you can go, miss Smith?" Gerhardt called after her, laughing all the while.

The cogs and gears in the hallway stopped moving in unison, coming to a stop with a single resounding *tok*. The larger gears swung inwards while smaller ones rolled out of the way, revealing a dozen hidden chambers set in the walls. From each of these chambers, a shambling monstrosity emerged, looking more flesh than artifice, all of them with moving gears.

She brushed past the first pair and ducked beneath the clumsy grasp of the next. By weaving and dodging beneath the clumsy attempts to grab her, she managed to get within arm's reach of the door to the Speaker's chambers.

A hand clamped down on her shoulder then, unyielding and controlling. It drew her backwards, forcing her to take several steps backwards before she was made to turn around. Expecting to find herself looking up at Gerhardt, she was shocked to instead see the face mask she'd given Pephe, his unblinking silver eyes - so much like Enaurl's and yet so different - starting down at her.

"Pephe," she said, breathlessly. "Pephe, please, you must let me go. The Speaker has gone mad. He intends to torture me, to convert me into... into..."

"Into a monster?" Pephe offered, his tone sad and defeated. "Like me?"

"Pephe, you're not a monster, you're a good man," Morri pleaded. "Please, let me go."

"Sorry, kid," Pephe said, using his grip to force Morri to finish turning around and begin walking back towards Gerhardt. "This is what I am now. This is what I have to do."

"I'll never go along with it," said Morri. "He's insane! I'm not a scion. Please,

Pephe, I'm begging you!"

Pephe sighed, the sound amplified by his face mask.

"Sorry," said the former black priest. "Here, this will make it easier."

Pephe's free hand suddenly appeared over her face, covering her mouth and nose with a foul-smelling cloth.

"It's okay, just take a deep breath. It'll make you sleep, that's all."

Morri screamed into the cloth, kicking and punching and scrabbling every which way she could in an effort to get away.

Don't breathe, she told herself, *don't breathe, don't breathe, don't breathe.*

She held her breath for as long as she could, still squirming and fighting to free herself. Her lungs burned, and her shoulder ached where Pephe's grip kept her trapped.

Finally, she could resist no more. She inhaled, and darkness came for her. She was dimly aware of Gerhardt's manic laughter as she was enveloped by nothingness.

Chapter Forty-Four

Somewhere beyond the reality that she knew, Voldani stirred. To her great surprise, she found that she felt no pain, no agony. The crushing weight of the stone had been lifted away, leaving her lying on ground that was as smooth as polished glass. The sensation, so different from the stone of the cavern floor, brought to mind the memories of the cave in and the dragon. In her mind's eye she saw the ceiling collapsing all over again, the earth roaring as it slammed down in an effort to claim her for itself.

Voldani's eyes snapped open and she sat up, breathing in sharply as she did. She found herself surrounded by the emptiness, lying atop a what seemed like gigantic pane of darkened glass that stretched into eternity. Light twinkled up at her from beneath its surface, shining through the cracks of her fingers. Moving her hands away, her breath caught at the wonder of what she saw; a sea of stars, as vast and impossible to comprehend as infinity itself, shimmered and sparkled beneath her.

Galaxies swirled and nebulae glistened, suns and stars whose names Voldani couldn't even begin to guess twinkled beneath her feet, shining their light up at her as they illuminated the vast void from below.

"What manner of place is this?" Voldani whispered to herself.

Rising to stand, she spun in a slow circle to assess her surroundings. The stars stretched on forever, as did the glass between them and her. Her mind churned to process what she was seeing, struggled to fully comprehend the truth. She suspected she knew, suspected she was dead and this was some sort of astral limbo, but she wasn't sure of anything.

Reeling as if physically struck, Voldani staggered backwards, accidentally backing into something solid that hadn't been there a moment before. Acting on instinct, Voldani drew both of her swords and whirled around, bringing her blades across in a practiced double slash. The steel of the swords connected with a large triangular mound of white marble, the blades protesting with a clink.

"No need to be so hasty," said a woman's voice, at once as strong as a waterfall and as smooth as the softest silk. "We've all the time in the world here, my dear Voldani. No need for haste at all."

The voice seemed like it was coming from all directions at once, confusing

Voldani. The warrior's eyes followed the edge of the marble upward to where it meet another piece of stone, then another, and another. Each was a varying shade of grey, and each was in a precise geometric shape - each fit into place to form a titanic woman sitting cross-legged. She was ageless and impressive, and so much more than Voldani had ever imagined. Her heart felt as if it might burst from a mixture of awe and love and amazement. She raised her hands to make the sign of the crossed roads, only to realize she still had her swords in her hands. She gasped and dropped them to the ground.

I have drawn my blades and struck against my goddess.

"Forgive me, my lady," said Voldani, kneeling low to bow in reverence.

"Never," said Perrus, the titan's playful words seeming at once soft and booming as she spoke them. "What sort of god would I be if I made my followers feel the need to apologize for being who they are?"

As Perrus spoke, the texture of the stones changed before Voldani's eyes; clouds of deep purples and blues appeared on its surface, which became clear and glassy like the floor. Brilliant stars occasionally peeked out through the clouds, making them glow with their light. The brightest of the stars were those that formed where her eyes were.

A silence filled the void, settling gently over the two women in the place beyond.

"You may ask it now," said Perrus, looking down at Voldani as she sat.

"My lady?" Voldani asked, looking up with uncertainty.

"The question you wouldn't let yourself ask in life," said Perrus. "The one that nagged you from your childhood until your last moment, the one that nipped at the heels of your faith and you, ever dutiful, pressed it down and refused to say it out loud in hopes I wouldn't hear it."

"Did you?" Voldani asked.

"I did," said Perrus. "You were thinking it so very loudly."

"Forgive me, my lady," said Voldani.

"No," said Perrus. "Not until you ask it, not until you've learned the answer."

"My lady, I couldn't--"

"Voldani," said Perrus, the woman's name spoken like a spell, binding Voldani to comply.

"Where were you?" Voldani asked, gasping and covering her mouth even as the words came out, trying to catch them and take them back.

Perrus smiled down at Voldani, immeasurable sadness and colossal weariness creasing her glassy features.

"There is no need to be ashamed of your question," said Perrus. "No need to be embarrassed by your wondering, especially given its honesty. It is, after all, a fair question."

"My lady, I…" Voldani started, attempting to mount a defense of her faith.

The stars beneath her boots caught her attention, making her remember where she was, what had happened to her, who she was speaking to. Her shoulders slumped. There was no reason not to be honest now, least of all now.

"My lady, I have struggled in your name. I have bled for your honor. I have killed your enemies and guarded your faithful, I have done so *much,* and yet for so many years you were silent. I received my gifts from you, but all my direction came from your priests and emissaries, not once since my childhood have I heard your voice. I have learned more about you from the slathering mouths of mange-infested timbergnolls than I have from you. Why? Why, after all I have done, did you ignore me when you knew how much I needed you?"

"I'm afraid that's where you're wrong," said Perrus. "In fact, it was quite the opposite."

"I don't understand," said Voldani.

"You didn't need me," said Perrus. "The children, the ones who cry for me to ease the burning of the fevers that wrack their bodies, need me. The homeless, those who weep and pray that I numb the hunger pains in their bellies and ease the sores in their feet long enough for them to walk, need me. The dying, the nearly dead who linger on in agony who beg that I mend them or summon my brother with haste, need me. You have never *needed* me, Voldani. You have struggled, yes, but always you have been *strong.* You have been a beacon of light in a world grown ever darker, a star burning against the hungering black of the consuming void. That is why I have needed *you* for all these many years."

"You… have needed *me?*" Voldani asked, stunned by her god's words.

Perrus's expression softened into one of a saddened mother, and as she did her form changed once more. The clouds and stars within her dimmed and became a blue blur, her edges softened and rounded, looking like great pieces of seaglass. With great care, a colossal hand reached down towards Voldani and cupped Voldani's face in a giant palm.

"More than you can imagine," said Perrus. "There are so many who need me, Voldani, so many who require my aid in the struggles of their lives. Some combat illness and fate, others combat tyrants and dragons. All who do so under my name ask for my protection, my guidance, my healing magics and my divine power for their various uses. The power they ask is an extension of my being, and so what they ask for is nothing less than pieces of my own existence. I give it to them, of course, as any loving parent would for a much-beloved child. You, Voldani, with your fate-touched ancestry, your god-blooded heart pumping with traces of my own divine light, have never needed my power. Instead, your actions and strength have given *me* strength. Your devotion to me, acts of goodness and mercy, and all the glorious things you have done in my name, the very nature of your existence - all these things have given me a great hope for you, a hope that you possess a might that is much needed in times such as these. Strength that I fear may yet be tested in the times to come."

Voldani digested Perrus's words at length, absorbing them, letting their meaning and weight be examined at length in her mind before she spoke again. Perrus spoke first.

"What am I to you, Voldani?" Perrus asked.

"You are a god," Voldani whispered. "My god."

"Yes, but what does that mean?" the Lady in White pressed. "'God' is just a word mortals give to things they can't understand. Does it truly have a meaning? Does it hold any inherent truths, or is it simply an explanation for things mortals can't control? Titans. Storms. Dragons. Beings such as myself. All have been called gods, either now or in the past, but they are not the same. My brothers and sisters, divine all, are as different from me as I from them. We do more than exist, Voldani; we live. In a way, we are as mortal as you are, though perhaps not in any sense that you could comprehend. For the most part, that is. Like you, we can be bound, imprisoned. Like you, we can be silenced. Like you, we can be killed."

"Are you in danger, my lady? My swords are yours, as in my life."

"I am not in peril, and your life has already ended, Voldani, it is already mine. Although…"

The White Lady paused, seeming to contemplate deeply for a moment. The swirling galaxies that formed her eyes blazed and shimmered within the onyx pools of their surface.

"Perhaps it should not be so."

"I do not understand."

"Do you trust me, Voldani?"

"Yes, my lady."

"Do you love me?"

"With all of my heart, my lady,"

"Would you do as I asked without question?"

"Not a one, my lady."

"That is your weakness," said Perrus.

"My lady?"

"Beings of divinity we may be, but we are not omnipotent, Voldani, nor are we omniscient. Were any of that true, there wouldn't be so many of us. And yet, we are as plentiful across the realms as the stars in space. Sometimes I wonder why that is…"

The Lady seemed lost in reverie, staring out into the starry void that hung above them like a mobile.

"You need not be all-knowing to make the right decision," said Voldani. "Nor do you need to be omnipotent to choose the correct course of action. I cannot speak to much of what you say, my lady, but I can speak to those respects; as I said, my swords and my life are yours."

Perrus smiled, looking down at Voldani the way a proud parent might look down at an eager child.

"I am blessed to count you among my faithful, Voldani," said Perrus. "I accept your offering, and to you I return them; I give you the gift of new life, a life that is your own. I ask simply that you walk upon the path that I will set for you."

"I swear it, my lady."

"Good. Your companions will soon find themselves in greater peril than they can possibly imagine: peril that threatens to shake your plane asunder. Even now, they follow the trail of the Iron Prophet. He will lead them to where the machine god slumbers. There he hopes to use the child to bind the god to his whims."

"To what end?"

"Would that I could know. To reshape the world as he sees fit, to exact vengeance on his enemies, to bring about an end to Odellia? It could be all or none of these things; whatever it may be, it will not end well. Gods do not bind easily, nor to they take to it kindly."

"What does this mean?"

"If the Iron Prophet attempts to bind Kine to his will, there will be a calamity such that has not been known for many ages. There is a reason the dwarves call him the Hammer of the Earth; if angered he will strike, and woe to those in his path."

"I will do all in my power to prevent this, my lady."

"I know you will. I also know you will need these," said Perrus, reaching into the suspended starscape above her.

Her fingers plucked a pair of falling stars from the abyss and pulled them down to her mouth. She exhaled onto to them, exuding a glimmering vapor.

Satisfied, she lowered her colossal hand to Voldani, revealing the items held within it: a pair of gleaming swords, each curved like a falling star and glowing with internal light, was offered.

"My lady, I... could not possibly," said Voldani, eyes wide.

"You can, and you will," said Perrus. "When I was a mere godling, I was told the tale of Iskwielg, the Dual Star, and how the very nature of its existence caused its own extinction. Driven by curiosity and tenacity of youth, I sought to reclaim the dual hearts of Iskwielg. It took centuries, but I succeeded. Now I present them to you, in the form which they will be of the most use. Take them and wield them in my name. With them, you shall bring me glory and yourself great honor. With Iskwielg, you may yet save your world."

"I... am unworthy of such a gift as this."

"Do not for a moment misrepresent your value, Voldani. You are a proud warrior, a relentless champion, and a powerful woman. For all of these reasons and more, I have deemed you worthy of this. Unless... You mean to question me?"

"No, my lady, of course not, my lady, I would never--"

"Hush, Voldani. There is not much time. Already your soul flies away from this place. Do you feel it? I sometimes wonder what it is like to be so irrevocably tied to a single physical form. Perhaps we can discuss it when you return to me next."

"When shall I return to you, my lady?" Voldani asked, taking the Iskwielg swords into her hands.

Perrus smiled softly.

"When your battles are fought and won," said Perrus. "When you are old and gray, when you have cleansed the church of the corruption that afflicts it, when you have instilled order and found an heir to teach all of your strengths and to gift with all of your wisdom. Then, and only then, will you return to this place."

"Corruption, my lady?"

"A great deception, one which you will end."

"Yes, my lady."

"Farewell, Voldani. Know that I am always with you."

Voldani's vision faded to white before going black, flashing white once more. She heard a sound like a rockslide, and suddenly found herself staring up at a cavernous ceiling. All around her was piles and piles of boulders.

Rising to stand, she recognized the place she now found herself; this was the lair of Orionatsaron, the tunnel that had been collapsed. For a moment she wondered if it had all been a dream, a fantasy created by her own unconscious mind. Turning in place, she found herself looking northward towards a spot of light; the opening to the cavern, she suspected. Patting herself down for injuries, her hands stopped at the jeweled swords that rested comfortably in her sheaths; the sister swords Iskwielg sat there, fragments of netherglass teeming with stars that were at once more radiant than the world around them and darker than the blackness of the night sky.

She bowed her head and whispered a silent prayer of thanks to Perrus. When she was done she opened her eyes and began walking southward.

She had many miles to cover to return to Zelwyr.

The events in The Graverobber's Sword will
continue in The Dragon's Contract